Three River Valleys Called Home

The Rhine, The Mohawk, and The St. Lawrence

The Life Story of German Emigrants, Settlers, and United Empire Loyalists

VICKI HOLMES

Suite 300 - 990 Fort St
Victoria, BC, V8V 3K2
Canada

www.friesenpress.com

First Edition — 2019

Credit for Cover Design Vanessa Ooms www.vanessaooms.com

Credit for Cover Author Photo C.W. Hill Photography Ltd.
(Philip and Catrina Eamers' 6th great-grandson-in-law)

ISBN
978-1-5255-4465-1 (Hardcover)
978-1-5255-4466-8 (Paperback)
978-1-5255-4467-5 (eBook)

1. *Fiction, Historical*

Distributed to the trade by The Ingram Book Company

TABLE OF CONTENTS

They had grit.

LIST OF MAPS

PREFACE

Years have past since my grandmother gave me a copy of a page from the family bible. In 1982, her gesture of passing on the information prompted me to explore my family history. At that time, I worked without computers, internet, or email. Regardless, in 1984, the result was an Eamer family history book and a wonderful reunion of over 300 Eamer descendants from all over North America. What an honour it was to meet so many relatives at Cornwall, Ontario and to celebrate the 200th anniversary of the Eamer's settlement. As sometimes happens, school, family, and many moves interrupted my genealogical hobby. I did not reconnect with my hobby until 2010, when my passion for researching my family history was reignited. I have not let much interrupt my work since.

Philip Eamer and Maria Catherine (Catrina) Leser were my sixth great-grandparents. Their lives and the lives of those near and dear to them were filled with rich and fascinating stories. Therefore, I set out to create a genealogy that was more than just lists of names and dates. I wanted to tell their story which included families such as: Alguire, Carman, Casselman, Cline, Crites, Cryderman, Eaman, Empey, Farlinger, Fykes, Gallinger, Hartle, Jeacocks, Link, Myers, Runnions, Silmser, Warner and more.

Living in a small city without access to large libraries meant that a virtual library was the primary source of my research. I was not disappointed. I located far too many original documents. I was captivated and often found myself reading documents not entirely related to the task at hand. As I read, I imagined what my ancestors' lives were like and asked myself many questions. From where did they come in Germany? Where did they live before they came to Cornwall? How did they get there? Who were their friends and neighbours? What did they eat? In what kind of home did they live? What did they farm? What clothes did they wear? I imagined them within the context of the broader history I was reading. Soon, I wanted to share with others what I had learned. I wanted to put eight years of research on paper. Realizing that, in genealogy, the search for information is never finished I began to write.

Much is written about the emigration of Germans to North America in the eighteenth century, and much is written about the experiences of settlers during the French Indian War or about American experiences during the Revolutionary War. However, not much is written from the perspective of the common farmer or tradesman who remained loyal to the King during the Revolutionary War, especially those who lived in the Mohawk Valley.

As I wrote each chapter, I came to know Philip and Catrina's friends and neighbours and the hills, valleys, and creeks of places they lived. I came to know the depth of challenges, fears, and successes that Philip, Catrina, and their children faced. Often, I felt as though I was with them living their journey. I read many stories in documents related to Loyalist post-war claims for losses and stories related to post-war American pension applications. Each of these documents contained not only rich genealogical information, but also personal accounts of experiences during the war. My understandings of extended family relationships made it difficult to write about their conflicts, sorrows, injustices, and struggles during the Revolutionary War.

I admired the Eamer's journey across the ocean arriving not only to much uncertainty, but also during the French Indian War. I admired their building a thriving farm with few resources and most often under threat of life and limb. I equally admired all the settlers for building a thriving community. Their tenacity humbled me. I was happy and intrigued when reading through church baptism and marriage records and sad when reading about illness, injury, or death. It was most difficult to write the fictional deaths of Philip and Catrina's sons and daughter. In fact, it took me several days to shake the sorrow I felt.

Challenges I encountered were few. There were two that stalled my writing for some time. First, in Philip's Loyalist claim for losses in 1788, his witness John Farlinger declared, "remembers claimant in Charlotte County. He was always loyal." To my knowledge, Philip never lived in Charlotte County, New York. He arrived in America in 1755, and the baptismal record of Philip's son Mattheus in February 1756 identifies his residence as 'Mohawk'. If Philip arrived in America as early as late spring of 1755 (ships did not usually sail during winter months), he had less than one year to travel from Philadelphia to take residence in Charlotte County and then move to the Mohawk Valley with a good portion of this year occurring during winter months. This route seems unlikely. I suspect that John Farlinger was speaking of the area near Lake George, which in 1788 was in Charlotte County, New York. John was a soldier of the 60th Regiment which was stationed at Lake George and fought for the British during the French Indian War. Sir William Johnson's militia were also at Lake George and also fought for the British. Philip lived very near Sir William's land; therefore, it is likely that Philip belonged to Sir William's militia. There is a muster roll of Captain Peter Service's Company dated 9 July 1758. The men on this roll lived very near Philip. Finding muster rolls that puts both John Farlinger and Philip at Lake George in Charlotte County between 1755 and 1763 will help solve this conundrum. Or, the answer to the conundrum could be that the scribe meant to write Tryon County and not Charlotte County in John Farlinger's statement in Philip's 1788 claim.

The second conundrum was that of the 'fifth child'. In Philip's Loyalist claim of 1784, two of his witnesses, Martin Alguire and Christopher Gallinger, (both knew Philip well, one was his son-in-law) stated that Philip was "now in Canada with his wife and five children". I could only account for four children arriving safely in Canada and still alive in 1784. However, Philip and Catrina had five sons (Mattheus, Martin, Johannes, Philip, Jelles) who I assumed were dead because no records of any of the five were found after 1780. One of these five must have been the fifth child. For the sake of the story, I chose Martin as the fifth child. Locating records of a fifth child in the early years of their settlement at Cornwall, Ontario could solve this conundrum.

Other challenges involved the various spellings of surnames. For example I found Eamer spelled as Amer, Aymer, Beemer, Emer, Emmer, Wemer, Weemer and Alguire spelled as Algire, Alcajer, Ahlgeyer, and Allgeyer. Silmser was spelled as Simser, Somser, Simpser, and Sellimser, Service was spelled Servis and Servos, Fykes was spelled Fikes, Fix, Fiex, or Fyx and Any spelled as Eny, Enie, Eneeg, and Ehni. Also, in many families, brothers often had sons and daughters whom they gave similar names. Subsequently, in just two generations there could be four or five different Jacobs, Johns, Margarets and so on. In addition, there was a variety of different spellings and names for villages and forts along the Mohawk River. For example, Stone Arabia was often referred to as Stone Raby, which I used throughout the story.

I found eighteenth century language fascinating and exasperating. Terms used to describe some groups of people were often derogatory, such as Negro, Indian, Savage, Rebel, or Tory. To be true to the context of the story, I used eighteenth century terms. Finally, there was the challenge of incomplete or absent records I so desperately wanted or finding conflicting historical information from different sources. I endeavoured to collect as many sources as I could to ensure accuracy; however, there are sections throughout the story that relied on my imagination to give depth to the story. In spite of the challenges, I made every effort to be as accurate as possible.

Fact and fiction in this story are differentiated by following the superscript numbers to their sources at the end of the book (endnotes). If readers want to explore the source, they can search the documents on the internet. About 85% of sources are online. Because it was impossible to search and know the genealogies of all the families in the book, readers can review previously published genealogies. For example: William Barker, *Early Families of Herkimer County, Descendants of the Burnetsfield Palatines*, Maryly B. Penrose, *Compendium of Early Mohawk Valley Families.* Andrew L. Dillenbeck & Karl M. Dallenbach, eds. *The Dällenbachs in America. 1710-1735.* Alvin Countryman, *Countryman Genealogy.* Johnathan Pearson, *Contributions for the Genealogies of the Descendants of the First Settlers of the Patent and City of Schenectady, from 1662-1800.* Henry Z. Jones, *The Palatine Families of New York: A Study of the German Immigrants Who Arrived in Colonial New York in 1710.* (2 vols.).

Finding and exploring documents was one of the most exciting parts of writing the story. I could not have written this book without the assistance of archivists from Darmstadt, Hesse and from Auerbach, Hesse. From the hundreds of sources I found, there were some I consistently utilized. I am indebted to the works of the following: Gavin K. Watt, who writes meticulously researched accounts of British and Provincial military events and experiences during the Revolutionary War. The website "The King's Royal Yorkers" and Tod Braisted's website "The Online Institute for Advanced Loyalist Studies". I am grateful to archivists at The Library and Archives Canada who provide incredible historical documents online and to the archivists at the U.S. National Archives and Records Administration. The enormous map collection of the New York State Archives was a guide as I followed Philip and Catrina's journey. A key resource was The Church of Jesus Christ of Latter Day Saints who continue to expand

Fig. 1. Map of Hesse adapted from: NordNord West: Lencer CC BY-SA 3.0 https://creativecommons.org/licenses/by-sa/3.0

PROLOGUE

Thursday, 14 February, 1788 – Montreal, Quebec

Philip slid the tattered paper across the desk toward Colonel Thomas Dundas, the British Commissioner receiving Loyalist claims. Philip knew he would need that piece of paper;[1] it was the lease to his New York farm. In October, seven long years ago, he pressed it into his pocket as he and his wife Catrina fled north, driven from their home by neighbours wielding firelocks and bellowing "damned Tories get out"! As a refugee Loyalist, he made sure the tattered paper never left his pocket during the 370 kilometre journey from Johnstown, New York, along the Sacandaga River to the north branch of the Hudson River, through the thick forests of the Adirondack Mountains to Schroon Lake, past Lake George, over Lake Champlain and down the rushing Richelieu River to the refugee camp at Montreal.[2]

As Philip stood in front of the Commissioner's desk, he noticed that the fireplace framed Colonel Dundas like a fine portrait. Warmth from the dying flame couldn't sneak past to warm the chill in Philip's bones. "How much longer could these old bones hold me up?" he wondered. Philip's old friend John Farlinger and his son-in-law Martin Alguire stood with him.[3] A sixty five year old man needs that kind of support when shattered by loss and burdened with all that needs doing. Philip was as worn as the paper. He stood stiff in the drafty room trying hard to manage each question Dundas fired at him.

"When did you come to America? Where was your farm? How many acres were cleared? How much rent did you pay? Who has your land now? Tell me what else you claim? With what regiment did you serve? How long? When did you arrive in Canada? Why didn't you leave sooner?"

"Oh, good grief!" Philip thought. "I've done this before in '84 in Montreal and '86 with Captain Anderson,[4] with the same inquests, the same questions, the rooms were cold there too. What happened to those claims?" Right now, Philip was tired, very tired, and he needed the money this claim provided. Loyalists Andrew Summers and Daniel Fykes just defended their claims, and Jacob Waggoner, John Farlinger, Michael Warner, and Michael Gallinger Sr. were next.[5] Philip waited while Dundas dipped his white feather pen.

The feather caught Philip's attention, drawing him back thirty three years to the dock in Rotterdam where he stood for hours with Catrina and his children, Elizabeth, Mattheus, and Catharina. On that dock, he remembered a man with a similar pen recording their names on the ship's passenger list. It was June 1755, barely a month since the family left their village at Auerbach, Hesse to sail up the Rhine to Rotterdam then to England and across the great sea to America.[6] Philip remembered waiting on the dock among crowds of passengers with his children clinging to his legs, stuck as firm as the barnacles on the ship's hull. Several times, he too wanted to cling to something. All the waiting and watching hatched his anxieties. His heart felt like pulp; his stomach pitched and sank. It was a sickening mix of hope, excitement, anxiety, and wrenching loss that churned through him. "How could they stay? How could they leave?" The records in Auerbach's little mountain church had tracked the Wiemer's presence like a schoolmaster taking attendance. 1708 – Wiemer? Here! 1722 –Wiemer? Here! 1752 – Wiemer? Here!

Fig. 2. Die Bergkirche (The Mountain Church) at Auerbach, Hesse. Courtesy of Armin Kubelbeck. https://creativecommons.org/licenses/by-sa/3.0/ And https://commons.wikimedia.org/wiki/File:Bergkirche_Auerbach_02.jpg

CHAPTER ONE
Home in the Upper Rhine Valley

As Philip stood on the dock at Rotterdam, an image of the little mountain church at Auerbach filled his mind. He wondered how many generations of priests, villagers, travellers, and soldiers had been there. He thought, "What kinds of things did they say about the village nestled at the foot of the mountain, or what kinds of encounters, good or bad, did they have there?" For centuries, the church stood among the hills that rose to the Odenwald Mountains. To the east, the church offered a view of these mountains and to the west, a view that stretched out across the open plains of the Upper Rhine Valley. Philip was born in Auerbach and baptized in the mountain church. In 1708, Adam, Philip's father, came to Auerbach from Eberstadt as a Miller. Milling was a trade Adam was familiar with as a young child watching his father Thomas. Sometime near 1680, Thomas Wiemer and his wife Ottilia moved to Eberstadt, a village just north of Auerbach and just south of Darmstadt.[7]

Philip found it easy to recount in his mind's eye the details of his parents' and grandparents' lives. Family stories nourished his memories. He remembered hearing these stories as he sat close to the fireplace in the evening with his family, or on long walks to the markets along the ancient Roman mountain road, or with his father and brothers herding their cows to the meadow, or collecting wood from the grand forests of the Odenwald. These everyday events demanded the telling of many stories. The details in the stories were now fixed firmly in his memory. He would carry them on his journey to America. As he stood on the dock, his memory fared well, but he craved to create a few memories of ages gone by. He believed that these ages of time were as much a part of who he was as was his muscle, bone, and blood. This belief and these cravings tested his imagination. As his imagination sped through centuries and through events, he understood why he found it so hard to leave this land. He understood his anxieties and why his stomach pitched and sank. Home was so much more than his own experiences. Since the time of the Celts, the vast experiences of so many people and the great changes in the land made this place he and his family called home.

The land that surrounded Auerbach and Eberstadt was once the home of the Celts until the Germanic tribe of the Chatti forced them westward in the second and early first century B.C. The Chatti were semi-nomadic people who farmed barley, oats, rye, flax, peas, and beans. Men spent some time tending crops, herding sheep and cows, or as carpenters or artisans, but most of the farming was done by women, slaves, or older men.[8] Roman writers described Chatti men as aggressive and fierce warriors with sturdy frames, strong agile limbs, piercing blue eyes, and flaming red hair. They were headstrong, intelligent, and cunning. Success in battle determined competence in this culture. Without doubt, preparation for, participation in, and the celebration of battle were primary efforts of Chatti men.[9] Unlike other Germanic tribes, the Chatti remained detached from the intruding control of Romans. Chatti engaged in some trade, only waging war when it was clear that the Romans wanted to dominate their lands and people. To ensure their domination, the Romans opened the Odenwald forest as a frontier defense area. They built many roads for the military and for trade. One of the most important roads was the 'mountain road' (Bergstrasse).[10] This road skirted the western edge of the Odenwald Mountains and passed through Auerbach, Eberstadt, and Darmstadt. Several lines of defense were created along this road. These defense lines were strips of cleared land with wooden observation posts at five hundred metre intervals. A Roman settlement was established at Eberstadt.

Although the Romans had large and highly organized armies, the Chatti were quite successful in battle against them. In fact, in A.D. nine the Chatti took part in the famous battle of Teutoburg Forest in which the Romans suffered their greatest defeat. Despite all the Chatti successes and their title as the single greatest threat to Roman dominance, the Chatti were eventually defeated in the third century A.D.. They were absorbed by two powerful Germanic tribes, the Alamani and the Franks.

As Roman power weakened in the third and fourth centuries, their lines of defense collapsed. The Alamani from the east and the Franks from the north took advantage of the weak Roman defenses and engaged in constant fighting for control of the land. For many decades, the Alamani controlled much of the lands until they lost the battle of Zulpich to the Frankish King Clovis in 497. During the reign of Clovis and his heirs, the people of Eberstadt and Auerbach were primarily tenant farmers, subservient to the Lords and Nobles of Manor houses.

Philip's imagination captured the eighth century when Catholicism spread through the country replacing Pagan worship. Only twenty five kilometres southwest of Eberstadt and thirteen kilometres southwest of Auerbach stood the famous Lorsch Abbey. Built by a Frankish Count in 764, this Abbey served as a place of pilgrimage for centuries. As a monastery, it housed a large library and scriptorium. Auerbach is listed in the Lorsch Codex, a document scribed by Monks about 1170. The first mountain church at Auerbach was believed to have been built in 1270 as a Catholic church with St Nicholas as its patron. Philip tried to imagine what this first church looked like. Was it built of wood or stone? How many people passed through its doors? Was it a place of sanctuary or pilgrimage? During early medieval times, the Catholic Church controlled every aspect of life, and feudal agricultural systems and serfdom were deeply rooted. Grain, particularly wheat, became a primary food source and economic product.

During the thirteenth century, a stronghold was needed along the mountain road to protect the resources of the ruling families, so Auerbach castle was built on top of the Meliobokus, the highest peak along the mountain road of the Odenwald.[11] Philip had no trouble remembering this castle. It stood like a loyal defender overlooking the village. Anywhere he was in the village, he could see the fortress. Hiking up the mountain to explore the ruins of the castle was an adventure that Philip and his brothers relished. Nothing outdid the days that they pretended to be soldiers of centuries past.

By the sixteenth century, there was a significant increase in the growth of villages, towns, and cities allowing many tenant farmers to become merchants or home based workers such as weavers. Landgraves controlled most of the political and economic activities of Hesse. Landgraves were Nobles and Lords accountable to the Holy Roman Emperor for administration of villages, towns, and cities. In 1521, Landgrave Philip of Darmstadt, known as 'Philip the Magnanomous' was one of the most famous administrators and a committed supporter of peasants and the merchant class despite the fact that he fought against the peasants during the great peasant revolt of 1525. Landgrave Philip was not only supportive of peasants and the growth of the new merchant class, but he also supported Martin Luther, the spread of Lutheran teachings, and the dissolution of a corrupt Catholic establishment. Lutheran Protestantism became the new faith in Hesse; Calvinism followed closely.

In 1528, the first Protestant Pastor began services at the little mountain church at Auerbach. Philip imagined the villagers at this first service and their delight at hearing the gospel in their own language instead of in Latin. He almost felt their exuberance at being able to participate in the service and sing songs of worship instead of watching priests and choirs from their seats. This sharing during the services, Philip thought, must have given the villagers great relief knowing they were to be a part of celebrations and that they could count on church support for their community. While imagining this significant event for the villagers, Philip found great comfort and pleasure in his memories of going to church with his family and neighbours. These comforting thoughts lessened his unease with all the bewildering sights and sounds on the unfamiliar dock. Philip felt his personal connection to God and the solid foundation that the church gave him. This connection and foundation was a gift he needed for the long voyage ahead.

Despite the new and less corrupt Lutheran religious leaders, the rise of the merchant class, the increased dependence on trade, and the support of the ruling Landgrave, the peasant farmers of Hesse struggled to provide the basic necessities of life. The land surrounding Eberstadt and Auerbach was not ideal for farming, which created a constant threat to their subsistence on a grain based diet. Any disruption of supply of grain from weather, increased taxes, and increasing populations made life very difficult and expensive. Often these disruptions created crises of hopeless poverty, disease, and starvation. These disruptions of poverty, starvation, and disease became the norm for farmers, merchants, and tradesmen during the Thirty Years War (1618-1648).

The Thirty Years War were known as the most horrifying and destructive in German history. Over these thirty years, religious and political conflicts provoked invasions into Hesse by Bohemian, Danish, Swedish, and French armies. As each relentless army invaded, they pillaged the countryside of wood, wildlife, and grains; they looted homes of food, belongings, livestock, and trade goods, and they committed indescribable torture and death on the Hessian people. Entire villages disappeared.

For those living in Eberstadt and surrounding areas, these invasions of armies and marauding soldiers forced many citizens to move within the seemingly safe walls of the city of Darmstadt; however, many citizens chose to stay and protect their homes and villages. In 1620, the Bohemians marched through Darmstadt and moved south to Eberstadt where the villagers tried to block their entry to the village. The villagers' efforts were to no avail, the army murdered, plundered, and ravaged.[12] Moreover, over these thirty years, Mother Nature frequently took her toll; severe cold and subsequent crop failures intensified the devastation. To escalate an already miserable existence, the plague swept through cities, towns, and villages ensuring death loomed in every household. No village or citizen was spared the effects of crushing armies or from nature's cruelties. Most peasants lived lives of despair.

In 1644, the misery of thirty years of war was ending. It was also about the time that Philip's grandfather Thomas Wiemer was born, most likely in Dusseldorf.[13] As an infant, Thomas was not only exposed to the common causes of infant death, but he also had to be kept safe from the devastations of war. The Swedes and the French just swept through Darmstadt, and now there was civil war between the Hessen states of Kassel and Darmstadt. As Philip thought of his grandfather's life as a young man, he wondered how he coped in the midst of a war. "Was he expected or pressured to join the army? How often was his life in danger? Were any family members injured or did anyone die? Did they have enough food?" However, for most of his youth, Thomas experienced relatively peaceful but active surroundings. The activity was aimed at rebuilding cities and villages and reviving farms and trade after three decades of war. Sometime near 1680, Thomas moved from Dusseldorf to Eberstadt, Hesse. In 1645, the population of Eberstadt was about 350. Peace was short lived in Hesse. This time war was against the Dutch (1672-1678), and Eberstadt was in the path of many armies. Thomas was subjected to the distress of war yet again. During this war, the French burned the Auerbach castle and the celebrated Lorsch Abbey was destroyed. Despite the plundering and constant threat of death, Thomas persevered.

His perseverance payed off. About 1678, Thomas married Ottilia. Their son George was born soon after their marriage. In 1680, Thomas received permission from the Landgrave to renovate and manage the Eschollmühle, a watermill in Eberstadt which was destroyed during the Thirty Years War and rebuilt in 1645.[14] Thomas saw an opportunity to build a good life for himself as a newly married man starting a family. Millers in Hesse made a good living and were prominent men in the community. Millers provided a critical function; they turned grain into flour. This good living was relative to most citizens struggling under heavy taxes and the harsh rule of Lords of the Manors.

The Eschollmühle at Eberstadt was located near the large meadows called Eschell. The mill was a collection of buildings built in the style of a country equestrian farm. The Eschollmüle consisted of a stable, riding area, pigsty, oil press mill, and grain mill. In 1686, on the large two storey main building, Thomas had the beautiful form of a 'life tree' carved into the main posts.[15] The mill used water from a brook called the Hetterbach, a tributary of the Modau River that originates in the Odenwald Mountains. Water from this brook came under the building creating the power needed to turn the massive stone grinders. 1n 1684, as a concerned businessman, Thomas objected to the petition of Hans Georg Frolich to build a ship mill at Erfelden, southwest of Eberstadt.[16]

Fig. 3. Copper Etching of Eberstadt Eschollmuhle 1767 by Heinrich Philipp Bossler. Inv. No. HO 686. Painting by Georg Adam Eger. With Permission of Hessisches Landsmuseum Darmstadt.

1681 was encouraging for Thomas and his wife Ottilia, not only as a Miller, but also because it was likely the year their son Adam Wiemer was born. In 1682, their daughter Christina was born, and in 1683 a son Johann Wendel was born. Two years later their son Daniel Melchoir arrived, and in 1687 another son Philip arrived.[17] Assurance of a stable income was secure for Thomas, but not assurance of a long life. On 12 Feb 1690, at the young age of forty six, Thomas died of the 'fever'. At his death, he was still grieving the loss of his wife Ottilia who died 3 Jan 1690 at the age of thirty eight and his youngest two-year-old son Philip who died in November 1689.[18] Thomas, Ottlia, and Philip died within three months of each other. It is likely they suffered from an infectious disease. Their children Adam just nine, Christina, eight, Wendel, seven and Daniel Melchoir barely five were left on their own. Thomas' brother Dieter inherited the Eschollmühle in 1693.[19] Perhaps Dieter Wiemer took care of his brother's orphan children.

To help the family, perhaps Adam worked at the Eschollmüle that his father Thomas renovated and his Uncle Dieter inherited. Gaining skill and knowledge in the milling trade was something Adam pursued. As a young man in his early twenties working hard to pursue a trade, he spent time at the tavern. During one of his evenings out, he and Elizabeth Dorothea Rau had a sexual encounter after drinking wine. This encounter was the reason they gave to marry in July 1706.[20] Adam and Elizabeth Dorothea had two sons while living in Eberstadt. George was born in 1707 and Daniel was born in 1708. Late in 1708, at the age of twenty-five, Adam moved to Auerbach to work in the mill. From 1708-1721, he and Elizabeth Dorothea had three more sons, Peter, Jacob, and Johannes.[21]

By 1722, Adam and Elizabeth had a family of five sons, George, Daniel, Peter, Jacob, and Johannes. Adam, now thirty nine years old, had the security of his work in the mill. This security lessened the burden of a large family. Adam and Elizabeth's sixth son, Philip Wiemer, was born 22 Dec 1722 and baptized in the mountain church 26 Dec 1722.[22] In 1726, with five older brothers, four-year-old Philip finally had a sister. Anna Elizabeth was born 17 Jan 1726 and baptized at the mountain church 20 Jan, 1726.[23]

Fig. 4. Die Bergkirche Auerbach (Mountain Church) Romanesque Church Door

Fig. 5. Die Bergkirche Auerbach (Mountain Church) Church Choir

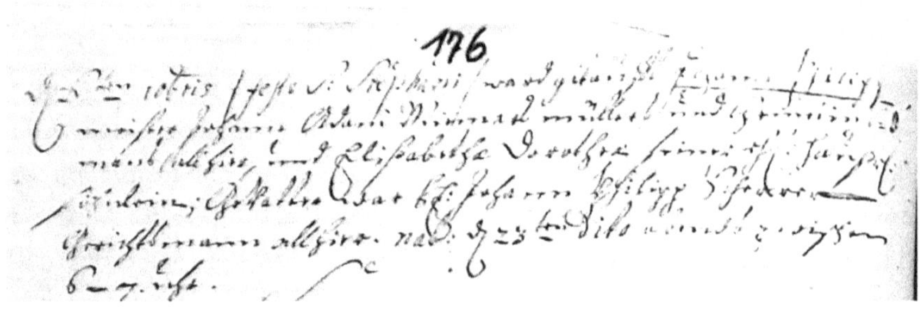

176

Fig. 6. Baptismal Record of Johannes Philip Wiemer, 26 Dec 1722. Courtesy of Die Bergkirche, Auerbach, Hesse.

Fig. 7. Baptismal Font at Die Bergkirche, Auerbach. The 1608 Bergkirch Auerbach baptismal font is carved from red sandstone in the renaissance form of a shell. Courtesy of Die Bergkirche, Auerbach, Hesse.

A short time after his sister was born and at the young age of seven, Philip suffered a great loss. His mother, Elizabeth Dorothea Rau, died in March 1729. Perhaps she suffered a difficult pregnancy, a problematic childbirth, postnatal complications, or perhaps she suffered from an epidemic infection such as typhus. Whatever the cause, Elizabeth Dorothea died a young woman. Adam now had seven children; George and Daniel were old enough to look after themselves, but the other four ranged in age from twelve to two. To be married again was perhaps Adam's wish, but with four young children it was also a necessity. In the little mountain church at Auerbach on 22 Sept 1729, Adam married Elizabeth Barbara Muetz, daughter of Conrad Muetz.[24] Adam was forty eight and Elizabeth Barbara was thirty one.

Philip remembered the death of his mother in ways that seven year old boys do. He understood that his mother was not ever coming back, and he was often preoccupied with thoughts of what had caused her to die. He hated seeing all his friends with their mothers, especially when these mothers did something warm and kind. He missed his own mother. Now he had to grow used to his new step mother. Just as he became content with the comforts of his new mother, he had a long succession of new brothers and sisters. The first was a little brother Johannes Valentin born in 1730, then Anna Barbara in 1732, and Anna Margretha in 1733, Johannes Mattheus in 1736, Johannes Mattheus about 1737, and finally Anna Catharina in 1739.[25] Philip now had seven brothers and four sisters. He remembered very well when he lost his little brother Mattheus in 1736. Philip was fourteen and Mattheus an infant. The Wiemers were a large family of twelve children.

Now, standing on the dock at Rotterdam surrounded with constant commotion and too many strangers, Philip missed his father, step mother, brothers, and sisters. When thoughts of never seeing them again seeped in, he felt the ache in his body and the tight sting in his chest. He wobbled and swayed a bit. He held Catrina's arm. Thoughts of reaching the dock across the great sea flashed through his mind. "Would that dock be like this one? Would his family be safe? Would people be kind? Would he be able to find shelter and food? Would their land be good? How many acres could he clear? How many chances would there be to build his dreams?"

To calm his escalating anxiety and relieve the pressing weight of responsibility, Philip turned his thoughts to early springs in Auerbach when the almond trees were blooming. He thought about the long sunny summers that were perfect for the rows and rows of grape vines spread across the mountain slopes, or the way the breeze encouraged the soft sway of the grain in the fields. Many times he watched the farmers unload that same grain at his father's mill. He thought about all the activity in the village square, a place where children played and adults talked about business or shared local gossip, and sometimes the village Bürgermeister (village master) read important news, new laws, or more taxes. He remembered how exciting it was to go to the market where he carefully inspected the carpenters', blacksmiths', hat makers', and silversmiths' tables. Now, he thought he could still smell the wagonloads of trout and salmon fresh from the Rhine.

Here at the dock, there were some of those familiar smells. But now, a grown man with responsibilities, Philip could no longer just think about sunny days and wandering around the market. His whole world and all that was important to him were here now. His small children needed him. Catrina needed him. He remembered when he was a young man at the market or the village square, and how captivated and fascinated he was with the young women. He and his brothers hoped there would be some young women who noticed their admiring glances. As a young man, it was always exciting to be noticed by young women! Philip knew that special day would come, but he had to make enough money to convince the village council that he could support a family.

Being the sixth son of Adam Wiemer, Philip knew he would not inherit much, if any, of his father's property. He might receive a small amount of money when he got married.[26] He often thought, "I'll never save enough for my own farm. Even if I did have my own place, farming here is difficult. The soil is pitiful and stony, and if I do harvest a good crop most of the profits go to paying the Landgrave's tithes, or I spend a lot of time working on roads, carting grain, and hauling wood. All that work just to help with tax and service debts of the village! Even with a good harvest, there might not be enough grain to sustain us to the next harvest." Some of the farmers Philip knew worked a second job as a tradesman, or their wives or children spun wool or made flax thread to make extra money.[27] Exasperated, Philip thought, "What's the sense of it all! There was always something, bad weather, lousy soil, taxes, and the threat of war! Or heaven forbid, I could be impressed into the army, which was common in Hesse for centuries!"[28]

Philip spent a lot of time thinking about his options as a young man wanting to get married and start his own family. "What options did he have? How could he be successful? What was standing in his way? Was there a trade he liked? Would there be enough work as a tradesman? No, as a tradesman I'd have to travel to different towns all the time![29] What about a sheep farmer? Sheep meant more taxes to graze them. I even need permission to own them! What about a vineyard? I still need to rent land, and there's not much available. Then there's always the weather!" Sometimes an alternative choice popped into his mind and stuck as an easy solution to all his exasperation. This choice allowed him to dream big without tax, land, or weather restrictions to smother his dreams. Philip thought, "I'll take the risk and go to America where I can buy my own land and be a successful farmer![30] My wife and family, everyone I know and some I don't, would someday consider me 'in a good way'! Right now, I need to work and earn enough money to marry and start a family."

That special day, when a young woman noticed his admiring glances, came while his mind was packed full of dreams. Philip married Maria Catharine (Catrina) Leser and their daughter Elizabetha Catharina was baptized on 29 Sept 1752 at Auerbach. Christina, the sister of Adam Wiemer and Philip's Aunt, was her godmother.[31]

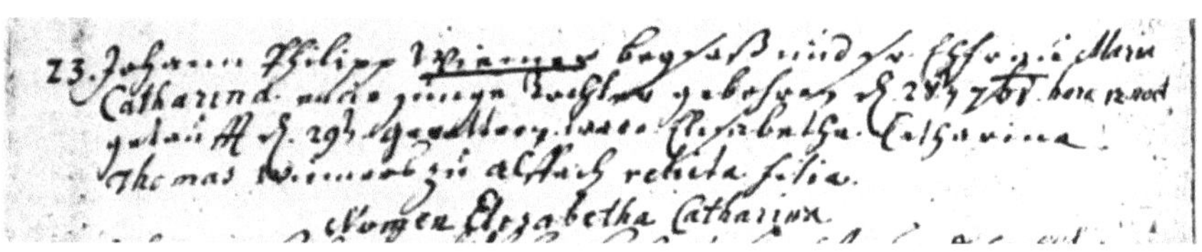

Fig. 8. Baptism Record of Elizabetha Catharina Wiemer, 29 Sept 1752.
Courtesy of Die Bergkirche, Auerbach, Hesse

All of Philip's thoughts about making a good living suddenly became more urgent. Philip and Catrina talked often about raising a family and wanting to provide for themselves and their children. They wanted to know that every year they would have more than just enough to eat. During one conversation, Philip asked Catrina what she thought about travelling to America to make a life there. Catrina gasped and answered with a flurry of questions, "What do you know about America? How will we get there and where will we live? Will the children be safe? Will we be safe? Do we have enough money? What about our parents?" Philip was certain he knew every answer in detail and had reliable sources for each answer. For decades, there were settlers who made the journey to America and who wrote home to give details of their hardship and success. These hardships often scared many into abandoning thoughts of this long, difficult, and dangerous journey. There were also recruiting pamphlets circulating in villages and cities throughout Germany that provided citizens with facts about America and about the journey. The recruiters wrote about the size of ships, the generous space between decks, and Pennsylvania's low taxation, rich soil, unlimited hunting, and fabulous weather. Philip remembered spending several hours talking to a recruiter for the shipping company of John Henry Keppele of Philadelphia. The recruiter recently visited Auerbach.[32]

Philip was very cautious of this recruiter, especially given the dreadful reputation many of them had for swindling innocent folks. This reputation earned them the name 'Soul-Sellers' or 'Newlanders' because they had been to America and returned to recruit countrymen. Often they offered Germans credit on passage in return for redeeming their debt in America through labor for a specified amount of time.[33] Eventually, Philip told the recruiter, "I'll give you our decision when you return from visiting villages south of Auerbach." After countless conversations, much exploration, investigation, and careful consideration, Philip and Catrina decided on taking the risk and making their life in America. Philip and Catrina not only weighed all the facts, warnings, and even some rumors, but they also weighed the exciting opportunities and the joy that comes with success in America, success that was especially good for their children.

To accomplish their plans, Catrina said "We need all our strength and all our caution and care! And, we must pledge to each other to commit to our purpose and to support each other." After making their pledge, they knew they needed the support of their parents. So, they brought their information, which included details of the extraordinary opportunities, to their parents.

When Philip and Catrina approached Philip's father Adam, Adam shared stories he heard over the years about people's experiences on their journey to Rotterdam, to England, and across the great sea. Many of these stories were of extreme hardship, poverty, disease, starvation, servitude, and shipwreck.[34] Adam particularly remembered the great migration of Germans to America in 1708 and 1709. He insisted that the reason they left Germany was simply because they were poor and hungry.[35]

Adam talked about a book that was distributed through the area. Everyone wanted to either read or listen to someone else read this book. He said, "They called it the Golden Book because it had gold letters on the front.[36] In those days, everyone thought that America was the answer to their constant prayers! In America, they were free; they owned their land and prospered!" He mentioned several people who went to America in 1709. "There was Adam Hartle Sr. He lived at Heppenheim, only fourteen kilometres south of Auerbach, and he was married at the little mountain church at Auerbach. There was also Johannes Barnhardt and his brother Jost who lived near Reichelsheim, only forty two kilometres west of Auerbach."[37] Adam tried to tell his son and daughter-in-law stories that would make their journey easier and not too expensive.

Philip and Catrina thought a lot about the cost of travelling to America. To collect enough money, they needed to sell all of their belongings and hope that Philip's father Adam could give them some money. They calculated the sailing time down the Rhine, across the North Sea and the great sea to America; they also allowed for time spent waiting at anchor for the best weather to sail, or on shore waiting for a sea worthy ship to board. In their calculations, they included their need for food and shelter, especially while in Rotterdam where they heard many people spent most of their funds leaving little or nothing to spend for the hardest part of the journey.[38] Their time in Rotterdam could be risky.

After all their calculations regarding the distance of the journey, they had to decide on the best time to leave. Philip considered the recruiter's information, the time of year when travel over land and water would be easiest, and when the weather might be most favorable. Philip decided to leave in May. Hopefully, they would arrive in Philadelphia in September or October. This arrival date gave them enough time to find a place to settle and build shelter for the winter.

If they left in May, they avoided the bad late fall and early winter sailing weather that Philip heard so much about. And, in late spring, ships sailed to England and America every two weeks, usually with good winds. Most importantly, Captains did not fill the ship's hull with passengers jammed together like fish, and they provided passengers with decent food and clean water.[39]

Philip finally collected enough money. He sold all of their belongings, and he sold his portion of inheritance to his brother.[40] His father also gave them some money. Philip was confident that he could cover their expenses. He met with the recruiter and agreed to the terms of the company. He signed the agreement and paid half of the cost. He would pay the remaining amount when they reached Rotterdam.

The recruiter instructed him, "You must be at Gernsheim the second Monday in May and contact the river boatman who works with John Henry Keppele."

Another cost Philip paid were state fees for his manumission. Manumission, or permission to leave the state, was difficult to get because most rulers were reluctant to allow their citizens to emigrate. Rulers wanted to keep their citizens so they could contribute to the growth of the state and to ensure there was a tax revenue. Not only did Philip require a manumission certificate, but he also required documentation of his birth and his good character which he received from the Pastor at the mountain church at Auerbach. This documentation was his 'passport'.[41] Once Philip received his manumission certificate, they were free to leave the state. And, he had his 'passport' which they needed at the border.

May came quickly, after the usual early spring in Auerbach. Philip, Catrina, and their children were ready. With commitment and preparation that took months, they packed basic supplies into two large linen knapsacks that Philip's mother made. Each knapsack was soaked in linseed oil for waterproofing and had leather shoulder straps and several buckles. They filled the sacks with one pot, one kettle, cups, bowls, spoons and knives, soap, combs, one extra skirt, shirts, pants, socks, one extra pair of leather shoes, one extra warm shawl, and they strapped three small woolen blankets to the top of the sack. Philip added a large empty hemp snapsack to carry provisions they would buy at Rotterdam. Catrina added dried fish, meat, and fruit, waxed cheese, rye bread, baked biscuits, oatmeal, and two leather costrels with 1 gallon of wine and one with water; there was enough to last three weeks. She would ration these precious provisions. Philip made sure his clay pipe and tobacco were safely wrapped inside. Their plan was to buy the larger items needed in America. Travelling light was important, and Philip did not want their belongings lost or stolen.[42] Packing was the easy part of leaving Auerbach

The most difficult part of leaving was saying goodbye. Philip and Catrina anguished at the mere thought of saying goodbye. Knowing there was no hope of ever seeing their family again fueled their agony. When this goodbye came, it carved a deep bed of grief in their hearts and was a burden they always bore. Even later in their lives, often this empty, wretched space emerged and did so until they died. There was also this empty and agonizing space in the hearts of their parents, brothers, sisters, cousins, aunts and uncles.

Philip's father Adam took them by wagon as far as Gernsheim, about fifteen kilometres northwest of Auerbach. At Gernsheim they paid for space on a Scow to take them down the Rhine to Rotterdam. The riverboat man would arrange for their clearance at the Dutch border. He was an agent for the shipping company of John Henry Keppele and worked closely with the recruiter.[43] As Philip and his father parted, Philip grasped his father's hand and looking down said, "I will write home as soon as we arrive in America. I will let you know of our safe arrival and our continuing health." This promise was the only way he could think of to ease the grief of goodbye.[44] Adam hugged Catrina and each of the children and turned to walk to the wagon.

That afternoon, Philip and Catrina boarded the Scow and settled in the small cabin space near the squared bow. Keeping the children distracted from their parents' obvious emotions was challenging. As Philip sat, he hoped they had enough money to sail safely and to get what they needed when they arrived in America. He counted 500 florins or £50, a small fortune for Philip. From everything he read and the advice he received, 200 florins was enough for their travel to Philadelphia. Philip and Catrina's fare down the Rhine was 16 florins. Their sea fare was 120 florins. Mattheus and Catharina, being under five, travelled for free, but Elizabeth had to pay a fare.[45] They had about twenty nine pounds left for supplies and travel when they reached Philadelphia. Philip packed the money and his documents in a hidden linen belt sewn into the waist of his pants. He gave several florins to Catrina in case his was lost or they were separated.

As the boat cast off, Philip and Catrina sat close to each other. With wide but stiff smiles, they gripped hands and remembered their pledge to support each other. With good winds, this 600 kilometre part of the journey could take several weeks.[46] While Catrina sat with the children, she looked out the small window beside her. She watched the waves splash the front of boat; as she turned to look back, she watched the shoreline slowly change. It would be a few weeks before she stopped looking back.

Fig. 9. Example of a Sailing Scow. Photo courtesy of the Alexander Turnbull Library, New Zealand. Photographer unkown on Wikimedia Commons

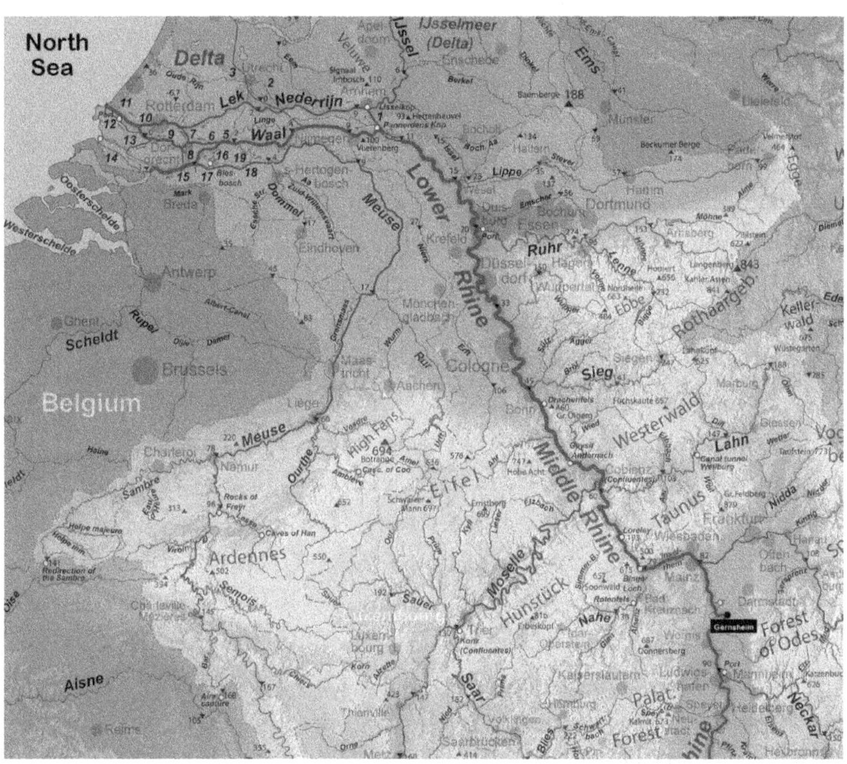

Fig. 10. Map of the Rhine River. Philip and Catrina likely started their journey at Gernsheim. Adapted from map courtesy of W. Wasser on Wikimedia Commons. https://creativecommons.org/licenses/by-sa/3.0/deed.en

CHAPTER TWO
The Journey to America (1755)

The Scow hadn't sailed far before it rounded the first of many bends in the river. The winds were good on the first two days, and the river's northerly current pulled them along the wide river. The familiar plains of the Upper Rhine Valley were comforting. Early on the third day, Philip was on deck, and he sighted the spires of an enormous red church on his left. To his right was a smaller river emptying into the Rhine.

The Captain described the scene, "We've reached the city of Mainz. The river here is 450 metres wide, and the smaller river on the right is the Main. The large church is the 700 year old Catholic Cathedral. It's red because it's made of sandstone." He continued, grumbling "This is the first of many stops to load cargo and pay our toll at the customs houses. You know, this constant stopping and waiting is what takes so much time to sail this river! They'll check the boat through when it's convenient for them!"[47] Abruptly, he added, "Your customs duties are included in the price of your ticket, unless they've increased the price." Catrina and the children came on deck and watched as the Captain maneuvered the boat into the small harbour. This was the first place that was new to all of them.

After almost an hour on deck in the cold wind, Philip was getting impatient. Shouting at the Captain, he said, "There's good wind, we're wasting time here. What are they waiting for?" Philip waited a few more hours on deck and then went back into the cabin. It wasn't until the afternoon of the next day that the boat made its way out of the harbour and back onto the river. The wind wasn't as good today, but it was warmer so the family spent the day on deck. Not far along, Philip noticed the landscape changing. The plains of the Upper Rhine Valley disappeared, and they were travelling through a deep valley. The hills on both sides of the river rose almost 200 metres. On one side of the river, vineyards swept up the steep slopes almost to the top, and on the other side were flourishing green forested slopes. They sailed slowly as the river carved a crooked path through the valley. Philip could see that they were approaching another harbour. As they got closer, he saw a large crane next to the dock. The crane, built in the fifteenth century, was evidence of the Rhine River having been a significant waterway in the history of transporting goods from the North Sea to the interior. In the distance, Philip saw a large white tower sitting on an island in the middle of the river. (The Mouse Tower). On the far side, on the steep slope, he saw a castle. They had reached Bingen. In four days, they only travelled about eighty kilometres.

On day five, they continued their crooked path through the deep valley. As they passed the town of Bacharach, the river narrowed. Philip could see the ruins of an old church on the slope of a hill (Werner's Chapel) and a very large castle very near the top of the mountain (Stahleck Castle). While Philip was studying the surroundings, Catrina spent most of the morning next to a large basin washing herself and the children. She was thankful for the hot water. In one of their pots, she was able to heat water over a small fire that the Captain lit on sand that filled the top of a brick frame. When they finished washing, Catrina sat outside with the children absorbing the heat as the sun's rays slipped through the clouds. She loved the way the breeze and clouds made shadows slide along the hills. Whenever she was on deck, the scenes of small towns, boats, barges, vineyards, trees, and rocks amazed her. She stared as long as the moving boat allowed. As she turned to watch the scenes fade away, she ached for home.

Their progress was slow as the Captain navigated around cargo barges, shallow areas, rocks, and the bends in the river. Soon they reached the town of Sankt Goar where they stopped again. As they approached the harbour on the west side of the river, Philip, taking occasional puffs from his pipe, stared up at the enormous castle (Rheinfels Castle) perched on the top of the hill above the town. With Catrina beside him wrapped in her woolen shawl, he stared at the huge fortress and said, "It looks like those ruins will tumble right off that hill into the river!"

With wide eyes she said, "I've never seen a castle that size!"

Philip looked at her and nodded, "I think we see a castle at least four times a day; this one is the biggest of them all! And, I think every time we see a castle, we have to stop so the Captain can pay the river toll! I often see him going into the customs house near the dock. That must be how the Lords of the castles make all their money." They moored at the dock for most of the day. Catrina set out portions of dried meat, fruit, cheese, bread, and wine for lunch and an early supper. Little Catharina played on her mother's lap with her little wooden doll whose name was 'Poppy'. Philip carved the doll for her before they left Auerbach; Catrina added a red linen cape with a hood. Elizabeth and Mattheus sat and enjoyed their fruit and bread.

Very soon after supper, the Captain requested that they stay in the cabin as he navigated past the narrows. He announced, "The river gets very narrow here (130 metres). It's fast as we pass through the rapids and by the large rocky hill overhanging the river (Loreley Rock). You'll see the rock on your right as we leave Sankt Goar. Please stay in the cabin until I tell you it's okay to leave!" While in the cabin, they felt the pull of the river and the roll of waves. Philip held Catharina close to his chest while he held tight to a secure ring on the wall. Catrina held tight to the edge of the bunk with Elizabeth and Mattheus next to her. They moved fast over the next few kilometres. Several hours later, they were allowed to come on deck and were surprised to see that they were no longer sailing through the valley. They moved much slower now. It was pleasant to see open space again. The hills were much lower and the river much wider. Late in the day, just before sunset, they saw the town of Koblenz. It sprawled along the river's edge for a long way. Near the end of the town was the Moselle River emptying into the Rhine. The Captain steered next to the dock and watched as men secured the boat. Philip and Catrina sat on deck for a while admiring the fortress (Ehrenbreitstein Fortress) high above the opposite side of the river. "What a view they must have from there," Philip announced. Happily, they spent the night at Koblenz. It had been a long and stressful day. They found it so much easier to sleep when the boat wasn't rolling and swaying.

In the morning, the sun shone on the grape vines that lined the slopes of the hills behind the town. It was a quiet morning on the river. Catrina knew they were going through their provisions too fast, so she rationed the cheese and bread at breakfast. To ease their hunger, Catrina often gave the children an extra biscuit. The Captain did have some provisions like wine, beer, salted pork and fish, peas, and biscuits. They had to pay extra for any of those provisions. Philip and Catrina would have loved a huge breakfast in the familiar and comfortable surroundings of home. But, at least they had food, and they were moving closer to their hopes of freedom and their own land. They had been on the river for eight days and travelled about 250 kilometres. The wind was soft today, but the stiff current dragged the boat northward at a steady speed. They passed several small towns.

The most eye catching was the town of Bonn. They approached the town on the west side of the river and of course sailed into the harbour to pay the toll. Philip talked to the Captain while he waited for the boat to be secured. Philip was curious about the age of many of the towns, especially the ones with the enormous castles.

The Captain explained, "Some of the larger towns, like this one, were built by the Romans and conquered by the Frankish Kings. The towns on this river were centres of trade and important for military control for many centuries. With all the side rivers, goods could be transported from France and the Netherlands as well as Germany." Philip knew well what the Captain was talking about. He remembered all of the goods, like salt and grain, which came to Auerbach from towns along the river.

On day eleven it was nearing the end of May and still chilly, especially in the evening. They needed their woolen blankets. The next morning, as they came around a bend in the river, they were still several kilometres from Cologne. From this distance rising into the sky, Philip saw twin spires of a church. This, he was told, was the great Catholic Cathedral of St. Peter. As the boat came closer to Cologne, the size of the cathedral was overwhelming. Straining his eyes at the monumental church, he noticed there was a crane at the very top. He learned later that construction of the cathedral began in the thirteenth century and it was never finished. The traffic of small and large boats at this harbour was also overwhelming. It took several hours to dodge boats on their way into the harbour. While at the harbour, the Wiese family with two children boarded.[48] They were also travelling to Rotterdam and then to America. The Captain declared, "I've taken thousands of families up this river to Rotterdam over the past twenty years, some I've even taken back down! They all wanted the same thing, freedom from regulations, land of their own, and a chance out of poverty." The cabin was already small and suddenly became much smaller with four more people. Even with this now crowded space, Philip and Catrina felt heartened because they knew they were more than half way to Rotterdam.

Since leaving Cologne, the river widened, the land was flat, and large meadows lined the banks. Over the next five days, they wound around the bends in the river. Sometimes feeling confused regarding which direction they were sailing, Philip depended on the rise and setting of the sun to maintain some sense of north, south, east, and west. Or he would come on deck at night to check the position of the North Star. After the sixteenth day, the Captain announced that they had reached Emmerich and the end of the Rhine. They had travelled about 550 kilometres. Now, they would travel on the Waal River into Rotterdam. Everyone went ashore and into the border office. The Dutch authorities inspected Philip's passport and letter of character. The Captain gave the border authorities the name of John Henry Keppele as the shipper who was providing passage for everyone.[49]

With only two more days of travel, Philip and Catrina spent the days and evenings planning their stay in Rotterdam. They talked about the provisions they needed to buy and how they would arrange to pay the final amount on their contract and have their names inserted on the passenger list. The Wiese family were eager to join their conversations and add important information or object to certain plans. Philip and Catrina were grateful to have others to share their excitement and their fears.

It was a sunny morning that welcomed them to Rotterdam. They spent the morning on deck scanning the many boats on the river. As they got closer to Rotterdam, they saw boats of all sizes, each with a purpose. There were barges, scows, sloops, merchant ships, some moving others anchored. And there were plenty of jolly boats being rowed between and beside the ships.[50] Philip leaned on the side of their Scow, straining his eyes for the best view. He was fixated on the progression of vessels. Mattheus had a chance to see all the little boats when finally they caught sight of their first sea faring ships. Their masts were perfectly straight, and enormous ropes were everywhere seeming to hang from nowhere. Each mast flew a flag.

Philip turned to Catrina while straining his eyes, "I wonder which one will be ours?" Mattheus squealed as the boats passed by. Groups of men, all sizes and shapes, bustled on decks and on the wharf moving wooden boxes and barrels on and off the ships while others moved up and down the wharf with carts and wagons. With an occasional break to view the passage of ships, Philip and Catrina spent the afternoon packing their knapsacks with their belongings and the remains of their provisions. Mattheus and Elizabeth tried to help, and little Catharina sat on the bunk clinging to Poppy. Before leaving the Scow, they spent time heating water for washing. They weren't sure how long it would be before they enjoyed hot water and a wash.

Philip, Catrina, the children, and the Wiese family came ashore late in the afternoon. On their way to find the Inn that the Captain suggested, they all weaved their way around sailors and merchants, past wooden crates and casks, wicker baskets, stone crocks, bales, sacks, and ropes wound and piled high. Catrina held Catharina close and Philip held the children's hands while they trudged through the narrow streets. The houses were two storied and close together. The streets were spotlessly clean. Catrina even noticed a young woman with her bucket and brush scrubbing the street. They finally reached a plain tall building tucked in the bend in the street. They knocked at the door. An elderly Dutch woman greeted them. She beckoned them inside with the entire top half of her body and her broad arm swinging in the direction of the hallway.

As she moved toward the stairs, she looked at Philip and said, "I'm Ingrid the Innkeeper, and I'm an agent for Mr. John Keppele's company.[51] Are there just five of you?"

"No, there is the Wiese family as well. We came from southern Germany and have been over two weeks coming up the Rhine."

"Ah, she said, you must be on your way to America! Well, follow me upstairs to your room." When they reached the stairs, Philip heard music and glanced into the large room on his left.

Windows surrounded the tables along the edges, and smoke filled the room with a thin haze. A man was playing a violin, and several men and women were seated at the wooden tables, each clutching a tankard. In the corner, children played with their dog. Philip and Catrina followed Ingrid up the stairs to two rooms at the end of the hall.

As he reached the end of the hall, Philip thought, "Hmm good, it's far enough away from the noise of the tavern."

Ingrid interrupted his thoughts, "I charge two florins per day for each room and that includes one meal at lunch, usually cheese, bread, cold meat, and cider."

Catrina dropped her knapsack and laid Catharina on the small bed at the back of the room. Mattheus and Elizabeth lay beside her. Philip and Catrina thanked Ingrid while closing the door. Too exhausted to do anything, they snacked a bit on some biscuits and dried fruit and the next thing they noticed was sunlight beaming through the small window. They had slept for more than twelve hours.

Philip looked out the window to make sure that they really were in Rotterdam; he hadn't been dreaming. Steering Catrina and the children to the door, he stated "We have to get to the wharf and find the shipping company's office. We can find out what ships are sailing to America and when they leave."

As they left the room, they met the Wiese family, and everyone filed down the stairs. They made their way through the narrow streets and wound through the commotion on the wharf. Along one walkway, there was a large sign on the door of one building, it read: 'John Henry Keppele, Merchant and Shipper, Philadelphia'. Philip stopped after seeing the image of a large sailing ship under the printed words. "This must be what we want. It will be a good start anyway," he thought. They all followed him into the room and stood in front of a small desk. A clerk was seated behind the desk sorting two mounds of papers.

The clerk looked halfway up, one eye on the papers and one eye on Philip. "Can I help you?" he asked in Dutch.

Philip didn't speak Dutch or English, so he answered the only way he knew how. He pointed to Catrina, the children, and to the Wiese family and made waving motions with his hands as if to mimic a ship sailing on the sea. He added the word America as best as he could. This was the first of many awkward and frustrating communication moments. He handed the clerk the receipt for the payment made to the recruiter at Auerbach.

"Oh I see, you want to go to America," the clerk said.

"Yes," Philip said, nodding his head vigorously.

After leaving for a minute to retrieve a translator, the clerk returned and began a long description of the ship, the voyage, the cost, and the contract. "There's a ship sailing in nine days for Gosport, England and then to Philadelphia. The ship is called a Snow. She's a 190 ton vessel and has a large capacity to carry provisions and emigrants. The ship's name is the Neptune and the Master is Captain George Smith.[52] Usually, the voyage to Gosport takes about eight days. The ship stops in Gosport to go through British customs and to take on provisions. The voyage across the sea takes about eleven weeks.[53]

Philip continued to nod his head as the translator related the clerk's description. When he heard the word Pennsylvania, Philip's shoulders dropped and his breathing slowed. Catrina held Catharina's and Mattheus' hands while tilting one ear in the translator's direction.

The clerk listed the items in Philip's contract: "Your contract includes provisions for twelve weeks and passage for two adults on the Neptune from Rotterdam to Philadelphia at 60 florins each. Your children at 2 ½ years and five years old travel free. The older one pays a fare. Your quarters are "tween decks", and you are guaranteed one bunk for each adult 1.8 metres long by 0.6 metres wide; the height of the deck is two metres. There are no separate areas for washing. You're allowed one bag per adult and one bag of extra provisions. We don't want you to bring casks or trunks onboard as we can't guarantee their safety, and they are stored in the hold so you won't be able to access them.[54] You have use of the fireplace on deck for cooking from seven in the morning until six in the evening, weather permitting. There's no smoking and no swearing allowed. Lanterns are out after seven in the evening. Passengers are allowed on deck in groups and at assigned times for purposes other than cooking.[55] The Captain will let you know how this time is shared among groups of passengers. There are slop pots located on each side of the deck. Passengers take turns emptying them overboard every morning. The companion hatch is closed when the weather is bad; otherwise, it is open for light and fresh air. The passenger deck floor is cleaned once a week with vinegar. You're required to follow all of the Captains orders at all times. If you do not, you will be arrested and thrown in jail when we reach America. Here's a list of provisions."

Monday	Tuesday	Wednesday	Thursday	Friday	Saturday	Sunday
Barley and Sryup 1 quart of beer 2 quarts of water	1 lb of wheat flour 1 quart of beer 2 quarts of water	1 lb of bacon with peas 1 quart of beer 2 quarts of water	1 lb of beef boiled with rice 1 quart of beer 2 quarts of water	1 lb of wheat flour and 1 lb of butter 1 quart of beer 2 quarts of water	1 lb of Bacon 1 lb of cheese and 6 lbs of bread for the whole week	1 lb beef boiled with rice 1 quart of beer 2 quarts of water Brandy if desired

Fig 11. Hope Brothers Shipping Company Menu 1752. This provisions contract is an example of the guidelines for contracts during the second half of the Eighteenth-century.[56]

"That's the contract, the clerk barked. Do you have any questions?"

Raising his eyebrows, Philip turned to the translator and asked, "Is the water fresh and stored in clean casks? Is the meat fresh and not over salted? Is there a doctor onboard?"

Catrina nodded, agreeing with his questions. These questions were important to Philip because he heard that one of the greatest dangers was to die of starvation or illness on the voyage. He also heard that the Captains and agents were less than honest when providing fresh and sufficient provisions.[57] He was being very cautious.

The clerk barked again, "Yes, the water is fresh, and the casks are cleaned before they are filled. We use only fresh meat that is lightly salted and recently packed in casks. There's no doctor, but many of our seaman know about common illnesses that occur while sailing, and they have experience treating minor injuries." He handed Philip a long and neatly folded piece of paper, "Here's one of our pamphlets that describes our services."

Pulling his pipe from his lips and pointing to a spot on the contract, Philip asked the clerk to write the answers to his questions. Then, Philip asked the translator to read the contract slowly and carefully. The translator told him that it contained everything Philip was told, nothing more and nothing less. Hesitating, Philip thought, "We've come this far. We can always turn back now. But, we want this chance. I've done all I can to keep everyone safe. I can only put my trust in these men and in God." Philip paid the clerk the remaining cost and signed the contract. After shaking his hand, the clerk told Philip that they must be at the wharf on Monday, June 16 with his contract, his documentation, and their belongings.

As the Wiese family dealt with the clerk, Philp and Catrina stood back and talked over their decision one last time. Catrina reminded Philip. "If we hold on to our faith in God and remain heedful, we'll be alright."

Standing tall and straight, Philip said, "Yes, God is our guiding light, and we are free travellers; we aren't travelling on credit! We can't be bought and sold!"[58]

After the Wiese family finished with the clerk, everyone left to go back to the Inn. On their way back, they stopped to look at the many food stands along the wharf and on some of the streets. They had time over the next nine days to find what they needed for a reasonable price. After deducting the 24 florins that their stay at the Inn cost, they only had 164 florins or about £16 left. They had to use some of the money they were saving for supplies at Philadelphia. These nine days at Rotterdam were expensive.

Over the next few days, Philip and Catrina visited with the Wiese family, rested, and took the children outside to play in the garden next to the Inn. They went for many walks and often had to find simple distractions to prevent paralyzing thoughts of home. The numerous simple distractions also helped to calm fearful thoughts about the ship and the sea that often brought on bouts of sweating, shaking, and shortness of breath. Catrina distracted herself with washing their few clothes, and Philip carved two small wooden spoons for Elizabeth and Catharina and a small boat for Mattheus.

On the Friday and Saturday before they were to sail, they went to the market not far from the Inn. They visited several merchants from London, France, Portugal, and Holland selling provisions, some looked a bit shady. Carefully and mindful of costs, they chose a variety of foods that kept for at least three months. Catrina also chose chamomile, sage, and lavender as medicinal herbs and wormwood to keep fleas away and rue to keep the mice away. On Sunday evening, Philip and Catrina packed all their clothing, pots, spoons, knives, bowls, and cups in their knapsacks. They purchased three extra woolen blankets for the wooden bunks and a small knotted rope bag to hang items off the floor, away from the rats and mice. In the extra linen snapsack they brought from home, Catrina sprinkled rue along the bottom and sides of the bag to keep the mice out. They packed several pounds of oatmeal, flour, salt, rice, raisins, dried apples, and dried meat, six loafs of rye bread, four pounds of cheese, biscuits, olive oil, and vinegar. They wrapped a two gallon stone cask of sauerkraut and a two gallon stone jug of cider and carefully placed them in each knapsack. They filled two one gallon leather costrels with fresh water and wrapped fresh tobacco in a pouch.

It was Monday June 16 when Philip, Catrina, Elizabeth, Mattheus, and Catharina left the Inn with the Wiesers and made their way to the wharf. Philip carried a knapsack on his back, the snapsack over one shoulder, and the two leather costrels over the other. Catrina carried Catharina close to her chest and a knapsack on her back. They carried all they owned and hopefully all that they needed for the next few months. With their heavy loads, they trudged through the city streets. They rounded a corner and caught sight of the wharf and the biggest crowd of people they had ever seen. There were hundreds of people, some standing and singing gospel songs, some weaving their way through the crowds, some sitting on a variety of different sizes and types of bags, and some with children, some alone.[59] Some were trying to sell goods to anyone who looked interested, even to those who were not interested. Sailors with knit or wide brimmed hats, short jackets, and baggy pants mingled in the crowd. Philip reached for the children's hands while juggling his load. Catrina held little Catharina tighter.

They walked toward the crowd and saw a very large ship with two masts and the British flag flying at the stern. They spotted a man at a table near the ship. People flocked around the man shouting and flapping their hands. On the table, Philip saw the sign of John Henry Keppele Shipping Company. They found a small opening in the crowd close to the table and stood still waiting for space in the lineup.

Through the noise of the crowd, Philip yelled in Catrina's ear, "I hope they're not all going with us on that ship!"

"Yes, it's unbelievable, but I think they are," she yelled back."

Philip waited among crowds of passengers with his children clinging to his legs, stuck as firm as the barnacles on the ship's hull. Several times, he glanced at Catrina while she cuddled little Catharina. He too wanted to cling to something. All the waiting and watching hatched his anxieties. The sickening mix of hopes, excitement, anxiety, and wrenching loss churned through him. His heart felt like pulp, his stomach pitched and sank. He thought, "How could they stay? How could they leave? He would miss the little mountain church at Auerbach."

Thoughts of the little mountain church were interrupted when he found himself in front of the table. A clerk with a white feather pen and a large log book asked, "Your name please and how many adults and children are travelling with you?"

"Philip Wiemer, I'm travelling with my wife Catrina and my daughters Elizabeth who is nine, Mattheus who is five, and Catharina who is 2 ½ years old," he replied." The clerk wrote their names in the log and asked Philip to present his documents and the receipt from the John Henry Reppele shipping company and place his signature in the log.

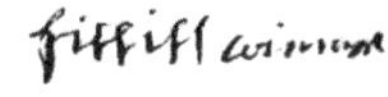

Fig. 12. Signature of Philip Eamer. American Loyalist Claims, 1776–1835. AO 12–13. Piece 079: Letters, Etc. Page 181.

Once the clerk was finished writing, he motioned to Philip and Catrina to move towards the gangway. Up they went. It was a long climb, especially with their loads. On his way up, Philip noticed a Pastor reciting a prayer to a group of passengers. When they reached the deck, a sailor looked at their receipt and pointed towards the companion hatch telling them to go below and find three bunks. They waited for the Wiese family to board and followed them down into the passenger deck.

The stairs were narrow and steep. There was a lantern at the bottom that lit the first metre; after that, Philip couldn't see a thing. Once his eyes adjusted to the darkness, he saw rows of wooden bunks along the sides of the ship. The bunks were made of slats about ½ metre wide with a narrow board along the edge. Almost one metre above the lower bunk was an upper bunk. Each was about two metres long. The centre passageway was dark and narrow with a small table about every 3 ½ metres. But, he saw the faint light of a lantern at the far end. The whole deck smelled like vinegar. Philip and Catrina chose an upper and two lower bunks about halfway down the starboard side. They liked this spot because it was away from the activity of the stairs but not too far. Also, there weren't any slop pots nearby. The Wiese family chose the bunks next to them.

As they set their belongings on the bunks, they noticed an endless stream of people coming down the stairs dashing off to choose a bunk. Some, they noticed, were tottering after consuming large amounts of the wine and beer being served at the wharf before everyone came aboard.

Philip thought, as he watched one elderly man stagger right into a bunk, "I guess feeling numb from liquor is one way of relieving fear." Once the bunks filled up, Philip said to Catrina, "It's a bit like being locked in the woodshed back home! I hope I don't have trouble breathing. Sleeping will be tricky."

Catrina nodded and said, "That's certain. But, with all these people, we're bound to make a few friends. I hope there aren't too many insufferable ones. In close quarters people get testy."

When the commotion died down, Philip, Catrina, and the children went to the upper deck. The space and air were refreshing. It was mid-morning and the weather was fair. They watched a group of singers finish a few gospel songs as the sailors raised the gangway. Behind them sailors were hoisting the sails and in rhythm hollered, "Heave, Ho." Others were hauling up the anchors. They watched the sails wave then billow. Philip heard someone yell "Fair wind! We're underway." He felt the ship sway slightly under his feet. Catrina held his arm tightly. They were slowly moving away from the wharf and the singing parishioners. At that moment, Philip felt as though they were the only ones on board and the only ones risking such a colossal adventure. His heart swelled into his tight throat; never before had he felt so in command of his life or felt such responsibility for the health and happiness of his wife and children. None of the 250 people below deck could feel the way he did now. He was grateful to lean on the strength, faith, and courage of the thousands of Germans who had made the journey before him.[60]

Fig. 13. Example of a Snow. Painting by Charles Brooking 1723-1759. Courtesy of Wikimedia Commons

During the commotion of setting sail, sailors were steering passengers to the companion hatch to go below. Philip and Catrina made their way to their bunk while trying to get used to the floor of the deck gently swaying. Catrina packed some of the food in the knotted bag, and Philip swung its rope over a slat in the top corner of the bottom bunk. Catrina sprinkled rue under the bottom bunk and laid out the woolen blankets, two on the bottom and one on the top.

Catharina played with Poppy, and Mattheus and Elizabeth watched the other children run up and down the deck. The Master of the ship came below and recited the rules. After delivering the rules, he arranged everyone in groups of seven which were to be the groups allowed to go on the upper deck in turns. Philip, Catrina, the children, and the Wiesers were group number four. They sat on their bunks until their group number was called at about six o'clock. They went above for their evening meal of barley soup and syrup and water or beer. Catrina brought a bit of their own cheese, bread, and fruit. There were only thirty five kilometres to the North Sea. They would reach it by morning.

Over the next few days, they were allowed on the upper deck with the Wiesers. The air and breeze was a great comfort from the stale air and smelly crowds below. They enjoyed sitting and watching the vast span of water that surrounded them. Sometimes they caught sight of land on the port side of the deck. This must have been Holland and then northern Belgium. Whenever Catrina came on deck, she brought a few of their blankets and gave them a good shake and some fresh air. The Wiemer and the Wieser's children played well together. Having each other was a blessing for the children. The Wiesers were also a blessing to Philip and Catrina. Philip made an agreement with Mr. Wieser that if anything happened to Philip, he would look after Catrina and the children. Philip made the same promise to Mr. Wieser.

On the evening of the third day, they were on deck just finishing cooking their day's rations when they noticed the sailors furling the sails, saw dark clouds, and felt the winds pick up. They hurried below to eat their bacon and peas. Suddenly, they felt the ship rolling and leaning hard, a voice hollered "Batten down!", and the companion hatch was slammed shut. After almost losing their supper from a sudden toss, they threw their empty dishes in the knapsack and leapt into their bunks. Wrapped tightly in their blankets, they heard waves slam hard against the ship's sides and hung on while the ship rolled, tossed, and leaned. They heard passengers scream, cry, pray, retch, and vomit. Everything was flying off bunks through the air onto the floor and in and under bunks.

Catrina yelled, "Philip, help!"

He yelled back, "Hang on tightly! We'll be okay!"

"Oh God help us!" she screamed.

This nightmare went on all night. Catrina prayed and tried to calm Catharina with quick songs. Catrina's gasps and groans interrupted her attempts to sing.

Through the night Catrina lay practically on top of Mattheus and Catharina just trying to keep them safe. Elizabeth was with her father, praying the only prayer she knew. It was not a rare thing to sail through weather like this in the North Sea. After all, sailors did call the sea 'Mad Dog'.

The pitching and tossing slowed to a constant roll, just enough for Philip to breathe deeply and reach for Catrina's hand. They laid there for a few hours whispering to each other amongst the other passengers' moans and sobbing.

Catrina pleaded, "Won't they please open the hatch! I need to breathe. I need some air!" In the middle of her pleading, the hatch opened and fresh air and light rushed down into the deck. "Thank God above!" Catrina shouted.

Philip raised himself up trying not to bang his head on the low ceiling. He hugged Elizabeth and swung over the side of the bunk and slid down onto the deck. With shaking hands, he grabbed Catrina, "Are you okay? Did you hurt yourself? How are the children?" He looked around to see a mess of clothes, bags, and dishes everywhere. A few others crawled out of their bunks, someone even crawled out from under the bottom bunk. Wrapped in blankets, with wide eyes and their heads hung low, they mumbled prayers of thanks. They were alive, and there was no water seeping through the sides of the ship. The Neptune was in one piece, still holding strong.

The constant roll and heave of the ship continued for another day, but at least they could lie on their bunks and not be pitched over the side. They hadn't been on deck for two days, so they couldn't cook any meals. Catrina handed out portions of dried meat and fruit, cheese and bread, and they sipped on their water and cider. Finally, on the fifth afternoon, group number four was called on deck. Philip, Catrina, the children, and the Wiesers crawled on deck.

"Oh, it feels so good to be out of that dark hole!" Catrina said. Just as she got the last word out she looked starboard and saw the most amazing solid white cliffs. At first she thought they were low clouds. She strained her eyes to make sure it really was white rock. "Philip! Look! There!" They stood and watched the endless white rocks as the ship sailed through the Strait of Dover. "Look, over there! An English Castle!" Catrina said pointing to the top of the cliff. (Dover Castle).

As the ship sailed into the English Channel, Catrina did her best to cook supper from yesterday's rations of beef and boiled rice. With today's flour and butter, she attempted to make dumplings. Cooking was difficult. Even getting a space at the fire took time. Everyone was pushing and shoving, and it was difficult to keep her pot of water from spilling with a rolling floor beneath. She was glad they bought a pot with a narrow rim and wide bottom, this meant less chance of spillage. The stove was a fire lit on top of a large iron cauldron filled with sand. The cauldron stood on brick and sand. Philip stood close by to help with carrying food and pots. The Wiesers watched the children until it was their turn to cook.

Good weather and wind made the last three days of sailing easier. They travelled an average speed of four knots and went about ninety kilometres every day except the two days the storm threw them zigzagging around the North Sea. When they were on the main deck, the journey was tolerable. Below deck was horrid. Seasickness had subsided for most of the passengers, but there were still several who retched and vomited. The stench of the slop pots was unbearable. Catrina had to wrap a small amount of lavender in a piece of cloth and drape it over her nose and mouth. It was clear that mice and rats were aboard and were getting into the passengers' provisions. The rue kept them out of their provisions.

On the eighth day, Philip watched as the ship sailed closer to the harbour at Gosport. It was a narrow channel to the harbour with Gosport on the port side and Portsmouth on the starboard. The Isle of Wight was behind them. Philip saw the large cannons on the hills at Portsmouth harbour. There was a lot of commotion on deck, so the passengers were sent below. From below, they heard the huge anchors being dropped into the harbour waters. From here, passengers and sailors got to shore in one of the ship's smaller boats, or someone rowed from shore. Right now, Philip and Catrina were enjoying the quietness of the water and the stillness of the ship.

The next day, some of the passengers went to shore, but Philip and Catrina stayed on board. To their delight, several sailors came below and cleaned the entire deck floors with vinegar. Catrina never knew that vinegar smelled so good! "I think for the rest of my life whenever I smell vinegar I'll think of swaying in this dark smelly wooden hole!" she confessed. They did go on shore one afternoon for a reprieve from boredom and to refill their bottle of cider and their costrels with fresh water. Catrina also wanted two small shawls for Elizabeth and Catharina; the breeze was cold on deck.

The days turned into weeks. This week was the third time the sailors washed the deck floor with vinegar. It was now almost the middle of July, and Philip spent a lot of time pacing the deck, grateful for the odd time he was allowed to smoke his pipe. Philip saw the sailors bringing provisions on board for weeks. "They must have enough food by now," he thought. While sitting with Catrina with his arms resting on his knees and wringing his hands, he said, "The longer we are here, the later we arrive in Philadelphia. That won't give us enough time to be ready for winter!"

Philip decided to approach the ship's Master, George Smith. "Why are we not allowed to go out to sea?" Philip asked.

The Master replied, "For two reasons, the customs officers have put us far down the list of ships to check over. We are only now at the top. And, even if customs was finished with us, we have to wait for the right winds to sail out of the harbour and back into the channel. It won't be long now. Two days at most."

Two long days later while sitting on their bottom bunk, Philip and Catrina were trying to entertain Catharina when they heard a lot of activity on deck. The Captain was yelling "Tides moving! Weigh anchors! Trim the sails!" As fast as they were able, the sailors heaved and climbed. "Anchors aweigh!" The winds were very good that morning, and the Neptune headed into the channel. Alongside the Neptune were four other ships that had been waiting for a morning like this. They all raced out to sea at a speed of about six knots (about 11 km/hr). It was Wednesday 16 July, two months since the family left Auerbach. They had travelled about 1100 kilometres and had 3000 more to go before they saw the shores of America.

After the excitement of the day and an evening meal of bacon and peas, Philip and Catrina sat on the edge of their bunk and talked about what it would feel like to lose sight of land. Not only were they leaving the land that would lead them back home, but it was land that could save them from death in the deep dark sea.

With her eyes fixed on Philip, Catrina said, "I don't think I can stand to see the land disappear. When it does, I might fall to pieces!"

Squeezing her hands, he said, "You won't fall to pieces. I am here, and you are tough! Let's lift our spirits and talk about what the land on the other side of the sea looks like."

They took turns describing what they would see when they reached America. Their keen imaginations created scenes of beautiful forests filled with berries, nuts, and wildlife and of crystal clear streams racing to fill sparkling blue lakes. Philip described the deep, rich, black soil and the meadows of tall grass that they would farm. Catrina described a huge garden filled with enough vegetables to keep them full and happy through winter. She talked about the berries and mushrooms she would pick in the meadows and forests. They relaxed and thought they could attempt to sleep while loaded with comforting thoughts.

It wasn't until late morning that Philip and Catrina's number was called and they were allowed on deck. It was so foggy they wondered how the Captain knew where he was going. There were only brief moments that they caught sight of the southern tip of England through the fog. As they sailed out of the English Channel and into the Atlantic Ocean, their lives were now entirely at the mercy of the Neptune, Captain, crew, weather, and of course the mercy of God.

Philip, Catrina, and the three children had been sailing for at least three weeks now and were trying hard to adjust to life trapped inside a ship that was constantly rolling up and down and side to side. They were tolerating the rolling, but the constant noise of passengers groaning, moaning, retching, and vomiting was not so easily tolerated. The stench was so overpowering Catrina gagged and wretched most of the day. Again, she found relief only when she buried her face in a piece of cloth sprinkled with lavender she brought, but even that was losing its effect. Many of the passengers cried out in the middle of the night praying for God to help them or cried out for someone to ease their seasickness. Children stopped playing. They lay on their bunks and whimpered most of the day and night. Husbands and wives argued; men argued and sometimes there were brawls in the middle of the deck or on the bunks. Every four hours, the endless noise was punctuated by the sailors' change of watch. When the hourglass completed a cycle every thirty minutes, a bell rang. At the eighth bell, Philip and Catrina waited for the noise of the sailors changing watch. This bell and the accompanying noise was often the only way to mark the passing of time.[61] The sun and moon sometimes weren't seen for days. Philip and Catrina were truly disconnected from what they knew as reality; now they lived in the world of the sea and wind with the Neptune and all its difficulties as their only saviour.

Adjusting to the noise and the ambiguous passing of time wasn't the only hardship. The smell of 226 passengers sweat, vomit, feces, and urine coalesced into the most indescribable putrid air. The stench was amplified when the sailors opened a cask of salted and sour meat. Catrina's and Philip's conversations were often interrupted with one or the other gagging or retching. The children were barely consolable for most of the day and only seemed comfortable when they slept. Vinegar couldn't even wash away the stench. Fleas and lice spread and became a standard appendage to their bodies despite the wormwood sprinkled on their clothes and blankets. It was over a month since they were last able to wash, and it would be another two months before the thought of washing could cross their minds. The lice and fleas found their way into the seams and corners of their clothes and blankets, and incessant scratching played havoc on their already stressed mental state. The rats had no trouble eating enough provisions to make multiplying easy, so much so that everyone considered them bunk mates. Catrina constantly brushed them from the children's bunk and watched them scurry under someone else's.

Meal time didn't add any relief from the distress of the hole below. For the first week, the food and water was tolerable, but after four weeks at sea the water became foul smelling and spoiled the taste of the food that was already intolerable. Catrina and Philip rationed the provisions they bought in Rotterdam. They were grateful that they at least had one meal a day that didn't cause them to heave. Clean fresh water was the only thing they didn't have.[62] Desperation for keeping the children alive was the only reason she allowed them to drink. Cooking and eating was always a challenge, but they were learning how to hold their spoons and cups so they wouldn't bruise their lips or bang their teeth while the ship rolled and tossed things around. It was harder for Catharina. She had only just learned to drink from a cup, and now she had to learn all over again. Before every meal Philip led their prayers, "Come Lord Jesus, be our guest, bless what you have bestowed. Oh give thanks unto the Lord, for he is good. For his mercy and love endureth forever."[63] Leaning on their faith in God and disciplining themselves to give thanks was their way of surviving this pit of hell.

During their fourth week at sea, Philip began to worry about Catrina. He watched her vomiting for days and tried to offer help any way he could. He didn't want to think about losing her to a horrible disease. They had come so far and were so close to their dreams.

Catrina didn't want to add to Philip's worry or anxiety, but she had to talk to him about her sickness. She waited until they were sitting quietly one evening and announced, "Philip, we're going to have a baby!"

Swallowing hard, Philip answered, "Oh thank God, I thought you were going to die! Are you sure?"

"Of course I'm sure,"

"When?"

"The middle of February."

As he held her tightly, he whispered, "Well, our family is growing; we are six now and one will be born in America!"

While on deck one day and spending at least an hour staring out at endless water and rhythmic waves, Philip asked the Captain where they were.

"We've sailed past Portugal and Spain and are close to the top of Africa where we will turn and head west."

With a tilt of his head and puff of his pipe, Philip said, "How do you know where to turn when there's nothing but water surrounding you?"

"I use my backstaff and hourglass to calculate the position of the sun at noon and my logline and hourglass to calculate speed. I also have my compass, and at night we use the stars to determine our direction. All the information I get from these tools I put in my logbook and use them to set the course of the ship. We want to find the right position to turn west and follow the trade winds and the sea current to the southern coast of America. Twenty degrees north is the position we want. We are very close to it. We've been lucky with the winds and are travelling at an average speed of four knots and ninety kilometres every day. Mr. Wiemer, let's hope we don't run into a storm that might set us off course!"[64]

It was now the middle of September, and they had been sailing for eight weeks. This evening's meal was boiled beef and rice with a bit of cheese and bread.

As they reached the top of the stairs and the freedom of the deck, Philip took in his routine deep breath and pulled Catrina to the side. "Let me cook the meal tonight, I don't want you among all those people pushing and shoving. You go and sit down with the children and enjoy the fresh air. I will bring our meal."

She replied, "I will enjoy sitting in the fresh breeze for as long as I'm able. Catharina and Mattheus don't have the energy they had a few weeks ago and will probably just rest beside me and play with their toys." They enjoyed at least one hour on deck when one of the passengers shouted, "Look, a fish that flies! Oh there's three more, look there!"

With their mouths wide open and gasping, Philip and Catrina said simultaneously, "How can that be? They are amazing!" Catharina pointed her chubby little fingers and giggled. Mattheus squealed and Elizabeth laughed. It was the most lively they had been for almost a month. They stood and watched the fish fly, dive and skim across the water as they took off into the air.

With a very straight face, Philip said, "I wonder if we could catch some and eat them? They would be fresh and tasty!"

Just as Philip was dreaming of eating a flying fish, another passenger called out from the other side of the ship, "Look over there, so many big fish swimming and leaping! They are so fast. They're all black on top with a bit of yellow near their tail!"

"Those are dolphins," one of the sailors replied.

Moving quickly to the other side, Philip and Catrina pointed at each dolphin they saw, "ooh, awe, ooh, awe!" Even the children were eagerly waving their little hands.

Three of the sailors were trying desperately to catch one for tomorrow's meal. "These fish taste fantastic," they hollered while suspended over the side of the ship.

Even though there were no fresh fish to eat the next day, those few minutes of watching the strange fish were the most pleasant moments they had had in over three months.

One afternoon near the end of September, Catrina was trying to rest on her bunk with Catharina when the ship leaned hard to starboard. Anyone standing in the middle of the deck was quickly thrown aside. One woman and her daughter were knocked unconscious, and anything on the port side that wasn't tied down was pitched to the other side. Just as the ship started to correct its lean, the companion hatch slammed shut. "Oh no," she thought. Not another storm. I barely survived the fright of the last one so many weeks ago." She held on so tight that her fingers went numb. She prayed through the evening and night as the ship heaved and water ran through the companion hatch, "Oh save us ..., or we sink, ...the winds and the seas are still high; Dear Saviour this moment appear, and say to our souls "It is I".[65]

From the top bunk, Catrina heard Philip, "The Lord is my Shepherd. I shall not want. ...." Amidst their own prayers, they both heard, "All is lost! Pray all, pray!" Eventually, the ship slowly stopped heaving and leaning and the companion hatch was raised. Catrina was exhausted. For at least twenty four hours, she put all her energy into prayer, hope, and holding on to Mattheus and Catharina.

It took three days for Catrina to recover from the distress of that storm. Being four months pregnant and at sea with horrid and scanty provisions for ten weeks, she existed on subsistence energy. Others were not so lucky. A young mother, about four bunks down from the Wiemers, suffered from seasickness since the journey through the North Sea. She was too weak to care for her infant and both were found dead after the storm. Her poor husband was filled with grief and left with two young children. The sailors removed them from the deck and, without ceremony, threw mother and child over the side into the wild ocean. After that day, Philip watched Catrina like a hawk and encouraged her to eat and drink whatever and whenever she could.

One week after the storm while Philip and Catrina were on deck, a sailor bellowed, "Land, Land ahead two points forward of the starboard beam!"[66] Everyone leapt to their feet and ran to the starboard rail straining to see a hazy dark mound on the horizon.

Philip grabbed the rail, and bounding up and down kissed Catrina and hugged the children, "Land, Land, Praise God! Land! Catrina, Land, we're here!" Every passenger praised God. The life left in them sparkled.

They sailed toward North Carolina and were heading north to Delaware Bay. It took two days to sail close enough to the coastline to see details of the land. For now, Philip and Catrina enjoyed their time on deck watching the shoreline pass and the birds and the fish appear. They still had to sail about 500 kilometres before they reached Delaware Bay and headed inland to Philadelphia. At the beginning of October, they reached the bay. As the ship headed northwest, the Delaware River was so wide they hardly saw both sides. On the port side, they saw several streams empty into the river and grassy marshes lining the shores. In the distance, they saw the Blue Ridge Mountains.[67] For now, they were at ease. They sailed safely 3000 kilometres across the great sea and 4100 kilometres from home.

Without strong winds, the ship sailed at a much slower speed, and by the end of the first day they noticed that the river started to narrow. The current was still strong, and they saw the Captain maneuver the ship carefully past several islands. As the river narrowed even more, Catrina and Philip spent hours on deck captivated by the beauty of the colorful forests of oak, birch, hemlock, and beech trees. Orange, red, yellow and green decorated the hillsides.

Philip said. "This is a beautiful but a very busy river. The large ships sure have to watch out for all those smaller Sloops. There must be a lot of merchant business on this river."

Catrina answered, "Good, that means there will be fresh food, and I hope lots of fresh water. I'm worried about a few of the passengers. They look poorly. The old woman and her husband haven't left their bunks in days." Just as she finished describing the sick, the ship swung wide to turn a corner. In front of them, spread out above the shore and up the hills was Philadelphia.

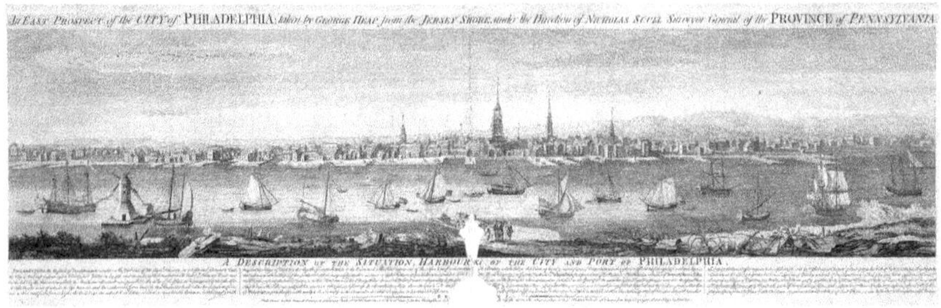

Fig 14. T. Jeffreys, Engraving. An east prospect of the city of Philadelphia; taken by George Heap from the Jersey shore. Library of Congress Prints and Photographs Division. LC-DIG-pga-01698 http://hdl.loc.gov/loc.pnp/pp.print

As the ship got closer to the city, the shore and a small island created a channel they sailed into. Still scanning the surroundings and the city, Philip and Catrina commented on everything they saw. Philip said, "That windmill at the tip of the island is a strange shape, there are so many angles. Of all the windmills we saw near Rotterdam, I don't remember seeing one like that." As he moved his finger across the skyline of the city, he added, "This city doesn't have any walls around it. I only see nice looking buildings, none look like the castles or ramparts on the Rhine."[68]

Catrina pointed to the tallest building at the northeast end of the city and said, "That must be an important church. It is the tallest building, and it has a beautiful steeple. Look. There are two other churches beside it. I wonder if there's a Lutheran Church." To the south of the churches, she pointed to the State House and the Court House.[69]

Philip was busy scanning the shoreline, "Look at all of the wharfs and all the boats landing. There must be one at every street!"[70] Elizabeth was pointing to the sailors rowing their boats. Mattheus was pretending to be a sailor. Catharina was pointing at the Dutch and Spanish flags flying on the ships anchored so close.

The next morning, Tuesday, 7 Oct 1755, the ship Neptune officially arrived at Philadelphia, according to the Pennsylvania Gazette which regularly announced the arrival of ships carrying emigrants and trade goods. That morning, a sailor came to the bottom of the deck stairs and announced, "Doctors from the city are coming onboard to make sure there aren't any infections or dangerous diseases among you. Without the Doctors' permission, no one is allowed on land, and everyone will be quarantined for several weeks. There're also men coming on board to deal with those of you who still owe your passage money[71]. If permission is given to enter the city, you'll all follow two of the sailors, and they'll take you to the Court House to swear the Oaths. Then, you are free to go where you will. You're all to come on deck when you hear the ship's bell ring twice."

As they packed their belongings in their knapsacks and rolled their blankets, Catrina was so full of doubts. "Where will we go tonight, tomorrow, and the day after that? We'll need food and a place to sleep at least."

Philip tried to calm her doubts. "There'll be people to help us find our way. I've heard so much about Germans in Philadelphia helping newcomers. I'll find a place to inquire about somewhere to stay until we know where we can settle. We have some money, and we have each other. Above all, we have our faith in the Lord to guide us to what is good."

As Catrina sat on the edge of the bed listening to some passengers moaning and some singing, she fidgeted with her knapsnack and entertained the children. She sighed, "Will that bell ever ring! We've been in this pit of hell for eleven weeks. Oh, these last few minutes seem so hard." She grabbed her knapsack, Mattheus, and Catharina the second she heard the first bell. By the second bell, she was almost at the stairway. Philip followed closely with Elizabeth, and they clambered up the stairs along with at least 226 other souls.

Standing on deck, they watched as a small boat was rowed toward the ship. Two important looking older gentlemen boarded the Neptune and talked to the Captain. When they finished talking, the gentlemen, who were Dr. Thomas Graeme and Dr. Phineas Bond, weaved their way through the passengers asking questions and looking in their mouths and eyes.

When Dr. Bond got to Philip and Catrina he asked, "How are you feeling? Are you vomiting? Do you have diarrhea? Do you have any pains in your stomach? Do you have any rashes or sores? Do the children have any rashes or sores?"

Philip answered, "We're feeling okay. We have marks where the fleas bit. My wife is four months with child and quite tired. The little children are tired too."

While examining their mouths and eyes, Dr. Bond said, "You're fine, nothing to worry about," and he moved on to others.

Philip and Catrina watched as the doctors went below, probably to check the older couple who hadn't moved from their bunks for days. Soon the doctors were on deck. The whole process took hours.[72] As Dr. Bond handed the certificate to the Captain, Philip heard him say, "Bring your ship to the Dock Creek wharf. Your passengers can enter the city, except those travelling on credit. People are coming aboard to make arrangements with those passengers."[73]

Four sailors directed the passengers who paid their passage toward the gangway, many others were directed to the centre of the ship. As the Doctors left, five other boats reached the ship, and merchants of all sizes, shapes, and dress came aboard. They went among the crowd of passengers in the centre of the ship. Philip watched the commotion.

He said to Mr. Wieser, "I wonder what kind of arrangements the merchants make with the passengers? I've heard awful stories about what happens to those who travel on credit."

Mr. Wieser explained, "They have to exchange their debt for a certain time of labour. Sometimes 't'is two years, sometimes 't'is seven. They're called indentured servants. The parents in that crowd might have to sell their children to the merchants which binds them to a terrible life. The children may'n't ever see their parents again! I wonder how fair the arrangement is when the passengers don't speak English."

Doctors' Certificate of the Ship Neptune.

> S^{r}
>
> Agreeable to Orders we have Visited the Ship Neptune, Capt. Smyth, Master, freighted with Palatines from Rotterdam and find the Passengers all in good health, except one Man and

> Woman, and that but very slightly ailing, so that we can not report any Infectious distemper being aboard the s^{d} Vessel, therefore there can be no objection to her being admitted to Enter the port. Tho. Graeme
>
> To his Honour the Governor Phineas Bond
>
> Philad^{ia} Octr 9th 1755.[74]

Philip and Catina were encouraged when they saw sailors scurry about raising top sails and moving very slowly toward the wharf. Some sailors were busy at the anchors. It all looked complicated, especially when they saw the wharf coming closer and closer. Several sailors climbed down to the wharf and were busy with ropes. Other sailors lowered the gangway. Philip, Catrina, the children, and the Wiesers followed two sailors down the gangway onto the wharf.

The passengers gathered on the wharf holding on to each other either for fear of losing sight of someone, or because they were too weak to stand alone. Philip held Catharina and, while firmly fixed to Philip, Catrina held Elizabeth and Mattheus' hands. The ground felt so strange. It was so long since they felt something solid under their feet. As they walked along the wharf toward Front Street, strangely they still felt the earth heave under their feet. Soon the group followed the sailors and the Captain up a small flight of stairs onto Front Street. This was one of the busiest streets Philip and Catrina had ever seen. There was a huge fish market, and men were making sails, barrels, and ropes; shops filled with boxes and barrels of all kinds lined the streets. They walked north along Front Street crossing several streets that led to the western end of the city. When they reached High Street (now Market Street), they turned west and walked down a wide street crowded with shoppers and merchants. Many ladies were dressed in beautifully embroidered wide skirts with lace neck kerchiefs and wide brimmed hats laced with colourful ribbons. There were tailors, grocers, and a large fish market in the middle of the street. The houses stood close together, looked so new, and were all built of stone or brick with cedar shingles.[75] Elizabeth and Mattheus stayed very close to their mother. They approached an impressive two story building with a balcony between two large plate glass windows. There were windows and doors on all sides of the building and a large bell perched on the roof.[76] Here they stopped at the front door near an organized crowd of Germans who called out, "Willkommen Heiben Philadelphia!" While calling out, the Germans walked among the passengers and handed out fresh apples. For Philip and Catrina, the first bite into the fantastic fruit was awkward. It was a long time since they chewed something so delicious. The children had large pieces to nibble.

In small groups, they walked up the stairs to the second floor. Each male passenger over sixteen stood in front of a table and placed their hand on a bible. One of the two Justices of the Peace, Benjamin Shoemaker or Septimus Robinson, recited the Pennsylvania Oath of Allegiance and Abjuration[77] After taking the oaths, everyone was required to sign or make their mark on the ship's passenger list.

> At the Court House at Philadelphia, Tuesday, the Seventh Day of October, 1755.
>
> Present: Septimus Robinson, Esquire.
>
> The Foreigners whose Names are underwritten, imported in the Ship Neptune, George Smith, Master, from Rotterdam but last from Gosport, did this Day take and subscribe the usual Qualifications. 226 Whole Freights. Shoemaker.[77]

As Philip, Catrina, and the children left the Court House, they met the crowd of Germans waiting outside. Almost immediately, a man walked toward Philip and Catrina. The man was dressed in a long black robe with a collar of two white bands hanging gracefully from his neck and lying on his chest. Philip recognized him to be a Lutheran Pastor. Beside the Pastor was his wife and another young man.

After taking a deep breath and exhaling a huge sigh, Philip thought, "Thanks be to the Lord. I knew there would be Germans here to help us!"

The Pastor reached for Philip's hand and said, "Good day Sir and Madam, my name is Reverend Heinzelman. I'm Reverend Muhlenburg's assistant from St Michael's Lutheran Church in this city." He hugged each of the children saying, "These three beautiful children must be yours. This is my wife Margaretha

Catharina, and this is Mr. Martin Silmser (See Appendix G).[78] He's here to provide you some comfort for a few days and to help you find a place to settle. He wants you to stay with his family for a few days. I must take my leave Sir, and I wish you Godspeed."

Martin Silmser reached for Philip's hand and said, "Yes, you're welcome to stay with us. You must be very tired. I know about the long hard journey. My wife and I came to Philadelphia only last year.[79] We live near Frankford about thirteen kilometres north of the city. I've a wagon, and the road to Frankford is fair. But, 't'is after noon now, and it will take us a few hours to get home, so we should leave soon. My wife is preparing a hot meal and a bed for you."

Philip shook his hand saying, "Thank you Sir. 'T'is a fine offer. My wife and I appreciate your generosity." Philip introduced Catrina and the children, and they started to collect their belongings. He asked Martin, "Is there somewhere I can buy a clay pipe and tobacco? My pipe was broken during one of the wicked storms."

"Yes, there's a tobacco shop on our way out of town."

Just as they were finished, Philip noticed that Reverend Heinzelman approached the Wiesers and talked to them for a few minutes. He was introducing them to another young couple. Philip and Catrina walked over to say goodbye. They hugged and gave each other blessings. It was a difficult goodbye. They had become friends.

Philip and Catrina walked with Martin to the side of the Court House, and Martin helped them put their few belongings in the wagon. He opened a cask that was sitting in the corner and offered each of them some fresh water. They all eagerly gulped the best water they had tasted in months. Just as they finished guzzling the water, Martin handed each of them a fresh pear. Philip said, "Oh heaven, 't'is the best fruit. It reminds me of home!" Catrina climbed in, and Philip passed her Catharina. Mattheus and Elizabeth climbed in beside them. They settled in the front corner of the wagon each wrapped in their shawls. Catharina squeezed Poppy close to her. Philip climbed in the front seat beside Martin, and the horses were urged on.

As they rode along, Catrina tried to doze off, but there were too many things to look at and too many things to think about. She just kept her arms snuggly around Mattheus and Catharina while the wagon jostled them about. Elizabeth managed to fall asleep. Philip and Martin talked about the journey, the ship, the passengers, and the land around Philadelphia.

Martin said, "We've only been here for a year, but I find the land here is not so good for farming, and it is very expensive. You have to go further into the interior to buy wild land which is much cheaper. I think it is better if you find land along a river like the Susquehanna toward the north or the Schuylkill toward the south. The land there is very good. But, I think we'll stay a while. If things don't get any better, we'll try and find another place to settle. Reverend Heinzelman says there is good land in northern New York along the Hudson and the Mohawk rivers. His wife is Mr. Conrad Weiser's daughter and Conrad Weiser knows a lot about the land in New York. He settled there when he first came to America. He's a very influential man."

"Other than the poor soil, there's a bigger problem here now. There's a recent Shawnese, Mingo, and Delaware Indian revolt in the frontier along the Susquehanna and the Schuylkill rivers. They're angry about unscrupulous land deals and the French claim to the Ohio Valley. Many settlers have been killed and their property destroyed. They're terrified of war. The government is building forts all along the Kittatinny Mountains; hundreds are starting to move back towards Philadelphia for protection from Indian attacks. They're afraid the French Indians are going to come down the Susquehanna River from Canada and kill everyone. [80] There's much talk about an impending war between the French and the English. It's a scary time for all of us. Even worse, the French and the Indians defeated General Braddock just north of here this past July. 'T'was was a major defeat. The soldiers who survived were just here last week on their way to New York. They camped on Society Hill; you passed by when you walked up Front Street on your way to the Court House.[81] I'm sorry you arrived in such horrific times."

Philip listened and thought carefully, "I'll have to make a decision about where to live soon, and I don't want to put my family in any more danger. I've many questions to ask before I decide."[82]

Despite all the frightening talk about the Indians and the French, Philip tried to pay some attention to the landscape, the farms, and the big beautiful country homes wealthy Philadelphians built. They hadn't been travelling far when they crossed over a creek on a sturdy stone bridge with three arches.

Philip commented, "'T'is a beautiful bridge and so well built for a wilderness bridge."

Martin nodded and said, "We're travelling on what's called the King's Highway which is a major road between Philadelphia, New York, and Boston. We're now crossing Pennypack Creek. The bridge is the Pennypack Bridge which was built in 1697, soon after William Penn settled here.[83] My wife and I often travel this road and over this bridge."

After a few hours of travel, they approached the village of Frankford and passed by an attractive two story stone house with a porch the full length of the house and many windows on each floor.

Martin saw Philip staring at the house, "That's the Jolly Post Inn," Martin said. "'T'is a favourite place to stay for travellers coming from Boston or New York. They say it was built about 1680. It's also a post house."[84]

"Oh, wonderful!" Philip replied. "I want to send a letter to my father in Germany."

"Of course you can send it at the Inn. Many people send letters home. Most of the time the letters arrive safely. I'll take you and your wife into the village in the next two days, and we can stop here and mail your post."

Martin turned the horses off Frankford road onto a small lane. They rode for about a kilometre and stopped in front of a good sized log cabin. A woman came to the door waving one hand while carrying an infant in her other arm. "Hello Martin. Welcome travellers," she said. They helped Catrina and the children off the wagon and started to unload the wagon.

As the woman came toward them, Martin introduced her, "This is my wife Elizabeth Margretha and my new daughter Christina Elizabeth." After wiping his hands on his trousers, Philip reached out to shake her hand.

"I have a big dinner fixed for you. And, I'm sure you'll appreciate a bed to sleep on that doesn't rock and roll," she said.

As Philip and Catrina picked up their belongings and went to walk toward the house, Martin interrupted them. "I'm sure you'd like to wash before our dinner. I know how terrible conditions are on the ships, and I know everyone is infested with lice and fleas. We were. My wife prepared lots of warm water and there's a private place behind the cabin where you can wash your whole body. We can help you get the lice out of your hair."

"Thank you," Philip replied. "We feel terrible. We haven't stopped scratching for months. 'T'is embarrassing to be so dirty and full of bugs. I'd like to cut my hair and this long shaggy beard. I'm sure Catrina wants to cut her hair too. And we must fix up the children."

They got busy over the next three hours. Philip and Catrina sat outside at the back of the cabin and emptied their knapsacks. They took off all the children's clothes and, with blankets wrapped round them, Catrina and Elizabeth cut their hair. After cutting their hair, they combed what was left and rubbed it with lye soap. Finally they wrapped it in a linen sheet to soak. The poor kids cried most of the time. Once they finished with their hair, they poured buckets of warm water over them and scrubbed with the lye soap. Even Poppy had a bath. Philip and Catrina were next. Martin kept hauling water from the well and kept a large pot over their iron stove full. Elizabeth looked after the children and gathered clothes that could be boiled, including Poppy's hooded cape. The wool blankets had to be burned.

When Elizabeth gave them all a set of new clothes, Philip said, "You've been so kind Elizabeth. I'll pay you for the clothing. Maybe there's a shop in your village where we can get a few things before we leave."

"There's no need to pay me Sir. Let's go and eat dinner. Your family is hungry and will want to sleep soon. You can rest for a day. Then we can talk about shops."

For two days the Wiemers (Eamers) slept and ate, and Philip enjoyed the freedom to smoke his pipe whenever he wanted. Catrina started to feel stronger, and the children enjoyed the fresh eggs, fruit, milk, cheese, bread, and meat. They were all grateful for every sip of fresh water. Philip and Catrina had many conversations with Martin and his wife about where to settle. With all the dangers present on or near the Susquehanna and Schuylkill rivers, that area would not be a good choice.

Philip questioned Martin more about land along the Hudson and Mohawk Rivers, "How many days travel does it take to get there? What is the land like? Can you buy or lease land? Are there many German settlers there now? Is there a city close by?"

Martin replied, "'T'is about two days travel to the Hudson River and another two days sailing up the Hudson to Albany which is the closest city to the Mohawk River settlements. They say the land there is the best farming land in the country, and the price for wild land is low. The soil is exceedingly good, rich, and not rocky, and there are plenty of streams, creeks, lakes and ponds. Many Germans and Dutch have settled there for over sixty years. The river valley is wide, flat, and surrounded by rolling hills. The thick virgin forests provide more wood than you could ever want. There's white pine, fir, spruce, ash, beech, chestnut, and maple. I've heard that you can lease land from a few Albany merchants. But, in the Mohawk Valley, I know of one man who is a merchant and trader in the area. His name is William Johnson. He's well known in Philadelphia. Several of his agents often come to Philadelphia."

Martin's description of the soil, forests, and streams captivated Philip's attention. "This area sounds great for us. With not much time to decide, I think this is as wise a choice as any. Would someone in Frankford know who to contact in Albany about land near the Mohawk River? And can we go into Frankford tomorrow and inquire about transportation to the Hudson River? I'd also like to post a letter to my father."

"Your choice is wise, and it's getting late in the season. We'll go to Frankford tomorrow. If you're lucky, there might be transportation to the Hudson. Tomorrow is Friday, October 10. Perhaps there's a boat on Saturday."

On Friday afternoon, Elizabeth Margretha stayed at the cabin with Mattheus and Catharina. Everyone else went to Frankford. When they got to the village, they stopped at a shop and Catrina bought caps, a set of pockets, shifts, jackets, petticoats, kerchiefs, shirts, trousers, wool stockings, wool capes, a frock for Philip and some wool blankets. These few things would be enough until they reached Albany. While Catrina was buying clothes, Philip went to buy tobacco and to the Jolly Post Inn to see about transportation to New York and sending a letter home.

Philip explained to the Postmaster that he wanted to take his family to the Mohawk Valley to settle. He asked, "Is there transportation available in Philadelphia that takes a family to Albany?

The Postmaster answered, "Yes, there is a Stage Boat that leaves every Saturday from the Crooked Billet Wharf that takes you by Stage Boat up the Delaware River to Bordentown. At Bordentown, there's a Stage Wagon that takes you to Perth Amboy, New Jersey, which is near the mouth of the Hudson River. You can hire a Sloop that'll take you up the Hudson to Albany."[85]

"How long does the trip take? And how much does it cost?"

"It takes two days from Philadelphia to Perth Amboy and another two days to sail up the Hudson. I think the trip to Perth Amboy is about six shillings for an adult. Or, you can go to Perth Amboy and then cross Raritan Bay to Manhattan. From Manhattan you follow the Albany Post Road. The road is rough and 't'is a long journey. It can be dangerous as there are often highwaymen who prey on travellers."

Philip was paying attention, but he was also thinking, "I don't think road travel is good for Catrina. She'll be so uncomfortable on that Stage Wagon. And, it sounds dangerous for all of us. The river route sounds better. If we leave on Saturday, we should be in Albany by October 16th. And by the 19th, we could be on our land getting ready for winter. He asked the Postmaster, "Can you help me with something else? I'd like to write a letter to my father in Germany, and I need some help." For a fee of one shilling, the Postmaster agreed to help Philip write a two page letter to his father and send it on the next ship to Rotterdam and forwarded to Auerbach, Hesse.

"It could take six months to reach Germany. There's a post house in Albany. You can write again if you wish. Most of the letters sent from Philadelphia arrive in Germany, but you might want to try sending another when you are in Albany." After thanking the Postmaster, Philip and Martin went to meet Catrina and Elizabeth and be on their way home.

Saturday morning was filled with the rush of eating, packing, and getting the children organized. They packed enough food in the snapsack to last about five days. It would be another long and strange journey. There was excitement and anxiety as before, but this time there was a sense of urgency. Philip was worried about getting settled before winter. He knew the trials of cold weather at home, and he heard that winters in America could be unforgiving. Saying goodbye to Elizabeth Margretha wasn't easy. She had been so kind. They had become friends.

After a familiar and long ride into Philadelphia, Martin pulled the wagon alongside a shop on the corner of Front Street and Chestnut Street. It was only a sixty metre walk to Crooked Billet Wharf where a Durham Boat was waiting to take passengers up the Delaware River. Philip paid the Boat Master Nicholas George eighteen shillings for their tickets, and Martin helped them load their few belongings into the boat. Philip didn't want to say goodbye to Martin. Philip enjoyed the conversations they had and the new friendship he made in this strange new place.

With a firm handshake, Philip said, "We're truly grateful for everything you've done for us. 'T'was a special gift to have a friend in such a time of need. We hope you might change your mind about living here and consider coming north to the Mohawk Valley. If you do, you know you'll always have good friends there to welcome you."[86]

"God speed friend." Martin replied. "Elizabeth Margretha and I will consider the Mohawk Valley and meeting our friends again."

While the Boatmaster waited for the tide water to rise and a good wind, Philip found himself studying the boat. He hadn't seen a boat shaped like this. It was similar to the Scow on which they sailed down the Rhine. It had a flat bottom and a pointed bow and stern. It was about twenty metres long, two metres wide, and the sides were about one metre high and almost vertical. On the inside, running along each side the length of the boat, were running boards with cross slats. It wasn't long before Philip knew the purpose of these running boards. There were three sailors including the Master. Each sailor held a pole about 5 ½ metres long with an iron tip on the end. As soon as the Master was seated at the stern to steer, the other two sailors jammed their poles into the bottom of the river and pushed hand over hand down the pole, walking low along the running boards as they pushed.[87] Philip was impressed at how fast the boat moved. The trip up the Delaware didn't take long. Being closer to the mouth of the river, they travelled down the more sluggish end. The power of the two men pushing made the forty five kilometre trip along this transportation thoroughfare to Bordentown go fast, about nine hours.

Early on the second day Philip, Catrina, and the children boarded a Stage Wagon that would take them to Perth Amboy, New Jersey. This was a new and difficult way for the family to travel. The Stage Wagon was similar to an ordinary wagon. A wooden box sat on top of the transoms, and it had benches, a top canopy, and open sides. The Stage had no springs to lessen the shock from the bumpy, rocky road.[88] The ruts were very bad in places. Philip was glad it wasn't raining. If it had been, the men would have had to get out and help the horses haul the wagon out of muddy furrows. Catrina suffered from the constant bouncing and jarring. Philip was worried that this was not the best way for his pregnant wife to travel. He was also worried about a possible Indian attack. With all the stories that Martin told him about the settlers in Pennsylvania, he worried that they might be caught in the middle of a group of unfriendly Indians. As they travelled along, he was vigilant in his surveillance of the countryside. He hadn't seen an Indian before, so this native group of peoples fascinated him. He didn't want to meet them in a hostile situation, but he was curious He wondered if there would be Indians where the family settled. Six large, strong horses pulled the wagon with great skill. They had thirty five kilometres to travel to Perth Amboy and, with a short stop at Cranbury at noon to eat, they arrived in about eight hours.

The cost of their ticket included one night stay at 'John Clark's House of Good Entertainment' opposite Perth Amboy.[89] They arrived at supper time and had a decent meal at the Inn. After supper, Philip went to find out about passage on a Sloop down the Hudson River. First, he needed to find someone who spoke German.

After a struggle communicating with Mr. Clark, Philip managed to locate a German man who ran the livery. He told Philip, "There are Sloops leaving for Albany every day. Just be at the dock next to the Inn early in the morning before the oyster boats go out into the Bay." Relieved and feeling uncomfortable being out near dark in a strange town, Philip quickly made his way back to the Inn. He knew they needed to be up very early, so it wasn't long before everyone was in a bed and asleep.

Philip felt better the next morning knowing they were closer to the end of their journey and that they'd be ready for winter. Everyone gathered at the dock watching the boats getting ready to row out to Raritan Bay to the oyster beds. Next to an oyster boat was a beautiful sailboat with one mast and two large and one small sail raised.

Philip approached one of the sailors and asked, in the best English he could and several hand gestures, "Are you sailing up the Hudson River to Albany? Can you take five passengers? We have our own food."

The sailor replied, "Yes, I'm Captain Samuel Pruyn and this is the Sloop 'Mary'.[90] Better climb on board we've good wind and the flood tide. We leave now. Sometimes it takes two days to get to Albany. Sometimes it takes five, depends on the wind and the tide. I charge five shillings for an adult, the children travel free. You can go and settle yourself in a bunk in the cabin."

Philip understood most of what the Captain said. So, he helped Catrina and the children on board. Everyone went to the Cabin at the bow of the Sloop and settled in their bunks. Philip went to pay Captain Pruyn who was already concentrating on getting the Sloop out into Arthur Kill (Staten Island Sound).

While standing close to the quarter deck watching the shore pass by, Philip heard the Captain say, "We can get as much as five kilometres an hour out of this flood tide, and with the wind we'll have a good day on the river!" Laughing, he said, "Maybe the flood tide will carry us all the way to Albany."[91]

"Hmm. That's all good to overhear, something about floods and a good day. We'll probably make it to Albany in two days," thought Philip. He took a few minutes to amble along the deck before he went to see Catrina and the children.

Philip, Catrina, and the children spent most of the morning on deck. They watched as the Sloop sailed through Arthur Kill. It was a beautiful morning, especially with the brilliant colors of the trees and the many small farms along shore to enjoy. Just after lunch they saw a large city on a point of land (New York City). As they got closer, they saw a battery with many canons surrounding the southern tip. As they sailed past the point of land, they saw a large fort, a beautiful church, and several wharfs filled with different sizes and types of boats. Finally at the end of the city, they saw a block house and a palisade that ran inland.[92] Soon they entered the Hudson River. The morning passed quickly. Just before noon the landscape started to change.

On each side of the river, mountains rose to about 300 metres. They were covered with the brilliant colors of the trees with rock visible only near the top. Streams flowed in on both sides of the river, and an occasional waterfall broke the cover of the trees. The Sloop took a turn and sailed past an island. With the strong winds and the fast river, it wasn't long before they sailed passed the mountains toward lower land still covered with the flush of the trees. By mid-afternoon, they sailed past Poughkeepsie passing several Sloops along the way. There were gusts of wind which made it very chilly on deck even with their blankets. Catrina and the children went into the cabin to warm themselves by the stove and to rest. Philip enjoyed watching the sails and the Captain manage the tiller at the stern. By the end of the day, they reached Kingston. As the Sloop approached the wharf, the Captain announced, "'T'is too dangerous to sail at night, too many sandbars and rocks. We'll stay the night. I'm going ashore for fresh fruit and milk."

After a comfortable sleep, Captain Pruyn had them on their way to Albany early the next morning. Philip, Catrina, and the children had gone ashore the evening before and bought some fresh milk, cheese, and fruit. It was another good day to sail. A breeze pushed the Sloop up the wide river while waves splashed against the bow and threw a light spray over the front of the boat. Bald Eagles flew overhead. There were small islands and many villages along the way. The shore was lined with meadows that met the base of low hills.

As they sat on deck, Catrina said, "This is a busy river. Look at how low the boats sit in the water. They must be heavy with cargo."

Philip answered, "I noticed the cargo when we were moored at Kingston. There were bundles, sacks, and boxes, many seemed almost too heavy to carry. They even unloaded stone and rock. Did you notice the fields of grain near the shore?" Philip knew this area flourished and not just with trees as far as your eye could see, but with trade and commerce. He thought, "There's a market for all the grain, peas, and apples I can grow."

It was early on Tuesday afternoon October 14th when they caught site of Albany. The Captain had to steer around obvious sand bars and maneuver into a small bay. The town sat on a flood plain and stretched along the shore then rose up the slope of a hill. They saw lush greenery and the shapes of low mountains in the distance. As the Sloop glided towards the shore, it headed for a small dock at the south end of the town. Behind them and to the north was a small island covered in meadow and a few small buildings.[93] Philip, Catrina and the children gathered their belongings and carefully stepped onto the dock.

After paying their fare, Philip asked the Captain, "Where can we find lodging for the night? And, do you know where I can inquire about settling along the Mohawk River in the area where Mr. William Johnson lives?"

Captain Pruyn replied, "Go to Richard Cartwright's tavern. 'T'is called the King's Arms." Pointing to the road ahead, he said, "Walk up Court Street until you see Beaver Street. Turn onto Beaver going west. You'll see the tavern sign. Mr Cartwright knows who you can talk to about land."[94]

The children were tired and didn't want to hurry up the street. Since they left Perth Amboy, they were fascinated with the many sights along the shores, and they spent hours on deck giggling. As the Sloop rolled up and down, the small waves provided plenty of splash for everyone. At least they weren't spending their time scratching flea bites. Philip carried Catharina, and Catrina towed

Mattheus and Elizabeth and walked up the sloping street. On their right was an imposing four storey stone building with windows lining each of the four storeys. There was a bell and a steeple with a golden ball perched right on top (City Hall). Just as they reached Beaver Street, ahead of them was a large stone church (Dutch Lutheran Church) with tall windows beautifully decorated and a bell tower on top.[95]

They turned onto Beaver Street and saw the King's Arms sign. People were coming in and out as Philip, Catrina, and the children made their way inside. Standing with Catrina at the entranceway, Philip said, "I feel uncomfortable standing here with a barely grown beard and my short hair. We need to find someone who speaks German." They walked to a desk near the door, and Philip asked in German, "We need a room for two nights."

A man standing near the desk approached them and, in German, said, "We have a room for you and your family. Are you here doing business?"

"No, we're travelling to the Mohawk River to settle on land near Mr. William Johnson. My name is Philip Eamer. Can I speak to Mr. Cartwright about land near the Mohawk River?"

"Oh yes, He knows people in that area. He's sitting at that table over there. My name is Jost. I'll take you to your room, and then we can talk to Mr. Cartwright."

After settling in their room, Philip and Jost went to talk to Mr. Cartwright. "Good day Sir. This is Mr. Eamer. He's wanting to settle on lands near William Johnson. Do you know anyone who has land to sell?"

Mr Cartwright shook Philip's hand and said, "Yes, Mr. Harmans Wendell has land on the Sacandaga Patent.[96] In fact, Lewis Clement is in Albany now and is on his way home soon to Tribes Hill which is only about six kilometres from Mr. Wendell's land. I'm sure he'll take you there. It's not safe for you to travel that road alone. He'll be here tonight. I'll tell him there's a family who needs transportation to the Mohawk. I'll tell him you'll be at the City Hall in the morning. While you're waiting for Mr. Clement, you can see if Mr. Wendell is there. He's an Alderman of this city."

Philip nodded and said, "Thank you Sir. My family and I are grateful for your help. We want to settle before winter sets in and it's approaching fast."

"Oh yes, 't'is cold at night now. You probably have two weeks before snow comes. If you need supplies, I've a store. Good luck to you Mr. Eamer."

Philip rose early the next morning, but he let Catrina and the children sleep. The tavern at the Inn was noisy last night, and it was difficult to sleep. It was only one block to the City Hall, so Philip was early. He stood looking east towards the river and saw the harbour busy with all kinds of boats, many he'd never seen before. There were narrow boats that looked like they were carved from one large log. At each end of the boat, there was an impressive sturdy man with dark skin kneeling on one knee and paddling. They maneuvered the boat easily. These two men were the first Indians Philip saw. Each of them wore a hat adorned with feathers that covered the entire top of their heads. There were two tall feathers, one pointed upwards and one downwards. Their chests were half covered with a blanket over one shoulder. To Philip, they wore what looked like a skirt and some leggings and shoes made of animal skin.[97] Surrounding these log boats, there were flat bottomed row boats, different from the Jolly Boats he'd seen at Rotterdam. There were four Sloops at anchor in the bay. And, men were unloading cargo onto wagons that were brought very near the Sloop. It was a busy waterfront so early in the morning.

From behind, Philip heard someone call his name. He turned and saw a man about his age approaching. "Hello, do you speak Dutch?" the man said.

"No, German," said Philip.

The man replied in the best German he knew, "Well, I'll try German. I'm Lewis Clement. Are you wanting transportation to the Mohawk River?"

"Hello, I'm Philip Eamer. Yes, I need transportation. I'm anxious to get settled before the snow comes."

"I can offer a ride. I'm on my way home to Tribes Hill tomorrow. 'T'will take us two days. We'll have to stay overnight at Schenectady and travel most of the next day." I've a wagon and a man to help me.

"Thank you. My wife and children will be grateful. I'm looking for Mr. Harmans Wendell. I was told he has land to sell. Do you know him?"

"Yes, I know him. Come in. He's probably here now."

Philip and Lewis entered City Hall and walked up two flights of stairs. In a small outer room in a large chair sat a well-dressed man. Walking towards him, Lewis said, "Good day Mr. Wendell. This gentlemen, Mr Eamer, wants to settle and farm near William Johnson. He's heard that you've land to lease. We're going that way tomorrow, and he wants to settle before the snow falls. Can you help him and his family?"

"I can," replied Mr. Wendell. "I've lot fifty nine on the Sacandaga Patent that should satisfy a hard working farmer. It's about sixty six acres. There's some meadow and a small creek running through, and there's plenty of woodland to clear for grain. I charge a quit rent of four pounds per year.[98] 'T'is 6 ½ kilometres northwest of your place Lewis. Can you take him there? I'll give you a map and some details. Mr. Eamer, you can walk the land. If you approve, I'll be up that way next spring. Mr. Wendell sketched a map for Lewis.

"Sir, may I have a written note as to our agreement until spring?" Philip asked.

Philip walked out of City Hall with the note in his hand. Even though things were working out very well, Philip was still anxious to get moving. He knew how much work still had to be done. After agreeing to meet Lewis in front of the King's Arm at dawn, Philip went to see Catrina and the children. He walked in their room with a huge grin and waving the note.

With a gaping smile, Catrina said, "What happened? Did you find a place to settle? Is it what we wanted? Can we pay for it?"

"'T'is just fine. Everything is working out okay. I've an agreement with Mr. Harmans Wendell that we'll finalize in the spring. For now, we've a ride to the land with Mr. Lewis Clement. We leave in the morning. It'll take us two days, so we need to gather our energy and make one last push. It hardly seems possible that we've been travelling since May, and we've come safely over 5000 kilometres! But, as you said back at Rotterdam, 'if we keep our faith in God and remain heedful we'll be alright'. Well, here we are with only fifty kilometres to go!"

Catrina held the note in her hand and hugged Philip and the children. "They want to go to the market. They've hardly complained at all,"

"Okay, we deserve time to look about."

They walked down Beaver Street and turned north on Court Street toward the Dutch Lutheran Church. Just before the church, they crossed a bridge over the Ruttenkill (a stream that flows from the hills and empties into the Hudson). They stopped to admire the church which stood at the corner of Market and State Streets. As they looked west up State Street, they heard the noon bell of City Hall marking the hour, and they saw another large church. (St. Peter's Episcopal). Beyond St. Peter's Church, high on a hill stood an impressive stone fort (Fort Frederick). As they walked along Market Street, they saw all the stone and brick houses lined up closely with their fronts facing the street. The houses had steep roofs and gables and gutter spouts hanging well into the street. Each house had a porch along the front of the house. As they walked along, there were people shopping, strolling, or sitting on their porches.[99]

Mattheus and Elizabeth wanted to go to the shore and watch the boats; so, the family walked down Stueben Street to Quay Street. Large yellow elm trees and red willow shaded their walk down to the river. Along Quay Street, many things got their attention. There were coopers, cordwainers, tailors, and bakers.[100] Mattheus loved the boats carved from a log and wanted his Papa to carve one just like them. Elizabeth stared as the Indian men unloaded bundles from their canoe. Catrina couldn't help staring either, especially at their hats. She said to Philip, "What kind of bird feathers are they? I wonder if they all wear hats adorned with feathers. How do they keep those hats on?" She had many questions and no answers. Philip was curious about what was in the bundles they were unloading. He also stopped to watch fishermen unload enormous sturgeon from the boats on Maiden Street.

At dawn, the family met Lewis in front of the King's Arms. Lewis had a large wagon and two sturdy black horses. Philip walked over to the horses and stroked the neck of one, "These are beautiful horses you have. They look capable and calm and have such beautiful long manes and tails!"

Lewis walked up beside Philip, "Yes, they've good feet and are good in harness and under saddle too, not really meant for heavy farm work though." Pointing to each horse he said, "This is Greta and this is Ankie. The Dutch brought this breed to New York City over 100 years ago."

While Philip and Lewis were talking, a young muscular black man loaded their belongings in the wagon. Catrina and the children stood back while he worked. Lewis called out from the front of the wagon, "Harry help the lady and the children in the wagon; we need to leave soon."

Turning to Philip, he said, "That's my Negro man Harry. He's a good worker.[101] I bought him six months ago in Albany."

"You bought him?"

"Yes, we've slaves in New York. Many farmers along the river own slaves. To get the work done you need them."

Philip thought, "Sounds like the servants folks had at home, but they weren't bought or owned. I won't ask questions now. I'll wait."

Harry climbed into the driver's seat. Since they got to the Inn, he'd only spoken two words, 'Yes, Sir,' or nodded his head. Lewis and Philip climbed up beside him. Catrina sat near the front of the wagon. It wasn't such a rough ride near the front, and she wanted to be able to talk to Philip. Catharina sat on her lap with Poppy. Mattheus stood grabbing the sides and peered up and down the street and then over the side to examine the wheels. Elizabeth did as big sisters do, she rolled her eyes and poked Mattheus in the leg, "you'd better sit down or you'll fall on top of me!"

Suddenly Lewis bellowed, "Move on Harry, or we'll be in Schenectady after dark."

They headed north along Maiden Street and west along Eagle Street then through the west gate of the timber stockade that surrounded the city. Once passed the gate, they were on the ancient Indian path, now the King's Highway or as the locals call it 'the Albany Road or Schenectady Path'.[102] As they drove out the city gate, the road stretched uphill through the early morning fog and onto a sandy plain. Soon, the fog lifted across the plain flaunting fields of golden scrub oak, red sumac, blue lupine, orange black eyed susans and white yarrow. In the distance were patches of yellow aspen with their sparse leaves fluttering in the breeze. The road followed different bird songs among the rolling landscape and sand dunes. Catrina enjoyed listening to all the new songs; they were sweet and melodic, but one stood out. It was a loud and rhythmic song repeated over and over.

"What's the bird that makes that sound?" Catrina asked Lewis.

"'T'is a whip-poor-will. I'm surprised we're hearing it. Those birds sing all night long and are quiet during the day."

After a few kilometres, the road narrowed to a sandy heavily wooded path lined with crooked pine trees with multiple awkward limbs. As they drove through the trees, Lewis said, "We call this the pine bush because of all these pitch pine. 'T'is a sandy stretch of land. The trees aren't really useful for building because they're so crooked, but we use the pitch to make tar to seal canoes, boats, and ships. Or you can use its knots or cut slices to burn as a candle. The pine knots are much cheaper than candles. During the darkness of winter, you'll want to have these.[103] We'll look for them in Schenectady."

As they travelled through the pine forest, Philip thought about what they needed to buy when they got to Schenectady. He worried about forgetting something.

He asked Lewis, "Are there any stores near our lot? I don't want to be stuck without during the winter, especially with a baby due in February."

"Oh, your wife is with child, that's wonderful! Don't worry. There are several farmers settled within a kilometre or two of your lot, some have sleighs. Everyone helps each other whenever there's a need. They're good people. And Jelles Fonda, a trader and merchant, has a store at Caughnawaga about five kilometres south of you."

"Has there been problems with hostile Indians? There were problems near Philadelphia when we were there. I heard frightening stories about scalping, plunder, and slaughter."

"Not recently, but we keep our guard up. We haven't had problems in this valley for a long time. Until September when the French came down to Lake George from Canada along with hundreds of Abenaki and Caughnawaga Indians. The British didn't want the French claiming all of Canada and all the land in the Ohio frontier; so, they organized a plan to be rid of them. The defeat of Major General Braddock was part of the plan.[104] There was a brutal battle at Lake George between the French and the English and their Indian allies eighty kilometres north of here."

"In June, while Major General William Johnson was organizing the attack on the French, he asked my brother Jacob and another interpreter Arent Stevens to gather hundreds of Indians from the Iroquois League of Six Nations along the Mohawk River and bring them to Mount Johnson. They gathered there before the march to Lake George.[105] "My brother and I speak several Indian languages, and we often work as interpreters for General Johnson. My father Joseph Clement Sr. was a trader with the Indians since we were little. We played with Mohawk children, made many friends, and we learned their language. Philip hardly said a word. He was absorbed in Lewis' description of the battle and wondered if he could be friends with Mohawks. He doubted he could ever learn their language.

Lewis continued, "The great Mohawk War Chief and Sachem Tiyanoga, or King Hendrick as many Englishmen and Dutch called him, led the Mohawks alongside General Johnson. The General lives at Mount Johnson on the north side of the Mohawk River, about nineteen kilometres east of your lot. He has a strong relationship with many Nations of Indians from Canada to Philadelphia. He understands their language and fully knows their customs and ceremonies.

He's their brother and ally. Many years ago, the Mohawk welcomed him into their Nation as a Sachem and gave him a Mohawk name. He's called Warraghiyagey which, in Mohawk, means 'a man who undertakes great things'.[106] He's a friend of the Six Nations, but he's also a mediator for the British. In April, they appointed him Superintendent of Indian Affairs and just before the battle, he was appointed Major General of the New York provincial militia.[107] General Johnson and his militia won the battle at Lake George. After the battle, the General was a hero here and in Britain."[108]

"Do they impress men into the militia? In Germany, men often don't have a choice about being a soldier!"

"No, not usually, sometimes if they need skilled workers like carpenters, wheelwrights, joiners or if they need wagons or batteaux. The farmers join because they want to protect their families and their farms. At Lake George, there were farmers from all over the Mohawk River and Albany area who fought with General Johnson. Even though we won the battle, we lost many good men. Captain William McGinnis had a militia company of over 100 men from Schenectady and surrounding farms. John Hare Sr. was his Sergeant, and John's sons Richard Hare, William Hare, and John Hare Jr. were Privates.[109] William McGinnis was killed in the battle and so was his brother Teady McGinnis. Arent Stevens lost his son Johnathan Stevens. For General Johnson, the worst loss was the death of his friend the endeared and eminent Mohawk Chief Tiyanoga (King Hendrick). General Johnson says they all fought like lions."[110]

"Since the battle, we watch for Frenchmen and their Indian allies prowling around the valley trying to create fear and turmoil. As we travel this road, what you need to fear are the rascal highwaymen. They are known to ambush, rob, or murder people. Many people are required to travel this road with a military escort because 't'is so deserted. But, I thought we'd be safe enough travelling by daylight with three strong men and a couple of firelocks."

While looking to his right and behind him, Philip said, "I'll keep an eye out. Can we stop somewhere and have some lunch? I know my wife would like to rest, and the children can play a while."

"We can stop to eat at the tavern. It's the halfway point, but we can't waste time. We don't want to be on the road at dusk."

About 1 ½ kilometres down the road, Harry pulled up on the reins. "Whoa, Whoa," he said as he pulled over next to a small stone building that was someone's residence and a tavern. Lewis waved to Philip, "Come in and have some beer, or you could try some spruce beer or rum." Harry watered and fed the horses. Catrina stayed by the wagon with the children. It wasn't long before Philip and Lewis came outside to share lunch. A bit of food, something to drink, and a chance to smoke his pipe and walk around a bit was refreshing. Harry had his lunch by the wagon. Catrina lay on a soft sandy piece of grass while Mattheus built a road through a small section of sand. Elizabeth tried to create a castle, and Catrina had to keep Catharina from putting the sand in her mouth.

Soon they were on their way again. It was a quiet part of their journey, a nice change from busy cities and crowded wharfs. For the next few hours, Philip and Lewis talked about the supplies Philip needed to build the cabin and provisions for winter. Once in a while from her seat behind the men, Catrina called out a few things for the kitchen or bedding. Lewis was firm about his warm clothing suggestions.

When Lewis talked about the cold of winter, Philip started thinking about his fireplace and asked "Is there a blacksmith in Schenectady? I need some things for the fireplace."

"There's one there, but we can stop at William Bowen Sr. and his bothers Reyer Bowen and Cornelius Bowen's place on our way to your land. They're blacksmiths, and they live near Fort Hunter."

About mid-afternoon, the horses pulled the wagon up a slope to a plateau and through the gate of the stockade. They drove into the town of Schenectady and down Niskayuna Street (Union Street) past several stone and brick houses. With steep roofs and gables and gutters facing the street, the houses were similar to the houses they saw in Albany. Halfway down the street at the centre of a public square stood a small square stone church. (Dutch Lutheran) A cupola and bell rested where the four sides of the roof met. A graveyard surrounded the church.[111] As they drove through the public square and past the church, Lewis announced, "We'll stay at Arent Bradt's Inn on Albany Street (State Street) tonight and leave at dawn.[112] We've still about thirty two kilometres to travel. After we settle in the Inn, we can take the wagon along Trader's street (Washington Avenue) and pick up your supplies."

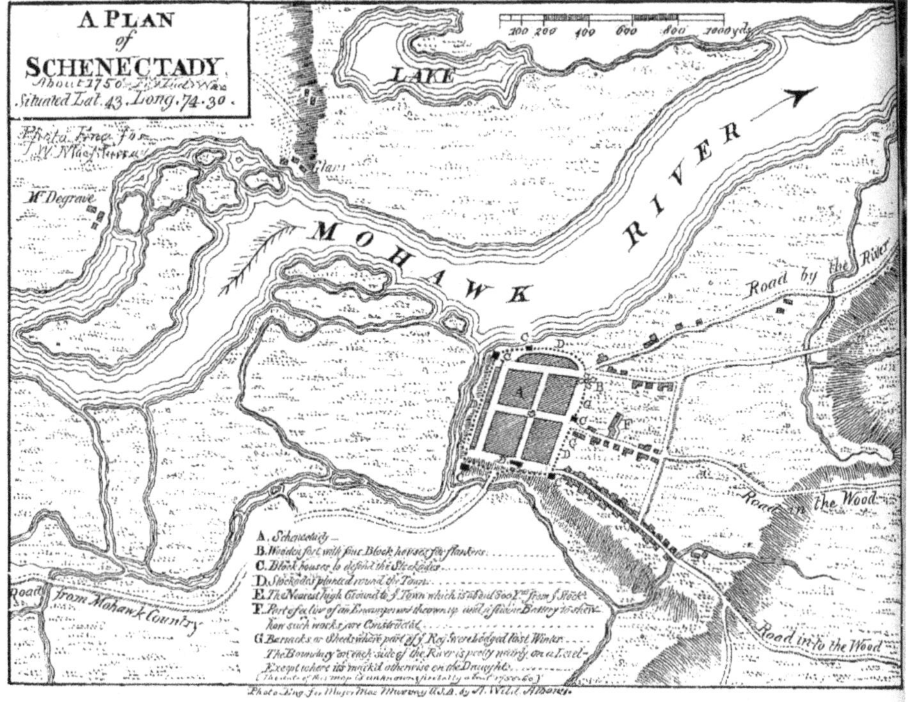

Fig. 15. Schenectady, New York and surrounding area 1750. Courtesy of Schenectady Digital History Archives on Wikimedia Commons. PD-US.

While Catrina settled the children, Philip opened the belt sewn into the waist of his trousers and counted the money that was left. There were £22. He thought, "That's okay considering what we spent in Philadelphia and the cost of travel to Albany. It was enough to get them through the winter. I'll pay Lewis something for taking us all the way to our land and for his suggestions and advice."

He said to Catrina, "We'd better go now. We've a lot of things to get, and I want to spend some time looking for a good horse."

"Good," she said, "We want to walk; we're tired of sitting." Mattheus and Lewis went with Philip to get buckets, a wash tub, rope, nails, a hammer, a plane, two axes, a barrel, four pounds of tobacco, a keg of rum, one window pane, and a chamber pot. The gunsmith was the next stop where they found a firelock, haversack, powder horn, powder, shot, flints, and two hunting knives. Philip chose a fowling piece (shotgun). It was a good piece and could be used for hunting birds and game. Harry loaded the supplies in the wagon and followed them as they walked to the livery to look at horses.

As they walked, Lewis gave Philip advice on what kind of horse to buy. "You'll want a good plough horse and one that you can ride to neighbours, Caughnawaga, or here. A Canadian horse is the best. They're tough little horses bred to work the fields, but they can pull a wagon or sleigh, and your wife could ride one. They're easy keepers too. Let's hope there's one here."

With eyes wide as plates, Philip said, "Wow, they sound perfect!" "I also need a milk cow."

"Don't get a cow here; it'll slow us down. You can get one from a farmer near your land."

As Philip, Mattheus, and Lewis went looking for a horse, saddle, halter, and bridle, Catrina, Elizabeth, and Catharina went to collect food and kitchen items. They still had a few dishes and a kettle they brought from Germany, but Catrina was still careful with the money she spent. She bought flour, sugar, butter, cheese, dried meat, dried fruit, raisins, molasses, salt, apple cider, a gallon bowl, wooden bowls and plates, mugs, knives, forks and spoons, a ladle, a broom, bed cord, three blue checked wool blankets, several yards of flannel, linen and bed ticking, two blanket coats, wool hats, worsted stockings, several skeins of mohair, knitting needles, thread, needles, buttons, scissors, a pound of spermaceti (whale oil) candles, and lye soap. Elizabeth helped her choose two bake kettles and one frying pan. The bill was £4, two shillings and nine pence.[113] Adding the cost of Philip's horse, gun, and other things plus what they'd spend at the blacksmith, they spent about £12, leaving them with £10, enough for a portion of the payment for their land, more winter provisions, and an ox and plough in the spring.

Harry stayed with the wagon all night. The family barely finished supper when everyone sunk into their beds and were asleep in minutes. Philip and Catrina rose before the sun. Catrina sighed and said, "This is our last day of travel. Soon we'll be home! I've been so tired that I haven't even had the energy to be homesick!"

Grinning, Philip said, "I know. We've been blessed have we not. We saw so many people suffer on the sea and so many looking so lost when we got to Philadelphia. But, there's still so much to do." They helped the children to the kitchen and enjoyed eggs, bread, cheese, ham, and milk.

With a mouthful of bread, Elizabeth declared the horse's name, "We'll call her Apple! She ate two apples after supper yesterday. She loved them."

"Okay Elizabeth, Apple sounds fine, don't choke on your breakfast," Philip replied.

Philip tied Apple to the back of the wagon, and Elizabeth sat close to her. They were soon on their way along Front Street. From that street, Philip could see the town fort inside the stockade. A blockhouse sat on each corner of the fort. Harry drove the horses out the town gate and down a hill about 125 metres. As they stopped at the flats next to the river, right away Philip noticed the rich dark soil on the flats. Pointing to a large field of harvested corn, he said, "Catrina, look at the size of that field of corn!"

Lewis replied, "The soil along the flat plains of the Mohawk River is outstanding. Every year the river deposits more soil and lots of driftwood. Right now the river is low, but in the spring it can flood, and down river there are lots of rapids and falls. The river starts in the Adirondack Mountains, about 242 kilometres west of here, and flows into the Hudson. 'T'is the only water route to the interior of North America. 'T'is been a major trade route for the Iroquois for hundreds of years. You'll see a lot of traffic on this river."[114] Harry guided the horses onto the rope ferry. Philip took Apple on and stood with her as the ferry was pulled about ninety two metres across the river. Harry drove the horses onto the King's Highway on the north side of the river. The road was wide enough and not too rough. As they rode along, Philip and Catrina studied the river and the land. There were several farms on both sides of the river, each one on the splendid soil of the flats at least sixty metres from the river. The flats rose to plateaus and hills covered with thick green forests strewn with fall colours, and the river meandered through the rich farmland and around several small islands. They'd driven about twenty seven kilometres when, about sixty metres from the shore, a large two storey stone house stood partially hidden by a stone wall and large willow trees. Philip could see several buildings, a grist mill, a blockhouse, and a rampart next to the house. A large creek entered the river close to the house. Lewis said, "The Mohawk call the creek Kayaderosseros. It means 'Valley of the Crooked Stream'. This is Mount Johnson the home of Major General William Johnson, but he's not here right now. He's at the army's camp at Lake George. In 1747, he bought the land from my father Joseph Clement Sr.. A few years later he built the house. 'T'was fortified this year because of troubles with the French and their Indian allies the Abenaki, Ojibwe, and Ottawa. We call it Fort Johnson."[115]

"You'll see Indians visiting General Johnson all through the year. There were up to 1000 at once, but usually only a few hundred.

Philip asked, "Where do they stay?"

"They camp on General Johnson's property, and he often has many stay in his home.[116] Most of the time they're from one of the six Iroquois Nations, sometimes Wyandot (Huron) or Nanticoke. My brother Jacob Clement was an interpreter for an Indian conference at Fort Johnson in May and June and a few weeks ago."[117]

Fig. 16. Traditional territories of the Haudenosaunee (Iroquois) Confederacy. Lionel Pincus and Princess Firyal Map Division, The New York Public Library. "New York province. Map of the country of the VI nations. Guy Johnson 1771." New York Public Library Digital Collections. http://digitalcollections.nypl.org/items/96fd0603-9b52-527c-e040-e00a18063f9b

Philip asked, "Do you have a family?"

"Yes, my wife's name is Caty Putnam. She's the daughter of Cornelius Putnam and Jacomintje Viele. Caty just delivered a baby girl a few weeks ago. Her name is Jacomintje.[118] She's a pleasure to watch. She's hard work for Caty though. And, I have two brothers and two sisters. My sister had a baby girl a few months ago, my niece Elizabeth Powell."

Pointing to the islands in front of Fort Johnson, Philip said, "Look Catrina. They even grow crops on the islands."

"I see them. Did you see the fine pastures and garden in front of the house?"

Lewis pointed to the other side of the river and said, "If you look over there you'll see the farm of Johannes Hough Sr.. He has land on both sides of the river, and he owns some of the small islands you see.[119] He has a son and grandson who can help with your cabin." Just as Harry drove around a bend, Lewis said, "We've only 6 ½ kilometres to travel. My place is north of here about 1 ½ kilometres. We won't have time to stop at William Bowen's.[120] We'd have to cross the river and then come back. If you tell me what you need for your fireplace, I'll tell him when I see him in a few days. He could make what you need and I'll bring them up."

"I need a crane and trammel, a ring pot stand, a shovel, tongs, ash rake, and a dog iron. I'll give you some money for Mr. Bowen. I expect I'll need it in about five or six days."

Lewis nodded, "'T'will take you about ten days to finish your cabin."

As Harry drove the horses around the bend in the river, Philip said, "Is that a fort on the south side?"

"Yes, that's Fort Hunter. It was built in 1711 to encourage the Mohawk people to convert to Christianity and to protect them from the French during Queen Anne's war. 'T'is about one kilometre down the Schoharie River on the east side. The Mohawks call the fort Teondalóga which means 'meeting of the waters, or two streams coming together'. 'T'is where the Mohawk River meets the Schoharie River. Teondalóga is one of three Mohawk villages or, as the English call them, Castles. Fort Hunter is the Lower Castle and home to the Wolf clan. Inside the palisades are four blockhouses and Queen Anne's Chapel. Reverend John Ogilvie is the Minister. He travels from St Peter's Episcopal Church in Albany. I hear there'll be a garrison there very soon. The British want to protect the Mohawks from the French, and the British want to make sure the Mohawks fight with them if they're needed."[121]

Philip asked, "Do the Mohawks live in cabins or tents?"

"Before there was a fort, their villages were about thirty longhouses made of wood and elm bark and surrounded by wood palisades. Some longhouses were 20 metres long and housed several families. Now, there's a village outside the fort palisades. Many families live in wigwams made of elm bark or in cabins.

They've come to depend on all the things that traders offer, things that make life easier for them like iron pots, knives, axes, and rifles. A newer stone church was built in 1741 near the fort, and there's a stone parsonage about 0.8 kilometres east of the Fort."[122]

Philip asked, "Are there any other churches close by?"

"Yes, about 6 ½ kilometres there's a Lutheran and a Reformed Dutch Church at Stone Raby (Stone Arabia)."[123] As they talked about the churches, Harry turned the horses north onto a narrow road. Lewis said, "This is the road through Tribes Hill past my place. We travel about five kilometres up onto that plateau and then northwest. I noticed that your little Canadian Mare is doing well. She's not too skittish, and your daughter loves her. You'll need some hay and oats to get her through the winter. I think Captain Peter Service Sr. can help with that and Adam Ruppert.[124] They live on the Kingsborough Patent about seven kilometres west of you across Cayadutta Creek.[125] I think you should stay with Michael Gallinger Sr. and his wife Agatha Ade while you're building. They live about four kilometres west of you on the Kingsborough Patent. They're a young German couple who came to the valley last year.[126] They're friendly people. I think you'll have lots to talk about. At least they speak your language better than I do."

"I wish there was a better way than intruding on people."

"Well, that's how it's done in the wilderness. It'll be a long time before there's an Inn here."

As they travelled north, Lewis looked east then said, "Harry turn onto this road. We'll stop about 1/2 kilometre. The road wasn't much more than a wide path, but the horses didn't hesitate. Mattheus was busy throwing pebbles that he collected on the pine bush road over the side of the wagon. Elizabeth kept an eye on Apple.

Lewis turned to talk to Catrina and the children. "Well, are you ready to see your home?"

"Really, you're tricking us!"

"No, I'm not. You must be grateful and proud that you endured such a long and hard journey! It takes great faith and courage to do what you did." Pointing to a large beech tree, Lewis said, "Pull over here Harry." Philip, Catrina, and the children got out of the wagon. In front of them were trees, lots of large trees. They couldn't see past them. Holding Catharina, Philip walked ahead to see if he could find a path through the underbrush. He waved and said, "Follow me Catrina. Bring Elizabeth and Mattheus."

With his family behind him, Philip managed to weave his way through the bush for about sixty metres when the trees gave way to a sizable meadow lined with birch trees. He stood for a few minutes looking in all directions. He spotted beech, hemlock, maple, and a few pine trees. He walked around and found a few bare spots in the grass. He dug several handfuls of soil. It was dark, soft, and had a fresh, sweet smell.

Catrina walked up beside Philip and smiled at the handful of dirt he was smelling. She smiled at him. Reaching for his hand, she said, "We are home! Our land, our home."

"Yes, we're really home, all of us. 'T'is impossible to believe we're standing here. I wish our parents could see this."

Elizabeth wandered into the meadow and played with the tall grass. Mattheus was close behind. Catrina picked a flower for Catharina. She clutched it in one hand and Poppy in the other. They walked a few hundred metres west where the meadow ended.

"I hear water. That is a good thing, a very good thing," said Philip.

Lewis appeared behind them and said, "We'd better go. It's long past mid-day. I don't want to greet the Gallingers in the dark, and I don't want to travel home in the dark."

"Yes, of course. We'll come back early tomorrow to walk the land and pick a site for our cabin."

As they headed down the narrow road, Philip's mind was filled with details of the work ahead. He imagined what the cabin would look like and what kind of shelter he'd build for Apple. He hoped there would be a few men to help. It was October 18th, and it was cool during the day with frost in the mornings. Snow would come soon. Despite all his worries and the heavy burden of such a dangerous journey, he felt fortunate to have had the help of so many people. His family was safe, and unbelievably he was now living what were once just thoughts and dreams in Germany. He took a few deep breaths hoping it would make things seem more real. On their way to the Gallingers' cabin, they passed a few farms not far from the road which, in the heart of this wild place, was reassuring. Lewis directed Harry, "Pull into this lane and up to the cabin."

The wagon hadn't come to a full stop when a young man came out the door of the cabin. A young woman followed with a bucket in each hand. The young man hollered, "Good day Lewis. I see you've brought guests."

Talking while he was climbing out of the wagon, Lewis said, "These are your new neighbours. We've just come up from Schenectady and stopped to see their land. Now I've come to ask if you can put them up for about a few weeks while they build a cabin and get ready for winter. They're over at the Sacandaga Patent."

"We certainly do have room, and we'd love to have them stay while they get settled."

Philip shook the young man's hand and said, "Hello Sir. I'm Philip Eamer. This is my wife Catrina and my daughters Elizabeth and Catharina and my son Mattheus. 'T'is a pleasure to meet you."

"Hello Philip. I'm Michael Gallinger Sr. and this is my wife Agatha. I'm glad to see you've arrived safely and that you'll stay with us. Let's get your things out of the wagon. We can store them in the loft for now. We can put your young mare in the pasture close to the cabin.

While Michael was helping Philip with Apple, Agatha set the buckets down by the door and offered Mattheus her hand. "Let's go inside," she said.

Catrina followed with Catharina and Elizabeth and said, "It's very kind of you to offer your home to strangers. Thank you."

"We're glad to help, and 't'is nice for us too. We now have a young couple and three children to get to know." Agatha took Catrina's knapsack and started up the steep stairs to the loft. "I think there's room for all of you up here. There's one bed big enough for you and Philip and the little one. I'll fix something on the floor for Mattheus and Elizabeth. The heat from the fire keeps it warm up here."

Resisting a pressing urge to lie down and after taking two deep breaths Catrina said, "This will be fine. We're happy to share our provisions while we're here."

Philip came into the cabin carrying a load from the wagon, and Elizabeth called from the loft, "We sleep up here Papa. Can I go see Apple Papa? Please, she'll be hungry."

"She's fine Elizabeth. She has hay. You help Mama."

Mattheus interrupted, "Are we going to build a cabin Papa? Can I help? It'll be really big, and I'll have my own bed!"

"Okay Mattheus. You can help in a few days."

Lewis and Michael followed Philip into the cabin. Lewis said, "I must take my leave now Philip. Michael tells me he knows a few men that he'll ask to help build the cabin. If I see Captain Service or Adam Ruppert, I'll ask about hay for your mare."

As Philip shook Lewis' hand, he said, "My deep gratitude to you Sir for everything you've done for us. Here's money for the fireplace items that Mr. Bowen will make. And, here's a small amount for you for all your trouble."

"Oh no Sir. I won't take your money. I'm sure there'll be many times you can offer me a favour. This is your home now, and we are your neighbours. I'll be off now. You can expect me back in about six days."

After a generous meal of rabbit, peas, bread, cheese, and apple cider, Philip and Michael sat by the fire and talked about their journeys to America. For Philip, it was a relief to tell someone about the hard parts of the journey without having to search for an English word or an appropriate hand gesture. Michael Gallinger eagerly shared his stories too. He and Agatha came from Hopfau, Baden-Württemberg about 241 kilometres southeast of Auerbach. Even though Michael came from a different part of Germany, many of his stories were similar. Catrina and Agatha offered their view of experiences that carried the conversation on for a few hours. But soon it was time to retire. It didn't take long before the only sound in the cabin was the crackle of the fire.

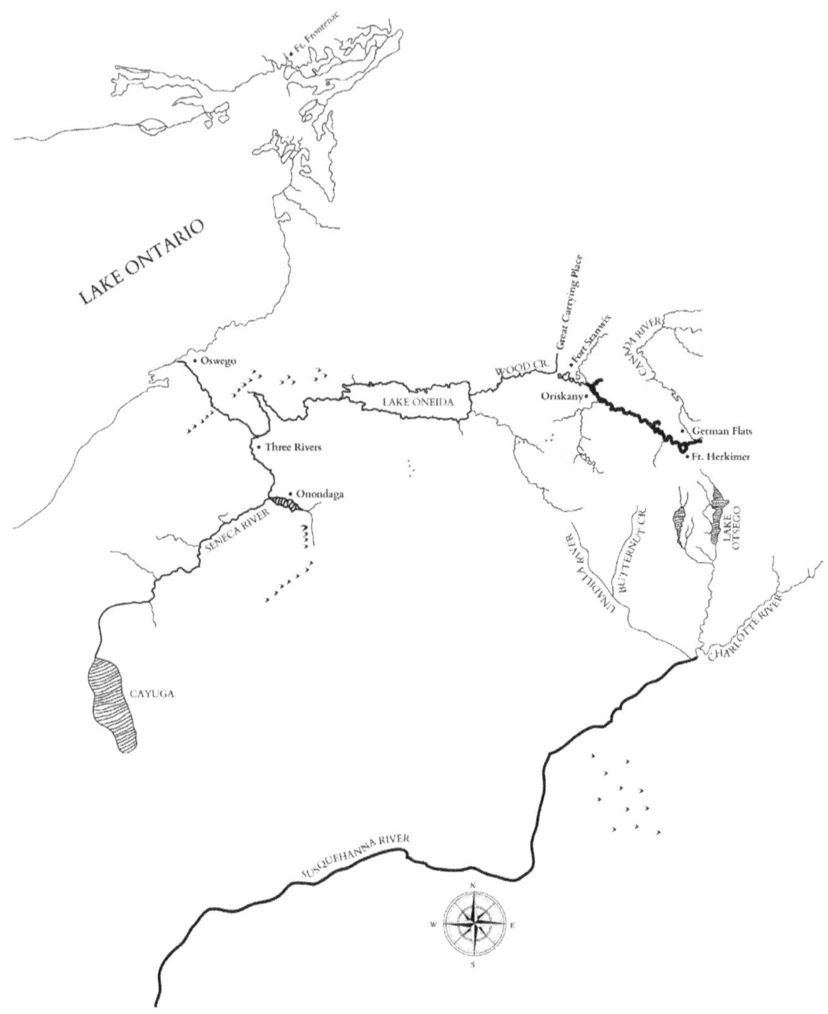

Fig. 17. Northwestern New York. Adapted from Claude Joseph Sauthier, A Map of the Province of New York, 1771. Library of Congress, Geography and Map Division, 74692660 http://hdl.loc.gov/loc.gmd/g3800.ar104702

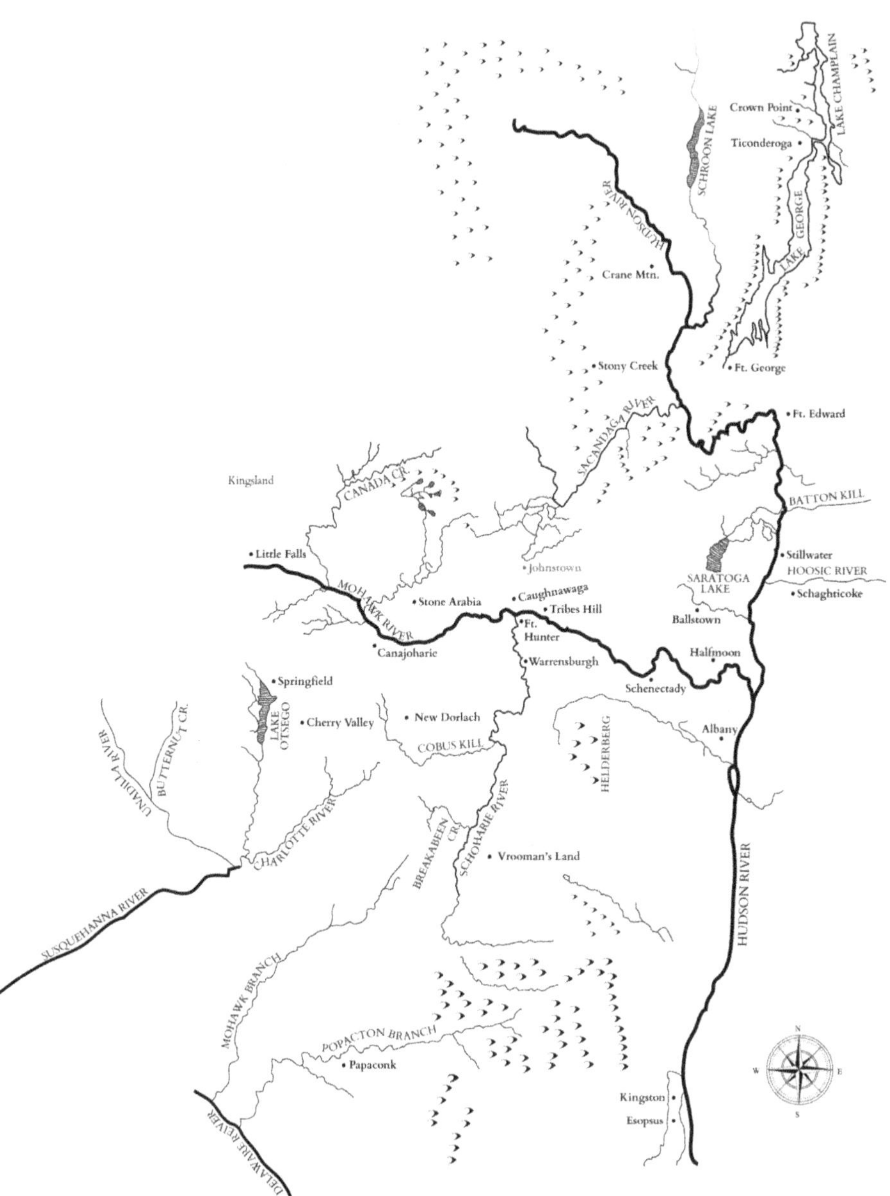

Fig. 18. Northeastern New York. Adapted from Claude Joseph Sauthier, A Map of the Province of New York, 1771. Library of Congress, Geography and Map Division, 74692660 http://hdl.loc.gov/loc.gmd/g3800.ar104702

Fig 19 Lot Map Kingsborough Patent West. Adapted From: New York State Archives, Albany, New York Collection #AO273, Portfolio E Map #859. And New York State Library's Special Collections Division, Manuscript Number XM20211.

See Appendix H for a list of the tenants of the Kingsborough and Sacandaga Patents

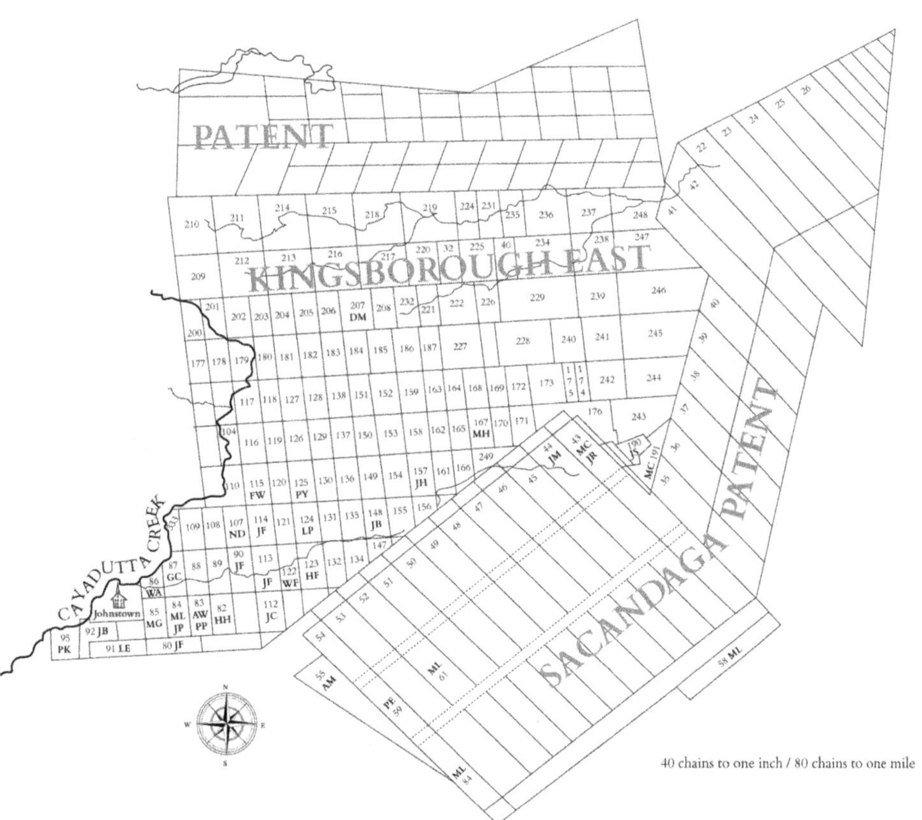

Fig. 20. Lot Map Kingsborough Patent East and Sacandaga Patent. Adapted From: New York State Archives, Albany, New York Collection #AO273, Portfolio E Map #859. And New York State Library's Special Collections Division, Manuscript Number XM20211.

See Appendix H for a list of the tenants of the Kingsborough and Sacandaga Patents

CHAPTER THREE

Settlement in New York (1755-1763)

Philip woke before the sun rose and tried to lie quietly for at least few minutes. He couldn't calm his mind and fidgeting was the consequence. Catrina woke when his wiggling leg bumped her feet. "Oh my, a restless husband! When you get to the lot what'll you do first?" she asked.

Laughing, Philip answered, "Well that's a good question. I think I've a plan, but who knows what'll happen when we get there."

It was Sunday, October 18 and a new moon day. This was a good sign. This new moon day symbolized a new start, and without question that was exactly what he was doing. Michael was up early and went to George Crites house on the lot behind him to ask him if he could help with the cabin.[127]As soon as Michael returned, they were organized and ready to go. Michael hitched his horse to his wagon, and they loaded what they needed for the day.

Philip gave Catrina and the children a hug and said, "As soon as all the trees we need are felled, you can come to the lot. I'll need help collecting stones and moss."

"We'll look forward to it. Today, I'll be busy sewing a tick for a mattress. I've two to make and one small one for a cradle. Enjoy your day husband."

As they turned out of the lane and onto the road, Michael said, "George Crites said he can help. He'll come by tomorrow. Now, we'll stop at the farm of Mattheus Link on our way to your lot. His farm is next to me. His wife's name is Maria Magdelena Kraft, and they've a new baby girl Maria. I was shocked when I learned we came from the same village of Hopfau, Baden-Württemberg. Like us, the Links only just arrived in America last year."[128]

Michael drove his horse up another narrow lane, and Philip saw a cabin almost from the road. Mattheus met the wagon as they came up the lane and said. "Good morning Michael. 'T'is a fine Sunday morning."

"Hello Mattheus. This is Philip Eamer our new neighbor. He's just arrived from Philadelphia with his wife and three children. We're planning to get a cabin built this week. Can you help us?"

"Good to meet you Philip. I'd be happy to help with the build. I'll come by tomorrow."

Michael nodded and said, "Many thanks Mattheus. George Crites will be there too, and I'm going to ask Jacob Henry Alguire (see Appendix D). That'll make five of us. I'm sure Philip will have his cabin before snow flies. Don't forget your axe, saw, wedge, and firelock."

When Philip and Michael arrived at lot fifty nine, Philip pulled out the map that Harmans Wendell drew for Lewis. On it were markers for the boundaries of the lot. Philip wanted to start at the nearest corner marker and walk their way diagonally to each corner and around the perimeters. After his walk, he should know where to build the cabin. He wanted it on higher ground and close to the creek with a good stand of white pine and fir close by. Lands on the south end of the Sacandaga Patent were known for their fine soil and many stands of hemlock and white pine. Lot fifty nine was at the most southerly end of the patent. White pine was Philip's best choice to build the cabin. It's soft and easy to work, but most importantly it's tall and straight.[129] The nearest marker was a large beech tree in the southwest corner. If the map was accurate, they should walk just past the creek. While Philip was reading the map, Michael collected their firelocks, powder horns, and haversacks. The chance of encountering a party of French and their Indian allies was possible, so carrying a firelock and knife was necessary.

Philip and Michael spent the whole morning walking the land stopping often to examine the creek, the trees, and the lay of the land. Philip chose a spot for the cabin close to the road in the southwest corner of the lot about sixty metres from the creek. He wouldn't have time to dig a well before winter, so the creek was their only water source. The creek was as essential as the trees, and it needed to be a short walk from the cabin. By late afternoon, they marked all the trees they needed, and they cleared brush for the cabin site and for a narrow lane from the road to the cabin. On their way home, Michael took a detour north on the

Sacandaga Patent. He wanted to stop at Jacob Henry Alguire's place to ask if he could help.

While navigating the narrow road along the western edge of the Sacandaga Patent, Michael talked about Jacob Henry's family, "Jacob lives in an area called Philadelphia Bush about four miles northwest of us. Two years ago, he came from the village of Ersingin, Baden-Württemberg with his wife Maria Salome Wahl and two sons Martin Alguire and Sebastian Alguire. His daughter Sophia Alguire was born at sea and baptized only a few weeks after they arrived.[130] Maybe his son Martin can help too. He's ten now and a good strong boy." They arrived at Jacob Henry and Salome's place just as Jacob was going out to feed his cow. Jacob agreed to be at the lot the next day, and he didn't hesitate to volunteer Martin's help. It was dusk when Philip and Michael got home. Everyone was eager to listen to Philp describe the cabin site and what they did that day.

On the fifth day of building, Catrina was up first on this frosty morning, and she was first in the wagon. For days, she heard all about the cabin, the land, and the new neighbours. She wanted to be there to see some of the building and meet the neighbours.

As the wagon moved toward the road, she asked Philip, "What can we help with today?"

"Well, we have to pack moss between all the logs, so you and Catharina can collect moss. You mustn't go too far from the cabin site. There's a chance that Frenchmen or Indians might be lurking near the cabin. Don't worry. We're well protected; we all have our firelocks. I'll keep Mattheus and Elizabeth with me. They can help pick stones. We've already placed the foundation stones for the cabin, but we need a lot of smaller stones for the fireplace."

Catrina added, "I've almost finished the ticking for the mattresses and pillows, and Elizabeth is learning to sew pillowcases. We'll need to have straw ready when we move in so I can stuff the ticks."

When they arrived at the cabin site, Catrina was amazed at the progress the men had made. They were ready to start the roof and the fireplace. The cabin was a good size and in a good position. It was six metres by 4 ½ metres with a front and back door, a kitchen with a window on one side of a large central fireplace, and a bedroom and sitting room on the other side. A steep staircase near the front door led up to a small loft. Catrina recognized the layout of their cabin from many small houses she saw in Germany.[131]

She said to Philip, "I like the window facing south. We'll get warmth and light from the sun."

Philip answered, "Our neighbours say there's a south westerly wind in the valley. So, if Apple's shelter is behind the house it'll block the wind. She'll be closer to the meadow too.

Catrina spent the morning collecting moss, and little Catharina helped her pack it into buckets. She was glad to take a break at lunch; her fingers were cold, and Catharina needed a rest. At lunch, she got to know her new neighbours. She met Jacob Henry Alguire's ten year old son Martin who was not only helping the men, but also playing with Mattheus and Elizabeth.[132] George Crites was a weaver so Catrina enjoyed talking to him about his loom, flax, linen, and weaving.

After lunch, Lewis Clement drove his wagon up the rough lane, waving he said, "Good day to you all. I'm amazed at all you've done neighbours." Catrina and Elizabeth greeted him at the wagon. "Good day Madam," he said.

"Good day to you Sir," Catrina replied.

Elizabeth ran to the back of the wagon saying, "Is all this hay for Apple!"

"Yes, Elizabeth. Mr. Peter Service Sr. and Mr. Adam Ruppert gave it to her."

"Oh Sir, please thank Mr. Service and Mr. Ruppert. Apple will love it."

"Where's your Papa Elizabeth? I've some things for his fireplace."

"He's been very busy. Now, he's making shingles with Mr. Alguire."

As Lewis was climbing off the wagon, Philip walked up. "Hello Lewis. So glad to see you."

"Glad to see you too Philip. I brought you the fireplace items you wanted and a welcome gift of hay from Mr. Service and Mr. Ruppert. I also have your special cargo. I see you're making progress on the cabin."

"Yes, there's lots of help. We're just finishing the shingles, and tomorrow we'll finish the fireplace. We should be able to move in on Wednesday."

It was early Wednesday morning October 28 when Michael and Agatha helped Philip and Catrina load their provisions and belongings onto the wagon and set out for the cabin. Elizabeth and Mattheus were settled in the back trying to keep the chickens calm. Catrina turned to Michael and said, "Thank you for these wonderful chickens Michael. They were a thoughtful gift and a treat for us to have fresh eggs every day!"

"You're welcome Madam. They're 'Dunghill' chickens. Some call them 'Barn Door' chickens. They're common round here. Not a fancy breed Madam, but they do give eggs. I expect a nice flock next year. I raise geese too."[133]

"Michael please call me Catrina. We're friends now."

The horses pulled their load over the light skiff of snow that defined the narrow road. In places they could see the sun shine through the trees, but for most of the ride trees hugged both sides of the road. As the wagon rolled along, Catrina thought, "The trees so close make me feel like I'm in a cage with nowhere to run. Sometimes, I feel like we're here all by ourselves. What a relief that we've met our neighbours. I'm certain if we need help our neighbours will be there, even if it does take a while."

Michael had barely halted the horses when Catrina practically leapt out of the wagon while keeping a firm grip on Catharina. Elizabeth and Mattheus followed. "Look Mama! There's chopped wood in that shelter, and there's an outhouse over there."

Elizabeth ran to the back of the cabin. Catrina couldn't believe she was looking at a log cabin with a front door, a window, and a chimney. She stepped in the front door and said as Mattheus was halfway up the stairs to the loft, "Oh, it's beautiful. The fireplace is perfect. There's even a crane and trammel to hang my pots over the fire. And look at these two sturdy tables and benches."

Philip walked up behind her, "Come around to the back room. I want to show you something."

She followed him to the room behind the kitchen. "Oh! It's a box stove. We'll sleep well in this warm room."[134]

Philip, Michael, Agatha, and Catrina spent the next hour unloading provisions and belongings. Some of the provisions went up to the loft, and Catrina put some on the shelves next to the kitchen window. Catrina unpacked the slapsack while little Catharina concentrated on putting spoons into several bowls.

As Catrina was emptying the slapsack, she found a package, and when she unwrapped it several pine knots fell out. "Philip did you buy these pine knots?" she asked.

"No, Lewis must have bought them for us and slipped them into our bag."

"How kind of him. He told us about using those pine knots for light instead of candles."

"Where did you get the bricks for the box stove?"

"William Bowen Sr. got them at General Johnson's kiln, and Lewis brought them. I wanted to surprise you with something special."

"This cabin is special, and the land is a gift from God. Praise God for bringing all of us safely here among such fine people."

"Yes, you're right Catrina. I'm relieved and proud that we got the cabin built in time. Since we left the English coast, I've worried about all of us freezing to death in the wilderness. Which was a possibility had it not been for all the help we received along the way, including the Lord's help."

Elizabeth came skipping in the back door saying, "Mama come and see the fine shelter Papa built for Apple. It has a thick roof of fir boughs, and she has a paddock to keep her safe."

"I'll come shortly Elizabeth. I want to look at the furniture your Papa made, and we need to unload the wagon." "Do we have straw for the bedding?" Catrina asked Philip.

"Yes, Mr. Alquire brought some. It's in the wood shelter."

"We'll need to stuff our bed and pillow ticking before it gets dark. After we unload the wagon, can you string the bed cord so that I can lay the straw ticks? Where's Mattheus?"

Pointing in the direction of the wood shed Philip replied, "He's outside making a temporary home for the chickens. I'll go get him and bring him inside. And, I'll get some water and start filling our barrel. When I get back, I'll start a fire with the coals that Michael brought."

As he went out the door, Catrina reminded him, "Don't forget your firelock."

That night, the family was glad to rest after a supper of leftover stew, biscuits, and apple pudding that Agatha Gallinger and Salome Alguire left for them. It was easy to rest after the gruelling ten days of work. There was a fire drawing well in the kitchen, coals in the stove box, and their water barrel in the kitchen was full. Elizabeth and Mattheus were in their beds in the back bedroom, and Philip, Catrina, and Catharina would soon share a bigger bed in the stove room. In the loft, they had enough provisions for winter and spring. Outside, there were about six cords of dry wood chopped, and Apple and the chickens were relatively safe from wolves or foxes. All was well. Catrina lay awake thinking of all the things she could do for herself and the family during the long winter months, especially preparing for their new baby. Philip already made hunting plans with Jacob Henry Alguire and Michael Gallinger.

Through November, Catrina was busy knitting badly needed bed socks and nightcaps. While sitting beside her, Elizabeth asked, "Mama, am I doing this right? Is the wool too thick?"

"You're doing fine with that hand whorl Elizabeth. Look how much wool you've spun this hour! We can knit two pairs of socks with that."

Even with a good fire in the fireplace and coals in the stove box, they all saw their breath in the mornings, and frost could be seen on logs on the inside walls. Any warm clothing was welcome. Philip kept busy making sure the water barrel was full and there was enough wood in the cabin for four or five days. Mattheus loved to help stack wood neatly beside the fireplace and collect the odd precious winter egg that a chicken would lay.

One early sunny morning near the end of November, Mattheus sat staring as Philip carved the rockers and hood for the new baby's cradle. They were so absorbed in the carving they didn't notice the wagon approach until it was halfway down their lane. The man driving wasn't someone Philip knew neither was the young man sitting next to him. "Good day Sir," the man said as he stopped in front of the cabin. "I'm Johannes Hough Sr. from near Fort Hunter and this is my son Henry Hough. William Bowen Sr. told us of your arrival. He lives about 1 ½ kilometres west of us. We've come with a load of dry wood and pieces of green deer hide."

"Good day to you Mr. Hough and Henry. We're always pleased to greet neighbours, and the wood and hide are needed. My wife Catrina is inside with our two daughters. This is my son Mattheus. Please come in."

Johannes and Henry sat on one of the benches while Philip poured them a bit of rum. Mattheus sat himself down right next to Henry. Turning toward Johannes, Philip asked, "Have you lived in the valley long?"

"I was born here. My father Henry Hough Sr. bought land along both sides of the river from Adam Vrooman about twenty nine years ago. 'T'is at Warrensburg near Fort Hunter.[135] We've seen a lot of settlers come to this part of the valley since General Johnson settled in Warrensburg back in 1737. There are almost as many as when the Germans from Schoharie settled German Flats and Stone Raby (Stone Arabia) in 1723.[136] Before I forget, I'm letting everyone know that there's good news about General Johnson. King George just granted him the title of Baronet for his work in settling this area and the magnificent defeat of the French at Lake George in August. We know him now as Sir William Johnson,

Knight and Baronet. He's a good man, very helpful to all the settlers and wants good things for the Indians."[137]

"Catrina and I'll be honored to meet him sometime."

"He's still up at Lake George. His army is helping to build a new fort. It's called Fort William Henry. It's just north of Fort Edward about twenty seven kilometres. The new fort will help protect the valley from the French coming down Lake George from Canada."

"I wondered Johannes, was there a specific purpose for the pieces of green deer hide?"

"Yes, I wanted to show you how to make snowshoes. You're going to need them to go hunting. By January there'll be a metre of snow. You can't walk very far in deep snow. I dried four frames for you, so you can make two pair, one for you and one for your wife. I'll show you how to lace them before we go. Henry is very good at making them."

"Thanks Johannes. I've been worried about the trip to the creek every day. There's a path now, but if there's a heavy snow, I'll have troubles. You're so kind to help us this way. And, we are beholden to you for the wood. 'T'is a blessing."

Very quickly, Philip was lacing several strips of hide on his own. Mattheus held the strips of hide straight while Elizabeth watched how her father wrapped the hide around the frame. Before Johannes and Henry left, they helped unload the wood from the wagon. As they climbed in the wagon, Catrina handed Henry a bundle of biscuits. Johannes said, "Maybe we'll see you in church at Stone Raby soon. Sometimes we go there instead of Fort Hunter. But for now, keep well."

"You also," Catrina replied.

Christmas past quietly, and January 1756 arrived with a heavy snowstorm. By now there was almost ½ metre of snow surrounding the little cabin. Paths to the outhouse, woodshed, Apple's shelter and the creek were well worn, and a column of smoke from the chimney rose softly through the trees. Philip, Jacob Henry Alguire, and Michael Gallinger set their snares just after Christmas and were ready to go out to see what was caught.

As Philip was putting on his snowshoes, Catrina stood at the front door and said, "Here's some bread and dried meat for the day. I'd be very happy if you brought us a few rabbits Philip. Their fur will line the hoods of our blanket coats, and I'll save some to line some moccasins. Rabbit stew will be nice too." She had to take two steps back to leave room for her very pregnant belly when she closed the door. It would be a busy day washing and baking bread, but she favoured the activity when Philip was away; otherwise, she'd worry about Frenchmen or Indians attacking their home, hurting them, or worse stealing the children. Those worries sent chills through her just like the sound of the wolves howling at night. It was a hideous sound she often heard too close to the cabin.

February didn't come soon enough for Catrina. She was ready for their baby. Elizabeth helped her cut and sew flannel for napkins (diapers) and a bed gown, and they used some of the linen to sew two shirts and caps. Catrina knit a nice mohair blanket. Philip finished the cradle with Mattheus' supervision.

One afternoon, Catrina was working in the kitchen when she turned and looked at little Catharina and said, "You love to sit in that cradle don't you. Why don't you put Poppy in the cradle? Catharina stop rocking so hard. You'll fall over! You can rock the baby when it comes."

Catharina replied in her little voice, "Boy baby, girl baby?"

"Mama doesn't know. We'll have to wait and see." When Catrina finished in the kitchen, she lay down on her bed with Catharina. Catrina wasn't comfortable. She tossed and turned, and then she knew. The baby was coming. "Elizabeth, call Papa!" she cried.

Philip raced into the room, "Now!"

"Yes, now Philip. Get Agatha!"

"Okay, I'll take Apple. I'll be back soon." As he left, he hollered, "Elizabeth put water in the kettle over the fire and watch Mama! Mattheus watch your little sister."

Martin Eamer was a beautiful little boy who was born soon after Philip brought Agatha Gallinger to help Catrina.[138] Philip held his new son while Agatha helped Catrina settle. He thought, "What a beautiful boy. A fine son and brother. He's travelled a long distance already, and he's the first to be born in America."

"Is he healthy?" Philip asked Agatha.

"He's just fine, and so is Catrina. You are a proud Papa again! Have you thought about his baptism? I just helped Salome Alguire deliver a fine baby girl yesterday. Her name is Elizabeth Alguire.[139] Both of you should arrange their baptism soon. Reverend John Ogilvie makes regular visits to Fort Hunter. Michael can send a message to the fort to let the Reverend know that two children have been born."

One of Reverend Ogilvie's regular visits to Fort Hunter was early in February, and he knew that the Eamers and Alguires had children needing to be baptized. So, Philip arranged for Jacob Henry, Salome, and their children to come to their cabin so Martin and Elizabeth could be baptized. On February 11th, Reverend Ogilvie arrived at the cabin in his sleigh. Everyone gathered in the kitchen. Young Martin Alguire sat on the bench holding Sophia, and Sebastian sat next to him. Elizabeth, Mattheus, and little Catharina sat on the other bench. The Reverend's German wasn't very good, but they managed to get through the baptisms. It was a quick service but important that the children would be in God's hands if they should pass on. Jacob Henry and Salome had met the Reverend when Sophia was baptized two years ago. Catrina and Philip were glad to meet him and comforted to know that there was one of God's servants close by.

As the weeks went on, Catrina felt stronger every day, but she relied on her faith to get her through most days. One morning while feeding Martin, she said to Philip, "I know we have each other and good neighbours, but I go to sleep thinking about French and Indian attacks, and I wake up thinking about them!"

"I worry too, and I'm constantly alert to noises and movement outside the cabin.[140] Michael Gallinger tells me General Johnson and most of his militia returned from Fort Edward in December, so we have militia here now. And, they've almost finished building the new Fort William Henry. Michael says General Johnson has a strong relationship with the Mohawks and many other Nations in the area. The King appointed him Colonel of the Six Nations and Northern Superindendant of Indian Affairs. In fact, he had more than 500 Indians from each of the Six Nations gather at Fort Johnson for the whole month of February.[141] Not only is he Sir William Johnson, but now he's an Iroquois Pine Tree Chief, an Iroquois Sachem. The Iroquois believe that his regard for their people is genuine, and they are impressed with his skill and knowledge about their ways. We hope they'll help protect us. They're not too keen on getting involved in fighting."[142]

Catrina stared blankly while Philip was talking and blurted out, "We need some kind of defense here in our own home!"

"Okay, we'll get a firelock for you, and we'll find a place in the forest for you and the children to hide. We'll have a plan if you should need to run. I'll talk to Michael Gallinger, Mattheus Link, Jacob Henry Alguire, and George Crites about a plan for our families. Maybe Lewis, Johannes, and his son Henry, or

William Bowen Sr. can help. They've experience scouting and fighting in the bush."

It was only the melting snow and the plans to clear land that held Catrina and Philip's anxieties at bay. Early in April another diversion occurred. Philip, Catrina, and the children were invited to attend the baptism of Mattheus and Magdelena Link's son Johannes Gottfried Link at the Trinity Lutheran Church in Stone Raby. This church was one of the first in the valley. It was a small log building on lot twenty of the first allotment of the Stone Arabia patent of 1723.[143] The church was about twenty two kilometres from their cabin. For about five kilometres, Philip led Apple with Catrina and baby Martin and little Catharina sitting atop and Elizabeth and Mattheus walking beside until they reached Michael Gallinger's farm. The rest of the way, they joined Michael and his family in their wagon.

Pastor Johannes Frederick Ries[144] conducted the baptism in the little church. The church was nearly full of parishioners from Stone Raby (Stone Arabia) and the village of Canajoharie just across the river. After the service, Philip and Catrina met several people from Stone Raby, most of them spoke German although their tongue revealed that they were from different areas of Germany. The men talked of the recent militia marches to Fort William Henry.

Michael wanted Philip to meet one of the earliest settlers in the area. He said, "I want you to meet Mr. Philip Empey Sr. His father Johannes Empey Sr. came with the first German settlers into this valley in 1723 and was one of the first lot holders in the Stone Raby Patent. He's also an Elder of the church. 'T'is good for you to know that he's originally from Königsberg, East Prussia but more recently Worms, Rhineland-Palatinate a few kilometres west of your home in Germany."[145] They walked over to a man who had just finished talking to Reverend Ries. Michael approached him and said, "Good day Mr. Empey. This is Philip Eamer, a new resident of the Sacandaga Patent. Michael asked, "How are you folks here at Stone Raby these past few months?"

Philip Empey Sr. replied, "Good day Michael. Things are very tense everywhere in the valley ever since our victory at Lake George. It seems the French don't want to give up their ideas of conquering the fur trade routes to Albany or the rich farmland of our beautiful valley. The militia has been called out for months now. As we speak, many men from this area are serving in Captain Robert McGinnis' Company. There are William Casselman Sr., his son

Severinus Casselman, Henry Frey Sr., and Richard Hare and his brother John Hare Jr. . Their father Sergeant John Hare Sr. and their brother Corporal William Hare just returned from duty in December.[146] And Lieutenant Henry Hanson has been on the march with his men since March.[147] They'll surely be a need for more men to be ready to march again any time!" Philip and Michael listened to Philip Empey with occasional nods of their heads until it was time to leave.

Despite their fears, Philip and Catrina had work to do. With Martin wrapped in the shawl she brought from Germany and slung over her back, Catrina spent three days clearing a small patch of brush for a garden. The girls' help was a blessing.

One afternoon during a short rest, she mentioned to Philip, "We need to go to Lieutenant Fonda's store at Caughnawaga and purchase a gun, lead, and powder for me. I'll feel safer when you're out in the bush. We also need some seeds."

"Okay, I'll see if Michael, Mattheus, or Jacob Henry are planning a trip there soon. It's not safe to travel alone. I'll get some provisions, and I want to ride over to Andrew Snyder's place. He's west on the Kingsborough Patent across Cayadutta Creek near Peter Service Sr. and Adam Ruppert. I hear Mr. Snyder has cows.[148] Maybe he has oxen too."

"We don't have much money left Philip, maybe not enough to last until we harvest a crop, and you still want to buy a plough and the oxen will need a yoke."

By May, settlers knew that Sir William led over 1000 militia to German Flats after he got word that 5000 French and Indian were within two days march of the settlement. Philip and Catrina knew German Flats was only about fifty six kilometres from their cabin, so they did what they could to stay safe. They chose a thick stand of trees near the creek as a place Catrina and the children could hide from attacks. The trees and thick green underbrush gave them cover. If they should make a noise, the sound of the water would make it difficult for anyone to hear them. Philip taught Catrina how to load and shoot the firelock. Mattheus and Elizabeth learned how to prepare the lead and powder for their mother. Soon, it would be difficult for Catrina to hide in any small space or run carrying an infant. She was pregnant and needed to tell Philip and the children that there'd be another baby in February.

Soon after Sir William sent troops to German Flats, two families arrived from Philadelphia to settle at Philadelphia Bush. Sir William kindly gave them money to get provisions.[149] Philip met one family when he went to help

Jacob Henry Alguire clear bush and cut firewood. Jacob introduced Philip to Johannes Alguire Sr. and his wife Catherine Margretha Müller. They had three children, Johannes George Alguire ten years old, Maria Elizabeth Alguire eight, and Catherine Alguire seven. Jacob Henry loved to tell everyone that he and Johannes lived only forty kilometres from each other in Baden, Württemberg, Germany. Johannes was from Ittlingen and Jacob Henry was from Ersingen. Philip knew how tired the family must have been. He travelled the same route only one year ago.

While Philip was out on the land starting to clear brush and trees, he chose an area as close to the house as he could and close to the meadow which gave him an easier start at clearing a few acres. He had bought a young oxen from Andrew Snyder and a yoke at the Caughnawaga store, and he started to teach Mattheus how to clear the land.

One morning, before going out on the land, Philip explained, "Some men take off a circle of bark around the trunk of a tree; they call it girdling. Eventually, the tree dies, but it's a slow death. We'll not do it that way son. We'll fell the trees with an ax and saw and remove each of the stumps.[150] T'is hard hard work, but the land is cleared sooner, and you don't have to plough around stumps. I'll need your help to clear brush and pick stones."

"I'm six now Papa, and I'm strong!"

Often, Philip had help from his neighbours. The men worked in groups, sometimes they worked at Philip's, sometimes at Jacob Henry Alguire's, Mattheus Link's, George Crites', or Michael Gallinger's place. Whenever they were out, one or two men stood guard and all had their firelocks close by.

One morning near the beginning of August, Philip sat on a log in front of the cabin cleaning his firelock. He was taking a break from clearing land to do some chores at the cabin. One of his chores was to go with Catrina to the creek to stand guard while she, Elizabeth, and little Catharina washed clothes.

While at the creek, Philip and Catrina talked about their hard work through the spring and summer and what was left to do before winter. Philip said, "I'm happy that we managed to clear about three acres and dig a well. Next spring, I can clear more acres and start ploughing and planting some wheat. I'm sorry that I haven't had much time to hunt. 'T'is too dangerous to go into the bush."

"I've nothing to complain about husband. I think you've done well with hunting. I now know many different ways to cook pigeon, rabbit, and wild turkey! The best prize was the deer you brought home. Maybe in the fall you'll bring another, or maybe a bear. We'll have a nice black rug on which Martin and Catharina can play. I hear bear meat is tasty and its fat will be useful. And every time I dip a bucket in the well, I praise you, our neighbours, and God. And, I love to stand and look at the open space you've made, even though it's still littered with branches and boughs. Could you ever have imagined having so many acres to plant! Wouldn't our parents be surprised and proud?"

Not long after their day at the creek, Lewis Clement's wagon rolled down their lane. Johannes Hough Sr. was with him. Philip was splitting wood when he saw Lewis halt the horses, wrap the reins over the seat, and leap out of the wagon.

"Hello Johannes, Lewis. What's wrong Lewis?" Philip asked.

Lewis planted his feet on the ground and said, "I'm letting everyone know that Sir William is sending militia out to Fort Oswego about 215 kilometres west of here to guard our fortification on Lake Ontario. I know 't'is far, but if the French take the fort, they'll have an open route into our valley. Sir William is asking anyone who can spare time to assist with cutting a road from German Flats to Oswego to meet at Fort Johnson. Hans Jost Herkimer, Hans Petrie, and Conrad Frank can't help, and they haven't been able to secure the help of anyone else at German Flats."[151]

"You'll be glad to know that Sir William is strengthening the garrison at Fort Johnson with men from the 42nd Regiment. The 42nd are men of the Black Watch or Royal Highland Regiment of Foot. They just arrived in Albany last summer. The 44th is planning to march to Oswego. Colonel Bradstreet just went there with 500 men, wagons, and batteaux to deliver supplies for 1500 troops. The French and Indians ambushed Bradstreet, but they got to the fort and kept the supply lines open for now."[152]

Philip put down his axe and said, "Things don't sound good even though we have troops protecting us. It's my wish to help, but I can't leave my family without defense. Do you think we should move our families to Fort Hunter?"

Lewis nodded and said, "You might have to if the French break through at Oswego or at Fort William Henry."

By the middle of August things got worse. Mattheus Link and George Crites came one day to help Philip clear logs. Mattheus said to Philip and George, "We need to sit for a few minutes and make a plan to secure our families!"

"What's happened?" Philip asked Mattheus while he poured rum into three cups.

Philip lit his pipe and sat down while Mattheus talked, "The French have taken Oswego.[153] At least Fort William Henry and Fort Edward are still in British hands, but there's danger the French will come down the Mohawk River from the west. Sir William is taking 1000 men to German Flats. Lieutenant Jelles Fonda is there now with Captain Thomas Butler. Two hundred twenty men are at Herkimer Church Fort, and Captain Gates and his men are across the river at Canajoharie."[154]

After a gulp of rum and a long drag on his pipe, Philip said, "Is there a place not far from here that would offer us refuge and safety?"

"Sir William's house is about thirteen kilometres from here," George replied.

"That's far when we might be running for our lives."

George added, "Captain Walter Butler's house at Switzer Hill is only about eight kilometres. But 't'is not well fortified. He and his sons Thomas and John are officers in the militia and with the Indians. They're always away. There's Fort Hunter. Captain Walter Butler is the commander there. But, I think heading for Fort Johnson is a better decision."

Mattheus sipped on his rum and said, "I think Fort Hunter is best, five extra kilometres to Fort Johnson might mean life or death."

Philip nodded in agreement, "Okay then, if the French come down the river, we'll meet at Fort Hunter. We'll travel in groups. I don't have a wagon, so we'll need help."

"There'll be room in a wagon for you," Mattheus said.

The month of September was spent getting ready for winter. Philip spent most days clearing the felled trees and branches and chopping firewood. Catrina and the children spent their time putting away vegetables from the garden and picking wild berries. In the spring, Catrina managed to plant cabbage, carrot, pea, and turnip seeds and some healthy young seed potatoes. With decent weather through the summer, the garden produced enough to put some away for the winter, and Philip dug and framed a small root cellar which was perfect for the potatoes, carrots, and turnips. Catrina even added some apples that Johannes Hough Sr. brought. She dried most of the peas and apples, along with wild gooseberries, saskatoon, thimbleberry and rose hips. Late September was a good time to collect rose hips. The night frost made them quite red and brought out the flavor when they were added to hot water. Catrina was most pleased with the cabbage. She shredded several large heads, covered them with salt, and placed them in crocks. They sat on a shelf in the root cellar with rocks weighing down the lids. Next year maybe they'd have a milk cow and lots of cheese and butter.

In the middle of September, Philip and Catrina were invited to the Trinity Lutheran Church at Stone Raby. Margaretha, the daughter of Johannes Michael Wick Sr. and his wife Anna Dorothea Koch, was to be baptized on September 13th. This afternoon of worship and visiting offered a reprieve from hard work and the constant worry about French and Indian attacks. Not long after the baptism of Margaretha Wick, the family visited the church again, this time for the baptism of Michael and Agatha's little girl Christian Gallinger.[155]

Catrina helped Agatha deliver the little girl at the end of September, and she was eager to see how Agatha and the baby were doing. Catrina brought apple dumplings hoping they'd be enjoyed. Philip and Catrina rarely saw anyone when they were home, so it was exciting to visit neighbours. This was the first time they'd met Philip Hendrick Klein who lived just south of Michael Gallinger on the south edge of the Kingsborough Patent and the northwest edge of the Butlersbury Patent.[156] Mr Klein was a sponsor for little Christian. They also met Johannes Albrandt and his wife Barbara. They lived very close to Adam Ruppert on the western allotment of the Kingsborough Patent.[157] Philip enjoyed talking to Johannes. He just settled in the area in 1754. They also saw Johannes Wick again and his children Catharina and Henry. Johannes' wife Dorothea was at home with their newborn daughter Margaretha.[158] The visit to the church was something Catrina and Philip talked about for weeks.

At the beginning of 1757, the days and weeks passed slowly, and the snow and cold weather kept the family inside the shelter of their cabin most days. Catrina's pregnancy was making her more and more uncomfortable, and it was difficult to keep the children from arguing with each other.

One day Catrina offered them some entertainment. "Mattheus and Elizabeth why don't you play a game of Jackstraws. I picked some perfect twigs for it this summer."

Elizabeth shouted, "Okay, as long as Mattheus doesn't mess up all the twigs!"

Catharina sat on a piece of deer hide on the dirt floor and watched them play. She was good at telling them which twig to choose. They played for most of the morning until Elizabeth got tired and wanted to finish the ties she was making for her mama's pockets. She picked up the spool knitter her papa gave her for Christmas and began knitting with purpose. Philip had carved a hole through the centre of a small piece of a thick pine branch. He placed four carved pegs on top around the hole. Elizabeth loved it. She spent hours making cords as belts or ties for wool caps.

Despite her discomfort, Catrina didn't have any trouble finding things to do to keep her busy. Little Martin was almost walking and always wanting to explore. Catharina was four and quite independent. Philip kept busy hunting on most of the warmer days in January bringing home a few more rabbits and a turkey. Catrina used the white rabbit fur to line two pairs of moccasins and mittens she made from the hide of the deer Philip shot in August.

Early one morning in February, he said to Catrina while gathering his willow fishing rod and snowshoes, "I'll be out ice fishing with Jacob Henry Alguire and Martin Alguire. We're going to Cayadutta Creek, can't wait for spring. 'T'is our favourite spot and only about three kilometres. I'll be back early afternoon."

Catrina nodded, "Some fresh trout and potatoes would be nice for supper![159] Be careful and don't be all day."

This was not a day Philip should have gone ice fishing. Early in the afternoon, he was walking down the lane feeling good about the load of trout he had slung over his shoulder. He saw Michael's wagon and ran toward the front door. While throwing the fish on the ground, he burst open the door and heard loud screams coming from the back room. The children and Michael were sitting in the kitchen. "The baby!" Philip yelled.

Michael replied quietly, "Yes, it won't be long now. We've been here about an hour. We came by to bring some fresh milk for you and found Elizabeth in a panic. Agatha is with her now and everything is fine."

Fifteen minutes seemed like an hour for Philip as he paced a small space in the kitchen puffing on his pipe. Finally, he heard infant cries.

Agatha appeared and said, "She has delivered a boy. You've a beautiful son."

Philip went to Catrina and saw her lying in their bed holding the tiny infant in her arms. "'T'is a boy Philip. We'll name him Peter Eamer (see Appendix E)."[160]

"He's beautiful, and Peter is a good name. 'T'is my older brother's name." Holding the tiny fingers with his large hand, Philip said, "Thank you Catrina. Now we're a family of seven, and we have two boys born in America!"

Being careful became infuriatingly normal behavior for Catrina and Philip. All winter word spread among the settlers that the French and Indians were lurking about the woods north of Fort Johnson. It was said they wanted to kill Sir William, destroy Fort Johnson, and attack settlements along the Mohawk River.[161] In February, Captain Mark Petrie's Company was mustered at German Flats.[162] Even Elizabeth, Mattheus, and Catharina knew what to do if there was an alarm. They knew how to move fast to their hiding place by the creek, or they could run to the river. Mattheus and Elizabeth had followed the path a few times when they went fishing with Philip. At the old black oak tree in the southeast corner of their land, the road crossed the property. It was only 2 ½ kilometres to the river.

An alarm did come by the middle of March. Michael Gallinger rode up to the cabin on horseback. Philip knew something was wrong. "What's happened," he hollered from the front door.

Michael yelled, "The French attacked Fort William Henry, and Sir William gathered sixty Mohawks and 1200 militia to go to their aid. They march tomorrow. Johannes Wick Sr., the Dillenbach brothers, and Philip Empey Sr. and his brothers William, Frederick, and Adam are with them. They're in Severinus Deygert's Company.[163] Peter Service, Adam Ruppert, Martin Waldorf, Peter Fykes Sr., and his sons Philip Adam Fykes and Daniel are scouting the western end of the Kingsborough Patent. We can organize several men to scout Albany Bush and Philadelphia Bush."

"Yes Michael. There's you and me, George Crites, Jacob Henry, and Johannes Alguire, Jacob Myers, Philip Hendrick Klein, Mattheus Link, Lawrence Eaman, Lodowyck Putnam, and Conrad Smith. I'm sure we can gather more."

The men were terrified of a repeat of what happened at Herkimer last November. There was a raid and the Indians killed George House and his wife Maria Gamal and took their daughter Mary Elizabeth House, just four years old, to Canada."[164]

For over a week, the men walked the areas closest to their land. Philip went out every day for a few hours with Lodowyck Putnam, Jacob Myers, and Jacob Henry Alguire. They walked along the road in front of Philip's land and along a path that led through the Sacandaga Patent to Philadelphia Bush. Most of the time, the only thing they heard were a few birds and their footsteps. There was still snow on the ground so footprints would be easy to see. But, the stillness was unnerving. When they did hear a sound its quake made their heads whip round in unison. Near the end of March, they got news that the French gave up their siege of Fort William Henry. The British managed to hold them back for four days. By the time Sir William, his militia, and the Mohawks arrived at Fort Edward, a few kilometres south of Fort William Henry, the siege was over. They headed back to the valley with great speed as there was rumors of an imminent attack on German Flats. Sir William rode all night and arrived at Fort Johnson early the next morning.[165]

For Philip and Catrina, the whole summer and autumn was spent slogging through daily chores and ploughing about six acres of land. Catrina was up from sunrise to sunset, always working, always watching, always cautious. One day a week she washed clothes and smiled every time she lifted a bucket of water from the well to fill the wash tub. She didn't miss the trips to the creek. Twice a week she baked bread, biscuits, and pie. Elizabeth helped with the chores, and Catharina helped with the babies. She loved to rock Peter in the cradle or entertain Martin with insects and wild flowers she discovered near the cabin.

Fig. 21. 1750's Dutch Plow Mohawk Valley. Copyright The Farmers' Museum, Cooperstown, New York, F0031.1975. Photograph by Richard Walker.

Philip and Mattheus worked from sunrise to sunset too, always watching and always cautious. They pulled stumps, picked rocks, and cleared trees and hundreds of branches, some of which were the size of small trees. Elizabeth, now nine, helped too when she wasn't in the kitchen with her mother. She handled

Apple well as the tough Canadian horse dragged tree trunks across the field. Philip used the oxen to pull the heavy trunks, roots, and the plough. It was gruelling work often in the heat of the day.

They came back to the cabin for a meal at noon, and Elizabeth brought two buckets of water to the field twice a day. Relentless clearing, ploughing, and seeding gave way to praying and watching. The whole family prayed regularly for good weather and watched the crop grow.

Philip had spent the last of their money on a plough, some wheat seeds, and a young milk cow.[166] Near the middle of June when the seeding was done, he sat on a stump at the edge of the field and thought, "I shouldn't have bought that milk cow. I should've saved some money for winter provisions. But my children need milk, and we could use it for cheese and curds." He calculated, "I'll need about two acres of wheat for ourselves and two acres could pay for winter provisions. I'll plant two acres in timothy grass for forage for the animals. Oh, I pray the harvest is good."

Catrina, Philip, and the children were grateful that a happy event interrupted their work. They attended the baptism of another baby. Mattheus and Magdelena Link's daughter Catherine Link (Caty) was born July 31.[167] But, happy moments were short lived. On August 10th, the settlers got word that the French had not only taken Fort William Henry, but their Indian allies had killed, scalped, or taken captive over 700 men. The men came from all over New York and the New England colonies and were attacked after they surrendered and while retreating with apparent safe passage to Fort Edward. Captain Robert McGinnis lost an arm and was taken to France as a prisoner.[168] Now, the eastern door to the valley was open, and with the fall of Oswego last autumn the western door was open too. The valley was exposed to attack. The French were winning the war.

While pacing the kitchen with Peter in her arms, Catrina said, "What are we to do Philip. We left Germany to get away from wars and death. 'T'is all around us every moment. We're right in the middle of it! I just want time to relax, to enjoy my babies, to enjoy our beautiful land. I can't. I'm always worried. Mattheus told me the other day that he couldn't sleep because he was afraid a Frenchman was going to come and take Elizabeth and Catharina."

"I know you're scared. We've come this far and had many terrible weeks and months. But, now we have our land, and our children are healthy. Surely, the soldiers will keep us protected."

Catrina did her best to hide her fears. But, she found herself being curt with the children; she couldn't sleep, and she only picked at her food. She found herself losing faith in their dream. She found herself thinking of home and her family. By November the difficult days far overshadowed the happy ones. Soon she'd be tested to her limits.

On 12 Nov 1757 early in the morning, the village of German Flats (Palatine Village) was attacked. Over 700 French and Indians ravaged and burned over sixty homes and outbuildings. Forty villagers were killed and over 150 taken prisoner. They took Magdelena Helmer, daughter of Johannes Adam Helmer Sr. and Anna Margaret Bell and wife of Marcus Reese, and her children. Their two year old boy Samuel stumbled and cried as the Indians dragged them through the forest. Samuel couldn't keep up, so the Indians hurled him against a tree, scalped him and left him to die. Marcus had been working in the fields and saw smoke from his house burning. Grabbing his rifle, he ran to save his family only to find everyone taken. He followed their trail finding Samuel near death. He quickly wrapped his little head in a cloth and carried him to the fort. Settlers along the valley were tormented. They were from German Flats, Stone Arabia, Albany Bush, Cherry Valley, and Schoharie, and they were in such a panic that they were moving their families and belongings to Schenectady and Albany for safety. It was just after the attack that Philip and Catrina attended the baptism of Margaret Alguire, Jacob Henry and Salome's fourth daughter, where they heard of the horrors at German Flats.[169]

After the baptism, Catrina spent most of her time in her rocking chair. She sat wringing both hands hard and said, "Dearest God Philip! There's nowhere to run or hide! They'll get our babies! I don't know how Salome copes with a newborn amidst this strain."

"Sir William is doing his best to get troops in the valley. He's asked for a company of Rangers who are skilled fighters and woodsmen. They're to be stationed at Stone Raby. I've heard that John Well's militia detachment from Cherry Valley, just south of German Flats, has marched. And Lieutenant Henry Hanson's Mohawk Valley militia detachment has marched.[170] We've lots of dried fish, and our share of the bear Jacob Henry and I shot this fall means that I won't have to leave you alone to go hunting very often. If the French reach Fort Johnston, Stone Raby, or Canajoharie, we'll go to Fort Hunter or Schenectady for protection."[171]

Philip and Catrina soon faced 1758, their third winter in the valley. Incredibly, the easy part had been the backbreaking work of ensuring there was food, water, shelter, and starting their farm. The toughest part was facing the constant threat of captivity, mutilation, or death. The backbreaking work continued, and the stress gnawed on them a while longer. In January, their tension eased a bit when they heard that Peter Service Sr. was given a commission as Captain in Sir William's 2nd Battalion of the New York Militia. Mr. Francis Ruppert Sr. was his 2nd Lieutenant.[172]

Both of these men lived about eight kilometres from Philip and Catrina. By April, the tension worsened when word spread that in March the enemy killed and scalped two settlers just east of German Flats, and by April 30th, the enemy ravaged the settlers near Herkimer Church Fort not far from German Flats. Lieutenant William Hare went out from the fort with his Rangers to follow the enemy. The settlers ran for protection at the fort, some were killed or taken and women were wounded.

In the midst of the stress of the past year and their ongoing tension, Philip and Catrina managed to harvest and sell about twenty bushels of wheat from two acres of cleared land. With money from the harvest, they bought a pregnant beef cow, a laying hen, and a rooster. Philip spent most of April and May constructing new pens for the animals. He wove a split willow fence for the rooster and chickens, and he built a more secure coop. Apple and the cows got improved corrals with wood rails.

In April, Philip came into the cabin one morning after showing Mattheus how to clean the corrals and the chicken coop. He said, "Catrina, today I'm going to George Crites' place. He has apple tree saplings that he got from Sir William's orchard, and I want to start our orchard. I've cleared ¼ acre in a nice sunny spot."

"Does he have any plum tree seedlings?"

"I'll see what he has. I'd like to start the apples this year. I'll try and get seven or eight saplings."

Later that week while Philip helped Mattheus weave the willow fence, Michael Gallinger and Andrew Snyder rode into the yard. After a quick greeting, the three men sat on stumps next to a pile of willows. Mattheus sat on the grass next to his papa. Andrew Snyder said, "Sir William has ordered the raising of detachments of militia from the County of Albany. He wants a company raised from men who live in this area. I've been commissioned as Corporal under

Captain Peter Service's Company, Francis Ruppert Sr. is 2nd Lieutenant, Adam Ruppert and Anthony Flower are Sergeants.[173] I'm here to recruit able bodied men who can participate in the campaign at Fort Ticonderoga between Lake George and Lake Champlain. We're to rendezvous at Schenectady. All men are to bring their own arms, a shot bag, powder horn, and something to keep the lock of their gun dry.[174] So far we've nine men volunteer. Are you with us Philip?"

"I want to serve, and I want to help protect the good people here. I must speak with my wife before I give you an answer. When do you need to know?"

"In a few days."

"Okay. Michael are you going?"

"Yes, I'm going and so are George Crites, Jacob Henry, and Johannes Alguire, Philip Hendrick Klein, Martin Waldorf, Peter Fykes Sr., and Martin Loefler Sr. and Lucas Feader Sr. from Tribes Hill.

Not soon after the men left, Philip went to talk to Catrina. "I've just seen Michael Gallinger and Andrew Snyder. Andrew is recruiting men for Captain Peter Service's Company. He's asked me to join and go to Schenectady and then on to Fort Ticonderoga to fight the French. I know this is hard, but I want to join the men and help protect this valley. I need your agreement and support."

"This was something I knew would happen and was so afraid of." Taking his hand, Catrina said, "Philip I can't lose you, and I certainly don't want you wounded or maimed. I don't know if I have the strength to be here alone with the children. But, I know you want to go and aid in the attack on the French. How long will you be gone? What about our harvest? We can't lose our harvest. We won't survive the winter."

"I'll leave in June, and I don't know when we'll be back. I hope it'll be a swift victory, maybe a few weeks."

"Okay Philip, you've my support. We'll tell the children, but not too soon."

"Mattheus knows; he was there."

"Well, sooner then, they'll be frightened, and Mattheus doesn't understand.

One afternoon near the end of May 1758, Philip was out in the orchard with Mattheus teaching his son how to plant apple saplings. Suddenly, he saw a man coming around the cabin and toward the field. He jumped for his firelock.

"Hold your fire Sir, I'm a friend," yelled the man.

"Your name Sir?" Philip asked while lowering his gun.

"I'm Captain Jelles Fonda from Caughnawaga." Jelles approached Philip and held out his hand.

While shaking hands, Philip said, "I'm Philip Eamer. This is my son Mattheus. What's your business Sir?"

"I'm travelling through the area recruiting Rangers for his Majesty's militia. I'm looking for excellent woodsmen who can speak one of the Indian tongues."[175]

"I do not qualify Sir. I do not speak an Indian tongue. I've been in this country only three years. I've just volunteered for service at Fort Ticonderoga with Captain Peter Service's Company. Your name is familiar Sir. Do you own the store at Caughnawaga?"

"Yes I do Mr. Eamer. We've many provisions you might need. Come by in the fall. 'T'is hunting season, and we have venison and furs. Good to meet you Philip. Thank you for aiding in protecting this valley. Captain Service is a good man. I'll be on my way now. Sorry to have startled you."

"Good day Captain Fonda."

It was the middle of June 1758 when Philip slung his haversack, firelock, and powder horn over his shoulder and walked down the lane to the road. He reassured his family that he'd be home soon and told Mattheus and Elizabeth to help their mother and look after their brothers and sister. He met Michael, George, Jacob Henry, and Johannes along the road. Francis Ruppert Sr., Andrew Snyder, Philip Hendrick Klein, Peter Fykes Sr., Martin Loefler Sr. and Lucas Feader Sr. had gone ahead with Captain Service. Philip and the others walked for two days to Schenectady, about forty kilometres. He remembered the town differently when he was there with his family and Lewis almost three years ago. Within the town stockade, there were hundreds of soldiers from different regiments and different parts of Albany, Connecticut, New Jersey, New Hampshire, and Massachusetts. They found their way to Fort Cosby, a fort inside the town stockade nine square metres with a stone foundation and blockhouses. There they found Captain Service. Many men were housed in the blockhouses, but Philip and Michael were billeted at a small house in the town.

The men of Captain Service's Company were assigned to maintain and guard wagons and supplies as they marched to Fort Edward under the command of Colonel Bradstreet. They marched along the west side of the Hudson River with a wagon train of supplies, ammunition, artillery, and 16,000 men spanning almost twenty seven kilometres. It was one of the largest armies of British and Provincial troops ever assembled in North America. Lord George Howe assembled the army, and General James Abercrombie was the commander of the American forces. The procession of wagons and men crossed the Hudson River at Fort Hardy and Batten Kill (Creek) and trudged the last kilometres on the east side of the Hudson with only one stop at the Halfway Brook blockhouse. There were men from the 27th, 44th, 46th, 55th, 80th, two battalions of the newly formed 60th Royal Americans, and the 42nd or Scottish Black Watch.[176] They marched sixty nine kilometres through mud, flies, mosquitoes, and fears of an Indian attack.

After muster at Fort Edward, Captain Service's Company were divided into messes of five men each. Each mess was given a tent, camp kettle, axe, wood, and straw for bedding. From the Quartermaster's store, each mess collected their rations, usually enough for a few days.[177] Philip, Michael, Jacob Henry, George, and Peter Fykes Sr. shared one tent. Philip and Michael set up the tent among hundreds of other men just outside the fort. Peter and George built a small fire, and Jacob sorted out rations for an evening meal. No one said a word as they devoured salted pork, peas, bread and beer. It had been a gruelling march.

After their meal while Philip was bent over a basin washing the mud from his face, neck and arms, Philip Hendrick Klein, Peter Fykes Sr., Martin Loefler Sr., Lucas Feader Sr., Johannes Alguire, and Corporal Andrew Snyder walked into their camp. Andrew Snyder called out, "Philip, you'd better leave that mud where it is. The flies and mosquitoes followed us into camp!"

"You're right Andrew. Come, join us for a gill of rum."

Later, as they sat around the fire, Michael said, "I've never in my life seen so many men and wagons in one place. I'm glad I wasn't charged with pulling one of those artillery pieces. They were always getting stuck. I guess they gave me charge of some wagons because I was a wagonmaker in Germany.[178] Everyone seems to be employed related to their skills or the size of their muscle."

Jacob Henry said, "The bread from the number of bread ovens near the Quatermaster's store will feed those muscles. There was enough bread to fill four wagons. A man could smell his way to the store."

Taking a puff of his pipe, Philip said, "I'm glad of the Sutlers' stores. There are some inside the fort and two just south of the fort run by a Mr. Pommery and Mr. Edward Best.[179] We can get tobacco, rum, molasses, soap, and candles if wanted. But, don't dare be caught near there after dusk T'is strictly forbidden. A flogging is punishment." Taking another puff, Philip added, "When we got here, the sight of all those tents took my breath, there were hundreds all lined up in rows, and there are thousands more on Roger's Island just south of us; that's where Major Robert Roger's Rangers live. They call them Roger's Independent Company of American Rangers, and I hear they're the kind of soldiers the army wants when fighting in the forest.

With a fixed gaze on the red embers of the fire, George Crites said, "I can't think about tents or molasses, rum maybe. I think we're to stay here and guard the wagons while the regular army goes up Lake George to take Fort Ticonderoga. I hope 't'is true."

Nodding, Peter said, "Hmm, me as well."

A few days later they began their trek another twenty seven kilometres to Fort William Henry and the shores of Lake George. It was near the end of June early in the morning when Captain Service's Company took their posts standing watch over supply wagons near the fort.

While on watch, Peter Fykes Sr. said, "You know, a few days ago some of Roger's Rangers were sent up Lake George on reconnaissance. Major Israel Putnam was sent and a man from our valley. The man from our valley is an officer in Robert's Rangers, Lieutenant William Philips Sr.. Billy Philips they call him. He's known as a skilled Ranger and has been on many scouts and in many battles. He was even taken prisoner and made a miraculous escape, and he survived the Rangers' famous life threatening journey home from their attack on the Abenaki at Saint Francois along the St. Lawrence River.[180] He lives just south of Fort Johnson on the north side of the river. Philip, you probably past his place coming up from Schenectady. He has four young sons, Peter, Cornelius, William Jr. and John Philips."[181]

As the men stood watch, they witnessed a constant procession of over 500 wagons, supplies, and soldiers arriving at Fort William Henry. The most spectacular sight was at the shore of Lake George. There, they saw the readying of the fleet of hundreds of bateaux, whaleboats, canoes, and enormous rafts onto which men were loading artillery. The display of force was overwhelming.[182]

Their view of the spectacular sight on the beach was interrupted with orders to assist men from the 60th Royal Americans Regiment in widening a road to the blockhouses. While Captain Service's men were guarding the wagons, the 60th Regiment were training close to them as Light Infantrymen under Colonel Henry Bouquet. Light Infantrymen were trained in forest warfare and travelled much lighter than regular soldiers. Even their uniforms were adapted to suit travel through difficult wilderness terrain ready to fight using bush fighting tactics. They cut their hair, wore brown gaters instead of white, had no lace trim, and cut their jackets short. They were seasoned woodsmen with excellent fighting skills much like Roger's Rangers. In fact, Robert Rogers trained many of them.[183]

Philip was assigned to work with a strong young man who just joined the 60th Regiment. His name was John Farlinger. While Philip and John Farlinger were working, Philip talked about his travels to America and his farm near the Mohawk River. John talked about the daily slog of a Light Infantry soldier. One day, Philip asked, "Do you expect to be part of the force that sails to Fort Ticonderoga?"

"Yes, I do. I expect we'll be part of Lord Howe's column".[184]

"My thoughts and prayers will be with you young John. I hope we meet again someday."

On July 5th, Philip woke before dawn hearing constant activity outside the tent. He shook those who didn't at least have their eyes open and said, "The men sail up Lake George today!" Philip no sooner opened his mouth when they all heard orders to muster. As they stood their watch over mostly empty wagons, they watched the army set sail over the calm and bright blue waters of Lake George. Robert's Rangers and General Gage and his 80th Light Infantry led the floating convoy. Colonel Bradstreet and his bateaux men followed. The final group comprised three columns of boats each with a colourful banner and carrying men from New England and New York.[185] Philip saw the colors of Lord Howe and knew that John Farlinger was among them.

Breaking the silence, Michael said, "Our prayers are with each soldier. Pray for a speedy victory for Lord Howe and General Abercrombie! You were right George. We stay, wait, and pray." Worry filled the waiting over the next few days. They hoped the army would return victorious, but they feared that the French and their Indian allies would follow close behind and take Fort William Henry. Memories of the slaughter at the fort in 1757 haunted the men.

On July 6th, Sir William Johnson arrived at Fort William Henry with 600 Iroquois warriors.[186] For months, Sir William struggled to convince the Iroquois Nations to break their position of neutrality and fight with the British. The 600 warriors were evidence of some success. The Indians were a stirring sight to see. Philip thought, "Their look is alarming. The red and black stripes are so intricately painted on their face. Through all the black, all I can see are the whites of their eyes! Their heads are shaven with only three braids with feathers at the crown."[187] Philip admired their readiness to fight in the bush. Each of them wore deerskin moccasins and leggings past their knees. Flaps of cloth covered their groins. Many wore shirts, but some only painted naked chests." They had weapons. Philip saw firelocks, tomahawks, and knives. The most fascinating was the two foot long wooden club carved in one piece with a six inch ball at one end. He saw the club hanging on one side of an Indian's belt. On the other side of his belt, Philip saw it. Suddenly, he felt his heart beat faster, and he lost his breath for a moment. He saw a large piece of gnarled dried skin with a long lock of black human hair. It was decorated with thin strips of deer hide and a feather. Philip thought, "A scalp! These men are fearsome opponents or formidable allies. Five hundred of them together are frightening! They are very different from the Indians I saw on the docks at Albany." Sir William and his warriors left for Fort Ticonderoga to rendezvous with General Abercrombie not long after they arrived.

On July 8th the garrison at Fort William Henry got the news of Lord Howe's death. There was a heavy mood through the encampment. Tension was high. On July 9th early in the morning, the men of Captain Peter Service's Company gathered for muster.[188] On July 10th, an express rider entered the gates with news of the stunning British defeat. Over 2000 soldiers lost their lives charging the fort head on through fields of logs and sharpened branches leaving them victims of slaughter. Many of the dead were from the Black Watch. During the battle, there was confusion amongst the men after losing the leadership of Lord Howe. The confusion worsened as they retreated to Lake George, and melancholy set in when they arrived at Fort William Henry.[189] As the horrific news spread through the fort, the men shuddered thinking of their comrades amidst that chaos. Philip thought of John Farlinger and of home.

It was mid-afternoon and Catrina was tending the garden with the help of all the children. She shuddered for a moment when she heard Catharina and Martin squealing. Instantly she thought, "Indians!" But as she glanced toward the lane, her hoe slid out of her hands. She scooped little Peter into her arms and ran to Philip. He picked up his pace when he saw Catrina and the children dash towards him. In a moment, the whole family wrapped themselves around Philip with Catrina crying in his arms and little Peter squeezed against his chest.

Between laughs and huge breaths, Peter said, "'T'is grand to be home. All the wee ones have grown, and I've only been gone a few weeks!" Looking straight at Catrina, he said, "You've done well. You look well."

"I've missed you so. 'T'was a worrisome time. We prayed each night for your safe return! And here you are! Praise God. You look well too, a bit worn and ruffled. Come into the cabin and rest."

"Not for long Catrina. I want to see how our crops are coming."

Philip hung his firelock above the fireplace and draped his haversack and shotbag over a hook behind the door. He sat near the door where a slight breeze cooled the kitchen. Elizabeth, Mattheus, Catharina, and Martin sat close, eager to hear their papa tell stories of his time fighting the French. Between satisfying puffs of his pipe, Philip told them about the long journey to Fort William Henry, the soldiers, the big guns, the many tents, and the formidable army setting sail on Lake George.

Mattheus squirmed in his chair and before his father finished a sentence he shouted, "Did we win Papa? Did we beat the French and the Indians?"

"Not this time Mattheus. Next time we will. Our soldiers need to rest. They want to see their families and take care of their animals just like you've been doing while I've been away."

Catrina handed Philip some rum and, with a sweep of her hands, she directed the children out the door. He tipped the mug and swallowed half the rum before he said, "So many men lost! T'was all a troubling sight to see. We were all so glad to head for home! Most of Captain Service's men have young children at home. Philip Hendrick Klein has two children, just nine and two; Jacob Henry has four and Salome will deliver another very soon. Michael has two and Agatha is just pregnant with their third."

"Yes, and I expect Magdelena Link will deliver any day now. She must be joyous at Mattheus' return. Are we still in danger? The British lost. The French are planning their attack."

"We are not in a good position now, but we have men to defend our valley, and Sir William has influence with the Indians."

Catrina was right. Magdelena Link delivered a girl on July 20th. They named her Catherine Link and called her Caty.[190] Michael Gallinger Sr. and Agatha brought their little sons Michael and Christopher to the baptisms; they now had two boys and one girl under the age of three, and Agatha was expecting in February. The summer and fall passed quickly. The long days of work ended in October with an abundant harvest from the fields and the garden. The root cellar was filled with vegetables, dried fruits, cheese, and sauerkraut. Good news was also abundant.

In September, news spread of British victories at Fort Frontenac at Lake Ontario, at Montreal on the St. Lawrence River, at Louisbourg at Nova Scotia, and at Fort Duquesne on the Ohio River. In October, Roger's Rangers successfully raided an Abenaki village on the St. Lawrence River. Robert Rogers and his men had proven that the British could strike in the wilderness at any time. Lieutenant William Philips Sr. of the Mohawk Valley was there and was one of only a few Rangers who survived the harrowing journey to safety, many died of starvation.[191] Despite the victories, Sir William Johnson was vigilant in protecting the valley. In October, he ordered the New York militia to march from Schenectady to the Mohawk Valley. And, he tells us that General Stanwix is overseeing the construction of a fort east of Fort Oswego at a place the Oneida call Deowainsta or Carrying Place. It's a portage from the Mohawk River to Wood Creek. The Six Nations have been using the portage for centuries when they travel west to east to trade. Sir William says it's a strategic place protecting the valley.[192]

Even with these victories, settlers were frightened of attacks. In December, Canajoharie farmers petitioned General Amherst for 100 soldiers to be quartered at their houses, and, in addition to the garrison at Fort Hunter, Sir William Johnson requested troops for Stone Raby and for his new blockhouses at Fort Johnson.[193] Sir William was also working hard to ensure that the Iroquois would commit to fight alongside the British. Until the recent British victories, the Six Nations of the Iroquois Confederacy didn't see any advantage to siding with the British and, as a Confederacy, they agreed they would remain neutral in any war between the French and the English.[194]

Despite the threat of French attacks, Philip and Catrina found more time to relax in December. The hard work of the harvest was over. Most of Catrina's time was spent sewing, spinning, or knitting. She wanted to make some special gifts for Christmas. Philip spent a lot of time outside tending the animals. He now had one milk cow and a little heifer, one ox, one horse, and six chickens. He was proud of his growing stock. Next spring he'd find a good stallion for Apple and a pregnant sow. Mattheus was eight now, and he loved to help his papa in the fields and with the animals. Soon he'd be old enough to swing an axe and chop wood. Martin was almost two and Peter just one. The girls were a big help to Catrina. Elizabeth was ten and Catharina, now six. Both girls loved to help with Martin and Peter.

Christmas was special this year. Everyone was so happy to have Philip home after so much worry while he was away in the spring. Soft snow fell lightly over the lane when Michael Gallinger Sr. drove his sleigh toward the front door. It was just three days before Christmas. He came to visit and leave gifts.

Philip opened the door and greeted Michael, "Good day Michael. 'T'is a splendid winter day. Just enough snow to cover our traps."

"Aye. Maybe we'll catch some fox, marten, or weasel this year. Agatha is at home with our little boys, and she is heavy with child. So, I've come to bring Christmas greetings." Michael reached into the bottom of the sleigh, dragged out two sacks, and made his way to the front door.

The children gathered around Michael. Martin clutched his trousers, Mattheus stared at the bulky bag he carried, Catharina wrapped her arms around his leg, and Elizabeth stood beside him with Peter in her arms. Michael smiled, ruffled Martin and Catharina's thick brown hair and said, "This is for your mother to prepare for Christmas dinner, and the contents in the other bag will keep her busy during the long January evenings!"

Catrina opened the bag and said, "Oh Michael, a goose! What a special dinner we'll have. Thank you." She opened the other bag and said, "Feathers, lots of feathers! And, they are goose feathers. They'll stuff a fine quilt for our little boys."

After Philip placed the goose on the table, he took two wooden bowls off the shelf and said, "These are for you and Agatha. I carved them from the old walnut tree I felled."

"Thank you Philip. These will get much use."

As Michael was ready to leave, Catrina asked, "How's Agatha? Your baby will arrive soon."

"She's fine. She sleeps well at night now that the threats of attack have lessened."

Catrina thought, "I'm glad she's resting. I know how tired I am as the sun sets and I crawl into bed. I'll be just as tired next year with my own child due in the early summer. I'll tell Philip soon."

On Christmas day, it didn't take long for the family to devour the goose. As Philip moved from the table toward the chair, he rubbed his stomach and said, "I'll sit for a while in my new chair and have a nice long smoke of my pipe, and I'll read us something from the bible. That goose was splendid Catrina. The only thing better was your berry pie! Thank you."

Catrina finished clearing the dishes and walked toward the corner of the kitchen. For at least one minute, she stroked the back of her new rocking chair and said, "Philip, I'll enjoy this chair every day for many years. It'll be so nice to rock Peter in my lap. How'd you ever make these two chairs without me knowing? And the settle bed for Martin and Peter!"

Philip smiled and said, "All those days I was out with the animals, I carved and sawed, and I hid them under the roof of the wood shed. You never go there! The hardest part was keeping the children from spilling the secret." As Catrina and Philip rocked in their new chairs, Martin, Catharina, and Elizabeth played with the little wooden horses that Mattheus carved for them. He was wearing the new trousers Catrina made and the woolen socks that Elizabeth knit.

As they crowded close to the fire, Catrina asked Elizabeth, "Do you think you could knit something for me this winter?"

"Of course, what do you need?"

"I'll need a baby cap and two pairs of little socks."

"For Peter Mama?"

"No Elizabeth, for the new baby that'll come early this summer."

Philip stopped rocking. Everyone else stared at Catrina. As Philip got up and stepped toward Catrina, he said, "'T'is splendid Catrina. We'll all welcome this new child."

Mattheus asked, "Where's Peter going to sleep? The baby will be in his cradle!"

"Well Mattheus," Catrina said. "Peter will sleep in the new settle bed with Martin. And, during the day it'll make a nice bench for your room!"

January 1759 brought deep heavy snow. There were four paths outside. One to the outhouse, one to the animal shelters, one to the well, and one down the lane wide enough for Apple. Often, driving snow made walking down those paths dangerous. So, Philip and Mattheus spent many hours clearing wide paths. Mattheus liked the path to the outhouse the best. He was proud of making the path safer when it was dark or when the snow blew. He said, "Look Papa. I've strung this rope from the house to the outhouse door, and this hollow piece of wood with pebbles inside is fastened to the rope. When you leave the outhouse, you grab the rope and keep walking. You don't have to see, just follow the sound of the pebbles."

"Wonderful Mattheus. We'll all be safer now. Let's check and make sure 't'is secure."

Philip and Catrina loved to visit with Reverend John Ogilvie, and they'd have the opportunity at the baptism of Michael and Agatha's new infant girl, Maria Catherine Gallinger.[195] Michael came to the Eamer's cabin with his large sleigh and drove everyone to his cabin. There'd been enough sleighs travelling over the road, and it was cold enough that Michael's two horses easily pulled the full sleigh along the hard surface. There were blankets and a bearskin rug to keep everyone warm. Everyone sang as the sleigh slid over the snow. It was Sunday, February 25th, and it was a beautiful baptism. Mattheus and Magdelena Link were there with their three children and so was George Crites, his wife and two sons, Johannes Crites and George Crites Jr.

On the way home, Philip asked Michael, "Will you help me build a sleigh this year? Catrina, Elizabeth and Mattheus learned to use snowshoes, but we need an easier way to travel during the winter, especially with two small children and a baby coming."

"Of course I can. I've put many wagons and sleighs together in my life. We'll get William Bowen Sr. or the blacksmith at Fort Johnson to make you some nice iron runners. You'll need a span of horses."

"I know. I'd like another Canadian. Apple is a good strong mare. She's done well hauling trees. I've cleared six acres now and hope to clear four more this spring. If the weather is good, I should have extra money for stock."

The melting snow always gave Catrina a little more energy. It was March, and she could smell the earth when she walked to the well. The birds were singing, and there were buds on the willow branches. One day after their morning meal, Catrina said, "Philip, the days are warmer, but there's still frost in the morning. 'T'is time to tap the maple trees. We've a good sugar bush near the creek. There are about ten trees of a good size for tapping. Let's ask Michael and Jacob Henry to help us tap and boil. Michael has a sugar bush too. We can help him next week."

"Okay, Mattheus can help bring wood for a good fire near the well so we can boil the sap. We've some good wooden buckets and a good size iron pot. Maybe next Saturday if the weather is fine."

On Thursday, Philip tapped three maple trees large enough for two holes in each tree. After drilling a hole, Philip gave two wooden spiles to Mattheus and said, "You tap the tree Mattheus. Make sure the spile tilts down a bit and make sure it's snug in the hole. The buckets will fill in a day or so." Elizabeth and Catharina followed behind hanging buckets under six spiles.

Early Saturday morning, Catharina and Mattheus were playing with their wooden horses when they heard a sleigh coming down the lane. They hollered simultaneously, "'T'is Mr. Gallinger Papa! We can make sugar now!" Mattheus ran to get his wool cap and coat. As he fumbled with his mittens, he said, "Come on Catharina. Mr. Gallinger and Mr. Alguire are going to build a big fire to boil the sugar water. They'll need our help."

They spent all day hauling sugar water and pouring it in a large iron pot. The men stayed alert in the bush always with their firelocks and knives close. Catrina and Elizabeth stirred the sugar water while it boiled. It had to boil down just right. Catrina handed Elizabeth a large wooden spoon and said, "You try it now. It looks ready. The bubbles are small."

Lifting the spoon out of the water, Elizabeth said, "Look Mama. 'T'is sticking to the spoon just a bit. I think it's ready. 'T'is a nice colour too."

Catrina smiled and said, "Yes, we need to strain it now to get out the sugar sand. We can strain it over this wool cloth. Then, we can pour it into these containers and put it into the root cellar." Just before dusk, Catrina measured one gallon of syrup. It was a good day.

Philip worked hard in March. As well as making maple syrup, he spent days oiling Apple's harness, fixing the oxen's yoke and bow, and sharpening knives, the axe, and scythe. He wanted to plough and seed three acres this year, and he'd need the animals to drag more logs from cleared land. He also began work on the box for the sleigh. It wouldn't be as fancy as Reverend Ogilvie's sleigh. But, there'd be two bench seats, enough room to take the whole family to church or to visit the neighbours.

It wasn't long before March became May and Philip and Mattheus started to plough the field and plant apple saplings and a few cherry saplings in the orchard. Everyone felt a bit safer this spring with the British victories last fall and knowing that Sir William strengthened his militia to 124 men and that they were in constant readiness. Many of the soldiers were billeted in farmers' homes at Stone Raby and along the Mohawk River. And, there was a new law that allowed the army to impress any man's wagon, sleigh or horses, or impress their services such as carpentry, artificer, or wheelwright. If a man refused, he'd be imprisoned for one month without bail, but if he offered his service he'd be paid twelve shillings every day.[196] Philip also knew that Sir William succeeded in convincing the Iroquois to support the British.[197] The British finally had the upper hand against the French.

By June, Philip had five acres of wheat sowed, one acre of peas, two acres of Indian corn, and three acres of timothy grass and oats. This would be a good crop. There'd be wheat to take to Johannes Veeder's grist mill and sell. And, there'd be peas and corn for the family and forage for the stock. While Philip and Mattheus were out every day and into the evenings working the land, Catrina worked all day and evening in the house and the garden. She was heavy with her sixth child and uncomfortable all the time. She loved it when some type of work meant that she could sit in her rocking chair for a few minutes.

One day late in the afternoon, she was sitting in her chair peeling potatoes and turnip when she felt familiar pains. She called Elizabeth and said, "Elizabeth, go get your Papa from the field. Tell Catharina to come and help me to my bed. The baby is coming."

"Yes, Mama. Should I tell Papa to get Mrs. Gallinger or Mrs. Link?"

"Yes, but hurry back. We might not have time to wait for them to come! This baby wants to be born!"

Johannes Eamer was born by supper.[198] He was a fine boy, fat and long, and he didn't wait for Mrs. Gallinger or Mrs. Link. Elizabeth and Catharina helped their Mama deliver him. Philip got as close as the girls would let him until Johannes was washed and wrapped.

Philip sat beside Catrina and said, "Another fine son. We are blessed. And two fine sisters who brought him into the world! Some of our neighbours are organizing a Protestant Dutch Reformed Church at Caughnawaga. Reverend Barent Vrooman from Schenectady will be the Reverend. I think they're holding services at Captain Butler's house. We can have him baptized there. It's closer than Stone Raby, six kilometres instead of seventeen."

"That's fine Philip. In a few days. I'm tired now and need to sleep. Can you give the children some milk, bread, and cheese?"

"Yes, I'll settle the children."

The children couldn't keep their eyes and hands off their new baby brother. Catharina often sat in her mama's rocking chair swinging her little feet while she held Johannes. Elizabeth worked hard in the garden doing the work her mama found so hard to do. She set new poles for the beans and peas, and she planted cucumbers, squash, turnips, potatoes, cabbage, carrots, and onions. Often during the day, Elizabeth walked through the forest close to home to fill her basket with wild onions and dandelions.

Philip found it hard to leave the children in the morning, but thoughts of blossoming apple and cherry trees and rolling wheat kept him focused on important work. It was the end of June when he heard of the opportunity to go to Albany with his friends and neighbours to secure his naturalization certificate.[199] This was something Philip had thought about for a few years. He wanted to be considered a citizen of this new land, not a foreigner. He wanted his family to have the rights and privileges that came with naturalization. He wanted to become a British subject.

Philip travelled to Albany with Michael Gallinger Sr., Jacob Henry Alguire, George Crites, Andrew Snyder, Lawrence Eaman, Adam Ruppert, Mattheus Link, Peter Fykes Sr., Francis Ruppert Sr., Philip Hendrick Klein, and Lucas Feader Sr.. He had come to know these men well, and he was grateful for their friendship. On this trip, he got to know a few more of his neighbours, Johannes Wert and Francis Ruppert's brother Adam Ruppert.[200] On July 3rd, the men gathered at the Albany City Hall at ten o'clock and were given the Oath of Allegiance, Supremacy, and Subjuration. The Judge of the court read the oaths to which they swore loyalty to King George III as the supreme Governor of the colonies, and they renounced allegiance to any foreign Prince. They received their certificates after each man paid the Court Clerk nineteen shillings, ten for the Speaker of the Assembly, six for the Judge, and three for the Clerk. Their naturalization afforded them the right to own property and vote. Now, they had the same rights and privileges of someone born in the colony of New York. As they walked out of City Hall and down the stairs, they heard the bell in the steeple toll.

For Catrina, it seemed as though Philip had been home only a week, but it was already the end of August, and he was out cutting and raking wheat with Mattheus. Elizabeth and Catharina already picked three bushels of peas from one acre and set them to dry. Now, they were picking the Indian corn from another two acres. Catrina had her hands full with two month old Johannes,

3 ½-year-old Martin, and 2 ½-year-old Peter while she tried to harvest the cabbage and turnip from the garden. Martin and Peter loved to throw turnip greens to the six piglets that were born in spring. Catrina didn't mind, the piglets needed to get fat. Three would be sold, one would be slaughtered and the meat shared with the Alguires and Gallingers, and some put in barrels of salt brine. The other two piglets Philip would breed with Andrew Snyder's boar.

One afternoon in September, Catrina was chopping cabbage and making brine for sauerkraut when Philip came in from the fields. He said, "I've heard great news from Mattheus Link. Sir William Johnson has captured Fort Niagara. Captain Jelles Fonda and Captain John Lotteridge were with him as were Lieutenant Henry Nelles and William Hare. Captain John Butler and many Mohawks went up to Niagara after the battle.[201] 'T'is wonderful news! The French can no longer reach us from the west! And the British have captured Quebec! That means the French are cut off from the northeast. Catrina, we are beating the French! Their routes into the valley are cut off."

Catrina dropped her knife on the table and said, "Are we really winning? Do you mean we don't have to take our firelocks with us everywhere we go? Do you mean I can go to sleep without thinking about who's going to come through the door or the window?"

"Yes Catrina, we can feel safer now."

The end of October brought a few reasons to celebrate. The Eamers' preparations for winter were all finished. Philip took about sixty bushels of wheat to Johannes Veeder's grist mill not far from Caughnawaga. He kept five bushels of ground wheat and sold the rest. He also finished the box for the sleigh. It had a front driver's seat for Philip and Catrina and a back seat for Elizabeth, Catharina and Mattheus. Little Peter and Martin would have to sit on the floor. It was a beautiful box with curved sides and a painted design that Philip and Elizabeth created with vermilion dye Philip bought at Jelles Fonda's store. William Bowen Sr. forged the iron runners, and Michael and Philip secured the box to the runners. Philip was also training Apple in her new leather harness. Elizabeth thought Apple looked grand in her new harness, and she wanted her to have some sleigh bells like Reverend Ogilvie's horses. Philip could wait for the bells. What he wanted was another bear skin to put on the seats. Maybe when he went out hunting with Jacob Henry Alguire and Mattheus Link in another week. The men often hunted late in the fall. They followed the Mohawks for a distance as they went north along their trails into the Adirondack Mountains.

The best celebration was on Sunday, October 28. The family rode in their wagon to Lieutenant Walter Butler's house just north of Caughnawaga where Reverend Ogilvie performed the baptism of Joseph Clement, son of Lewis Clement and Caty Putnam.[202] Lewis' brothers James Clement, Jacob Clement, and Johannes Clement were there and Caty's brother Arent Cornelius Putnam. At any baptism there was always plenty of food for everyone, and Catrina always brought something. Today, she brought corn cakes.

The Eamers enjoyed a productive fall, and for the first time in nearly five years they relaxed enough to really enjoy the colours of the forest and the cool fall days. Frost came early this year, and winter soon stretched over the valley. There were many opportunities for the family to enjoy their sleigh. They visited Jacob Henry Alguire and Salome and Johannes Alguire and Catherine at Philadelphia Bush and Michael and Agatha Gallinger on the Kingsborough Patent. One day late in February 1760, Philip had to drive Catrina to Mattheus and Magdelena Link's farm. She was needed to help Magdelena with the birth of her daughter Julianna Link.[203] Occasionally, Philip drove the sleigh further west on the Kingsborough Patent to visit Martin Waldorf and Peter Fykes Sr. and his sons Philip Adam, Daniel, and Peter Jr.[204] They'd become friends since their march to Fort William Henry with Captain Service's Company. Early in March 1760, there was still one metre of snow in the forests around the cabin. But, the road to Caughnawaga was passable with a thick layer of packed snow. Apple pulled the sleigh easily to Fonda's store. Philip often made trips to the store for provisions and to hear news in the valley.

In April 1760, on one of Philip's trips to the store, he talked to John Bowen and a young Mohawk. The young Mohawk was just at Sir William's house to deliver news that a party of the enemy was seen crossing the Sacandaga River on the northern end of the Sacandaga Patent. They must have come down from Montreal through the Adirondacks. John said, "Sir William has ordered out the militia to track down the enemy. He's trying to get as many Mohawks as he can but most are away hunting.[205] Your place is on the Sacandaga isn't it?"

Clutching his parcel and spinning toward the door, Philip said, "Yes, on the southeast end, about four kilometres from the Sacandaga River. I've got to hurry. My wife and children are home alone!"

Philip wasn't even in the sleigh's seat when he gave Apple the command to trot on. Soon she was pulling the sleigh at a full canter down the snow packed road toward home. He reached Michael's farm and steered Apple down the lane. In one leap he was knocking hard on the door calling for Michael. As the door opened, breathless he said, "The enemy's been sighted crossing the Sacandaga River. Be on alarm! Can you tell George Crites and Mattheus Link?" Philip hadn't finished his sentence when he was back in the sleigh driving Apple towards home.

Catrina was out on the small porch shaking rugs when she saw Philip come up the lane much faster than usual. He called to her while quickly removing Apple's harness and bridle. "Take all the children inside and close the shutter on the kitchen window. The enemy has been seen a few kilometres north of here." Without answering, Catrina knew just what to do. After putting Apple in her shelter and checking the other animals, Philip hurried inside. All the children were in the kitchen sitting on the benches. All heads and eyes were on their parents. Philip took the firelock and his shot bag off the fireplace mantle and opened his cartridge box and powder horn.

"Are you going to shoot someone Papa?" Martin asked.

"No Martin, I'm just being prepared to keep us all safe." Philip turned to Mattheus and said, "Go and get your Mama's rifle, we'll load it together, you've been practicing."

After the hurried preparation was complete, the six children sat at the kitchen table frozen with fear. Philip and Catrina tried to settle their fears. They all sat and ate cheese, bread, corn cakes, and drank apple cider while Philip and Catrina told stories of their grandparents, uncles, aunts, and cousins in Germany. Martin and Peter loved to hear about the big castle near Auerbach. Elizabeth had a few memories to share too. She remembered the sheep that grazed in the meadows and hearing the church bell ringing.

For the next few days, Philip and Catrina were cautious. The children weren't allowed outside very often, and Philip always had his firelock with him. Catrina had one close by too. Although May brought some relief, they still slept lightly.

At breakfast one morning Philip said, "The militia has been called out. They mustered at Albany on May 5th. George Crites, Jacob Myers, Johannes Empey Sr., William Casselman Sr., Joseph Powell, Henry Fetterley, and Conrad Smith were there."[206]

Catrina answered, "I know some of those men, but I don't know Joseph Powell or Conrad Smith. Do they live close by?"

"Joseph Powell is Lewis Clement's nephew. Lewis' sister Elizabeth is married to William Powell. William and his wife are very close to Sir William. They were sponsors at the baptism of Sir William's son John. The Powells live close to the Clements.[207] Conrad Smith lives about two kilometres southwest of Philip Hendrick Klein on the Butlersbury Patent, but he also has land on the eastern side of the Kingsborough Patent.[208]

"Is Johannes Empey Sr. related to the Philip Empey that we met at the church at Stone Raby?"

"Yes, Philip Empey Sr. is his son."

"I know the Casselman family lives at Stone Raby too."

"Yes, William Casselman Sr. settled there in 1723 with his father Dieterich Casselman Sr. He was a young boy then. They were one of the first families to settle at Stone Raby."

In July, Philip and Catrina felt more relief when they attended the baptism of Martin and Margaret Waldorf's daughter Catherine Waldorf.[209] Baptisms were a blessing to the family, but they were also a blessing to their friends and neighbours who came to celebrate. While everyone talked, the children played. At this baptism, they talked about the militia, British victories, the condition of the roads and crops, or about Sir William's brother Warren who was coming to visit.[210]

August and September brought hard work for the whole family. Philip, Catrina, Mattheus, and Elizabeth spent most days in the field cutting, raking, and piling the wheat and oats. When they finished those fields, they picked rows and rows of corn. It was expected that German women and girls worked the fields alongside the men.[211] Elizabeth, Catharina, and Martin helped when it was time to harvest chestnuts, walnuts, and hickory nuts from the forest. The work didn't stop there. The children spent many hours hulling, washing, and drying basketfuls of nuts. When they finished that work, they helped husk corn.

One afternoon when Philip finished checking the apple and cherry trees, he walked up the path to the small front porch where Catrina was sorting baskets of corn cobs. He sat down beside her and started sorting through the cobs. He said, "'T'is Catharina's birthday soon. Can we do something special? 'T'is hard to believe, but she'll be eight. I noticed that she still carries Poppy around, the little doll that she brought from Germany. Can we make her a new doll?"

"Of course, her birthday is September 28th. I'll make her a nice corn husk doll with a skirt and a white linen cap and apron."

Nodding, Philip added, "I'm sure Apple won't mind giving up some of her tail hair for the dolls braids! We can invite the Alguires and Gallingers and roast corn and ham."

The happiest news came a few weeks before Catharina's birthday. General Amherst had taken Montreal with help from Sir William, Captains Butler, Lotteridge, Fonda, Lieutenant Nelles, and almost 200 Iroquois. General Amherst gave all the Indians silver medals and one gold one for Sir William.[212]

As soon as Philip heard the news from George Crites. he said to Catrina, "The British control all of Canada. It's only a matter of time before this war is over! Now we can live in the valley without fear. No more burning, killing, scalping, or kidnapping. Wouldn't our parents be proud that we didn't give up? They knew the hardships of war."

Catrina said, "I'm not sure I know how to live without fear or worry."

"It won't be long before you feel at ease. Your only worry will be the children, your garden, and staying warm in the winter!"

Philip dropped into his chair and lit his pipe. Through the early months of winter, Philip was right. Catrina didn't mention the hiding place or her firelock once. She fussed over and played with the children, and she finished sewing two quilts.

Early in February 1761, icicles were forming along the cabin roof, and there was ½ metre of snow surrounding the cabin. There wasn't much snow this winter, but it was cold. Everyone wore their wool socks and caps to bed, and the children were snuggled together in their beds wrapped in down filled quilts. Elizabeth and Catharina shared one bed in the loft. Downstairs, in one room, Mattheus had his own bed, and Martin and Peter shared the settle bed. In the box stove room, Johannes slept with his parents or in the cradle. Often Philip woke in the middle of the night to make sure the fire was stoked in the kitchen and in the stove box. Philip always put on two pairs of wool socks before slipping on his moccasins. A thin layer of ice covered the snow along most paths so walking to and from the cabin was dangerous.

One night late in February, Philip was up stoking the fires. He couldn't sleep. Warnings the men gave at church on Sunday kept swirling in his head. Over and over, he heard them say, "Johannes Adam Helmer Sr. and Lorenz Herter's wife told Sir William that, after the sermon at the Herkimer Church Fort, Old Mr. Herkimer told us to put ourselves in a way of readiness because he'd heard that the Five Nations would destroy the river with bow and arrow." The only thing that interrupted Philip's persistent thoughts was the bright light of the full moon through the kitchen window. The light had a different glow than any Philip remembered. He slipped on his coat and moccasins and stepped outside. He stared at the night sky for almost a minute before he realized he was looking at the most amazing sky he'd ever seen. He thought, "Maybe there'll be a horrific storm? Maybe the sky is on fire? Maybe poison will fall from the sky! He didn't know what to think. He shivered. He wasn't cold. He shivered more. "I have to get Catrina to see this, maybe Elizabeth, Mattheus, and Catharina too. No, they'll be scared. But, I don't want them to miss this beautiful sky. The red and green waves are moving like water in the creek!"[213]

Several days later Philip, Catrina, and the older children still found it hard to contain their excitement over seeing the moving colours in the sky. They talked about it at every meal for weeks. Mattheus and Catharina were constantly asking their parents where the colours came from and what made them move. Several neighbours had seen it also and were adding their opinions to the growing local conversations. Two events seemed to alleviate these curious and alarming conversations.

First, on March 27th, Sir William and thirty nine settlers, including many from the Kingsborough Patent, petitioned Cadwallader Colden Esq., Commander in Chief of the Province of New York, for almost 10,000 acres of land on the north side of the Mohawk River west of the Kingsborough Patent and near Teady McGinnis' Patent. This petition was for the patent known as Kingsland. Among the patentees were: Peter Fykes Sr., Philip Hendrick Klein, Michael Gallinger Sr., Lucas Feader Sr., Lawrence Eaman, Mattheus Link, Peter Service Sr and Christopher Service, Francis Ruppert Sr. and Adam Ruppert, Johannes Wert, Andrew Snyder, Conrad Smith, and Johannes Ault.[214]

Although this was a promising time for these settlers, the Mohawks of the Lower Castle (Fort Hunter) and the Upper Castle (Canajoharie) were confused, frustrated, and angry at other white settlers' recent land deals. For months, the Indians petitioned Sir William about these fraudulent purchases. In fact, on March 1st, many Chiefs and Sachems of the Lower Castle visited Sir William at Fort Johnson to talk about being cheated out of their lands. Several days later, at Sir William's summer house called Castle Cumberland, twenty one Upper Castle Elders came to talk about Canajoharie fraudulent land purchases. Sir William had never known the Indians to be so 'uneasy in their minds'.[215] So, the settlers' petition for lands near Canajoharie came alongside tension and suspicion among the Mohawks.

The second event happened on March 28th. Sir William gave a gift of fifty acres land to the settlers of Kingsborough as a Glebe for the use of the church to support a Priest.[216] Philip saw the notice at the end of March when he was at Jelles Fonda's store at Caughnawaga.

At supper, Philip told Catrina what Sir William wrote on the notice.

Catrina replied, "That's so exciting for our community. For so long we've had to travel to Stone Raby to attend the Lutheran or the Dutch Reformed Church to worship or to receive blessings from the Reverends, some of us had to travel as far as Schenectady. And, we were never sure when Reverend Ogilvie would be this way from Albany. Where's the land?"

"'T'is right next to Captain Peter Service Sr. and his brother Christopher Service on the east side of Cayadutta Creek. That's only about 1 ½ kilometres west of Michael Gallinger Sr.."

"We'll be happy enough with an Episcopal Church. We're used to Lutheran, but 't'is so nice to have our own village church. When will it be built?"

"I think they'll start building this summer. 'T'will be built near the bridge over Cayadutta Creek."

Fig. 22. St. John's Episcopal Church, Johnstown, New York ca. 1761 From: Flick, Alexander. *The Papers of Sir William Johnson, Vol VIII*, 927.

Not much snow fell through the winter, so there wasn't much moisture in the ground this spring. The river was as low as Philip had ever seen. Philip and Mattheus got the wheat, oats, and corn in as soon as they could. Even Martin helped this spring. After all their morning chores and household work was done, Catrina, Elizabeth, and Catharina got busy sowing the garden seeds every day during the last week of May. Catrina would have to ask Philip to weave more willow fencing to keep the pigs and chickens out.

In early June, Philip drove his wagon to visit Michael Gallinger Sr.. He needed help fixing the axle. While they worked, Michael talked about his visit to German flats a few days earlier. He said, "I took one of my cows to sell to George Adam Bowman and have it butchered. George is a skilled butcher. He learned the skill from his father Johannes Adam Bowman. While I was there, George and his brother Jacob Bowman were talking about the good news for the Miller family. George said that young Jacob Miller, now fourteen years old, and a young Daniel, whose parents are dead, and Daniel's little cousin were found hidden among the inhabitants at La Chine, a small village on the island of Montreal. Jacob was stolen during an Indian raid at German Flats in 1759, and Daniel and his cousin on the Mohawk River in 1756. Apparently, Mrs Miller went to see Sir William in March pleading with him to find her boy and bring him home. General Amherst just returned them to Albany. Apparently, eighteen others who were found are also at Albany."[217]

"That's fantastic for the Millers. Most families who've lost their children, wives, or husbands never see them again. I'd wonder till my last breath what had become of them. I've been so terrified of that thought. I couldn't bear to lose Catrina or any of my children. I'm glad they've mustered the militia again only a few weeks ago. Did you hear that Peter Fyke's young son Philip Adam Fykes has joined?"

"He's twenty one years old now. 'T'is time he joined the militia. I hear that Joseph Powell has mustered too. He's the same age as Philip Adam."[218]

"Yes, and I'd imagine that Peter Fyke's other sons Daniel Fykes and Peter Fykes Jr. will be joining soon too. 'T'is good to have those young men in the militia."

Even though there was still a risk that there'd be a French or Indian raid, Philip felt more confident knowing that the militia had been called out. He still took his firelock to the field when he went out to work. Trying not to scare them, Catrina and Philip made the children practice their escape route all the way to their hiding place or to the trail to the river. One day while Philip, Mattheus, Martin, and young Peter were bringing water to the apple and cherry trees,

Philip made them show him what they'd do if Indians were seen in the forest beyond the orchard. Mattheus was to scoop Peter into his arms, and Martin was to run as fast as he could behind Mattheus. Catrina practiced with Elizabeth and Catharina too while they worked in the garden.

The summer went quickly this year. Philip was pleased with his growing orchard. He had twenty apple trees that would give apples this fall and the six cherry trees gave plenty of fruit in July. Next year he'd plant a few more apple trees and some plum trees. He worked hard on enclosing the orchard with a sturdy post and rail fence. Digging the post holes was backbreaking work for Philip. Mattheus worked just as hard for an eleven year old as he laid the rails between the posts. Philip was planning on buying a stone horse (stallion), so he wanted to fence three acres of grass pasture this year.[219] And, Catrina already asked for a larger wattle fence for her garden.

September was one of Catrina's favourite months. The summers were hot in the valley, and she enjoyed the cool fall air and the beautiful colourful trees. One early morning in the middle of everyone's chores, Michael drove the horses up the lane at a canter and stopping hard called for Catrina. "Come quickly, 't'is Agatha's time. She needs your help!"

While untying her apron, she grabbed her cloak and yelled to Elizabeth, "Tell your Papa I'm going to the Gallingers to help Agatha. I'll be a few hours. Watch the children."

It was Friday, September 4th. Henry Gallinger was born quickly. He was Agatha's sixth delivery and fifth child. All her children were under the age of five.[220]

Only a few days after Henry Gallinger's birth, a group of settlers from the Kingsborough Patent went to Albany, and, on September 11th, they obtained their naturalization certificates. All settlers of foreign birth in New York were required to pledge allegiance to the King. This group of settlers petitioned the representatives of the colony of New York on 10 March 1761 and included Peter Service Sr. and his brother Christopher, Johannes Wick, Johannes Ault, Conrad Smith, Johannes Albrant, Johannes Eberhart Van Koughnot Sr., and several others.[221]

On November 15th, two months after the naturalization of many Kingsborough settlers, Philip, Catrina, and the children rode the wagon to the Dutch Reformed Church at Stone Arabia to watch the baptism of Henry

Gallinger. Henry's namesake and sponsor was Henry Dachstadter of German Flats, his daughter Barbara was also a sponsor. Henry Dachstadter's father George Dachstadter Sr. came to New York with the Palatine immigrants in 1709 and was one of the first settlers on the Burnetsfield Patent of German Flats. Because the family were celebrating the baptism of their friend's son, Catrina thought this was a good time to tell Philip that their family was going to be larger next spring. She whispered the good news to him as they took their seats in the pew. Philip spent the whole service sitting a little taller than usual.

During the early winter months. The family went about their daily chores as the snow drifted up and around the small cabin. For everyone every day, there were animals to feed and water, corrals to clean, and wood to bring in. Catrina, Elizabeth, and Catharina spent long hours cooking, sweeping, and washing clothes. Often shirts, trousers, and petticoats were covered in frost even when hung close to the fire. There were a lot of new clothes to sew or old clothes to mend. Philip spent most evenings reading from the Bible as Catrina and the children listened attentively. Once the sun set, with the exception of one candle for each bedroom, the only light by which to read was the flame of the fire. Philip had bought three pewter candlestick holders the year after they arrived. Elizabeth was responsible for carrying the candle to the room in the loft, and Mattheus was responsible for the candle in the back room. The pine knots Lewis Clement gave them their first year in their cabin weren't as easy to find here as they were near Schenectady. So, the women spent many days in the fall dipping cotton candlewicks in tallow and making enough soap to last until summer.

Just about every Sunday, the family attended church services at either the Dutch Reformed Church or the Lutheran Church at Stone Raby. Catrina loved the ride in the sleigh, especially with Johannes snuggled under the weight of a bear skin on her lap and the children squirming and giggling in the rear seat. Catrina always baked some corn cakes for the ride to church. On Saturday November 28th, they attended a special service. It was the baptism of Mattheus and Magdelena Link's son Mattheus Link Jr.[222] Philip and Catrina loved the opportunity to visit with friends and neighbours. This Saturday, they spent a lot of time with Jacob Henry and Salome Alguire. Their son Martin was there too. He was growing into a fine young man, almost sixteen now and approaching an age that he could start thinking about a wife and his own family. They also met

Phillip Miller and his wife Anna Visbach who lived near Caughnawaga and were friends with Jelles Fonda.

Near the end of January 1762, Philip sat at the kitchen table one evening finishing writing a record of the crops he grew last year and the profits he'd made taking his wheat and oats to Johannes Veeder's grist mill near Caughnawaga. Catrina came up beside him while his head was down and the light of the candle barely lit the paper. She said, "Did you see any Indians when you went to William Bowen's to fix the iron runners on the sleigh?"

"No, I didn't, but William told me over 100 passed along the road to Fort Johnson just last Monday, the 25th. He saw Canajoharie, Mohawk, Onondaga, Oneida and even some Tuscaroros. They were going to Fort Johnson for a conference with Sir William and Lieutenant Guy Johnson Sir William's nephew. The Indians are troubled about fraudulent land claims, and Sir William is troubled about the Seneca promoting an uprising against the British near Detroit. I think Sir William will do his best to deal with the land claim issue. He'll want each tribe to confirm their allegiance with the British. Why did you ask?"

"I saw four Mohawks walk past our lane a few days ago and wondered if something was happening. I'm not afraid of the Mohawks. They're our friends. I recognize them right away. I hear also that men of the valley were on the road to Albany to be naturalized. From Stone Raby there was the blacksmith Casper Koch and his son Rudolph Koch, and near Warrensburg along the Schoharie River there was Johannes Klein, a neighbor of Harmanus Mabee. And there were sons of Johannes Peter Frederick and his wife Anna Veronica, Philip, Barent, Johannes, Jacob, Lodowyck and Conrad. And I hear Ernest Frauts and David Eny."[223]

"Hmmm." Philip replied. "I thought you were going to ask me how my extra work for Sir William is faring? For over a week, Michael, Jacob Henry, George, Lawrence, and Mattheus had been driving sleighs hauling lumber and mortar stone to Fort Johnson"

Catrina replied, "What's the need for all those sleighs?"

"Sir William is building a new house just north of the church land across Cayadutta Creek. He needs to gather mortar stone and timber so he can build as soon as the ground thaws."[224]

"I hope some of it's for the new church! Maybe even a school. The children learn their numbers at home, but I'd like them to learn to write English."

Catrina had reason to be thinking of children and school. Four days ago, she delivered a daughter, Anna Margaret Eamer. Elizabeth's comments surprised both Philip and Catrina, but they understood the dreams of children. They still hear Elizabeth say, "We've a sister! Yay, a girl. We've too many brothers."

March was certainly an exciting month. Everyone was enjoying little Anna Margaret, and they felt the warmth in the air and heard the birds singing. As Apple pulled the sleigh along the soft snowy road, Catrina noticed the sun starting to melt the snow. It was Thursday, March 18, and they were on their way to a baptism. This time, Philip and Catrina had been asked to be sponsors for Philip Jordan, son of Stephen Jordan and Margaretha. The service was held in a small building with Reverend Barent Vrooman from Schenectady providing the service. Philip was very proud to not only be this infant's namesake, but also his sponsor. It was a great responsibility to undertake. By being sponsors, Philip and Catrina pledged to make certain that little Philip Jordan was raised in the Reform faith and that he led a good and successful life.[225]

April chores were much the same every year. There were maple trees to tap and sugar to make. And, there were harnesses and tackling to oil. Last year Philip bought a new leather riding saddle for Apple. It needed a bit of oil too. Elizabeth and Mattheus were good young riders bareback. But, Philip wanted them to get used to riding faster; so, to be safe, they needed a saddle. Catrina, Elizabeth, and Catharina brought out the quilts and coats to hang in the sun, and all the bed sheets needed washing. And, of course, everyone in the family had their turn at a bath in the large wooden tub. Mattheus built a large fire outside to heat lots of water. The tub was filled with warm water, and everyone got a square of soap and a comb. First, Catrina got her only pair of scissors and cut everyone's thick brown hair about four inches. The knots and tangles had to be combed out before the oil and dirt were scrubbed away. All the scrubbing reminded Elizabeth of the scrubbing they got when they arrived at the Martin Silmser's house in Philadelphia. Even Mattheus remembered that scrubbing.

During Philip's turn at the bath, he tried to tell Catrina about his days hauling timber for Sir William while she poured water over his head. He managed to say, "I've never in my life seen so many Indians as I did last Wednesday. While I was at Fort Johnson hundreds of Indians arrived, most in groups of at least ten or twenty. There were some dressed in ways I'd never seen. They must have come a long way and are from tribes I don't know. George Schenck Sr. said he recognized some as Cayugas and Onieda, and he said he thought some might be Seneca. He said that Sir William was meeting with them to ensure peace in the valley like he did in January, and that they were complaining about settlements on their land along the Susquehanna River. Being at Fort Johnson was like being in Philadelphia. There was so much activity I was afraid I'd run over someone with the sleigh. We were asked not to come back for a few days, too much activity."[226]

"I'm glad you were careful. You could've started another war! Where do they all stay? What do they eat?"

"There's an Indian Council house on the grounds, but there were almost as many tents as there were Indians. Sir William feeds them. I saw some roasting meat and fish over a fire. And, one of Sir William's slaves was roasting a pig!"

Catrina sighed and said, "Well, as long as they're all talking about peace."

By July, Philip was watching his crops grow and was nearly finished enclosing the meadows, the three acre grass pasture, the orchard, a good piece of the eight acres of wheat, and three acres of oat fields. He'd been on the land for almost seven years and had fourteen acres cleared. Eighteen if he counted the three acre orchard. Catrina was walking through the orchard one afternoon filling her basket with herbs along the way and checking the apple trees. "I'm glad I don't have to walk among the bees now that the blossoms have fallen," she said to Philip as he walked up behind her.

"I know. I'm certain there must be a hive with honey close by. Mattheus, Martin, and I'll have to go look one day. Some honey would be nice."

Catrina bent over, picked up her basket, and said, "I've sweet news. We're going to have another baby."

Wrapping his arms around her and her basket, Philip said, "That's wonderful news. I'll always welcome a new child into the family! When can we expect this baby?"

"February."

"Oh, I'm sorry for you. 'T'is hard to bring a child into the world when it's so cold. I'll work hard this year to get another bear so that you've a good warm blanket, and Michael Gallinger and I are going to buy some sheep. I want to buy one ram for meat and a few lambs. I'll take the skin to Adam Loucks at Stone Raby. He can tan it for me, and you can sew a warm sheepskin coat and slippers to keep your feet warm. And, we'll have mutton through the winter."

One hot muggy day, Philip was driving his wagon along the road to Schenectady. He was on his way to buy sheep and lambs from Sir William. Along the way, he met Henry Hough driving the opposite direction. His wife Catherine was with him, and she was cradling a tiny bundle. Philip waved, and Henry slowed his wagon.

They stopped in the middle of the road. Resting the reins on his lap, Philip said, "Good day Henry. Good day Mrs Hough. I see there's a tiny bundle in your arms. Is this a new babe?"

"Yes, she is!" Henry replied. "She was baptized Maria Hough last Wednesday at Caughnawaga."[227]

"My best wishes to you both. I'm on my way to buy sheep from Thomas Flood, Sir William's farm manager."

"Thomas Flood is a careful overseer when he's not been drinking. When he has he's harsh. Mind his prices. Sheep'll do well in this valley. And, Mutton is good. 'T'is a good choice Sir."

Late in July, Philip was putting new hinges on a gate when he saw Michael come riding around the back of the cabin. Michael dismounted in a hurry and said, "I've been riding to the neighbours to sound the alarm that Indians attacked German Flats again. Last night, Sir William got a message from Henry Frey Sr. that the town was burnt. Sir William is now at Mr. Frey's at Canajoharie, and Sir William thinks that Mr. Frey's alarm was without foundation. He's ordered the troops to Canajoharie and to Nicholas Herkimer's house at German Flats anyway. They're to protect the area and to send out scouts. Goshen Van Alstyne's Company is there. Henry Seeber and Peter Casselman are in that Company, so are William Casselman Sr. and his sons John, Severinus, and William Jr."[228]

While looking at young Martin, Michael said, "'T'is a nice looking gate. Did you build that young fellow?"

"I helped Papa and Mattheus Mr. Gallinger! Papa and Mattheus cut the rails."

"Well done Martin! You can help me make a gate for my chickens. I see you've some sheep now Philip. Good, we can shear together when the time comes!"

Only three days later, Michael came riding down the lane. Meeting Philip at the corral, he said, "Well Philip, it seems that the Indian attack at German Flats was a false alarm!"

"What happened?" Philip asked.

"Well, t'is a splendid story. After Sir William investigated the event, he found that an Indian was drunk and wanted more liquor, so he stripped off all his clothes and swam across the river to the Tippling House where two young girls had been left to attend the house. Being naked and drunk, he scared the girls, and they ran out. The girls ran to a field where people were mowing and yelled to them that there was a naked Indian at the Tippling House. Everyone was terrified. I'm not surprised. We know they've experienced Indian cruelty. Anyway, they all ran to the river, swam across, and frightened everyone on the other side. "The alarm was sounded," Philip asked.

"Oh yes, and the settlers added that the settlement had been destroyed![229] A militia man was dispatched to Sir William right away. That was when I came to see you. T'is all cleared up now. But, I still think we need to keep vigilant. The war's not over yet."

With a good chuckle Philip replied, "Aye, 't'is a splendid story. Funny, if I didn't feel for the frightened girls and farmers."

"I'll take my leave now. Agatha needs me to help with the young ones. Good day Philip."

Late in the fall, Philip butchered the ram and shared some of the meat with Jacob Henry Alguire and Johannes Alguire and Michael Gallinger. Catrina roasted a shoulder and leg and the rest she salted and put away in the root cellar. Philip took the beautiful dirty white wooled skin to Adam Loucks at Stone Raby to cure and tan. He also took a deer hide. Philip wanted Catrina to have a warm coat and slippers this winter. And, he wanted Mattheus and Martin to have a pair of leather breeches. Catrina worked on her slippers first. Having only two bear skins to ease the chill in her feet, she wanted warm feet while walking on the dirt floor. Her fingers hurt from spending many hours cutting and sewing sheepskin and deer hide, but she was pleased when she finished her coat and the boy's breeches.

One evening in late October, she was showing her slippers to Philip and said, "I'll need some wool cloth to make Elizabeth and Catharina warm jackets and skirts for the winter. Does Jelles Fonda have any at his store?"

"Yes, he does. Jacob Henry Alguire was just there buying kersey, flannel, buttons, and thread for Salome. And, I saw him with a new wool hat."[230]

One December evening, Catrina sat in her rocking chair beside the fire. The cabin was chilly, and she could hear the wind howl passed the doors and window. But, her wool cap kept her head warm, and her feet were almost sweating propped up so near the fire and inside her soft sheepskin slippers. Philip was warm enough in his wool cap and wool breeches and comfortable in his rocking chair. Puffs of smoke from his pipe drifted above his head every few seconds as he watched Martin, Peter, and Johannes playing on the bear rug by the fire. He could hear Anna Margaret nursing and Elizabeth, Catharina, and Mattheus at the table getting chestnuts ready to roast. It was crowded in the little kitchen.

Between puffs on his pipe, Philip asked Catrina, "I think we should try and write home again. I know we didn't get an answer from our letter last year, but I've heard that some people have asked Sir William to post letters for them, and they did get an answer. I'd like everyone at home to know we are well and that we have so many wonderful children and one on the way."

"Yes, I'd like to try sending a letter again. It seems like only a few years since we left Germany, but it's been seven years! T'is hard not knowing how our parents are. They could be sick or have died. Or, maybe your brother Johannes Mattheus is married now with children!"[231]

Catrina rarely went outside this January. Philip was always up first lighting the fire and then out the door to fetch water for Catrina. The older children weren't far behind. They did their chores every morning helping their papa feed the animals and gather wood. Early one morning, while Catrina handed Elizabeth, Mattheus, and Martin their wool caps as they went out the door.

Elizabeth asked, "Are you coming too Mama?"

"No Elizabeth, it's too cold for your little sister, and I'm afraid I might fall on the ice. And, I have to stay and watch your cornmeal pudding that's over the fire."

After about an hour, everyone came in banging snow off their coats and moccasins and rushed to the fire to warm their hands. They always looked forward to their hot cornmeal pudding, bread, and cheese.

At the end of January and the beginning February 1763, there was a wicked winter storm. For days, Philip and the children struggled when they went outside to care for the animals. The cold wind blew snow straight at their faces taking their breath away and making their cheeks and chins burn. Even their eyelashes froze. Everyone was grateful for Mattheus' wooden rattle on the string to the outhouse. It would've been easy for one of them to get lost and hard for others to find them. The cabin was colder than it had ever been even though Philip stayed up most nights making sure there was constant fire and coals.

One morning early in February, Catrina went to lay down after their morning meal. She knew it was time and had only Elizabeth and Catherina to help. She hoped the baby would come easily. Late in the afternoon after hours of struggle, Catrina gave birth to a small fragile baby boy. He was so tiny. He almost disappeared when wrapped in Catrina's sheepskin coat. They laid him in the cradle and placed it beside the iron stove, and they moved Catrina and Philip's bed next to the cradle.

Catrina woke from a short sleep and said to Philip, "We must name him Philip Eamer and baptize him right away. He's so tiny and 't'is so cold. I'm afraid for him."

"Yes, we'll take him to Caughnawaga as soon as this storm has past. I think Sunday will be fine. You'll be more rested in a few days." Little Philip Eamer was baptized at the little log Caughnawaga Church on Sunday, 6 Feb 1763. Philip Miller and Anna Visbach were his sponsors.[232]

March 1763 brought a terror unlike the ones the family experienced with the French and Indians. It was a terror that Philip saw in Catrina's face when she ran out to the woodshed early one morning. "Philip, come now! Philip is very sick. Please come now!"

Catrina started back to the house as Philip caught up to her. "Where is he? I know he wasn't feeling well these past few days. And, he's so tiny."

"He has a fever, and he won't suckle! He's breathing so hard and fast. Oh dear God, he's going to die!"

"He'll be alright. How are the other children?"

"Elizabeth and Catharina are tired and picking at their food. Peter has been crying a lot since yesterday. I think t'is the long winter and the cold."

"No one comes in or leaves until the children are better." Catrina was with little Philip for two days. She prayed constantly. Early in the morning while she quietly rocked him, he died. He lived not even two months.

The next day, Philip and Mattheus built a small coffin and dug a hole near the oak trees behind the orchard. Catrina wrapped little Philip in a wool blanket they brought from Germany. She thought of her own mother as she tried to stand beside the small hole in the ground. She held Elizabeth's and Mattheus' hands, and she wept. Reverend Barent Vrooman came to bless the baby after his services at Caughnawaga. Philip recited several prayers then spread dirt over the little box. He said, "Little Philip will rest peacefully under the oak trees." His hands shook as he spread the dirt. And, in a low soft voice he said, "We'll be near you son. God's hands, being full of grace, will lift you to heaven."

It was a blessing that March was a busy month. All the activity helped ease the grief of losing little Philip. For several weeks, wagons continuously passed along the road from Tribes Hill passed the lane to their little cabin. The wagons headed northwest several kilometres to the site of Sir William's new house. It was to be a magnificent two story wooden house called Johnson Hall, seventeen metres long and 11 1/2 metres wide with a stone foundation, two fireplaces, and a large cellar. There would be a grist mill, a coach house, and other outbuildings. Samuel Fuller was the architect.[233]

It wasn't long after work began on Johnson Hall when the congregation of the Dutch Reformed Church at Caughnawaga started building a suitable church. This church would be a square structure built of rough limestone. It stood on the Caughnawaga flats along the Mohawk River at the east end of the village of Caughnawaga. The building of this new church was a welcome announcement not only for Philip and Catrina on the Sacandaga Patent, but also for more than 100 tenants on or near Sir William's Kingsborough Patent. Their journey to a new church was five kilometres along a good road.[234]

Fig. 23. Reformed Dutch Church at Caughnawaga (no spire until ca. 1795)
From: Benson, J. Lossing, Pictorial Field Book of the Revolution. Volume 1 Chapter X, 233.

News during the summer months centered around the construction of Sir William's grand house, the new church at Caughnawaga, improvements on well-travelled roads, or plans for the clearing of new roads. Everyone knew there would be roads to improve and new public roads to each of these building sites. This spring and summer would surely be a busy time for the Commissioners of Highways of the area. They were responsible for the clearing and better laying out of new highways and public roads. The Commissioners were Sir William Johnson, Johannes Vrooman, and Douw Fonda.[235] If clearing was needed, the men and young boys in the area were required to offer their help for a certain number of days per year. This meant more trees to fall, stumps and rocks to move, and branches and bush to clear.

Philip, Mattheus, and Martin spent their days clearing and fencing more land, planting the crops, and planting about ten more apple trees. One afternoon, Philip was out near the meadow admiring the lambs that he bought last summer. They had wintered well. While standing and resting against the fence, he thought, "T'was a good purchase. Of the four lambs I bought, there are three ewes and one ram. In the fall, I'll slaughter last year's ram, and we can enjoy more mutton and another sheepskin. As long as the crop is good this year, I'll buy another ram from Mr. Flood and breed my three ewes. The wool will be nice this fall. It'll fetch a good price. Catrina can knit socks and sweaters, and, I think it's time Catharina learned to knit. George Crites weaves nice cloth. I wonder if John Friel, Sir William's tailor, needs wool. I'll ask if I'm at Lodowyck Putnam's, John Friel lives next to him on lot 114."[236]

While Philip was busy thinking about wool, wool cloth, and wool socks, Catrina was thinking that Philip and the boys needed new shirts, and she wanted to make three aprons. She thought that blue check linen would be nice. It was Saturday, July 17th when she and Philip harnessed Apple and headed to the store at Caughnawaga. This would be a nice outing for them since little Philip died. Elizabeth was fifteen and Mattheus thirteen; they could look after the little ones for a few hours.

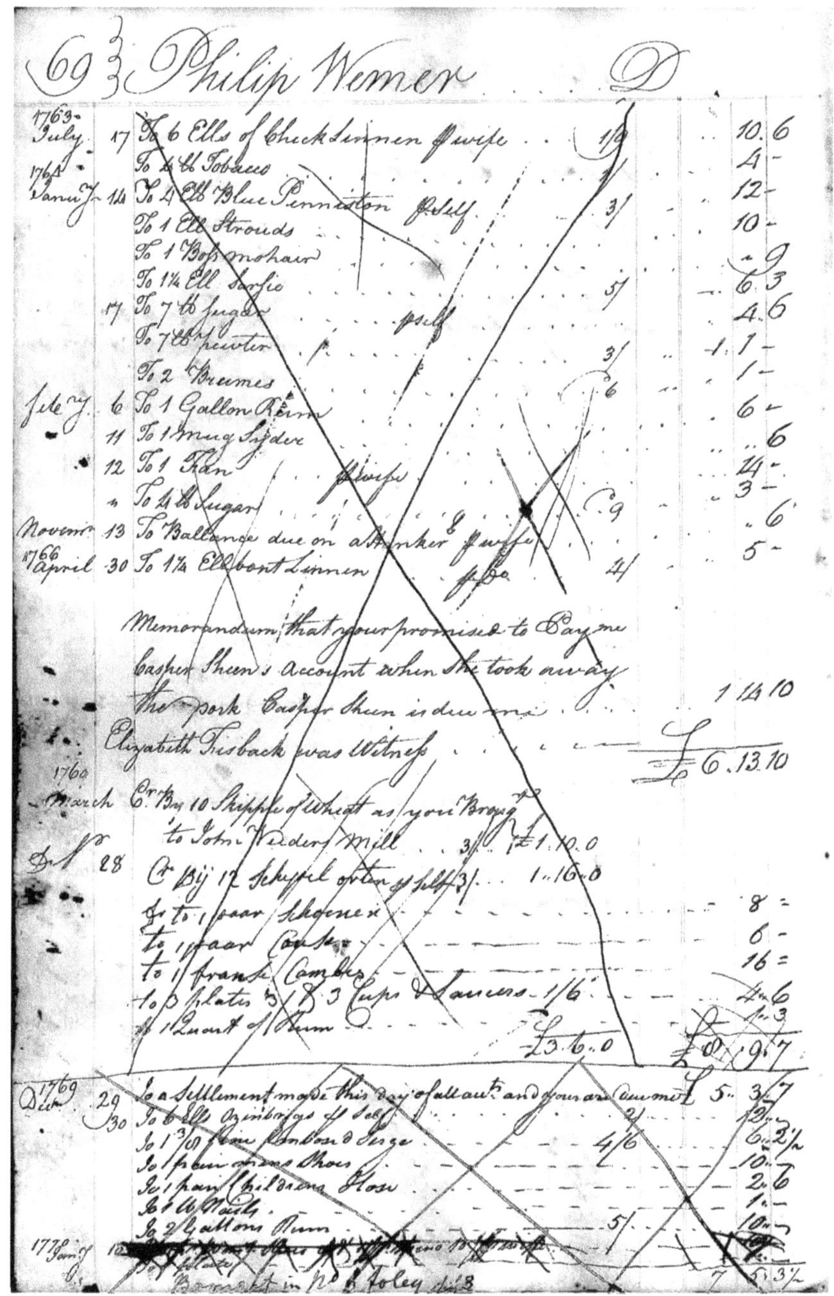

69 Philip Wemer Dr

Date		Item			£ s. d.
1763 July	17	To 6 Ells of Check Linnen p wife	1/9		10.6
1764		To ¼ lb Tobacco			4-
Janry	14	To 4 Ells Blue Penniston p Self	3/		12-
		To 1 Ell Strouds			10-
		To 1 Box mohair			9
		To 1¼ Ell Sarfie	5/		6.3
	17	To 7 lb Sugar p self			4.6
		To 7 lb pewter	3/	1.	1-
		To 2 Breemes			1-
Feby	6	To 1 Gallon Rum	6		6-
	11	To 1 mug Syder			6
	12	To 1 Fan p wife			14-
		To ½ lb Sugar			3-
Novemr	13	To Ballance due on a Ankker p wife	9		6
1766 April	30	To 1¼ Ell bont Linnen p Do	4/		5-

Memorandum that your promised to Pay me Casper Sheen's account when She took away the pork Casper Sheen is due me — 1 14 10

Elizabith Fisback was Witness

£6.13.10

1760 March Cr By 10 Skipple of Wheat as you Brought to John Veeder's Mill 3/ £1.10.0

28 Cr Bij 12 Skepel ... p self 3/ 1..16..0

Item		£ s. d.
to 1 paar Skoenen		8 =
to 1 paar ...		6 -
to 1 frank Cambes		16 =
to 3 plates & 3 Cups & Sauceers	1/6	4.6
to 1 Quart of Rum		1.3
	£3.6.0	£0.9.7

Date		Item		£ s. d.
1769 Decr	29	To a Settlement made this day of all acct and your are due me	£	5.. 3.7
	30	To 6 Ells Oznibrigs p Self	2/	12..
		To 1 ⅜ ... Sarge	4/6	6..2½
		To 1 pair ... Shoes		10..
		To 1 pair Childrens Hose		2.6
		To 4 lb Nails		1..
		To 2 Gallons Rum	5/	10..
1770 Janry	10	...		
		To 1 plate		
		Barnard in No 8 folio	7	5.3½

Fig. 24. General Store Ledger, Courtesy of Special Collections Fenimore Art Museum Library, Cooperstown, New York. Jellis Fonda Papers, Coll. No. 157, 1750-1791. Wemer, Philip: 69A.

When Catrina went to the counter, Philip asked her to get 4 lbs of tobacco and, seeing Philip Empey Sr. of Stone Raby, he went over to find news of the French and the Indians. "Pray Mr. Empey, have you news of French or Indians near us?"

"Good day Philip. Captain Severinus Deygert's Company from Stone Raby and Captain Jacob Klock's Company were called out on an Indian alarm at German Flats. Apparently, fourteen men didn't show. Some of them were Adam Empey Sr., and Christian Dillenbach, Martin Dillenbach, and Lieutenant William Dillenbach, all sons of George Martin Dillenbach and Anna Elizabeth Casselman."

With a shrug of his shoulders, Philip replied, "Hmm, 't'is a difficult thing to go on a moment's notice leaving your families unprotected and your fields uncut. 'T'is confusing times in which we live. Even though we all hold our families dear, and we must have grain and hay for the winter, they'll be trouble for those men for their absence. Maybe even fines or jail!"[237]

Philip and Mattheus were out in the yard sharpening the scythe and plough blade when Philip saw two soldiers at the end of the lane. He recognized the uniform right away. Philip remembered what the Light Infantrymen of the 60th Regiment looked like. They were trained and dressed for forest warfare. These men wore red collarless coats cut short with blue facings and a white shirt. Their breeches were blue, and their brown gaiters reached their thighs. Their hair was cut short, and their black tricorn hats sat firmly on their heads. They wore their knapsacks high on their backs just like the Indians. Each of them had a Brown Bess firelock. In the middle of the leather belt that secured their coats was an ammunition pouch. Philip wondered why soldiers from the 60th Regiment were in the area. Then, he recognized one them. It was John Farlinger. Quickly, Philip set down his tools and walked toward them.

Philip and John reached out to embrace and Philip said, "'T'is so good to see you! I've thought of you since we left Fort Edward years ago."

John replied, "I'm fine, but tired of war and want to farm now. I've served in the 60th for seven years. We've just been discharged a few days ago and found land on the Kingsborough Patent very near you. This is Anthony Walliser, another private in the 60th. I've settled on lot eighty and Anthony on lot eighty three. Michael Gallinger told me where you lived."[238]

Philip smiled, "You're in a good spot, right next to Michael Gallinger Sr. and Mattheus Link. They're good men with fine families and we're very good friends! Come and sit for a while and have some rum. I want you to meet my wife Catrina and my children. While waving Mattheus over, he said, "This is Mattheus, my eldest son."

It wasn't until November 1763 that Philip and Catrina heard news they could hardly believe. It was Christmas Eve when Philip flung open the door of the cabin. Everyone was in the kitchen and the cold air coming through the door got their attention.

Reaching for her shawl, Catrina said, "What's happened?"

"The war is over!"

"What do you mean? Is that true?"

"Yes, Yes, Yes, it is true! The French have surrendered. There won't be any more butchery in the valley. No more scalpings or settlers taken! We can live in peace." The children jumped up and down, elbow to elbow, clapping, and yelling Hurrah, Hurrah, and Hurrah!

Catrina wrapped her arms around Philip saying, "Hallelujah and praise our God!"

"King George proclaimed the treaty in October, and Sir William just proclaimed his obedience and the obedience of all the inhabitants of this area to the conditions of the treaty."

"What are the conditions?"

"Most of them have to do with trading or buying land from the Indians. No one is allowed to trade without a license, and no private person is to buy land from the Indians. Transactions are all made through the Governor or the Commander in Chief of the colonies. I'm glad of that. There's been much cheating and abuse. "[239]

"Sir William has a lot of knowledge of Indian beliefs and customs. He gained the Indians' trust and worked on their behalf. That was crucial to peace. We owe him a great deal."[240]

Fig. 25. Edward Lawson Henry, 1903. *Sir William Johnson Presenting Medals to Chiefs of the Six Nations at Johnstown, N.Y., 1772.* Courtesy of Wikimedia Commons: Original Source Canadian Museum of Civilization. PD-US.

Fig. 26. *Sir William Johnson, ca. 1760.* Courtesy of the Library and Archives Canada, Acc. No. 1989-407-1

There couldn't have been enough celebrating over the next few days. So many of Philip and Catrina's friends attended church service on Christmas Day. It was a beautiful winter morning when they arrived at the new church at Caughnawaga. Philip and Catrina sat between Michael and Agatha Gallinger, and Jacob Henry and Salome Alguire. And, they saw George Crites, Lawrence

Eaman, Martin Waldorf and Margaretha, Captain Peter Service Sr. and his wife Magdelena, Philip Hendrick Klein and Anna Margaretha, Lodowyck Putnam and Elizabeth, Johannes Hough Sr. and Catherine and his sons Henry Hough, and Johannes Jr., Lewis Clement and Caty, Adam Ruppert Sr. and Barbara, James Crosset, and Peter Fykes Sr.. After the service, about twenty sleighs headed north toward Johnson Hall where they all joined Sir William and nearly 100 Mohawk Indians. When Philip, Catrina, and the children rode up the lane to Johnson Hall, they could see a grand fire in the front yard where crowds of people gathered. The children leapt out of the sleigh and headed straight toward tables that were covered with all kinds of meats, tasty lemon cakes, apple pies, and hot chocolate. At the rear of the house, there were two more fires. Near one of the fires, Philip and Catrina sat on a bench next to Johannes and Henry Hough. Michael Gallinger had gone to get each of them a gill of rum.

While Philip sat savouring each puff of his pipe, Johannes Hough Sr. and his son Henry told stories about their first years in the Mohawk Valley. They talked about the beauty of the valley. As they described their experiences, each of them drew deep breaths which, after a few minutes, gave way to heavy sighs. Just as Johannes finished, Henry saw two Mohawk friends. He waved them over. Henry spoke the Mohawk language. He learned the language playing with the Mohawk children who lived near Fort Hunter.

As the two Mohawks sat down next to Philip and Catrina, they spoke to Henry, and he translated, "They said, Sir William has chocolate, nice hot drink." Henry introduced the Mohawks,

"This is Tehodinayea, Seth in English and Teyorheasere, Abraham in English. They are of the Wolf clan at the Lower Castle near Fort Hunter. They both fought with Sir William at Montreal in 1760." Henry spoke to Tehodinayea and Teyorheasere telling them about the stories they just told of living along the Mohawk River.

Tehodinayea talked with Henry Hough for a long while. The young man entranced Philip and Catrina. They couldn't keep their eyes off him as he spoke. His hair fascinated Philip. The sides and front of Tehodinayea's head were bare, and three braids dyed with red ochre stood atop a square patch of hair.[241] He decorated it with many feathers. Catrina admired the beading on his moccasins, and she noticed the grease smeared all over. She thought, "The grease must work well to keep his feet dry. I'll have to put some on our moccasins."

As Tehodinayea spoke, Henry translated, "Before the Mohawk lived in the valley, the great ice melted, and a lake was created. The Appalachian Mountains surrounded the lake which was as large as this whole valley. The water from the lake eventually carved a gorge through the mountains separating our northern hunting grounds in the Adirondacks from the lands of the Oneida and Onandaga in the southern Catskills. The water raged through the gorge and carved great holes in the rock. As it raged, it left waterfalls, rock caves, and potholes. That is how our great river and valley were born. We call it Tenonanatche, which means 'a river flowing through the mountains'. With this great river, all the Haudenosanee (Iroquois) peoples could travel by canoe from the great lakes in the west to the great ocean in the east. We could follow the creeks and rivers that ran south to the lands of the Delaware and the Shawnee or north to the Wyandot's and Ojibwe lands."

When Tehodinayea finished, Teyorheasere talked, and Henry translated, "He says that the Mohawk River gives many gifts. The fish, eels, birds, and turtles feed our people. When the river floods it leaves rich soil along the flats so we can grow plenty of corn, squash, and beans. We're grateful for the forests in the valley and the game they keep. Even the rocks give purpose. Without the flint we would have no arrows for hunting, and without ochre we couldn't paint our bodies for war."

Philip had his own memories and his own regard for the valley. He understood a little why Tehodinayea and Teyorheasere talked about the valley with such reverence. Philip thought, "As I stand on a high point on my land, I can see the rolling hills gently rise from the winding river. They tell me 't'is 240 kilometres long. In my few years here, I've travelled the road east and west through the flats that stretch out from its shore. From this high point on my land, I see the thickest forests I've ever seen. As the forests spread up and over the valley, they bring life to the mountains. In the fall, the red, yellow, and orange leaves decorate the mountains in ways that take my breath away. Sometimes I think the valley is on fire. Even my yellow and gold fields bend in the wind, and the stalks of corn bow their feathered tips. It's all more beautiful and plentiful than I ever imagined so many years ago in Auerbach."

Philip took a swig of rum and then a puff of his pipe. He leaned back, blew the smoke straight up and thought, "Despite the horrors of the war, people here accomplished so much. There are over 500 homes along this valley, all with good cultivated lands.[242] We're blessed. I'm blessed. Catrina and I have seven healthy children. At fifteen, Elizabeth is a young woman and Mattheus, at thirteen, a young man. Catharina is eleven and growing so fast. Hmm, Martin is seven, and Peter is six. They'll soon be able to manage heavier work in the fields and around the house. At four, little Johannes is no longer a baby and Anna Margaret is not yet two." Philip took another puff of his pipe as he thought about little Philip that they buried not so long ago.

Catrina reached over and clasped Philip's hand. She had seen his face soften and his eyes sparkle. She knew he was full of gratitude. She said, "Through all the long journeys, long days, and sleepless nights, I've always believed in your strong heart and your big stubborn dreams. Despite the fears, the cold, and the relentless work, we've made a good life here."

"We have," he said squeezing her hand. Indeed, we have. Together, we have."

CHAPTER FOUR
Home in the Mohawk River Valley (1764-1774)

The gruelling work of daily life welcomed 1764 in such a familiar way. It was January and the Eamers huddled in their cabin among snowdrifts and enormous tree branches that bowed under the weight of the snow. One afternoon, Catrina sat at the kitchen table cutting woolen stroud and penniston into a pattern for warm waist jackets and petticoats for Elizabeth, Catharina, and herself.[243] She had already cut two patterns for undershirts for Philip and Mattheus. While Catrina cut, the girls stitched the beginnings of their winter clothes and argued about using the blue penniston for their waist jackets or their petticoats.

Just as Catrina finished cutting the back of an undershirt, Philip came in from feeding the chickens. "Sure are busy women in this kitchen," he said as he unlaced his moccasins and slipped off his blanket coat.

As he bent over, the snow in his hair melted and dripped onto his leggings. Catrina said, "Stand over here husband. I want to measure this shirt." As Philip stood still beside the table, Catrina measured and asked, "Can you go to Caughnawaga tomorrow? We need 7 lbs of sugar, and I need a new broom."

"'T'is fine. I need pewter to make bullets."[244]

Early in the morning, Philip harnessed Apple to the sleigh and, under a soft fall of snow, drove down the road to Fonda's store. While he was looking at the brooms, William Empey Sr. from Stone Raby walked over, "Good day Sir," Philip said.

"'T'is a fine day Philp. I've not seen you since the celebration at Sir William's house. I hope you and yours had a festive Christmas and New Year."

"We did William, thank you. How are things at Stone Raby this early in the year?"

"Well, he said while lighting his pipe. In a matter of a few weeks, there's been much commotion in our community. Just before Christmas, Henry Frey got a complaint from Mrs. John Abeel. She said her husband finally lost his mind, and she was terrified of him. Apparently, he's chased everyone out of the house including her, only the Seneca and a few Negroes were allowed to stay. He even takes his gun to bed with him! After a few puffs, he continued, Gysbert Van Alstyne went to find his brother Cobes, and old John Abeel came after Gysbert with a hatchet missing him and striking a post at the door. As Abeel hollered for the Indians, Gysbert jumped onto his sleigh and sped down the road! Whew! Now, Henry Frey applied to Sir William to come to Mrs. Abeel's aid."[245]

With lowered brows, narrowed eyes, and a slow shake of his head, Philip stared at William as he continued, "Things just calmed down with Mrs. Abeel when Martin Dillenbach Jr. was arrested at the home of William Dillenbach for assaulting William Loucks, a Sergeant in the militia." Philip's eyes widened and his jaw dropped. William added, "He's to come before Justice Henry Frey to answer to the charge of assault and battery.[246] I'm not sure how he'll come through that. Surely, not a good thing to assault a Sergeant in the militia!" Just as William was finishing his sentence, his wife Margaret came to fetch him. "Sorry Philip, I must be off now!" Philip waved and continued looking at the brooms. One batch was well made. He chose two from that batch thinking one will wear out sweeping those dirt floors.

Just as Philip was leaving, he met George Crites at the door. "Good day George. I'm glad to see you friend."

"A good day to you Philip. How does all at home?"

"All are well, and you?"

"Fine Sir. I've come to get paper for shot cartridges. I've just heard that the militia has been called to muster and march to the Schoharie valley. There's been a lot of Seneca and Delaware Indians rising up in that valley. To pass muster we have to be well supplied with ammunition.[247] That means Jacob Myers, Conrad Smith and I'll be gone for a while."

"I know you'll be well supplied George. If you ever need powder I have extra. Good luck to you and return soon."

It was an early spring in 1764. There were huge ice floes and much flooding along the flats.[248] The snow melt quickly late in March, and much of the land along the flats flooded badly. Philip worried about the land being too wet to plough and seed. He thought about Henry Hough and Lewis Clement being so close to the river. One day while Philip, Mattheus, and Martin were chopping and stacking wood, Catrina and Elizabeth came out, each with a basket of meat, bread, and corn cakes.

They asked Philip to harness Apple to the sleigh. Catrina said, "We're quite sure Magdelena Link will deliver her baby very soon, maybe today. 'T'is a good idea if we go and check on her and bring some food. Catharina is watching Martin, Peter, and Johannes."

As Philip finished fastening the harness, he said, "Will you stop by John Farlinger's place and tell him Mattheus and I'll be by to help him and Anthony Walliser with their clearing. John is next door to Lawrence Eaman.[249] This'll be their first spring on their land. I'm sure they'll need help."

Mattheus and Magdelena welcomed their new daughter Anna Link on the 22 March 1764, and Michael and Agatha welcomed a new son Johannes George Gallinger on the 5 April 1764[250] One thing that Catrina was frequently prepared to do was to help women with their labour and the safe delivery of their children. It was scary for women. To them, the risks were clear. Thoughts of death were never far.

Early in the day on the first Saturday in May, Catharina couldn't stop fidgeting at the kitchen table and repeating, "I love lemonade. I love lemonade!"

"How do you know you're going to get lemonade," Elizabeth replied.

"Because Sir William always serves lemonade at his house."

Catrina interrupted, "You girls get your jackets and petticoats on and make sure to wipe the dirt from your shoes! Hurry, or we'll be late."

As he slouched by the smoldering coals of the fire, Mattheus yawned, "Do we have to go to this baptism?"

"Yes. We're all going. 'T'is a special day. Reverend Abraham Rosencrantz is going to baptize seven children at Johnson Hall. We must be there to see little Anna Link, Johannes George Gallinger, Conrad Smith, and Peter Ruppert baptized."[251]

Apple pulled the wagon and the whole family up the lane to Johnson Hall. Elizabeth and Catharina loved coming to the Hall. It was so grand. There were two storeys with large windows on each story, and two stone guardhouses sat on each side of the house. The garden was beautiful, and the sweeping green branches of the willow trees swayed in the breeze. Elizabeth surveyed the crowd at the front of the hall. When she saw Jacob Myers and Michael Myers (see Appendix C), she jumped out of the wagon to greet them. With quick steps, Catharina followed, but she went to the front door with her mama and papa and her brothers; she wanted to get inside to see if there was lemonade!

As they walked into the main hall, instead of lemonade, two enormous paintings captivated Catharina. She stood staring at one that she knew was a map, of what place she didn't know. The other was a picture of some soldiers with metal hats that were the colour of their pewter plates at home. They wore red skirts and had the longest spears she'd ever seen, much longer that the ones her Mohawk friends used for fishing.[252] Everyone in the picture looked very sad, but the baby was nice and plump. Catharina stood by her brothers until it was time to go into the great room. Glancing through the two big doors, she tried to see if the lemonade was in that room, and she wondered if everyone would fit. She saw Elizabeth walk in with Jacob and Michael Myers. Behind them came Captain Peter Service and his wife Magdelena, Sergeant Adam Ruppert and his wife Anna Barbara, then George Schenck Sr. and Magdelena. Catharina looked for Mr. and Mrs. Link and their new daughter Anna, but she couldn't see them in the crowd.

As Catharina stood waiting, she saw a Mohawk man and woman at the doors to the great room. With her mouth wide open, she stared. The woman had black shiny hair that flowed over her shoulders, and the muscles in the man's arms and chest were so big that they lifted the red cloak draped over his shoulder and across his chest. Catharina turned to Mattheus, "Who are those two Mohawks by the doors?"

"That's Molly and Joseph Brant. Molly is Sir William's Mohawk wife and Joseph is a War Chief. He lives across the river at Canajoharie."[253]

Catherine was close enough to Molly Brant to hear her tell Jenny and Juba, the two Negro women standing beside her, to get Cork and Cato to set more chairs and two tables in the back courtyard.[254] Catherine thought, "That must mean there'll be cake and lemonade in the courtyard."

For weeks, there didn't seem to be anything that would outdo all the excitement of the baptisms but there was. Philip had to make a trip to Albany to meet with Harmans Wendell to finalize and sign the lease to his land.[255] Philip gave Mattheus strict instructions about what farm work needed to be done so that they could get to planting as soon as he returned. Martin, Peter, and the girls were told to look after the animals and help their mama ready the garden.

Philip was gone only three days, and when he rode up the lane he saw Catrina and the children busy in the garden. He dismounted next to the fence, leaned over and said, "A very good day to you wife! And, look at my fine children all covered in dirt."

"'T'is a fine day husband, now that you're home. Come and help us with these potatoes we bought from Sir William. They're called Munster potatoes. They're all the way from Ireland. Sir William loves his garden and is always bringing in new kinds of trees, flowers, and vegetables. These potatoes are supposed to be the finest ever. We'll see come September."

"I'll help you after I get Apple some water and put these important papers in the cabin."

That night, Philip was grateful to sleep in his own bed without the noise of the Inn. He lay next to Catrina telling her about the ride to Schenectady and the dry sandy pine bush just outside of Albany. He talked about the things he saw in the city and his meeting with Harmans Wendell. The meeting, he told her, lasted about one hour and, he said, "Harmans Wendell signed the lease and so did nine other proprietors of the patent!" As she listened, Catrina remembered Albany and all the fine houses, shops, and busy streets. She remembered Richard Cartwright's Tavern, The Kings Arms, and how glad she was that she didn't have to travel on any more ships.

As Philip finished a sentence, she said, "I've heard that Lieutenant Nicholas Herkimer is building a fine house like the ones in Albany. 'T'is not far from Little Falls on the south side of the river. It's to be a very large brick house almost as large as Sir William's house. Do you think we should start thinking about building our own house? Not a brick house, but one with two storeys and at least one more bedroom. We've seven children in two bedrooms, and they're growing, almost too big to sleep so many in a bed! And, there'll be one more child early next year!"

Philip reached out and squeezed Catrina's hand, "'T'is good news dear wife. You're right. Our crops have been good, and the orchard is giving good fruit. We've made some profits. I've been looking on our land for hemlock trees that would make good timbers for a larger house. We could start digging the cellar in June and hope the house is finished next year for our new baby."

By the end of May, Philip and Catrina chose the site for their house which was not far from the cabin. From the front, there would be a good view of the lane, and at the back a view of the fields and the orchard. The house would be six metres by 9 ½ metres with two floors and a large stone fireplace. There was room enough for four rooms downstairs and four upstairs. The exterior would be clapboard with three windows on the top floor and two windows plus one door on the main floor. A front porch would extend half the length of the house.

When there was any spare time, Philip, Mattheus, Jacob Myers, and Michael Myers, Johannes Alguire Sr. and his son Johannes George Alguire, and Jacob Henry Alguire and his son Martin dug the cellar and lined it with rough limestone. They transported limestone from Jelles Fonda's quarry at Caughnawaga and lay the stones in courses along the cellar walls.[256] To get the work done before harvest, Jacob Henry Alguire brought Michael Carman and Jacob Sheets, both lived at Philadelphia Bush.[257]

Fig. 27. Representation of Philip and Catrina's House. Sketch by Anne Hill, sixth great-granddaughter of Philip and Catrina.

While they worked, the men shared opinions on managing their fields, planting their crops, or handling their stock. It was also a time to share local news. Recently, the men from Philadelphia Bush heard of new tenants who came from North Britain (Scotland). They had unusual accents, which were hard for the German men to understand, and they practiced the Catholic faith. One settler was Lieutenant Hugh Fraser. Mr Fraser lived just south of Lodowyck Putnam and close to Jacob Myers. Next to Hugh Fraser was William Fraser and his sons William Fraser Jr. and Thomas Fraser, and there was John Fraser of Boleskine, Inverness, Scotland. All these men fought in the last war with the 78th Regiment (Fraser Highlanders) and with the 60th Regiment.[258]

With eight men working, the cellar was finished by the end of June. It took Catrina's constant attention to keep the children away from the hole. For the next few weeks, several men helped Philip fell massive hemlock and white pine trees. The hemlock timbers would be hewn as beams and the white pine for rafters, floor boards, window and door frames. For now, the trees would lie until next spring.

As the summer wore on, the Eamers worked hard in the fields or on the house. They worked through hot humid days and the heavy driving rains that thunderstorms brought. Not a day went by when, at the end of it, they did not all flop into their beds. When Mattheus wasn't in the fields, he spent many hours training Apple's young colt to stand in the harness next to Apple. He named him Scout because he was so brave. Scout did well pulling the wagon around the yard and down the lane. By summer's end, the young colt was reliable. Pulling the sleigh in winter would be another challenge.

Construction on the Kingsborough and Sacandaga Patents flourished in 1764. New tenants were building cabins, barns, and fences, and established tenants improved their buildings. Sir William now had a saw and grist mill and a lime kiln. And, he finished construction of St. John's Episcopal Church. All of these buildings were within one kilometre of Johnson Hall. All tenants were required to assist in the maintenance and improvements of roads, and all tenants participated in some kind of commerce in the area, even if minor. After ensuring that they had enough to sustain their growing families, they sold their grain, wood, furs, and wool. Francis Ruppert Sr. was one who began a larger business venture. He entered into a contract with Peter Remsen to supply potash for a certain sum and the labour of one Negro for one year.[259] Making potash was a labour intensive process that required large amounts of timber to fuel the fires and create the ash used to make potash.

For decades, acquiring land was a major business in the valley. Wealthy Dutch and English landowners and merchants bought large tracts of land to reap the profits from tenants' rent and to utilize the land's resources which was primarily timber. Sir William was undoubtedly the largest landowner in the valley. Through his acquisition of lands, he controlled most of the business and farming activities in the valley. His relationship with the Indians was central to his success as a landowner. It was a reciprocal relationship that benefited Sir William and the Indians. Many tenants sought to obtain land to expand their farms or gain access to timber as so many of the Kingsborough tenants did with Sir William in 1761.[260]

The end of 1764 came with many blessings for Philip and Catrina. Their harvest was good, especially the apples. And with the purchase of two more milk cows, their stock was improving. Blessings came to everyone in the valley with not only a peace treaty with the French and their Indian allies, but also with the Seneca, Shawnee, and Delaware nations who, after the peace treaty with the French, continued to fight because of settlers' encroachment on their lands. Destruction and death south of the Mohawk River was widespread. Philip often thought about Martin Silmser and Elizabeth Margretha in Philadelphia. He wondered if they suffered through all the Indian troubles. Many of the militia had marched south to scout and protect settlements. Sir William's son John, Captain Henry R Hanson, Gilbert Tice, and Lieutenant William Hare were sent south with others to the Susquehanna River to protect the settlers.[261] After many months of fighting, Sir William travelled to Niagara in July and, over a few weeks, negotiated a peace treaty with the Seneca, Shawnee, and Delaware.[262]

During the month of January 1765, when Philip travelled to help friends chop firewood, or when they went hunting, he always saw a lot of tenants in their sleighs flying along the winter roads. For Philip, all those tenants on their way to the store to buy goods for one purpose or another, or just enjoying a bit of free time to visit friends was evidence of their successful harvests and many blessings. More evidence of success was the copious amounts of foods brought to the church to celebrate Christmas. One Saturday late in January, the Eamers went to the church at Caughnawaga to witness several baptisms. Everyone arrived in their sleighs and brought food to celebrate.

Catrina loved this little church. When she entered the church, the inscription on the stone tablet over the door comforted her. In German, it read, "Komt laett ons op gaen tot den Bergh des Heeren, to den huyse des Godes Jacobs, op dat hy ons leere van syne wegen, en dat wy wandele in syne paden." ("Come ye, and let us go up to the mountain of the Lord; to the house of the God of Jacob, and he will teach us his ways, and we will walk in his paths.")[263] As the family entered, Reverend Barent Vrooman greeted them. They made their way to a pew and sat next to Lodowyck Putnam his wife Elizabeth and their sons Aaron, Richard, Frederick, and their daughter Anna Margaret.

To Catrina, it seemed more crowded in the church when everyone dressed in their thickest warmest clothes. During the service, the children fidgeted and squirmed in their seats. Philip sent a few steely stares at Martin, Peter, and Johannes while Catharina flipped through most of the pages of the prayer book. Catrina started to get uncomfortable, but she loved to see so many children welcomed into God's family. There was Johannes, George Schenck Sr. and Magdelena's son. John Smith and his wife Anna were his sponsors. There was Johannes Richtmeyer, son of Johannes Richtmeyer Sr. and Gertruad Conrad. Jeremiah Quackenbush and his wife Jannetje were his sponsors. Finally, there was Anna Margaret, Lodowyck Putnam and Elizabeth's little girl. Margaret, Francis Ruppert Sr. wife, was her sponsor.[264] These baptisms were a celebration of new life not only for the parents and sponsors, but also for the community.

March 1765 brought more signs of life. Two of Philip's ewes had lambs, sap ran in the maple trees, and the apple trees were sprouting blossoms. Catrina could smell dirt as the ground thawed. Certainly, there was a lot of life at Johnson Hall on March 17. Because of their Irish heritage, St Patrick's Day was always a grand day for Sir William and some of his close friends. There was Sir William's doctor Patrick Daly, William Adams a doctor too, and his brother Robert Adams, a merchant. There was Bryan Lefferty Sir William's lawyer, and Michael Byrne and his brother John Byrne. Finally, there was Thomas Flood. Many of Sir William's tenants were Irish too, John Friel a tailor, George Crites Sr. a farmer and weaver, and Edward Foster an old soldier and farmer.[265]

Early Saturday morning March 17, Mattheus was at the front of the cabin with Apple hitched to the wagon and Scout tied to the rear. As he paced, all he could think about was the horse race he'd be riding with Scout. Elizabeth and

Catharina were the first ones out the door fresh and clean and dressed in their best jackets and petticoats.

Teasing them, Mattheus said, "In those clothes, I bet neither of you is going to be the one who catches the greased pig Sir William lets loose!"

"Ha," Catharina replied. "No, but we can run a race in these clothes and win too."

"What are you going to win Catharina?" Philip asked as he came out the cabin door.

"A foot race Papa. Are you going to be in a wrestling contest Papa?"

"Maybe Catharina. After I've finished cheering for you at your foot race and for Mattheus and Scout in their horse race."

Peter piped up, "I'm going to enter the scariest face contest Papa. I scare Catharina and Johannes all the time. Remember when Sir William had the party for the Indians at the Hall and Mr. Gallinger won the grinning contest. He won tobacco!"[266]

"Aye. Michael Gallinger Sr. did well."

Catrina and Elizabeth came out with two large baskets. Holding the baskets while they climbed into the wagon, Philip peered under the cloth cover, "What's in here? Ohhhh apple pies!"

"Yes. Elizabeth made them for the contest."

Philip handed Catrina and Elizabeth the baskets, "You'd best hold these in your laps. You wouldn't want the boys to get hold of them in the back of the wagon. There'd be none left for the contest."

Giggling Catrina said, "Yes, and careful husband that you don't drive too fast or one of the pies will land in your lap!"

Philip drove the wagon northwest along the Tribes Hill road towards Johnson Hall. As soon as they neared the bridge at Cayadutta Creek, they met several other wagons with children in the back waving, giggling, and hollering hello. When they arrived, the yard was full of tenants and Indians. Philip strained to hear Catrina asking him to help Johannes out of the wagon. The whole family made their way to the courtyard at the back of the house. A large pole was set in the centre of the yard, and there was a young Mohawk boy trying hard to climb to the trinket at the top of the pole. He was having trouble; the pole was greased! At the far end of the yard, Philip pointed to a group of tenants and Indians in a football game.

Catharina walked up to a Negro woman at one of the tables and asked, "Please, when are the foot races, and where can my Mama and sister put their pies?"

"The foot race is in one hour at the front of the Hall, and your mama can put the pies over there."

As Catrina watched Mattheus lead Scout to the southwest corner of the Hall, she reached for Philip's arm, "Please watch that the children don't get to close to anyone whose been drinking a lot. There're always so many men drinking beer or rum. And, will you help Mattheus with Scout. I worry about him riding in Sir William's field with so many other horses."

Mattheus let Scout graze while he waited for the other riders to come along. Soon, he saw Martin Alguire leading his mare and then Johannes George Alguire with his mare. Mattheus kept a distance from the mares as Scout was starting to prance. Philip stood close by to help. Soon, everyone was mounted. People crowded near the start line. Everyone was whooping and hollering. Philip was right there. Ten horses were swirling and prancing. Their riders focused on the start flag. The ½ kilometre race lasted less than thirty seconds. As Philip raised his arms high and pumped his fists, he also took a deep breath and thought, "At fifteen years, my son is a fine rider. Ah, he finished safely, and he wasn't last."

With strong, long strides, Mattheus led Scout back to his father, "Papa, he was amazing. Did you see us go?"

"I did son. You had good command of your horse." Philip took the lead rope while Mattheus went with George and Martin to watch the men play football. As Philip led Scout back to the wagon, he saw John Farlinger and Michael Gallinger Sr. leading their horses to the starting line of the men's race.

At the Eamer's house, tales of the activities at Johnson Hall started and ended most conversations long past tapping the maple trees and tending to newborn lambs and piglets. Mattheus told a few variations of his ½ kilometre race on Scout, and Elizabeth loved to show off the linen handkerchief she won for the best apple pie. Catharina didn't talk much about her footrace, but she sure loved to brag about her papa's win in a wrestling match.

Most of the time, Catrina sat quietly and listened to the children's exciting tales, but one day she talked about the muddy children, "There were so many of them scrambling in the mud puddle. Sir William must have hidden a lot of coin in that puddle! I'm glad none of you decided to scramble. You would've been washing your own clothes."

Martin sat straight up and said, "I didn't want to do that Mama, but next year I want to catch the greasy pig! I catch our piglets all the time."

It wasn't long after their visit to Johnson Hall when Philip and Catrina heard news that put fear in their hearts. An epidemic of smallpox had hit the Mohawks of Fort Hunter hard. News spread of many deaths at the village. Molly Brant got the disease, but she was lucky to survive with only the marks of the dreaded disease. Joseph Brant, her brother, was spared the lifetime marks.[267] Terrified of the disease, Philip and Catrina watched the children for illness and kept them close to home.

As spring wore on, Catrina felt more and more uncomfortable with the growing child in her belly. She was used to the awkward way she had to move around. This was her eighth child, and she thought not her last.

Late in April, she was out hoeing the garden getting ready to seed. "Ohh," she thought rubbing her back, "I can hardly bend over with my large belly in front of me and my aching back behind me!" She sat down on a log. Soon, her legs were wet, and she looked down to see her water create a puddle of mud. She hollered, "Elizabeth! Catharina! Come and help me."

They both came running from the chicken shed and saw their mother sitting on a log and leaning against the fence. As she caught her breath, Catharina said, "Is it the baby Mama?"

Between fast and deep breaths Catrina managed to say, "Yes, Catharina."

Catrina was only in her bed for about ten minutes when loud baby cries were welcomed.

Catharina peered at the newborn wrapped tightly next to Catrina, "A girl Mama! We've another sister. She's beautiful. Her lips are so tiny!"

Catrina turned, and holding Elizabeth's hand she said, "Go get your Papa Elizabeth."

Just as Catrina gave Elizabeth the order, Philip walked into the room. "A daughter husband. She's pink and has a good cry."

"How beautiful Catrina. What will we name her?"

"Dorothy, after your mother."[268]

"Yes, she would like that very much. How are you?"

"Good husband. I want to rest now."

Elizabeth and Catharina looked after their new sister while their mother slept. Philip went to get the boys so they could see their new sister.

Soon after little Dorothy Eamer's baptism, Philip went out on business. He wanted to talk to Johannes Veeder about bringing his apples to put through his press and make cider.[269] He also went to Fonda's store at Caughnawaga to buy a few sheets of paper for keeping his business accounts and flour and sugar for Catrina.

He walked through the door at Fonda's store nearly bumping into Thomas Flood. "Good day to you Sir. How are the fields up at Johnson Hall?"

"Fine Mr. Eamer. 'T'is a busy season. We always need supplies. We've got a new potash works and laboratory near the Hall now. I've come to order a potash kettle."

"Aye, yes." Philip said. "Mr. Francis Ruppert Sr. and his sons George and Adam are making that a business with Peter Remsen."

"Yes. Mr. Peter Hasenclever, a merchant from New York, has written to Sir William about Mr. Ruppert's business. Mr. Hasenclever has begun a new settlement east of Herkimer. It's called New Petersburg.[270] Mr. Hasenclever is even talking about mining."

"There's much demand for potash in the colonies. They make a lot in Pennsylvania and North Carolina. 'T'is a pleasure to see such business here. Philip tipped his black felt hat to Thomas, "Good day to you Sir."

Philip walked to the counter to order his paper and flour. "Good day to you Jelles. 'T'is a fine spring day. I'm happy to tell you my Catrina and I've just had a baby girl. We've named her Dorothy. How's your family Sir?"

"Congratulations to you and your wife Philip. Our family is fine. Our new son is now one year old, and Jannetjie is with child. What would you like today Philip?"

"Four sheets of paper, four pounds of flour, and three pounds of sugar."

Jelles looked straight at Philip, "You've heard about the new tax on printed paper haven't you? Any printed paper items like newspapers, pamphlets, cards, or licenses are to be taxed. This tax begins on November 1." Running his hands through his hair, and shaking his head he continued, "Newspapers are one penny for each page, and you have to pay with coin not paper currency. Not many people are happy about this. They call it theft, and they're stirring up trouble in the streets, sometimes in mobs!"

With a creased brow, Philip answered, "'T'is not a good thing to tax us without our say, but trouble in mobs is worrisome."

Tapping his fingers on the counter, Jelles said, "They'll be trouble if the King's government doesn't listen! 'T'is never enough. Last year they prohibited us from buying sugar and molasses from our own merchants. We must buy from the British! King George needs to pay for the war with the French.[271]

"I'll be back in a few weeks. Pray tell me what news there is of taxes." Philip walked out holding his goods close to his chest and shaking his head.

Early in May, Philip and Michael Gallinger Sr. hitched their teams of horses and oxen to chains and moved the hemlock and pine they'd cut last summer. They set the logs close to the building site and spent the next few weeks hewing them. Philip took some of the pine they logged to Sir William's mill to be cut for floor boards, lathe for the walls, clapboards, and shingles. He'd collect the cut wood after planting was done. Philip spent his evenings drawing plans for the house, making sure that he and Michael would carve the correct mortise and tenon joints.

One evening while at the kitchen table bent over his plans, the children sat with eyes glued on his drawing. Their questions flew at him like a swarm of hornets, "How many windows Papa? Where are the stairs? How many stairs? Why is the fireplace so deep? Will there be heat upstairs?

Grabbing his pipe from his lips, he pointed the stem at each of one the children saying, "All right now. I can't think. Stop asking so many questions please!" This went on most evenings until whenever the pipe stem came off his lips the children went quiet.

Philip wasn't the only person building in the spring of 1765. Before planting season began, Sir William had almost all the male tenants of Kingsborough and their sons busy helping him fulfill his dream of building a town with at least the basic necessities that a growing community needed. The men dug holes and built foundations for ten 1 ½ story houses. Everyday there were wagonloads of stone and timber coming up the road to the little town site. Sir William hoped tradesmen and a schoolteacher would occupy most of the houses. John Fraser, a weaver and an old soldier from the 60th Regiment and Fraser's Highlanders, occupied one house. Two others were for his friends Dr. William Adams, and William's brother Robert who would use his house as a store. Donald Ross had a 15 acre lot with 10 apple trees. And, Randel MacDonnel had a lot where he kept horned cattle, sheep, and hogs. Sir William's lawyer Bryan Lefferty rented lot six. Finally there needed to be a tavern. Captain Gilbert Tice would be the owner of the tavern.[272] Sir William had already built a grist and saw mill, a lime kiln, and a stone church with a graveyard and a glebe set aside for a clergyman. He also had visions of a Court House and Jail. For now, the men just kept building.

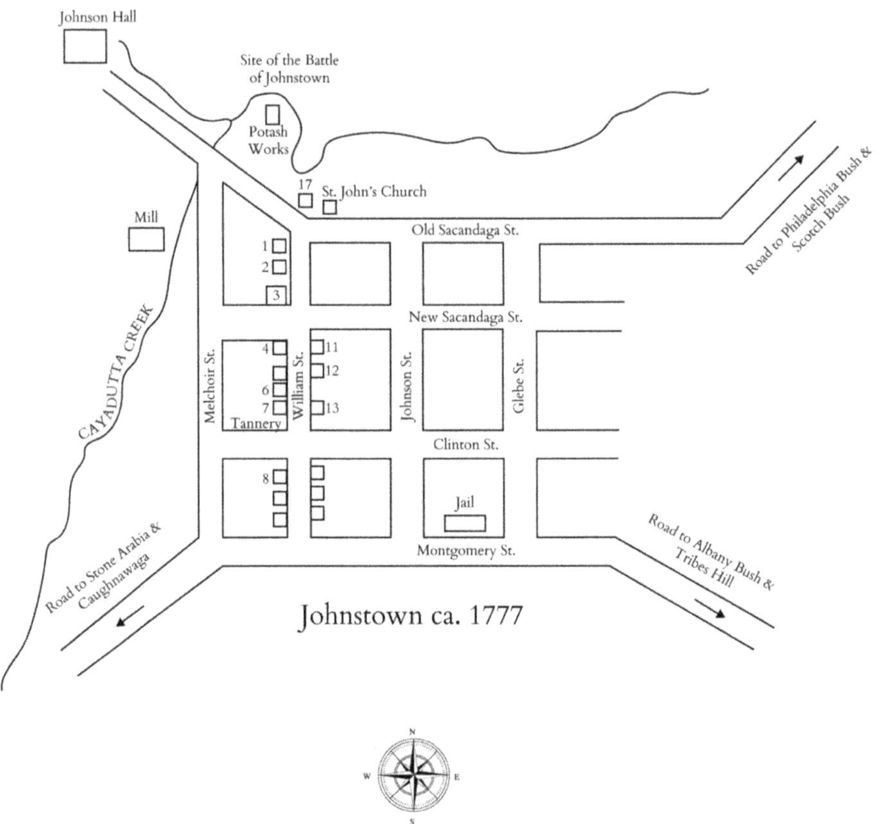

Fig. 28. Village of Johnstown, Tryon County, New York ca. 1777. Adapted From: New York State Archives, Digital Collection. Plan of village of Johnstown, Fulton, Co., on the Cayadutta kill. 1784. Map #890. Identifier: NYSA_A0273-78_890. New York State Archives, Digital Collections. Map of the village of Johnstown, Fulton County. Map #880. Identifier: NYSA_A0273-78_880. "Fulton County NYGenWeb" Johnstown Historical Visitor's Guide.

See Appendix I for a list of the tenants of Johnstown

In the midst of all the building, many settlers in the valley found time to participate in an annual event to celebrate the great German immigration to

New York in 1709. Families from this great migration were the first to settle in the Mohawk Valley. They settled near Fort Hunter along the Schoharie River and near German Flats, Canajoharie, and Stone Raby along the Mohawk River. The event was called 'Immigration Day' and it was celebrated on June 14th.[273] This year, they celebrated at the Lutheran Trinity Church in Stone Arabia. Many tenants from Kingsborough joined the celebration, including the Eamers, Gallingers, Alguires, Eamans, and Crites.

After the church service, they gathered outside to visit and enjoy all the food the women brought. They had a chance to see all the new children in the community, and they heard news of who was to be married and who had passed. These events not only enabled everyone to give thanks for their blessings and to express their commitment to God, but these events were also, unquestionably, a time for accomplishing business, learning new farming and domestic practices, and for nurturing friendships and forming new ones.

While sitting and enjoying the blue sky and the warmth of the valley sun, Catrina noticed Jacob Henry and Salome Alguire talking to a man with whom she wasn't familiar. Taking hold of the bottom of her skirt, she rose and walked over to the group. "Hello Jacob and Salome. Hello Sir. My name is Catrina Eamer. I'm Philip Eamer's wife. You are new here Sir."

"Hello Madam. Yes, I've just arrived in Johnstown from Germany. My name is Michael Cline. I settled on one of the new lots in town. I'm a gunsmith, but I make most things a blacksmith would make."[274]

"How wonderful to meet you. Do you live in one of the new houses?"

"Yes, I do. 'T'is a perfect size and a good lot. I'll be building a shop soon, and I hope to hire an assistant and a journeyman."

Catrina smiled and said, "Wonderful. This is a growing community with many young men who might want to be gunsmiths rather than farmers."

In all places one went during the summer, talk of the growing new town site was the focus of conversation, even at the construction site of the Eamer's new house. During June and July, the men set the foundation posts, finished the fireplace, and raised the framing. At the end of July, Jacob Henry and Johannes Alguire Sr. and their sons Martin and Johannes George were helping Philip place the trusses for the roof. Michael Carman offered to do the joinery work and help build the window and door frames. Young Martin liked the joinery work, and he helped Michael make the dowels for the framing. The men talked most of the morning about the different buildings in town. Philip contributed his own opinions about the roads and where buildings were situated. Most of the afternoon was spent debating about what type of roof was better, a German roof or a Dutch roof. By mid July, they were ready to make shingles, finish the clapboard, and plaster the lathe strips with lime plaster Philip purchased from Sir William.[275]

On a warm July afternoon, Mattheus sat with his hands in a large bucket of plaster. He said to his papa, "'T'is a dirty job building walls!"

Philip laughed as he wiped some of the plaster from Mattheus' forehead and said, "'T'is dirty, but 't'will be a fine house, and you can say you helped to build it."

"How many more buckets do I have to mix Papa?"

"Oh, if I tell you you'll quit! We'll finish this first layer and then let it dry for a few weeks. Then it'll need another layer. So, there'll be plenty more buckets. Martin and Peter will help. You can be the big brother and show them how it's done." Philip sat with Mattheus, Martin, and Peter as they mixed several buckets.

As Catrina came out the door of the cabin, she giggled, "You four look like ghosts. There's more on you than in those buckets!"

Philip had to wait for the plaster to dry before he could finish any work on the inside of the house, so he spent his time constructing a hay barrack for this year's harvest. Philip continued working on the barrack until the second week in August when all the tools were put away, and he went out to the fields with the whole family. Everyone had a job. Philip, Martin, and Mattheus cut and raked wheat, oats, and grass hay, and Elizabeth, Catharina, Peter, and Johannes stacked it into sheaves. Catrina looked after Dorothy and Anna Margaret and brought much needed food and water to the fields.

One afternoon after finishing three rows of hay, they sat in the middle of the field to enjoy lunch. Catrina lay down on a blanket while nursing Dorothy. She said to Philip, "Does't thou know what's better than the breeze that's playing with my hair?"

"No, what's better?"

We've no worry about someone rushing from the woods. We sha'n't be attacked or kidnapped. You've no need to bring your firelock! We can sit quietly without fear and watch our children play and the animals graze."

"Indeed, we surely are lucky. The valley is a different place when peace surrounds us. But, we'd best get back to the field, or we'll be very hungry, happy people."

Mattheus stood at the door of the hay barrack with one hand directing his father, "Just back them up a few more feet Papa. We can unload the hay from there." The wagon creaked and groaned as it rolled back into place.

Philip pulled up on the reins, "Whoa. Whoa," He secured the reins over the seat and climbed down while asking Mattheus, "Have you two pitch forks?"

"Yes, they're here Papa." Mattheus climbed on top of the pile of hay in the wagon and started pitching it down.

"Keep piling it here son. I'll spread it." Philip and Mattheus pitched and spread hay for over an hour. Finally, they stopped and rested before getting another load. Leaning against the wagon and rolling a swig of cool water in his mouth, Philip looked up and saw two young men coming down the lane, both carried firelocks.

Mattheus looked toward the men walking down the lane and said, "Who's that Papa?"

"It looks like Johannes George Alguire and young Martin Loefler Jr.. Hello Johannes George. Hello Martin. What brings you here today?"

"Hello Mr. Eamer. We've been tracking a wild cat. Johannes George's father heard its raspy chirps and screams last night. There's no mistaking that sound. Thought we'd come by and let you know there's one about."

Mattheus laid down his pitch fork and said, "Papa, a wild cat. Can I go track with them?"

"Not this time Mattheus. We've got to get the hay in while it's still dry." "Thanks Martin and Johannes George. Good luck and keep watch in all directions, up too. Those cats come out of nowhere." Before they left, Philip reached out to shake their hands. "How's your father Martin?" I haven't been to your place for a while. We're right next to each other, but we've been so busy building and haying."[276]

"He's well and busy with the harvest too. Well, we're off now up the Sacandaga trail at the south east end of your lot."

"Tell your father good wishes." Philip and Mattheus watched as the two young men walked toward the Sacandaga trail.

"We'd best get that last load of hay son." The pitch fork landed with a thud as Philip threw it in the back of the wagon. He grabbed the wagon seat to hoist himself up, and as he rolled into the seat, he saw a man and two young boys walking down the lane. Squinting hard and shaking his head, he said out loud, "I know that man!" In one leap, Philip was out of the wagon and heading down the lane, "Martin Silmser! It can't be! So many years." Brisk strides led both men to each other. They reached out with a two handed handshake and an embrace that lasted, it seemed, for minutes, Philip caught his breath, "What? How? You are here!"

With a grin as wide as his face, Martin answered, "I know. 'T'is difficult to believe. We arrived yesterday and acquired land at Philadelphia Bush. Johannes Alguire Sr. and his wife Catherine Margaret told me where I could find you."

"And Elizabeth Margretha?"

"Yes, she's here too at home with our three daughters. You remember Christina as a babe and there's Anna Maria. She's eight now. And our four-month-old daughter Anna Margretha. These are my two boys. Henry who's nine and Nicholas who's seven."[277]

"They're fine boys Martin. I'm so glad everyone is well and that you've such a fine family. I've been thinking about you over the years, especially during the war and the trouble with the Indians. We got news of the troubles near Philadelphia, but it wasn't much news. Catrina and I spoke of you often over the years." "This is my son Mattheus." As Philip rested his hand on Martin's shoulder, he said, "Come inside."

As Catrina saw the men walk through the door, her mouth fell wide open. Throwing both hands to the sides of her head, she said, "Oh Martin, how wonderful!"

Martin Eamer and Peter led Nicholas and Henry outside right away to show them their fishing rods. Martin picked his rod up and pretended to cast his line into an imaginary river. "Did you fish in Pennsylvania?"

"Oh yes," Nicholas said with his shoulders back and his chest out.

Looking at Henry, Peter asked, "Do you know how to swim?"

"Of course I do. I learned at the creek by our farm when I was five."

"Great. We'll all go to the river; there's a swimming hole near Tribes Hill, or we can go to the Cayadutta Creek swimming hole. We just follow the Indian path along the creek. 'T'is not far."

It seemed like a very short visit for the boys when Martin came out of the cabin calling, "Come boys, we must go."

Reaching for his felt hat, Philip said, "I'll take you all home in the wagon. And, I can see Elizabeth Margretha and your girls. We can plan a day together soon. There's so much to talk about. And, I want you to meet some tenants."

Over the next few weeks, Philip and Catrina visited Martin and Elizabeth Margretha often. Catrina helped Elizabeth with the children and assured her she'd be there to help her when her baby came. Philip and Mattheus made sure they had enough wood for winter. Many times it felt as though they'd never been apart, but it had been ten years since they said goodbye in Philadelphia. Philip never forgot their kindnesses.

In September, the two families spent many hours together picking apples. One afternoon, Philip and Martin Silmser loaded forty pecks or ten bushels of apples onto the wagon. After the last peck was loaded, Philip leaned against the wagon, smiled and said, "'T'is a fine load. That should get at least one barrel or maybe two rundlets of cider. There's enough here for both our families. We still have apples for two more wagonloads and some leftover for Catrina to dry or make apple butter. I'm glad I bought the extra rundlet from our cooper, Conrad Smith.[278] If I need more, I can stop at his farm on our way to Johannes Veeder's mill."

While Philip was busy taking the apples to the mill, Catrina, Elizabeth Margretha Silmser, and the girls were coring and slicing apples and stringing them to dry. Catrina loved the Roxbury Russet apples Philip got from Sir William. They were so sweet, and they lasted well past fall. The best apples for cider, she thought, were the Hughes Crab.[279]

Peter and Johannes quickly grasped two buckets of apple scraps and said, "Come on Henry and Nicholas we've scraps to feed the horses, pigs, and chickens."

As they threw scraps over the fence, Peter hollered, "Wait Johannes. Pick out the seeds!"

"What for?"

"Mama says no seeds. They'll get sick." For at least fifteen minutes, the boys happily leaned over the buckets picking seeds out of the scraps.

By the time the barrack was full of hay, two barrels and four rundlets of cider were put away, and the root cellar was full, it was time to get ready for the fall fair at Johnson Hall. Johannes and Peter were in the garden one day walking through the patch of pumpkins.

Pointing to one pumpkin, Johannes said "Ohhh look at this one. 'T'is the biggest. That'll win the prize. Papa will have to lift it into the wagon."

As the boys were trying to figure out the best way to get the pumpkin out of the garden, Catrina arrived with her basket. "Did you find the best pumpkin boys?"

"We did Mama. 'T'will win! What are you picking Mama?"

"Cucumbers Johannes."

"We get potato salad!" Johannes said flapping his arms against his thighs."

"We'll all have some, but I'm bringing most of the special salad to the fair. 'T'was my mother's recipe. I remember her teaching me to slice the cucumbers very thin. 'T'was the secret to the special salad."

It was near the end of October 1766 when the family made their way through town and over the bridge to Johnson Hall. As they road along the road, Catrina held her nose a little higher than usual. Philip asked, "Do you smell something strange Catrina?"

Smiling and resting her hand on his knee, she said, "I just love the smell of the wet leaves on the ground and the light that comes through the bare trees. 'T'is a perfect day for the fair." Once at the hall, Philip and Mattheus maneuvered the pumpkin to the end of the wagon, and with extra care and effort they lifted it out of the wagon and carried it to the back of the hall. The girls followed, watching carefully. Yelling simultaneously with their hands on their hips, Johannes and Peter said, "Don't drop it Papa. Mattheus mind your way. Mattheus!"

With little Dorothy in her arms and Anna Margaret clutching her hand, Catrina made her way through the crowd to the back of the hall. As she looked for a place to sit, she saw Jacob Henry Alguire. What caught her eye was the blue check linen trousers he was wearing. She hadn't seen those on Jacob before and thought, "There must have been blue check linen at Jelles Fonda's store this summer."[280] Her eye moved to the woman standing beside Jacob. She hadn't met this woman. There must be new tenants near Jacob.

Jacob and the new couple walked over to her. Smiling, Jacob said, "Good day Catrina. A good day for a fair. This is Johannes Hartle and his wife Regina Falk. They arrived from Athens, Greene County last month. 'T'is just north of

Kingston near the Hudson River. They've settled on the Kingsborough Patent near Peter Fykes Sr."[281]

"Good day and welcome. I'm Catrina Eamer, Philip Eamer's wife. We live about five kilometres east of Johnstown on the Sacandaga Patent. Do you have children?"

With the palm of her hand resting on her large belly, Regina replied, "We have three sons and a daughter and one to be born in November. Our sons are eleven, ten, and eight. Our daughter is near six."

"Your children are the same age as ours. Perhaps they'll meet each other at church soon."

Philip joined the group and said, "Good day Sir and Madam. I'm Philip Eamer."

Johannes reached to shake Philip's hand and said, "Hello Sir. We're Johannes and Regina Hartle. I see you had a big job to finish carrying that oversized pumpkin to its resting place."

"Ahh yes. My young sons kept a close eye on me. Your last name sounds familiar Sir. Where in Germany did you live?"

"I was born here in New York colony. But my father often talked about his village in Germany. It was in the Landgraviate of Hesse along the Bergstrasse (Mountain Road) to Darmstadt. The village was called Heppenheim."

Just as Johannes was finishing his sentence, Philip's eyes opened wider and wider. "Oh! That's only a few kilometres from our village of Auerbach. When we were leaving Germany, my father told me stories of the families near us who travelled over the great sea about 1709. I think he mentioned your father."

"Yes, my father Adam Hartle Sr. left his village in 1709 and arrived at New York in 1710. He used to attend the little church at Auerbach."

"And is your father with you now?"

"No. He died many years ago at Georgetown, New York, the original West Camp German settlement. 'T'is what the settlers called the Tar Bush.[282]

As Philip heard Johannes talk of the church at Auerbach, he felt his throat tighten, and his eyes welled with tears.

Catrina quickly put her arm under his and pulled him close to her. She said, "'T'is a wonderful church with a beautiful view of the town. Our daughter was baptized there." Catrina and Philip visited with Johannes and Regina until it was time to gather the children and go home. Their smiles never left their faces on their way home. They were happy they now knew someone with a connection to home.

Just as the frost started to gather on the window panes, the family moved into their new home. Philip loved to watch Catrina move about so freely in her kitchen, and he loved to watch the children scamper about on the fine wood floors. There was so much space Philip had trouble keeping track of all eight children. Often he'd sit in his rocking chair in front of the fire with his pipe and the Bible thanking God for helping him provide this home for his family. When he looked over at Catrina rocking little Dorothy and watched Anna Margaret on the bear rug at his feet, he knew it would be a good winter.

Good weather in January 1766 made it easier for Philip's boys to learn more about hunting and fishing. Philip, Martin, Peter, and Martin Loefler Sr. and his son Martin went out towards Philadelphia Bush several times early in the month. One morning, after they set their traps, they made their way along the Indian Path that followed Cayadutta Creek. The creek widened at one bend. Here, the boys made an opening in the ice. Philip and Martin Sr. spent time helping them with their bait and made a small fire while watching the boys fish.

While they watched, they talked about trapping and the best kinds of furs. Martin Sr. was describing a marten he trapped last winter, "'T'was a good day to trap, nice and warm. This marten had beautiful thick brown, silky fur just like the ones I saw Henry Hawn, Godfrey Shew, and Nicholas Shaver bring in to Fonda's store last week. They'd traded some blankets and powder for a bundle of marten fur from the Mohawk hunters near Canajoharie. 'T'is hard to believe the distance they travel as traders. They often go all the way to Fort Detroit.[283] For two beavers, the Indians get two yards of stroud or a man's penniston coat. They can even get a silver brooch for one racoon. If the King decides to tax furs, they won't get that much for their furs!"

Martin Loefler Sr.'s face turned red, and he clenched the stick while jamming it into the coals, "You know, Jelles Fonda told me about an incident in Albany with men from the 'Sons of Liberty'. Jelles read about it in the New York Gazette.[284] Apparently, the men were suspicious that Henry Van Schaick, a merchant and the Albany Postmaster, was offered the position of Stamp Tax Collector. After offering Mr. Van Schaick an opportunity to swear he'd never apply for or accept the position, he refused. This enraged the Albany 'Sons of Liberty'. So, four hundred of them went looking for him and ransacked his house, busting furniture, breaking windows, and finally dragging his sleigh away and setting it on fire. In all their fury, they finally realized Mr. Van Schaick wasn't home. In their hot state, they went looking for him. Along the way, they scared the life out of everyone who had anything to do with Mr. Van Schaick. It was quite a mob. Finally, they found him and forced him to sign a deposition that he'd never apply for or accept the tax collector position."[285]

While setting a log on the fire, Philip said, "I can't imagine such a mob marching in the streets of Johnstown! And to demolish a man's property at will. I've heard these 'Sons of Liberty' have acted in Boston and have groups in other cities. 'T'is dangerous to have so many men, willingly and with malice, parade about burning or stealing property and threatening citizens. Yet, the newspapers say that the 'Sons of Liberty' are the only guardians of the rights and liberties of America. I know they say this. John Farlinger brings a newspaper when he rides the post to Albany. Mr. Van Schaick gives it to him to read to his countrymen."[286] Philip and Martin Sr.'s conversation was cut short when the boys brought four shad and dropped them, still wiggling, next to the fire.

With a booming whoop, Martin came into the kitchen. While dangling four fish from the end of a rope, he almost stepped on Anna Margaret and bumped the cradle while Dorothy slept. He proclaimed, "Here Mama, we've fish for dinner! Peter and I caught three fish, and Martin Loefler Jr. caught four. He took three home and gave us one. And, Papa has two rabbits!"

"Shh, Martin. You'll wake your sister. 'T'was a good day for all of you. Now, we'll be busy in the kitchen fixing rabbit stew and frying fish."

"Can we have corn dumplings with the stew?" asked Peter.

"Even with dumplings, the four fish won't be enough the way my brothers eat." Catharina said while rocking in her mama's chair mending wool socks.

Elizabeth looked up from the bats of wool she was roving and suggested, "Maybe we could mix the fish into the rabbit stew!" Peter's nose crinkled as he turned his head.

Catrina interrupted, "Maybe the Silmsers would like one of the rabbit furs. I'm sure Elizabeth Margretha would make something with the fur."

"Can I have one Mama?" Elizabeth asked. "I want to line the hood on my blanket coat. I can wear it to church next week."

With her rabbit lined hood blocking her vision, Elizabeth flipped it off her head as she helped Anna Margaret into the sleigh. Everyone was wrapped in wool and fur when Apple and Scout pulled the sleigh out of the yard onto the road to Stone Raby. Today, Johannes Ruppert, son of Sergeant Adam Ruppert and his wife Barbara, was to be baptized.

Leaning close to Philip's ear, Catrina whispered, "'T'is good to see Adam's brother Johannes and Sophia Lepper as the little boy's sponsor. Sergeant Adam Ruppert has four sons now. 'T'is so much work for Barbara without daughters to help her. Maybe the next child will be a girl."[287]

Michael Cline and the Silmsers joined the Eamers for several days work in the sugar bush. Nicholas Silmser and Henry Silmser helped Martin and Peter stoke the fire while the girls took turns stirring the sugar water in the huge kettle. Peter peered into the kettle and said to Elizabeth "Make sure it's just right. We want to make snow candy. Turning to Catharina and Anna Maria, he ordered, "We need sticks to roll the syrup. Can you find some please?" Even though the morning passed quickly, their lunch break seemed to never come. Finally, while barely tasting their food, the children gulped down the bread and cheese. The quicker lunch was gone the quicker they'd get their snow candy. Michael Cline helped Martin pour rows of syrup onto the snow they'd collected. The children lined up to roll the syrup and snow onto their sticks. It was a gooey mess, but it tasted so good, and it was so much fun.

One afternoon in March, Peter came into the house looking for Mattheus, "Mattheus!" He hollered. "The pigeons are back. Will you take us hunting? Please. Please. Martin and I want to go."

"Okay, but I have to help Papa with the lambs first. We need your help too. Come to their pen." On their way back to the house they met Elizabeth gathering eggs at the chicken coop.

While scurrying behind Mattheus and out of breath, Peter stared at Elizabeth and proclaimed, "We're going hunting."

"Papa won't let you fire the musket Peter. You're too young."

"No, but I can help Mattheus load the powder and ball."

After collecting his musket and shot bag, Mattheus and his brothers made their way toward the Sacandaga trail. Mattheus stood tall in his new hunting frock Catrina made for him. He filled out the loose linen frock with his broad shoulders, and the fringe on the collar emphasized his thick neck. Mattheus led the way toward the Sacandaga trail. As the path narrowed, he entered the forest with Martin and Peter close behind.

Mattheus heard the boys marching behind him. Then he heard, "Mattheus, we're Iroquois making our way north to Quebec on the ancient great Iroquois trail!"

"Oh, we are? I bet we'll find lots of venison for the long long trip! You'll need more paint on your face if you're to scare your enemies. You remind me of Catharina and her fancy stories of Frau Holle, the fairy forest protector. Mama tells her stories of Frau Holle all the time. One day I saw Catharina coming out of the forest with her hair covered in chicken feathers. She told me she had fixed her hair just like Frau Holle!"

Near the end of April, Catrina visited Fonda's store with Elizabeth Visbach. As they drove along the road to Caughnawaga, they talked about the spring work they'd done and the things that were left to do. As they walked into the store, they had to weave their way past several people to the counter. Catrina waited her turn to get the ells of linen for which she came.[288]

As Catrina and Elizabeth Visbach stood waiting, Elizabeth Shaver, Philip Shaver's wife, walked over, "Good Day Mrs. Eamer and Mrs. Visbach. The store is so full today."

"Good Day Elizabeth. The store is full now that the weather has cleared. We just came for linen so I can make hunting frocks for Philip and my boys."

"Well, let's hope there isn't a tax on that! It seems that's all the men can argue about these days. But, my husband tells me that the King repealed the Stamp Tax due to the relentless harassment and disturbance it's caused!"

"Oh, let's hope that puts an end to the burden of the extra taxes and the disturbances. 'T'is much nicer to enjoy the apple blossoms I see on everyone's farms instead of carrying the burden of taxes or worse colliding with a bitter mob in town."

"'T'is so Catrina. A mob it might be. Settlers are coming in so fast. I see many new faces each week. We've two new tenants on the Kingsborough Patent. There's a Mr. George Bender and his wife Maria Gertruad Hagedoorn. They're from south of Albany at the flats along the Hudson near Rhinebeck. They live now on the western allotment of Kingsborough with two young sons and a daughter. And, there's a Mr. Jacob Crieghoof and his wife Benedicta Ruff. I think they're very near you Catrina."

"Aye. They are. A fine family who've come up from the Schoharie Valley with their two girls and two boys.[289] 'T'is good to know we've neighbours so close. Our children and theirs are close in age."

A few weeks into May, Philip had Apple at a nice easy trot along the wagon road to town. It was early in the morning. He first smelled the apple blossoms at Jacob Crieghoof's place, then on Henry Hawn's,[290] then John Farlinger's, and Michael Gallinger's. As he got closer to town, he could smell the blossoms at Lawrence Eaman's place. Philip loved May not only because of the apple blossoms, but also because the roads weren't quite as muddy as they were in April, his pastures were green, and most striking were the flowers on the chestnut trees. Philip loved the way the white flower clusters stood on the branches like candles. He reached town and rode down Montgomery Street to William Street. He was on his way to Michael Cline's home to help him finish his gunsmith shop behind his house. Michael had started building in late March; so the men only had finishing work to do. As they worked, Michael and Philip described their preference of life in town versus life on a farm.

Philip said, "I favour life on the farm. I've seen enough of cities in Germany, and I've always dreamed of owning a farm."

Michael replied, "Living in town is more profitable for business, and I enjoy the company of others. William Philips Sr., the Ranger and wagonmaker just moved here and so did James Davis, a hatter.[291] Sometimes, the noise of horses, wagons, carriages, and rowdy men bothers me. Just last week, several carriages drove up to Tice's tavern on Main Street, one of which was Sir William. I think the others were Sir William's son-in-law Daniel Claus and his nephew and son-in-law Guy Johnson. Captain John Butler arrived too. Later in the evening, I heard the raucous in the tavern. The next day, Corporal Andrew Snyder came by to have his musket repaired. He told me the men were celebrating the first meeting of the new Masonic Chapter and Sir William's station as a Master Mason. I also heard that while his son John Johnson was in England, the King knighted him. He's now Sir John Johnson.[292] I agreed with Corporal Snyder. The men had much to celebrate."

Philip and Michael continued working until late afternoon. As Philip was tacking up Apple, he asked, "Will you come by in June. I want to start building my barn and a summer kitchen for Catrina?"

"'T'will be a pleasure. I'll be by as much as you need me. I wish you a good afternoon Philip."

"A good afternoon to you Michael."

Philip made his way home, set Apple loose in her pasture, and went to the house for a noon meal before heading out to the orchard. As he sat, he listened to Elizabeth and Catrina chatter.

"'T'is a wet June this year," Elizabeth said as she set the plates on the kitchen table.

"Aye. 'T'is good for the garden and the fields, but the mud is constant and it's everywhere. Your brothers will bring in plenty when they come for their meal."

"Mama, the squash and beans are coming up nicely, and the lettuce and onions will be ready for picking soon. I'm happy Papa made this new big table for our new kitchen. There's more room for vegetables and for children."

"'T'is a fine table with proper chairs too. They won't be sitting at it long. There's much work to be done in the fields and on the barn."

"I like the work they're doing on the summer kitchen! We can fix our sauerkraut and apple butter out there on those terrible muggy summer days, maybe even bathe in the winter. There's never room in the house." Elizabeth barely finished her sentence when there was commotion at the door. Catrina was right. There was plenty of mud at the back door when Mattheus, Martin, Peter, and Johannes came in. It wasn't long before two adults and eight children were seated at the big table.

Noisy chatter carried on over the clatter of shuffling bowls and plates. While pouring milk into his tin cup, Mattheus said, "Johannes George Alguire told me there are new shops opening in the village. He says Christian Sheek has two houses, a blacksmith shop, and a barn on lots one and two. He also has a farm at Johnson's Bush.[293] And, Johannes George says there's a new shoemaker from Ireland who's just building his house. The land was a gift from Sir William. His name is Mr. John Lonie."[294]

Catharina interrupted, "New shoes Papa! Can Elizabeth and I have a pair with buckles? Maybe you could go into town and meet the new shoemaker."

"You can have a new pair when they're needed. I think you need new winter cloaks before you need shoes."

As she started to clear the bowls and plates, Catrina added, "Yes, last year all you had were blanket coats, and they didn't fit well."

It was August when Mattheus Link and Philip went into Johnstown to pick up locks and latches for Philip's barn at Christian Sheek's blacksmith shop. On their way home, they stopped at Captain Tice's tavern for some beer.

As they sat at a table next to Martin Waldorf and George Schenck Sr., Mattheus tipped his hat and said, "Good afternoon Martin and George."

George raised his tankard and said, "Good day to you Mattheus. I hear you've a new fine young son."

"Aye. My Jacob was born only a few weeks ago and baptized last week."[295]

Placing his hat on the table, Philip added, "'T'was a fine baptism. The church was full of Kingsborough tenants. We met new neighbours and saw friends from Stone Raby. Michael Cline, our new gunsmith attended. And Johannes Michael Wick Sr., Casper Koch, and Christian and Lieutenant William Dillenbach were there with their families."

As the men continued their agreeable conversation about the conditions of farming and necessary improvements.

Martin Waldorf leaned back in his chair and said, "Well, we've many new roads, some are narrow and rough, not much more than a wagon path, but we can still get our grain to the mill. I think it wasn't so long ago that the only way to travel through this area was by foot on the Indian paths. Sir William does a lot to improve our way. He brings in new grass and wheat seeds for us to plant and animals for us to breed. I can remember when there were few sheep in the valley.[296] All of this makes good business for us."

"Johannes Eberhard Van Koughnot Sr., one of Sir William's tenants from the Kingsborough Patent, has a tanner's shop in Johnstown. He has seven sons and one daughter! His sons also work as shoemakers. He'll do a good business."[297]

George Schenck nodded his head and said, "Aye, and Francis Ruppert Sr. and his sons George, Adam, and Johannes are kept busy with the potash business. But, I hear Francis and Peter Remsen had disagreements with Mr. Hasenclever about the price of potash."[298]

Philip said, "Trade is always a risky business, even harder now with all the taxes."

"You're correct indeed Philip," Martin said while taking a swig of beer. "Acquiring land is a better business. Francis Ruppert Sr., Lucas Feader Sr., and Michael Byrne received a deed from the Indians for 10,000 acres between Brickabeen Creek and Stony Creek in the Schoharie Valley.[299] And, I hear Sir.

William is interested in having some of his tenants trying to grow hemp and make a business out of it. A good idea if we can get seeds. And certainly possible now that there's peace in the valley. We can work our land without fear of injury or ruin."[300]

Philip and Mattheus slid their chairs away from the table saying, "We must take our leave now friends. Yes, there's the last of the corn to bring in, and these locks and latches must go on the barn doors."

It was early in the morning at the end of September 1766, Philip had finished his chores and was sitting on the porch watching the leaves float off the trees. He watched as a gust of wind blew the leaves like rain all over the yard. The harvest was finished and so was the barn and the summer kitchen. Catrina had spent many hours in the summer kitchen fixing her sauerkraut and apple sauce. This year, she taught Elizabeth and Catharina how to pickle cucumbers and squash. They took some to the fall fair along with some of our finest apples. Philip was proud of his daughters. Elizabeth was a fine young woman now, and Philip noticed she paid a lot of attention to Michael Myers who didn't waver in responding to her attention. If it was to be, it would be a good match. Catharina was almost of age to attract a young man, but right now it didn't seem that important to her. She loved the garden and walking in the forest. A gust of wind brought Philip's attention to Mattheus, Martin, and Peter standing beside his chair.

Mattheus had his firelock in one hand and his shot bag thrown over his shoulder. "Let's go hunting Papa."

"Okay, which way shall we head?"

"Up the Indian path towards Sir William's Fish House."

"Hmm, good. A likely spot to find a deer. There are open meadows that border the forest."

A few hours later, Johannes sat at the kitchen table fiddling with a piece of wood he was carving. He'd had his head down most of the day, but occasionally lifted it, leaned forward and with wide eyes said, "I'm old enough to hunt Mama!"

"You're very skilled in the forest Johannes, but five people hunting at once are too many. You'll scare the deer away. Soon, it'll be your turn."

Several hours later, Johannes leapt out of his chair and went out the door running towards the field. Soon Catrina heard, "Mama, they've got a deer!"

She put the potatoes in the pot that was hanging over the fire, and as she wiped her hands on her apron she walked toward the back door. "Superb!" She thought. "All that meat for winter, tallow for candles, sinew for moccasins and snowshoes, and a hide for new breeches. And, the boys will be so proud."

Philip, Mattheus, Martin, Peter, and Johannes spent the next afternoon gutting and quartering the deer, making sure to keep the hide intact. As the boys helped separate the meat and cleaned the hide of fat, they spent a lot of the time talking about what part of the deer they liked best to eat.

As Philip set aside some of the meat for Martin and Elizabeth Margaretha Silmser he said, "They've four children to feed and one infant that needs good milk from her mother. I'm sure they'll be glad to have venison. I'll take the hide to Johannes Eberhard Van Koughnot Sr., our new tanner in Johnstown, and I'll save the brains for him to use for tanning. We'll have to take the hide to him tomorrow."

With his eyebrows raised, Peter asked, "Can I go with you to Mr. Van Koughnot's Papa? I want to see how he fixes the hide."

"Okay Peter. We'll leave early in the morning after your chores."

"I'll be ready Papa!"

Late in the evening, Philip laid two large logs on the fire and lifted the candle from the kitchen table. As he walked towards the stairs. He turned to Catrina and said, "'T'is time to retire dear wife. 'T'was a long day. I'll check on the boys and Elizabeth, Catharina, and Anna Margaret." Catrina rose from her rocking chair and followed him up the stairs. Philip opened the door to the boys room just enough to peer in. Mattheus and Martin were whispering, each in their own bed near the window. Johannes and Peter were just two bumps under the blankets, still and quiet. Philip whispered, "Mattheus, Martin, shhh. You'll wake your brothers. Sleep now. Morning comes early."

"Good night Papa." Philip closed the door and walked across the hall to check the girls. Not a sound came from the room when he cracked open the door.

Philip peeked into Dorothy's cradle then pulled his night cap down over his ears, lifted the quilt, and quickly slid his legs under. "Brr," he said as he nestled into Catrina.

"I know husband. 'T'is why I give thanks for our sheep and the thick wool socks they provide. I think I'll knit some mittens for Anna Margaret for Christmas, and Johannes and Peter could use another pair."

Philip rolled over and slid up to Catrina's warm body saying, "I wanted to make some Christmas gifts from the deer hide. I think Peter and Johannes would love deerskin mittens and Martin a new pair of moccasins. And, I thought I'd have some hide cut and make saddlebags for Mattheus and sewing kits for Elizabeth and Catharina. You could sew clasps onto the saddlebags for me and fill the sewing kits with some needles, thread, and sinew."

"I started to embroider pockets for Elizabeth, Catharina, and Anna Margaret. I hope they're ready for Christmas. I can only work on them when the girls are asleep."

It was just before Christmas when Philip rode to Fonda's store for butter and flour. He always knew he'd see someone he knew. Today, Henry Hough was there with Samuel Runnions.[301] He'd only met Samuel once before at the fair at Johnson Hall when Samuel joined Captain John Butler, Captain Jelles Fonda, and Philip for a gill of rum while they waited to watch the football game.

Seeing Henry and Samuel at the store counter, Philip walked over. "Good day Henry. Good day Samuel. Doesn't all the snow make it so much easier for the horses and sleighs?"

Henry replied, "Hello Philip. The snow is welcome on the roads. Travelling is so much harder through mud. The ice on the river is welcome too. My Negro and I've been travelling to Schenectady for Jelles. We've put in a week's work and three days with the horses and sleigh."

Philip noticed Henry's mound of purchases on the counter. He had tea, snuff, two french blankets, and nails. "I see you've some fine Indian shoes (moccasins)."

"Yes, I'm here to pay the Onondaga woman who made them and get some leather for mittens."[302] Samuel is here to get more calico and checked linen for his wife Tangulus. Jelles didn't have enough in the summer, so he's back again."[303]

As Henry sorted through his goods on the counter, he said, "Jelles usually has most everything that's needed. Maybe he has a bit of chocolate. My children would love a chocolate drink."

Samuel turned to leave and said, "I wish you and your families a merry Christmas season. I hope to see you for the St. Patrick's Day celebration."

During January and February of 1767, Philip spent most afternoons finishing a kitchen pantry and blanket chest for Catrina. With the furniture he'd made, living in the house was so much more comfortable. In the spring, he'd start cutting wood for two blanket chests, one for the girl's room and one for the boys. When he wasn't working on furniture, Philip and the boys were out in the recently cleared fields burning enormous piles of branches and stumps. It was difficult getting the fires started, but once they caught the flames were fierce, and plumes of black smoke billowed high above the trees.

One morning, after burning two piles, Philip and the boys came in the house to eat. When he took his cap off, Catrina stared straight at him and said, "Philip what have you done to your hair! She looked closer and took a handful of his thick curly hair. It's singed! You've been too close to those fires."

Running his hands through his hair, Philip said, "We were always at least twenty feet back. It doesn't take long to singe curly hair."

"Well, we'll have to cut the ends off. You can't go to church for Daniel and Anna's wedding with your hair like that.

Like baptisms, marriages were events that provided tenants opportunities to celebrate and socialize. On March 9th, Philip, Catrina, and the children set out on the chilly sleigh ride to the Dutch Reformed Church at Stone Raby to attend the marriage of Daniel Fykes, son of Peter Fykes Sr., and Anna Ruppert, daughter of Francis Ruppert Sr..[304] As Catrina watched the ceremony, she realized Elizabeth was of age to marry. Catrina's shoulders dropped, and while yielding a sigh she thought, "How did Elizabeth reach that age so fast? Soon, Catharina and Mattheus would leave home too. All my children will soon be gone."

The swift passing of time perplexed Catrina. As she tried to focus on something or someone uplifting, she noticed Francis Ruppert was distracted from his daughter's smiles. She turned to Philip and said, "What do you think has put that frown on Francis' face?"

Philip shook his head and said, "He must still be bothered with his troubles with Mr. Peter Remsen and Mr. Hasenclever. I hear Justice Henry Frey has examined him about his contract and his relationship with those men."[305]

Shrugging, Catrina continued to check for uplifting faces. She glanced to the pew ahead of her and to her right. She noticed that Michael Cline was sitting with Johannes Michael Wick Sr. and his daughter Catherine. Michael looked very pleased with the service, but more pleased when he frequently glanced at Catherine Wick. "Hmm," she thought. "I wonder if Mr. Cline has found a match in Johnstown so soon." Catrina was right. Within two months, Michael Cline and Catherine Wick, daughter of Johannes Michael Wick and Dorothea Koch, were married.[306]

The apple and cherry blossoms in the Eamers' orchard brought colour to their farm. The scent and colour made it easier to ignore the wet muddy fields and roads. Philip and his boys spent many hours preparing their hoes, shovels, axes, harnesses, plough, harrow, cart, and wagon for summer's work. At eleven and ten years of age, this would be Martin and Peter's first year handling the harrow and the ox and cart. They had much to learn from Philip and Mattheus. Elizabeth and Catharina planted potatoes and squash, and Anna Margaret helped them tend to the newborn piglets and lambs.

Philip and Catrina now had forty acres cleared and a six acre orchard. It was mid-May before all the peas and corn were planted. Philip planned to clear five more acres this year, and he wanted to improve his herd of sheep and purchase one more mare. Having Apple and another mare haul the wagon and sleigh was easier than putting Scout in harness. Once the seeds were in the ground and the roads dried, Philip and Catrina travelled to Fonda's store for a few supplies.

As they walked into the store, Catrina saw Tangulus Runnions at the counter. "Good day Tangulus. Have you seen the plentiful seeds and plants from Sir William's garden? Last year there was a special kind of bush bean I tried. It filled out nicely and gave a good picking of beans. He's cultivated so many varieties. I'm hoping he'll get plum trees. I'd like some in our orchard."

"No, I haven't tried any new plants this year. I'll ask Jelles what he has. I'm just here for butter."[307]

At the end of the counter, Philip was talking with Samuel Runnions, Henry Hough, and Gideon Marlet. Philip asked, "Gideon, what news is there of taxation in the colony?"

Shaking his head and waving his hand as if to brush a fly off the counter, Gideon replied, "Our King and his government might have repealed the Stamp Act, but now they've imposed duties on most everything that's imported to the colonies. There's duty on glass, lead, paint, paper, and tea! They think we won't notice that duty is still unfair taxation imposed on us."

Thumping his fist on the counter, Samuel added, "Aye, and we're required to quarter British soldiers in our homes and Inns. That includes food and drink! All of this costs us, and we've no say in the British parliament."[308]

While lifting the quart of rum that he'd just bought for Nicholas Philips.[309] Henry Hough said, "I hope there's nary a day when they tax rum. We'll have to make our own."[310]

Philip gripped his pipe, and after a long drag he said, "I expect we'll hear more about the 'Sons of Liberty' protesting."

Gideon nodded, "Oh yes. They've organized. We'll see it in the newspapers soon."

As the men continued their conversation, Michael Dorn walked up to the counter. Jelles Fonda reached for his pay register and said, "Michael, I've your payment of ten schillings for the bateau trip you made to Schenectady for me. I expect there'll be more trips soon. And, I hear Sir William is looking for men to improve the wagon path from Philadelphia Bush to Tribes Hill."[311] Jelles turned to Gideon, Philip, Henry, and Samuel and said, "You men can spread the word about the work needed on the road. And, if you're up by Nicholas and Elizabeth Shaver's place, you can stop at the next lot and see if the new man from the Hudson Highlands wants to assist. His name is David Jeacocks Sr.. His wife's name is Margaret Grietje Keuning, and I think they've three boys who could help."[312]

At the beginning of July, Philip and Mattheus joined other tenants to widen and maintain the road from Philadelphia Bush to Tribes Hill. There were trees to fall, stumps to clear, stones to move, dirt to haul, and ruts to fill. Early one morning in July, Philip hitched Apple and the new mare Bess to the wagon while Mattheus hitched the ox to the cart. It would take them about one hour to make their way down the road towards Tribes Hill where they'd meet others who were working on the road. As they drove up to a group of men, Philip saw Martin Loefler Sr. and his son Martin, and Samuel Runnions, Gideon Marlet, Henry Hough, Lewis Clement, and his brother Jacob Clement.

Philip pulled the wagon to the side of the road. While swinging himself onto the road, he said, "Good day Martin. Mattheus and I've brought axes and shovels and the wagon and cart to haul brush, tree limbs, rocks, and dirt. I see you've got a good start on the work."

"Good day Philip. Aye. We're all here fulfilling our required few days of road work. We know too well about the law and our obligations to clear the roadways. With this work, I'll have put in two of my six required days this year. Just bringing your wagon, ox, and horses will count for two of your six days."[313]

"My son Mattheus tells me that Lodowyck Putnam and his sons Aaron, Richard, and Frederick are working on the road up at Philadelphia Bush. I expect that Jacob and Michael Myers, Johannes Alguire Sr. and his son Johannes

George, and Jacob Sheets, Michael Carman, and William Schuman will be busy up there too. It won't be long before we're finished."

As he carried two shovels to the side of the road, Martin replied, "Oh there'll always be more ruts to fill and roads to build or widen."

"You're right Martin, especially with all the new tenants these past few years and with Sir William bringing all the new storekeepers and tradesmen to Johnstown."

By noon, the men cleared the brush and tree limbs from the side of the road, removed stones, and filled the ruts.

Just as Philip unloaded a pile of brush from the wagon, he heard Henry Hough call out, "Okay men, 't'is time for nourishment and a gill of rum! I've been to Fonda's store and brought us a gallon of rum to share."[314] The men sat at the side of the road, grateful for the rest and the rum.

Lodowyck Putnam raised his cup and said, "Here's to a good harvest and hunting season this fall. I see Henry's ready with his new grass scythe!"

"Aye. I got it when I was at Fonda's store. It's been useful this morning cutting grass at the side of the road. Heard some useful news at Fonda's too. We're getting a new schoolmaster at Johnstown this fall, a Master Edward Wall from Ireland. He'll be living next to the church on Sacandaga Road just before the bridge at Cayadutta Creek."

Jacob Myer's eyes widened when he said, "A grand thing for the children here. We'd like one up at Philadelphia Bush. Our children learn numbers and letters at home, but we don't know how to help them with their learning. A schoolmaster is most welcome at Johnstown except at harvest. I know several families who'll send their children to school. I'm certain Captain Peter Service Sr. and Martin Waldorf will be of those counted."

Work on the road halted in August as the harvest progressed. With so many acres of corn to pick, oats and wheat to cut, apples to pick, and winter wheat to plant, Philip needed the help of all his sons and daughters. Before the sun rose, Catrina and Elizabeth were in the kitchen preparing a meal, and Philip and Mattheus went out to prepare the animals for the day's work. As the sun rose, the family was at the kitchen table. Philip began the meal with a prayer, "Oh Lord, bless this food for which we are so grateful. Bless us with dry weather for a time, and keep us all in good health."

Reaching for the bowl of corn meal, Catharina said, "Papa can we go to the creek to swim tomorrow?"

"Not tomorrow Catharina, maybe on Sunday. We must work every minute to get the crops in before it rains or there's an early frost."

"But Papa my hands are so sore from picking blades off the stalks of corn. Swimming will help them heal!"

Looking at his own hands, Peter said, "Look at the blisters on my fingers from wielding the scythe. Papa's right. We can't be idle until the hay is stacked, the corn is shucked and shelled, and the oats and wheat are standing dry in the barn ready for threshing, fanning, and cleaning."

With her little chin raised high, Anna Margaret lifted the sleeve of her white frock and raised her arm over the table, "Look at the sore on my arm. 'T'is blue!"

Catrina reached over and lowered Anna Margaret's arm, "'T'is just a bruise little one. 'T'will be gone soon. You'll be more careful not to trip over piles of squash."

One morning, after two weeks of work from sunrise to sundown, Catharina came out the back door and looked onto the bare corn and wheat fields. She squinted, trying to see in the distance, then called to Philip, "Papa, there're Indians walking through the fields. I see six men and two women, and they've a dog with them!"

Philip squinted for a minute and said, "'T'is all right Catharina. They're probably on their way to the Sacandaga trail then north to their hunting grounds in the Adirondacks or west to Kayaderosseras. I think they're some of our Mohawk friends from the Lower Castle (Fort Hunter). Maybe it's Tehodinayea (Seth), or Teyorheasere (Abraham) and their families. They'll be gone 'til snow comes."

Snow was still a month away when the Eamers made their way to Johnson Hall to attend the baptism of several children. Anna Margaret, now five, had tasted the lemonade that Catharina loved so much. But, Anna Margaret seemed more interested in the musical instruments she'd heard at the Hall. As the wagon rolled up William Street, she said, "Listen Mama, can you hear the harp that the blind man plays? Or maybe someone will be playing the trumpet?"

"'T'is too far to hear anything now Anna Margaret, maybe when we're closer."

Catharina sat forward and said, "I want to see the monkey and the parrot and the peacock with the plumes of feathers on his tail!"[315]

Catrina and Philip always enjoyed their visits to Johnson Hall. There was, of course, a chance to see friends, but there were always so many other things to see and do. It was a welcome change to the work of the farm and the challenge of tending to eight children, even if three of them were now adults. Today, many of Catrina and Philip's friends welcomed their children into God's hands. On 24 Sept. 1767, William Philips Jr. and his wife Jannetjie baptized their daughter Hannah. Captain Peter Service Sr. and his wife Magdelena were Hannah's sponsors. They also sponsored Maria Lena, daughter of Peter Young and Marlena Service and Anna, daughter of Lucas Feader Sr. and his wife Maria Eva. Daniel Fykes and Anna Ruppert baptized their daughter Margretha. Francis Ruppert Sr. and his wife Margretha were her sponsors. Finally, there was a new family to the area who came from northwest of Albany, Johannes Adam Pabst and his wife Eva Maria Hamm. They baptized their daughter Margretha. Peter and Maria Margretha Ziegler were her sponsors.[316]

By the end of November, the gruelling work of the harvest had passed, and enough food was stored in the barn, the root cellar, and the cellar in the house. Snow now covered the fields and the orchard. During the winter months, Philip's trips to Fonda's store were fewer, but he did make one trip early in December. During each trip, he picked up news of trade or troubles in the colony.

This particular trip, he met Christopher Service, the brother of Captain Peter Service Sr.[317] "'T'is good to see you Christopher. How's your son Daniel Service? My Martin speaks of him often as they are of the same age and the same interests."

"Good day Philip. Daniel is well. He works for Sir William off and on. The other five children keep my Clara busy. I'm here for spelling books and a school primer to help the young ones with their letters. In November, when I was here to get shoemaking tools, I forgot the books. Clara soon reminded me."[318]

"Have you news of any disturbances related to taxes?"

"Aye. 'T'is still a topic that starts arguments and plenty of trouble. A farmer in Pennsylvania just published some letters to countrymen of the colonies.[319] Jelles has this pamphlet. I expect we'll see copies of it circulating at Captain Tice's tavern. Many have strong opinions about the liberties of the colonies." Philip and Christopher talked and smoked their pipes for many minutes after others had left the store.

1767 ended with a celebration. The new tenants George Bender and Gertraud's son Anthony Bender was born on October 25th and baptized on December 19th. Godfrey Shew and his wife Catherine were his sponsors. And Michael and Agatha's daughter Dorothy Gallinger was born on December 9th and baptized on December 28th. She was their eighth child. Dorothy's sponsors were Johannes Deygert and his wife Anna Dorothy Schumacker of Stone Raby.[320]

While gliding across the snow in the sleigh and snuggled under the bear rug, Catrina thought, "This year has been one of the best for our crops, and 't'is a sight to see the community grow. I wonder how many baptisms and marriages there'll be next year. Maybe our Elizabeth will be one to marry. I've noticed that Elizabeth has seen a lot of Michael Myers at church, and she spent most of the day with him at the fall fair."

1768 hardly began when Philip and Catrina attended another baptism at the Reformed Dutch Church at Stone Raby. This baptism was special because Jacob Henry Alguire was a sponsor for Catherine, daughter of William Schuman and his wife Margaret.[321] William and Margaret were tenants on the Kingsborough Patent and neighbours of Jacob Henry and Salome.

January was cold, and the snow was deep, but Philip needed to get his firelock repaired at Michael Cline's and Catrina needed some things from the Fonda's store at Caughnawaga. He'd been out early in the morning feeding the animals and now struggled with the sleigh. The cold bit into his fingers making them sting and not easily work the harness. He gave Apple extra hay and a bit of corn fodder to keep her warm, and they set off. Philip drove the sleigh up Montgomery Street then onto William Street and halted Apple in front of Michael's shop.

He felt the warmth of the forge as he opened the door, "Good day Michael. How does Catherine and your son George Cline?"

"Good day Philip. George is not one yet, but well. Catherine is heavy with child and expecting next month."

"You've made a good business here, and you've a few acres for a garden. If you want wheat or corn ground, I had a good crop this year."

"'T'is good to know Philip. Have you a firelock for me to repair?"

"Aye. The lock isn't firing."

"I'll have it fixed for you in a few days."

"A few days is fine. I have to go to Fonda's at Caughnawaga now."

"Well, you soon won't have to go all that way to the store. Mr. Robert Adams is opening a store soon on this street."

"I'll be glad to visit his store, and I know Catrina will be glad it's closer to home." Philip left the warmth of the shop and set off for Caughnawaga.

Before carrying on to Caughnawaga, Philip stopped at Captain Tice's tavern for a slice of cheese and bread, a tankard of beer, and any news anyone had to tell. He walked into the tavern through a haze of smoke that masked the orange coals in the large fireplace. In one corner, he saw Nicholas Shaver and his sons George Adam Shaver, Johannes Shaver, and Nicholas Shaver Jr.. Next to the Shavers sat William Casselman Sr. and his sons Johannes, William Jr., Severinus, and Warner Casselman.[322]

Philip joined the Shavers and ordered a tankard of ale. While lighting his pipe, Philip asked Nicholas, "How many kilometres did trading with the Indians take you this fall?"

"Many kilometres summer and fall. Game here is scarce. I must go west toward Oswego and Niagara or north toward Montreal where the Indians have more game to hunt. There's competition among traders and much cheating and abuse of the Indians. I fear Sir William will set harsh regulations at all trading posts.[323]

While chewing on the end of his pipe, Philip said, "Hmm. Aye. This fall, my daughter saw a group of Fort Hunter Mohawks heading towards distant hunting grounds. The settlements are growing so fast they've less hunting grounds from which to choose."

Nicholas nodded and said, "The Indians are badly treated at all the trading posts. They're cursed, kicked, and beaten. 'T'is worse than it ever was. Indians everywhere hate the posts.[324] I fear the cheating and abuse could lead to violence, maybe even war with the Indians. And, the French are still hoping to recapture the lands and forts they lost during the last war."

Nicholas Shaver's son George Adam leaned toward Philip and said, "The Governor, Sir Henry Moore, has ordered the militia to be reorganized north and west of Albany. That means, as Colonel of the Albany Militia, Sir William will reorganize his regiments from Albany to west of Little Falls. Sir John Johnson and Captain Peter Service Sr. will have regiments as will Colonel Guy Johnson, Colonel Daniel Claus, and Hans Jost Herkimer from Burnetsfield Patent. Captain Jacob Sternberger's Company from south of the Mohawk River in the Schoharie

Valley have already organized. Men from the Chrysler, Bauch, Bauman, Merckle, and Shaver families are among those enlisted. And Captain Thomas Ackeson's Company have men from the Mattice, Frymire, Uzille (Ziely), Crieghoof, and Le Roy (Laraway) families.[325] I've enlisted with Lieutenant John M. Veeder as has Johannes Casselman." Philip puffed and chewed on his pipe as he listened.

From the next table, William Casselman Sr. leaned over and said, "Aye. My son Johannes enlisted, and I hear two families have just come to Kingsborough Patent from the Schoharie Valley. One family is David Eny and his wife Anna Maria Frautz. David and Anna Maria have four sons and three daughters. None of the children are old enough to enlist. The other family is Michael Warner and his wife Margaret Schrey. They've but two children, one boy of five years and one girl just four.[326]

Philip picked up his hat from the table, stood and fastened the belt around his blanket coat and said, "I'll say farewell friends. I must get to Caughnawaga and home before dark."

George Adam lifted his tankard saying, "Aye Philip, farewell. Be ready this spring for more work on the roads to Johnson Hall."

It took Philip ½ hour to travel from the tavern to Fonda's store. He was feeling the chill in his bones as he walked in the door. Philip stood at the counter next to Christopher Service, and as he took off his mittens and lit his pipe, he said, "Good day Sir. I see you'll be busy with your shoemaking tools."

"Good day to you Philip. Aye. I'm making shoes for the new schoolmaster, and they need buckles. These knee buckles are for me."

As Jelles Fonda walked up to the counter, Christopher asked, "Jelles, I need the Onondaga woman to make a pair of moccasins for the schoolmaster. Her shoes are exceptional."

"Indeed they are Christopher. I'll order you a pair."[327]

Lifting Catrina's supplies from the counter, Philip said, "Good day Jelles and Christopher. I must be on my way. My mare is anxious with the sleigh, and 't'is well past noon."

Spring 1768 was just as busy as the fall harvest last year. Philip, Mattheus, and Martin taught young Peter and Johannes about planting cherry and apple seedlings. And, Philip bought a few plum seedlings from Sir William that he wanted to get in the ground. He knew Catrina would love the smell of plum blossoms. They would remind her of the sweet smell of almond blossoms in Germany. The spring work carried on as other years, but this year Peter and Johannes were responsible to care for the tender seedlings. The only interruption to the family's work was attending the St. Patrick's Day celebration at Johnson Hall and the baptism of Michael Warner and Margaret's daughter Maria Margaret Warner. Jacob Kuhlman was her sponsor.[328] Both Jacob and Michael lived at Albany Bush.

One early morning in July, Catrina, Elizabeth, and Catharina were watering the garden. Anna Margaret, and Dorothy were chasing each other round the wattle fence. Elizabeth stood with a bucket in each hand and hollered, "Stop all the running and the noise! We can't watch you when you're behind the fence."

Anna Margaret stopped, put her hands on her hips, and said, "Don't holler Elizabeth. I'll tell Mama what I saw!"

"What did you see Ann Margaret?" Catrina asked.

"Michael Myers gave Elizabeth flowers from the meadow."

"Well, there's nothing wrong with that."

"But Mama, Michael likes Elizabeth."

"Michael is a nice man Anna Margaret."

Elizabeth glared at Anna Margaret and said, "You shouldn't be spying on me. Mama, Michael was thanking me for helping him with his spelling. He said he'd weave me saddle pads for Apple and Bess."

"All right girls get back to fixing the garden, and Anna Margaret don't tattle on your sister. All that chatter can get you into trouble."

Late in July, Catrina came into the kitchen to start her morning chores. While seeing Philip trying to shave, she said, "Careful husband. If you stand any closer to that looking glass, you won't be able to see, and you'll cut yourself."

With barely a smile Philip replied, "I'm forty six years old, and my sight isn't what it used to be. I need to be this close."

"Aye. I know. I can't see my embroidery as I used to. No bother. We still manage all our chores just fine. Where are you going this early?"

"We've work to do on the road from Stone Raby to the mill near Johnson Hall, and a group of men are working on the road to Philadelphia Bush. We'll be two days at it.[329] Mattheus and I are meeting the men at William Street near the potash works.

Philip and Mattheus arrived on William Street with Apple and Bess pulling the wagon. Christopher Service waved and directed them to the side of the road, "Good day Philip and Mattheus. 'T'is a good day to work on these rough roads," he said as he pointed to the ruts the wagons and carts made. My son Daniel and my brother Captain Peter Service Sr. and Martin Waldorf are here as are George Schenck Sr., Johannes Albrandt, Johannes Hartle, and Adam Ruppert. I think David Jeacocks Sr. is the only one you haven't met. He's just moved here from the Hudson River area."

Philip and Mattheus laid their axes and shovels at the side of the road. Philip nodded saying, "Aye. William Casselman told me of David's arrival. And indeed, I see this road needs repair. How far does Sir William want us to work?"

"All the way to Rudolph Koch's place near Stone Raby. We'll work along the patent lines of Kingsborough. At Stone Raby we're to meet Henry Merckle Jr., William Casselman Sr. and his sons Johannes, Warner, Severinus, and William Jr."

With his shovel resting on his shoulder, Captain Peter Service Sr. waved us all on saying, "C'mon men let's get this work done, and we can soon enjoy that quart of rum my brother bought from Fonda's store especially for this nasty work!"[330]

For most of the day Philip and Mattheus worked alongside David Jeacocks Sr. and Adam Ruppert. Adam had much to talk about. He told us about the potash business and the long hours he and his brothers spent chopping wood to produce the ash needed. He told us about his brother Francis' trip to Philadelphia last month on business for Sir William.[331] Francis visited a Mr John Baynton, a well-known merchant and trader, and Captain George Noarth. As Adam finished talking about Francis, his eyes lit up when he told us of his newborn daughter Margaret.[332]

Finishing the road work, picking cherries and apples, and harvesting vegetables from the garden and harvesting beechnuts, chestnuts, and walnuts from the forests meant that the fall fair at Johnson Hall was drawing near. While cutting, stacking, and hauling hay, wheat, oats, and corn, the children talked about what games they'd play and all the food there was to eat. Anna Margaret was old enough to play in the games. She was bringing the Hotchpotch doll that Catrina made for her. There'd be a game to see how many different letters into which the children could shape the doll. Anna Margaret loved her letters. At seven years old, she could form the doll into A to Z. Johannes and Peter had been practicing 'hoops' with an old barrel hoop and sticks. They could roll the hoop down their lane and along the road. They were good at steering the hoop around the rough spots that made it tip over.

Early one morning in September, Catrina stood at the bottom of the stairs and called to the girls, "Elizabeth, Catharina, Anna Margaret come now, we're leaving soon."

Catharina came bouncing down the stairs saying, "Elizabeth is still fixing her hair in her cap and putting a blue ribbon round her straw hat. She's fussing Mama!"

"Well, you take Dorothy to the wagon, and I'll call her down."

Soon the family was on their way up William Street past the church toward Johnson Hall. As soon as the wagon stopped, Elizabeth was climbing out saying, "Oh, I see Jacob Henry and Michael Myers and Martin, Sebastian, and Sophia Alguire. I'll find you later Mama."

"Don't go far Elizabeth. I'll need your help with Dorothy and Anna Margaret."

"I won't Mama." With one hand on her straw hat and quick steps, Elizabeth almost tripped on her way to see the Myers and Alguires.

Michael Myers walked toward her with a hand forward and said, "Good day Miss Elizabeth. I'm so glad you came. You look fine this nice day."

"Good day to you too Michael and thank you. 'T'is a splendid day for the fair. I can't stay long. Mama needs help with my sisters."

"'T'is no problem. Will you walk with me to that stand of trees?"

Michael took Elizabeth's hand, and they walked to the stand of beech and maple trees at the edge of the grounds. They sat against the trunk under the canopy of a beech tree. "Do you know what they call the beech tree?" Michael asked.

"No. What do they call this most beautiful tree?"

"They call it the lovers' tree because it's so easy to carve names in the smooth grey bark of the tree. I want to carve our names in this tree Elizabeth. I want to mark my love for you here. Will you be my beloved wife Elizabeth?"

Elizabeth gripped his hands and with a very wide smile said, "Yes Michael. With great joy now and forever. Yes! Oh, but my mama and papa?"

"'T'is alright Elizabeth. I've asked your father's permission just yesterday. He's given his blessing." Michael and Elizabeth sat under the tree. With Elizabeth's head on his shoulder, they held hands, said nothing, and watched the beech and maple leaves float to the ground.

"We must go Michael. I must tell my Mama and Papa and my brothers and sisters. There's much to plan and do. When will we marry?"

"After the harvest, maybe in December. I still have work to do on our cabin. And, I want to make a few pieces of furniture. And, I'm weaving two rugs for our home. Michael Carman taught me. Now, I've my own loom."

That evening Elizabeth and Catharina were in their bedroom. Catharina was already stretched out under the covers while Elizabeth slipped into her night-gown and was folding her petticoat and shift. Catharina had let out a spirited squeal when Elizabeth told her the news of her engagement. All afternoon she pestered Elizabeth with questions about Michael, their new home, and house-keeping. Now, Catharina lay still and staring at her sister. Finally, she said, "I'll be sad when you leave. I'll miss you so. We've always been together, especially since we left Germany. What am I to do? I have only Anna Margaret and little Dorothy for company. Won't you be lonely Elizabeth?"

"I'll miss you dreadfully too. But, I won't be far, only a few miles away. We'll always see each other. And, I'll be so busy keeping my own house and looking after Michael that I won't have time to be lonely. Besides, it won't be long before you're married too. You and Martin Alguire have been friends for many years. And, I see his eyes sparkle when you're around."

Catharina reached over her head to the far corner of her bed and picked up Poppy. She held Poppy out towards Elizabeth; the doll's tattered wooden arms and legs stuck out under the worn red cape. "Here sister. You must take Poppy to comfort you."

"Don't be silly Catharina. I won't take your Poppy from you. You can give her a tighter squeeze if you feel lonely."

For most of October and November of 1768, Catrina was busy sewing a new jacket, petticoat, and white linen cap for Elizabeth's wedding day. Catrina bought some soft blue ribbon to trim the border of the cap and the edges of the blue penniston jacket and the petticoat. Catharina embroidered new pockets. Martin, Johannes, and Peter went out several days late in November to trap a rabbit so Catharina could line Elizabeth's new muff and the collar of her wool cape with the soft white fur. Philip and Catharina decided that they'd give the couple £2, one sow, two ewes, two chickens, and some linen sheets, pillowcases, and towels.

One evening, Catrina lay next to Philip under the weight of several blankets and a quilt, happy that her feet and fingers were finally warm. She reached for his hand under the quilt and said, "Our eldest daughter will be making her own home in just a few weeks. I'm happy with young Michael as her choice. He's a hard working young man who has a good start to a small farm, and he seems to be doing well weaving. They certainly are in love. Remember those days dear husband."

"Well, I know them now my dear wife; we still work hard, and we're definitely in love!"

"At least they won't be raising their family and building their farm with the terror of French or Indians attacking."

"Aye. Things are so much better now. Especially since Sir William signed the treaty in November with over 2500 Indians at Fort Stanwix. I heard about the great procession of bateaux down the Mohawk River. Joseph Brant was with them and Philip Philips, even Reverend Samuel Kirkland, Minister and friend of the Oneidas, and the Seneca Chief Kaieñˀkwaahtoñ of the Turtle clan. Now, there are clear boundaries between white settlements and Indian hunting grounds. I hear from Captain Peter Service Sr. that the Indians gave up, for a sum, a vast area in Ohio country, parts of Pennsylvania, New York, and Virginia all for the promise that no white man would settle on these western Indian lands. They want to live in peace away from marauding settlers and traders who steal their land, hunt their game, and cheat them at trade. Even the treaty signed in 1763 didn't prevent illegal squatters and violent acts and murder against Indian nations. Nor did the law stand in justice for wrongdoings against the Indians. So, the treaty is signed, and there's an agreement on the boundary lines. Let's hope the lines are respected."

Catrina squeezed Philip's hand under the blanket and said, "Aye. Sir William knows the Indians and their ways, and he knows the wrongs that have been done without redress. He also knows there'll never be peace so long as the Indians' honour, life, or land is held with such contempt. 'T'is always been one of their fears that the white man would be rid of them forever, or turn them into slaves like the Negroes."[333]

It was only five days into December when Elizabeth finished packing her things into her haversack. The last thing she dropped into the bag was the spool knitter her papa made her so many years ago. With it, she knit many cords, mostly belts for her brothers' breeches or hunting shirts. She pulled a new handkerchief from her pocket, folded it, and placed it on Catharina's pillow, then straightened the blue ribbon on her new cap, brushed the front and sides of her new petticoat, and tugged her jacket flat against her hips. With her hands pressed against her stomach, she thought, "Oh why does my stomach flip and my heart seem to skip a beat? I must breathe deep through this day or else the day be ruined." Grasping the stair railing, she made her way down the stairs. Philip and Catrina stood closest to the door and reached for her hand as she walked into the living room.

With a wide open smile, Catharina said, "Elizabeth, you are beautiful! The blue fabric suits you well, and your hair twists sit nicely below your cap."

"Thank you sister. Mama spent time with me this morning fixing my hair and pressing the wrinkles out of my petticoat with the flat iron." Elizabeth turned to her brothers who stood as an arc in front of her.

Peter was the first to speak wise words of a twelve year old, "Ahhhh, my big sister is to be hitched! He's lucky Michael Myers is." Martin and Johannes nodded and stared.

Nineteen year old Mattheus bowed so low that his thick black queue fell over his shoulder, "'Good lady, 't'is indeed a fine day to see my sister so happily married." Elizabeth blushed and wiped a tear from her cheek. Catrina held Elizabeth's haversack while Philip helped her with her new red wool cape and muff.

It was just before noon when the family arrived at the Trinity Lutheran Church at Stone Raby. Reverend Theophilus Engeland, a visiting Reverend from Philadelphia, greeted them. Catrina and the children took their seats in the pews near the front of the church. Elizabeth and Philip stood at the back waiting for the Reverend to take his place. Philip helped her remove her cape and muff. From where she stood, Elizabeth's eyes met Michael's. He nodded and smiled. She saw that the church was full, and she began to search the room for familiar faces, for her friends. She saw Charlotta Loefler with her new husband George Hough, and Eva Service with her husband Jacob Kitts, and Eva's sister Marlena Service with her husband Peter Young. Sitting beside Eva and Jacob Kitts were Anna Kitts and her husband Gerritt Van Brakelen and Elizabeth Kitts and her good friend Henry Boshart. Elizabeth grew up with all of these women. For almost twenty years, they swam in the creeks, played in the meadows, and celebrated at all the fall fairs. Elizabeth felt her face and neck soften and her shoulders drop. She reached for her papa's hand.

Catrina heard every word of Reverend Engeland's service. She saw Philip nodding frequently, so she knew he heard every word too. More than once,

Catrina wiped tears from her eyes and reached over little Dorothy to clasp Philip's hand. As Catharina watched, she wondered when she'd see her sister again. She knew they were to live in Michael's cabin at Philadelphia Bush, which was only a few kilometres from home. It would be an easy walk on a nice summer day. Catharina wondered how Reverend Engeland managed to find so many things to say when all Michael and Elizabeth wanted was to be married. Catharina's mind wandered. She found herself examining the length of Michael's hair queue and the black ribbon tied round it. She noticed the cut of his white linen shirt and wool breeches. Most definitely, she noticed that Michael and Elizabeth didn't take their eyes off each other.[334]

Catharina needn't have worried about her chances of seeing Elizabeth. In just over one month, she'd seen her sister and her new brother-in-law twice, each time at the Trinity Lutheran Church at Stone Raby. On December 28th, Reverend Theophilus Engeland delivered the same service he had for Elizabeth and Michael for George Schenck Sr. and Magdelena's daughter Eva Julia Margareta Schenck and her husband Balthasar Brietenbucher. The Reverend was busy once again on January 17th for Jacob Henry's son Sebastian Alguire and his wife Anna Barbara Wekeser's wedding.[335] After each service, Catharina was happy to talk to Elizabeth about her new home and what occupied her days.

Near the middle of May 1769, Philip made a trip to Johnstown to Robert Adam's store. And, he wanted to talk to Michael Cline about buying a firelock for Martin. By hunting season this fall, Martin would be almost fourteen years old and wanting his own gun. Philip also wanted to pay a visit to William Philips Jr. at his grist mill.[336] After visiting Michael, Philip drove down William Street passed the church and the house of Edward Wall, the schoolmaster. The grist mill was next to Cayadutta Creek, just off William Street. Philip quieted Apple as she pulled the wagon into the mill yard. The noise of the stones grinding the wheat always spooked the horses.

Seeing William in the yard, Philip waved, "Good morning Sir. My wife sent me with a basket of a few fine provisions."

"'T'is kind of you and will be enjoyed for certain. Come in and sit. I haven't seen many this long winter except for my new Miller, Peter Young. There've been many solitary days. I look forward to the coming birth of our child."

"Soon, you'll be busy enough with our neighbours bringing in their winter wheat. I'm sure there are constant wagons and carts to Johnson Hall."

"Aye, and to the church and the school."

"I saw several children on their way to the school as I drove by this morning. There were Christopher Service's children, John, Jacob, Margaret, and Catherine, and Martin Waldorf's children, Eve, Catherine, and Helena."

William smiled and added, "Too, I think the Runnion boys Henry Runnion and Peter Runnion, and George Bender's son George Bender Jr., and Johannes Dorn's children, Johannes, David, and Jeremiah. 'T'is good to see so many children attend."

"Aye. Jacob Myers tells me they have a schoolmaster up at Philadelphia Bush, and I hear the Mohawk school at the Lower Castle (Fort Hunter) has thirty children attending from the Bear, Wolf, and Turtle clans. My daughter Anna Margaret plays with Catherine and Susannah of the Wolf clan whenever there are gatherings at Johnson Hall. They are of those attending the Mohawk school."[337]

Philip and William continued talking about events nearby. Taking a few puffs of his pipe, Philip said, "Did you hear Sir William supports the building of a wooden church for the Mohawks at the Upper Castle (Canajoharie). 'T'is near Joseph Brant's homestead, near Nowadaga Creek just east of Little Falls on the sixth allotment of the Canajoharie Patent. It's to sit on the slope of the hill next to the King's Highway. I'm sure you'll be able to see it from the flats near the river.[338] They start building early this fall. Daniel Miller is taking charge of the building, and George Klock is supplying the boards. I know Johannes Nelles and Henry Nelles are supplying some of the provisions. There're many men building. I only know of Balthasar Dillenbach, Rudolph Fuchs, and Johannes Walradt and some of Sir William's Negroes.[339] I saw one of his new slaves when I was getting squash seeds at Johnson Hall last week. He's a young man about nineteen years. Apparently, he came up from Richard Cartwright's home at Albany."[340]

William added, "I imagine there'll be Adam Young and William Casselman Sr. and Anna Margaret's boys Johannes, Severinus, and Warner working on that church. They all live in that area."

"Aye, and Conrad Countryman Sr. boys, George, Frederick, Adam, and Jacob."[341]

"With all of the arguments over land surveys and purchases the Mohawks and German settlers have had over these past few years, 't'is indeed surprising anything gets built at Canajoharie."[342]

William nodded, leaned back in his chair, and said, "We mayn't see many huge tracts of land bought and sold as we have past days. But, I've heard that Sir William received a warrant for a tract of land on the north side of the Mohawk River. The land was a gift from the Canajoharie Mohawks in 1760. A survey was complete in 1764, and it's only just now that the King approved ownership. The track is 66, 000 acres and is called the Royal Grant or Kingsland. It runs on the north side of the Mohawk River from old Fort Hendrick at Canajoharie west to German Flats. I know that George Schenck Jr. is a tenant on that land. Many of your friends have quit claim interest in the property."

"Indeed. Michael Gallinger Sr., Philip Hendrick Klein, Lucas Feader Sr., Francis and Adam Ruppert, Peter and Christopher Service, Mattheus Link, George Crites Sr., and Peter Fykes Sr. have an interest.[343] I wonder if Mr Robert Picken, our new resident of Johnstown, surveyed that land. Mr Picken has come from Schenectady and lives along William Street."

"I know Mr. Picken talked with Sir William and Captain Butler regarding the land. Sir William requested a survey."[344]

"While filling his pipe with tobacco, William said, "There's another patent that's been surveyed. The Indians gave a deed to the Englishman John Bowen, Dr. Robert Adams, Captain Gilbert Tice, Michael Byrne, and Jelles Fonda for 20,000 acres along the Schoharie River.[345] And, Captain Peter Service Sr. was granted 25,000 acres north of Cosby Manor near Fort Stanwix."[346]

Shaking his head, Philip said, "I fear t'will never end, this thirst for land. The only things talked about in the valley are land, wheat, and furs. I've heard of another deed given to Samuel Runnions and Achilles Preston, 120,000 acres next to the Sacandaga River."[347] Philip rose, and as he put on his black felt hat he said, "I must take my leave Sir else Catrina will worry. Good day Sir,"

"The like to you and Catrina."

Philip, Martin, Mattheus, Peter, and Johannes spent most of June tending the winter wheat crop and the orchard. Sometimes the boys went hunting fowl with Martin Alguire, Nicholas Silmser, Christopher Gallinger, John Loefler, and Frederick Putnam. The meadows on the Sacandaga Patent were a nice place to flush grouse or pheasant. Or, they'd go to the river for mussels and eels. Often, they met David, Paul, Isaac, and Joseph, Mohawk boys from Fort Hunter. Sometimes, Mattheus and Martin went to help Michael Myers put wood up for the fall and visit their sister.

One day late in June, Catrina and Philip harnessed Apple to the wagon for a trip to Fonda's store. Catharina stayed home to finish the laundry she'd started with her mama early in the morning. Anna Margaret and Dorothy giggled as they climbed into the back of the wagon. As expected, Catrina and Philip saw several of their neighbours. They saw Christopher Service, Michael Dorn, and Henry Hough.[348]

Philip stopped to talk to Henry while Catrina watched Anna Margaret and Dorothy study everything in the store. "Good day Henry. How does your father?"

"Good day Philip. He's fine Sir, but he complains of his rheumatism."

"I haven't seen you for several weeks. Have you been away?"

"Aye. I've been on a few trips for Sir William. I'll be away again soon with Philip Miller. I expect for a few weeks. I've come for my payment and some tea. I think Michael Dorn is due payment for trips on the bateaux to Schenectady. Christopher, it seems, is here for something stronger than tea. He's got a stock of brandy and tobacco of course."

"Have you seen much of William Bowen Sr.? I don't get to the south side of the river often."

"Aye. I do see him. He's a busy smith with much work for Sir William this past year."[349]

"Catrina and I'll pay a visit sometime soon."

"Yes, do come to Warrensburg. The river crossing at Fort Hunter 't'ain't difficult, and there are several tenants there with whom to make acquaintance. Of course, William Bowen is there as is Jacob Rombaugh. Mr. Rombaugh grows and spins flax, and their apple orchard is impressive with over 100 trees."[350]

As Henry and Philip finished talking, Catrina stood beside Philip and said, "We must take our leave Philip. We've two baptisms to attend tomorrow at Stone Raby, and I must help Catharina with the washing."

"Who's to be baptized?" Henry asked.

"Jacob Alguire, the son of Jacob Henry Alguire and Salome and Maria Margaret Warner, the daughter of Michael Warner and Margaret."

Smiling, Henry said, "Severinus Casselman of Canajoharie just baptized his son Conrad Casselman. And his brother Warner Casselman baptized his son Henry.

"'T'is many Sir. Our friends Michael Gallinger Sr. and Agatha sponsored Johannes George Koch, the son of Johannes Koch and Magdelena Dillenbach."[351] 'T'is certain there's much new life in the valley."

At the time, Catrina didn't realize the significance of Henry Hough's statement about new life in the valley. It wasn't until one day late in July when the family was in the orchard picking cherries. Elizabeth and Michael came to help pick. Martin Alguire came too. Over the last few months, Martin was visiting a lot.

While the family was having a rest, eating cheese and bread and drinking apple cider, Elizabeth said, "Michael and I have important news for all of you. Mama and Papa, you're to be grandparents sometime late December!"

Catrina leaned over and rested her head on Philip's shoulder, clasped his hand and said, "Oh a sweet babe! That's blessed news for us and for you both. We must prepare. You'll need help making blankets, napkins, caps, and a few new petticoats and aprons for you." Everyone spoke eager words filled with blessings.

After hugging her sister and brother-in-law, Catharina stood next to Martin fidgeting with her apron. "Shall we tell them?" she whispered to Martin.

"Aye. 'T'is a good time."

"Mama, Papa, Martin and I have news too!"

As her mouth opened and her chin dropped, Catrina said, "What news is yours?"

"Martin asked me to be his wife."

Elizabeth hugged her sister saying, "'Blessings to you sister. 'T'is such good news for all."

Catrina leaned back against a tree and said, "Well, my fingers, needle, and thread'll be busy this fall. Catharina will need her wedding clothes." Anna Margaret and Dorothy couldn't stop giggling while they skipped in circles around their sisters. Mattheus, Martin, Peter, and Johannes firmly shook each of their brother-in-law's hands.

The news at the day in the orchard spurred extra activity at the Eamer household for weeks. But still, the harvest took most of their time. Also, Philip was never surprised when his time was required working on the roads. Other than the King's Highway that ran from Schenectady to German Flats on the north and south shore of the Mohawk River, there were many other shorter roads between villages. That kind of work had to be done between the spring melt and harvest. So, early in August, he and Mattheus headed to Stone Raby to help maintain the road from Rudolph Koch's home to Johnson Hall.[352] There'd been new regulations passed regarding building and maintaining roads in the county. Henry Merckle, the Commissioner of Highways in that district, was responsible for organizing workmen.[353] Philip expected to see the many sons of Christian Dillenbach Sr. and Philip Empey Sr. working that day because they all lived on the Stone Raby Patent.

Not only were the men of the valley required to build and maintain roads, but they were also required to muster for their district's militia. In 1768, the militia for the county of Albany had recently been reorganized into several different regiments. Sir William Johnson remained the Brigadier General of all militia north of Kingston on both sides of the Hudson River. Colonel Guy Johnson was the commander of the 3rd Regiment, whose area spanned from Schenectady to Stone Raby. Lieutenant Colonel John Butler, Major Jelles Fonda, Captain Peter Service Sr., 1st Lieutenant Achilles Preston, 2nd Lieutenant Peter Service Jr. and Ensign Barent Frederick were his officers. In all, there were 491 men of the Mohawk district enlisted in the 3rd Regiment. The Kingsborough and Sacandaga areas were included. Other regimental officers were Captain Gilbert Tice, 1st Lieutenant William Bowen Jr., 2nd Lieutenant Daniel Service, 2nd Lieutenant Henry Hare, and Ensign Walter Butler.[354] The districts of the valley were well protected with over 1900 men enlisted in various regiments.

During the fall, Catrina spent many hours sewing clothes for her new grandchild and for Catharina's wedding. Anna Margaret and Dorothy helped as seven and four year olds do. The boys spent time hunting for a few rabbits or a marten or fox so they could provide a bit of fur to line the hood of Catharina's cape and her new muff. Philip knew Michael and Elizabeth didn't have much time away from the work of their farm, so he spent time building a cradle from pieces of a fallen maple tree. At the end of September, the family also attended the fall fair at Johnson Hall. This year, Philip brought some of his apples to sell, and Catrina brought squash and turnips.

By the end of October, getting ready for winter weather was the most important task on everyone's mind. The men and boys of Kingsborough and Sacandaga shared the work of cutting and splitting wood, filling the animals' shelters with plenty of clean straw, butchering cows, sheep, or pigs, and often they went out hunting. The women and girls spent most of their time in the kitchen pickling and drying as many fruits and vegetables as they could. Making sauerkraut was always important for Catrina as was making sure the apple cider casks were full and casks of pork were well salted. Many days were spent using the fat from the butchered animals and ash saved during the year to make soap and candles. There weren't many minutes of rest.

Late in October, the family attended the Dutch Reformed Church at Stone Raby for the baptism of Maria Waldorf, daughter of Martin and Margaret Waldorf.[355] After the service, Philip and Catrina spoke to Adam Ruppert and heard of his brother Francis' difficulties in Charlestown, South Carolina.

Adam related the story, "In August, my brother Francis Ruppert Sr. traveled to Charlestown on business and became quite ill. He wrote to Sir William requesting his pay as he had to pay for doctors, lodgings, and care. And, he asked if Sir William could please send me to South Carolina with his wife, whom he was greatly wanting.[356] As my sister-in-law Margaretha is aged and could not take the journey alone, I went with her to tend to her husband and to bring him home. It was a long and tiresome journey, but we arrived home safely. My brother still mends."

"You do your brother and sister-in-law a good service Sir. I hope Francis is well again soon."

Snow came early in 1769. Catharina woke early on Sunday, November 26th. Today, she would marry. She'd slept less than one hour the entire night with thoughts of all kinds whirling through her head. She heard noise downstairs. So, she rose and put on her wool stockings.

With her kerchief wrapped over her shoulders, she made her way to the kitchen. "Good morning Mama."

"'T'is a fine marrying day dear Catharina! You'll be a lovely bride, and I'll certainly be a proud Mother." After managing to eat a few bites of cornmeal, some dried apple, and some milk, Catharina went upstairs to put on her new shift, petticoat, and jacket. Catrina stayed in the kitchen to finish sewing the bit of fox fur around the hood of Catharina's new cape. There was much chatter and noise as Philip, the four boys, and two girls ate breakfast.

It wasn't long before everyone was in the sleigh gliding over the first snowfall. Reverend Theophilus Engeland met the family at the door. The wait wasn't long before Catharina was standing beside Martin.[357] Like Elizabeth last year, Catharina saw many of her friends from Kingsborough and from Stone Raby.

She saw her new brother-in-law Sebastian and his wife Anna Barbara, and she saw her new sister-in-laws, Sophia, Hanna, Margaret, and Elizabeth. Many church elders were there too. Catharina saw Johannes Empey Sr., Martin Dillenbach, and William Nelles Sr. and his son William Jr. and Henry William Nelles. Michael Carman, Jacob Sheets, Jacob Myers, William Schuman, and George Cough, all tenants of Philadelphia Bush, came to celebrate with Martin and his father Jacob Henry Alguire.

Martin Alguire and Catharina settled into their cabin at Albany Bush where Martin leased 100 acres.[358] Their possessions were sparse, but Philip and Catrina had given them a gift of two chickens, two sheep, two piglets, and £2. Catrina had also sewn them a quilt, and Martin's mother Salome gave them sheets and pillowcases. Martin spent most of his time between weaving and farming while Catharina tended to the animals and the housekeeping. Some days, the winter weather left them feeling isolated, but they were just a few kilometres southeast of Philip and Catrina, and they knew Christmas would come soon. The Eamers would celebrate together.

Christmas day in the valley was always a time of joy and good cheer, particularly for the Eamers this year. Early on Christmas day, the family met at the Caughnawaga church for the divine service and to celebrate the birth of their savior. There was plenty of time after church to celebrate with neighbours and friends with food, drink, and dancing. Everyone was in a festive mood.[359] After church, the family enjoyed a quick but generous meal at the farm. They ate ham with apple and sausage stuffing, sauerkraut, and potato dumplings. Catrina baked lots of cookies and even fruit bread that resembled the Stollen she remembered so well in Germany. Their meal was quick because, with newborn Philip too young to travel and Elizabeth still recovering from childbirth, everyone was to travel to Elizabeth and Michael's cabin.[360] Catrina brought them a basket of Christmas dinner, and while fussing over the tiny Philip, the family exchanged a collection of gifts of woolen socks, mittens, kerchiefs, carved bowls, and leather pouches.

On the last evening of 1769, Philip and Catrina sat in their rockers in front of the fire. It was quiet in the house. Anna Margaret and Dorothy were asleep, and the boys were upstairs. While gazing at the fire and puffing on his pipe, Philip said, "'T'is a good day I had at Fonda's store. I cleared my account with Jelles, brought home two gallons of rum and a new pair of shoes, and I'm happy he had all the items you wanted. I think you're to sew a new waistcoat for me with the fine embosed serge I bought and some new trousers for the boys with the ozinbrig. They'll be fine trousers for working in the fields or out hunting. And, I see the girls have new woolen hose."

"You're correct on all of those items husband. All I need are some pewter buttons to finish your waistcoat."

"'T'was also good to see Henry Hough. I believe he's to have a new great coat as he left the store with 6 ½ ells of blue coating along with a box full of buttons, mohair, knives, forks, and a couple of handkerchiefs. He'd done well with his pay from Jelles for a few trips to Schenectady."[361]

"I'm pleased you don't have those long trips away from home, only long days in the fields. We must be able to help Elizabeth and Michael with little Philip. And with Catharina and Martin's news of a baby expected in July, we'll be busy parents and grandparents."

"Aye, we will, but 't'is all a blessing."

January 1770 was remarkably cold. Every time Philip sat down in his office at the back of the house to work on his accounts the ink was frozen, even if he kept it near the box stove in the sitting room. Many more times than usual, Philip and the boys were out at the wood pile gathering fuel to keep the house warm. One day near the end of January, Philip braved the cold and travelled to Elizabeth and Michael's at Philadelphia Bush to make sure they had all they needed, and, of course, to see his grandson Philip. After his visit to Philadelphia Bush, he headed into Johnstown to stop at Robert Adam's store and at Tice's tavern to catch up on community news.

This day at the tavern, Philip sat with David Jeacocks, Michael Gallinger Sr., Johannes Eberhard Van Koughnot Jr., Jacob Van Koughnot, John Farlinger, Anthony Walliser, and Frederick Goose. With tankards of beer covering the tables and pipe smoke filling the air, the men discussed politics, the behavior of the schoolmaster and the minister, and conveyed recent news in the valley.[362] Johannes Michael Wick walked in carrying a box filled with six ells of black callico and one large blanket he'd bought at Fonda's store. He'd just traded 16 lbs of butter and 25 schipples of wheat.[363] Right behind Johannes came Michael Cline.

Michael dropped into the chair beside Philip and said, "'T'is good to have work, but Sir William keeps me too busy! I've no time for anyone else."

"Aye, Jacob replied, Johannes Wert worked a day and gave two fowl as dues."[364]

After a gulp of beer and depositing his tankard firmly on the table, John Farlinger said, "Mr. Adams says that John Wells of Cherry Valley is wanting to start potash manufacturing, and Sir William has had several men hauling freight this winter. Johannes Petrie, Lewis Clement, and others hauled many loads past Little Falls and into Seneca territory."[365]

Anthony answered, "Aye, and the men are still working on the Indian church at Canajoharie. I heard Balthasar Dillenbach and Jost Fuchs are cutting and hauling wood. And, I hear a Reverend John Stuart from New York is to be their Minister,[366] and Goshen Van Alstyne is contributing to the work. On the north side of the river, the community of Palatine started work on a large stone church. 'T'is only a few kilometres from Fort Plain. 'T'will be a big job; it's made of limestone. They're naming it the Palatine Evangelical Lutheran Church.[367] Henry William Nelles donated the land, and everyone in the community is donating something." "I wonder who the minister'll be?" Anthony asked. "Probably, Reverend Theophilus Engeland," answered Johannes Michael Wick.

Philip listened and swallowed his beer, then he said, "More churches will mean a need for more roads and work to keep them passable. I hear there's work to be done at Butlersbury Patent soon."

David Jeacocks Sr. turned to Philip, raised his tankard and said, "That work'll come soon enough. Right now, we've much to celebrate. My newborn daughter Sarah is baptized, and my good wife is healthy and strong, and Jacob Van Koughnot has a new wife, Miss Catherine Fykes, daughter of Peter Fykes Sr.. The biggest news is that there're many of us to be naturalized at the end of this month!"[368]

Sitting straight up in his chair Frederick Goose said, "Aye. There's three of us old 60th Regiment soldiers, me, Anthony Walliser, and John Farlinger. And, there's George Crites Sr., Johannes Ault, Johannes Albrandt, George Ruppert, Johannes Hartle, George Bender, George Schenck Sr., Henry Hawn, Johannes Eberhart Van Koughnot Jr., Conrad Smith, and Godfrey Shew. This bunch'll be heading to Albany on January 27."

Late in April 1770, Philip and Mattheus loaded the wagon with shovels, axes, and saws and headed toward Gilbert Tice's tavern in Johnstown. They were to meet others to work on a road from Tice's house south to the road that runs through the Caughnawaga Patent (Edward Collin's Patent).[369] At the tavern, they met Michael Cline, Christian Sheek, Johannes Van Koughnot, William Philips Jr., and John Lonie. The road would run close to Lieutenant Colonel John Butler's home. Philip expected John Butler's sons Walter Butler and Thomas Butler to be there, as well as Philip Hendrick Klein, Henry Hart, and Philip Shaver. At least six times during the morning, the men stopped work to let wagons pass. Philip tipped his hat to Andrew Snyder, Marcus Reese, Peter Service Sr., and Adam Ruppert as they rolled by carrying freight for Sir William. One wagon that rolled by was Johannes Dorn on his way to Fonda's store to deliver ashes and peas. Another wagon was George Crites Sr. delivering wheat to the mill.[370] It was near the end of the day when Philip and Mattheus returned home to tend to the fields and animals.

Returning from the fields one morning at the end of May, Philip walked into the summer kitchen while Catrina and Anna Margaret were baking bread. He announced, "Mattheus and I are going to town. The plough blade is broken, and I think Christian Sheek can repair it."

"Fine husband, we need cornmeal. Will you get some from Robert Adam's store?"

Philip and Mattheus loaded the plough into the wagon and set out for town. Philip struggled as he urged the horses through the muddy ruts along Montgomery Street and down William Street. Finally, they stopped in front of Christian's shop.

"Good day, Christian. I've a broken plough blade. Can it be fixed?"

"Good day Philip. 'T'is a fine weather day. Good day Mattheus. Aye. It can be fixed, but it will be a few hours. Just unload it and set it at the back of the shop."

After chatting with Christian about news around town, Philip and Mattheus walked down William Street to Adam's store to get Catrina's cornmeal. When returning to the wagon, they met John Lonie on his way to Tice's tavern.

With a slight bow, Mattheus said, "Good day Sir."

"The like to you. Will I see you at Tice's?"

"Aye. We'll come along soon."

Now twenty years old, this was the first time Mattheus was at the tavern with his papa. The noise of talk, laughter, and the crackle of the fire was the first thing he noticed. In one corner next to the bar were men at a table playing cards and smoking their pipes. At another table, men were playing a game with dice. Mattheus sat with Philip Service, Christopher and Daniel Service, John Farlinger, and John Lonie.

John Farlinger raised his tankard to Mattheus and said, "Young Mattheus you must have a pint and share news with us."

"What news is their John?"

"I've this newspaper from Mr. John Monier in Albany. He's replaced Henry Van Schaick as postmaster. 'T'was given to me yesterday when I rode post for Sir William. I've much news from my day at Albany. It seems Mr. Monier is angered with me for pounding at his door to wake him. He's reported to Sir William that I, not in my right mind, damaged his front and kitchen door. Mr. Monier exaggerates and calls me insolent. I was trying to wake him and had to knock loudly. I've sent a note to Sir William explaining and begging his forgiveness for any trouble I might have caused. I was just at Mr. Monier's last Saturday with no troubles at all. In fact, I've made twenty trips there these past months."[371]

"Perhaps Mr. Monier overdoes his recollection!"

Christopher Service leans over to read John's newspaper, "How does all in the colonies? What news is there of troubles?"

Daniel leaned forward clutching his tankard, "Tempers flared in New York City in January over handbills British soldiers posted calling the 'Sons of Liberty' enemies of society. There was a scuffle and drawing of swords, several soldiers and town folk were wounded.

"Were there liberty poles?" John Farlinger asked.

"Does not say in this newspaper. But 't'is worse in Boston. Several town folk were killed when British soldiers fired on a mob of angry citizens."

"Pray tell, what incited such violence from the soldiers?" Philip asked.

"Not said here. Perhaps the soldiers felt threatened with so many coming at them with fury in their eyes and at the ends of their sticks. Or, town folk were overwhelmed with so many British soldiers about. It seems there are more and more soldiers whom we pay to billet now that the French vacated their frontier posts. Sha'n't know what the cause until after the soldiers' trial. No doubt 't'will give fire to flaring tempers."

"Indeed, God knows there's usually trouble when mobs are in the streets or with liquor in the taverns. We've our own places where trouble brews, here or at Christian Nelles' tavern west of Fort Plain.[372]

Gulping the last of his beer, Daniel Service said, "Sir William has enough trouble keeping peace among the Six Nations and keeping an eye on settlers pushing into Indian land. There're many settlers along the Delaware, Susquehanna, and Ohio Rivers. They don't respect Indian land. And, Sir William ha'n't been well this past year. His stomach and old war wound bother him greatly. I was just at Johnson Hall getting our pay from Thomas Flood for ploughing done. Martin Waldorf, Peter Crouse, and I worked seven days in Sir William's fields at nine shillings per day."[373]

John Lonie nodded, "Sir William is busy each day. I've orders for shoes for his family, his gardener and bricklayer, his Negroes, Mr. Flood, and many Indians, and I repair harnesses for horses and his sleigh and chair (chaise).[374] Even with leather from Johannes Eberhard Van Koughnot Sr. our tanner, I've not enough. Soon, Sir William will be giving you orders Christopher, or we'll need another shoemaker in Johnstown. And Michael Cline is busy day and night, as are William Bowen and Christian Sheek with blacksmith work.

After three swigs of beer, John belched and continued, "Then there's more land to clear. Sir William claimed another patent along the Adegeghteinge (Charlotte River) with James Davis, Michael Gallinger Sr., William Philips Sr., John Friel, Lucas Feader Sr., Mattheus Link, James Bennet, and William and Robert Lotteridge."

Raising his tankard, Daniel Service said, "Aye, and my father just completed a land deal with Sir William. He traded Sir William a piece of his land for 1500 acres along the Charlotte River. We're to move there soon."[375]

At the evening meal that night, Mattheus told everyone the news he'd heard at the tavern and what he thought of the men's popular gathering place in town.

Martin nodded and leaned back in his chair, "Well, while you were out with Papa, I fixed the fence around the orchard. I found two pigs roaming through the cherry trees. They were on their way to the road. Was the plough able to be fixed Papa?"

"Aye Martin. 'T'will hold well this season."

As Anna Margaret and Catrina cleared the plates and bowls, Catrina said, "We must go down to visit Catharina and Martin at Albany Bush. I want to know that she's feeling well. Their baby is due in a few weeks. 'T'is good they've asked Michael and Elizabeth to be the child's sponsors."

Fixing fences, cutting wood, and repairing outbuildings kept Philip and the boys busy until the end of June. One day, the last week of June, Martin Alguire came riding fast up the lane hollering for Catrina, "Come quickly Mrs. Eamer. Our baby! 'T'is to be born!"

Catrina yelled for Anna Margaret, "Tell your Papa I've gone to help Catharina. Please watch Dorothy."

All afternoon, Catrina did all she could to ease her daughter's pain and fear. It wasn't long before a healthy baby girl was swaddled in a linen blanket and placed next to Catharina.

"Mama, she's beautiful. I'd forgotten how tiny new babies are. We're to name her Maria Salome. One name for each grandmother. Maria for you and Salome for Martin's mother. Martin come and see your daughter![376]

Catrina leaned over to kiss her daughter, "Thank you Catharina. Your Papa will be so happy, as am I. You need rest now."

Catrina heard the wagon pull up next to the cabin, and minutes later Philip walked in. "How is she dear wife?"

"She's fine and so is your new granddaughter, Maria Salome Alguire. We must watch them both closely for the next few days. Martin, you must fetch me if Catharina or the baby are with fever or sluggish. We'll go now but will be back tomorrow."

Philip and Catrina visited Elizabeth and little Philip and Catharina and Maria Salome as often as they could. In the middle of August, Philip and Catrina payed another visit to Catharina, Martin, and their new granddaughter. Catrina always brought meat, bread, milk, and vegetables when they visited. She knew babies demanded energy from their mothers, fatigue was never absent. But, with all her worry, both her daughters and their husbands were doing well. The babies were already growing. On their way home that August day, they stopped at Fonda's store.

The store wasn't crowded as most tenants were busy in the fields. But, Catrina saw Martin Waldorf and Margaret at the counter and went to talk. "Margaret, 't'is a fine day to be out. Catharina has given birth to a fine baby girl."

"My good wishes to you and Philip. 'T'is comforting to know a new life has safely arrived."

As Margaret and Catrina chatted, Jelles placed the indigo on the counter and said, "There're two ounces for you Mrs. Waldorf. I'll get the stocking garters and the three cups and saucers you wanted. I've given your husband Martin the deer skin he wanted and the two gallons of rum he wanted for Captain Service. I've a good fox hide and marten hide that Severinus Casselman brought in. Is Martin interested?"

"We've no need for skins now. Thank you Jelles."

As Margaret and Catrina waited, Samuel Runnions walked to the counter and ordered 1 ½ ells of white linen, 1 ell of red stroud, and a plough share.

As Jelles' Negro lifted the plough share onto the counter right in front of Henry Hough, Jelles took Henry's order for two gallons of rum and asked, "Did you get the two cows delivered to Martin Van Alstyne? 'T'is a task to get them across the Mohawk River and down the rough road to Canajoharie."

"Aye. They're delivered some time past."[377]

Curious and uneasy, Philip asked Jelles and Henry, "There've been hundreds of Indians at Johnson Hall since the beginning of August. What is their business with Sir William? Is it of concern to us?"

Henry answered, "In July, Sir William held an Indian congress with many Nations at German Flats. Colonel Claus, Colonel Guy Johnson, Lieutenant Colonel John Butler, Hans Jost Herkimer, and others from German Flats attended. The congress lasted one month. Near two thousand attended from many Nations. After the congress, many of the Indians came to Johnson Hall to meet with Sir William. There's no alarm. 'T'is usual for Sir William to ensure the covenant chain with the Six Nations remains unbroken and that their concerns are heard."[378]

"Sir William ha'n't a moment to himself these past few months. Just a few months ago, Reverend Charles Inglis, from Trinity Church in New York City, visited Johnson Hall to discuss the history, character, traditions, and moral and spiritual qualities of the Six Nations Peoples. Reverend Inglis is to publish a book to memorialize the Indians. He's come to the only man I know who has complete knowledge of these things and a close relationship with Six Nations People. I saw the map of Indian country that Sir William drew for the book. 'T'is the most detailed map I've ever seen."[379]

Jelles nodded, "'T'is true. For thirty years, Sir William has been everywhere in this country many times. He knows the Indians like no other white man."

Philip raised his eyebrows and took a long drag of his pipe, "I sha'n't argue with that Jelles. We see so many Indians pass along the roads and their old paths, and their canoes travel the river all the time. Their trade aids all. I only worry when there's news of discord and threats of uprising or war. Many of us remember the horror of the past war and look to actions for any problems that prevent a recurrence of those times."

September brought mild weather and colour to the valley. But, most tenants only paid attention if rain came. They were too busy to notice that the fall fair would soon be upon them, except for Jacob Myers, Jacob Sheets, and George Cough. These men had extra work with which to attend. Early in the year, the tenants at Philadelphia Bush hired Christian Furtenback, a school teacher, who created much tension and discord among the settlement. In fact, the relationship between the teacher and some of the inhabitants got violent. The wives of some tenants beat the teacher until he was disabled and couldn't attend school. He demanded his pay for the entire six months, of which he only taught four. The tenants couldn't afford this, and they objected to the fact that he wanted pay without work and that their children would be without schooling. There'd be no time to find and hire another school teacher before harvest was finished, and they couldn't spare the children's help at harvest. The three men wrote a letter to Sir William for advice on how to solve their problem as they were poor and not litigious.[380]

Jacob Henry Alguire's troubles at Philadelphia Bush were still bothering him at the fall fair. Philip and Catrina arrived at Johnson Hall with Martin, Peter, Johannes, Anna Margaret, and Dorothy. Mattheus was coming later with Sebastian Alguire and his wife Anna Barbara. Philip and Catrina invited Jacob Henry and Salome to come and sit with them while they watched the musicians play. The noise of the trumpet seemed to agitate Jacob, but soon there was more soothing music with guitars, flutes, violins, and an Irish harp. Jacob Henry was impressed when he heard Peter Johnson, Sir William and Molly Brant's son, play the violin. Jacob Henry even started to smile when he heard the Irish pipes.

Of course, there were the usual games and competitions. This year, there was a horse race where the riders were mounted backwards. Mattheus raced Scout again and did well. Anna Margaret wanted her mama to be in the sack race with her. Catrina knew Philip would chuckle as he watched her hop along with both feet inside a sack. Anna Margaret thought it was the greatest fun, and Dorothy couldn't stop giggling as she sat on Philip's lap.

Just as the sack race ended, Dorothy threw her arm toward the Hall, pointed and said, "Papa look at that chicken! It's so big. Its feathers Papa, there're huge and so colourful!"

"That's a peacock Dorothy!" he said while he laughed and wrapped Dorothy in his arms. "Sir William brought it from England."[381]

"Can we have one Papa? We'll have coloured eggs!"

There were many things for Dorothy to gawk at and many children her age with whom to play. Anna Margaret Silmser, Godfrey Shew, George and Elizabeth Gallinger, Anna and Jacob Link, Margaret and Catherine Service, and Eve and John Waldorf were all there. As the sun got low on the horizon, the family slowly made their way to the wagon. Apple and Bess pulled the wagon down William Street, and as they turned onto Montgomery Street, Dorothy and Anna Margaret were asleep.

Even as the snow fell early in December, events at the fair were recalled at many meals and around the fireplace in the evenings. 1770 was another good year for Catrina and Philip. Their crops of wheat and corn were good, and they always had plenty of food in the root cellar and in the cellar of the house. They were grateful for their blessings, but most decidedly, they were grateful for six healthy children in the house, two married daughters settled on their land with good husbands to look after them, and two strong and beautiful grandchildren.

The month of January 1771 lingered under the relentless snow and cold winds. The days were long, but daylight wasn't. As during most winters, the family spent most of their time inside occupied with sewing, mending, spinning, and knitting, or repairing fishing rods, haversacks, cartridge boxes, or sharpening knives and hatchets. Two outings took the family to the Reformed Dutch Church at Stone Raby. On January 6th they attended the wedding of Barent Frederick, son of Peter Frederick and George Schenck's daughter Dorothy Schenck. Again, on January 27th they made their way to Stone Raby for the baptism of several children whose parents lived across the river from German Flats near Fort Herkimer.[382]

Sitting comfortably in the sleigh snuggled under bear skins, they followed the road south to Caughnawaga and then west to Stone Arabia. Reverend Abraham Rosencrantz greeted everyone as they entered the church. Philip and Catrina took their place in a pew at the side of the church. Right away Catrina noticed several prominent settlers and officers in the militia. Many of these prominent settlers came to German Flats with the first Palatine settlers in 1730. Catrina saw Major Peter Ten Broeck and his wife Anna. They were sitting with Nicholas Herkimer Jr. and his wife Maria who were to sponsor Major Ten Broeck's son Johannes Nicholas. Sitting next to Nicholas Herkimer Jr. was his brother Captain Hans Jost Herkimer Jr. and his wife Maria. Nicholas and Jost were the sons of Colonel Hans Jost Herkimer Sr., commander of the 5th Regiment of militia. Nicholas Herkimer and his wife Maria were to sponsor Captain Herkimer's son Nicholas. There was also, Philip Frederick Helmer, the son of George Frederick Helmer, baptizing his daughter Anna Barbara, and Dieterich Wolleben, the son of Johannes Nicholas Wolleban, baptizing his daughter Kunigunda.[383]

After the service, Philip and Catrina enjoyed visiting with friends and neighbours. Johannes Dorn was there with all his sons, Johannes Jr., Jacob, Peter, David, and Jeremiah. Philip and Johannes spent a while talking about their fall hunting trips. Johannes had gone out with all his boys and brought home two deer that he traded at Fonda's store.[384] They talked about how fast the town was growing and how much traffic there was on the roads. Johannes saw James Davis and his brother Isaac Davis three times with loads of boards heading north to Sir William's Fish House on the Sacandaga River. Johannes wasn't sure what Sir William was building or repairing. And, he often saw Samuel Runnions collecting tenants' ashes and taking them to Fonda's store. Sometimes, he had almost twenty five schipples.[385] Philip said he'd heard talk that a Court House and Jail were to be built in Johnstown. On their way home, Philip and Catrina revisited the many things they saw and all the conversations they'd had.

Catrina wasn't surprised when she'd learned the family would make another trip to the church next week. After the loss of his wife, Sebastian Alguire was to remarry on February 5th. His bride was Christina Kuhlman, the daughter of Philip Kuhlman Sr. of Albany Bush.[386] In a few months, Philip and Catrina attended a different kind of service. Christian Casselman, Henry Koch, Johannes Empey, and Johannes Dorn Jr. were to be confirmed.

A more important event occurred for Philip and Catrina only two days after the service at the Reformed Dutch Church. On January 29th they travelled to the Lutheran Trinity Church at Stone Raby for the baptism of their third grandchild, Elizabeth Margaret Myers, daughter of Michael Myers and Elizabeth Eamer. Martin Silmser and his wife were her sponsors. And, they learned that Catharina and Martin Alguire were expecting their second child in December.[387]

Not too long into February, several men from the Kingsborough area celebrated as they became naturalized citizens of New York. On February 15th, they'd made the trip to Albany that so many made in the last few decades. They paid their fees, took the oaths, and heard the bell in the steeple ring as they left city hall. Those who celebrated were: Jacob Crieghoof, Martin Silmser, Philip Kuhlman Jr., Martin Loefler Jr., Daniel Fykes, William Schuman, Michael Myers, Christian Sheek, George Schenck Jr., Jacob Waggoner Sr., and Godfrey Eny.[388]

During March 1771, construction began on a bigger Episcopal Church in Johnstown. The original St John's Church built in 1761 could not accommodate all the settlers of the growing community.[389] Tenants of the Kingsborough, Sacandaga, and the new Mayfield Patent still found themselves travelling to churches at Stone Raby and Caughnawaga for their spiritual needs. Many of the tenants and their sons worked long hours digging the foundation, hauling soil, stone, logging and sawing timber, and framing a church that could hold '1000 souls'. On their way to school, the children were often late because they stopped to watch the men work.

Amidst the building of the church, there were always spring chores to be done. One of the most challenging chores was shearing sheep. Philip had several lambs and ewes to shear. Knowing this was a good day for everyone to be out shearing, Mattheus, Martin, Peter, and Johannes were up early.

After a few mouthfuls of breakfast and wanting the day to be organized, Peter said, "Whose going to hold and whose going to shear? We all know that Mattheus has the job of washing."

Martin answered, "Well, our good brothers-in-law Martin Alguire and Michael Myers will be there. They can help wash. Papa'll shear."

Rubbing his chin, Peter said, "I hope the corral we put up by the creek holds them all. When Mr. Gallinger and his sons Christopher Gallinger and Michael Gallinger Jr. drove their sheep here yesterday, the corral held. Maybe they can wash?"

"The corral'll hold fine while we wash and shear. Mr. Gallinger can help Papa shear."

"Martin Alguire will surely love the wool to weave."

"Maybe Mama'll make a quilt with some of the batting, or Anna Margaret can make some nice soft lambswool socks!"

The jobs of church building and shearing lasted well into April 1771, then it was time to plough and plant. One morning, mid-May, Philip drove to George Crites' to deliver some wool he wanted woven into rugs. Being so close to Anthony Walliser, John Farlinger, and Michael Gallinger, he paid them a visit. When he got to Michael's farm, he stopped long enough for a bit of rum.

Michael met him as he rolled down the lane. "Good day friend. How does Catrina and your grandchildren?"

"All are well this day. Catrina and I often go to see little Maria Salome, little Philip, and our newest granddaughter Elizabeth Margaret."

"Aye. Proud grandparents ye are."

While the two men shared bread and cheese and a gill of rum, they talked about local happenings. Michael sat back in his chair telling Philip about his trip to Jan Baptiste Van Eps, a merchant in Schenectady. "Johannes Richtmeyer is bringing a bateau load of goods from Mr. Van Eps to Fonda's store for Sir William, and I brought back Sir William's post, some glue, and six pairs of worsted stockings for his children. Riding post to Schenectady takes me a full day, but the pay is worth the time. Last year, I was paid £8. I've ridden forty seven times."[390]

"I'm glad to see 't'is good business for you."

"Aye. There's good business for all along the river. There're so many boats on the river as soon as the ice is gone."

"I've heard many talk of wanting our own county with local men representing us."

"There are inconveniences being so remote from the county seat. 'T'is why there's talk of a Court House."

All the tradesmen and farmers kept busy through the summer keeping up with the demands of providing for their families, making a bit of profit from their grain, corn, fruit, wool, and meat, and ensuring there was enough food and wood put away for winter. Although they did hear about rumblings in other colonies about tensions with the British government and its representatives, arguments and tension in the valley among tenants was not their greatest concern. Tradesmen and farmers enjoyed the opportunities that peace provided. Too many remembered the horrors of the frontier war with the French. Their greatest concern came whenever large groups of Indians came to Johnson Hall.[391]

Tensions and alarm rose in August when about 350 Indians came to Johnson Hall for a conference with Sir William. There had been trouble in the south with the Shawnee and Delaware Indians and Sir William wanted to confirm that there was peace among the Six Nations and reaffirm the Confederacy's friendship with the British.[392] Philip knew there was also trouble north in Canada. He had talked to William Philips Jr. at the grist mill. William told him that his Uncle Philip Philips, brother of William Philip's Sr., had been to Montreal about nine times as an interpreter. And, he was told that Daniel Claus, Sir William's son-in-law and Deputy Secretary of Northern Indian Affairs, was having troubles with the Indians in Canada.[393] All of this made Philip more alert whenever he was on the roads or in the fields. He made sure Catharina and Martin and Elizabeth and Michael knew of the troubles and that they had all they needed to be safe.

Philip's worry continued through the fall harvest well into November until the focus of his and other tenants' attention turned toward creating a new county. After not hearing a reply from their first petition to the General Assembly at Albany, Sir William spread news by way of the Town Crier at Johnstown and Caughnawaga that tenants could sign a second petition. This second petition not only requested the creation of the county, but it also offered alterations in the proposed county boundaries and requested Johnstown as the county seat. These new boundaries spanned across the Mohawk Branch of the Delware River, parts of the Susquehanna River, the Mohawk River, and west of the Schoharie River. In addition to Philip, Lewis Clement, William Nelles Sr., Jelles Fonda, Henry Frey, Christian Sheek, John Wells, Gilbert Tice, Goshen and Martin Van Alstyne, Jacob Eberhard Van Koughnot, Peter Service Jr., Martin Loefler Jr., Philip Kuhlman Sr., James Davis, Marcus Reese and many more signed the petition.[394]

Sir William wasn't the only one with grand visions for Johnstown and the new county. A Mr. John Cottgrave was staying in Johnstown and had a private conversation with Thomas Flood about his grand designs for the town. He asked Thomas to keep the plans he was about to tell him a secret before he proceeded to describe alterations to the church and the building of a new free school. He also described his desire to buy Michael Gallinger's farm so that he could divide it into lots and bring in new 'refined' settlers of his choosing. He also wanted to purchase a large piece of land on the Sacandaga patent and build a new store. All of his ambitious ideas began with his dislike of boarding at Tice's tavern and having to tolerate the roaming peacock. His ideas arose from beliefs the tenants and their children were lazy, poor, crude, and desperately needing refinement. He believed the inhabitants' "vice arrived at perfection".[395]

After the tension of anticipating an Indian attack during the summer and fall and waiting for word on the petition for a new county, Philip was glad of the stillness of winter. Of course there were Christmas festivities to look forward to, but the birth of his fourth grandchild was most on his mind. Near the end of December, Catharina and Martin Alguire welcomed a healthy baby boy whom they named Philip Alguire. It was early on a Friday afternoon when the Eamer, Alguire, and Myers families met at the Lutheran Trinity Church at Stone Raby. Throughout the baptism, the Reverend Theophilus Engeland kept everyone's attention except Catrina and Philip. Their gaze was constant as they smiled with their chins up watching Catharina and Martin hold their little boy. As sponsors, Mattheus Eamer and Sophia Alguire were a fine looking pair standing beside them.[396] For two years, there was much change for Philip and Catrina. Even with a few less people in the house, they were still needed, sometimes much more than past years. Their time was well spent and rewarded with many happy moments.

Spring came early in 1772. Near the end of February, heavy rain and winds caused water in the Mohawk River to rise and ice to break up causing severe jams.[397] Wherever it could, water ran fast or it just flooded the plains. It was a dangerous time near the river and connecting creeks.

Late in February, after their morning meal, Mattheus, standing near the front door, collected his musket and shot bag and turned to Catrina, "I should be home by mid-day Mama. I'm meeting Martin Loefler Jr., and we're heading toward Tribes Hill to hunt."

Catrina handed him some biscuits and cheese and said, "A good hunting day to you son. I'll expect you home this afternoon."

Mattheus met Martin Loefler Jr. near the road to Tribes Hill. They headed south towards the river. It was a warm but windy day with rain that came and went as they walked. About 1 ½ kilometres from the river, Mattheus and Martin met Lewis' son John Clement, William Bowen Jr., and the Putnam brothers Peter, Garrett, and Victor Putnam. They walked along the King's Highway toward Fort Johnson and then headed north along Kayaderosseras Creek. As they walked, Peter Putnam said, "Let's move away from the shore of the creek. 'T'is slippery and the water is fast. Mind the brush hanging low."

Just as Mattheus turned toward the forest, he slipped and fell backward into the creek. He struggled and slipped on the rocks. The fast water pulled him farther into the creek. Martin turned to grab Mattheus, but couldn't grip his coat. The boys ran along the creek following Mattheus as far as they could. Martin Loefler Jr. hollered, "Faster boys, we must catch him! Lord help us! I can't see him!" The boys followed the creek south and reached its mouth at the river. They searched along both shores. Finally, they saw Mattheus' body caught in the willows on the edge of the river. Martin turned to Garrett and said, I'm going for Mr. Eamer and Martin and Peter. They'll help us."

Martin Loefler Jr. ran east and within ½ hour reached the Eamer farm. With little breath left, he hollered, "Mr Eamer quick, come quick!"

Hearing Martin, Philip ran from the barn, "What trouble Martin?"

"'T'is Mattheus. He's fallen into the creek and taken into the river!"

Philip hitched Apple to the wagon and, with Martin Loefler Jr., Martin, Peter, and Johannes in the back, raced down Tribes Hill road. As they reached the shore, Philip leapt out of the wagon toward Mattheus. Holding his son's wet, cold body, he shook him calling, "Mattheus! Mattheus wake son, wake!" There was no movement, no breath from the body. Philip held him close, rocking and sobbing, "My son! Mattheus!"[398]

Martin, Peter, and Johannes wrenched their brother from their papa's arms and lifted his body into the wagon. The ride back to the farm was like rolling through fog in a bad dream. Martin, Peter, and Johannes wept and moaned as they sat close to their brother. Apple pulled the wagon without any direction while Philip just sat with a glazed stare.

Catrina, Anna Margaret, and Dorothy ran from the house grabbing the sides of the wagon as it rolled toward the barn. Catrina's knees buckled as she followed the wagon. Tripping and grasping, she wailed, "My son! My son!" Mattheus was laid in a bed of straw. Kneeling next to him, Catrina stroked her son's hair and gripped his lifeless hand. Philip knelt too. And, while lifting his hands to his head, he pulled at his hair as his hands ran over his head. He rocked and sobbed. Anna Margaret and Dorothy sat close to their papa. Soon, their moans drenched the barn. Peter saddled Bess and rode to fetch Martin Alguire and tell Elizabeth of the accident. Martin and Johannes headed north on foot to fetch Michael Myers and tell Catharina.

It was the end of March 1772 when Catrina was walking among the cherry and apple trees with their thousands of blossoms placing a sweet scent against her weary face. As she walked, Catrina's empty gaze didn't rest on anything in particular.

Philip met her as she reached the edge of the orchard and said, "Are you to visit our son?"

"Aye. I want to speak to him and our Lord."

They walked together toward the oak trees and sat beside the graves of Mattheus and little Philip. With her head low and with soft eyes Catrina said, "He rests with his brother. He was a fine man and to be even finer yet with years taken from him. I thought he might choose Sophia Alguire as his bride. They'd've lived a long life together with many children. Why Philip? Why?"

"'T'will never be an answer. Our hearts break and so does Sophia's heart. Jacob Alguire and Salome tell me Sophia says little and eats less. We'll keep him in our hearts till we meet our Lord."

Catrina and Philip worked hard through March and April looking for any chore that would keep them busy. In fact, they were so occupied that news of the new county came and went without much attention. With about 10,000 inhabitants, the new county was to be called Tryon County, after New York's Governor William Tryon. Johnstown was declared the county seat. The boundaries were laid out, and new districts created. The districts were: Mohawk, Stone Arabia, Canajoharie, Kingsland, and German Flats. Each year on the first Tuesday in April, inhabitants of each district were to elect two tax assessors, one tax collector, two overseers of the poor, two fence viewers, two constables, and a clerk. Justices for each district were appointed, a County Sheriff was chosen, and Dr. William Adams was appointed Coroner.[399]

The first week of May, Michael and Agatha Gallinger came by to visit Catrina and Philip. They hadn't seen them at the St. Patrick's Day celebrations at Johnson Hall. They worried. They brought two goslings from their stock hoping that the babies would keep Anna Margaret and Dorothy smiling and occupied since the loss of their brother. Agatha helped the children fix a shelter for the fluffy white goslings and left them to play and went into the house to join Michael, Catrina, and Philip. Michael was sitting near the fire with Philip talking about his recent trip to Albany. Agatha heard him say, "I was riding post to Albany for Sir William. For my return trip, Mr. John Monier, the Postmaster, gave me letters and some advertisements that Mayor Abraham Ten Broeck wanted posted at various places along the Mohawk River.[400] 'T'is a long ride that takes about six hours down the King's Highway and over dry dusty lands past Schenectady. But, I've a good horse who has a steady trot."

Philip asked, "What news is there in Albany of the quarrels with the British?"

"Men still argue at any taverns I visit from here to Albany. For now, there're hot exchanges, but 'tain't violent. But, Albany has a new newspaper called the Albany Gazette, 'T'is written that in Boston there are plans to organize the 'Sons of Liberty' and other colonists to commence town meetings. I expect like- minded colonists and their leaders will share grievances and communicate news of resistance to British tax and oppression. 'T'is certain these ideas of town meetings will spread."

Fig. 29. Johnstown Court House. From Max Reid, The Mohawk Valley. Its legends and its history. 215. Photographs by J. Arthur Maney Courtesy of Flickr Commons.

"Aye. We must hope that grievances are resolved peacefully before talk turns violent and spreads into our valley."

"Sir William believes there's a good chance of war, at least in the south and the east. For us, he worries that confusion and uncertainty will agitate the Indians."[401]

Michael and Philip sat silent for a few minutes smoking their pipes. Then Michael said, "Our new Governor is to organize a new militia in the valley. He's to visit in July to celebrate the creation of our new county and inspect the militia.

By then the new Court House should be finished."[402] Our Judges have been appointed. They are: Colonel Guy Johnson, Lieutenant Colonel John Butler, Ensign Peter Coyne, and Lieutenant Colonel Henry Frey. Assistant Judges are: Sir John Johnson, Colonel Daniel Claus, Major Jelles Fonda, and Major John Wells. Our Justices of the Peace are: Peter Ten Broeck, Hans Jost Herkimer Jr., Conrad Frank, and Henry Frey Jr. Esq. And, I hear a new Sheriff is coming from New York City. His name is Alexander White. Apparently, he was in command of Fort Herkimer in 1764, so he knows our valley well."[403]

After a long drag of his pipe Philip asked, "What is there of local news?"

"With the creation of our new county, we have new Highway Commissioners and new highway laws as of March, 1772. Commissioners for the Mohawk District are: Sir William Johnson, Sir John Johnson, Lieutenant Colonel John Butler, Ensign Peter Coyne, and Major Jelles Fonda. For the District of Stone Raby they are: Severinus Deygert, Arent Brower, Adam Loucks, George Coppernol, and Henry Merckle. Some of the highway laws are what they've always been, but there are a few new laws: The Highway Commissioners are to hire an overseer who is sober, discreet, and capable. And, they're to create a list of inhabitants for their districts and assign a quota of days we're obliged to work on the highways and the tax we must pay toward maintaining our roads. The lists and quotas will be posted at Tice's tavern and Fonda's store. If you provide a sleigh, wagon, cart, horses, or oxen, you're credited with three day's work. If anyone refuses to work, they'll be fined ten shillings, or their goods, worth ten shillings, will be confiscated and sold. And, no one under the age of sixteen is allowed to work. No one is allowed to alter roads or place gates to block any road. If you want to take a shortcut, you're not allowed to go through any private gates onto private land. And, if one of your trees falls on the road, you've forty eight hours to remove it. If you don't, they'll fine you ten shillings.[404.] So, it seems we've much to pay attention to regarding our roads. I've seen the list and quotas posted at Tice's tavern. Your name is on it Philip. You must pay one shilling, six pence tax, and you're to work four days. Other names I saw were: Johannes Clement and Lewis Clement, Martin Loefler Sr., Johannes Wert, Andrew Snyder, Johannes Dorn, and Johannes Albrant, James Davis, and Captain Peter Service Sr..[405] Happier news is that Sir William ordered the bell and organ for the church. I expect we'll hear that bell ring, and we'll sing to the tune of organ pipes next year."[406]

It wasn't long before Philip worked a day off his quota for 1772. With young Peter, he drove the wagon into town to help fill ruts along Sacandaga Road and William Street. Peter came along because David Jeacocks had met Philip at Fonda's store while he was picking up one gallon of rum for the men at Sir William's lime kiln.[407] David asked if any of Philip's sons were interested in learning to make lime.

Philip and Peter arrived at St. John's Church where John P. Service and his brother Peter Service Jr., George Crites, Lawrence Eaman and Philip Hendrick Klein had already started working. Peter took his haversack from the back of the wagon and walked west on Sacandaga Road towards the lime kiln. He waved and said, "I'll be back mid-afternoon Papa."

As the men dug and raked filling ruts and potholes, they talked about the sheep and horses Sir William brought to the valley. George Crites said, "There's a new family at the Sacandaga Patent on the eastern edge of Kingsborough Patent close to Joseph Hanes and Jacob Sheets. They're the Cryderman family, Valentine Cryderman and his wife Catherine and seven boys and three girls! For certain, a big family. They come from Livingston's lands on the east side of the Hudson River south of Albany. Valentine has 120 acres, and he's started to clear.[408] He's talking about raising sheep."

Peter Service nodded, "He's in a good place near Jacob Sheets. Jacob's got about thirty sheep."

Just as the men were finishing at the south end of William Street, they saw Peter Eamer walking past the Court House. As he reached the men, he threw down his haversack, slumped to the ground, and let out a groan saying, "'T'is hard work making lime. We spent hours breaking limestone and heaving it into the kiln. Mr. Jeacocks was there with his sons Francis Jeacocks, David Jeacocks Jr., and Johannes Jeacocks, and Mr. Flood didn't miss a chance to be severe with Sir William's Negroes. They were working the same as everyone, but Mr. Flood didn't seem to think so. Mr. Philip Empey Sr. sons, William, Philip Jr., and Adam were there too with Mr. Empey's Negroes. Peter laid back in the grass and said, I believe one earns the good money paid for lime."

Philip handed Peter his canteen of water and said, "You look worn son."

"I'll be much mended after a good meal Papa."

Near the end of June, Catrina was in the kitchen mending Philip's linen shirt and his oznabrig trousers. While Catrina mended, Philip started to clean his firelock. After a few minutes, he set down his firelock, lit his pipe and said, "I expect most of the men in the valley sha'n't forget to spend time preparing for Sir William's celebration of the new county, Court House, and Governor William Tryon's visit. I hear the Governor is to inspect the regiments at Johnstown and German Flats."[409]

Catrina nodded saying, "You know there'll be hundreds of people there. Not just tenants, but Sir William's family, soldiers, distinguished people of the valley, and of course Indians from many Nations. I think that's what's getting the children excited. They look forward to the fancy carriages, uniforms, dresses, and eating lots of food. I know 't'isn't the speeches."

As Philip polished the wood on his firelock, he said, "I hope there's no trouble with the King's representative and the King's soldiers. Seems like a perfect opportunity for those who support the cause of liberty to voice their opinions, or worse to place their opinions at the end of a fist."

Catrina examined the buttons on Philip's shirt, shook her head and said, "There'll be many there to keep the peace. I'm more worried about someone bringing smallpox to the village. I hear they're inoculating about fifty Indian children soon, I hope before the gathering."[410]

Late in the morning on 26 June 1772, Philip turned Apple and Bess onto Montgomery Street. They hadn't even reached the building site for the new jail when Philip pulled back on the reins, "Whoa! We sha'n't be getting to the Hall quickly. It seems everyone in the valley is going that way. I've never seen so many wagons. Let's go north on Glebe Street and see if we can move along."

"There're not just wagons Philip. There are so many people walking that way. I see tenants from Butlersbury and Albany Bush. Look ahead of us. I'm sure those are groups of Cayuga, Seneca, and Onondaga. They've come a long way. I don't see any Oneida yet."

Philip and Catrina, Anna Margaret, Dorothy, Martin, Peter, and Johannes finally crossed the bridge over Cayudatta Creek and rolled down William Street to the Hall. As Philip pulled the wagon under a willow tree, Catrina said, "Look! Over there. I see Martin and Catharina with Maria Salome and Philip, and there are Michael and Elizabeth with little Philip and Elizabeth Margaret. Once the family wound their way through the crowd to the back of the Hall, they faced a bigger crowd. Tables loaded with food and drink were set up at one end of the

Hall. From the Hall, waving over the crowd, were two striking red, white, and blue British flags and one that fluttered at the top of a pole.

Catrina caught Anna Margaret's and Dorothy's attention and pointed to the flags, "Look, aren't they beautiful on Sir William's grand hall."

Philip turned to Catrina and whispered, "Just keep an eye out for a flag with 13 horizontal red stripes. If you see one, there's likely to be trouble. 'T'is the flag of the 'Sons of Liberty.'"

The family found a place away from the crowd to sit and listen to the speeches and watch the festivities. Martin Silmser and Elizabeth Margaretha, Jacob Henry Alguire and Maria Salome, Jacob Myers, and Johannes Alguire Sr. and Catherine Margaret sat with them.

Before lunch and the speeches, Catrina pointed out more dignitaries and prominent people. There were more than she'd seen at any other event. She saw Nicholas Herkimer Sr., Lieutenant Colonel Hans Jost Herkimer and his brothers Henry, Nicholas Jr., and Captain George. From Bultersbury were Lieutenant Colonel John Butler and Ensign Walter Butler, Philip Hendrick Klein, and Henry Hart. There were Gideon Marlet and Samuel Runnions from Fort Hunter and Lieutenant Colonel Henry Frey from Canajoharie. And, there were many she saw, but didn't know.

With Elizabeth Margaret on her lap, Elizabeth tapped Catrina's knee and said, "Look over there Mama. I saw that man arrive in a large coach with his wife and two Negroes. Catharina tells me that is Mr. Philip Schuyler, a government assemblyman from Albany. And, the gentleman with the white wig and gold braided tricorn I'm told 't'is Mr. Robert Livingston; he's a Judge who lives along the Hudson River in a grand house."

Touching her sister's shoulder, Catharina said, "I see Captain Peter Bellinger and Lieutenant Frederick Fisher. Oh, look over there. 'T'is Joseph Brant talking to Molly Johnson. They're with Chief Steyawa, the great Mohawk Sachem and King Hendrick's brother. Papa tells me King Hendrick was a great leader, a peaceful man full of honour. He died the year we arrived in America. And over there, I see Tiagoansera (Little Abraham), son of King Hendrick's brother Abraham. I'll tell Martin and Peter, they'll be glad to know he's here."

Elizabeth pointed towards the back door of the Hall, "Look. Martin and Peter are there talking to Major Jelles Fonda. They're beside Sir John Johnson, Colonel Guy Johnson, and Colonel Daniel Claus. It seems most of Sir William's family are here."[411]

Conversations that started at the celebration continued through fall and into winter. The talk varied from how many new buildings and roads were needed to guesses about when the brick Court House and the stone jail would be finished. Finally many tried to guess how many new settlers would come to Johnstown. Some said they'd come from the New England colonies others said there'd be more coming from Germany. Sometimes the talk turned to arguments about what kinds of businesses yielded the best profits. Consistently though, there was talk about politics, taxes, and liberty. The talk often got loud and was punctuated with an occasional scuffle and a lot of bitter feelings. Even with rising tensions and bitter feelings, many of the prominent citizens of the valley remained committed to their new county and seemed to support the Protestant faith and the government of King George. They demonstrated this support when, in December 1772, they signed an Oath of Allegiance.[412]

Early in February, the overseer of roads called out several tenants to clear snow from the streets in Johnstown. Philip was one of those called. He knew he must go because a new law meant a fine of ten shillings for every day he refused to oblige.[413]

As he left the house to hitch Apple and Bess to the sleigh, he turned to the stairs and called out, "Martin, Peter, we've to go clear the roads of snow. Come now with your muskets. You can hunt wolves this afternoon."

Martin and Peter were halfway down the stairs when Peter answered, "We sha'n't miss a chance to collect a bounty on wolves; there's a reward of twenty shillings for an adult wolf or fifteen for one under a year! We've only to go before Justice Henry Frey and, in front of him, cut off the ears of the wolves. After that deed, he'll give us a certificate."[414]

Along the Tribes Hill road to Johnstown, Philip heard his sons talk about their schemes for hunting wolves and means of keeping their powder dry if it snowed. As they rode onto Montgomery Street, they passed a group of men working on the Jail. Martin pointed to the thick stone walls and said, "I hear the walls are four feet thick and that Sir William is hiring more men to quarry the stone and haul it from Mr. Fonda's quarry, and they need to haul stone to make lime. Mr. Henry Merckle and Mr. Adam Loucks are organizing the sleighs."

Philip blew a sigh and said, "May'n't be enough sleighs son. Men from all the districts are coming to haul next week. They also need 3000 bushels of sand. They've organized forty sleighs every day for ten days from each district in the county. I'm certain the cost is rising."[415] And, there's still work to be done on the

Court House, but I think they've hauled all the bricks needed. I'm hauling for one day from Caughnawaga to Johnstown."

Fig. 30. Johnstown Jail. From Max Reid, The Mohawk Valley. Its legends and its history. 207. Photographs by J. Arthur Maney Courtesy of Flickr Commons.

Martin and Peter brought stories of hunting wolves to tell at the family's evening meal, and Philip brought home news that Domine Romine, pastor of the Reformed Dutch Church at Caughnawaga, married Sebastian Alguire to his third wife Maria Weaver.[416] His second wife, Christina Kuhlman died after only two years of marriage.

While finishing his ham stew, Philip continued the conversation, "I think I'll buy two head of horned cattle from either Jacob Waggoner or George Bender, both of Kingsborough Patent. 'T'was good listening to the men talk about their cattle while clearing snow today. It sounded like each of them have fine stock.[417] But, my visit to Waggoner will have to wait until mid-March as several men from these parts are going to Albany to receive their naturalization certificates."

"Is it a long journey to Albany Papa?"

"Aye Johannes. 'T'is a day's ride. The men stay at an Inn and then come home the next day."

"In what Inn do they stay?"

"There're many in Albany. They all have signs on the front door, and they choose the one they want."

"Are they nice Papa?"

"Aye. 'T'is the law that Innkeepers must have feed for the horses, a good feather bed, food, and always something to drink. Sometimes, there's singing or music."[418]

On 8 March 1773, men from the Kingsborough and Sacandaga area made the trip to Albany and received their naturalization certificates. Some of these men were: Michael Cline, Michael Warner, Henry Hawn Jr., Jacob Waggoner, George Schenck Jr., Michael Carman Jr., Jacob Sheets, Jost, John, and George Cough, and Balthasar Breitenbucher.[419]

Just after the men received their naturalization certificates, even more settlers came. Andrew Millross, a carpenter from Durham, England, leased 100 acres at Salmon Bush on the Kingsborough Patent, and David McEwan, an Irish farmer, settled on 100 acres on the Kingsborough Patent[420] But, the greatest influx of settlers in 1773 came when a group of Scottish Highlanders arrived near the end of May. The Clan leaders of 425 Highlander men, women, and children were: John MacDonnel of Leek, Allan MacDonnel of Collachie, Alexander MacDonnel of Aberchalder, John MacDonnel of Scotus, and their Catholic Priest Peter McKenna. Most of them leased 100 acre farms in the northeastern area of the Kingsborough Patent which became known as Scotch Bush.[421] Like the tenants of the Kingsborough Patent, the Scottish settlers knew the hardships of war and were frontier farmers. Unlike the Kingsborough tenants, they were Roman Catholic, and they spoke Gaelic. These differences gave purpose to nurturing their own Gaelic community under the patronage of Sir William. Their Gaelic roots appealed to Sir William and helped shape their strong relationship.

One afternoon at the end of June, Philip met several of the Scottish settlers. Philip was at Fonda's store getting salt, sugar, and tea for Catrina when a group of Scotsmen came into the store.

Philip tipped his black felt hat to one as he entered and said, "How do you do Sir."

"I'm well, Sir.'T'is a fine weather day."

Even with so few words, Philip noticed the man's lilting accent. It was pleasing to Philip's ear, but he thought it would be hard to follow if a few more words were spoken.

As Philip encountered the Scottish settler, one of Sir William's Negroes entered the store. Philip tipped his hat to the man and said, "Good day." He received a nod but no reply.

The Negro handed Jelles a piece of paper and said, "Please Sir. May I have six grass scythes and some oznabrig for Sir William?"[422]

While putting his items in a sack, Philip said to Jelles, "How is Sir William? Daniel Service tells me he hasn't been well."

"Aye. He's been away at the seaside to rest. His stomach plagues him constantly. Nothing seems to ease his sufferings not even the warm springs at Saratoga."[423]

"May'nt be a while before Sir William recovers. 'T'is harder for him with all the disturbance among the settlers. What news is there from the colonies?"

"'T'is no better. I see you bought tea. There's now a new Tea Act. Our tea merchants must buy their tea from the East India Company and still pay a tax. 'T'is not enough to tax our paper, lead, and glass. There're protests at ship yards across the colonies. Most are not buying tea."

"Aye. 'T'is the talk at Tice's tavern for certain. 'T'is also talk that one of Colonel Daniel Claus's Negroes is to be burned in a fortnight."

"Aye, a branding. For what crime I don't know."[424]

"There've been several who've spent time in the pillory at the new jail. One can see plainly as the wagons roll along Montgomery Street. 'T'is such horrid talk Jelles. I've better news."

"My new grandson John Alguire is to be baptized this week. Martin and Catharina welcomed him into this world only a few days ago. Everyone is well. We're blessed."[425] And, our blessings are greater! Catrina is with child and to deliver in December."

"That's good news. Am I correct? Your youngest Dorothy is about eight years now, and you've four grandchildren."

"'T'is true friend. How does your father Mr. Douwe Fonda and your sister Peggy and her husband Mr. Barney Wemple? I hope their Inn, tavern, and mill are providing well for them."

"Mr. Fonda is well. His milk cows keep him busy as does this store and our trade. The Inn and tavern are full most days, and there's always grain to grind."

"I must take my leave friend. A good day to you."

"And to you friend. I hope Catrina is well and that Jannetjie and I will see you at the spring fair."

"You'll see us this Tuesday. Since the new law passed this March there are regular fairs twice a year lasting three days, one in June and one in November."[426]

After days of work washing, shearing, and sorting wool, Philip, Martin, Peter, and Johannes loaded 130 lbs of fleece in the wagon. Catrina added a bushel of dried peas. Anna Margaret and Dorothy brought a basket of corn biscuits and three jugs of apple cider. Once at Johnson Hall, the Eamers sat with Martin and Elizabeth Margaret Silmser and their children, Christina Elizabeth Silmser, John Henry Silmser, Anna Maria Silmser, Nicholas Silmser, and Anna Margaret, and they sat with Johannes and Catherine Margaret Alguire and their children Johannes George, Johannes, Maria Elizabeth, Catherine, and Philip. It wasn't long before David Eny and Anna Maria joined them with their children Godfrey, Mary Margaret, Anna Maria, John, George, Jacob, Christine and little Jessie Eny. This crowd of adults and youngsters spent all day fussing over the newest babies, enjoying the games and entertainment, and making sure to describe all they knew of the most current happenings in the community. Of course Catrina and Philip's news of their baby due in December was a surprise for many. More surprises were that Christina Elizabeth Silmser was to marry John Chrysler son of Heronimus Chrysler of Vrooman's Land, and that Jacob Henry Alguire and Maria Salome announced that their daughter Anna Alguire was to marry David Jeacocks Jr. on the first of December.[427]

Lucas Feader Sr. and Jacob Myers soon joined the men in the group. As Lucas sat down next to Philip he said, "How does your crop of winter wheat Philip?"

"It fares well. We've had a good spring. How does your crop of tobacco?"

"It does well. I sowed my patch around stumps in a field just cleared. The seed is so fine I had to mix it with dirt or it just blew everywhere. I'll transplant the plants to the field when they're big enough. Mayn't get a good price for tobacco this year, prices are falling."

"Aye. Wheat brings the best price."

Jacob Myers added, "George Cough and I can't use a good portion of our land, and we don't want to pay rent while we improve another piece. We've asked Sir William to decrease our rent 'til we get a start on another piece of land.[428] We pay £9 per year and use only half our land, about sixty acres."

With a furrowed brow Philip said, "'T'is a lot for land not used. I pay £4 for seventy acres."[429]

Philip and his sons were busy through the summer tending the fields, orchard, hogs, sheep, and horses. Early fall was spent cutting wood, harvesting grain and apples, and selling a few pigs and sheep. Harvesting the garden kept Catrina, Anna Margaret, and Dorothy busy from sunrise to sunset. Despite her growing belly and the constant ache in her legs, Catrina spent many days in the summer kitchen cutting and boiling cabbage for the winter supply of sauerkraut. Anna Margaret and Dorothy brought fresh milk and helped their mama make cheese. Sometimes, Philip and Catrina went to Albany Bush to visit Martin, Catharina, and little Maria Salome, Philip, and John. Or, they'd go north to Philadelphia Bush and visit Michael, Elizabeth and little Philip and Elizabeth Margaret. It was during one visit in October that they learned Michael and Elizabeth were expecting another child in the spring.

One early morning in July, Philip was mending the shingles on the roof of the house. He noticed a man working in the field just south of their place. Philip decided to walk over and greet the man. He walked across the road and soon saw there was a woman working too. And, he noticed the man was wearing a kilt. "Hmm, he thought. "They must be of the Scottish group that just arrived."

He raised his hat to them and said, "Good day to you. I'm Philip Eamer your neighbour. As the man approached him, Philip recognized him as the man he'd seen at Fonda's store a few weeks ago.

"Good day Sir. I'm Angus McDonell and this is my wife Mary. We've just leased this land and started our improvements."[430]

"I remember those days. Now, there are daily proofs of satisfaction in our planting and improvements."

"Aye Sir. A puir man is fain o little."

Philip turned his ear toward Angus and thought, "Hmm, I think I hear something about poor and little." "My wife Catrina and our children will help any way we can. 'T'is good to have another family close.

The work continued late in October with several hunting trips and preparations for the fall fair. Philip decided to take a trip to Fonda's store before the snow fell. He needed rum, tobacco, salt, and two ells of stroud and two of linen for Catrina. He also had some wool to take to Samuel Runnions across the river. Philip could take Douwe Fonda's ferry at Caughnawaga to get to Samuel Runnion's farm. The river would be easier to cross all along the Mohawk River now that there was a law to establish and regulate eight ferries. Ferry operators must keep their ferries in good repair and not charge inhabitants ferriage beyond what the law indicates. If they neglected the regulations, they could be fined £5, half of which goes to the informant.[431] Philip also wanted to visit Jacob Rombaugh and William Bowen Sr. at Warrensburg. Once at Samuel Runnion's farm, Philip just had to cross the Schoharie River at Fort Hunter. The river was low now which made the crossing easy.

In just a few weeks, the Mohawk River was covered in ice and snow. Christmas was approaching and so was the birth of Philip and Catrina's tenth child. The family prepared for Christmas as they did each year, baking and making presents. Philip spent many hours carving toys for his five grandchildren, and Catrina spent as many hours knitting socks, mittens, and hats. She'd already sewn clothes for the coming infant and a down quilt for the cradle. She was glad she'd kept the cradle even though there were several times when she thought of giving it to Catharina and Elizabeth.

Very early on Christmas day after Catrina put the goose in the iron pot over the fire and mixed dough for dumplings, fatigue overtook her, and she went upstairs to their bedroom. One hour later the pains began. Anna Margaret sat with her while Philip hitched Bess to the sleigh and sped down the lane to get Agatha Gallinger. Early in the afternoon, Catrina gave birth to a boy.[432] She was exhausted. The baby was small with a frail cry. He could only suckle for a few minutes. She nursed him almost constantly.

Despite the fatigue, Catrina and Philip felt blessed this Christmas. Their many prayers that day and over the next few weeks were proof of their gratitude for the bounty in the lives and were proof of their concern for their son. They named him Jelles Eamer after their friend Major Jelles Fonda who, with his wife Jannetjie Vrooman, would be his sponsors. Because Catrina and little Jelles were weak and tired, his baptism at the Caughnawaga Reformed Dutch Church would not be until January 14th.

For the first week of January 1774, all of Catrina's energy was spent looking after Jelles. Anna Margaret and Dorothy did the cooking and housework while taking great care to be sure their mother had all she needed. A few afternoons, Catrina had enough strength to step outside the front door. She loved to feel the crisp, fresh air and a bit of sun on her face. One afternoon while standing at the door, one by one Philip, her boys, and Dorothy walked passed her toward the sleigh. They were going to the Caughnawaga church to the marriage of Johannes George Alguire, son of Johannes Alguire Sr. and Catherine Margaret, to Mary Margaret Eny, daughter of David Eny and Anna Maria Heuschmid.[433]

Even though Catrina would not attend, she knew there would be support for Johannes George and Mary Margaret. Many of their neighbours from

Philadelphia Bush would be there, the Myers, Carmans, Sheets, Coughs, Hanes, Reeses, and of course, Johannes George's sisters Maria Elizabeth and Catherine and his two brothers Johannes and Philip. Mary Margaret's brother Godfrey Eny would be there too.

Early in February after stopping at Fonda's store, Philip went to Barney Wemple's tavern. That day Philip Miller, Philip's friend and sponsor for his departed son Philip, was at the tavern with Anthony Van Vechten. So were all of William Casselman's sons, John, William Jr., Severinus, Warner, Conrad, and Frederick Casselman, and Christian Dillenbach's sons, Balthasar, Christian, Thomas, Martin, and Henry Dillenbach. Johannes Veeder and Catherine Mabie's sons Volkert, Simon, and Abraham were there too. It was a rowdy crowd so early in the afternoon.

Philip walked in and hung his blanket coat and beaver fur hat by the door and said, "Good day friends." As he sat next to Phillip Miller and Anthony Van Vechten, he ordered a tankard of beer. Philip glanced towards the fireplace and said, "It seems Severinus Koch and Rudolph Koch are heated over some topic. Their faces are apple red, and their voices are booming. Why are they so angry at the Casselmans?"

Philip Miller replied, "Balthasar Dillenbach and Warner Casselman raised their glasses to King George and cursed the 'Sons of Liberty' for disrespecting private property and destroying all that tea. He said they should go to jail for breaking the law."

"What tea?" Philip asked.

Anthony described the tea calamity, "Several weeks ago, hundreds of men dressed like Indians threw about 300 chests of tea belonging to the East India Company into the Boston harbour. The men were protesting Britain's tax on tea and the East India Company's monopoly on tea. Tea merchants in the colonies can't compete. With British support of the East India Company and the tax on tea, the British have gone too far! Tyrants they are."[434]

Taking his pipe out of his mouth, Philip answered, "These fights and protests are coming to close to our homes. Look how angry they get! 'T'is happening at Tice's, Frey's, Loucks, Shoemakers, and Nelle's taverns too, and at William Schuman's public house at Philadelphia Bush. There're uncertain and dangerous consequences to these disputes."

Philip Miller nodded, "Aye. Sir William says 'that a storm of civil unrest is gathering, and he fears a terrible war'. 'T'is still much worse in Boston."

As Rudolph Koch shoved Balthasar Dillenbach against the bar, Philip rose from his chair and walked to the door. "I must take my leave friends. Tempers are too hot. Commotion and trouble are rising."

The taverns were not the only place where there was commotion and trouble. During the first week of March, Gitty, the Negro slave of Johannes Nelles, set fire to Johannes' barn and was arrested and stood trial at the Court House. For what reason she lit the fire no one knew. On March 7th, Adam Loucks, Justice of the Peace, took her statement and heard her plea of not guilty. On March 11th, a trial was held before Justices Adam Loucks, John Butler, and Joseph Claus. Johannes Nelles, Jacob Klock, John Thompson, John Fonda, Peter Hanson, and Harmanus Smith were some of the prominent inhabitants called as witnesses. James Clow, a free Negro and one other Negro belonging to Johannes Nelles were also called. Henry Walradt was one witness called on behalf of Gitty. On March 28th, members of the Jury, John Thompson, Christian Sheek, William Bowen, and Peter Bowen found Gitty guilty and sentenced her to be burned until she was dead. This sentence was carried out on March 30th.[435]

Through March and April 1774 despite rising tensions everywhere, Philip planned the annual spring shearing, planted the spring crops, and tended to the lambs and piglets. Some of these animals he took to the market in June along with most of the sheeps' fleece. He helped Catrina as much as he could, but he depended on Anna Maragaret and Dorothy to help their mother. Catrina was finally gaining strength after Jelles' birth in December. Jelles was still weak, so Catrina nursed him as often as she could. By June, she had enough strength to attend the baptism of her newest grandson, but could not because Jelles was so weak, and the weather was cool and wet. So, on 26 June 1774, the Eamers went to the Caughnawaga church without Catrina and little Jelles and met Michael and Elizabeth for the baptism of five day old Godfrey Myers. Godfrey Eny and his sister Margaret were the child's sponsors. Also at the church that day was Major Jelles Fonda and his wife Jannetjie who were sponsoring the baptism of Jelles Fonda Van Vechten, son of Anthony Van Vechten and Maria Fonda.[436]

A few days after the baptism of Catrina's grandson Godfrey, she was sitting in her rocking chair by the fire trying to nurse Jelles. While she rocked, she fussed with his white cap, his wool blanket, his linen bedgown, and she stroked his hair. She kept rocking.

Finally, while throwing her head against the back of the chair, she called out, "Philip, we must try and get Dr. Adams here! If he can't come, maybe Sir William's doctor Patrick Daly can come."

As he rushed into the kitchen just hearing the end of her sentence, Philip said, "I'll go to town now and get Dr. Adams."

She kept rocking as she heard the front door close. While she waited, Catrina sat with Jelles held close. Nothing she did seemed to arouse her son. She brought her head down and placed it on his forehead. She gasped. Holding Jelles tighter to her chest, she cried, "Blessed Lord take my son. He's been so loved these six months."[437]

The house was quiet all week after Jelles was buried with his brothers Philip and Mattheus. If Anna Margaret and Dorothy found themselves without housework to do, they found sewing or gardening to keep busy.

One day while in the garden, Anna Margaret was weeding the strawberries. Bending low, she said, "This little flower reminds me of Jelles. 'T'is so tiny and white. I hope Mama feels well soon."

Dorothy laid her hand on her sister's shoulder and said, "She'll mend. Don't worry. Why don't we go to Philadelphia Bush and pick wild asparagus with Anna Margaret Silmser and Jacob Eny and Christine Eny. Mama loves asparagus."

"Maybe Margaret Alguire will come. And, we can go see Catharina and Martin and little Maria Salome, Philip, and John."

While the girls spent their time in the garden or picking wild asparagus and wild onions, Catrina spent her time in the kitchen or tending the fruit trees. One afternoon, after returning from town, Philip found her in the orchard. Together, they walked down each row of trees pruning tiny apples from heavily weighted branches.

As they stood among the branches, Catrina said, "I haven't been to town for a long while. What news is there?"

"On July 6th, John Miller came before Justice Peter Bowen and Judge Sir William Johnson at our Court of Common Pleas for trespassing on John Lipe's land.[438] Just as Johannes Seeber was taken before Justice Henry Frey last spring for trespassing, or in December when Henry Bowman was taken before Justice Jelles Fonda and Judge John Butler for trespassing on Evert Van Ep's land.

Catrina smiled, "Alas, the doors of our court swing wide."

"Aye, and the court has a new Justice, Mr. John Marlet."[439]

"Hmm, the Marlets who live next to Samuel Runnions?"

"Aye. 'T'is the family."

"What news is there of Sir William? Is he well?"

"Not so well. But he still works. In a few days, several hundred Indians arrive at Johnson Hall. Sir William will do what he's always done. He'll listen to their complaints and try and ease their minds. John Friel is tasked with making many coats for them, some laced and some plain."[440]

"Is there great unrest among them?"

"Aye. There's much unfair trade and much liquor in their villages, but the worst of their complaints are the murders of their people as they try to protect their hunting grounds from white settlers moving onto their lands. There're great pressures for Sir William these past months. The Indians are always his concern, and there's so much unrest in the colonies. The Commander in Chief, General Frederick Haldimand, tried to ease the Indians' concerns with a proclamation that protects their lands and hunting grounds."[441]

"How are the British responding to losing all that tea?"

"With fury. They implemented new laws in response to the colonists' behavior. They've closed the port at Boston until the tea is paid for, and they've brought in more British soldiers. In all of Massachusetts, town meetings are severely limited which means the colonies' Committees of Correspondence can't meet. But the worst law, in the colonists' minds, was the passage of the Quebec Act which gave the Canadian French the right to settle on lands that the colonists wanted."[442]

"So, there's nothing but escalating anger from all."

"Aye. The colonists have called for a conference of the thirteen colonies to redress grievances and find ways to restore the union between Britain and the colonies that's based on fair principles."[443]

"It mayn't be safe for me to be out husband!"

"'T'is safe. We'll ride through town on our way to see our grandchildren.

On July 11th, even late in the afternoon, it was hot, but Philip wanted to take Catrina out for a few hours. They drove up to Philadelphia Bush and spent a few hours playing with their three grandchildren. They ate and visited with Michael and Catharina. They left the cabin and took the Sacandaga Road to town. For an hour, they enjoyed the red glow of the setting sun.

Just as their wagon rolled along Sacandaga Road slowing to turn south onto Johnson Street, a rider flew past spooking Apple and Bess. Philip gasped, "'T'was Sir John Johnson. He's ridden hard all the way from Fort Johnson. That horse will expire. 'T'is wet with sweat and frothing at the bit!" Catrina saw Michael Cline, John Fraser, and Robert Picken come out their front doors, and several men stood on the porch of Tice's tavern. In a few minutes, the horses settled, and Catrina and Philip sat in silence. As they approached the lane to their house, another rider galloped past the wagon hollering, "Sir William has died!"

With his eyes focused on his horses and his mouth wide open, Philip held the reins tighter as Apple and Bess spooked. "What did he say?"

Catrina buried her face in her hands saying, "Lord have mercy! Sir William is dead! It can't be. What's to become of our village! 'T'was Sir William's generosity and proud efforts that built this village."

As he brought the horses under control Philip replied, "'T'is a sad day for us all, but I fear the saddest for the Indians. He was their true friend, protector, and brother, and a Mohawk Sachem whom they gave the name Warraghiyagey. For the Indians and for us, he was most decidedly 'a man who undertook great things."

The next morning, Michael Gallinger Sr. saw Philip standing on the porch as he rode up the lane. He dismounted, tied his gelding to a rail and walked toward Philip. "You've heard?"

"Aye. I've heard. And, we heard the wails of the Indians through the night.

'T'is their custom. Their people embrace grief and express it most piercingly."

"I'm certain they've sent their wampum throughout their lands to tell of their loss."

"I expect we'll see hundreds along the roads soon."

"T'is happening already. They're at Johnson Hall."[444]

"Is there news of the funeral?"

"Aye. 'T'is at St John's on Wednesday. Reverend John Stuart from Fort Hunter is giving the service."

Catrina, Philip, Martin, Peter, Johannes, Anna Margaret, and Dorothy left the house early on Wednesday to attend the funeral. Philip stopped the horses a distance from the church. There were just too many people. He turned to

Catrina and said, "We must leave the wagon here and walk. I hope we can find Catharina and Elizabeth in this crowd!" The church was full when they arrived, so they found a place on the grass in the front yard. Martin and Johannes found a comfortable spot for their Mama while Peter went to look for Elizabeth and Micheal and Catharina and Martin. In just twenty minutes, the crowed swelled to over 2000 people.

Catrina could barely see down William Street towards the Hall. She pulled Philip's arm saying, "Look, they come with the casket. There are hundreds of Indians surrounding the wagon. Look at their paint and dress! 'The red and black 't'is so marked. I see Joseph and Molly Brant and all of Sir William's children. The pallbearers must be of great importance."

Philip replied, "They say 't'is Governor Franklin of New Jersey with Goldsbrow Banyar, a Judge of the Supreme Court, and Stephen De Lancey, a New York merchant and member of the New York Assembly."[445]

"I see so many tears, so many embraced."

Sir William was buried that day in the family vault under the altar, and early the next morning the Six Nations Sachems performed the sacred ceremony of condolences.[446]

Only a week after Sir William's burial, the Eamers met their friends and neighbours at Michael Gallinger's farm. Having the chance for all to share their grief was important to Michael and Agatha, so they invited their friends to eat, drink, and share stories of the past and uncertainties about a future without the steadying force of Sir William. Some of those who came were: George Schenck Sr. and Magdelena, John and Sophia Farlinger, Lodowyck Putnam and Elizabeth, Benjamin Crosset, Jacob Henry and Salome Alguire, Johannes George Alguire and Margaret, and Martin and Elizabeth Margaret Silmser. While enjoying roast pig, rum, and the many other foods the women brought, there were many stories of first days and months on their farms, first fairs, first St. Patrick's Day celebrations, and always of Sir William's generosity.

While sitting next to the fire with Martin Silmser and Johannes George Alguire, Philip said, "Who's to take Sir William's place as negotiator and liaison with the Indians?"

Martin replied, "'T'is Colonel Guy Johnson. He was appointed almost as soon as Sir William died. The Indians were anxious to know what would become of their relationship with the British and settlers without Sir William. They were pleased to accept Colonel Guy Johnson."[447]

Filling his pipe with tobacco, Philip said, "We'll rest easier if the Indians can trade and live in peace. I only hope peace is what we can maintain among ourselves. For three years, we've heard so many stories of unrest in newspapers from Boston and New York."

Nodding, Martin added, "At the meetings of the Committees of Correspondence in most of the colonies, news of protest is collected and distributed. 'T'is a network of information. When John Farlinger brings his paper from the postmaster at Albany, I myself saw some of the letters from a farmer in Pennsylvania."[448]

Pointing the tip of his pipe at Martin, Philip said, "Aye. The Whigs who organize and manage the Committees of Correspondence are gaining popularity and much influence, not only among the people, but also within the colonial governments. Soon, they'll form their own government. They stir the masses against King George and our union with Great Britain."[449]

"'T'is a way for folks to speak their grievances."

"Aye, but they'll hear no other point of view." said Philip.

"'T'was a Committee of Correspondence that organized the conference of the thirteen colonies to respond to the British Intolerable Acts. 'T'is soon to be held in Philadelphia. I hope differences are resolved there. The British must remedy the recent acts against the colonies. There must be a way to provide rights and liberties and remain loyal to King George."[450]

A morning attending a baptism at the Caughnawaga church was a good excuse to take an afternoon away from the kitchen. On September 11th, the Eamers attented the baptism of Martin Becker, son of Arent Adam Becker and Elizabeth Swart. Martin and Catharina Alguire were little Martin Becker's sponsors.[451] Again, one Sunday early in October, the Eamers attended the Trinity Lutheran Church at Stone Raby. Reverend Theophilus Engeland died last year, and the congregation were waiting for their permanent Pastor to arrive. Today, they would hear the sermon of Reverend Frederick Ries. There were two baptisms that day. First was Dieterich Loucks, son of Adam and his wife Dorothy Fuchs who baptized their son Dieterich Jr.. Johannes Hess and his wife Ann were Dieterich's sponsors. And second was Adam Empey's Negro and Philip Empey's Negro who baptized their daughter Anna. Philip Empey Sr. and his wife Elizabeth Barbara Schultz were the child's sponsors.[452] That day Philip and Catrina enjoyed their respite from the harvest and their opportunity to give thanks for their blessings. But their ease was shaken when they met with friends and neighbours after the service.

For many weeks, conversations at churches, in taverns, and in the stores focused on the death of Sir William, but today the focus shifted. At the back of the church, Philip Empey Sr. and Elizabeth Barbara chatted with Philip and Catrina.

As he spoke, Mr. Empey kept glancing over his shoulder and pointing the tip of his pipe toward Philip's fine embossed serge vest as if he would stab him. He said, "'T'is known that at Adam Louck's tavern on August 27th several men from this area met to organize a Tryon County Committee of Correspondence. The men drafted resolutions in support of Whig protests against British taxes and British oppressive acts in Boston. They also sent delegates to the conference in Philadelphia.

"Pray can you tell us who was at Louck's tavern?"

"Some of the leaders of the meeting were Christopher Yates, Isaac Paris, John Frey, and Andrew Fink Jr."

"I'm thankful that they stated their continued allegiance to King George."[453]

"If ye are sure of that, I'm heartily glad to hear that news. I fear there'll soon be a time when we'll all be forced to choose a side."

The drive home was quiet. Neither Catrina nor Philip spoke as they passed Anthony Van Vechten's and Colonel John Butler's homes. Johannes and Peter jostled around in the back annoying Anna Margaret and Dorothy. Martin rode Scout well ahead of the wagon; he was anxious to get home and repair the corn house.

It was November, soon time for the fair at Johnson Hall. As they did each year, Catrina and Philip brought their finest sheep fleece, pumpkin, squash, and corn. That day, Catrina and Philip spent time with Captain Peter Service Sr. and his wife Magdelena and with Peter's brother Christopher Service who had come up from Charlotte Creek. All of Captain Peter Service's sons were with him, Johannes Service and his wife Maria Catherine Schenck, Peter Service Jr., and his wife Magdelena Miller, and Philip P. Service with his wife Maria Catherine Seeber. Captain Peter Service's daughters were there too. Maria with her husband Lucas Feader Sr., Eva with her husband Jacob Kitts, Mary Magdelena with her husband Peter Young, and Annatjie with her husband John Kitts. There too were Martin and Elizabeth Margaret Silmser and their children, Christina, John Henry, Anna Maria, Nicholas, and Anna Margaret.

It was a fine day at the Hall with the usual games, music, food, and drink. As Catrina shared a piece of lemon pie with Philip, she said, "'T'is a different fair this year without Sir William. But 't'is nice to see Sir John.

"Aye. He's moved into Johnson Hall with his wife Lady Mary Watts." I hear his long time love Miss Clarissa Putnman moved to Schenectady with their two children."

"I expect that's the way with aristocrats."

"Aye. I was on the Tribes Hill road, and I met Clarissa's father and mother, Arent Victor Putnam and Elizabeth Peek. They didn't look happy."

"Seems a small trouble compared to the troubles talked about these days or the risk we take in threatening peace with the Indians.[454]

"We can only listen and not provoke, or we'll find ourselves in jail."

"Aye my husband. Thou hast always been a great leveller. I hope we make it through the cold dark days of winter and feel warmth in the valley again."

CHAPTER FIVE
The Revolutionary War (1775-1781)

The frigid days of January 1775 did nothing to cool the red hot mood of revolution in the colonies. In Albany at Richard Cartwright's tavern, a meeting was held to organize a Committee of Correspondence. Sixty eight delegates, some of whom were from Schenectady and Schoharie, signed a resolution binding them to vigorously carry out measures that assured the safety of citizens during the dissolution of British rule. This resolution supported the delegates' countrymen in the eastern colonies and reflected their resistance to the slavery of past arbitrary and oppressive acts of British parliament.[455]

Although Philip read many liberty pamphlets, heard arguments among his countrymen, and witnessed many brawls, the enormity of their significance didn't hit him until early March when he rode to Johnson Hall and was stopped by four armed Scotsmen after he crossed the bridge on William Street.

The Scotsmen hollered in unison, "Halt! Sir, what's your business here?"

Philip responded to their shouting by pulling hard on Apple's reins hollering, "Whoa girl," "I'm Philip Eamer, a tenant on the Sacandaga. I'm here to bring sheeps' fleece to Mr. Flood."

As the Scotsmen searched his saddlebags, Philip caught sight of the yard of the Hall. It was unlike anything he'd ever seen. In the front yard between and in front of the guard houses, he saw several swivel cannons and at least twenty armed Scotsmen parading around the yard. Those swivel cannons, he thought, could easily spray a crowd with enough grapeshot to kill several men.[456] Philip didn't waste any time dallying as he might have done a few months ago. He delivered his sheep fleece, mounted Apple, and cantered down William Street toward home.

When Philip came through the front door and walked into the kitchen, he saw Catrina standing beside Peter washing blood from his face. Martin sat next to them with a bandage around his head. "Well, he said. "Pray, dear wife with what trouble have these boys met?"

Peter moved his mother's hand from his face and said, "Martin and I met John Davis and Thomas Davis on our way home from Philadelphia Bush this afternoon. They stopped us on the Sacandaga road and carried on with the most disagreeable charges. They asked if we were for the King or for liberty. I answered that I stand firm for neither. Thomas looked me straight in the eye and said "Damn rascals. You're not siding yourself with our cause!" "The next thing I knew his fist landed in my face."

Martin added, "Aye Papa. As Thomas threw his punch, John tackled me to the ground. We scuffled. I rose and hollered, "We've no quarrel with you!" We're friends are we not? Papa, we've spent so many days through the years hunting and fishing with John and Thomas. And, their father Lewis Davis is your friend. Is he not married to Maria Clement, Mr. Lewis Clement's sister? They're our neighbours here on the Sacandaga Patent.[457] 'T'is too much confusion and bitter feelings these past months. The other day I passed Lodowyck Putnam and his sons Aaron, Richard, and Frederick on the Sacandaga road. I waved and wished them good day. They passed me by without a word or a nod."

"Hmm," Philip said while stroking his chin. "Catrina call Anna Margaret, Dorothy, and Johannes. We need time together to talk about days ahead. I fear we need to be prepared."

As Martin hollered out the back door to Johannes, Anna Margaret and Dorothy came down the stairs and into the kitchen. Catrina laid bread, cheese, and cider on the table. Within ten minutes everyone was around the kitchen table.

As Philip was slicing the bread, he said, "It seems that the Continental Congress, as those who stand for liberty, are losing patience with British taxation and their measures prohibiting us from purchasing goods from anyone but them. I've just been to Johnson Hall, and Sir John and the Scottish Highlanders have fortified Johnson Hall and are preparing for violent confrontations. We must all be ready for any kind of confrontation."

"Papa, Mr. Gallinger rode post to Albany not long past and brought news home. Christopher Gallinger and Michael Gallinger Jr. tell me that the Albany

County Committee of Correspondence issued a new law. They say that whoever acts in opposition of the Congress are deemed violators of the Association and are enemies to the country. They call violators Tories!"

"And what do they call those who support Congress?"

"They call them Whigs or Rebels. Papa, anyone is seized and fined or jailed if they aid those suspected of being an enemy, refuse to sign the Association Oath, reject continental money, or even drink to the King's health! This is the law now Papa. They say this even after the General Assembly of New York pledged to pursue redress of their grievances calmly and with hopes of reconciliation with Britain."[458]

As he reached for some cheese, Peter said, "Johannes Hough Jr. and his brother Henry Hough say that Colonel Guy Johnson is fortifying his new house too. They say he fears Rebels from New England will abduct him and take him to a New England prison. And, they say, a court was held in Johnstown where many who are loyal to King George prepared a declaration that pledged their opposition to Congress and the Association. All the magistrates signed this declaration."[459]

"Son, I fear that declaration only fuels the fires of discord. When in public, we must say no more than is necessary. Those who've been our friends may not be so now. Others may be watching and listening to what we say and do. This is true when we are along the roads or trails, in the taverns, in the store, at church, or even visiting our friends. Rebels might try to rile us with eager words of freedom or vile words against the King or our countrymen."

Catrina's gaze fell on Philip at the end of the table. She said, "What of Catharina and Martin and Michael and Elizabeth. They do not know of all of this."

"I suspect that Jacob Henry Alguire and those at Philadelphia Bush have heard and seen as much as we have. Scotch Bush is not far from them. They must've seen armed men on the road. Even so, Peter and I will travel there tomorrow and advise them to keep guard."

"Elizabeth must not be troubled. She's to deliver within a few weeks. I'm going to Albany Bush in two days. I'll stop and see Elizabeth and Michael.

Anna Margaret gripped her cup of cider and asked, "What of the Indians Papa? Are they opposing the Continental Congress? Does all this stir their anxiety or anger?"

"Colonel Guy Johnson and Sir John Johnson will continue as Sir William did. They know how to keep peace with the Indians."

"But Papa, the Indians fought with the French many years ago. They could fight with the Rebels."

"I'm sure the Indians don't want violence near their villages."[460]

Nodding his head, Peter shrugged and said, "But Papa, Thomas Butler says that he heard his Papa, Lieutenant Colonel John Butler, say that during a conference with the Six Nations in January, Colonel Guy Johnson was angry with Reverend Samuel Kirkland for encouraging the Oneida to support the activities of the Continental Congress."[461]

"T'is not the business of our missionaries to involve themselves in advising any of the Six Nations. We all must mind what we do and leave the Indians to Colonel Johnson."

Philip, Johannes, Peter, and Martin stayed busy with farm work during April. But, whenever they were in the yard or the fields, they kept their firelocks close by. Those first weeks of determining who was with the King and who was with the rebels took great caution and patience and seemed to drag on forever. Wherever they went, it was a hard task to mind who they talked to and what they said. The only thing that seemed normal was the excitement of seeing Elizabeth and Michael's new baby Christian Myers.[462] They had five children now. At least their oldest, Philip, was able to help his mother with the younger children.

Even though helping Elizabeth kept Catrina's mind from anticipating trouble with any of their neighbours, her unease built from the time she thought about leaving the farm until she returned home. Philip insisted that he or one of the boys accompany her, Anna Margaret, or Dorothy if they left the farm. One difficult day came on March 7th when Catrina had to miss the marriage of Martin Loefler Jr. to Anna Catherine Feader, Lucas Feader Sr. eldest daughter. It must have been a difficult time for those families. They came to America together in 1754 and now Martin Loefler Sr. was supporting the Rebel cause and Lucas Feader was supporting the British.

Philip's caution was affirmed near the end of April 1775. Philip and Peter were returning home after visiting Henry Hough at his new farm on lot 61 next to Johannes Wert on the Kingsborough Patent when they heard gunfire and horses from behind their wagon. As Peter reached for his firelock, six men came riding alongside the wagon. They were hollering and waving whatever they had in their hands so vigorously it took all of Philip's strength to hold the horses from bolting. "We've won!" they hollered. "We've beat those scoundrels! The Boston Whigs have beat the British!" One of the men leaned toward Peter and, with only six inches between them, his eyes pierced Peter's like daggers. The man said, "Best be a friend of the cause, or we'll bind you in irons and parade you round town in tar and feathers! The old man too!" Peter froze, but his anger rose. He lifted his hand to swing at the man. Philip grabbed Peter's hand just as it left his side. "Let them be," he whispered.

Through the month of May, this public display of confidence in the cause of liberty and the Rebels' threatening behavior toward suspect or confirmed Tories continued. Daily displays increased after word spread that Ethan Allen and militia from the New Hampshire Grants and Colonel Benedict Arnold had taken Fort Ticonderoga. This was a strategic victory that would cut off the British route from Canada into New York and provide a place from which Rebel forces could invade Canada. To support the actions of the Continental Congress, Rebels throughout many counties took action and set up more Committees and Subcommittees of Correspondence.

In May, the Eamers spent many hours sharing stories and news during supper and in front of the fire until late in the evenings. To be informed, they believed, could save their lives.

One evening, Peter shared the names of those he knew had formed the Mohawk District Committee, "Be cautious, these are ones who'll certainly be watching us, Adam Fonda, Volkert Veeder, Sampson Sammons, John Marlet, Frederick Fisher, and Abraham Yates. And Papa, Mr. Harmans Wendell is on the Schenectady Committee!"[463]

Martin spoke of a new law that required all citizens of Albany County to produce any arms or ammunition that could be used in the defense of the country. He said, "Anyone not producing these arms or ammunition or not reporting persons known to have arms or ammunition would be considered enemies. The effect of these laws was to stockpile arms for the new army and to disarm Tories." Martin also told them that the Committee in the Palatine District held a meeting on May 18th. They condemned the Johnson family and its branches for having ruled the area for too long and for arming over 150 men who are ready to march. They also proclaimed their support of the Continental Congress. Many at a similar meeting at Cherry Valley signed an Article of

Association or a loyalty oath and ensured this oath would be circulated throughout Tryon County for all to sign. Those refusing to sign would be marked as Tories and enemies of the country.[464]

After hearing his son speak, Philip added, "Aye. Michael Gallinger Sr. tells me that the Second Continental Congress has taken control of the government and are now taking charge of the war effort. They're raising money and appointing officers to raise a Continental army.

As they sat around the fire, most of the family recounted stories told by others or news relayed through close friends. Johannes, however, had his own experience. He sat closest to the fire gripping his tin cup between his knees and while tapping his feet as he leaned forward, Johannes recounted what he had seen, "This past Thursday May 11, I was on my way to Canajoharie to pick up a barrel for our apple harvest from the cooper William Casselman Jr.. I passed Johannes Veeder's Mill just west of Caughnawaga. I heard a great raucous. I saw as many as 300 men cheering as they gathered to raise a tall pole. I pulled my wagon to the side of the road and watched as the men began to raise the pole. Just then, Sir John, Colonel Daniel Claus, Colonel Guy Johnson, Lieutenant Colonel John Butler, and many armed Scotsmen arrived and halted the proceedings. Colonel Johnson dismounted and stepped upon Johannes Veeder's porch. In a booming voice, he began a vigorous speech. I've never heard such vile language from Colonel Johnson. He shamed them for denouncing the King, warned them of the foils of their actions, and called them tykes and many more vicious names. As Colonel Johnson stood shouting and shaking his fist, Jacob Sammons fired an insult at him. Jacob called him a liar and a villain. Instantly, Colonel Johnson sprang off the porch calling Jacob a damn villain and seized him by the throat. One of the Scotsmen swung at Jacob with the handle of his whip knocking him to the ground, and straddling him he pinned him to the ground. Jacob struggled, swung and landed a blow to the Scotsman. He leapt to his feet, threw off his coat, and raised his fists to the Scotsman who promptly struck Jacob back into the dirt. He rose again to find two pistols aimed at his chest and knocked down again and beaten badly. In the midst of the commotion, most of Jacob's countrymen dispersed, frightened by the swords and pistols. Jacob was left face down in the dirt. None of the countrymen were armed that I could see. Relieved I was as there seemed to be no chance of escalating violence. 'T'was a nasty sight. Many of the men fled past my wagon. I heard them all muttering vulgar attacks against the King, the Johnsons, and the Scotsmen. The Fondas, Fishers, and Veeders stayed behind to assist Jacob. Last I saw, Jacob's brother Frederick Sammons and his father Sampson Sammons were helping him into their wagon."[465]

After the episode at Johannes Veeder's farm, Guy Johnson's suspicions about a plot to kidnap and imprison him rose. He rallied several Mohawks to assist in guarding his home and sent a letter to the Oneidas for help. The letter was lost on the road and fell into the hands of the Rebels. Having read the letter not meant for their eyes only intensified their growing fear that Colonel Johnson had offered the Iroquois the hatchet and that they accepted, meaning that the Indians would invade the valley. Everyone was paranoid. Tension in the valley grew. It didn't help when the Albany Committee received a letter from the Mohawk Chief Little Abraham reminding them of the long held Mohawk covenant chain with the British and their support of their Superintendant Colonel Johnson. Little Abraham also reminded them of the significance of not only maintaining peace, but also maintaining their ancient Iroquois Confederacy. In a letter to Colonel Guy Johnson, the Rebels reasserted their rights to liberty and their indignation at Colonel Johnson's insistence on stopping men on the road and searching them, fortifying his house, and arming guards. They promised to support him in any efforts to keep the Indians from interfering in the affairs of the county.[466] None of their words lessened Colonel Johnson's suspicions. So, he made the decision to leave the valley and seek safety in Canada.

For several weeks, Philip was rarely out on the roads. But, on the last day of May he rode down to the King's highway at Caughnawaga. As he approached the road along the shore of the river, he saw dozens of boats moving fast along the high waters of spring. He dismounted and reached beside him pulling his firelock from its bucket. He looked closer, and in one bateau he saw William Fraser Jr. from Ballstown, and John Friel and James Bennet from Kingsborough. In another larger boat with a canopy, he saw Colonel Guy Johnson, Colonel Daniel Claus, Lieutenant Colonel John Butler and his son Walter. In one canoe, Philip recognized the Mohawk leaders Joseph Brant and Chief Odeserundiye John Deserontyon from Fort Hunter. Philip stepped back and leaned against Apple. He tried hard to see who was in each of the boats as they passed swiftly. He tried hard to understand what was going on. He thought, "Where were Colonel Johnson and Colonel Claus going? Many of the people he recognized as Sir John's Scottish Highlanders. Why were so many with him? Who's left to protect us from any mobs?" Philip guessed there were over 130 men, some women and children too.[467] Others who stopped along the shore to watch the parade of boats were smiling and waving. There were no worried faces.

When he returned home to tell Catrina and the children, he found Johannes and Peter in the midst of an animated conversation with their sisters.

"Where on the river did you see them?" Anna Margaret asked.

"We were close to Fort Johnson. The boats must've just left Colonel Guy Johnson's home."

With eyes as wide as plates, Dorothy asked, "Was Sir John Johnson and Lady Johnson with them?"

"No, I didn't see them."

Philip interrupted, "I didn't see Sir John either. He must still be at Johnson Hall. I'm going to ride to Michael Gallinger Sr. and John Farlinger's to see what they know. Maybe we'll ride up to Johnson Hall."

Catrina pulled her hands out of a washtub and said, "Not now Philip. I need to go to Martin and Catharina's and help her with our grandson. You'll need to accompany me. At just a few days old, little Peter Alguire is a fine baby, but his mother needs my help. I know they want him baptized at Caughnawaga in a few days. Peter and Martin's sister Margaret Alguire are to be his sponsors."[468]

"Peter or Johannes can take you. I need to see Michael and John soon."

Philip rode up John Farlinger's lane and found Michael Gallinger Sr. and Lawrence Eaman already there. "Good day friends. Have you seen or heard of Colonel Johnson's departure? I was at the river and saw the convoy of boats."

Lawrence replied, "No, but Jacob Crieghoof was there, and he's been by to tell us. We only know that Colonel Johnson thought he was to be taken, so he fled. Jacob also saw John Hare Jr., our Under Sheriff, at Fonda's store posting a proclamation from Governor Tryon prohibiting Committee meetings. Sheriff Alexander White posted one at the Court House and at the churches at Caughnawaga and Stone Raby."

With one hand holding the stem of his pipe and the other rubbing the nape of his neck, Philip replied, "I know Sheriff White already arrested some men for meeting. He has little patience for offences against the King. This proclamation will spur the rabble on."

John added, "I've heard there've been mobs in Schoharie Valley. The magistrate, Alexander Campbell, refused their offer to command a regiment and refused to sign their oath. When he refused, Committee men and 104 others mobbed his home and store telling him never to return. At Cartwright's Inn in Albany, they were celebrating the King's birthday when a mob surrounded the Inn, beat Richard, and plundered his goods. Later, they arrested Abraham Cuyler, the Mayor of Albany, ousted him from office and threw him in jail. Apparently, he drank to the King's health and damned the King's enemies, all illegal activities according to Committee men. The King's laws are replaced so fast. The Continental Congress say what is law."

"The King and Governor Tryon reached out with many attempts to reconcile. 'T'is not to be."[469]

In June and July 1775, despite constant tension and the chance of confrontations, Philip and his sons continued their work ploughing, seeding, and shearing. Philip often spoke to his sons about his decision to remain loyal to the King. They supported their father knowing it was difficult to make choices like that and knowing the dangerous consequences his choice might bring to him and to their whole family.

One mid-July afternoon while they were picking and sorting cherries, Johannes asked his father, "Will you fight Papa? Will you join a King's regiment?"

"I'm almost fifty four years old. Most armies don't want a man my age. But, I'll defend my property and family if forced. I defend what is rightfully mine. We've fared well in our allegiance with the King, Sir William Johnson, and his son Sir John Johnson. 'T'is been more than twenty years that your Mama and I've been in America. We travelled many miles knowing we'd never see our families again. I ache inside for them some days. We're too citizens of this great country, even though I've different ideas of how things should be. I don't always agree with the King's taxation and his hold on our trade, but we're comfortable here. We've made a good life, and there's nothing so bad that could disturb that." Philip turned to his sons and asked, "Would you fight? Would you join a King's regiment?"

Johannes and Martin said, "Aye Papa. We would."

Peter nodded and said, "Aye. I would."

With his head low and while lifting a bushel of cherries, Philip said, "Don't talk about this in front of your mother or sisters. They've enough to worry about. I know their hearts would break if any of us went off."

Peter leaned forward and said, "A Captain John Munro was here recruiting men to complete a Royal Highland Regiment, the men could be Highlanders or any loyal men. 'T'is the 84th. The recruits are paid a guinea and a crown to join, then sixpence per day. The 84th is in Canada and Captain John Munro is to travel there with the recruits and Sir John's brother-in-law, Stephen Watts."[470]

Philip shook his head saying, "'T'is too early to commit yourself to service. Bide a bit more time."

"But Papa, so many are signing, and the Rebels are recruiting their militia now. Each county is to form a militia with able bodied men between the age of sixteen and sixty. They're to elect their own officers. Each man gets a good musket that carries a one ounce ball, a bayonet, priming wire, brush and steel ramrod, a cutting sword or tomahawk, a cartridge box that holds twenty three cartridges, twelve flints, and a knapsack. The men are to supply their own gunpowder and 4 lbs of ball. In each militia, seventeen of sixty eight men are to be Minutemen, ready to march without notice."[471]

As the boys loaded the willow bushel baskets into the wagon, Martin grabbed a handful of cherries and said, "There're four regiments from Tryon County, one for each district. The Mohwak district is the 3rd regiment. Mr. Frederick Fisher is to be their Colonel, and he's recruiting. We know a few he has recruited. There is John Davis, Gerrit Van Brackelen, Gerrit Putnam, Abraham Veeder, Adam Fonda, and Gideon Marlet."[472]

"'T'is true. We know them all. Enough now of armies. We need to get these cherries down to Fonda's store. And, we need extra salt this fall. I want to put plenty of pork in brine. I'll need two of you to come along. I want to buy some shot and gunpowder, and I know 't'is difficult with the new laws. At present, I'm not a known or suspect Tory, so we shouldn't have any problems. And, Jelles and I have been friends since the war with the French. You remember that he and Jannetjie stood for your late brother Jelles not two years ago."

One day early in September 1775, the harvest work slackened, and Philip managed to get gunpowder and lead at Fonda's store. Now, he found time to tend to their three firelocks and shot bags. He sat in the barn and cleaned each one. After he finished with the firelocks, he went outside to start a small fire so he and the boys could melt lead and make some shot.

Just as he struck his flint, Johannes and Peter rode up to the barn. Peter leapt off Scout, pulled the reins over Scout's head, and walked toward Philip saying, “Papa, we’ve just rode past town on Montgomery Street right through a skirmish! Sheriff White was holed up at Robert Picken’s house, and there was much firing from all directions. The windows in Mr. Picken’s house shattered. The Rebels have about 500 men. And, we saw Sir John and his men ride down William Street to defend the Sheriff. As we rode near the jail, I saw several men arguing with the Jailkeeper John Hare Jr.. They wanted him to release Mr. John Fonda and others. I saw them break down the door of the jail.”

“I hope you were riding as fast as you are now talking son.”

Peter carried on, “Papa, ‘t’is a blow up because of Sheriff White’s vigilance and enforcement of the King’s law. Folks want him gone! They say he’s obnoxious. Major Jelles Fonda testified against him when his brother John Fonda was arrested. Dr. William Petrie complained about the Sheriff’s disgraceful and rough behavior after he was arrested. Mr. Petrie and Johannes Veeder testified to him cursing against the cause. William Seeber Sr. says the Sheriff forced his way into their house and cocked his pistol at his son Jacob while saying, “Damned Rebel. If you say one more word I’ll blow your brains out!” And, Mr. Anthony Van Vechten complains that the Sheriff says he’ll have to hang a good many in this country before long.”

“Where do you hear all of this Peter?”[473]

“From Michael Gallinger Jr. and Jacob Eaman when we were out hunting.”

“My sons, speak only to your family of your opinions on any of this.”

In October, while taking wheat to Sir John’s mill, Philip met Lawrence Eaman. Lawrence waved hailing him to the side of the road. “Good day friend. How does your wheat crop this year?”

“Well, I’ve a load here for Sir John’s mill. I’ll be sowing my winter wheat soon. In these uncertain times, I want to keep as much ground wheat and salt at home as I can.”

“Aye. ‘T’is wise.” “Have you heard that Sheriff White is now in Canada? He fled for his life a few weeks back. The Rebels threatened him and plundered his home. ’T’is wise he left, but they’ve taken him on Lake Champlain on his way to Canada and sent him to jail in Albany.[474] Now they’ve arrested Lewis Clement, and Frederick Sammons captured Peter Bowen. Anthony Van Vechten testified against Mr. Bowen, and according to Lodowyck Putnam’s testimony, Lewis Clement was angry he had to leave on account of the damned Fonda’s. He threatened to bring a good number of Indians back with him and destroy all the people here about. The Tryon Committee found Mr. Clement guilty of being a dangerous enemy to the cause and Mr. Bowen guilty of refusing to sign the Oath of Association. They were given a choice of paying a fine of £25 or being held in close irons for three months at their cost. Mr Clement refused to pay a copper as did Mr. Bowen. The Committee men sent them to the Albany Jail, but they've been returned and are now at Johnstown Jail. As soon as Jacob Seeber and eight men brought them to the Johnstown Jail, John Hare Jr., George Cook, and Robert Picken threatened to shoot Seeber. They've arrested those three too, but didn't hold them long. The Mohawk Chiefs met the Committee at Goshen Van Alstyne's house and want Mr. Clement and Mr. Bowen released. The Committee refuses unless they admit their wrongs and end their resistance to the cause."[475]

Philip rested the reins on the seat of the wagon and said, "I knew not of Sheriff White's confinement, nor of my friend Lewis Clement or Mr. Bowen. But, I do know that they arrested Philip Shaver and charged him with threatenings against the cause. They had no evidence; so they demanded he reappear before the Committee at another date. If he fails to appear, he's fined £100. Amidst all this, incredibly we've two new families come up from New York City to settle on the Kingsborough Patent. Mr. John Peascod Sr., a stone mason, and his wife Mary Johnson and five children all under the age of ten. With them, on the same ship from England, came Mr. John Waite Sr., his wife Jane and six children.[476] 'T'is a hard time for them to come to this beautiful valley."

"Aye. They must keep a close watch. I know I watch Jacob and John."

"And, I keep a close watch on my sons' and my daughters' families."

Lawrence nodded and said, "We best not idle here too long lest anyone think we're conspiring against the cause. Good day to you."

"The like to you friend."

On a crisp November morning, Catrina walked to the woodshed to collect kindling she knew she'd need for a long day of baking bread. Setting down the jug of warm cider she carried, she sat near the growing wood pile with her wool cloak wrapped around her. She watched as Philip and Peter swung their axes. This was an essential task. The family could go through near thirty cords of wood through the winter. Catrina didn't want to delay their work, but she thought this was good time to be informed of all incidents in the community. After all, she thought, "I'm the keeper of the house when the men are away. I must know who to trust and who to fear. I must apprise my daughters equally." Catrina reached for the jug of cider and said, "Sit with me a few minutes, rest your axes and drink. I want to know of our community." Philip and Peter sat and described what they'd heard and saw over the past few weeks.

Philip finished telling her of Sheriff White's escape from Johnstown and his confinement in Albany and about the confinement of Lewis Clement and Peter Bowen. Tilting her head and pursing her lips she said, "How does Sir John cope as his authority is stripped away without just cause?"

"He does persist in trying to maintain some control. Recently, the Committee men asked Sir John if they could use the Court House and Jail to conduct the business of their cause. Sir John thought their request unreasonable. His reply was that the Court House and Jail have always been for lawful public use, but they remain his property. If they paid him £700 as the buildings are worth, they could use them for any cause they wanted, and he said, he'd rather have his head cut off before he did anything to support actions against the King. He suggested they use a private house for their jail.[477]

Peter sighed and said, "Even with Sir John's constant efforts, I hear that Captain George Herkimer, General Nicholas Herkimer's and Hans Jost's brother, took George Crawford of Butlersbury, John Friel, John Picken, and John Cameron prisoners. Captain Herkimer suspects they were in Canada in September with the Kings' men, Chief Odeserundiye John Deserontyon, and some of our Fort Hunter Mohawks. He believes they willingly fought against the Rebels during recent attacks on Montreal and Quebec and returned to the valley. Affadavits from Rueben Simmons and John Dennis were sent from the Schenectady Committee to our new Sheriff John Frey. John Dennis, having returned from Canada, gave evidence of happenings in Montreal and against John Friel. Sheriff Frey has had John Friel in irons with nothing but bread and water for twenty one days.[478] Now, they've posted guards along the river at Little Falls and German Flats to arrest anyone returning to the valley by way of Oswego."[479]

By December, the snow in the valley was ½ metre deep. Regardless, the Eamers attended the baptism of Jacob Henry Alguire's grandson Jacob Kuhlman Jr.. He was born to Elizabeth Alguire and Jacob Kuhlman on 2 Dec 1775. As Catrina listened to the service, she thought, "'T'is only been a few months since Sir William died. So much has happened. 'T'is strange sitting here amongst this congregation. Our neighbours and friends don't look different, but everyone and everything is different, so terribly different. How can things ever be what they were? At least 't'is nice that Elizabeth and Jacob asked Catharina to be a sponsor, and 't'will only be a few days before we return here to celebrate the wedding of Elizabeth's sister Margaret Alguire to Johannes Hough, Henry Hough's son."[480]

At least for a few days in December, the Eamers took pleasure in old friends celebrating new lives and new beginnings. Small pleasures faded in January 1776. First, a small event on New Year's Day didn't go unnoticed. For years on New Year's Day people went out in their sleighs to visit friends or to Tice's tavern or to one of the taverns along the river. All day long there was gunfire to mark the beginning of the New Year. This year was different. Not only had Captain Tice left the valley with Colonel Guy Johnson, but there was a new law prohibiting the firing of guns on New Year's Day. The Committee decided it was a waste of ammunition. Such was the small event.[481] However, a second shocking and disruptive event threw the valley into eight long years of a vicious, devastating war. No one escaped the carnage, not Tory, Rebel, nor Six Nations.

What couldn't go unnoticed happened one Wednesday afternoon early in January. Philip and Peter were out in the barn tending to the milk cows and sheep when Philip saw Lucas Feader Jr. and Martin Silmser walking swiftly toward the barn. Lucas set down his firelock and sat on a stump by the barn door.

Looking straight at Lucas with a furrowed brow Peter said, "What brings you both here at such a pace?"

In a shaky voice Lucas replied, "We've been at the river near Caughnawaga."

"Yes. Go on Lucas."

"There are 3000 men of the militia with General Philip Schuyler. They've camped on the river since yesterday. And. And. General Nicholas Herkimer, 900 with him! There're tents, hundreds of them in rows almost a mile long, fieldpieces too, and banners flying everywhere! I saw George Dachstader, Adam Everson, and Richard Putnam of John Davis' Company and others of Colonel Frederick Fisher's 3rd Tryon Regiment." Lucas, now out of breath, gasped and continued, "Little Abraham and the Fort Hunter Mohawks are with them."

"For what purpose is such an army there?"

Martin leaned toward Peter and said, "They've come for Sir John and his Highlanders. Congress and General Philip Schuyler are convinced Sir John is arming his men to attack the valley. They presume him a great danger to the cause and demand certain conditions or they'll arrest him."[482]

Nodding, Peter said, "Since January 14th, they've had guards on both sides of the river near Warrensburg to intercept any correspondence coming through for Sir John. A few months back, I know they intercepted a runner from magistrate Alexander Campbell of Schoharie. He sent news to Sir John warning him of the danger he faced.[483] We must be away now to Johnson Hall. My brothers and I will follow." Peter turned to his father and said, "Papa, we must go and assist Sir John."

"Peter, there's no hope of defense against thousands. You must stay out of harm's way. I'm certain we'll hear how we can help."

That evening Dorothy swept every corner of the floor at least twice while Catrina and Anna Margaret scrubbed dirty and clean pots. Philip, Johannes, and Peter sat by the fire fidgeting with anything their hands could find. Often Peter opened the front door to listen for sounds of gunfire. Martin paced across the kitchen floor while Dorothy swept around him. It wasn't until mid-morning the next day that they heard any news. Finally, Michael Gallinger Sr. and John Farlinger knocked on the front door and started talking as soon as Philip opened the door. Michael said, "'T'ain't a fair day for Sir John or any of us loyal to the King.

Fig. 31. Sir John Johnson 1777. Library and Archives Canada Acc. No. 1938-34-1

"Yesterday, Sir John, Allan MacDonnel, and several Mohawk Chiefs met with Colonel Philip Schuyler on the road to Johnstown. Without resources against Schuyler's army or an avenue of retreat, Sir John was forced to capitulate. Colonel Schuyler demanded that Sir John not travel west of German Flats nor go to any seaport, if he did they would take him prisoner to another part of this county or another. He also demanded that Sir John deliver up all cannon arms and other military arms and ammunition that would be used to arm inhabitants or Indians. And, he demanded that the Scotsmen not only immediately deliver up their arms, but that they were also to deliver up six of their men as prisoners to ensure the security of the capitulation. General Schuyler expressed that the sole purpose of this treaty was to prevent the horrid effects of a civil war betwixst those who might be brethren. If Sir John refused, force would be met with force without distinction.[484]

"And how did Sir John respond?" Philip asked.

Sitting in the rocking chair next to the fire Michael replied, "The next day, Sir John replied. He refused to restrict his travel nor give up hostages. General Schuyler and Sir John corresponded until finally terms were agreed upon. Arms are to be surrendered by the Scotsmen and other inhabitants, Sir John's travel is restricted, and six hostages are to be presented. The six were Allan MacDonnel and Allan MacDonnel Jr. of Collachie, Alexander MacDonnel, Randel MacDonnel, Archibald MacDonnel, and John MacDonnel. These six are allowed six days in Albany to sort out their affairs and will be taken to Reading or Lancaster Pennsylvania where they are to be maintained according to their station in life. Another hostage taken was John Thompson of German Flats. John lived among the Indians since 1759, and he speaks their language well. He had a good trade with all the Indians along the Mohawk River and a fine farm. His good relationship with the Indians is threatening to the Rebels. They've looted his store of goods, liquor, and furs and will send him to prison in Albany. His wife Dorothy McGinnis and their five Negroes escaped to Niagara, but they've taken Dorothy's brother George McGinnis."

"General Schuyler's army, Sir John, the Scotsmen, and other inhabitants of the area are to come to Johnstown on Saturday, January 20 at 12 o'clock to deliver up their arms and prisoners. General Schuyler arrives this afternoon."

"What of our Mohawk friends? Did they not defend Sir John?

"Little Abraham and the Fort Hunter Mohawks did object to any sign of force or violence. Little Abraham says that the path to the valley is one of peace and was made so by a Treaty with Congress many months before. He begged General Schuyler to take care and not spill blood on this path, nor to take Sir John. He says the Mohawk remain mediators between both sides. He insisted that their Sachems attend the meeting with Sir. John. I fear their words were ignored."[485]

At 12 o'clock on Saturday, January 20, Philip, Peter, Martin, and Johannes stood at the corner of Clinton and William Street among hundreds of other tenants of the Kingsborough, Sacandaga, and Mayfield Patents. They watched as General Schuyler marched his men into Johnstown. For over an hour, they saw their friends and neighbours, over 300 Scotsmen, and Sir John surrender their arms and ammunition. But, it wasn't only the Scotsmen that General Schuyler disarmed. Peter saw two soldiers approach David Jeacocks Jr. who was standing near the Court House. They demanded he surrender his gun, powder horn, and cartridge box.[486] With his brothers, Peter leaned on the fence that surrounded Tice's tavern. All three brothers, with their arms crossed tightly around their waists, watched in horror as six hostages surrendered and Sir John was intimidated into accepting a parole of honour.

Weeks passed slowly for Catrina, but she managed to keep Anna Margaret and Dorothy busy combing and spinning wool. One morning in the middle of March 1776, Catrina found herself thinking of how they were to get the trees tapped and sugar made with all these soldiers about. She strained to see out the kitchen window. Rubbing the frost from a spot on the window, she stared at the entry to their lane. For several minutes she saw soldiers marching side by side past the lane, each one with a musket over his shoulder. She knew that after General Schulyer had been at Johnstown, the Committee men and General Herkimer's men rounded up at least 110 inhabitants loyal to the King and tracked the whereabouts of the wives of leading Loyalists. They took Michael Carman Sr. to Albany. She worried about Jacob Rombaugh. He was taken but escaped and was taken again on his way to Canada. Now he's on trial for his life.[487] She wondered where the soldiers were going now.

Anna Margaret laid her comb on the pile of wool and said, "What do you see Mama?"

"'T'is nothing. Keep combing. We need to get this wool to Martin. 'T'will soon be time to shear more wool. And, I want to take some to William Schuman for his stocking loom. I expect with all the trouble these days he doesn't get many customers at his public house."[488]

"Maybe soldiers stop at his place? Catharina tells me she sees soldiers marching along the road towards the Sacandaga River."

With a strained smile Catrina replied, "Perhaps the soldiers do stay with Mr. Schuman. I hope Catharina doesn't venture far from home as I told her."

As Catrina gently placed the spun wool into a linen bag, Peter and Martin walked into the kitchen. Peter said, "There's news from Jacob Henry Alguire today."

"What news? We were just talking about Martin's weaving."

"Sebastian enlisted in Captain Andrew Finck's Company. They march to the barracks at Saratoga soon. Martin tried to talk to his brother, but Sebastian is committed to the Rebel cause. And William Feader, Lucas Feader's brother, enlisted in Emanuel De Graff's Company."[489]

Catrina set the bag of wool by the kitchen door and said, "There'll soon be many more fathers, sons, and brothers on different sides of this fight. Not even blood kin can make reason these days. Kin are watching kin, and I expect eager to report what they know to the Committee men."

"Hmm, Aye. There're many words secretly pass between men lately. I know that Colonel Frederick Fisher's men are patrolling the Kingsborough, Mayfield, and Sacandaga Patents. They've been seen near Sir William's Fish House watching for anyone entering the area from the north. And, General Schuyler is restricting traders from entering or leaving the county unless they have a pass. The Indians want trade goods and get anxious when the white man's arguments interfere with their trade."

Martin nodded and said, "I know Nicholas Stevens, from Alplaus Kill across the river near Schenectady, is watched. Not long ago, he went north without a pass from the Schenectady Committee, and Nicholas has not signed the Association Oath either."

"They're looking west too. There're patrols west to Fort Stanwix, Oswego, and Niagara. They watch the Mohawks pass there and back. They suspect them of taking communications for Sir John to Captain John Butler at Niagara."[490]

"Enough talk of watching and secrets. I need to get this wool to Martin Alguire and to William Schuman. Can you take me Peter?"

"Aye Mama. We'll go now."

"We'll have good things to talk about on the way there. We can talk about John Henry Silmser's marriage to David Eny's daughter Anna Maria Eny.[491] Maybe we can stop and see the newlyweds."

April brought the spring melt and the usual mud. But Catrina didn't mind so much. After the long silent days of winter, the sound of birds singing all month long made her smile despite the rising tensions and chaos in the valley. She had to search for things to smile about. Everyone knew that Sir John Johnson and many more were watched closely. She worried because Sir John had visitors from Albany who had been before the Albany Committee and in jail recently. His visitors were a Major James Gray and Mr. Thomas Gummersal who had recently fallen ill.[492] Michael Gallinger Sr. told her that John Monier, the postmaster at Albany, appeared before the board and was disarmed for refusing to sign the Association Oath. Others from the area were taken too. There was John Lonie, a shoemaker from Johnstown, Julius Bush, a tanner from Stone Raby and Jacob Rombough, a farmer from Warrensburg, Lewis Clement's boy Joseph, and John Annable and James Massie from the Butternuts along the Susquehanna, and on May 12th Hans Jost Herkimer Jr., the brother of General Nicholas Herkimer, was taken.[493] It wouldn't take much for General Schuyler to throw Sir John in jail indefinitely or banish him from the county.

On Tuesday, May 7th, Catrina was hanging her wash by the summer kitchen when she heard a wagon roll into the yard. She held her breath for a moment, put down the sheets, and went to see who arrived.

Waving vigorously, she greeted Jacob Henry and Martin Alguire. Puzzled at their arrival, she said, "Good day. What brings you here today?"

Jacob Henry and Martin slowly climbed down from the wagon. Martin replied, "We've bad news from Saratoga. My brother Sebastian died at the barracks."[494]

After embracing Martin, Catrina looked toward Jacob Henry and said, ""T'is so sad. Jacob Henry I'm so sorry. What happened?"

"Those scoundrels killed my son!"

Martin held his father's arm and said, "There was great sickness at the barracks. Since the Continental army retreated from Quebec many men have died from hunger, cold, and disease."

Jacob Henry raised his fist saying, "We shall see who prevails in this wretched fight! Sebastian's dear wife of only two years is destitute. She's with Salome now and will stay with us for a while."

"Oh dear," Catrina said as she sat down on a stool on the porch. "We must take good care of each other now. Who knows what distress we must confront? We must tell Philip and the children; they were fond of Sebastian."

It wasn't long before distress was palpable. General Schuyler had intelligence from scouts and affidavits from informants who reported that Sir John was gaining the Indians' support and rousing them against the rebellion. As a Magistrate of Tryon County and a Captain in the 3rd Tryon County Regiment, Jelles Fonda received several of the affidavits.[495] On May 10th, General Schuyler sent a letter to Sir John pointing out Sir John's hostile intentions and advising him he was to be taken prisoner and sent to Albany then to General Washington.[496] On General Schuyler's orders, Colonel Elisha Dayton arrived in Johnstown on May 20th with 300 soldiers. He set up quarters at Tice's tavern and immediately sent Major Barber with a letter to Johnson Hall. Colonel Dayton wanted to know at what day and time he could expect the Highlanders assembled so that he could escort them and their families to Albany. On Major Barber's return from Johnson Hall, Colonel Dayton learned that, after receiving the letter of May 10th from Colonel Schuyler, Sir John, furious over the illegal activities of Congress and their army, assembled about 200 Highlanders and escaped through the woods to Canada.

As Colonel Dayton and his soldiers chewed on the loss of their captive, they couldn't help but notice several Mohawk warriors walk passed their tents in full war paint and dress holding an expression that displayed their dissatisfaction with the presence of Dayton's army. They were on their way to Johnson Hall. It wasn't until the next day that Colonel Dayton held council with Little Abraham and the Mohawk warriors and heard their warnings about spilling blood on the path of peace. On May 22nd, Captain Joseph Bloomfield went to Johnson Hall with orders to retrieve the keys to the Hall and outbuildings and to confiscate Sir John's papers. He was also to instruct Lady Mary Johnson that the army was to possess Johnson Hall, and she was to pack her things as she, now with child, and her infant son William were to be escorted to Albany.[497]

Word spread of Sir John's escape. Now more than ever, Philip wanted to meet with Michael Gallinger Sr., Lawrence Eaman, Jacob Crieghoof, and John Farlinger to find out who had fled with Sir John and how they could be protected from the Rebels constant harassment. Philip left word with Michael and

Lawrence to come to his farm the day after Lady Johnson was taken to Albany. He'd also left word with his sons-in-law, Martin Alguire and Michael Myers.

When the men arrived at the farm, Catrina hustled them in the front door, saying, "Philip, all of you can't meet in one place like this. Suspicions will be aroused. You'll be in jail for certain!"

"We won't be long Catrina. Next time 't'will only be two or three of us."

The men sat around the kitchen table, some talking at the same time and some taking swigs of the rum. While Philip filled his pipe with tobacco he said, "I see John Farlinger isn't with us. I assume he must have fled with Sir John. Who can tell us which other men have gone?"

Michael answered, "My boys Christopher and Michael Gallinger Jr., Anthony Walliser's boy John, and Johannes Albrandt's boy Francis, George Crites Jr., David McEwan, and David Jeacocks Jr.."

Martin Alguire added, "Jacob's boy William Sheets, and Michael Carman Jr., John Coons and his brother Jacob Coons of Butlersbury have gone too. And Joseph Hanes boys Michael, George, and Christopher Hanes." Shaking his head he added, Henry Hough and young George Bender Jr., just fourteen years.

Michael Myers spoke out, "The Putnam boys, Richard, Arent, and Victor from Tribes Hill are gone too."[498] Jacob Myers tells me that over 100 men from Scotch Bush have gone. I know the Scotsmen John and Duncan Murchison and William and Hugh Fraser went, and George Shaver, Nicholas' boy. And, there's news from the west. George Dachstadter and Johannes Adam Helmer Jr. from near Herkimer are gone."

Reaching for more rum, Jacob Crieghoof said, "There're so many who assembled with only a few hours notice. Captain Peter Service's boys Philip and Peter Service Jr. said that the group set out towards Sir William's Fish House at dawn on Tuesday, May 21; their brother John P. Service went with the group. They're going north to Canada through the Adirondacks to Raquette Lake then along the Grasse River. They've Mohawks Odeserundiye John Deserontyon and Onoghsokete Isaac Hill from Fort Hunter as guides. With the Mohawks as guides, 't'is the only way they'll survive. They've few provisions and are trekking through hunting territory that the Fort Hunter Mohawks have used for centuries. We must take great care. The Rebels are searching for them. Sha'n't be a moment we can let down our guard."[499]

Philip nodded and said, "Aye. They've scouts on the road to Albany Bush and Tribes Hill, and some passing on the trail through the Sacandaga Patent. General Schuyler and the Committee men from Albany and Tryon want to oust all Tories and secure Tryon County. General Herkimer and Colonel Fisher have rallied their regiments to assist, and Colonel Dayton occupied Johnson Hall.[500] And, I've heard they've taken Valentine Cryderman."[501]

Martin added, "Mr Cryderman's farm is on the Sacandaga, only about ½ kilometre from my place. I know soldiers were seen on their way to Sir William's Fish House with plans to erect a defense there."

"What of the Scotsmen?" Lawrence asked.

Michael replied, "Many are gone, but those who remain are called to assemble at Johnstown for questioning. General Schuyler will take five hostages for every one hundred Scotsmen, and if anyone dares to take up arms against the cause or assist the enemy, the hostages will be put to death."

"We need the assistance of Thomas Gummersall!"

"Aye, but there's been a reward offered for his apprehension. He's been secreted in the woods or in Loyalist houses since Sir John left. He was too ill to travel. Now he's to travel to New York. 'T'is too dangerous for him here."[502]

By June, Philip and the boys had pruned the fruit trees, sheared twelve sheep, and seeded Indian corn. As they worked, they spent several hours discussing ways to make sure they had enough provisions till next spring. They decided to butcher one extra hog this year, keep extra flour, and turn more apples to cider. Some of their provisions went in the house cellar, but knowing their situation could suddenly turn bad Philip constructed a small, well hidden cellar under the barn. Catrina and the girls planted as many vegetables as they could, and made extra cheese and corn cakes. With all the soldiers nearby, going into the forest to collect berries or mushrooms wasn't an option. One day in June, Philip, Martin, and Peter reluctantly ventured out onto the roads to Fonda's store for salt and flour.

They drove the wagon the long way bypassing Johnstown. It was too risky to go into town. So, they drove south down the Tribes Hill road and turned west onto the King's Highway toward Caughnawaga.

As Philip and the boys entered the store and approached the counter, Jelles said, "Awe. There're some fine young men to enlist in Colonel Fisher's regiment. Good day Philip. Are your boys to enlist for the cause?"

"Not as yet friend. 'T'is the start of planting season, and I need their help managing hogs for breeding."

"Well, we'll see them soon and you as well friend. Have you signed our Association Oath yet?"

"'T'will be done soon as I stop at the Court House." Philip fidgeted with his hat then laid it down on the counter and said, "Can I have 40 lbs of salt and flour?"

"'T'is a lot this trip."

"Aye. Catrina will have pickling, and I'm to slaughter a hog."

The boys carried the goods out the door, and Philip quickly tipped his hat to Jelles and followed the boys. As the horses hauled the wagon to their lane, they saw Michael Gallinger Sr. riding toward them.

Michael stopped his mare beside the wagon. Breathless, he said, "Colonel Dayton's men are fortifying the jail for their defense and to house all the prisoners recently taken. There's no room at Albany for all their prisoners. John Hare Jr. lives close to the jail, so they've plundered John's place, taken his belongings, damaged his fields, and taken his stock. They're even using timber from his house to fortify the jail and his fence wood for their fires. John's boy William Hare and his wife Margaret Davis were home when the soldiers came. They watched horrified as the soldiers looted their home. John escaped but wants to take his family to Canada. The soldiers are building two forts west along the River, one called Fort Plain the other Fort Dayton. Stay safe and keep off the main roads. You young boys don't draw attention to yourselves."[503]

"'T'isn't easy to work our farm when we're secured to it each day. We've missed the spring market at Johnson Hall this year. 'T'will be hard to sell our goods!"

Only a few days later, Philip was working in the barn. From there, he heard a great raucous on the road near their lane. He looked out into the fields and saw the boys working. He hurried to the house to find Catrina, Anna Margaret, and Dorothy. "Stay inside!" he yelled through the half open front door. He walked through the trees to the edge of the road and saw at least twelve soldiers whooping and hollering, "The damn British are finished now! We're free of the tyrants!" With each holler, a shot was fired up into the trees. Philip walked back to the house. Soon the boys joined everyone in the kitchen. They sat there until dusk. The next day Philip discovered that the Rebels had their own constitution signed and were now independent of Britain. "'T'was a grand day for them." Philip thought.

The summer dragged on with farm work and constant news of Rebels harassing neighbours or friends. Philip kept a close eye on Angus McDonell and his wife and children across the road and was able to walk to Jacob Crieghoof's place once in a while for news. Philip avoided visiting the Loeflers' farm. He knew they supported the Rebel cause. One day while talking with Jacob, Philip learned that Philip Shaver, who had returned from Oswego with Colonel Guy Johnson's leave, was harassed and finally taken prisoner. Mr. Shaver needed to be with his family because his wife Elizabeth Angst was to deliver very soon, and he had several young children. So, he signed an oath promising to remain quiet as long as he was not disturbed.

Philip also learned that Valentine Cryderman was released from jail after being held there three months. He suffered the worst abuse because he refused to sign their Association Oath, and he became so terribly ill that he lost his senses. He was now home on his Sacandaga Patent farm with his wife Catherine and their ten children. He is bedridden, and they must tend to him constantly.[504]

Through the cool days of October, Catrina, Anna Margaret, and Dorothy often walked the Sacandaga trail or the road through Albany Bush. They wanted to bring whatever help they could to the Cryderman family, or they wanted to be sure Michael and Elizabeth and Jacob Kuhlman and his wife Elizabeth Alguire were okay. One day, they stopped to see Johannes Hough, Henry Hough's brother, at Albany Bush.[505]

Johannes met Catrina and the girls coming down his lane. With a smile, he said, "'T'is a fine weather day ladies."

"Aye Mr. Hough. We hope all does well with you. Do you have news for us from your brother Henry?"

"I do Madam. He's come home two days past by way of Lake Champlain and through the forest past Split Rock.[506] He brings word of Sir John and his men."

"'T'is fine news I hope. We've many young men who went away with Sir John. Their families need word of them."

"Indeed Madam. Henry told Major Fonda he deserted from Sir Guy Carleton's army, but Fonda's men watch him, so he's hid away in the woods at present. I can relay to you his words. Come sit inside and hear the story."

Johannes sat at the kitchen table while Catrina and the girls sat around the fire. He began, "About 170 men left Johnstown before dawn and headed to the Fish House. In their knapsacks, they carried provisions for about nine or ten days, some had muskets others only knives. They moved fast knowing General Dayton's men might be close behind. A few loyal Mohawks guided the men northwest along the Sacandaga River then overland to Lake Pleasant. Following the Raquette River, they reached Raquette Lake where the men not only collapsed from exhaustion but also ran out of provisions. Now forced to eat roots and beech leaves; they hunted what they could, but they could not fire their muskets for fear of attracting the attention of possible patrolling soldiers. Earlier, knowing his men might perish in such an arduous journey, Sir John sent runners north to St. Regis to bring help. When the exhausted men reached Raquette Lake, about twenty five St. Regis Mohawks were there constructing elm bark canoes to carry the group along the Grasse River to St. Regis. 'T'was a miracle they were not discovered or did not perish from hunger, fatique, or cold. After nineteen days, the men arrived at St Regis along the St. Lawrence River and rested under the good care of the St. Regis Mohawk."

"How does Sir John? Does he know they've taken Lady Johnson?"

"Aye. He knows. He's uneasy of mind after losing all that was most dear to him and each day fatigued from looking after his men. His anger is expressed when he calls those who exiled him and took his dear wife and child wretched, ungrateful, rebellious miscreants, many of whom, after so many years, were under the greatest obligation to the family.[507] After a few day's rest, the group reached Montreal and the safety of the British garrison."

"On June 19th at Chambly near Montreal, Sir Guy Carleton gave Sir John an order to raise two battalions of men, the 1st Battalion very soon. The regiment is the King's Royal Regiment of New York (KRRNY), and it was raised for the defense of their frontier. Sir John was appointed Lieutenant Colonel Commander of the Regiment."[508]

"Do you have news of the Gallinger boys?"

"Aye. They've enlisted in the 1st Battalion."

"Will our men come back to protect us from the Rebels' constant torment and maltreatment?"

"'T'is certain that Sir Guy Carleton will send troops south. Now, he's just driven the Rebels out of Quebec. He must continue to defend Quebec."

"We'll pray our men return home soon. Till then will word come to us of their well-being?"

"Aye Mrs. Eamer. Scouts often come south through the woods."

That evening Catrina told Philip and the boys everything that Johannes Hough told her about the men who had left Johnstown.

As they sat around the kitchen table, the boys had many questions about the new battalion. Peter asked, "How strong is the battalion Mama?"

"'T'is over 200 men. Most of them from near here, some from Canada."

"Do they have uniforms and muskets?"

"Aye. Johannes says that Sir John supplied them with all they need. Their uniforms are green coats cut long with royal blue facings. They even have royal provincial pewter buttons. They wear white woolen waistcoats and breeches."

"And gaters Mama?"

"Aye, button up canvas gaters."

"What of their musket and ammunition. They're soon to be fighting men."

"Each has a musket with a thirty six hole cartridge box and, of course, a canteen and haversack."[509]

Peter leaned back in his chair and said, "I know Sir John will look after his men."

Johannes replied, "I hear the Rebels run low on ammunition. Several have been moving through the patents looking to take windows and use the lead therein for bullets! There're many of us who've been chased out or fled so some homes with windows are empty.[510] Perhaps Peter, Martin, and I'll soon join the battalion too."

Philip lit his pipe and said, "You're needed here now. We must farm so we can eat and give to those who've had their belongings stolen."

For a short while, Catrina, Anna Margaret, and Dorothy attended to something other than the harvest. It was November 1776 and snow was on the ground. Their work now was to knit enough wool mittens and socks for winter. They were also knitting wool blankets and caps for Martin and Catharina's newborn son and fifth child Daniel Alguire and for Johannes George Alguire and Mary Margareta Eny's newborn son Johannes Alguire.[511] Sometime in November, the family took time to travel to Albany Bush to visit Martin, Catharina and their new grandson Daniel. Even in these difficult times, Catrina and Philip boasted about their nine grandchildren.

On other trips to Philadelphia Bush, Philip and Peter stopped at Martin Silmser and Elizabeth Margaretha's farm. Philip and Peter sat at the kitchen table while Martin poured them a cup of rum and laid a plate of jerky on the table.

Martin reached for the jerky and said, "I've news from Albany."

"Is it news of Lady Johnson?"

"No. 'T'is news of prisoners at old Fort Frederick at Albany. There were so many prisoners there that many were sent to Connecticut. Among them was Owen Connor Jr. from Fort Hunter. He's a friend of the Butlers and godson of Walter Butler Sr. Others sent to Connecticut were Johannes Hartle, Jacob Rombough, Nicholas Shaver, Adam Snyder, Philip Cook, John Lonie, George McGinnis, Christian and Henry Dachstader, Richard Loucks, Truman Christie, Peter Pruner, Daniel Fyke, Conrad Smith, Adam Helmer, Jost Petrie, and Peter Service. Others, imprisoned many months were Magistrate Alexander Campell, John Munro, Joseph and Samuel Anderson, and Henry Van Schaick the Postmaster at Albany.[512] And, they took Henry Hare from Fort Hunter and are sending him to Hartford, Connecticut. Pray 't'is not the Newgate Prison. Most do not survive that prison."[513]

"Aye. Henry lives on the south side of the river near Fort Hunter. I've seen him at Johnstown visiting his brother John Hare Jr.. Their brother William is a trader with the Six Nations and another brother Peter was a batteauman for Sir William."

"Now, they've taken William Cornelius Bowen from Warrensburg. Henry Hough, and George Ramsey along with William Cornelius Bowen stood before the new Committee for Detecting and Defeating Conspiracies. The Committee men, with evidence from Isaac Paris and the Tryon Committee, found them dangerous, desperate, and disaffected from the cause and ordered they be sent to Poughkeepsie on the Hudson River!"[514]

By the end of 1776, hundreds of men had fled the valley or been taken prisoner. Fear permeated the Eamer house. Philip spent most days in December busying himself with whatever small chore that would occupy his mind and his time. He spent time in his office at the back of the house calculating the profits he managed to make during the year's harvest. Often, he hoped the volatile situation might change and allow his farm to continue to prosper. However, doubt slipped into his mind most hours of the day and night. The children had their own way of coping, usually with many questions that most of the time couldn't be answered. Catrina focused on daily chores and on how she could stay in contact with her daughters and grandchildren.

1777 barely began when Michael Gallinger Sr. and his fifteen year old son Henry Gallinger trudged up the Eamers' lane carving a deep path with their snowshoes. Leaving their snowshoes resting against the house, they entered the warmth of the kitchen.

"Good day Philip. 'T'is a crisp day and the snow is still deep and soft as we passed the front of Jacob Crieghoof's place. Often, we take back trails to avoid the roads and the soldiers. We're glad of a rest, and we've brought news of the activities of Committee men and militia."

"Glad to see you and Henry. Sit by the hearth and warm yourself."

Michael reached for the back of the rocking chair, and, turning it towards the flame, he sat and began talking, "There's news that Henry Hough, William Cornelius Bowen, and George Ramsey escaped from Poughkeepsie jail. And, Major John Butler has been at Niagara for months as the Superintendent of Six Nations. Maybe Henry, William, and George are making their way to Niagara.[515] Major Butler's work is to keep the Six Nations loyal to our King. And, for many weeks, Joseph Brant has been at his village Oquaga on the Susquehanna, but he arrived at Niagara with Gilbert Tice on December. I expect he'll join Major Butler and the other King's men. The Committee men and militia think Joseph is still at Oquaga, and being suspicious of Joseph and frightened of his influence with the Indians, they've ordered that Joseph and Gilbert Tice be found and arrested. They aren't sparing any men or cost to this end.[516] And, Hans Jost Herkimer Jr. escaped from jail and is right now making his way through the woods to Niagara. If any of us need to flee, Niagara offers safety."

"'T'was hard to hear that Lieutenant Major Butler's family were taken after he fled with Colonel Guy Johnson in '75. 'T'was also hard to hear that Hans Jost had to leave his family behind. I hope they're reunited soon. I hear that John Fraser of Johnstown and Philip Shaver and his family have left for Canada."[517]

Henry reached forward to move a log in the fire and said, "Papa, tell Mr. Eamer the news Mr. Hare brings from Canada."

"Aye. After seven months at Hartford jail, Henry Hare made his way to Canada and has now returned to the valley. He brought news that Sir John's 1st Battalion of the KRRNY is at Pointe-Claire on the western end of the island of Montreal. The men are lodged in barns near the village and, for now, spend their days busy with camp life of soldiers. Francis Albrandt, Johannes Albrandt's boy is in the Colonel's Company and assists the Quatermaster. The tailors are kept constantly busy outfitting the men. Another Corp of King's men, called Jessup's Corp, was raised at Crown Point in November 1776 and is to join the KRRNY at Pointe Claire."[518]

"'T'is good news Michael and means your boys Christopher and Michael Jr. are safe."

Just as the conversation changed to talk of necessary spring work, Anna Margaret and Dorothy came into the kitchen. "Good day Mr. Gallinger and Henry." "How does Mrs. Gallinger and Elizabeth and Dorothy?"

"They're well and hoping to see you someday soon."

Early in March 1777, Philip and Johannes returned home from a necessary trip to Fonda's store. As Catrina helped them bring the flour, tobacco, and oznabrig to the house, she asked, "Any troubles at the store or on the road today?"

"Nay, all was quiet. 'T'is a good time early in the morning. We did see a disturbing notice tacked up at the store."

"What notice was given?"

"It seems another law has passed. Only a week ago, representatives of the State of New York passed an Act of Confiscation and appointed Commissioners of Sequestration for each county." Catrina listened as she set the oznabrig on the table.

"What's confiscated? From whom?"

While emptying the sack of flour into the crock, Philip answered, "The Commissioners can lawfully seize and sell the personal property of anyone who has joined the enemy of the cause. That includes land, stock, grain, hay, tools, and personal belongings. Or, they can rent the properties. If 't'is not seized or rented, they believe 't'is wasted or used for some wicked purpose, so they distribute it to their army and the poor and distressed."

Catrina sat down hard in a kitchen chair and rubbed her face with both hands. "Do you mean all a person's worldly goods belong to the state!"

"Aye Catrina. But, they're supposed to leave the families of those gone to the enemy with enough to sustain them for three months."

"And then what after three months? Have they lost all sense of decency?"

Philip shrugged and shook his head saying, "Harmans Wendell is a Commissioner for the city of Albany and Colonel Frederick Fisher, John Eisenlord, Peter Deygert, William Harper, and John Harper for Tryon County."[519]

Early in May, Philip and Peter walked the kilometre along the back trails to Jacob Crieghoof's farm. When they arrived at the back of Jacob's house, he greeted them with a gesture to go to the barn.

As the men sat on the tail of the wagon box, Philip asked, "What word have you about the Commissioners of Sequestration taking John Farlinger's farm? I worry about his wife Sophia and his daughter Elizabeth Farlinger only seven and his son John Farlinger Jr. only five."[520]

"I've no word on Farlinger's place, but much of Sir John's property is for sale or rented as are some of Colonel Guy Johnson's, Walter Butler's, Lewis Clement's and Henry Hough's.[521]

Peter asked, "Is there word of any of the King's men coming to the valley to protect us from the Rebels' daily abuse?"

"Aye. Christian Dillenbach Sr. of Stone Arabia, Johannes Ault of Kingsborough, and Michael Carman Sr. of Philadelphia Bush often provide victuals for scouts coming into the valley or help others find guides to Canada. The Rebels think Christian's sons Martin Dillenbach and Henry Dillenbach obnoxious and resistant to the cause. In fact, just the other day, Martin raised a stick with a linen handkerchief tied to the end, and waving it said, 'Huzzah for King George!' I fear he'll soon be arrested."[522]

Jacob continued telling Philip and Peter what he knew, "Christian tells me that the Fraser boys William Fraser Jr. of Ballstown and his brother Thomas Fraser of Johnstown had instructions from Captain Daniel McAlpin to recruit men for a Corp. They recruited about 40 men when an informant alerted the militia. They were forced to hide in unfamiliar woods for considerable time with no food. They hoped a guide would take them to join the British troops, but 400 men of the militia pursued them, and they were overtaken, arrested, and sent to Albany. William, Thomas, and Donald Fraser were sentenced to die. With good fortune, they escaped and are now with General Burgoyne at Fort Edward."

"What of Mr. Fraser Sr.? He gave such loyal service to Sir William as a trader at Niagara for so many years"

"Through all of this, the old man suffered unimaginable torment. They plundered all his farms and sold what was left. They left him with nothing of any value. William Jr. and Thomas' wives and children were forcibly and violently turned out and driven away."[523]

Peter sighed and said, "Many men are leaving to join the British, but it sounds like soldiers mayn't come to the valley to protect us. What are we to do Papa? It sha'n't be long before they find a reason to arrest us and throw us in jail. We've avoided signing their oath or enlisting in Fisher's regiment for almost a year. We cannot keep failing to muster. We'll be arrested. 'T'is the law.[524] And Mama is so nervous all day long. She paces. She doesn't sleep. I hear her up at night."

"I know son. I see her worry. We must yet be strong and patient. I sha'n't leave this farm 'til they drive me out!"

Jacob nodded and said, "Aye. Many of our friends and neighbours left and more have recently followed. Henry Hare and an Indian guide had the task of carrying letters and intelligence from Johnstown to Quebec. They were discovered and fled into the woods. The Rebels swiftly followed on horseback and on foot. 'T'is the last we know of them. We hope the deep snow was to their advantage and that they escaped pursuit. Peter Davis from west of Caughnawaga and Anthony's Nose and Frederick Dachstader and John Dachstader are also on their way to Quebec."[525]

With his lips pressed tight, Peter nodded then said, "Aye. And I hear John Waite's boys Joseph Waite and George Waite fled too."

Jacob answered, "And about eighty five men march to Canada as we speak. Michael Warner, John Peascod, Philip Klein, John Friel, Jacob Waggoner, Johannes Hartle Jr. and Johannes Ault's boy Michael Ault and David Jeacock's boys Francis Jeacocks and John Jeacocks are among the eighty five."[526]

Philip leapt off the wagon and started pacing near the stacks of hay saying, "If any more have to flee all who are left will be too young or too old to resist the rebellion. This leaves so many families exposed! The women are frightened and rarely leave their farms. They don't even have the comfort of their church. Reverend John Mckenna of Scotch Bush escaped last month, and I hear St. George's Episcopal Church in Schenectady was closed, and they've arrested Reverend John Doty. They accuse him of plotting with the Negroes against the state and think he wants to destroy the town. He was acquitted but taken again and refused to sign their oath. He's now at Albany Jail."[527]

Jacob jumped off the wagon and, with his arms clutching his sides, he paced too saying, "Take heart friend. Troops will come to assist us. There's word that soon Sir John will come into the valley from the west at Fort Stanwix and General Burgoyne from the north. They'll take Albany and cut off the Rebels' supplies from the Hudson Valley and New York City and take possession of our rich farmland and supply of grain. Sir John has sent John Mcdonell of Charlotte River into the valley to recruit troops for the KRRNY. At Kingsborough, Johannes Ault's boys Nicholas, Frederick, and Henry have gone, and Lucas Bowen at Philadelphia Bush. And near Anthony's Nose, William Casselman Jr. and his brother Severinus Casselman have gone. Their brother Warner Casselman of Canajoharie went too."[528]

Philip continued to pace. Peter turned to Jacob and asked, "What's the strength of Fisher's Mohawk District 3rd Regiment?"

Jacob Crieghoof replied, "There're many volunteers and every day Lieutenant John Marlet and Lieutenant Henry Hanson enlist more recruits. Captain Jelles Fonda has recruited men over fifty for his Associated Exempts. He's recruited John Kitts Sr. and Jacob Kitts, Conrad Smith, and Johannes Richtmeyer. 'T'is hard to know for what reason some of the recruits joined the regiment. Some are harassed or threatened into compliance, some join to keep their families safe, others really haven't yet decided if they believe in King over rebellion, and some wait to see which side offers them the best chance of retaining their farms and possessions. Many just want to preserve their life's work and their children's birthright. 'T'is a question to which I'm quite sure I know the answer when I see Johannes Ault Sr., Johannes Hartle Sr., Jacob Eberhart Van Koughnot, Jacob Henry Alguire, and Lawrence Eaman as recruits."[529]

Philip replied, "I'm sure I know what pushes Jacob Henry Alguire to join. He's my daughter Catharina's father-in-law, and if his decision keeps her safe we're better for it. 'T'is not my place to judge. There may be a day when we must choose."

"Papa, we must be on our way home. We promised Mama we'd get some chicks from Mr. Gallinger."

Philip nodded and said, "Good day Jacob. 'T'was much needed news. If ever need be, our home is a place of safety for you and yours."

'T'was mid-June and a breezy warm day when Catrina asked Philip to hitch Apple and Bess to the wagon. She finished planting the garden several weeks ago, and there was plenty of maple syrup put away this spring. Now, she wanted to travel up to Philadelphia Bush to visit Michael and Elizabeth. Elizabeth was five months pregnant with their fifth child. Catrina worried. There were always soldiers along the road through Philadelphia Bush. As she filled two baskets with crocks of syrup, dried meat, loaves of bread, and apple dumplings, Anna Margaret and Dorothy came in the back door holding a basket stuffed with four chicks from Michael Gallinger Sr..

Anna Margaret lifted the basket toward Catrina saying, "We want to bring Elizabeth these chicks."

"That'll be a nice, but we can only spare two. Take two back and come to the wagon. We'll be on our way soon. I want to stop at Mrs. Cryderman's."

After stopping to check on the Crydermans, Martin drove the wagon north toward Philadelphia Bush. For a year now, whenever the family was out in the wagon or sleigh, they headed toward their destination without stopping and with very little giggling or jostling from anyone in the back. The joy of getting out had all but disappeared. Martin steered the horses up Michael and Elizabeth's narrow lane into the yard. Down in the gulley behind their cabin, he saw Michael, Johannes George Alguire, Martin Silmser, Nicholas Silmser and his brother John Henry felling trees. Catrina and the girls took their baskets into the cabin, and Martin and Peter walked down the gulley toward the working men.

Peter called out, "Hello Michael. We've no axes today, but we can roll logs."

Waving his hat, Michael called back, "Come and sit with us while we have some rum and rest a while." The men laid down their tools and sat together away from the fallen logs.

Johannes George Alguire tipped back his cup of rum then said, "I've news from Schoharie valley and beyond. My father-in-law David Eny has family there, and they tell him of Joseph Brant's efforts to gather White men and some Six Nations from the Schoharie valley and even as far away as the Delaware and Susquehanna Rivers. Joseph wants to move the Fort Hunter Mohawks to safety. He raises the British flag at his village to show his loyalty to King George. His men are known as Brant's Volunteers and were eager to find someone to lead them as they struggled against the persecution of the Rebels."[530]

"Henry Hough and his brother Johannes Hough joined Brant and John Glasford from the Susquehanna, Henry Bush from the Delaware, and another named George Barnhardt and Johannes Barnhardt from Popachton on the east Delaware. Three others were taken prisoner and are at Esopsus, Ulster County on a prison ship, Jonas Wood from the Hardenburg Patent and Jacob Middagh and John Middagh of Stone Ridge, Ulster County. Jacob Middagh and others were sentenced to death by hanging."[531]

Peter asked, "What of Brant's Volunteers now?"

"More than 100 men gathered at Unadilla west of Charlotte River where General Herkimer met with Joseph to try and ease the tension between settlers and Brant's men and ease the settlers' fears of Indian attacks. Daniel Service, son of Christopher Service Sr. of Charlotte River, was taken prisoner for declaring his loyalty to the King. Now, Brant's Volunteers are on their way to Oswego to join the King's troops."[532]

"Aye. I know Daniel's Uncle, Captain Peter Service Sr." Philip puffed a few times on his pipe then said, "Hmm, now there's John McDonell of Charlotte River, Major Butler, Sir John, Joseph Brant and his volunteers, and even Hessian Jaegers all at Oswego. They'll soon have enough men to come into the valley to recover their lands and their families and to assist us. They best come soon most folks are losing hope."

It was the end of July and the Eamers needed to get into the fields. Peter, Martin, and Johannes spent days checking the horses' and oxen harnesses, sharpening scythes, and repairing rakes. Philip joined them in the barn one afternoon to ready the wagon for the fields. Martin rose from his work, dipped the ladle into the bucket, and gulped back cool fresh water.

As Martin set the ladle back in the bucket, he looked up and saw Jacob Henry Alguire and Martin Alguire ride into the yard. "Good day friends. Is it news you bring or offers of assistance as we ready for the harvest?"

Martin Alguire dismounted and said, "'T'is news of troops at Fort Stanwix, now called Fort Schuyler by the Rebels, and a cry for Tryon County militia."

"Pray, what are the militia demands now?"

"General Nicholas Herkimer and the Tryon Committee of Safety issued a plea for men to rouse up and crush the British tyrants who are now at the western door of the valley. They speak of the tyrants and their savages murdering and scalping innocent children."[533]

"'T'will be a difficult task for General Herkimer and Colonel Fisher to rouse many. Most men are discouraged with news of General Burgoyne advancing from the north and the gathering of men under Joseph Brant. They fear all will be lost under the tomahawk and knife of the Iroquois. Frederick Helmer warned the Tryon Committee of Safety that the Iroquois will join Colonel Daniel Claus, and William Seeber Sr., the Chairman of the Committee, laments the deplorable situation in the valley and has sent for help."[534]

"I've seen men on the march toward German Flats. They are to muster with General Herkimer. His plea seems to have stirred their fire for liberty."

Jacob Henry nodded and said, "Aye. Even Captain Jelles Fonda marches with his Associated Exempts and Captain Gerrit Putnam of Kingsborough Patent with his Company. And, Captain John Davis of Sacandaga Patent. To not follow will fall hard on those who do not muster. These men leave their fields at a most unwanted time. They cannot leave their crops sit for long."

Martin sat next to his brothers Peter and Johannes and said, ""'T'will be noticed that we did not muster. We'll risk taking the mark of Tory."[535]

It was early in the morning on 7 August 1777. Catrina was preparing a meal, Anna Margaret was in the barn milking the cows, and Dorothy was collecting eggs. Philip and Peter were harnessing the horses to the wagon when Michael Gallinger Sr. galloped up to the barn.

Philip dropped the harness and said, "Michael you've been riding fast. Your horse is wet! Pray what trouble is there?"

Michael leapt off his mare and barely hit the ground when he said, "There's news from Fort Schuyler! 'T'was carnage! A few men have returned with the news."

"Slow down Michael. I can barely understand what you're saying. What happened at Fort Schuyler?"

"Not at the fort, but near. In a wooded ravine at Oriskany. General Nicholas Herkimer's troops were on their way to Fort Schuyler to support Colonel Peter Gansevoort. There was an ambush and General Herkimer's troops were slain by General St. Leger. Men of the KRRNY, Joseph and his Volunteers, and Major Butler and the men of his Indian Department led the ambush. There were five companies from Colonel Fisher's 3rd Regiment in the midst and more at the rear of the march. General Herkimer is gravely wounded. His Captain, John Davis, is dead. And, William Seeber Sr. and his sons Severinus and James Seeber are killed. Jacob Empey, Philip and William's brother, was killed. Henry Fetterley of Guilderland was taken prisoner and killed. His brother Peter fought with Major Butler. Captain Andrew Dillenbach, Christian's nephew was killed. Hundreds others killed, too many badly wounded and left to lose their scalp and die.

"The ground was red with blood and bodies. The men fought hand to hand, brother against brother, cousin against cousin. Joseph and his men chased those retreating and finished them with hatchet or spear. The Tryon militia are ruined! Casualties near 500."

"What of Sir John's KRRNY. Our boys!"

"Their losses were less. The 1st Battalion was there. Our Jacob and William Sheets, Michael Ault, Christopher Hanes, and Mattheus Snetsinger were there. As were Captain Richard Duncan's Company, Captain Alexander MacDonnel, and Captain Patrick Daly's Company. Sir William's dear friend, Major James Gray and Captain Stephen Watts were wounded. Captain Lieutenant John McDonell of Charlotte River was killed, and John Hare Jr. is dead."[536]

Peter leaned heavy against the wheel of the wagon and said, "Mr. Gallinger, what of the Mohawks of Fort Hunter. Little Abraham has always wanted peace."

"'T'is no more."

"What's no more?"

"The great Iroquois Confederacy. The central council fire of the Iroquois at Onandaga was extinguished several months ago, and the Oneida fought with the Rebels. Most others fought with the British. The Oneida and Seneca lost many in the battle. They seethed with revenge, howled and clamoured to kill as many as they could find."[537]

After the battle at Oriskany, Catrina willed the warm days of August away. There was always talk of the battle among tenants and talk of the wounded and dead. Lucas Feader Sr. had thrown his son William Feader out of the house for his work with the Rebels in preventing General St. Leger from passing along Wood Creek to Fort Stanwix. Many of the crops were left to rot on the ground. Except for Little Abraham, most of the Fort Hunter and Canjoharie Mohawks fled to Sorel near Montreal. Fort Hunter was plundered and became a tavern for the rebels. Reverend John Stuart was arrested. Tempers of the Oneida, militia, and Committee men were fierce. For anyone with a slim connection to a known or suspected Tory, the slightest misstep got them harassed, fined, or jailed. Many fled to the woods and hid, others enlisted. Several men from the Schoharie Valley enlisted including John Chrysler, Nicholas Mattice, and Christian and Frederick Bauch of Cobus Kill. Captain Walter Bulter, Lieutenant William Reyer Bowen, and Captain Peter Ten Broeck were arrested.[538]

Near the end of August, the Eamers learned of the suffering of the family of Philip Empey Sr.. The Empeys were targets of Rebel fury when Philip's wife Maria Elizabeth Barbara Schultz and their youngest children were thrown in Johnstown Jail after Philip and his sons escaped from jail for refusing to muster at Fort Dayton. The Rebels also offered a £50 reward for the capture of Philip dead or alive. When Maria and the children were released and sent home, Maria found Rebels there. She was beaten, and four men dumped her on the road, leaving her for dead. Philip came out of hiding to save his wife while his sons Philip Empey Jr., Adam P Empey, William Empey, and Jacob Empey went to join the British. Only Christopher, Peter, Henry, and Anna Maria Empey were left at home with their father and mother. Their suffering was more difficult knowing that Philip Empey Sr. brothers Adam, John, and Jacob were soldiers of Colonel Jacob Klock's Regiment of the Palatine District.[539] Warner Casselman of Canajoharie and his brother William Casselman Jr., whose wife Anna Margaret Empey was Philip's sister, went north soon after the Empeys.[540]

Weeks passed before Catrina, Anna Margaret, or Dorothy dared spend time outside of the house. They picked and dried their apples and made their own cider; a trip to Johannes Veeder's mill was too risky. The men brought in their crops, but most of it was confiscated at the grist mill. The Eamers were left with a little ground wheat, but their corn remained safe in the barn.

Catrina noticed the musty smell of the fallen leaves on the ground when she ventured out to the wood lot with a meal for Philip and the boys. On her way along the path, she tripped several times over tree roots almost losing the basket of food and drink. She turned a corner in the path and saw the men working. Waving the basket in front of her, she hollered, "Some food for your weary selves." Finding a spot under a large maple tree, she sat and broke a piece of bread and cheese for herself. "We must get to see Elizabeth. She's soon to deliver her baby. I don't know how well they fare, and I worry."

Philip replied, "'T'is too dangerous for you to walk the roads or the forest paths. Fort Schuyler is still under siege, General Burygoyne fights to our east at Saratoga, and the militia scours the woods through Kingsborough and Sacandaga for our hiding men. Most here are terrified of an Indian war. Martin and I'll go and check Elizabeth and the children."

Martin set his tin cup on a stump and said, "We've news that Major John Butler raised a Corp of rangers, most are from the Susquehanna and Delaware

Rivers, but some are from here.[541] And, there's word that many assist British scouts from the west and the north. William Philips Jr. gave shelter and provisions to Henry Hough's and Henry Hare's scouting parties for more than a week."

Catrina shook her head and answered, "Aye, and William is now confined in the Johnstown Jail where he must pay for his own fire and water!"[542]

It wasn't many days later when Catrina was washing the morning meals pots and readying food for the evening. She had a pot in her hand when she heard the noise. She whirled around dropping the pot as she stared at Philip. Placing his large hand on her shoulder, he whispered, "Be easy dear wife. 'T'is just me."

With her voice raised, Catrina replied, "I've not been easy for months husband. The only thing that settles me is knowing that my Elizabeth safely delivered a baby girl. I can only hope her baptism will be as planned. Anna Margaret and Daniel McGregory are the baby's sponsors!"[543]

"I hope all goes well too. But, it might not happen. News has spread that General Burgoyne surrendered, General St. Leger and his men have withdrawn from Fort Schuyler towards Oswego with General Benedict Arnold in pursuit, and France has entered the war against Britain."[544]

Catrina gripped the edge of the table, lowered her head, and sobbed, "Philip what are we to do. They'll take our farm! They've just taken everything of Philip Empey's, and he sits with his wife in Schenectady as she lay dying!" Catrina gasped and sobbed as she blurted out the last words, "The Oneida have plundered Miss Molly Brant's home at Canajoharie!"[545]Philip held her close as she sank into his arms. She buried her face into his shirt and mumbled, "There's nothing left for us to do."

"We must be strong for our children. Winter has begun. The fighting will ease. The British will recover and come again.

It wasn't until February 1778 that Philip and Catrina were able to take the sleigh up to Philadelphia Bush to see Michael and Elizabeth and their new granddaughter Margaret Myers. As the horses pulled the sleigh down Montgomery Street and turned the corner onto Glebe Street, they passed the jail. Anna Margaret and Dorothy sat low in the back of the sleigh covered with a black bear hide.

The bear hide muffled Dorothy's voice when she said, "Papa look at the soldiers and the pickets all around the jail."

Looking straight down Glebe Street, Philip answered, "Shh Dorothy. We mustn't stare. Those are Colonel Frederick Fisher's men. They're the garrison guarding the prisoners." Dorothy slipped further under the bear skin as the sleigh passed the jail.

Catrina whispered, "Philip, I saw Henry Shew. He's a Sergeant. Frederick Sammons too, and I think that's John C. Service, Christopher Service's boy. Captain Peter Service Sr. nephew."

"I saw them too, and Captain Jelles Fonda, and Adam Ruppert with Lieutenant Henry Hanson.[546]

When they arrived at the Myer's cabin, Philip took a chance and went to Jacob Myer's cabin to learn news of scouting parties and activities of the Tryon County militia. At Jacob's, they shared a cup of rum, and Philip learned that there were scouts near Johnstown not long ago.

Jacob recounted all that he knew, "Aye Philip, there've been scouts. Christian Dillenbach Sr. near Stone Raby and Philip Cook of Canajoharie offer them provisions and secret them in the woods.[547] They say there're militia up at the Sacandaga River, and they're constructing a Blockhouse. So, they frequent the roads and paths through the Mayfield Patent, Philadelphia Bush, and Kingsborough. I've seen them pass our farm a few times. Johannes Alguire Sr. saw them too. The scouts tell me that Sir John's 1st Battalion is on the south side of the St. Lawrence River at LaPrairie, Quebec. Most of our men are in Captain Patrick Daly's Company. Some, who are now at Longueuil, Quebec, are in Captain Lieutenant Joseph Anderson's Company. John Farlinger is a Drummer, John Smith a Sergeant, and Francis and John Jeacocks are Corporals. And, Reverend John Doty is their Chaplain. Captain Tice, Henry Hare, Robert Picken, and Lewis Clement and the rest of the Indian Department are at Montreal. For now, some leave Quebec and come south on scouting parties, most wait out the winter."[548]

Through the spring of 1778, Philip, Johannes, Martin, and Peter rose early as they always had, but now a distinct difference to their morning routine was a discussion about how they would maneuver there activities to get the most work done while avoiding being seen, stopped, and questioned by passing militia or suspicious neighbours. They always saw militia moving along the road, passed the farm toward Johnstown, or north toward Philipdelphia Bush. It was most difficult when they were called out to do their share of road work.

Johannes noticed a few Oneidas pass by and said to his father and brothers, "'T'is noticeable there are few Six Nations men who travelled to Johnstown to speak with General Schuyler."

Martin agreed, "Aye. Mattheus Link tells me the Seneca still fume after heavy losses at Oriskany and refused to meet with Schuyler. Seneca warriors replied to Schuyler's invitation saying "'No, the Rebel axes still stick in their heads.'"[549]

"'T'is a great fear of the Rebels that the Six Nations side with the British. When armed for war, there's little that can be said or done to lead the warriors away from their ways of revenge and their ways of fighting. 'T'is said that Joseph Brant and John Butler recruit more and more each day."

It was morning near the end of June. Philip was in the barn checking a litter of piglets when Catrina walked passed one the large doors with red and green star motifs that Catharina and Elizabeth painted so many years ago. Catrina entered the barn and walked across the threshing floor. She peered over the rail to the lower level where she saw Philip in a stall amidst six piglets.

Leaning over the rail, she smiled and said, "'T'is a rare day that we all go to visit Michael and Elizabeth with Martin and Catharina joining us. Have you chosen a piglet for each of them?"

"Aye. There are two fine ones in this litter. I'll be at the wagon soon."

"Fine husband. We all wait."

From the back of the wagon, Dorothy called out, "Papa hurry. Those little ones will wiggle right out of your hands, and 't'is no fun chasing pigs!"

The Eamers arrived at the Myers cabin and saw Martin Alguire and Catharina with all five of their children. Maria Salome and Philip scampered about the yard trying to keep up with John and Peter. Catharina held Daniel as he squealed and giggled at the sight of the piglets. Everyone gathered at the back of the cabin out of sight of patrolling militia. Philip sat with his sons and sons-in-law around a small fire. He set out his tobacco and pipe like he was erecting a shrine then gulped back a swig of rum. This past year whenever he anticipated hearing difficult news, he wanted to be prepared. Today would be one of those days.

Martin Alguire leaned back in his chair and said, "There's much news over the whole valley these past weeks. The British sent scouts and small raiding parties from the north. Major John Butler and Joseph Brant retaliate for Rebel cruelties and are determined to rid the valley of any possessions or property that might aid the rebellion, or they take what might aid the British. Just a few weeks ago, Butler and Brant swept through Cobleskill killing nineteen people, burning ten houses and barns, and driving away at least 200 cattle. Jacob Frymire, son of Johannes and grandson of Michael Frymire was killed and scalped. Jacob's Uncles Philip Frymire and Nicholas are said to have been with Butler. I think Lucas Feader Sr. and Francis Ruppert have land just south of Cobleskill"[550]

Peter set another log on the fire and said, "Aye, and a raiding party was just north of Herkimer in the spring. They say Jacob Countryman son of Conrad of Canajoharie, Severinus Casselman, and Lucas, William, and West Bowen were with Butler."[551]

Martin nodded, "So many settlements destroyed. I hear Springfield and Andrewstown. There's nary a house standing, cattle, oxen, and horses taken, crops burned, and all the settlers huddle in the forts for protection, or they flee as far as the Hudson."[552]

Philip reached for a hot stick in the fire and while lighting his pipe said, "Johannes Alguire tells me he and his son Johannes George were trapping beaver in the wetlands near the Sacandaga River the first days of June. They spotted a large raiding party of near 200 Indians with Loyalists between the Sacandaga River and Johnstown. Johannes and Johannes George flew the area for fear of their lives. They heard later from Michael Carman Sr. that Michael and several others had been working on the roads and were taken by the Indians. The Indians took them as far as Sir William's Fish House where they were released. Henry Wormwood of Mayfield and Edward Connor of Kingsborough were with Michael. The raiding party of Major John Ross, Loyalists, and Indians destroyed much in their path towards Johnstown. Godfrey Shew and three of his sons Jacob, John, and Stephen were taken, and an alarm was raised at Caughnawaga. Settlers flew to the church for safety."[553]

Michael Myers leaned toward the fire and said, "Next will be German Flats or Canajoharie. All their grain will be burned, and the crops will lie on the ground. Those south of us are short of food and in great distress. Sha'n't be long before we'll need food. The men of Mohawk and Palatine districts are anxious to get the crops in and refuse to muster."[554]

"Aye. It seems the British swarm the valley. 'T'is good for us who are loyal and want this revolt crushed. But, the fighting is too close. Our families are in danger. And soon they'll come for us to sign their oath, enlist, or throw us in prison."

Almost in unison, Peter, Johannes, Martin, and Martin Alguire said, "We'll go to the British lines and enlist in Sir John's battalion."

It was nearing the end of August 1778 when Philip and his sons managed to finish the harvest, get a few hundred pounds of grain ground, fill the corn and grain bins, and put away some cider. One afternoon, they were out near the summer kitchen carving the carcasses of a pig and sheep they'd just slaughtered when Johannes Hough, Henry's son, emerged from the bush just north of the house and walked into the yard. Philip turned quickly with his saw raised and ready to strike.

Johannes raised his hand and said, "Mr. Eamer. 'T'is only me. I cannot stay long and must stay out of sight. They've taken your son-in-law Martin Alguire at Albany Bush. He was on his march to join the King's forces when he was taken. He's held at the Johnstown Jail. I fear they'll take him to Connecticut. Your daughter Catherine and their children are well. My father is near Johnstown with a scouting party and brought news that Johannes George Alguire of Philadelphia Bush was also taken to Johnstown Jail, and Jacob Henry Alguire has been called to muster for Captain Jelles Fonda's Company."[555]

Peter dropped his knife and wiped his hands saying, "Papa, we must tell Mama and go fetch Catharina and the children. They're in danger if the Rebels come to plunder their farm! I'll harness the horses now!"

Philip nodded and said, "Johannes you go with him. Martin stay here with your mother and sisters. We'll need to make room for Catharina and the five children."

Only a few minutes later Philip heard the back door slam and saw Catrina running toward him. "Philip! They have Martin! Catharina needs us. She's with child."

"Aye. Peter and Johannes leave soon."

As Philip picked up his hat and firelock, he turned toward Johannes Hough and said, "What other news does Henry bring?"

"He tells me men from several Companies of KRRNY at Montreal wish to be here defending their families. They've heard of the devastation in the valley and are worried for our safety. They've all signed a petition to their Commander General Guy Carleton. David McEwan, John Friel, Jacob Waggoner, Philip and Adam Empey, Michael and Christopher Gallinger of Captain Daly's Company all request to go to New York to recover their families and defend the province to which they belong."[556]

"We see and hear of defenders coming from the North, but what of Joseph Brant and Major Butler in the south?"

"They've raided areas along the Susquehanna and up to Unadilla and the Butternuts. A Rebel scouting party went along the Charlotte River to the house of Christopher Service Sr.. After much abuse from resisting arrest for aiding the British, a member of their party shot him dead in front of his wife and daughters. His young sons Christopher Service Jr. and John C. Service were taken prisoner. John is now ill at the prison in Albany.[557] To avoid prison or death, Christopher Service Sr. son's Daniel and Jacob Service fled to join Major Butler. I must go. I put you at risk if the militia find me here. Good day to you Sir."

Two weeks past and Catrina couldn't find a moments peace. Usually this time of year, Philip finds her in the summer kitchen pickling or making cheese and sauerkraut. He opened the door to the summer house and found Catrina pacing in front of the fireplace muttering to herself.

He walked toward her and rubbing her arms he said, "We'll get Martin out of jail."

"With all speed husband. But what of Catharina. She refuses to leave the farm for fear they'll raid her home and take their stock."

"We'll go as often as we can. There's soon to be a baby born to Johannes Hough and Jacob Henry's daughter Margaret Alguire.[558] We'll go when the baby comes. Johannes's father Henry has men scouting Albany Bush. They'll watch over her."

Catrina stood wringing the towel she had in her hands and said, "Our men are being taken. We've just enough food to get through the winter and hardly any occasion to cut wood for heat! There's no end to this horror!"

Over the next few days Philip and the boys spent their time felling trees and cutting firewood. One day while at their woodlot, Peter caught sight of a man coming toward them. He reached for his firelock and motioned to his brothers to do the same.

Peter called out, "What's your business Sir?"

"I'm a friend. I know your place to be safe. My name is William Kennedy, and I come as a scout for Sir John to bring back intelligence."

"Aye. Our place is safe. Come and rest Sir. We've a few provisions. What news is there from our south?"

"The Rebels have built three forts in the Schoharie Valley for settlers' protection from our raids. Pickets now surround the stone church at Schoharie and at two other stone houses."

"Have any of our Loyalists been taken?"

"I know of a father and son near Duanesburgh near the Helderberg Ridge. They are Adam Pabst and his son Rudolph Pabst. They were arrested for going to the Indians and taking several men with them. Also at the Helderberg Ridge near Rensselaerville, an old soldier with General Wolfe at Quebec Mr. John Becksted and Christopher Bern were marked for death. The Rebels came and shot Mr. Bern in the head and body, but John being not at home escaped. The Rebels later came, plundered his house, and took him and his wife and five young children, one an infant. They took them forty eight kilometres east across the Hudson River to Greenbush. Mr. Becksted was a loyal man who often secreted soldiers in his house or took provisions to them in the forest. And Janet Clement, the daughter of Lieutenant Lewis Clement, lies dangerously ill in prison."[559]

"Pray, who else?"

"Many men of Butler's Rangers were taken along the Susquehanna and Delaware."

"What other news Sir?"

"Mr. Jacob Crieghoof of Johnstown provided bail to release Mr. John C. Service from Prison. Major Butler requested he be released to assist John's widowed mother."

"Aye. Mr. Christopher Service Sr. was murdered at his home only a few weeks ago."

William Kennedy sighed and continued his story, "And, Christian Sheek sent his apprentice and journeyman to join Sir John.[560] At German Flats, Joseph Brant and his volunteers and Captain Caldwell of Butler's Rangers burned sixty three houses, fifty seven barns full of grain, and herded away many cattle. No captives were taken. The settlers took cover at Fort Dayton and Fort Herkimer."[561]

"Thank you Mr. Kennedy. If you pass again we've provisions."

"Take care Mr Eamer. Your sons are needed in the King's service."

"Aye. I fear soon enough."

Through the fall of 1778, Catrina paced, fidgeted, ate little, and slept less. She thought of not much else but Martin and Catharina. It would be a long winter for Catharina with five children and one due in March. As Catrina grew more anxious, the war raced through the valley like the plague. Everyday there was news of homes and crops burned and settlers captured, wounded, or killed. Hundreds of families fled to Schenectady or the safety of forts at Schoharie. The constant presence of the King's men quieted Loyalists' fears of abandonment but awakened their fears of starvation or revenge. News of the attacks at Springfield, Andrewstown, German Flats, and Cherry Valley consumed Catrina with the torment of guilt and despair. One reprieve, late in December, freed her from agonizing emotions. At the Caughnawaga church, Catherine Snyder, daughter of Adam Snyder and Catherine Link was baptized.[562] Catrina always enjoyed seeing Mattheus and his wife Magdelena. Mattheus Link, Catherine's father, was good friends with Andrew Snyder, Adam's father. There was tension in the church that day when Rebel and Loyalist families gathered. Gysbert S. Van Brakelen, Francis C. Putnam, and John Little, all soldiers in the 3rd Tryon County Regiment, baptized their children that day.[563]

With the constant strain of conflict, 1778 ended with the suffering of many whom Catrina, Philip, and their children once knew to be good neighbours and friends. Catrina no longer recognized the once pleasing valley she called home. It was as barren of friend and civility as it was of comfort.

On the last day of January 1779 just as day lit their room, the smell of fried pork and cornmeal roused Peter, Johannes, and Martin. Johannes was the first to slip out of bed and draw on his woolen trousers and shirt. "Up now brothers. Papa will be out in barn ahead of us." As they followed Johannes down the stairs into the comfort of Catrina's kitchen, Peter and Martin heard Anna Margaret and Dorothy stir in the room across the hall.

Catrina stood in front of her new iron stove tending the meat in the frying pan. As the meat fried, she gave the contents of the iron pot a stir then lifted it onto the middle of the table. She turned to Peter and asked, "Is the sleigh in good order? Tomorrow we must travel to Stone Raby to celebrate the baptisms of Johannes George Alguire and Margaret Eny's daughter Dorothy Victoria Alguire. Margaret's brother Godfrey Eny and his wife Maria Moore are the child's sponsors.[564] And, Henry Gallinger is to be a sponsor for Michael Swobe's daughter Dorothy."

There were still occasions at church when the Eamers spent a few hours enjoying the company of old friends. On this snowy winter day, Philip and Catrina visited with Michael and Agatha Gallinger and Mattheus and Magdelena Link. They were careful not to draw attention to themselves knowing they were always watched. Catrina noticed that Margaret Waldorf was there with her toddler Elizabeth on her lap and her son John Waldorf and her daughters Catherine, Maria, and Helena next to her. Sitting next to Margaret was Eve Clark. Margaret and Eve were neighbours on the Kingsborough Patent, and their husbands Martin Waldorf and Simon Clark were away with Colonel Daniel Claus and his Indian Department. Catrina hoped that Margaret and Eve avoided harassment by the Rebels.[565]

It was nearing the end of March 1779, and Catrina's memories of mountains of snow and the chill in her bones faded. She'd already made one trip to Albany Bush to visit Catharina and her new granddaughter Elizabeth. Catrina's visit was especially joyous because Martin was released from jail only a few weeks before Elizabeth's birth. Catrina was grateful that Martin was safe and that his release made the baby's birth so much easier for Catharina.

One morning soon after her visit, Catrina woke to see a sun beam cross the foot of their bed. She rolled closer to Philip liking the warmth of his body. It took several minutes to gather the courage to swing her legs out from under the covers and place her feet on the cold floor. She didn't usually rise before Philip but today was special. Their new granddaughter Elizabeth Alguire was to be baptized at Trinity Lutheran Church at Stone Raby.[566]

Catrina gently shook Philip and said, "'T'is time to rise husband. 'T'is better to move your aging bones before they stiffen for good."

She heard Philip's muffled sounds from under the bedding. He rolled over and said, "I'm awake dear wife but not sure I want to rise. I dread the discord that might come to our door."

"'T'will be a good day. There's a baptism."

Only a week after Elizabeth's baptism, Philip was in the orchard when he saw Martin and Nicholas Silmser walking towards him. He waved and called out, "Good day Sir."

Martin approached with Nicholas not far behind, "Good day Philip. Might Nicholas speak to you of something important?"

"Aye. 'Not troubling news I hope."

"No Sir." Nicholas replied. Martin sat on a nearby log leaving Nicholas and Philip next to a large blossoming Apple tree. As Nicholas removed his hat and reached out to shake Philip's hand, he dropped his hat and fumbled to retrieve it.

With a tilt of his head Philip said, "No need to shake my hand. Ye know me well."

"Aye Sir, since I was a boy." Standing stiff and still fumbling with his hat, Nicholas continued, "I've come to ask permission to marry your daughter Anna Margaret.[567] She's a fine woman, and my father is to give me thirteen acres of good farmland near my brother John Henry at Philadelphia Bush. Father and I've near finished a sturdy cabin."

Philip reached out placing his hand on Nicholas' shoulder and said, "You're a fine young man from a good family. I've known your father and mother over twenty years. My daughter will be in good hands during these fearful times. I give you both my blessing. When is this wedding to be?"

Nicholas blew out a huge breath dropped his shoulders and said, "At the end of this month Sir. There sh'an't ever be anything for you or Mrs. Eamer to worry about. I must go tell Anna Margaret the news!"

As Nicholas spun around towards the house, he dropped his hat, and Philip said, "Mind how much jumping about there is in the house. 'T'is too early for dancing!"

"Nay Sir, but sing we might."

Philip turned toward Martin and with a grin gave him a nod.

Martin rose from the log, and in a firm embrace with Philip he said, "'T'is a fine day when we can embrace as family!"

"Sha'n't be a day when we'll not be joyous about this union. I expect Anna Margaret, Dorothy, and Catrina are jumping about the kitchen now."

"Aye. Elizabeth Margretha was joyous when Nicholas told her his desires. I'm only sad that so many couples are married and babies born during these times of cruelty and deprivation."

"Well, we're living proof that unions and babies don't wait for peace and prosperity. They come regardless. We meet our challenges with God's help."

Martin nodded and said, "Sit Philip. I must tell you what I know of Rebel activities and the militia. They have orders to seize any stored grain from last year's harvest. Their army and destitute Rebel families need clothing and provisions. Michael Gallinger Sr. was obliged to surrender his wagon and horses to carry provisions to distressed families. And, he stabled twenty two span of horses for two nights.[568] We must find ways to secret our grain this harvest, or we'll find ourselves with nothing, and our families will starve for want of flour."

"'T'is a worry Catrina and I have most days. This year, as soon as the crops are off the field, 't'will be hid in several places. Catrina has already harvested mushrooms from the forest. They dry now."

"If there are safe opportunities to fish or hunt, dry as much as you can. Some of the best fishing is near Sir William's Fish House near the Sacandaga River, but the militia guards that point constantly. They're building a blockhouse for permanent guards and patrols. They call it Fort Fisher. The settlers fear that Sir John and the Indians will come again as they did last year, and they want protection."

"Aye. 'T'is a favourable entry and exit point for our scouts, soldiers, or those escaping confinement or harassment.[569] Captain Solomon Woodworth and Captain Samuel Rees are there with their Companies. I saw Christopher Service Sr. son John C. Service on his march there this winter. You can notice John most anywhere. He wears a yellow linen frock and pantaloons and has a white feather cockade in his hat. Young John is one of Captain Woodworth's best scouts, an enterprising young man. "Do you know Philip Helmer at Fonda's Bush? He lives not far from Sir William's Fish House near the blockhouse?"

Puffing on his pipe, Philip said, "Aye. I know of him."

"Philip's son John P Helmer was taken back in '77 at Ballstown with Henry Runnions on their way to join the King's service. They were imprisoned on a ship at Kingston, New York. After John's release, he joined Sir John's secret service in the KRRNY. Sergeant Henry Shew captured him while he was at home on parole at Fonda's Bush. Now they have him at Johnstown Jail."[570]

"Hmm, Peter Prunner, a scout for Sir John, must have come down the Sacandaga River. He frequented Albany Bush only a few days ago and told my son-in-law that Daniel Fykes was taken to Albany Jail."

"And how is Daniel's wife Anna Ruppert and their 5 young children, two young sons I'm certain? It must be a difficult time for her as her brother-in-law Philip Adam Fykes is with Jacob Klock's Regiment."

"Aye, the Fykes men, George, Henry, John, and Peter Fykes Jr. live on the Kingsborough patent close to Anna and the children. They are watched closely. Her sister-in-law Catherine Fykes and her husband Jacob Eberhart Van Koughnot live at Kingsborough too and help her."[571]

"Another King's patrol must have come down the Sacandaga River. The Fort Hunter Mohawk Peter, having but one hand, and two white men captured James Kennedy's son, young Samuel Kennedy of Corry's Bush (Princetown), along the King's highway near Fort Johnson. They'd two others and pinioned them all, but one escaped."[572]

"Keep a good eye friend. Too many are being taken and often sent to Connecticut or Kingston. That's too far for us to be of any assistance to them and leaves wives and children here in great distress."

"My hopes for Nicholas and Anna Margaret is that they can enjoy some kind of wedding celebration. Perhaps a few close friends can celebrate with us in our barn."

One day early in May, Philip and Catrina stood at the back of the house near the fence that surrounded their pasture. Each of them fixed their eyes on the field for signs of their winter wheat sprouting.

Catrina stood with her hands clasped in prayer and said, "Blessed Lord, have mercy on us and provide us with a bountiful crop. May your blessings pass over this valley and help those in need."

As Catrina prayed, Philip stared, nodded, and murmured, "Hmm. Aye."

Just as they turned to walk the fence line, Peter and Johannes came running from the barn hollering, "Papa, Catharina's Martin has gone!"

"What!" Philip yelled.

"He's gone with John Kuhlman, Henry Gallinger, and Philip Shaver's sons Adam Shaver and John Shaver, and Lucas Feader Sr. and his son Lucas."[573]

As Philip stomped and huffed toward Peter and Johannes he said, "Damn those Rebels, they just wouldn't leave him be. Ever since Martin was released from jail they've badgered him and Catharina! They've chased him out. Peter Prunner must've recruited those boys. Peter lives at Albany Bush near most of them."

Catrina grasped her skirt high as she trudged over the wagon path. When she caught up to Philip, Peter, and Johannes, she stopped and threw her skirt down saying, "Catherina is home with five children and little Elizabeth not even three months old! What's she to do?"

Putting his hand on her shoulder, Philip replied, "The Kuhlman's at Albany Bush are close by. They'll watch out for her."

Johannes nodded saying, "Aye. They can't forget that John Kuhlman's sister Christina was once married to our departed Sebastian Alguire."

Catrina answered, "But also know that John Kuhlman's brother Henry is with John Casselman's Company of Rangers!"[574]

June 1779 dragged along with work and worry. Catrina and Dorothy spent their time in the kitchen, outside doing laundry, tending the animals, or in the garden. One day, after spending a few hours tending the hogs and chickens, they sat near the barn doors talking about the star motifs painted on each of the doors wondering if the motifs' magic would protect them from the soldiers and Indians. From where they sat, they watched Philip help Peter train the new mare Philip bought in the winter from Michael Warner at Albany Bush. Martin Alguire told Philip about Michael's horses and his good stock. Apple was over twenty now and couldn't manage the hard work of the fields; so, they bought the young three year old mare and named her Star. She would have to pull the wagon and sleigh with Bess. They were lucky to have her given the army's hard use of horses.

Near the end of June, Catrina put what extra food she could in the back of the wagon while Philip hitched up Star and Bess. Soon, the wagon rolled along the road through Butlersbury south of Johnstown towards Elizabeth and their grandchildren. After seeing Elizabeth for a few hours, they stopped to see Lawrence Eaman and his sons John and Jacob Eaman hoping there'd be valuable news. Lawrence met them coming up his lane and helped Philip hitch the horses. Catrina said good day and went toward the cabin to visit Regina. With a wave of his arm, Lawrence pointed to chairs on the porch.

The two men sat for several minutes before Philip said, "The Rebels have been relentless in their retaliation for the ruin waged upon the valley last year. 'T'is early in the year and many Loyalists have been imprisoned or fled, and the militia impress our horses, wagons, and grain. What reports do you hear that might change our troubles?"

"None that will change it for the better. I fear much worse. I heard news of Rebel revenge on the Six Nations for their part at Wyoming and Cherry Valley. They think the cheapest way to secure the frontier is to wage expeditions against the Indians. General James Clinton and General Sullivan lead the expeditions. With 500 men, Lieutenant Colonel Marinus Willet's army just destroyed the village of Onandaga. They burned over fifty houses and all their corn and beans, fine horses and all other stock were killed and thirty three were taken prisoner and twelve killed. The army made plans months ago for destruction of other villages. No one knew. Surprise is to their advantage and the Indians' annihilation. The armies march as we speak."[575]

"This will do nothing to secure the frontier. 'T'will only add to the Indians' bitter resentment after false accusations at Wyoming and the White man's relentless disregard for their hunting grounds. This, I fear, draws upon the Indians an infinite hatred and revenge and sets fury in motion."[576]

"Rebel revenge is plain to see when so many of our friends and neighbours are taken prisoner, most dealt harsh treatment and some dealt a sentence of death."

"'T'is true. Lieutenant Henry Hare of Captain Tice's party of the Indian Department and Sergeant Newbury were arrested as spies only a few days ago. They came down from Montreal to visit their families, and their neighbours thinking they were acting as spies alerted Captain William Snook of their presence. At night, Sergeant William J. Newkirk's men surrounded Hare's home near Fort Hunter and took him and Sergeant Newbury for trial before General James Clinton at Canajoharie. Both were found guilty and hung at Canajoharie only a few days ago!"

"May God keep their souls. And what of Henry's wife Alida Vrooman and their six children? I think the oldest is a son Johannes not yet thirteen."

"Alida and her children are now prisoners."[577]

"Conditions in our jail remain cruel. All the prisoners, some in irons for months, must pay for their own wood and water, and food is inadequate, only bread and milk for some. Our jail at Johnstown is full of prisoners and they've not enough guards. They're sending prisoners to Albany or to Connecticut. Philip Helmer of Fonda's Bush is confined, and Henry and Jacob Merckle of New Dorlach, Julius Bush, Dieterich Merckle, Philip Empey Sr., William Empey, Randel Hewit, Dieterich Loucks of Stone Raby, George Fykes and Peter Fykes Jr., Nicholas, Adam, and John Shaver, Johannes and Nicholas Ault, and Michael Van Koughnot of Kingsborough and George Eny of Albany Bush. They've taken Julius Bush to Hartford, Connecticut. A few prisoners were released on recognizance after Johannes Ault and Johannes Shaver paid their bail of £100. Godfrey Eny paid £200 bail for the release of his brother George as did John P. Empey for the release of his father Philip."[578]

Philip looked at Lawrence then lowered his head and said, "'T'is scandalous to force us to sign an Oath of Allegiance, force us to fight for the cause of liberty, or to place us in jail for the smallest of infraction of their rules and then ask us to pay the price of a small farm to be released on supervision! All of this after ten to twenty years as their neighbours or friends. Dear Lawrence, there is no sense to any of this anymore. This is all too much. Most days I trudge through my work, making no plans for days ahead. My firelock and knife are with me everywhere I go. We hide our food. All in our household know where to hide. I worry about my sons. Will they be taken, mutilated, shot, or hung! Our countrymen run for their lives to the nearest fort or fortified house.[579] And, my dear wife ages before my eyes. When I look at her, I see no smile in her eyes or on her face. And of our farm I have great fears."

Lawrence leaned back in his chair and shrugged, "Our valley dies before our eyes. I fear we'll be forced to fight or flee."

A week after his visit to Lawrence Eaman, Philip and Johannes were herding sheep to pasture. All ten sheep were headed in the right direction when suddenly they scattered. Dorothy's screams frightened them. Philip turned and saw her running toward him, "They've got him! They've got him! Mrs Gallinger sent Mattheus and Magdelena Link! Mama sits in her chair. She doesn't talk. She doesn't move!"

"Where's Mr. Link? What did Mr. Link say Dorothy?"

"He's at the house with Mama. They've arrested Peter and Johannes George Gallinger and the Carpenter Mr. Andrew Millross.[580]

Peter and Johannes collected the sheep and quickly moved them into the pasture then raced to the house. Philip burst through the kitchen door and hollered, "Where is he? Where's Peter?"

Mattheus Link stopped Philip as he came in the door and said, "He's at the Johnstown Jail. A couple of Lieutenant John Little's men arrested him on the road to Tribe's Hill. He must have been on his way home."

Philip pulled a chair next to Catrina. With his hand resting on her leg he asked, "Why? Why did they take him? For what reason?"

"He told the soldiers harvest was approaching, and he was needed at home so could not enlist. He sits now in irons waiting to go before Captain Jelles Fonda." Philip sat with his head low and his hands running through his hair.

Mattheus pulled a chair next to Philip and said, "All will be well Philip. Jelles Fonda has been your friend for many years. He knows your family. We'll get Peter out. But, we must keep Johannes and Martin safe. They are at risk of jail too. We know 't'is law since '78. All men between sixteen and fifty must enlist. Captain Fonda's been pushing for improving protection in the valley. Increasing enlistments is his aim."[581]

Catrina rose from her rocking chair and facing the men said, "Why my Peter? William and Michael Van Koughnot were only fined £5 and £10 when they refused to bear arms.[582] 'T'is not right. Maybe there's something else! Something more serious! Philip we must go. I'll bring food and water, for Johannes George too."

"Git on!" Philip called out to the horses as he urged them toward town. One after another, Catrina mumbled prayers as she bounced on the wagon seat and held the basket of food tightly in her lap. In the back of the wagon, Agatha gripped Maria Catherine Gallinger's hand with one hand while the other gripped her basket of food. Agatha's daughter insisted on coming. She was frantic with worry about her brother and Peter.

Michael bellowed over the noise of hooves, tack, and wheels, "Philip, when we get to the jail, you stay with the horses. Agatha, Catrina, and Maria Catherine and I'll go into the jail. You've not enlisted. That'll aggravate them. You risk harassment. They'll be easy with me. I've enlisted with Fonda's Company as have many others."[583]

Catrina, Agatha, and Maria Catherine followed Michael up the small hill to the jail. As they reached the top of the hill, Michael tipped his black felt hat to the guards at the door and said, "Good day. We've heard there are two prisoners taken today along Tribes Hill Road. Their mothers and I've brought some food, and we've come to inquire of their well-being and the charges brought against them."

With their muskets at the ready, the guards stepped toward Michael and said, "Aye Mr. Gallinger. Your son is secured along with his friend Mr. Peter Eamer. You cannot pass beyond this point."

"What of the food we've brought."

"'T'will be delivered to them."

"I've your word?"

"Aye, our word."

"When do the men go before Mr. Fonda, and what are the charges against them?"

"They're charged with resistance to the cause and won't be before Mr. Fonda for a few weeks. He's at Albany and won't return until the end of July."

"We'd be grateful for a few words with them."

"Not allowed. None of our Tory scoundrels are allowed visitors."

Maria Catherine held onto Michael's arm and said, "Please Sir. I want to see that my brother and my friend are well."

"No Madam. No! Not even family."

Catrina took Maria Catherine's hand and turned to walk toward the wagon. As soon as their backs were to the guards, Maria Catherine burst into tears, "They'll be ill used or sent to Connecticut. I'll never see my brother or dear Peter again!"

"T'will not happen dear. Mr. George Schenck Sr. is with Captain's Little's Company, and he's a dear friend of ours over twenty years. And, he's Johannes George's godfather. He'll not let harm come to them."[584]

Wiping her tears with Catrina's handkerchief, Maria Catherine replied, "We cannot trust that they'll do that. Some things are no longer certain in the valley."

Every other day through the month of July, Philip, Catrina, Michael and Agatha paid the guards to deliver water and baskets of food to Johannes George and Peter. Time dragged on as they waited for Jelles Fonda's return and a hearing at the Court House. Philip knew the Rebels needed evidence against Peter, but he also knew that without Peter's signature on the Oath of Allegiance and a promise to enlist there would be a heavy fine and harsh treatment. Johannes George was only fifteen. Even though the law required men aged sixteen to fifty to enlist, they often took boys younger than sixteen. Too young, Philip thought, to be a soldier. And, Michael's son Henry Gallinger enlisted in Fisher's Regiment last year, but he went off and joined the British in May. And the Rebels knew that Michael Gallinger Jr. and his brother Christopher had already gone to the British.[585] This evidence would not hold well for Johannes George. None of Peter's brothers had yet joined the British nor enlisted in the militia. Reluctance to commit to the cause was almost as damaging as going to the British. Some men even took to hide in the forest for months. Philip knew that to avoid harassment, imprisonment, or confiscation of property one had to take a stand for the cause. So far he'd avoided enlistment. Each day, his avoidance put his family at risk.

Even continuous farm and house work couldn't keep Catrina distracted from worry. Philip witnessed her daily and sometimes hourly in fits of panic. One day, she even proposed the idea of bribing either Jelles Fonda or the guards to set Peter free. Finally, news came at the beginning of August 1779 that Johannes George was released with the promise he'd enlist next year when he turned sixteen. His release was both a curse and a blessing for Catrina. At last she and Philip had news of Peter. They didn't waste any time visiting Johannes George and questioning him about Peter's well-being.

The Eamers' anguish lingered during the long slow days of September as they waited for word of a hearing for Peter. Finally, it came. One early morning at the end of September, they all arrived at the Court House. Philip and Catrina sat in the front row behind the prisoner's box and waited. Two guards brought Peter into the court room, and with needless vigour they slammed him into the prisoner's box. Catrina couldn't help but notice the irons on his wrists and legs and that he'd lost weight. It was an agonizing hour that passed as they listened to the charges, the evidence, and the verdict. Despite the fact that Jelles and Philip had been friends for over twenty years and little evidence, there was still a harsh penalty. Peter was ordered to enlist in Fisher's Regiment and his bail was set at £4.[586]

September 1779 had been a hard month, but Peter's return home offered great relief. While Philip and Catrina were effecting Peter's release, many women of the Kingsborough Patent petitioned the Governor for passes allowing them to travel with their families to Canada to join their husbands. The Commissioners of Sequestration confiscated the cattle and belongings of the men who had gone to the British. Catrina knew that Sergeant John Peascod's wife Molly was of this group of women. The women's desperation escalated when the Governor refused their petition unless those taken at Cherry Valley in '78 were returned. Hoping that permission to travel to Canada would be granted, the women had not planted crops for winter food.[587]

Starvation for them was now ever more probable. To make matters worse, a law was passed on October 22nd that required the forfeiture and sale of property of anyone who adhered to the enemy of the state. Philip and Catrina knew many who were indicted and whose property was confiscated. There were: Simon Clark, Lucas Feader, Henry Albrandt, William Schuman, Peter and Philip Service, Christopher Empey, and Michael Byrne. Sir John Johnson, Daniel Claus, Guy Johnson, Hans Jost Herkimer were indicted for treason and banished forever from the State.[588] For everyone, the fall offered no rest from the struggle to carry on amidst the fear and deprivation in a valley torn apart by war.

One afternoon in late October, Philip was secreting away a barrel of cider and the last of the dried fish and beef he had so purposefully prepared through September and October. Catrina added a few crocks of sauerkraut, two rounds of cheese, some corn cakes, dried fruit, potatoes, and squash to their stash. They just finished securing the door and hatch to one of their food pits and were spreading straw when Michael Gallinger Sr. appeared at the side of the barn. Philip yelled, "Michael announce yourself. You startled us!"

"Aye. 'T'is time we agreed on a secret signal."

"You and I and all of our sons know a good short wolf howl."

"How about two short wolf howls, one right after the other then silence."

"'T'is good Michael. I'll let Johannes, Martin, and Peter know."

"And I, Johannes George, Mattheus Link and Lawrence Eaman."

"What news have you of your sons with Sir John?"

"I only know that the men have gone to their winter quarters at Sorel, Coteau-du-Lac, and Montreal. And, there're almost 1000 refugees victualled near Montreal. They're housed in small camps on the Richeleau and St. Lawrence River. I hope the British provides them with shelter and a wood supply that shields them from the harsh winter."[589]

"We must prepare for winter. It seems there is not a time that the Rebels wouldn't come to drive us from our homes."

"May'nt be an issue during the winter months, but we must prepare ourselves for anything. I've readied two haversacks filled with food, flints, and warm clothes. They sit by the door next to my firelock and cartridge box."

"We'll do the same this day. Has Major Fonda called his Associated Exempts to serve?"

Michael nodded saying, "Aye. We were called to garrison Fort Plain and to go out on scouts. I excused myself on the grounds that the harvest work needed to be finished. Jacob Shew is acting as a substitute for me."[590]

"Peter hasn't been called out, and I hope 't'is the same during the winter months."

It was early November and the snow hadn't fallen yet, so Michael, Agatha, and their daughters Betsy, Dorothy, and Maria Catherine took the wagon to visit the Eamers. A few weeks ago, Michael offered to help Philip fix the iron runner on his sleigh. It needed to be in top working order in case it was needed for a journey to the British lines. The women were always glad of a chance to visit. Dorothy and Elizabeth hadn't seen Dorothy Eamer since Johannes George was released from prison, and this past year Maria Catherine never missed a chance to visit Peter. Michael pulled the wagon up to the side of the house, and there was a flurry of activity as Johannes George and Michael unloaded the food they brought.

Philip strolled across the yard, and while taking the pipe out of his mouth to accommodate his huge smile, he said, "Michael, those are two fine geese you've brought. We're in your debt! I've some dried mushrooms and salt pork to offer you."

"Mushrooms are always nice to find in stew. Thank you. One of these geese is for Michael and Elizabeth. I know you'll be to visit them at Philadelphia Bush before winter takes hold. I know they're to have a baby early in the year, and mothers need meat."

All afternoon the men carried on fixing the sleigh while the women shared news of recent births and weddings. But most importantly, they counselled each other about fitting actions and words if they happened upon the ornery nature of Rebel soldiers or neighbours supportive of the cause. They knew well of many occasions of robbing and bullying, and they never forgot what happened to Philip Empey's wife Maria Elizabeth Empey nor to Valentine Cryderman. Maria Catherine was the only one absent from the conversation. Almost as soon as they arrived, Dorothy saw her step out the back door and walk towards Peter who was waiting next to the summer kitchen. "Hmm," Dorothy thought as she watched them clasp hands, "If my brother doesn't marry that woman soon, he'll be much too hard to live with." When the time came for the Gallingers to leave, everyone gathered at the front of the house offering embraces and encouraging words that were meant to get each other through the tension of these troubled times. They all enjoyed the time spent together even though the intent of each of their tasks was to provide them all with a measure of safety and security.

Catrina welcomed the light of the moon in their bedroom. She felt secure knowing she wouldn't have to stumble about if she had to rise and dress in a hurry. Having Philip next to her was equally comforting.

She reached for his hand under the quilt and said, "'T'is always on my mind."

"What occupies your thoughts?"

"When and how we'll have to leave our home and farm. Will we be spared our dignity and our possessions? Or even our lives."

"Those are distressing thoughts dear wife. We sha'n't have to worry about any of that."

"Oh yay, 't'is possible. Hundreds of others have over these past few years. And, what if we're driven out in the cold of the coming winter. How will we ever survive? How will we be certain our children and grandchildren are safe? I don't know what to ask our Lord anymore. I've asked so many times for his mercy. Maybe we make the decision to leave or not leave and not wait for someone with a firelock pointed at us?"

"We shan't leave yet. 'T'is a long way to the British lines and we've no pass to travel the roads to Schenectady and Fort Edward. The trails to the Sacandaga and Lake George are too dangerous in the winter and we've no guide. We must hold hope that this horror ends soon, and we'll be safe in our home once again."

It was Christmas Eve 1779, and for a brief while Catrina felt safe in her home. Michael, Agatha, Johannes George, Maria Catherine, Dorothy, and Betsy were all at the Eamers' house this Christmas Eve. Much of the evening was spent praying for the men in their families who had joined Sir John's Regiment. Although separated from those they loved, their sons and husbands were now safe somewhere near Montreal. In April, Martin Alguire told Jacob Henry and Philip of his plans to join Sir John.[591] They supported him knowing he had already been imprisoned once in '78 for five months, he'd never take arms against the King, nor would he sign the Oath of Association, and he was watched closely. Thus, if taken again they knew his fate would most likely be a long prison sentence in Albany or Connecticut. Since Martin left, everyone spent as much time as they could looking after Catharina their six children and their animals.

When prayer for the divine celebration and for the safety of their men seemed exhausted as did everyone in the crowded sitting room, Peter rose from his chair and reached for Maria Catherine's hand. She rose and stood beside him. Peter turned and faced his family and said, "I know, even with the joy of the season, we all bear the burdens of this terrible war. There sha'n't be a better moment than now to reveal our joyous news. With the blessings of our parents, we are to be married at the Church at Caughnawaga in January."[592]

Dorothy rose, lifted her cup of cider and said, "Dear brother and sister-in-law. May your life together be long, blessed with many children, and filled with joy. 'T'is about time you decided on this union." Everyone rose and, each with wide smiles and sparkling voices, gave a toast that filled the room with delight.

By the end of January 1780, Peter and Catherine were settled in the little cabin on the Eamer property. They agreed it was safer for them to stay close to their families. For years Philip used the cabin as an office and kept it in decent repair. Despite repairs, the cabin had seen better years. Peter spent several weeks in the fall fixing timbers, building a bed, a table, chairs, and chopping their own supply of wood. Peter wanted to be prepared for a long winter. It was long and bitterly cold. For weeks, they both wore their wool coats from the time they rose until sunset when they crawled under the bear rug thrown on top of their bed. It was as severe a winter either of them had ever known. They were glad of the wood and the warmth of the fire.

Most of their days were spent near the warmth of the fire. Often Philip, Catrina, or Dorothy walked the few hundred metres from the house to bring food or share news. Peter and Catherine learned that Jacob Merckle of Stone Raby was released from prison with £100 bail and was to appear before the Commissioners when summoned. Also, as a result of his bail conditions, Philip Empey Sr. was granted permission to visit his relatives at Bowman's Creek and was to return in two weeks.[593] They also learned that several distressed families of men who joined the British were detained and were now offered in exchange for Rebel prisoners. The families would go by sleigh to Isle Aux Noix, Quebec. Most of the family names were familiar to Peter and Catherine. They were: John Friel, William Fraser Sr., Philip Shaver, the widow Hare, Robert Pickens, Colonel John Butler, Lewis Clement, Eve Clark, Hans Jost Herkimer, and Warner Casselman. Mr. Peter Hanson, a Rebel prisoner and brother of Lieutenant Richard Hanson of Butler's Rangers and brother-in-law of Jelles Fonda, was to be exchanged for one of Colonel Butler's sons, either Thomas or Andrew."[594]

Despite the welcome thaw in March, the Committee men and militia continued to terrorize suspect tenants or vigorously flush out known Tories to strengthen their numbers or banish them from the valley. Tenants in or near

Johnstown were ordered to form three Companies of Rangers by May. If they refused and did not take up arms against the British, they would be sent to Albany in irons, their houses destroyed, and all their property sold for the use of the cause.[595] A large group of Loyalist families who had their property confiscated and who were held in confinement finally received permission to go to Canada under the flag of Christopher Yates. Among the group were the families of Lieutenant Lewis Clement, Colonel John Butler, John Friel, Simon Clark, Hans Jost Herkimer, and Warner Casselman.[596]

Men of Captain John Casselman's Company and Captain Gerritt Putnam's Company were often seen patrolling Johnstown. Philip Empey Sr.'s brothers, Adam and John Empey, were among Captain Casselman's men. George Schenck Sr., George Schenck Jr., Nicholas Shaver, Johannes Alguire, and Philip Adam Fykes were recruited in Ensign Peter Vrooman's Company. Even with threats and harsh punishments for refusing to support the cause, the Scotsmen remained stubborn and did not join.[597]

Somehow in the midst of the tension and chaos, Catrina, Philip, Martin, and Dorothy made their way to church at Caughnawaga. It was a special service because Johannes was asked to be a sponsor for the baptism of Johannes Service, the son of Philip P. Service and Maria Catherine Seeber. At the same service, Daniel Fykes and Anna Ruppert baptized their son Jacob Fykes.[598] The Eamers did not stay long. They had their own news to celebrate. Peter and Maria Catherine announced they were expecting a baby in November.

April 1780 brought little relief from daily threats and torment. As Catrina prepared the family meal early one morning, she stood near the kitchen window stealing a glance at the blooming cherry and apple trees. There was a time when she would have stopped to give the brilliant trees a long and proper gaze. Today, as most days, she kept her head low, and her hands shook as she peeled the breakfast potatoes and tried to cut even slices of cheese.

Philip walked up quietly behind her. As he let his hands fall on her shoulders like a wool blanket he said, "'T'is a good morning wife. Are you well?"

"Not so well dear husband."

"What's ailing you?"

"'T'is fret and fuss that never leaves. Only yesterday I heard a past friend say, 'A Tory is a thing whose head is in England and its body in America, and its neck ought to be stretched.' T'is a raging fever of loathing towards those who were once friends and family. They say those loyal to the King wish to see them enslaved."[599]

"Keep heart dear wife. You're strong and brave, and we've fared better than others. Soon, you'll have relief. Only a month ago Mr. Walter Sutherland, one of Sir John's scouts, was here and heard our fears and our request that guides be sent to take us to Canada. We must hold ourselves ready for the journey."

"You're right husband. They'll come. We must ensure the children and their families are ready too. Ohh, there're so many little ones, and Catharina's Martin is away. And Maria Catherine is with child."

Philip put his finger to his lips and turned toward the kitchen entry way. Catrina motioned to Johannes and Martin to sit and eat their meal.

Johannes rose from the table and took a last gulp of his cider. "I'll leave now and fill the cart with the hay for Michael and Elizabeth's milk cows."

Martin looked toward his brother and said, "Don't be all day with that. Papa and I need you in the field."

"Nay. I'll be home before the midday."

"Wish our sister well Johannes. She's carrying a new life and will be in need of extra rest."

"Aye Martin. Michael and I can help with what she needs."

Johannes walked alongside Star as she pulled the cart along the road to Philadelphia Bush. It wasn't long before he reached the northern section of the road that led to town. Ahead, he saw a group of men at the side of the road. They walked toward him jeering and shouting, "A Tory's brother! Catch the wicked scoundrel!" Johannes froze. He counted ten men. His heart pounded. His eyes darted, looking for a path away from the crowd. Star pranced and blew. He held her tight. Before he could do anything, three men grabbed him and threw him to a clearing by the road. Their voices pummeled his ears.

Johannes struggled and screamed, "Let me be! I'm only to my sisters with this hay!"

"We'll teach him. Your brother-in-law Martin Alguire is a traitor, a villain! Won't this one make a fine goose! Just like Gallinger's geese! Get the tar!"

Johannes tried to wrestle free, but grew weaker with each punch they landed. He struggled to breathe as they stripped him and tied him to a tree, his hands and feet bound. He was dizzy, and the men around him grew to a foggy mass of deer skin and wool that smelled of rum. All he heard were his own screams and their grunts, hoots, and snorts. The pain sliced through him like knives as they covered his chest, arms, legs, and feet with hot pine tar.[600] As his head dropped to his chest, feathers flew everywhere.

Johannes felt someone's breath on his face and heard his name called then let out a moan heavy with pain, fear, and fury

"Johannes, I'm here. 'T'is Jacob Henry. You're safe. Lie still boy."

Jacob Henry and his son Jacob Jr. spoke softly to Johannes as they cut the ropes that pinned him to the tree. Jacob Henry turned to his son and listed clear instructions, "Run, get your mother! Tell her to bring two blankets, rum, and water. Then go to Mr. Sheet's farm and get young Jacob. Bring a horse and wagon. As fast as you can son!"

Catrina sat on the bench in her garden for a rest. She'd been in the garden all morning and took a minute to survey the seeds she'd planted. She saw the wagon turn into their lane and wondered why Jacob Henry and Maria Salome would be visiting today. She wiped her hands on her blue checked linen apron as she walked toward the wagon.

She knew something was wrong when Jacob Henry leapt off the wagon seat with purpose. "What's happened Jacob Henry?"

"Johannes has been hurt badly Catrina. They've beaten and tarred the poor boy! Get Philip and Peter. I need help. We'll need hog fat and water! Now Catrina. Hurry!"

Catrina hollered for Philip and Peter as she ran to the back of the wagon. "Dear Lord. My boy! Does he speak or move?"

"Not as yet. Hurry Catrina. He needs a bed and care!"

Catrina ran toward the house passing Philip and Peter as they ran to the wagon.

It was near sunset when they finished removing most of the tar. Mercifully, Johannes lay unconscious as they pulled and scraped the tar from his body. There was too much raw skin to wrap with bandages, so they lay clean cotton sheets over his chest and limbs. Peter sat at the edge of his brother's bed and prayed as Dorothy and Maria Salome tended to each limb. Catrina sobbed as she dipped cotton sheets in boiling water and spread them over a chair to cool. Knowing Johannes would be bed ridden for days, Philip, Martin, and Jacob Henry filled clean ticking with fresh straw.

After fixing the mattress, the men went to see if Jacob Sheets had returned with Star and the wagon. Just as they went out to the yard, they saw Jacob driving the wagon down the lane.

Philip walked toward the wagon and said, "'T'is one blessing that the horse and wagon are found. There seems to be no other blessings while vigilantes walk the roads."

Jacob Henry nodded and said, "Aye. 'T'is a sad and cruel act that's been known for years and little restraint on it or other vile occurrences."[601]

A week passed, and Johannes remained in bed lapsing in and out of consciousness. Catrina feared he had been struck on his head. However, these past few days she worried more about his fever and the festering wound on his chest. She never left his side and insisted Philip lay blankets for her on the floor next to Johannes. His condition grew worse each day. His fever raged, and his breathing laboured. One afternoon, Philip sat with her at the side of the bed. They were silent except for their soft prayers.

With a trembling voice and quivering breath Catrina said, "'T'is the Lord's wish to take him dear husband. Our prayers must be for his merciful parting. I cannot stand to see my boy endure this agony. I cannot endure this agony."

Philip took Johannes hand and said, "My dear son. My son of good nature and fine manner. Go to God now and be at peace."

With their hands in prayer, they kneeled and lay their heads on his bed until long after Johannes breathed his last breath.[602]

The next day they buried Johannes near the orchard next to his brothers Jelles, Philip, and Mattheus. The house was filled with silence or sobbing most hours of the day. Peter spent many hours sitting next to Johannes' grave. As he sat, he whittled pine into myriads of shapes. There were birds, beavers, fish, and even flowers. All of these, he arranged beneath the cross their papa made. The whittling helped tame Peter's rage toward the men who did this to his brother. At times, he felt he could have whittled the pieces of pine to dust. Even Maria Catherine and thoughts of his child coming soon did not console him.

One afternoon after chores, Philip came to sit with Peter. Philip lit his pipe, and leaning against the oak tree, he said, "You know Sir John sent two men with a Mohawk guide to advise those of us who want to come off to Canada to make ourselves ready. Sir John's scouts tell us that 500 men left St. John's on the St. Lawrence River and made their way down Lake Champlain to Crown Point.

The men now make for Johnstown through the woods at Schroon Lake. Captain Lieutenant Thomas Gummersal commands Sir John's Company. That means that John Farlinger, Francis and David Jeacocks Jr., John Service, and Francis Albrandt are among them. There's also Captain Richard Duncan's Company with Severinus Casselman and Philip Cook in that Company, Captain Samuel Anderson's men and Captain John McDonell's Grenadiers. Sir John asked that Luke Bowen, Michael Carman, Jacob Coon, and Nicholas Shaver's boy George Adam should be among the men who come to Johnstown. They know the land, trails, and roads well and will be of great service. The scouts expect many tenants will be desirous of joining the Companies and their wives and families desirous of going to Canada. They say that vessels await us at Crown Point on Lake Champlain."[603]

"We'll leave soon Papa. I want Maria Catherine and me to go with Sir John's men. I want you, Mama, Dorothy, and Martin to come too."

"Your Mama and I cannot go as yet. Elizabeth is with child, and Catharina can't handle so many young children with her Martin not there. They need us here."

"Papa, I worry you'll both be harassed or sent to jail. You cannot stay."

"Your brother Martin is with us. We'll be cautious."

'T'is not safe, not after what happened to Johannes. And, I've heard too that Mr. Valentine Cryderman died. They've just buried him at the graveyard in Johnstown. And, Jacob Cryderman went to join Sir John. I think Joseph will join his brother soon. If Johannes, Harmanus, Thomas, and Henry Cryderman weren't so young, they'd join too."[604]

"Aye. The boys avenge their father's death. Even your Mama's mutton stew and apple pies did little to calm Mrs. Cryderman at the loss of her boys." "As it is with me Papa. There'll be a day of reckoning for the crime of Johannes' death."

Since Johannes' death early in May, Philip was aware that Rebel militia gathered near Johnstown. He'd had a visit from Jacob Crieghoof who, living close to Johnstown, was able to keep watch over militia activity. Jacob described who garrisoned the jail and who were seen as scouts early in May. He'd seen Captain John Little, Thomas Sammons with Lieutenant William Wallace's Company, George and Leonard Dachstader with Abraham Veeder's Company, and Captain Jelles Fonda and most of his Company. Jacob also told Philip about the militia searching his house looking for Captain Andrew Wemple who deserted from Colonel Fisher's 3rd Regiment. They went to the Butlersbury Patent where Captain Wemple lived. Philip Hendrick Klein's house on the Butlersbury Patent was a house they searched."[605] By the third week of May, Philip learned that the Rebel companies assembled at Johnstown were dismissed so that the men could plant their crops.[606]

Late in the afternoon on Sunday May 21st, Philip, Catrina, Martin, Peter, and Dorothy gathered in their parlour for an hour of prayer and to share happenings of the day and news in the community. It was easier to settle for their evening meal and a nights rest when they had this chance to be together and share their worries and their hopes.

Dorothy was up the same time as her mother on Monday morning. She knew her chores were to milk the cow and gather eggs before the morning meal. She stepped out the front door and made her way along the path to the barn. For the first few metres, she was lost in daydreams about the last time she saw Henry Gallinger. It was almost one year to the day that he left for Canada. The smell of smoke interrupted her dreaming. It smelled like the smoke from the wood that burned under the maple sugar pots, but it was thicker, and it made her cough. She turned to the south and saw a thick grey haze fill the sky. She squinted in hopes of spotting the source of the haze but saw nothing.

She turned and quickened her step back to the house, flung open the door and rushed into the kitchen saying, "Mama, there's smoke filling the sky to the south near the river."

Philip came up behind her saying, "We'll go to the lane and look for its source."

Catrina, Peter, and Martin came out to the lane. Pointing towards the southeast, Philip said, "Looks as though there's fire burning as far east as Tribes Hill and to the west at Caughnawaga. 'T'is certain Sir John's men are laying waste to the Rebel farms along the river."

Peter turned to Catrina and Philip and said, "I must get Maria Catherine and our provisions. Duncan Murchison prepared all the Loyalists. We're to meet Sir John's men at Scotch Bush to make the journey to Crown Point."[607] As Peter turned and ran toward their cabin, Catrina reached for Philip's hand and put her head on his chest. "It was best that Peter and Maria Catherine make their escape," she thought.

Peter rushed in the front door and hollered, "Gather our knapsacks Maria Catherine! We must go quickly. Sir John's men are attacking the settlements along the river and will soon make their escape. We meet them at Scotch Bush." Maria Catherine dropped the apple she was peeling on the floor, grabbed her skirt high and ran to the bedroom. She filled their knapsack with one extra shirt, skirt, stockings, and kerchief. She knew they had to travel light. They'd need food more than extra clothing, and in the fourth month of her pregnancy she could not carry much. As she ran into the kitchen carrying both knapsacks, Peter was at the table filling his cartridge box and powder horn. "Catherine, your sturdiest shoes must be worn and a warm cloak. Take extra jerky, cheese, and dried apples."

Within thirty minutes, Peter and Maria Catherine were sitting with Philip, Catrina, Martin, and Dorothy at the kitchen table. Catrina dug through their knapsacks making sure they had enough for at least ten days. She added dried yarrow and wintergreen and a pewter cup of witch hazel and slippery elm bark salve that she made in the fall.

Peter sat with Philip and Martin by the fire. Resting his cup of rum on his knee, Peter said, "We're meeting Mattheus Link Jr., Johannes Gottfried Link, and Peter Service Jr. and his brother Philip Service at the trail behind Jacob Crieghoof's farm. 'T'is the safest route north to Scotch Bush."

Martin asked, "Is Lena going with Peter and Maria Catherine with Philip."

"No, they're staying to care for their infant sons William Service and Johannes. Lena has little Thomas only three and Philip just five to look after, and Maria Catherine has five young children. There are other families who are coming, but they must be able to travel the distance."

While lighting his pipe, Philip said, "Try to get word to us about your safe arrival and housing at Montreal. We'll not rest well until we hear that you and Maria Catherine are well and the others are safe."

"Aye Papa. I'll try."

By noon, Peter and Maria Catherine made their way to Scotch Bush. Over the next few hours, they waited as others entered the camp. They saw the armourer Michael Cline, William Bowen Sr., Michael Carman Sr., Jacob Sheets Jr., Jacob Cryderman, Peter Fykes Jr., Andrew Millross, Philip Empey Sr., William Philips, George and Jacob Eny, David, Jacob, and Jeremiah Dorn whose brother Johannes Dorn stayed behind with their father, and Jacob Eaman whose brother joined only a few days earlier, and Johannes and Nicholas Ault and Adam Ruppert's boys Francis Ruppert and his brother Pader Ruppert.[608] It was nearing sunset when a great commotion stirred at the south end of camp. Peter left Maria Catherine sitting next to a small fire and walked toward the crowd. Peering over the shoulders of two men, he saw six Mohawks and Philip Shaver, Michael Carman, Peter Dorn, and John Farlinger leading prisoners whom he recognized. He saw Lieutenant Sampson Sammons and his sons Jacob, Thomas, and Sergeant Frederick Sammons, and he saw Robert Adams and Captain Abraham Veeder.[609]

Peter instinctively raised his hand and covered his open mouth when a line of soldiers and Indians entered the camp behind the group of prisoners. There must have been hundreds of men each with disheveled uniforms, breeches, hunting shirts, and a variety of caps. Some collapsed on the ground in any vacant spot next to a fire, some flung their cap hats off. The lock of red horse hair on their cap hats caught Peter's eye as the caps hit the ground. As soon as they could, the men rifled through their knapsnacks for food and slumped on the ground to remove their moccasins or high-low boots. Peter noticed the boots had been polished with 'black ball' but were now scuffed and caked with mud and soot. He made his way back to Maria Catherine weaving past women fraught with filling cups with cider or rum as fast as the men could drink.

It was still dark when Peter opened his eyes and pulled his wool blanket over his shoulder. He heard the dim sound of men's voices, coughing, groaning, and the crackle of a fire as he rolled over and saw the still shape of Maria Catherine. He thought, "'T'will be light soon, and she'll wake. 'Sha'n't be long before the whole camp comes alive. I best be up and ready our packs." He lay there a few minutes then raised himself up and laced his moccasins. As the dappled dawn broke over camp, Peter stood beside the fire. Through the filter of smoke, he saw Maria Catherine stir. "Wake my love." he whispered. 'T'will not be long before we're on the march north. You must eat. Our baby needs nourishment."

"I'm awake sweetheart but am already longing for the familiar warmth of our cabin and the sound of your father and Martin making their way to the barn." She sighed and pulled her blanket close to her chin. "How long will it be before we see our dear ones? Will we ever see them? How will they fair? Those against us are roused to seek revenge?"

Peter knelt beside her. Finding her hand beneath the blanket, he grasped it as he placed a soft kiss on her lips. "We'll all be well and together again soon. 'T'will be my promise."

Barely an hour after dawn, Abijah, Truman, and Simeon Christie of the Mayfield Patent were among the men leading the group from Scotch Bush north toward the Sacandaga River. The Christie brothers lived in the area and knew it well. Maria Catherine and Peter walked among a group of Loyalist men, women, and children who numbered 143. In front and behind this group were about twenty slaves and 500 soldiers of the 29th 34th, 53rd Regiments, the KRRNY, Jessup's King's Loyal Americans, Peter's Queen's Loyal Rangers and McAlpin's American Volunteers, Von Kretzenberg's Hessian Hanau Jagers, and Mohawks. With them were thirteen prisoners who were what remained of the twenty seven prisoners taken. Sir John released Captain Abraham Veeder in exchange for one of his soldiers and released Sampson Sammons and his son Thomas, Myndert Wemple, and John Fonda on their word they would not take up arms against the British and that they would protect the loyal families left behind.[610]

When the forest path opened into a meadow, Maria Catherine hoped for a clear sky so she could look to the position of the sun to tell her how long they had been walking. For over an hour, her legs and feet seemed a great weight on her stride. It was her arms that drove her forward. She tried to get used to her belly growing and had to change her stride. She kept her eye on Peter whose steady pace in front of her was a rhythm on which she relied. Each root and rock she stepped over or skirted was one she could put behind her. For a moment, her eyes scanned the meadow; she lost her rhythm and tripped on her skirt.

Peter heard her moan turned and said, "'T'will not be long now. Must be just past noon, and I expect we'll stop for a rest."

"'T'is a good thing husband. I'm weary and thirsty, and my thoughts remain at home with Mama and Papa and my brother and sisters. I know not what horrors await them."

"Keep faith my love. Your father and brother are strong and able as are your mother and sisters. They've friends who remained behind. The soldiers will be busy looking for us. For now we must keep moving. Our trail must be skirting the road near the Blockhouse. 'T'is too close to militia."

"I may'n't have dry shoes when we camp tonight. 'T'is marshy here. All I see are swamp willow, alder, and birch trees."

"Aye Catherine. 'T'is the Sacandaga Vlaie. We're closer than not to the Sacandaga River."

"Will boats await us?"

"Aye. Luke Bowen told me that we canoe up the Sacandaga then cross the Hudson and march north to Stony Creek, Crane Mountain, and Schroon Lake. Once we're at Schroon Lake 't'is not far east to Bulwagga Bay at Crown Point where ships await us."[611]

Peter and Maria Catherine sat close to the fire trying to dry their wet stockings and shoes. Catherine kept her naked feet covered hoping they would warm by the fire. "Everything is damp husband. I fear my shoes will still be wet tomorrow. My back is sore. How many days must we walk?"

Peter reached over and covered his shivering wife with his blanket. "'T'will be maybe seventeen more days." As Peter moved Catherine's shoes closer to the fire he said, "Break some bread and cheese for yourself. The nourishment will warm you."

"I shiver not just from the cold but from thoughts of militia following us and of our families and how they fare."

"Sir John has many scouts keeping watch. You need not worry. And, remember that at our homes this time of day is spent with a cup of warm cider by the fire. Think of them in that way dear wife. We'll pray this evening for their safety."

At home, Philip sat in his rocking chair sipping his cider. The fire hissed as the water in the iron pot began to boil. Catrina was preparing squash and potatoes for their pork stew. Suddenly, Martin and Dorothy jumped from the kitchen table when a knock at the back door broke the silence in the room.

"Wait." Philip said.

As he rose slowly from the chair a familiar voice said, "'T'is safe. 'T'is Martin and Nicholas Silmser."

The door creaked as Philip peered out. "Come in quickly. Since Sir John's raid, we don't know whose eyes are upon us. And, we've not had contact with any friends of the King to tell us what chaos and carnage was unleashed."

"We've come to convey what we know."

"What of those who joined Sir John? Have the militia overtaken them? Pray tell us. Peter and Maria Catherine are with them. Two days have passed. Please sit."

Philip took two pewter cups and a crock of rum from the shelf. His hand shook as he poured the rum while Martin Silmser said, "Near 530 men, 200 of them Indians, swept eastward twenty one kilometres through the valley from Tribes Hill to Anthony's Nose. One hundred and twenty houses, barns, and mills were set aflame. Caughnawaga lies in ashes. Eleven men were killed. Some of those dead are two old gentlemen we know well, Captain Jelles Fonda's father Douw Fonda and Henry Hanson of Tribes Hill. The Fischer brothers John and Harmans are also dead. Their brother Colonel Frederick Fischer suffered a near mortal wound to the head and half his scalp. Much of his belongings were plundered, and his house, barn, barracks, and crops all burned. They took his horses and Negroes. Johannes Veeder's cider, saw, and grist mill were burned as were his house, barn, barracks, and cider mill. They took many horses and killed his cattle, sheep, and hogs. He is ruined. Barney Wempel's widow Peggy escaped death, but her home and tavern are ashes, and her son Myndert was taken prisoner. Near her, John Fonda's place burned and he a prisoner. Nearer us, Isaac Davis lost his home, barn, and barrack. His cattle gone as are all his possessions. And Lodowyck Putnam and his son Aaron both killed. North of the Mohawk River to Anthony's Nose at Little Falls much of the flour, grain, and corn are destroyed. The Indians and Sir John's men spared women and children, but their sons, husbands, and fathers were objects of their vengeance. Now the Rebels hear rumours that Joseph Brant follows with equal vengeance. Their militia couldn't muster enough men to strike back, and Sir John and his party of hundreds are safely on their way to Crown Point with enough recruits for Sir John's 2nd Battalion of the KRRNY."[612]

Philip puffed hard on his pipe then said, "What plans have you and Nicholas?"

"We'll stay low for now. 'T'is certain the Rebels will be at the ready and hunting for those who played any part in the raid. I've enlisted with Captain Fonda's Associated Exempts. We're not suspect. And, I hear John Dachstader harboured one of Sir John's soldiers at his home. For disguise, he dressed the soldier as a woman!"[613]

Nicholas turned to Philip, nodded and said, "Sir. Anna Margaret is safe at home, but she worries about Peter and Maria Catherine on their way to Canada and you so far from us."

"Have you seen Michael and Elizabeth? They have five young children, and she is with child to deliver this fall."

"They're not too far north of us. We'll check them as soon as we are able. Martin, you should not be out on the roads. They'll want you for the militia. 'T'is dangerous. Even here at home, you're exposed to danger. Many have taken to the woods to hide."

"Aye. And I worry about Catharina at Albany Bush."

Martin rose from the table. As he picked up his musket he said, "We musn't linger. 'T'is slower travelling through bush paths, and we must be home before dark."

"We thank ye friend for bringing us news and for visiting my daughter and her husband."

Through the month of June 1780, the militia were frequently seen along the road in front of the Eamers' lane. Several times, Philip saw the wagons or carriages of the Commissioners of Sequestration. The property and possessions of Loyalists were quickly taken or sold for a pittance. Philip heard that William Fraser Sr. sold his remaining possessions and went to Governor Clinton for a pass so he could send his wife and his daughters-in-law and their children to Canada. They did go by sleigh to Fort George last winter, but they had difficulties crossing the ice. The drivers left them overnight, and poor young Thomas froze his feet. They turned back home where they now survive on the mercy of Loyalists. They hope that William's sons Lieutenants Thomas and William Fraser, now commanding the Loyalist blockhouses on the Rivière Yamaska, can secure a pass to take them to Canada.[614]

At twenty four years old, Martin Eamer feared arrest or doing anything that provoked confiscation, so he was never out in the fields or the yard during the day. At dawn and dusk, he did what he could to help his father. Otherwise, he kept to the barn, the barracks, or the summer kitchen. At fifty eight years old, it was safer for Philip to be out; however, he remained cautious. They were all cautious. They wanted to come safely through the horror of the war and save their farm. With Peter and Martin Alguire joining the British, extreme caution was essential.

One afternoon in July, Catrina and Dorothy were in the garden thinning carrots and tending to the squash and beans. Seeing Conrad Warner, Michael Warner's son, racing down the lane, Catrina dropped her basket and ran toward him. "What is it Conrad?

'T'is Catherina!"

"What's happened?"

Holding his chest, Conrad burst out, "They've taken Martin's farm. Catherina and their six children are thrown out and are making their way here. She needs your help. She has little Elizabeth to carry, and Daniel barely walks."[615]

"Were they hurt?"

"No, but terrified and confused."

Catrina didn't have to call Philip; he saw Conrad and the commotion in the lane. Catrina called out to Philip, "Hitch the wagon. They've chased Catherina off their property. She's on the Albany Bush Road. Hurry Philip."

Catrina and Dorothy scrambled into the wagon and Conrad leapt up on the seat next to Philip. He barely sat when the horses pulled ahead. Catrina leaned over the side of the wagon staring down the road. Suddenly, her arm raised as stiff as an arrow. Pointing she said, "There they are. Philip slow!" Catherina was crying and holding Elizabeth next to her chest. Maria Salome walked beside her mother grasping the hands of Peter and Daniel. John stumbled along behind and Philip ran toward the wagon shouting, "Grossmutter, Grossvater!" Before the wagon came to a complete stop, Catrina and Dorothy were on the road clutching Philip and John.

Catrina reached for Catherina as she trudged forward sobbing, "Mama, 't'is all gone! They've taken our horses, cows, and sheep. Two men loaded Martin's loom into a wagon! We've nothing but what we wear. They called us traitors and enemies of the cause and threatened to burn everything."[616]

"You and the children are not hurt. We'll take you home."

Catrina took little Elizabeth and waited while Catherina climbed into the wagon. Dorothy lifted the boys. "Philip, we must take Conrad home. 'T'is not safe for a young man to be on the road. His mother will worry."

"Aye. 'T'is not far. Then we're headed home at good speed."

Only a few days after Catherina and the children settled at the house, Philip spotted Martin Walliser, Anthony's son, walking to the barn by way of the path from the creek.

Martin called out, "I've news from Agatha Gallinger. They've arrested Michael at his home. Five militia men and two men from Hartford Connecticut came this morning and placed him in irons. They say he's disaffected from the cause and has refused to sign the Association Oath."

"For what reason are Connecticut men there?" Philip asked.

"They came to know his crimes. He's to go to their jail.[617] Agatha is distressed and calling for help."

"Aye. Catrina and I will go now and do what we can."

Catrina and Philip sat with Agatha, Johannes George, Betsy, and Dorothy for most of the afternoon. They talked of evidence the Committee men might have against Michael, but they knew the fact that his sons joined the British might be enough to send Michael to prison. Certainly, not signing the Association Oath was enough evidence. All Philip and Catrina could do was offer comforting words and some pork stew and corn cakes.

Not many days passed before Michael was taken from the jail to the Court House and was found guilty and sent to Hartford Connecticut. Over the next few weeks, Philip and Catrina did what they could to help Agatha. They ached for their friend who had no way to know if her husband was injured, dead, or alive. They prayed for Michael's safety. Agatha tried to find someone who could secure his release or take him money for provisions, wood and water but all failed.

Each day that the Eamers evaded a catastrophe was a good day. Their thoughts were often of Peter and Maria Catherine. Everyone prayed that Maria Catherine was warm and fed and able to rest and that the unborn child was at no risk. The house was full again with Catharina's little children, and Catrina was careful with their consumption of provisions. It was the beginning of August and Philip would soon need to be in the fields harvesting the little grain he was able to plant in the spring. Martin was his only son left to help. It was too dangerous for him to be seen in the open fields. Dorothy helped her father and so did Catharina's two boys Philip and John. The boys were old enough now to help their grandfather. And, the Rebels wouldn't dare bother nine and seven year old boys.

Philip walked the field with his scythe while the others behind him gathered the wheat into sheaves. As he walked, Philip glanced toward the edge of the field and saw a man and a young boy emerge from the bush and jump the fence. As he looked closer, he recognized Michael Cline and his ten year old son Johannes Cline.

As they stood near the bush along the fence line, Michael said, "Good day Philip. We've walked the back way from my shop at Johnstown to bring you news of Joseph Brant's raids, and I've brought extra powder and shot. I thought you might need use of it."

"Where's Joseph? Do you know if he comes this way?"

"Joseph Brant, Lieutenant Joseph Clement, Old Smoke, and Cornplanter the Seneca war chiefs, and the Tuscarora War Chief Sagwarithra with over 300 Indians swept ten kilometres along the river near Canajoharie. They burned all the grain, almost 100 houses and barns, the church and mills, and they drove off or killed that many cattle and horses. Most of the men were in the fields harvesting and couldn't defend their homes. Some families got away to Fort Plank. But, twenty nine were killed and about fifty taken prisoner. Among the prisoners were Christian Casselman and his wife Catherine Loucks and their children Margaret, Elizabeth, and their infant Anna, and George Schenck Jr.'s wife Barbara and their children Margaret and Christina just nine months old. The Indians scattered into small groups killing and burning wherever they went. All the crops are now or soon will be ashes. Take care to collect and hide as much food as you can. There'll be no grain but some perhaps at Kingsborough, Sacandaga, and maybe Stone Raby. What grain there is will go to feed the militia and those left destitute by Brant. The Colonel Jacob Klock, Captain John Casselman, Sergeant Adam Countryman and others petitioned the Governor for relief."[618]

"Is that Jacob Countryman's brother Adam?"

"Aye. Jacob is with Sir John's 1st Battalion. Jacob is the only brother in that family who fights with the King."

"There are many families who suffer that torment. Captain John Casselman is the only brother who fights for the Rebels."

"Joseph Brant is headed southwest to the Schoharie River Valley and Vrooman's land."[619]

"That valley is rich with grain and has many grist and saw mills. Hieronymus Chrysler has land at New Dorlach near Cobus Kill and along Breakabeen Creek. He has many sons who farm there also."

"Aye, as does William Bauch Sr., Frederick Bauch Sr., Ury Richtmeyer Sr. and Nicholas Mattice Sr.[620] Many of their sons joined Colonel Butler or Joseph Brant, but some are commissioned with the militia."

"Is there any word of Sir John and the KRRNY?"

"Aye. Sir John raised a 2nd Battalion with many of the men who went to Canada with him in May. I hear they are at Coteau-du-Lac on work duty improving the works and building canal locks so boats can bypass the rapids on the northern shore of the St. Lawrence River. Sir John sent a party of men south to Johnstown to ready us for another raid. The men are asking Loyalists to ready provisions for over 2000 men. Many are baking extra bread and will slaughter some hogs and sheep. Be warned. The militia know about the need for provisions and the plans to make a supply of bread for Sir John's men. Colonel Harper's men will apprehend anyone with a supply of bread. If Catrina, Dorothy, or Catharina make loaves, be sure to disguise the process and keep the loaves concealed.[621] Johannes and I must conceal ourselves in the woods as we make our way back to Johnstown. Fare well Philip and spread this news to any you can."

On the last day of August 1780, Philip and Martin were in the barn packing corn husks and dried peas into a rundlet. As they rolled the rundlet into its hiding spot behind the milk cow's stall, Catrina ran in with Joseph Hanes Sr. close behind. She yelled, "Philip hitch the wagon. We must go to Elizabeth. She's having pains and it's too early."

"Did something happen to bring this on?"

Joseph stepped in front of Catrina and said, "It did. Colonel Harper's men were around Scotch Bush and Philadelphia Bush looking for anyone stashing provisions. They ransacked our house and barn and went to Johannes Alguire's, Jacob Henry's, Michael Carman's and Michael Myer's place. When they were at Michael's, they held him and threatened him with a bayonet. Your daughter suffered a huge fright and became ill as soon as they left. I fear she is to deliver her baby. You must come."

In ten minutes, Catrina was at the wagon carrying an armload of linen, lye soap, a jug of rum, and some herbs wrapped in linen cloth. Dorothy and Catharina were close behind. Bess pulled the wagon out onto the road to Johnstown. As they got to Montgomery Street, two soldiers stopped the wagon and searched the box.

Catrina held out her bag of herbs to be searched and said, "Please, I must get to my daughter. She is with child and is in danger."

The soldier waved his arm and said, "Let them pass."

The wagon rolled down Glebe Street to Old Sacandaga Street then east on the road to Philadelphia Bush.

Catrina, Dorothy, and Catharina jumped out of the wagon as soon as it entered Michael and Elizabeth's yard. Catrina ran and burst open the front door snapping commands as soon as she entered, "We need boiling water and lots of blankets. Dorothy I need your help. Michael take the boys outside! Where is she?" Michael pointed to the room behind the kitchen. For hours, Catrina sat with Elizabeth and held her hand or gave her sips of water or rum. Elizabeth's moans never ceased until finally she reached for her mama, screamed and said, "Mama! 'T'is come away! My baby is gone."

Catrina lifted the tiny lifeless child, wrapped her in a blanket, and placed her on the table near the bedroom door. She returned to Elizabeth and helped her deliver the afterbirth. Elizabeth sobbed and moaned for several more hours, and Catrina grew more and more anxious. This was not normal. Something was wrong. All night Dorothy and Catherina never left her side. Catrina sponged her and fed her sips of water. Nothing eased Elizabeth's discomfort.

The next day Catrina awoke from a fleeting nap to continue her watch over Elizabeth. Philip returned from telling Martin of his sister's tragedy and was in and out of the room all day. Michael never left her side. Elizabeth shivered and moaned of a terrible headache and stomach pains. As the day wore on, Elizabeth called out for Michael and became incoherent. He tried to calm her, but she shivered, tossed, and turned while clasping Michael or Catrina's hand.[622] When Catrina wasn't wiping the sweat from Elizabeth's face, arms, and hands, she was wiping her own tears or pacing the room. Often she sat in the rocking chair with her arms tightly wrapped around her waist, rocking so hard the chair almost tipped. At other times, she sat still and stared.

At dawn on the third day, Philip came into the room and walked toward his daughter's bedside. For a moment, he dared not touch her or even look at her. He thought, "This cannot be. My sweet Elizabeth. She was so brave crossing the great sea. She was Catherina's keeper on that long journey. Such a fine mother and wife she was." Tears poured down Philip's face as he knelt beside Elizabeth.

He rose and went to Catrina sleeping in the chair. He touched her arm, and as she opened her eyes he said, "Our dear Elizabeth has passed on."

Catrina's hand clung to his. Her red shiny eyes looked towards Elizabeth as she slumped into the chair. She gasped then paused then said, "Dear God why have you taken her?"

Dorothy placed her hand on her mother's shoulder then knelt beside her sister's bed and said, "How could you leave me? Dear sister don't go."

Catharina wept as she tidied her sister's nightgown, blankets, and hair. Later that morning, Michael brought their four oldest children to their mother's bedside to say goodbye.

Just before dusk, Dorothy and Catrina wrapped Elizabeth in a woolen blanket and carried her to her grave at the edge of the forest. They placed Elizabeth's infant girl next to her and began to cover the grave. With each shovelful of dirt, Catrina sank closer to the ground. Michael placed two crosses at the head of the grave, and Catharina placed a crock of purple asters and goldenrod next to the cross. To ease the children's confusion, Philip knelt with them beside the grave and recited a prayer. Each of them gently laid a flower next to the cross.

For a week after Elizabeth's death, Martin grew more agitated at the restrictions to his liberty at his own home. He wanted to help his father in the fields; he wanted to help his mother with the garden, but most of all he was angry that he wasn't able to be with Elizabeth as she lay dying. One morning Philip greeted Martin at the kitchen table. Martin's shot bag lay on the table, and he was packing a knapsack with bread, cheese, and dried meat.

Philip stared at the table and said, "Where are you going? What's happened?"

"Nothing's happened Papa. I can't sit here and watch you work. I must feel of use. I'm going beaver hunting with Lucas Feader Jr.. We're heading east toward Ballstown."

"'T'is too dangerous to be out in the woods now!"

"'T'is safer than staying here, and I must do something."

Catrina walked in and saw the knapsack, "What are you doing Martin? You can't leave us too."

"I'm going hunting Mama. I'll be back in two weeks. If the militia is to seize all our grain, we need all the food we can get." Martin lifted his woolen hunting coat from its hook then placed his black felt hat over his thick black hair. As he opened the front door he said, "Tell Dorothy and Catharina I'll bring them some beaver fur for a winter muff."

September 1780 left gaping holes in time as the Eamers passed each day with only memories of Elizabeth. Their grief intensified every time they visited Michael and their grandchildren. There were many nights when at least one person in the house paced the floor or sat in one of the rocking chairs by the fire. Even Philip spent several early morning hours next to the fire smoking his pipe. He wondered how his family could endure more loss. His thoughts drifted to the early days on the land and in the forest when he worked side by side with his sons who were no longer here. When he thought of the farm, he felt his heart beat faster and his breathing become shallow. Then he thought of Martin. It was now seventeen days since he left to go hunting. Why was he not home? What could have happened? With every day that passed, Catrina peered out windows, stared down the lane, and fumbled preparing meals. Philip tried to comfort her with countless reasons why Martin had not returned. None seemed to sooth her.

Even with the help of his grandsons, it was the middle of October before Philip finished stacking wood for the winter. Catrina, Dorothy, and Catherina put away twice as much sauerkraut as usual, and they dried most of the apples. When they could, the women went to friends' farms to see what news they could gather. They always asked for any news of where Sir John's men were stationed and when they were expected to come to Johnstown. Although many scouts had been in and about the area, no one could give them any definite news. But they warned Catrina, Dorothy, and Catharina that the militia were suspicious of Tory wives and would arrest them. Maria, the wife of Adam Helmer, was one they watched. It was not just the women they suspected. They were convinced that many family members harboured the enemy and provided intelligence daily.[623]

In the evenings after the children were in bed, they gathered at the kitchen table and argued about whether they should leave the farm. They all winced when the long and dangerous journey by foot and boat was mentioned. Every evening, similar questions were repeated. How would they obtain a pass? How would the children fare? What possessions would they take? Would they find Peter and Maria Catherine? Would they find Martin Alguire? Would Nicholas and Anna Margaret go too? What about Michael Myers and the children? Where was their brother Martin? Would Philip and Catrina's age prevent them from embarking on such a journey? Always, there were more questions than answers.

Early in the morning of 18 Oct 1780, Dorothy went out to the barn to milk the cows and collect eggs. Just as she had done in May, she saw the sky filled with smoke. "Where now?" she thought as she ran to the house. She raced into the kitchen yelling, "Smoke! Papa! The sky is filled with smoke!"

Philip ran to the end of the lane and saw the red glow on the southern horizon. "Fort Hunter? Caughnawaga? Where are they?" he thought as he tried to squint through the smoke. Philip went back to the house and ordered the girls to gather belongings for themselves and the children.

He didn't have to ask Catrina; she was already in the kitchen cutting bread, cheese, and dried meat. "It must be Sir John. Peter could be with them! We must ready space in the barn and cellar to harbour any soldier."

With all their belongings near the door, the family waited and waited and waited.

The night passed and daylight brought nervous anticipation of what the day would bring. Just after noon Philip heard distant gunfire. He went on the porch and saw smoke rising in the west. While he stood wondering what would come about, he saw young Hermanus Cryderman and his brother Johannes walk up the path from the creek.

As they ran toward the house, Philip called out, "Hurry boys. Come in the house." As Philip held the door open as the two rushed into the kitchen he asked, "What news have you from your mother? Brother?"

"We've come with a message from one of Sir John's scouts. Any able bodied man who wishes to join Sir John is to meet west of Garoga Creek at the old Dillenbach farm. They must carry their own musket, cartridge pouch, and powder with provisions for six days and be able to travel fast through woods and across water."

"Where's Sir John? Where has his army been? Peter might be with him?"

"Of the KRRNY there are Captain John McDonell's Grenadiers, Captain Samuel Anderson's Company, Captain Richard Duncan's Company, Major James Gray's Company, and a platoon under Captain James McDonell."[624]

"My son Peter is with Captain John McDonell's Grenadiers as are many of his friends. I know of Jacob Sheets, Michael Gallinger Jr., Nicholas Ault, Balthasar Dillenbach, Adam P Empey, and David Jeacocks Jr.."[625]

"Since yesterday, Sir John led over 900 troops and Indians on a raid up the Schoharie Valley to Fort Hunter then along the Mohawk River to Anthony's Nose where they crossed the river and attacked Stone Raby. They're now headed west from George Klock's farm near Canada Creek. 'T'is not far from Leonard Helmer's farm, Adam Helmer Sr. brother."

"How does their army fare?"

"They've laid waste to the Schoharie Valley and both sides of the Mohawk River to Anthony's nose. Near 200 buildings and every bushel and acre of grain for eighty kilometres is ash. 'T'was the armies' goal to rob the Rebels of grain to feed their army and destroy places from which to attack Canada. And, Sir John gained recruits.[626]

"They were victorious at Stone Raby but met formidable forces under Lieutenant Colonel Volkert Veeder and Captain Abraham Veeder at Klock's field. Now they move towards Oswego and home."

"Do you know of any men killed or wounded?"

"Of the KRRNY, three privates killed, one lieutenant wounded, and thirteen privates missing. The lieutenant wounded was George McGinnis. He was shot in the knee and carried to an Oneida Castle on horseback"[627]

"We hoped to hear of our son Peter.

"None of the men have come near Johnstown. If Peter were here he might have found a way to send word to you."

"Aye, but 't'ain't easy to wait."

"We must take our leave Sir. There's not much time for us to tell those who might want to get to Sir John."

"I cannot join Sir John. At 58 years, my age prevents me from being of use to him, and I cannot leave my family. These marches and battles require youth and a vigour of which my time has passed."

"It mayn't be of concern to you Sir. Good day to you."

"The like to you Hermanus. You also Johannes. Tell your mother we're close by should need be."

It was two weeks before the sky cleared of smoke. The smell of it lingered, and with the right wind a fine layer of ash covered anything exposed. For two more weeks, Philip spent most days and evenings chopping enough wood for winter. Late one November evening as Philip and Catrina lay in their bed grateful for blessed sleep, Philip turned to Catrina and said, "We sha'n't be overcome dear wife. Even when every muscle in our bodies ache from worry and work. We'll hear word of Martin and Peter, and Maria Catherine will safely deliver their child soon."

"Work and my aching body helps me to believe you. At least I feel alive. But, I've lost faith in our Lord. Each day and night I pray, still no answer. Only word of suffering."

"But, we've good news from Michael Myers. He's to marry Jacob and Benedicta Crieghoof's daughter Elizabeth."[628]

"'T'is a blessing that our grandchildren will have a new mother."

"And, we've more good news that Nicholas Silmser and Anna Margaret expect their first child next summer." And, Margaret Waldorf heard that Martin is safe and victualled at Montreal. And, John Jeacocks and his brother David Jeacock's wives Helen and Hannah are safe and victualled at Lachine as are Robert Picken's family, Conrad Shaver, and William Casselman Jr. wife Catherine Hepple. Margaret says there are about 280 souls at Montreal and Lachine, about 162 are children."[629]

"These are good things husband, but my heart aches for what's gone. We've no word of Peter and Maria Catherine or Martin. There seems little life in the valley. No green fields, no wagons or sleighs filled with families, no farmhouses that once spread along the river, no animals grazing the meadows, and no friends at the taverns or stores. 'T'is empty. Sir William would weep. Not so long ago the edge of the frontier was Herkimer, now it's Schenectady. And the happenings this year gives the Rebels a deep red rage. They'll never be peace. Hearts break."[630]

Philip reached over and as he laid his arm across Catrina's stomach he whispered, "We sha'n't break Catrina. We cannot yield to despair. We'll overcome this wretched war."

Catrina woke earlier than usual one March morning. She was anxious and needed to move, so she gently lifted the quilt, swung her feet to the floor and reached for her stockings and shoes. She quietly rose and dressed. She opened the front door and walked toward the edge of the garden. The sun was bright and its warmth was melting what snow was left. As she walked along the fence, the smell of the dirt and the sight of the red columbine and yellow arnica helped shreds of hope surface. She straightened, and her steps felt lighter. The misery of a long winter was over. Her thoughts of the great number of friends who were taken prisoner or fined for going off to join the British didn't seem such a burden.[631] Maybe, she thought, this year would be different.

April and May 1781 passed amidst a flurry of work in the fields and the gardens. With the help of Catherina and her children, Catrina planted more cabbage, squash, beans, and peas, and Philip was able to cut winter wheat and sow corn and wheat for the fall.

One afternoon at the beginning of June while Philip was repairing the fence around the sheep pasture, Michael Gallinger Sr. walked toward him.

Philip dropped the fence rail and said, "Are you well since your release from Connecticut jail? Are you bringing news? How does Agatha fare?"

"I mend slowly since my return, and I bring news of our friends in Canada and of Sir John."

"You've news of Peter? Martin?"

"Your Peter is at Point Claire. He's enlisted in the KRRNY 2nd Battalion. I've no news of Martin. But, others are safe at Quebec camps. Sergeant George Barnhardt's wife Catherine, Catherine Casselman, and Helen and Hannah Jeacocks are at Point Claire. Luke Bowen remains at Sorel, John Lonie's wife Catherine and John Friel's wife Deborah are at Montreal. And, I've a hand bill with a proclamation from Sir John. He asks us to join others to suppress the rebellion and save our farms."[632]

> Sir John Johnson's Proclamation to the People of the Mohawk River
>
> The Officers & Soldiers of Sir John Johnson's Regiment present their affectionate and loving wishes to their Friends & Relations on the Mohawk River & earnestly entreat them to assemble themselves and come in to Canada or the upper posts, where under that Gallant leader, they may assist their countrymen to quell and put an end to the present unnatural rebellion, in hopes soon to return to their native homes, there to enjoy the happiness they were formerly blessed with under the best of Kings, who is willing to do everything for his subjects.
>
> May 22nd 1781

"With so much devastation in our valley, this war must soon be over. Catrina and I think we can wait a little longer before we seek the British lines. 'T'is a long journey from which we might not recover."

"Agatha and I hope for an end to this war soon too, but 't'is getting more difficult to escape the wrath of the Committee men and the militia. They've inflicted great pain on John Waite and his wife Jane."

"What insults have they suffered?"

"'T'was greater than insults. All their property was burned and their stock taken because their sons were with the British, and they're accused of harbouring the enemy and providing them with provisions. Both John and Jane are now prisoners. Jane was allowed to return home only for what possessions were left. 'T'is a tragedy. They came to the valley only five years ago from England."[633]

"The Rebels are relentless. They hunt us down like animals. Right now, they're on the prowl near the Helderbergs for Henry Hough and anyone else who proves suspicious of harbouring the enemy."[634]

"There's no safe place anymore. Whether in your own house, yard, barn, or the woods hunting, none of us are safe not even the women."

"I fear my wife and daughters can't suffer much more tension and harassment."

"Aye, mine as well.

It was the middle of June 1781 when Philip and Catrina took the risk and drove the wagon up to Philadelphia Bush to visit Nicholas and Anna Margaret. Catrina wanted to be sure that Anna Margaret was coping and not sick. In two months her baby is due. Philip, Nicholas, and Martin spent a few hours sharing news of scouting, militia activity, or news of Sir John's men. They all knew that Lieutenant Colonel Marinus Willett was the Commander of the Continental forces near Johnstown and was quartered at Canajoharie. And, Colonel Moses Hazen's Canadian soldiers were to relieve him, meaning there would be plenty of scouts in the area.[635]

Philip told Nicholas and Martin that he had seen Captain Gerritt Putnam, Captain Anthony Whelp's and Colonel Fisher's men at Fort Hunter and that he'd heard Colonel Willett was challenged with keeping enough militia men to repel Loyalist raids. It seems, Philip was told, that the men were more concerned about harvesting their crops or staying close to their own families and homes. Food was scarce since Sir John's raids and the arrival of soldiers into the valley. Most of the Loyalists were warned that Colonel Willett directed his soldiers to expropriate grain and stock to feed his men.[636]

Martin shared news of the men of the KRRNY which boosted their spirits and hopes that their own forces would come to the valley and defeat the Rebels or pilot them to Canada. He said that some of the soldiers of Sir John's regiment sent a petition to Sir John informing him of the daily abuses to which their families were victims. They requested that he obtain passes for them to come to Canada. Frederick Goose and Andrew Millross were among those who petitioned.[637]

August 1781 brought very good crops and at least eased fears of a hungry winter. But even a good harvest did not ease the Loyalists' daily fears of harassment, apprehension, jail, fines, or confiscation of their property. News that the French army joined forces with the Continental army at Yorktown, Virginia did nothing to ease tensions, neither did the defeat of Loyalists at an uprising in the Schoharie Valley near New Dorlach and Currytown.[638]

One morning at the end of August, Catharina and Dorothy were picking squash and digging potatoes when Martin Silmser cantered down the lane, stopped at the garden fence, and hollered, "Bring Catrina, Anna Margaret will deliver soon!" Before Catharina and Dorothy could put down their spades, Martin turned his mare and headed back down the lane.

Catrina saw Martin ride up the lane, but by the time she was on the porch, he was gone. She walked toward Catharina and Dorothy as they hollered, "Mama, Anna Margaret will soon deliver!"

Catrina lifted her skirt as she whirled around and ran to the barn calling, "Philip! Harness the mare! We must go to Anna Margaret!"

It was early in the afternoon as Nicholas, Catharina, Dorothy, and Catrina stood at Anna Margaret's bedside gazing at the tiny child in her arms.

Dorothy reached and touched the boy's soft cheek and said, "How blessed you are Anna Margaret. You've a beautiful boy. What will you name this little one?"

Touching Anna Margaret's arm, Nicholas said, "We'll call him Martin after his grandfather."[639]

Catrina smiled and said, "Aye. Martin is a fine name. There was another Martin just born in December. 'T'was Johannes Hough and Margaret Alguire's little boy and Jacob Henry such a proud grandfather."[640]

Dorothy looked to Catrina and said, "There's much that brings some happiness during these troubled times. Little Martin's baptism and other news that Johannes George Alguire will know some happiness after the death of his wife Mary Margaretha Eny. He's to marry Anna Maria Silmser on the 19th of September.[641]

Catrina was always happy in the fall. It was the season she most loved. The work of harvesting was done, the corn was in the crib, the wheat cut and threshed, the apples turned to cider or dried, and the root cellar was full of vegetables, fruit, sauerkraut, and cheese. In the fall, she cherished the trips the family made to church at Caughnawaga or Stone Raby taking pleasure in the magnificent view of the valley from the heights of Stone Raby. She often asked Philip to stop the wagon to enjoy the view of the river winding through the valley and the brilliant red, orange, and yellow of the tree tops covering the hills.

On Monday, September 10, Catrina was sitting on the pine bench on the porch when she saw Joseph and his son Johannes Hanes ride up the lane. It had been weeks since she saw the Hanes. Even though they lived at Philadelphia Bush and close to Jacob Henry Alguire and Martin Silmser, she did not always visit the Hanes when she was at the Alguires or the Silmsers. "What could they want?" she thought as they came closer.

Joseph called out, "Good day Mrs Eamer. We bring news."

"Come in for cider Joseph. I'll get Philip."

They sat at the kitchen table, resting for a moment and taking pleasure in their cider.

Catrina asked, "What news have you Joseph? And who brings you news?"

"My son Michael has come scouting for Sir John. He's a Sergeant with Captain Richard Duncan's Company and brings news of the men of the KRRNY for all of us at Kingsborough and Sacandaga.[642] Your son Peter is at Coteau du Lac with the 2nd Battalion. They are employed on the works under construction. They've not seen battle since '77."

"Even John McDonell's Grenadiers? My son is with them."

"I know not. The men sometimes transfer to different companies. The Grenadiers have seen battle and are at Carleton Island."

"Is there news of Peter's wife Maria Catherine Gallinger?"

"No news of the women or where they are victualled. But, many wives follow their husbands to the place they are quartered. Perhaps Maria Catherine is with Peter at Coteau du Lac serving as a laundress and nurse."

"Do you have news of Martin Alguire?"

"Aye. He's with Major Ross' Company at Lachine."[643]

"Any news of pilots being sent as guides for us to Canada?"

"None yet. But, there're always scouts in the area. I'll bring news as soon as I know."

Catrina felt the frost of October late into the morning and always donned her wool cape when she went to the barn to milk the cows or collect eggs. These past two years, she noticed her fingers, hips, and knees were stiff. Chores that she completed quickly years ago now seemed to last well into the morning.

On Wednesday October 10, she walked toward the house with the bucket of milk just collected and saw soldiers in three wagons pass their lane. She thought, "They're travelling fast? With a heavy load too. It looks like wheat. From where have they taken that wheat?"[644] Catrina quickened her step into the house and called Philip, "Philip, the soldiers passed by with wagonloads of wheat? Have we hidden ample corn and wheat? I expect the soldiers are impressing wheat!"

"Aye. We've put away enough corn and grain for our family till spring. 'T'is well hidden near the barn and in the cellar."

As he spoke to Catrina, Philip thought, "Hiding has become ordinary. At the beginning of this terrible war, I hid my loyalty to the King and I tried hiding my shock, anger, sadness, and fear. These past two years, I hid food and men." All this hiding, he thought, was the only way he'd keep his farm and the only way he'd keep his family safe. Yes, even keep them alive. He'd just heard that Sergeant Michael Hanes was discovered hiding at his father's farm, so he and his father left for Canada. Joseph left his wife and three children behind else he'd be thrown in jail again.[645] Philip was tired of hiding, tired of the suffering, tired of seeing his wife tormented with worry. He was tired of war.

At noon on Thursday October 25, 1781 Philip finished pitching hay to the sheep and checking their shelter when he smelled it. Smoke! It was coming from the south near Fort Hunter.

"Another raid. There's not much left to burn or take," he thought as he moved fast toward the house. "Catrina, Dorothy! Fix your knapsacks and put them by the door!" Philip opened the cupboard where he kept extra powder and shot. He grabbed his shot bag and was checking its contents when Catrina rushed into the kitchen and started cutting jerky and cheese.

She looked at Philip and said, "Do you think 't'is Sir John and his men again? There's been no word to expect them, not even rumblings from the Rebels."

"We must prepare no matter what we're guessing. There's too much at stake to be wondering. Pack your knapsack Catrina and don't forget woolen socks and cap."

Not long after he first smelled smoke, Philip heard gunfire. It was close. The soldiers were coming up Tribes Hill road towards Johnstown.[646] They'd pass right by their house! Philip gathered everyone at the kitchen table and around the fire.

As she sat at the table holding little Elizabeth, Catharina gasped, "Papa! I hear wagons and men marching."

"I hear it too. Be still."

Catrina rose and peeked out the back kitchen window. "Philip! There's someone behind the summer kitchen!"

Philip grabbed his firelock and peered out the window. He opened the door and hollered, "Who are you? Do not lurk about. Show yourself!"

He heard a voice he recognized. "T'is me Mr. Eamer. Martin Alguire."

"Martin here quickly!"

Catharina leapt out of her chair when she heard the name Martin. Martin barely got in the door when she embraced him with every ounce of her strength. They held each other tightly. Catharina sobbed. Philip gently pried Catharina's arm from Martin's waist and motioned him to sit. "I've only five minutes Mr. Eamer. I'm with Major Ross' company, and I've leave for only fifteen minutes. I've come to be a witness to my family's good health and tell you that Peter is here with the Grenadiers, as are Michael Gallinger Jr., Jacob Sheets, David Jeacocks, Michael and Nicholas Ault, Francis Albrandt and Adam P Empey and Sergeant John W Empey.[647]

As Martin talked, five of his six children huddle around him. From Catharina's lap, even Elizabeth reached her chubby arms toward him. "Our troops and Indians came from Oswego southeast through Onondaga. We've over 250 of the Six Nations, 100 KRRNY, 150 Butler's Rangers, thirty Highlanders, eleven Hanau Jägers, and many British soldiers. The west side of Schoharie is burned, Currytown and Warrensburgh too. We've been in the valley a few days, and now the Rebels pursue us. Captain Abraham Wemple and Captain John Little's company are close behind. Our forces are on their way to Johnstown then west to Oswego and the British lines. I must go now. But before I go, I warn you to be wary. Major Finck still hunts those disaffected from their cause."[648]

"Catrina reached for Martin's knapsack and shoved corn cakes, jerky, and cheese wherever she could find a spot. "Share this food with Peter and keep well. 'T'is cold and wet, and you've marched a long way. 'T'is still a long way to safety through wild forests. Give our love to Peter and God willing we'll all be together again."

Catharina had hold of Martin's arm as he turned to go out the door. She couldn't let go. He grasped her hand and kissed it firmly. "Be safe my love. When I am able, I'll come for you and the children."

All afternoon, the family gathered in the kitchen saying little to each other except to raise their voice when the children wriggled or fidgeted. Catrina, Dorothy, and Catharina tried to knit while Philip puffed hard on his pipe. As minutes crawled on, the sound of repeated gunfire kept them rubbing their arms, tapping their feet, or pacing the kitchen floor. A heavier sound of cannon fire rolled through the trees and down the lane. They sat there through the night till the break of dawn while nibbling and sipping on whatever nourishment they could. Before Philip crept out to the barn to feed the stock, he went to his office at the back of the house and opened his locked tin box. He folded the deed to their farm into a piece of linen and placed it firmly in his pocket along with a bag of silver coins. After feeding the stock, he returned through the kitchen door and said, "Make ready for an escape. I fear this battle will raise the fire in the Rebel heart so that we mayn't ever cool their fever."

It was midday, the day after the last sounds of gunfire when Catrina caught a glimpse of ten Rebel militia walking down their lane. She screamed, "Philip! The militia. They near our front door!" Just as she turned to find Catharina and the little ones, there was pounding at the front door. Fearing the door would free itself from its hinges, she backed against the kitchen wall with her arms wrapped around the children.

Philip stood by the door and bellowed, "Who strikes our door?"

"Open damned Tory. Open or we'll strike you and your family down. Every one of you villains come out. Make haste!"

"Stand away. We are unarmed!"

Philip opened the wobbling door and faced two men whose eyes glared white against the red of their faces.

"Now! Out!" they said pointing their bayonets at Philip's chest. The back of Philip's coat shook as Catrina's grip tightened. She heard him whisper, "Take hold of your knapsacks on the way out the door." With her sack over her shoulder, she followed him out to the yard. As she stood beside Philip, their familiar yard seemed like a place she'd never been. The colours of fall were dim. It smelled of smoke and reeked of fury. Dorothy followed, and Catharina held Elizabeth as she steered her five children into the yard.

"You've fifteen minutes to quit this valley you filthy traitors.[649] We know your son and son-in-law take arms against liberty. We've cause to string you from that tree, your wife too. As we did with Mr. William Kennedy. He rots in our jail at Fort Plain and watches his gallows erected, but not after we practiced hanging him at his home and left him for dead for his wife to cart him home on her back. Or we've cause to search your house and haul off your cash and goods as we did Mr. Michael Carmen Sr. We hauled all his cows, calves and horses, furniture, and £8! Or, Mr William Parker, demolished his buildings and plundered the rest of his property! And, we've just been to Mr. Michael Gallinger Sr. Last we saw he was heading north.[650]

Catrina's knees vibrated. The men stepped closer and closer. She recognized most of these men. They were Kingsborough tenants. She'd known them as children and known their fathers and mothers. Catrina struggled for a deep breath but none came, just tears flowing down her cheeks. Her hands trembled as she lifted her kerchief to wipe the tears while the sounds of her crying grandchildren deadened the Rebel cursing.

Philip tried to talk through the cursing and thrusting bayonets, "To stand a chance, we must get warm clothes and food. 'T'is on the cusp of winter. Food Sir, else my grandchildren will starve!"

When Philip saw the Rebel's clenched jaw thrust forward with the simultaneous thrust of his bayonet, he knew they must leave now else death was eminent. There would be no mercy.

"Quit this land now! Out! And never return else you take pleasure in our vengeance!"[651]

Philip grasped Catrina's hand and motioned Dorothy and Catharina to follow with the children. They walked toward the woods and the path to the creek. Catrina strained to tighten her throat and hold back her wail, all that surfaced were silent tears. She noticed the smell of harvest as she walked past the wattle fence around the garden and caught a glimpse of the orange and yellow pumpkins and crookneck squash she hadn't picked. For a moment, her gaze toward the east and the orchard triggered memories of the sweet smell of thousands of apple and cherry blossoms. No one spoke a word. They walked amidst the sound of their front door slamming, the whinnies of Apple, Bess, and

Star, the squealing hogs, the bawling cows, and the clucking and squawking of the chickens. "Don't look back. Keep walking!" she heard Philip say loudly. She turned only to encourage Dorothy to follow swiftly. She didn't dare fix her eyes on their home.

Philip did not stop until they crossed their creek and found the start of the trail through the Sacandaga Patent. They gathered together and trembled as they cried and hugged. The children only whimpered while grasping pieces of anyone's clothing.

As she wiped the tears from her eyes, Dorothy asked, "Where will we go Papa? 'T'is so cold."

"We must walk north to Jacob Henry Alguire's farm. We'll stay until we know where we can go. Walk swiftly and quietly. Do not draw attention to our presence. We know not who travels this trail or these woods." As he motioned everyone to keep walking, he thought, "I hope we'll find Michael and Agatha Gallinger on our way. Michael knows this trail well. They'd visited Valentine Cryderman's family many times."

It was late afternoon when the family stumbled down Jacob Henry's lane. Maria Salome ran out the door towards them, "Philip! Catrina! What's happened?"

As Catrina sobbed in Maria Salome's arms, Philip replied, "We've been used poorly and near died. Driven from our home. Animals and belongings gone. Perhaps the buildings too. I dared not look back."

"Come inside and warm yourselves. Michael and Agatha Gallinger arrived before noon with Johannes George and Dorothy. Betsy stayed behind with James Thompson and his family. And, John and Jane Waite have secreted in the woods since they escaped jail and their cattle were taken and property burned. They've waited since October 21st for a guide to take them to Montreal. Three of their sons are with the KRRNY, one was killed. Joseph Hanes, his wife, and young son John Hanes must flee also. They've been persecuted and Joseph fears for his life.[652]

"Is a pilot secured?"

"Aye. Peter Prunner, Sir John's scout, is now finding two Mohawk guides. They leave in the morning."

"We'd best travel with them. God knows we must be gone."

'T'is a heavy frost in the morning and soon snow. Michael and Agatha wish to travel too."

"What of Martin Silmser and his family?"

"Martin left yesterday to join Edward Jessup's Rangers.[653] Anna Margaret and Christina Elizabeth stay with their mother Elizabeth Margaret and their brother John Henry Silmser. And, Nicholas and Anna Margaret are safe at their home as are the newly wed Johannes George Alguire and Anna Maria Silmser.

At dusk as everyone supped on bits of mutton soup that Maria Salome prepared, Michael Gallinger Sr. recounted what he knew of the battle at Johnstown. "Major Ross and his men came up to Johnstown by Tribes Hill road after burning everything on the west side of Schoharie creek, past Gideon Marlet's place, then to Warrensburg. They've destroyed the Rebel scout John C. Service's house even went after his mother with a musket. At Johnstown, Major Ross met the Tryon County Militia and Colonel Marinus Willet's men. For a while, they fought in near dark. Many were wounded on both sides, some killed. Wounded was Henry Richtmeyer, cousin of Dorothy Richtmeyer wife of Christopher Rettig and grandson of Conrad Richtmeyer one of the first settlers in the Schoharie Valley. Killed was John Bowman of Corrysbush who leaves four orphans, the youngest Lewis is not yet one month old. And dead is a Butler's Ranger named William Bush, husband of Catherine Casselman. He too leaves three orphans. Major Ross and his men turned for Oswego that night with Colonel Willet in pursuit. 'T'is said that Walter Butler was killed as they crossed West Canada Creek."[654]

Jacob Henry came into the kitchen with Peter Prunner and two Mohawk warriors. As they found a place at the kitchen table Peter said, "I and these two warriors will guide you to Crown Point, Fort St. John, and Montreal. We leave at dawn. I tell you now how and with what we travel. We've over 190 kilometres to travel to reach the ships that'll take you up Lake Champlain, so at least thirteen kilometres is needed every day.[655] All eighteen of you must travel with speed. The smallest children must be carried. Men bring what weapon, shot, and flints you have. Wear your warmest clothes. 'T'is cold and wet. Only one pair stockings and shirt in your knapsacks and one blanket roll. The rest must be food. We've near eighteen days travel. Rest tonight. The trails and woods are toilsome, and Rebel scouts lurk in the woods."

That night everyone had a bed in which to rest their shaken hearts and bodies. Some might have even slept. Catrina rolled, tossed, and cried most of the night. The only comfort she found was when she nestled into the crook of Philip's back. The sound of Catharina's little Elizabeth crying woke her. Catrina saw frost on the window as the tiny bit of dawn shone through. She rolled out of bed and grasped her wool cape draped across a chair. She heard Catharina scurrying about her bedroom rolling clothes for the children and stuffing her knapsack. She took a deep breath and sighed. There'd be plenty of hurried preparation soon. As Catrina sat by the fire, the motions of pouring Jane Waite a cup of hot cider seemed mindless. Catrina felt numb all over, but especially her thoughts. There was activity all around her, but she could not say with what everyone was busy.

Philip came and put his hand over her shoulder and said, "'T'is time now dear wife. We must go."

"But, my things? I'm not ready."

"Yes, you are. We're in great danger if we stay. I pray we may come back someday and reclaim our farm."

"Oh yes! Dear husband. Our orchard, the garden, the animals, our home!"

Peter Prunner motioned the group out into the yard and the chill of the October morning. The two Mohawks stood at the head of the trail that led north to the Sacandaga River. Johannes George Gallinger positioned five year old Daniel on his back with instructions to the sobbing boy to hold tight to his woolen jacket. Dorothy took time to position three year old Sarah Waite in a kerchief sling on her back. Catharina did the same with two year old Elizabeth. Anne Waite, Dorothy Gallinger, and Maria Salome Alguire gathered in a group with nine year old Philip, eight year old John, and six year old Peter Alguire. The four elderly couples, all just shy of sixty years, gathered in front and behind the group. They were ready. The Mohawks started moving. Over her shoulder, Catrina stared at Jacob Henry, Maria Salome, and Jacob Jr. standing on their porch. Catrina's tears poured down her cheeks. She could not speak. She turned, and one foot moved forward followed by the weight of the other.

CHAPTER SIX

Home in the St. Lawrence River Valley (1781-1784)

At dusk on the first day of their journey north, the twenty one refugees and their three guides stopped in a grove of hemlock and white pine. The grove was good cover for their small camp where smoke from their fire was concealed, and a small tumbling twisting creek flowed through the forest. As soon as they arrived, Agatha and Jane placed blankets near the large roots of three hemlocks. The blankets barely touched the ground when the young boys nestled into the groove of the roots and fell asleep. The girls gathered fire wood while Philip and Michael started three small fires. Jane and Catrina laid out cheese, bread, and dried fruit and put jerky in water setting it to boil in their only tin pot. Catharina sat by the fire with her blanket draped over her shoulders and little Elizabeth in her arms.

Her fixed gaze into the fire softened when she asked, "Papa, how many kilometres tomorrow?"

"At least ten. One of the Mohawk guides tells me 't'is a good trail through the woods."

With her eyes half closed, Catharina said, "Dorothy and I'll sleep well even if it snows. Our feet or arms cannot move again until morning."

"Aye daughter. 'T'will be cold. Stay close to the fire."

She mumbled as she lay on the ground with Elizabeth nestled next to her, "Are there Rebel scouts in these woods?"

"There might be. The Mohawks are out now looking for signs. There'll always be someone on guard through the night. Sleep now."

At dawn, Catrina woke to the crackle of the fire. She saw Philip carefully place sticks over the coals and watched as the flames rose. She asked, "How must we survive so many days of this?"

"The trials of the trail will be different each day. We must only look to the end of the day not to the end of our journey."

"Aye husband. But, I look ahead to the thought of seeing Peter and Maria Catherine. I want to know they are well. And, I look ahead with the hope we might find our Martin."

For two more days, Catrina followed Philip along the path through groves of red maple, deep green spruce, and golden tamarack. She kept pace, but sometimes she stumbled over roots or slipped on leaf laden rocks. With each stumble, she moaned and tears flowed, freeing the heavy heartache she carried. At the end of the third day, the group followed the path along the edge of a large meadow. She knew dusk would fall soon. She listened for the children. The sound of rushing water dampened the sound of their whimpers.

She reached for Philip's knapsack, and giving it a tug she said, "Is that river water I hear?"

"Aye Catrina. We're very near the Sacandaga. 'T'is dusk soon. We'll cross in the morning. Our guides know the easiest spot to cross, and we've six men to help the women and little ones."

As soon as she woke, Catrina combed the forest at the edge of their camp for three or four walking sticks. They would need them to steady their tired legs as they crossed the river. The children just finished eating their corn cake when Peter Prunner led the group along the path that descended to the rocky shore of the river. Catrina saw one of their Mohawk guides on the other side. The other guide was motioning them to step into the river and follow him across. As she stepped into the water, she lifted her skirt and tied it to one side. Catrina's feet went numb. A chill moved through her body. She gasped, planted her stick into the river bottom, and stepped forward. As she moved slowly across, she was grateful that the water was low and that the soft current barely pushed her. Once across, she realized it was easier to cross than to stand soaking wet on the other side and watch the children cry and cling to whomever struggled to keep their balance.

It took hours that morning to cross the Sacandaga River and even more time to warm everyone enough to safely continue on the trail. For four more days, they walked north to Stony Creek then around the western base of Crane Mountain and north again to cross the Hudson River. Once across the Hudson River, a clearing among bronze beech and red maple trees provided a perfect spot to set up their camp. Crossing the Hudson River drew the last ounce of strength from everyone. The children lay listless on the ground wrapped in their blankets. As Agatha, Jane, and Catrina felt the warmth of the campfires around the perimeter of the fire, they managed to feed each child spoonfuls of a broth of wild onion bulbs and beech leaves. Once the children were settled, the women set what damp clothes they could next to the fire and huddled close enough to see the steam rise from their shoes. Catharina held Elizabeth close to her breast and sipped on broth while Catrina broke a few small pieces of bread from a loaf and passed them among the women.

Catrina's hand shook as she brought the bread to her mouth, but the weight of Philip's hand on her shoulder eased her shivering. She looked up and said, "We must find a way to carry the children. They cannot walk much farther."

"We'll make a travois for the knapsacks and carry Daniel and Peter."

"What about the older boys?"

"Philip and John are strong enough. We've no choice. Our guides tell me that the trail around Schroon Lake is well worn, but the area is rocky and has many hills."

"I sha'n't make too many uphill kilometres husband."

"I'll fasten a rope round my waist to give you aid. We've not much farther to go, only five more days to Crown Point."

The mist in the trees woke Catrina early the next morning. She lay quiet and unable to move without pain in her back and her knees. She shivered as she watched her breath flow into the frosty air. Her tears warmed her cheeks. She lifted her blanket and rolled to her knees when she saw their Mohawk guide sit next to the low embers of their fire. Once up, she paced around the fire until she felt her blood warm her fingers and toes. As her fingers warmed, she was able to set the tin pot over the coals and heat water. At least the children would have something warm in their bellies.

A distance of forty kilometres took the refugees near the end of Schroon Lake. For three days, the rocks, trees, roots, streams, and hills passed as if in a dream. Even warnings of Rebel scouts nearby seemed trifling. The only blessing was a few bass and lake trout that Michael and Philip caught on their second day along the western edge of Schroon Lake. As they turned east toward Fort Ticonderoga, the group shared mumblings of safety, hot food, and rest. They followed the path along creek beds and valley meadows and past Paradise and Eagle Lakes.

Catrina gripped the rope tied to Philip's waist as they climbed the slope of a hill. Despite the shelter of the hills, Catrina felt cold, wet sleet strike her face. As they began to descend, Catrina's knees buckled, and she stumbled. Philip turned and eased her to her feet. Catrina moaned as she tried to catch her breath.

As she bent over, she heard Peter Prunner calling out, "The path opens to the road to Fort Ticonderoga! Sha'n't be long now before we've warmth, a bed, and some food! There's still a small garrison at the fort who'll guide us north to Bulwagga Bay and a ship to Montreal."

Still bent over, Catrina prayed aloud, "Our dear Lord and Saviour has brought us to safety. Praise God! Praise God we all live."

After a meal of salt pork, bread, and dried apples, the group settled next to the warmth of an iron stove in one of the barracks. Catrina set her worn, wet coat and kerchief at the end of the bed and helped Catharina wrap little Elizabeth in a tattered wool blanket. There was no talk of what the next day would bring, only talk of finding their camp beds, lie down, and murmur gratitude for instant sleep. Michael Gallinger, John Waite, Joseph and John Hanes, and Philip stayed awake long enough to listen to Peter Prunner talk of plans to walk north along the shore of Lake Champlain to Crown Point and Bulwagga Bay to catch a schooner heading north to Montreal. It was the first week of November. The wind was strong and the water choppy, but the lake was open all the way to Fort St. John.

For three days and 134 kilometres, the group of twenty one sat huddled in the hold of a British cargo schooner bound for Fort St. John. Catrina thought she'd forgotten how the swell of waves rocked a ship. Their journey across the great sea was so long ago, but her memories flooded back. She sensed the smell of vinegar, urine, and rotting pork. Her stomach rolled each time the ship listed. She tried to retrieve memories of cherry and apple blossoms, but she only managed to break a tiny smile and thank God for the safety of her husband, daughters, and grandchildren. For now, with God's blessing, she might find Peter and Maria Catherine and Martin, and Nicholas and Anna Margaret would someday soon travel north to safety. Perhaps Michael Myers and his new wife Elizabeth would bring her grandchildren to her. Someday, she only hoped they survived the journey to return and enjoy the pleasures of their New York farm again.

Early on the third day, Catrina heard the sailors' footsteps thump across the main deck as they hollered, "Port ahead, raise the sails! Ready anchors!"

Philip grasped Catrina's hand, glanced at Catharina and said, "Fort St. John. 'T'will be strange for us all. Nothing familiar here except each of us. We've only a day or two 'til we arrive at the safety of the British camp at Montreal."

One by one, the group staggered onto shore. Philip steadied Catrina as she made her way onto the rocky beach. He helped her balance herself as she sat on a large rock and went to aid Catharina with the children. As Catrina sat on the rock, she watched the soldiers walk past. Their green coats with blue facings and their cocked black hats were unfamiliar to her.

A deep voice startled her, "Madam. I'm Henry Ruiter of Robert Leake's Company of the 2nd Battalion KRRNY. Is this the group of Loyalists aboard the schooner from Crown Point?"

She wobbled as she rose to speak to him. As he grasped her arm to steady her, she replied, "We are those from Johnstown and Crown Point Sir. My son is with the Grenadiers or the 2nd Battalion. Peter Eamer.[656] Do you know of him Sir?"

"No Madam. We're stationed at many places along the St. Lawrence River. Perhaps he's at Montreal. We've barracks and rations for you a short distance from here."

Pointing toward the schooner Catrina said, "I must wait for my husband and daughters. Look. They come now."

"Aye Madam. Then kindly follow me."

In the barracks, there was barely a sound from the twenty one refugees. Catrina and Jane slept. Catharina lay on her camp bed with Elizabeth beside her while Philip, John, Peter, Daniel and Maria Salome sat on the floor playing Jack Straws. Michael, Philip, Joseph, and John sat next to the iron stove, each with a tin cup of rum. The silence broke when Peter Prunner entered the barrack with Barnabas Hough of Captain John Peter's Corp. of Queens Loyal Rangers. The two men stood by the door, and Peter Prunner bellowed, "We've secured transportation for you tomorrow morning. Supply wagons leave at dawn for the garrison at La Prairie. 'T'is about twenty four kilometres west on the south shore of the St. Lawrence River. From there, a batteau will take you across the river to Montreal where you'll be housed and provisioned."

Casting his eyes at each of the refugees, Peter Prunner saw some not react at all to his message. Each of them lay still without eye contact. They didn't even raise or turn their heads when he entered the room. As he looked, he thought, "They're all near collapse from fatigue of body, mind, and soul. Poor souls, I must give them a bit of hope." He announced, "May you find solace knowing that the Reverend John Stuart, your ever faithful man of God from Fort Hunter, is here at the garrison having arrived from Schenectady only a few days ago. He's offered to come to this hut and give you God's blessing."[657]

Daylight barely lit the skiff of snow on the ground while the group of refugees huddled near three wagons. As soldiers harnessed the horses, each person clutched the blanket wrapped over their shoulders until they heard a soldier say, "Children aboard first. Move to the front of the wagon!" Philip and Michael lifted Catharina's boys onto one wagon. Philip held Elizabeth while Catharina climbed up. The Hanes family, John Waite Sr., Jane, and little Sarah Waite boarded another wagon. Catrina tried to manage herself, but she didn't have the strength. Philip lifted her aboard, and Dorothy followed. After Dorothy, Michael, Agatha, and Johannes George clambered up, Catrina walked to the front and slid down the side of the wagon between bundles of cloth, too tired and cold to care where she sat.

She laid her head on Philip's chest, and pulling her blanket tighter she said, "Are Catherine and the children aboard?"

"They're in the next wagon. I see young Philip holding Daniel. 'T'is not long now. With no mud, the horses will make good speed. We'll be there at the end of the day. Montreal is only a few hours across the river."

"My heart aches to see our new grandchild. She or he must be nearing their first birthday. My stomach turns, and I'm weary. Where will we live? Will they feed us? Maybe there'll be others there we know. Will we ever see our home again? Will Peter be there? What of Martin Alguire? And our Martin? Dear husband we must find our Martin." She sighed as Philip pulled her closer.

Late in the afternoon, the wagons rolled into the garrison at La Prairie. Catrina woke to the sound of several men talking, each had deep, strong German accents. She looked to the tail of the wagon and saw three men helping Michael and Agatha onto the road. The men, she thought, were soldiers but in uniforms unlike she had ever seen, and their language and accents reminded her of home. They wore black wool tricorn hats with a cockade of ribbons on one side. Their coats had long tails and were a deep green trimmed with red crimson on the lapels and cuffs. She wondered if these men belonged to the German troops she knew fought with Sir John. Still curious about the men, she rose and walked to the tail of the wagon, allowing one soldier to lift her down.

She steadied herself and in German asked, "With what regiment are you Sir?"

"I'm Private Bernhard Doenges with Lieutenant Colonel Karl Adolf Cristoph von Creutzburg's Hesse Hanau Jägers."[658]

"Hesse was our home Sir."

"We've many soldiers from Hesse Hanau Madam. La Prairie is our headquarters. I've been in America since the spring of 1777. We fought with your Lieutenant Colonel St. Leger at Fort Stanwix and General Burgoyne at Saratoga." Reaching for her arm, he said, "We must move to a barrack. 'T'will be dark soon. At dawn we're to transport you to Montreal by batteaux."[659]

Fig. 32. A New Map of the Province of Quebec, according to The Royal Proclamation of the 7th of October 1763. Johnathan Carver, Robert Sayer, and John Bennett, 1776. Courtesy of Library of Congress, Geography and Maps Division, 74694799. PD-US.

Positioned near the front of the bateau, Catrina huddled under her blanket and watched the sun rise above the horizon. As the sun's rays spread across the river, sparkles atop the waves mesmerized her, and she gazed at the small mountain that rose behind the city. The bateau, with its heavy load of cargo and passengers, was familiar to Catrina.[660] They travelled on a similar boat when they left Philadelphia, and she saw many like it along the Mohawk River. This one, she thought, was longer and made of oak and fir. She leaned against the side of the boat and watched as four oarsmen pulled them closer to shore. She watched bateaux and schooners dip and rise as they passed by their rolling battteau. Soon, she saw the steeple of a large church above the stone ramparts that surrounded the city. Carefully, she scanned the buildings along the western shore that led to the wharf and the city gate.

She listened as Philip and Michael talked. She heard Michael say, "We must find a barrack for us all and then look for the Quartermaster. We must secure rations."

Philip replied, "I managed to hide a few shillings in my shirt pocket when we were forced out, and Jacob Henry gave me £2 the morning we left."

"Agatha and I've £2, but the Rebels robbed John and Jane of everything they had, and Joseph has nothing."

Agatha leaned forward and said, "We must find someone from Captain Patrick Daly's 9th Company in the 1st Battalion KRRNY or the Grenadiers. They'll help us find Michael, Christopher, and Henry."

Catrina added, "Peter too and Maria Catherine. And someone from Major James Gray's Company who might know the whereabouts of Catharina's Martin." Catrina covered her face with her hands and said, "Oh, everyone is so strewn about! 'T'will be months before we're together again!"

Dorothy and Johannes George were the first to climb out of the batteau. They stood waiting, and one by one they gathered the children.

Philip spoke to Bernhard Doenges while the group stood shivering. "Where can we find the Quartermaster of the KRRNY? We must find shelter and rations."

"Go through St. Mary's gate and past the hospital to the parish church Sir. Then turn west and go out the Friar Recollets' gate. The military barracks are there."[661]

With one arm around Catrina, Philip tipped his hat and said, "Obliged and good day to you Sir."

As the group walked through the Recollets' gate, they saw lines of tents and clusters of small buildings to the north. Philip and Michael led the group to one noticeably large hut. Soldiers with recognizable KRRNY scarlet uniforms stood outside.

Philip approached one soldier and said, "Quartermaster Sir?"

"Inside Sir. 'T'is Captain Thomas Gummersall."[662]

As Philip and Michael entered, Captain Gummersall's assistant motioned them forward saying, "Newcomers?"

"Aye, this hour."

"With what regiment do you belong?"

"None Sir as yet. My daughter's husband Martin Alguire is with the 1st Battalion Major James Gray's Company, and my son Peter Eamer is with Captain John McDonell's Grenadiers, and many of our friends and neighbours are with Captain Patrick Daly's Company."

Philip and Michael entered Captain Gummersal's office and sat before him, each in a rickety chair. The Captain asked, "Gentlemen, tell me from where and how you've come. What are your needs?"

Philip replied, "We've been chased from our home near Johnstown because of our loyalty to our gracious King. We've travelled weeks with Peter Prunner of the KRRNY. Our journey took us hundreds of kilometres through dangerous woods. Our wives are old and fatigued, and the children are cold and frightened. Please Sir. We require housing and rations for our subsistence."

"How many in your party Sir?" "Twenty one in all. Four men over fifty five, one man of seventeen, another about thirteen. The rest are women and children."

"Sir. All able bodied men are considered fit for service, and therefore are required to enlist to receive rations. Otherwise, they must find their own work. The women and children are allowed provisions and shelter, but they must provide washing services to the army."

"But Sir, we have and are suffering. One man of our party is old and infirm and not fit for work or service."

The Captain leaned toward Philip and said, "Provisions are low and we've almost 1700 refugees in camps along the Richelieu and St. Lawrence Rivers. There're 266 in Montreal alone."[663]

"Aye Sir. We're grateful for what you can provide. The woman can wash and sew, and Mr. Gallinger, Mr. Hanes, and I will find work."

Philip and Michael joined the group huddled outside the Captain's hut. Michael pointed towards a cluster of huts nearby and said, "This soldier will get us wood and take us to our lodgings. I'm afraid not all of us are allowed provisions. Philip and I'll find the Sutler or a market and bring food."

The soldier brought them to an empty hut at the end of a row of twelve. When Philip got closer, he stood in front of the hut rubbing his chin and thought, "These huts are small, made only of pine slabs, and seem hastily constructed. They can't be more than six by twelve metres." When he entered, he realized the hut provided shelter from the wind and snow but not much shelter from the cold. He looked up and whispered a prayer when he saw a large iron stove at one end, but when he saw eight camp beds squeezed along each wall he stiffened and thought, "How are twenty one people going to live in this small space? They'll need more huts. Thousands have left the valley without homes to which they can return, and there're thousands more to come."[664]

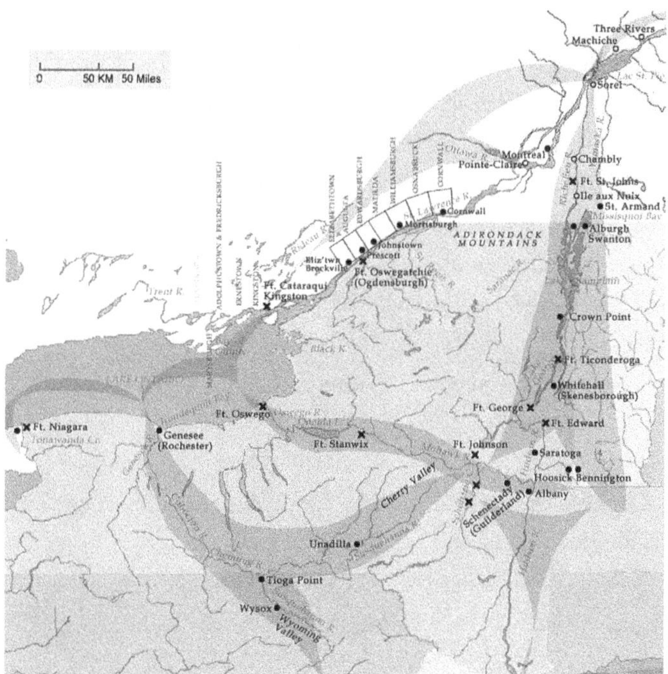

Fig. 33. Loyalist Migration to Canada, 1780s showing Townships settled in 1784. Courtesy of Lisa-Ann Rance©. (Township #1, Charlottenburg, at the far east of the Townships is missing on this map)

That evening Dorothy braved the cold and took the young children for a walk. She stopped to warm herself near one of the fires built in front of the row of huts. As she rubbed her hands over the flames, she looked to a group warming themselves at the next fire. Her heart beat faster as she thought, "I know that woman! 'T'is Mrs Empey, William Empey's Sr. wife." Rushing the children back to the hut, she called out to Catrina, "Mama. Mrs Empey! I saw her. She might know where we can fine Peter and Maria Catherine."

Catrina grabbed her cloak from the hook near the door and raced down the steps of the hut saying, "Where? Where? Dorothy Where?"

Pointing she said, "There Mama."

Catrina rushed to the next fire. Waving her hands, she called out, "Maria Margaret! Maria Margaret Empey!"[665]

A woman turned, and with her hands raised she replied, "Catrina Eamer!"

As the women embraced, Catrina said, "We've just come. Chased from our home! Are you well?"

"Aye. The children and I came with Sir John after their valley raid in May. Many of our friends came. Some are here. Martin Waldorf came last year as did Henry Hare's widow Alida Vrooman. T'was dangerous for her to stay after the family's imprisonment and Henry's hanging in '79. They suspected her of providing intelligence.[666] And, there's John Lonie's wife Catherine and their four children and Peter Service Jr.'s wife Lenah and their six children. Newcomers are George Adam Dachstadter's wife Eva with their five children, Johannes Adam Helmer's wife Maria Barsch with their four children, and John P. Service's wife Catherine."[667]

"We look for Peter and Maria Catherine. You must know where they are? They came with Sir John too."

"Aye. Peter is with the KRRNY at their camp at Point Claire.[668] Maria Catherine is with them. And, a new baby! A son! They named him Peter Eamer Jr.."[669]

"Ohhh! A grandson. Where is Point Claire? How far?"

"'T'is only twenty four kilometres west. They've supply wagons going regularly."

"I must get Philip. We must go to the camp."

"They might not have lodgings there."

Catrina barely heard Maria Margaret's last words as she turned and hurried back to the hut. Out of breath and nearly tripping on the steps to the door, Catrina burst into the hut saying, "Philip we must go to Point Claire! Peter and Martin Alguire are there. 'T'is only twenty four kilometres."

"'T'is too late Catrina. Tomorrow we'll ask Captain Gummersal how we can contact Peter and Martin."

Catharina stood listening. Then she said, "Martin will want to see his children."

"We must go Papa!" Catharina begged.

"May'n't be possible Catharina."

Early in the morning, Philip, Catrina, Catherina, and Michael and Agatha walked to Captain Gummersal's hut to inquire about going to Point Claire. They learned that refugees must stay where they are provisioned, and there was no room on a supply wagon. But, Captain Gummersal thought it possible that Peter and Martin might obtain leave to come to Montreal. He promised to get word to Captain Daly and Major Gray at Point Claire.

Two days dragged on while Catrina, Catherina, and Agatha occupied their time with cooking, washing, feeding the fire in the iron stove, and keeping the children busy. Every time they heard footsteps near the hut, one of them opened the door with hopes their sons or husband had arrived. One afternoon, Catrina was stirring pork broth and peas and checking the biscuits in the frying pan when there was a knock at the door. She turned, rested her spoon on the pot, and watched Catharina walk to the door. The next moment she was watching Catharina hug her brother as he stood in the doorway. My son has grown, Catrina thought as she dropped her spoon and rushed toward him. She hardly noticed his full length bright scarlet coat with blue facings and his smart red waistcoat.[670] At 5'11", Peter was a tall, handsome soldier. As Catharina hugged Peter, she gasped when she saw the man standing behind him. It was her dear husband Martin Alguire. Peter stood aside and let the two embrace. His chin dropped as he watched five children rush to the door and cling to any part of Martin their hands could grasp.

Peter set down his 'short land Brown Bess' musket and his round black felt hat and embraced Philip saying, "Papa, thank God you're here and you are well."

"And thank God for your health too son. Nary a day has gone by when your Mama and I didn't think or speak of you and your dear wife."

Catrina hugged Peter and did not let go as she led him to a chair near the stove. The crowd of children, still clinging to Martin, moved toward the middle of the hut. When they moved, Catrina saw her enter the doorway. She carried a small bundle in her arms.

Catrina's words followed a gasp and squeal, "Maria Catherine! And our grandson Peter!" With her arms stretched toward the bundle, Catrina said, "Are you well? Is the boy well? May I cuddle him?" Philip walked forward and smiled as he stroked the infant's chin. Peter Eamer Jr. wiggled, gurgled, and smacked his lips as Catrina held him close. She stared into his eyes as she removed his wool cap and blanket to examine his head, arms, feet, and hands.

The room was crowded. Dorothy finally got close enough to Peter to give him a hug. He took her hand and turned her toward the door, "Look sister who's come with us."

Dorothy's grin spread ear to ear as she walked toward him. She had not expected to see Henry Gallinger and certainly not in such a handsome scarlet uniform. Henry's grin was equally wide.

He took her hand, kissed it, and said, "'T'is a grand day when I can see you again and see you safe and well."

"'T'is my heart's wish to see you too, safe and healthy. We tried to get news of your regiment, but news came in small amounts and not often."

"Well, there're many ways to get news now, and we're closer."

Finally, Michael, Agatha, and Johannes George were able to interrupt the young couple and embrace Henry.

It was well past dusk when Peter set down his cup of rum and said, "'T'is time for us to leave. We cannot be away from camp much past dark. We'll come again tomorrow. We're expected back at Point Claire. We've only two days leave."

Catrina rose and began to help Maria Catherine wrap little Peter in his wool blanket. She said, "Maybe we can move to the refugee settlement at Pointe Claire? I want to be closer to you."

Peter shrugged and said, "'T'is best you all stay here Mama. When winter is over, the regiment will probably move again. In fact, soon, 100 of our men are to proceed to Carleton Island. We're to replace the 150 men who went to the Mohawk Valley in October with Major John Ross and Major Butler. One of us may be included in that detachment of men."[671]

Philip passed Peter his musket and hat and said, "Take good care son. Send word as often as you can. 'Twill be hard for your mother to be at a distance. This upheaval takes a toll on her."

"Sending word will be first on my mind, but the cold and snow are severe here and communication slow."

Joseph Hanes rose to shake Peter's hand and said, "Send word to our sons that we're well and wish to see them as soon as they can come."

"Aye Sir. I'll see them. Your son Michael Hanes is a Sergeant in Captain Duncan's Company and Christopher is with the Grenadier Company."[672]

Michael, Agatha, and Dorothy hugged Henry and said, "Send word to your brothers of our well-being and our arrival here. Tell them to make their way here at the soonest possible time."

"Aye Papa. They'll be glad you're safe and victualled so close."

As Johannes George shook his brother's hand, he said, "As soon as I'm satisfied that Mama and Papa are taken care of I'll enlist with Sir John's regiment. John Waite Jr. will also. You'll see us by spring."

John and Jane Waite approached Martin and said, "Relay a message to our sons George and Joseph. George is with Captain Daly's Company, and Joseph is a Corporal in Captain John Munro's Company. Tell them we are safe, fed, and resting and that we desire to see them soon. We've lost one son to this war. We fear losing another."[672]

Through the final weeks of 1781, keeping hopes high was difficult for everyone. Except for a few hundred refugees, some soldiers, and Canadians from surrounding villages, the refugees were isolated within their hut. Days were long, dark, and cold. Snow fell constantly, and without snowshoes or warm winter clothes, they seldom ventured outside. A few days a week most of the women walked to the regiment tailor's hut and spent the day sewing blanket coats, jackets, and breeches. The others stayed to look after the seven children. The men were called on to travel to nearby woods to fell trees, haul logs, and chop firewood.

Near the end of November, delayed, devastating news circulated through the camp. Astonishingly, they learned that General Cornwallis surrendered to General Washington and General Rochambeau at Virginia. It seemed the British lost the war. Peace was imminent. Soon, fighting in the Mohawk Valley would cease. For all the refugees, the cost of losing the war was feared. For Philip,

Catrina, their children, grandchildren, and their many friends and neighbours, their losses were inconceivable and most of the time unspeakable.

One afternoon, most of the group were wrapped in their wool blankets sleeping and some crowded near the iron stove. No one spoke.

Philip sipped his ration of rum slowly and said to Michael, "We'll keep faith that ruin is not our end. We'll wait for word from our General Haldimand. Surely our loyalty and service brings us hope."

Michael replied, "We must circulate through camp and stay abreast of any news. There'll be happenings of our concern."

"Aye. Our readiness to respond will work in our favour."

Johannes George spoke out, "Papa, John Waite Jr. and I still want to enlist. We're fit and old enough now, and we want to be of service."

"May'n't be possible if General Haldimand disbands our troops."

"Papa, the General will always need troops."

During the first weeks of 1782, Philip listened for news of the KRRNY 1st and 2nd Battalions' movements when he was chopping wood or helping to unload supplies at the army camp. He often took his ration of rum with men familiar with the regiment. One afternoon as he took his break from work, he thought, "I must keep track of the whereabouts of Peter and Martin Alguire. 'T'is likely General Haldimand will disband his troops soon, and if thousands of Loyalist refugees cannot return home, they'll resettle somewhere in the province. Ohh, 't'is a vast land. Finding the boys amidst the chaos could be difficult. And what if they're sent on a scout or raid? The dangers to their life are not yet over."

Philip also watched for the arrival of men, women, and children from the colonies. There was still the possibility that he might learn the whereabouts of his son Martin or hear of his arrival in Canada. He kept note of all he learned during the day and brought his news to Catrina at the end of the day.

Early in February, the refugees did nothing else but surrender to winter's grip. The snow and frigid wind had hold of them day and night and made travelling the narrow path to collect their provisions a daunting task. Philip and Joseph volunteered one afternoon to make the dreaded trek and collect their ration of pork, flour, butter, and peas. The only benefit to the trek, other than ensuring they had food for a week, was that it was another opportunity to gather information about the troops and the state of the British army in Canada and in the colonies. On this day, they gathered useful but upsetting news.

While in line, Philip stood behind Catherine Lonie, John's wife and Lenah, Peter Service's wife.

When the women turned to acknowledge him, Philip said, "Good day to you both. 'T'is a harsh cold day. I hope this line moves quickly."

Catherine Lonie replied, "Good day gentlemen. The line moved some before you came. I must move quickly too. Moving keeps me warm, and my three sons and daughter await me."

Lenah Service added, "And, my six boys await me. Hunger is always their greatest complaint."

"Have you ladies any word on the regiment?"

"Aye Mr. Eamer. Major Ross and most of the 2nd Battalion are to move to Oswego and Carleton Island. The army fears a Rebel invasion. The men are to fortify the works, transport goods by batteaux to the upper posts, and go to the colonies on scouting and secret service missions. Men of the 1st Battalion are at Lachine and Coteau du Lac. Only those men with illness or injury are exempt. Christian Sheek remains at Coteau du Lac, Peter Service Jr. is at Montreal ill and remains behind, and Nicholas Barnhardt Sr., the brother of Sergeant George Barnhardt of the 2nd Battalion, is too old to serve.

"I know the Barnhardts. Their grandfather Johannes Barnhardt lived only a few kilometres west of my village in Germany. That family is from Gross Zimmern and Reichelsheim, Hesse."

"Michael Warner is our armourer and is at Montreal.[673] The women and children with the 2nd Battalion winter in the barracks at Ile Jesus north of Montreal."[674]

Carrying their week's rations and with news of the KRRNY Battalions, Philip and Joseph made their way back to the hut.

Quick to enter and keep the cold out, Philip set down the food and removed his blanket coat. "We've news of our boys! They're ordered to Oswego."

Catrina collapsed into her chair. She raised her hand to cover her chest and said, "What! 'T'is hundreds of kilometres along a treacherous river! 'T'will be months before we see Peter and Martin again, perhaps years!"

"Months maybe Catrina, but sha'n't be years. We've to wait for a communication from the boys."

Catrina's hand pressed hard on her stomach, and squeezing her eyes shut she said, "With such news I doubt dear husband that I'll survive this brutal winter.

At least I'm comforted to know that Maria Catherine and our grandson Peter will be close. Ile Jesus is only an hour north of us."

"Aye. We're often there cutting wood."

"We've other problems Philip. Some days 't'is too much to bear. The children cry most of the day and night with hunger. Their gums bleed, and they bruise. They need fresh food, and there's no milk. Today while sewing, I met a Mohawk woman, the wife of Caleb Peck. Joseph knows him. His farm was on the Kingsborough Patent and close to Joseph. Caleb's wife Catherine tells me we must get the bark of white spruce or pine and make a tea or get more spruce beer. We'll all die if we don't get these things. We must conquer the scurvy. There's also measles, smallpox, and jail fever of which I fear most every day. I worry that Maria Catherine does not know these things and our little Peter will die. Now what does she do that Peter is to go to Oswego."[675]

"We'll get these things. I promise. We'll go tomorrow to the woods, and I'll ask of spruce beer at the Quartermaster's store."

Early April 1782 brought relief with the thaw. Despite the mud, mosquitoes, and black flies, at least there was warmth. One day, the men were called out to a sugar bush to tap maple trees. While boring holes and placing buckets throughout the bush, Michael and Philip met a soldier of the 1st Battalion KRRNY who just came from Coteau du Lac where Captain Daly's men are quartered.

Michael approached the soldier to learn what he could of the battalions. Michael said, "Good day Sir. Our sons are with the KRRNY. We wish to learn of their location. Have you knowledge?"

"Aye. The 1st Battalion is at Lachine and Coteau du Lac and the second is at Carleton Island and Oswego."[676]

"Have you knowledge of the arrival of Loyalists fleeing the colonies?"

"Aye. A Mr. William Kennedy just arrived from Skenesborough with directions from over 100 distressed families quartered at Skenesborough. Members of the families tell us that in February, in the dead of winter, they were ordered off their land. After Major Ross' attack at Johnstown 25 Oct 1781, the Rebels discovered that these families' sons and husbands were in Canada in the King's service. The Rebels chased them off their land. As refugees, the families arrived at Skenesborough lacking every necessity of life. Now, their sons and husbands in the King's service wrote a petition to General Haldimand requesting a flag be sent with provisions and clothing to nourish them and protect them from the inclement weather. When the weather permits and they are strong enough, they can be sent under the protection of a flag to Canada."

"Aye. I know Mr. Kennedy. He's a tenant of Kingsborough Patent and a scout for Sir John. Do you know the names of the soldiers who wrote the petition?"

"Aye. Most of them are men from Sir John's Kingsborough Patent. They are: Martin Waldorf, William Shuman, Jacob Waggoner, Conrad Snyder, Adam Cline, Johannes Shaver, John McWilliam, Daniel Smith, Andrew Kumerling, William Hare (for his mother Margaret), Thomas Ross, Hugh Gessina, and John Cough."[677]

"I know the Cough family. They lived near Jacob Henry Alguire, William Shuman, and Michael Carman at Philadelphia Bush."

Seated against the limb of a maple tree, the soldier said, "Poor William Kennedy. In March 1782, he was released after five months in the Albany prison. As soon as William went home he found his house plundered, his cattle gone, and his wife and six children thrown out into a metre of snow without essential clothes. He managed to hire a sleigh to bring them to Montreal. Another man, Mr. Michael Carman Sr. was charged with harbouring Kennedy and the aging farmer, tanner, and scout William Parker near the time they were taken prisoner. I think late October 1781. Poor Mr. Parker. They executed one of his sons. Well, the Rebels ordered Michael Carman Sr. into the woods, and while he was away the Rebels from Warrensburg plundered his home, stole his horses, calves, and cattle. They broke into his chest and stole £6 sterling silver along with all his clothing and his household furniture. As they did to Mr. Kennedy they did to Mr. Carman, chasing him off his property at the point of a bayonet without permitting him to carry anything away. Mr. Carman and his wife and children made it to Schenectady where she suffered a broken wrist from which she has not recovered."[678]

The soldier continued his story, "The widow Margaret Hare, wife of the late John Hare Jr. who was killed at the battle at Oriskany, has also suffered. She is of the Davis family. She and her six children were also plundered and robbed. They tried to get to Canada, but procedures and rules hindered their travel until she finally got as far as Schenectady. She was turned back to Johnstown due to Major Ross' raid near Schenectady. At Johnstown, she was not allowed to enter under any roof on account her son was a volunteer with Major Butler. So, she and her six children returned to Schenectady. She stayed there until February when she finally made her way to Skenesborough to await a ship."[679]

Philip picked up his sugar buckets and said, "Thank you. We wish you well. 'T'is sad news of the suffering that continues for our friends and neighbours still in the valley, but 't'is good news that we can await the arrival of so many families. Hope remains for my wife and I that our son Martin might be among them. We've not heard of him for over one year. Perhaps our daughter Anna Margaret and her husband Nicholas will also be among them. Sir, now we must return to our work."

In April and May 1782, most of the women in the hut spent their days at the tailor's hut or the washing hut. One day in May, Dorothy and Anne Waite were assigned to the wash hut. About six women were bent over large wooden wash tubs scrubbing shirts and breeches while several others carried the clean clothes to hang on the line outside.

While Dorothy rested a moment rolling her neck side to side, she spoke to the woman sitting next to her, "A good day to you. I'm Dorothy Eamer. 'T'is a warm spring day. Have you been at Montreal long?"

"Good day. I'm Catherine Winter. We've been here since last fall. Before last fall, my family was quartered at Point Claire with many others from the Susquehanna River. We're from the settlement of Wyalusing in Pennsylvania."

"With what regiment is your husband?"

"My husband Henry Winter was with Butler's Rangers since '77, but he was taken prisoner with our son Nicholas in '78. Now, we're here with my daughter Elizabeth. My three sons are with the 2nd Battalion KRRNY, the youngest Peter is a drummer."[680]

Dorothy turned as she heard the hut door open. Her chin dropped, and she laid the wet shirts on the table next to her. It was Philip and Michael walking through the door.

As they entered, they said, "Ladies 't'is good news. Our countrymen from the valley just arrived. We're going to the Quartermaster's hut to greet them. I'm sure you'll want to come too and see who's arrived."

Before Philip walked to the Quartermaster's hut, he went to get Catrina. Together they walked along the rows of refugee huts toward Captain Gummersal's hut.

With his arm supporting Catrina as they walked, Philip said, "Mr. Kennedy says there were over 100 families. Let's pray that Anna Margaret and Nicholas are among them."

Catrina nodded and said, "I pray also that Michael Myers has brought our grandchildren too."

As they approached the hut, they saw an enormous crowd of people. Some in the crowd were sitting on whatever was available, others talked in groups, and still others leaned against the walls of the hut. Catrina's eyes darted across the crowds. First she scanned the groups, next as many seated as she could, finally her eyes skimmed those leaning against the walls.

Without warning, she grabbed Philip's arm and pulled it hard towards her, "Philip, I see him! I know it's him. He's so thin, but 't'is him!"

"Who Catrina?"

"Our Martin!"

"Where?"

"Against the wall, there!"

Her arm was still pointing as she rushed toward the north side of the hut calling, "Martin! Martin!"

She could hear Philip's footsteps behind her as she struggled to get her breath.

Then she heard, "Mama! Papa! I'm here." Martin stood straight against the wall of the hut frantically waving both hands.

Suddenly, the three were locked in an embrace and shedding tears.

Philip stepped back and said, "Are you well? Were you injured? Were you lost? Were you a prisoner of the Rebels? The Natives?"

Martin looked for a place to sit away from the crowd. "Here Papa. Let's sit here, and I'll tell you."

Catrina clasped Martin's arm as they walked together to a small log near the hut. As they sat, Catrina wiped her tears and took many deep breaths. She said, "Before you talk son, please tell us if Anna Margaret, Nicholas and their children are among the 100 families. And what of Michael Myers, his wife Elizabeth and our grandchildren?"

"No Mama. They're not among the refugees. Mrs. Waldorf is among them with her eight children. She can bring you any news of the Silmsers and Myers and maybe our farm."

Catrina winced and said, "Okay. We'll inquire tomorrow."

"Jacob Crieghoof and his son John are among the refugees. He can tell you of Michael Myers and Elizabeth. Jacob's son John Crieghoof deserted from the 2nd New York Regiment of Foot and has come to Canada with his father and mother Benedicta."[681]

Martin began to tell his story, "After I left to go beaver hunting that fall, Lucas Feader and I made our way towards Ballstown. We made it as far east as Alplaus Kill when we were separated. Not familiar with the woods, I wandered for several weeks and was taken prisoner by Lieutenant Phylo Hulbert of Captain John Peter's Corp. of Queens Loyal Rangers. Another man, John Gibson was taken at the same time. 'T'was a difficult time. I was near frozen and starving. At the time I was taken, there was great commotion near Ballstown when Major John Munro made his raid. We were suspect."

"Eventually, we secured our identity as loyal to King George. But not of any Corp., we enlisted in the 2nd Battalion KRRNY.[682] Over several weeks, we travelled north with Lieutenant Hulbert and his men. For the next year, I worked at the shipyard at Ile aux Noix building bateaux. I attempted to reach home or even send word, but by either weather or ability was never able. I expected I'd at least find Peter's regiment, and always prayed that you had found a safe way north. I wondered too of Lucas Feader. I pray he found his way home or to the British lines."

"All of us prayed for word of you and your safety always hoping we would see you again. The Lord answered our prayers."

"Yes. Praise him Papa. I've longed for my family for months."

"You've a new nephew. He's almost two. His name is Peter and is your brother Peter's son. Peter is with the 2nd Battalion KRRNY at Oswego. Maria Catherine is at Ile Jesus. There's a bed for you in our hut. Come eat. 'T'is not much, but 't'is warm. Catharina and the children and Dorothy will be overjoyed.

When Martin entered the hut, Catharina froze. She looked puzzled and shook her head and said, "Oh, I hoped for so long. My dear brother you are here!" Martin was swarmed with hugs and kisses not only from his sisters, nieces, and nephews but also from the Gallingers, Hanes, and Waites. They sat and talked long into the evening as the children lay curled in their beds and some of the adults momentarily nodded off.

Not long after their morning meal, Martin headed to the Barrack Master's hut to ask about work. He qualified for rations, but he wanted to find work. Catrina walked with Martin not just because she hated to leave his side, but because she wanted to find Margaret Waldorf.

With her arm cradled in his, Catrina asked, "What kind of work do you hope for?"

"With 100 families having arrived and many more to come, I'm sure they'll be needing men to construct huts or chop wood. I know the army is often involved in husbandry, or with my experience in the shipyards, I can surely build or repair boats."

"Where do you think I'll find Margaret Waldorf?"[683]

"We can ask the Barrack Master. He'll know where the families are housed."

After speaking with the Barrack Master, Martin was hired to help construct fifteen new huts, and Catrina was directed to a hut west of theirs.

Catrina lifted her skirt and knocked the mud from her shoes before she climbed the stairs of Margaret's hut. She knocked twice, and the door opened revealing a woman that Catrina barely recognized. It had been many months since Catrina last saw her friend, but still she was shocked. Margaret looked old. Her hair was thin and entirely grey. Her cheek bones protruded leaving her eyes quite sunken. The torment of war and persecution and the harsh weather of the seasons clearly caused an aged face. For a brief moment, she thought, "I wish I had a looking glass. Perhaps my appearance would be as shocking to friends I hadn't seen in a while."

Regardless of Margaret's almost toothless grin, her smile and welcoming embrace warmed Catrina's heart. "Come in my friend. 'T'is been too long," she said as she swung open the door.

"I've brought greetings from Philip, Dorothy, and Catharina. They send their blessings and are pleased you've safely arrived."

"We are here and alive. For now, that's enough for me. I'll be satisfied when I can see my Martin. My eight children arrived with me.[684] Do you know where the men of the Indian Department are quartered? I want to find Martin, but my daughter Ann Eve wants also to know the state of Simon Clark"[685]

"Nay. But the Barrack Master could help you find him. Can you tell me what news you have from home? I worry so about my daughter Anna Margaret and Michael Myers, Elizabeth and our grandchildren."

"A few weeks after Major Ross and Captain Butler attacked Johnstown, I saw Anna Margaret and Nicholas Silmser at Jelles Fonda's store getting flour and salt. Anna Margaret was carrying her infant son Martin."

"Aye. Martin was just a few months old when we left. Did they look well?"

"As well as any of us who've had to work hard to put small amounts of food on the table. The Rebels continue to impress our flour, corn, and peas to feed their army."

"And what of Michael Myers and his wife Elizabeth Crieghoof. I worry about my grandchildren."

"I've seen all five of the Myer's children. Young Philip is growing tall and a fine young man, and little Margaret is a strong little child."

"It gives me ease to hear they're well. And what of our farms Margaret?"

"They confiscate all property belonging to anyone loyal to the King or anyone whose sons or husbands are in the King's service. The property is either sold or rented. Our property was seized, but our son John stayed behind to purchase it at the public auction. He's to sell it for the best price he can and come north to join us in Canada."

"Have you news of our farm. Has it been sold? Have you seen the Commissioners of Forfeiture there?" Catrina held onto Margaret's arm, and squeezing it she said, "Dear Lord! Has it been burned?"

"I know not of your farm Catrina. I've not heard of it being burned. If it is forfeit, perhaps Mr. Harmans Wendell will rent it. He supplied the lease."

The days of summer dragged on with chores and listening for news of the KRRNY and its men. Talk among the refugees was always of new arrivals, news of the negotiations of peace, and obtaining food, clothing, fuel and managing the mud and bugs. Catrina, Jane, and Dorothy helped those Loyalists who were ill or too old to help themselves and those who recently learned that their property was confiscated. They gave aid to the cooper William Casselman Jr., his wife Catherine Hepple, and their thirteen year old son Adam Casselman. The women also helped Hannah Alguire the wife of Corporal David Jeacocks and Sophia Enckhold the wife of Nicholas Mattice Sr.[686]

Philip and Catrina managed a few trips to Ile Jesus to visit Maria Catherine and little Peter always bringing her what rations they could spare. By the end of August 1782, it was clear that the refugees would spend another winter in the camp with uncertainty about the year ahead. Because there were still threats of an invasion into Canada, many young men continued to enlist. Among the enlisted were John Waite Jr., Johannes George Gallinger, and John Crieghoof.[687]

Early in September, there was an event that interrupted the monotony of chores and the stress and boredom of camp life. Everyone in Philip and Catrina's hut attended the wedding of Martin and Margaret Waldorf's daughter Helen to Philip Mauk a member of the Indian Department and one of Brant's Volunteers. The wedding was held at the Anglican Church in the Parish of Montreal. The French Reverend Delisle conducted the ceremony with the assistance of Reverend John Stuart.[688]

Fall at Montreal stirred memories for Catrina. One cool evening she walked to the southern end of camp from where she could see the St. Lawrence River and the blanket of flaming red, orange, and yellow trees. For a moment the beauty took her breath away. Soon, her stomach sat heavy in her belly and tears welled in her eyes. The colours and the water reminded her of home. Flooding her vision were memories of Philip stopping the wagon on the hill after church. She remembered that from the heights of Stone Raby she could almost see the whole valley with the same flaming red, orange, and yellow trees. It was one of her favourite spots. "What if I never see my home again?" she thought. What of the fruit trees we nursed as saplings? Am I never again to visit the graves of my children? I cannot abandon them. Suddenly, the beauty of the water and the trees by which she stood disappeared. A wave of panic tightened her chest. She tried to get her breath. She was dizzy. She looked for a rock or a log on which to sit. With none that she could see, she tucked up her skirt and sat on the ground. "It just can't be," she said sobbing into her lap. She needed Philip. She needed his comforting voice and strong arms. She rose and dragged her body back to camp.

Even in the early days of winter, the labour of supplying hundreds of refugees and hundreds of soldiers never ended. The men in the hut always worked. One day, Philip and Michael volunteered to unload wagons arriving from the wharf. They met Adam Helmer and Philip Empey Sr. near the Quartermaster's hut and spent the morning unloading boxes and bales. Just before noon, the men were tired and were soon to break for a rest and cup of rum. Philip Empey and Adam Helmer were unloading a bale when it slipped from their grasp and fell on top of Philip Empey. As he rolled a barrel into the supply barrack, Michael heard a thunderous crash and screams. He turned toward the sound then rushed to see most of Philip Empey hidden under a 100 lb bale of cloth. Michael cringed when he saw Philip's twisted legs protruding from under the massive block of cloth.[689] Very few minutes passed before four men lifted the bale from atop Philip and stared as he lay twisted and semi-conscious on the frozen ground. Carefully, they lifted him onto a blanket and carried him to the Quartermaster's hut. One man ran to get a surgeon or his assistant. Work stopped as the men waited for word of Philip's injuries.

As the men waited, they gathered around the fire in front of the Quartermaster's hut and talked of the struggle of loading and unloading cargo. To most of the men it did not matter if the load came off bateaux or wagons; they agreed that the weight of some of the barrels, bundles, and bales could bend a man to his knees. Some of the men had been up the river and added their stories of the toils of rowing bateaux up the St. Lawrence River. Even with a few short canals built to bypass the Cascade and Coteau rapids, there were still the rapids at the Cedars and Long Sault to navigate. With his hand clutching his pipe and a furrowed brow, Philip listened. He had not experienced navigating through the kind of water these men described. As they finished their tales, Philip's attention turned to the fact that they had just been up river. That meant they would have been near Carleton Island.

Always wanting to know where Peter and Martin Alguire were, Philip asked of the location of the KRRNY 1st and 2nd Battalions.

One man answered, "The 2nd Battalion is at Oswego and Carleton Island, and the 1st is at Terrebone and Ile Jesus and soon to come to Montreal. Many of their families are to be lodged at Lachine.[690]

An hour passed, and the men had not heard word of Philip Empey. The day was late, so they moved the remaining cargo inside and made their way back to their huts.

It was mid-December before Philip Empey recovered from his accident. He had dislocated his knee and suffered numerous bruises and scrapes. He managed to hobble about using a cane, but he was unable to perform any work which meant there was no extra money for fuel, rum, or rations. As the weather worsened and more snow fell, activities for others in the camp slowed. The typical winter weather wore thin the spirit and energy of all the refugees.

One afternoon when least expected, Catharina and Martin Alguire's boys Philip, John, and Peter burst into the hut jumping up and down saying "Mama, drummers and fifers! The soldiers are coming."

Catharina threw her wool blanket over her shoulders and flung open the door. She stood at the top of the stairs peering down the row of huts. She saw them! They marched in pairs in their bright scarlet coats toward the Quartermaster's hut.[691] "It was officers and men of the KRRNY," she thought as she shivered, not from the cold, but because she realized she might see her husband Martin and her brother Peter. She had waited over a year to be in the same camp as the regiment. Now, she thought, "Christmas will be special this year."

As she watched the soldiers, Catrina crowded next to her daughter on the narrow step. Holding her daughter close she said, "'T'is them! I hope all of them!"

"'T'is Mama. They're to muster.[692] We must walk over to greet them."

It was as good a Christmas season as the refugees could expect given their cold, hunger, sorrow, and anxieties. The men were given furlough and spent time with their families. Because most families had barely enough to eat day to day and were always cold, some of the soldiers' furlough time was spent collecting extra firewood and looking for ways to improve their families' rations. Since early 1782, illness or distress entitled a few families to lodgings in houses nearby and an allotment of firewood. The widow Margaret Hare, Michael Carman Sr., William Kennedy, and the old and lame William Parker were among those families.[693] The approaching Christmas season motivated soldiers without these allotments to be resourceful.

Early in the day just before Christmas, Peter, Martin, and Philip shocked everyone when they hustled through the front door of the hut stomping the snow off their feet and waving their catch of fish.

Philip waved his and said, "A Christmas feast for all. Walleye, and lots of them!" Peter waved his catch saying, "Lots of pike too. But some I save for my dear wife and son at Ile Jesus."

Catrina's smile grew as she looked at the fish hanging from their hands. She said, "Ohh! What a blessing. Where did you get fresh fish?"

"We've been ice fishing on the St. Lawrence River. A few more soldiers were equally lucky. 'T'will be a fine Christmas dinner. Michael and Joseph have a catch too. There'll be plenty."

Christmas day 1782 saw many of the 295 refugees attend the Anglican Church service in Montreal. Even though they had difficulty understanding the French minister, they followed the service faithfully. Their prayers were deep and heartfelt and were directed to their family and friends still facing persecution and hostility in the Mohawk and Schoharie Valleys. Some prayed for their own strength and faith. They knew the days ahead would be full of uncertainty and gruelling work.

January 1783 brought the inevitable ice, wind, snow, and cold. The focus of every hour of every day was to stay warm and eat something. For most refugees, there certainly wasn't energy to expend feeling one way or another. Their emotions were as frozen as the landscape. Many surrendered to the loss and disappointments of the past few years and anxiously awaited to hear the terms of peace. Despite the bleak outlook, they did have a reason to celebrate. They celebrated the marriage of Henry Bowen to Andrew Kumerling's daughter Catherine at the Anglican Church at Montreal.[694]

Like everyone else, every day in February, Philip and Catrina waited for news of the terms of peace and checked for news of new arrivals from the colonies. One afternoon early in March, Philip sat next to the iron stove wrapped in his blanket coat. Catrina sat next to him trying hard to knit while wearing wool mittens.

As they quietly talked, clouds of breath drifted above them. Catrina leaned back, looked straight at Philip and said, "Will we go back? Will we try to reclaim our farm?"

"I don't know yet what is best. We need to know on what terms we stand. There's much talk of hostile action against Loyalists returning. Very few support the rights and liberties of all in this new nation. To them, we are venom and deserve the harshest of punishment. They call us wretches, robbers, murderers, and they say 't'is a crime to have any communication with us. They wish us to be vagabonds for the rest of our lives. 'T'is dangerous Catrina. We risk the mobs. They've new laws now that restrict the rights of anyone supporting the British or having taken arms against the Rebel cause."[695]

Catrina slammed her knitting onto her lap and said, "What can be more dangerous than staying here freezing and starving! And, without knowledge of a place to settle! How can we make a new home Philip? We're old and can barely complete the simplest daily chores."

"'T'is true, but Peter and Martin are young, and they have sons who can build and work a farm of their own. I hear that thousands of Loyalists fled New

York to Halifax and St. John in the east. Families apply for grants of land, some receive 500 acres."[696]

Catrina shook her head. As she picked up her knitting there was a knock at the door. Joseph pulled open the door, and Philip knocked the tobacco out of his pipe saying, "Jacob! Young Jacob Waggoner. So long since we've seen you. How is your father Jacob Waggoner Sr. and your mother Hannah Waite? Hello Adam Klein. Do you both come on business of the army? You Jacob are too young to be attached to the King's service. You're just a boy. And you Adam, your uniform tells me you're with the KRRNY."

Jacob replied, "Aye Sir. My father Jacob is a Private with Captain Patrick Daly's Company, and I serve as Captain Daly's servant. My father and Sergeant John Smith provide me with much guidance. I come because, as Captain Patrick Daly's servant, I hear of new arrivals and where they are to be housed.[697] Some come from the colonies and some from other camps. Your daughter-in-law Maria Catherine and her little boy Peter Jr. have arrived here from Ile Jesus.[698] She's at the Quartermaster's hut registering for provisions. Can you fetch her and the little one? Peter is assigned duty and can't get her."

"Of course. Thank you for telling us Jacob. We shall leave now."

When they arrived back at the hut, Catrina scurried about trying to find room for Maria Catherine while Peter Jr. walked from bed to bed touching everything and greeting everyone. Catrina held his chubby hand as he crossed the room wobbling and reaching for his mother. Catrina stood scanning the room and sighed, "We'll squeeze your bed next to ours and close to the stove." With John Waite Jr. and Johannes George Gallinger joining the regiment and Joseph and his wife moving to Lachine, the small hut was now home for nineteen family members and close friends.[699]

That evening Philip sat near the stove enjoying his pipe and talking to Michael. The two men talked of their journey north and of those in their family still in the valley. Rubbing his chin, Michael said, "I wonder if our Betsy will stay in the valley with her beau James Thompson? 'T'is so far away. We sha'n't ever see her again or know our grandchildren. Agatha and I can't ever go back. 'T'is too risky, and nearing sixty years of age we can't travel that far. Perhaps Betsy's brothers may visit."

"Aye. I worry about Anna Margaret and Nicholas and Michael Myers and the children. We won't see our farm again. But, I pray our children come. 'T'is impossible to think of not seeing them again."

"The terms of peace we've just heard give a bit of hope. Articles V and VI give assurance we can go to any state unmolested to regain our property with no other loss of person, liberty, or property allowed."

"Aye. But most states pass their own punitive laws that disregard these Articles. New York is one of those states.[700] So, it seems the fury against us and their quest for vengeance remains and will remain for many years. Since we were chased from our homes, I've kept the deed to our farm safe."

"And mine is close by too."

Our Mohawk friends are wronged as well. They're deprived of their homeland. The great Kanien′kehake no longer sit by the Tenonanatche, their beloved river that flows through the mountains. Tiagoansera (Little Abraham) calls the Americans 'a worm that cuts off the corn as soon as it appears.' That land was Mohawk traditional territory long before any White man came to the valley. 'T'is all taken. The Americans took from them and the British forgot them. The British gave away territory that was not theirs to give. Joseph and Molly Brant and our Fort Hunter Mohawk friends will be irreconcilable. I cannot conceive the betrayal and humiliation. The Mohawk will fight for their lands."

"They say Governor Haldimand is distraught and ashamed over the treatment of the Mohawk."[701]

"There are rumours that those who've remained loyal to the King and who've taken arms against the Rebels will be granted land in territory west of Montreal. I hope that includes the Indians."

"We must heed any news of land grants, but first we must heed news of any new refugees. Our children and grandchildren may be among them. I hear that several men of the KRRNY go into the Mohawk valley on scouts and secret service missions. They say Corporal Jacob Countryman, Severinus Casselman, Corporal Mattheus Snetsinger, and John P Helmer go frequently. Maybe they will bring us news of our children. I want to know how they fare and if they plan to come north soon."[702]

"We can go and ask at the regiment's camp tomorrow."

Through the warm days of spring and early summer, Philip and Michael waited patiently for word of scouts returning from the valley. Men of the

KRRNY were busy building new barracks for over 800 soldiers, 505 in the 1st Battalion and 384 in the 2nd Battalion. The men also built new huts for the hundreds of refugees continuously arriving. There were now 305 in Montreal and a total of 1678 in camps above and below Montreal.[703] Rations of pork, flour, butter, and peas were distributed with caution. Men, women, boys, and girls of an age deemed suitable for work were struck off rations. Catherine and young Peter received ½ ration each. Philip Alguire, now twelve years old, received ½ ration, John Waite Sr. and Jane received 1 ½, Margaret Waldorf and four children received 2 ¼, Michael, Agatha, and Dorothy Gallinger received 1 ½ rations. And, David McEwan's wife Sarah, a newcomer to Montreal, received ½ ration. At Lachine, Joseph Hanes and his wife received 1 ration. At Lachenaie near Terrebonne, Daniel Fyke's wife Anna and three children received 1 ½ rations. And Jacob Rombaugh's wife Mary and his son Amos' wife Elizabeth received even less rations. Amos and his brother John Rombaugh brought themselves in from Vermont in May 1782 and enlisted in the 2nd Battalion.[704]

Near the middle of July, Philip and Michael got extra work building huts for the increasing number of refugees arriving daily. For weeks, they rarely sat for any reason. The physical work helped restrain Philip's ever growing worry about his family who remained in the Mohawk Valley and his anxiety about where his family would settle once the terms of peace were confirmed.

One day after nailing lumber for the frame of a hut, Michael said, "Philip, come and sit a few minutes. Enjoy a smoke of your pipe and a gill of rum. Your mind will ease knowing that General Haldimand assures his soldiers that they will be discharged as soon as the terms of peace are confirmed. I'm glad we enlisted in the KRRNY in March. Not only did we ensure rations for our families, but we're now eligible for a grant of land. 'T'is said that provisions for granting his Majesty's loyal subjects lands are confirmed. John Waite Sr. tells me that every Master of a family receives 100 acres and each member of that family fifty. To every single man fifty acres. To every non-commissioned officer reduced in Quebec 200 acres and to every private soldier reduced 100 acres with fifty acres to each member of his family.[705] The survey of lands west of Lac St. François begins soon. Captain Justus Sherwood leaves with Lieutenant Solomon Johns, two men of the King's Rangers, and seven men of the Loyal Rangers. They're to travel down the St. Lawrence River to the Bay of Quinte on Lake Ontario."[706]

"Do you know of any of the terms for these grants?"

"There are no fees to register a claim, but the land is granted as fiefs or seigneuries with a quit rent of half a penny per acre, as it is now in this province. And, we must take an Oath of Allegiance to the King and the legislature of this province. 'T'is not good they organize these lands as they did in Germany so many years ago. Feudal tenure 't'is what it is. The men will not be pleased. But, I'm heartily glad of the news of land. I reckon you and I've lost everything because of our loyalty. Our whole life's work! We'll have comfort in knowing this land provides for us in our last days and sees our families secure in their future."

"Yes. 'T'was a good decision to enlist. Now, if only we had word of our families still in the valley."

It was mid July 1783 as Philip was finishing the sixth new hut when he saw Catrina running toward him hollering, "Come quickly! 'T'is John Chrysler with news of new arrivals!"

Philip dropped his saw and held Catrina as she ran into his arms gasping, "Where is John? And what news has he?"

"He says Mr Monier, the postmaster at Albany, arrived this morning with refugees from the valley. Our Anna Margaret and Nicholas Silmser are with him. As are Michael Myers and the children! Everyone has come."

"Catch your breath Catrina. All of them? Martin and Elizabeth Margaret Silmser? Jacob Henry Alguire? We'll go to Mr. Lewis Geneway the Barrack Master.[707] The new arrivals will be there."

Philip and Catrina walked as fast as they could following John Chrysler and winding their way through groups of refugees.

As they got closer to Mr. Geneway's hut, John Chrysler rushed to his wife Christina Elizabeth Silmser as Philip and Catrina turned their heads in all directions scanning the grounds for a glimpse of their children, grandchildren, and old dear friends.[708] "There! By the barrels and bundles!" Catrina started to run waving and screaming, "Anna Margaret! Anna Margaret! Nicholas!"

Nicholas saw her first and grasped two year old Martin's hand pulling him toward Catrina. Anna Margaret gasped and followed Martin. "Mama! Papa! Here! We're here!" She struggled to move faster with her pregnant belly and holding one year old Philip Silmser.

Suddenly a group of people moved toward Catrina and Philip. There was Martin Silmser Sr., Elizabeth Margaret, Jacob Henry Alguire, Maria Salome, and fourteen year old Jacob Alguire Jr.

As Catrina hugged Anna Margaret and Nicholas, Philip walked toward his old friend Martin. He squinted, not recognizing him in his Jessup's Corps uniform.

They grasped each other's hands and hugged. Philip said, "'T'is God's blessing you're all here. You've enlisted? With Jessup's Corps?"

"Aye Philip. We had to leave. 'The harassment was horrid, vicious at times. 'T'was not safe. We took the first guide we could. Mr. Monier was escaping the violence too. There's almost no one left in the valley."

"And what of your son Henry Silmser and his wife Anna Maria Eny?"

"They've stayed at the farm. Anna Maria's brothers Godfrey and John are with Fisher's militia and Godfrey's in-laws are with the Rebels. "

As the two men stood embracing, Philip saw an aged man hobble toward him. The man was gaunt and drawn. His clothes were torn and tattered. His head hung low and his arms limp. Philip thought, "It can't be! "T'is my friend of thirty years! Jacob Henry!"

Philip turned toward him holding him steady with his embrace. "My friend. I'm grateful you're here. Safe! You look worn my friend."

"Troubled times Philip, much suffering," he said as he wheezed. "Those tykes took me to Johnstown Jail then to Hartford, Connecticut. I was released at the notice of peace, made my way home, and travelled here with the rest of my family. I feared I'd die most days of this journey."

"You're safe with us friend. And, I see Johannes George Alguire and Anna Maria Silmser made the journey with their one year old Elizabeth Margaret Alguire. You've a fine granddaughter Jacob Henry."

"Aye, and Anna Maria is again with child. Philip, you too have a fine young granddaughter and a new grandson. Michael Myers and Elizabeth Crieghoof's daughter Maria Myers is now two, and their son Michael Myers Jr. was baptized only a few weeks after Elizabeth Margaret. And, Johannes Wert and Dorothy Eaman's son Nicholas Wert was baptized too.[709] Have you seen our Sophia Salome and her husband Johannes Dorn?"

"Johannes is here in Quebec with the 1st Battalion. I've not seen Sophia. But, we'll find them."

There were so many newcomers that three of the new huts are filled. Over sixty of Catrina and Philip's family, friends, and neighbours arrived. Many were at Montreal, but many were at other camps near Montreal. Lucas Feader Sr., his wife Maria Service and their son John Feader were at Ile Jesus. At St. Lawrence was John Farlinger Sr. wife Sophie and their daughters Elizabeth and Madlain, and Sergeant Michael Van Koughnot's wife Eve Empey with their son John and daughter Polly.[710]

The next morning, Catrina was one of the first to rise. Dorothy and Maria Catherine readied the children. They all marched out the door. Catrina followed announcing, "We're going to see what Anna Margaret needs and what we can do for Martin Silmser and Elizabeth Margaret and Michael Myers and Elizabeth. They'll need to know where the wash is done and where to collect their rations."

Philip nodded and handed Catrina a flask saying, "Bring this bit of rum for Jacob Henry. He has need of it."

August brought the refugees reprieve from fighting mosquitoes, black flies, and the hot humid air. They welcomed the cool air of fall. The cool air was a blessing too for Anna Margaret. Despite the crowded hut and the excitement of the new arrivals, her labour was quick, and she delivered a healthy baby girl. They named her Dorothy after her Aunt.[711]

One afternoon, just as Dorothy Eamer and Maria Catherine took the last of the shirts and trousers off the clothesline, Catrina brought another basket to hang.

As she handed the basket to Dorothy she said, "Your Papa brought me good news yesterday. It seems Henry Gallinger had something important to ask him."

"And! What was Papa's answer?"

"He's given his permission for you to marry, but he's not happy that you'll be going with Henry to the camp at L'Assomption."

Dorothy dropped the basket and hugged Catrina. As she turned to hug Maria Catherine, she said. "I'm so heartily glad Mama. Henry is a good man."

As she hugged Dorothy, Maria Catherine smiled and said, "I'm heartily glad to be your sister-in-law Dorothy. You're right. My brother is a steady and good man. I hope there are others at L'Assomption whom you know."

"There are. Henry tells me that Molly Johnson, Sergeant John Peascod's wife, Eleanor Allen, Corporal Francis Jeacock's widow, and Sophie Ault, Conrad Snyder's wife are all there.[712]

It was late October 1783, only a few weeks before Henry would be posted at L'Assomption. Michael and Philip sat at the front of their hut discussing how they would keep track of the young couple. There was much talk around the camp about the disbanding of troops and moving refugees to lands west of Montreal.

Philip reached for his pipe and said, "I hear they've stopped all recruiting and recalled all officers gone into the colonies. And, men were granted leave to return to the valley to collect their families."

"Aye. Those who remain in the Mohawk Valley are desperate. They must bring them north soon. And, I hear also that the surveyors who walked the lands west of Montreal have returned. Near a place called Mille Roche, they walked five kilometres back from the river and sixteen kilometres up the river. The land, they say, is some of the most beautiful they've ever seen. Beyond a pleasant shoreline, there's deep, black, rich soil with few stones or swamps. The woods are thin, but the trees are exceedingly large and tall, mostly beech, maple, elm, basswood, butternut, white oak, hickory, and pine."[713]

"'T'is good timber for building and fuel."

"Have they surveyed the lots?"

"Not as yet. In the spring, they're to send Patrick McNiff, a man from Saratoga and Albany, to lay out the fiefs and lots."

"Aye. The towns along the river are to be a mile square."[714]

"We must be ready in the spring to gather our families to make the journey. Batteaux travel the river all the time. I expect they'll be many making that journey as soon as they can."

"We must find a way to send word to Henry and Dorothy when the time comes. And, we need news of the birth of their child expected soon."

Philip puffed hard on his pipe, and while tapping both feet on the frozen ground he said, "Knowing we'll never regain our property and possessions is the most grievous situation. Do you know what is said about our claim to the British government for compensation?"

"We're told that because of our loyalty and our loss of rights and possessions, we have a claim to compensation that is measured in proportion to services rendered. They've appointed a Board of Commissioners to hear our claims. We must find out what details and documents are required regarding property lost and services rendered. I'll give my claim to Sir John. When the Commissioners review your claim, priority goes to those who helped the army or bore arms against the Rebels. But, they'll consider those who took the Oath of Allegiance or took arms with the Americans but who later joined the British. Acceptance of our claims closes on 24 March 1784."[715]

"I'm relieved that I managed to secure the deed for my land in my pocket before those wretches threw us out! We can ask our Captain for further guidance."

Winter came fast and with fury. It worried Philip that the cords of wood were diminishing faster than expected. If December was cold, February would not be kinder. When they had time away from the regiment, Martin and Peter did what they could to improve the wood pile, but Philip knew it would not be enough. Most days were spent inside the hut close to the stove.

Philip sat one afternoon with Catrina, each with a child in their lap. Catrina was wrapped in two blankets with mittens, hats, and wool socks. She said from beneath the mounds of cover, "'T'is severe this cold, and we've few rations. I worry about sickness taking too many this winter, especially the little ones and the aged."

"I hear that Daniel and Peter Fyke's brother Henry died of sickness at Carleton Island."

"He was just twenty nine years old. Henry Fykes had a fine family. Sarah Runnion's was his wife, and they've three children, John, Marie Elizabeth, and Catrina. I remember Catrina's baptism. Adam Hartle was her sponsor.[716]

"These sicknesses come fast and spread with fury. With so many newcomers, disease will easily overcome us. We're not strong enough nor do we have enough food. And what of Henry Gallinger and our Dorothy's new baby girl Catherine?"[717]

One day, as Philip filled the stove with wood for the fourth time, Michael burst into the cabin covered in snow. 'T'is a blizzard out there. I've been to the regiment camp, and there's news that the 1st Battalion is to be disbanded on 24 December. The 2nd Battalion will be disbanded in the spring. All men are to report to their Captains for their discharge certificates and pay. Your discharge certificate states the amount of land to which you are entitled. Christopher and Henry will get their certificates from Captain Patrick Daly and Michael Jr. will get his from Captain John Mcdonell of the Grenadiers."[718]

During the Christmas season, the regiment and the refugee camps at Montreal were buzzing with chaotic activity. On Christmas Eve the situation worsened. Tensions rose when British regular and provincial soldiers and German soldiers received word they were to be disbanded. They were to receive housing and rations through the winter but no pay. To add to their anxieties, no one knew for certain where they were to settle in the spring. Everyone was impatient and short tempered. In fact, it was so chaotic and potentially dangerous that a military patrol of a Corporal and six soldiers along with several Montreal citizens were called out to patrol the streets and apprehend any soldiers or any suspicious persons found out of barracks.[719]

Philip and Catrina were no different than others. They thought that their children and grandchildren were near and safe. All that changed one afternoon after Christmas when Peter arrived at the hut. Philip opened the door, looked at Peter, and knew something was not right.

Peter shuffled into the room, and in a soft shaky voice said, "I've bad news about Martin. He's very ill. Dr. Charles Blake, the surgeon, quarantined him and won't let anyone see him.[720] I talked to the assistant surgeon outside the hospital, and he told me that Martin has smallpox. There are others afflicted too."

Philip gasped, "Smallpox! How bad is it?"

"'T'is bad Papa. I could hardly walk him to the hospital. His head ached terribly, and he was with fever. He could not drink any liquid."

Catrina flew from her chair screaming, "Smallpox! Is he conscious?"

"Aye Mama, when I last saw him."

Catrina shouted, "I knew there were many Loyalists nearby with the smallpox and measles too. Oh dear God in heaven. The curse of this disease will kill us all! We should've been inoculated. Our Reverend Stuart appealed to all to protect ourselves from this killer.[721] When can we see him?"

"We can't Mama. We have to wait. The Doctor will tell us how he fares."

"What about you Peter? You've been near him."

"The Doctor is watching me and others."

"We must have the children inoculated!" "Oh Lord have mercy. We've not the money to pay for the surgeon!"

It was quiet in the hut that December evening. The sound of the raw winter wind as it battered the windows buried any spoken words. Philip, Catrina, and Maria Catherine sat still and silent by the iron stove. Others shuffled about beside and behind them. John and Jane Waite silently passed a gill of rum to Philip and cups of cider to Catrina and Maria Catherine.

The cold wind drove in the first days of January 1784. Twice every day, Philip and Catrina wrapped themselves in their blanket coats and lumbered through the deep snow to the barrack hospital. Between short shallow breaths, they prayed as they walked. Catrina struggled to keep her eyes wide open, but her eyelashes were fastened shut with icy tears. They brought a small pot of soup and some bread each time they visited, but they were told Martin would not eat or drink. Each visit brought no encouraging news. They heard only that their son was not always conscious. They counted that as a small blessing after hearing agonizing moans drift from the walls of the hospital.

Amidst this wrenching horror, Philip prepared his claim for the loss of his New York property and possessions. On 7 Jan 1784, he stood before the clerk James Finlay and swore an oath on the Holy Evangelist Bible that his account of losses was, to the best of his knowledge, just and true. He presented himself as a private soldier of the 2nd Battalion of the KRRNY who now lived in Canada. He described his loss of property as seventy acres of land near Johnstown of which sixty acres were cleared and well enclosed. He swore that there were no encumbrances on the property save a yearly rent of £4 a year forever. This property, he claimed, was worth £350. In addition to the property, he claimed an orchard, a new dwelling house, and other buildings on the property. His possessions he described as thirty three skipples or twenty four bushels of spring wheat. Sowing of winter wheat in the ground equaled £24 and 15 shillings. He claimed farming utensils, a sleigh and harness at £20, four cows at £18, four horses at £25, nineteen sheep at £17 and 16 shillings, and ten hogs at £4. His total loss was valued at £449 and 11 shillings. As Philip swore his oath and recounted his loss, Martin Alguire and Christopher Gallinger stood beside him as his witnesses. Martin and Christopher also swore an oath that Philip's losses were incurred as a result of his loyalty to King George and his attachment to the government of Great Britain. They swore that Philip, his wife, and five children were now in Canada.[722] Philip signed his claim and was told it would be given to Captain Joseph Anderson and sent to the Board of Commissioners in England.

181

To the Honble Board of Commissioners appointed by Act of Parliament to enquire into the Losses and Services of all such Persons, who have Suffered in their Rights Properties and Possessions during the late unhappy dissention in America in consequence of their Loyalty to his Majesty, and Attachment to the British Government &c — — —

The Memorial of Philip [illegible] late of Johnstown in the County of Tryon and Province of New York, Private Soldier in the Second Battalion of the K^s Royal Regiment of N York Commanded by Brigadier General Sir John Johnson, and now in Canada —

Humbly Sheweth

That the Losses sustained by your Memorialist in consequence of the Premises Amounts to the Sum of Four Hundred and Forty Nine Pounds, Eleven Shillings Halifax Curr^y according to the following Account of Particulars which he hereby Claims. — — — Whereas may be allowed him — — — —

70 Acres of Land lying Situate near Johnstown of which Sixty Acres was Cleared and well Inclosed with an Orchard, a New Dwelling House, and other Buildings thereon — — —		350-00-0
33 Schipple or 24¾ Bushels Sowing, of Winter Wheat in the Ground — —		24-15-0
Farming Utensils as Waggon, Sley, Harrow, Harness		20-00-0
[illegible] Cows — — —	@ 90/ each	18-0-0
[illegible] Horses — — — —	12£ — 0°	25-0-0
[illegible] Sheep — — — —	12/ — 0°	4-16-0
[illegible] Hogs — — — —	8/ — 0°	4-00-0
		449-11-0

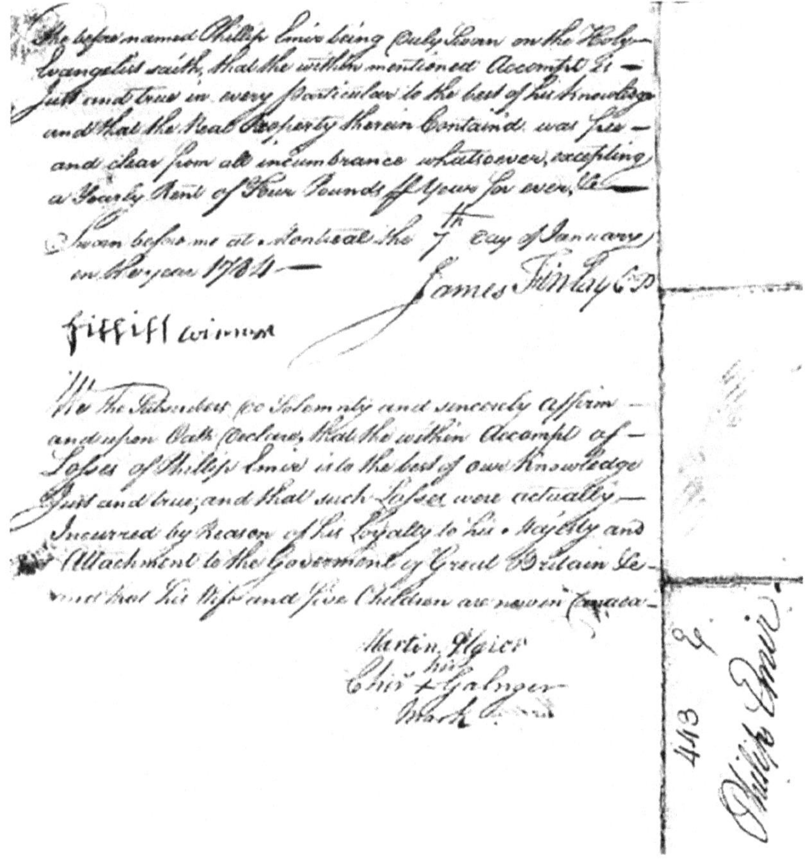

The before named Philip Emis being Duly Sworn on the Holy Evangelist saith, that the within mentioned Accompt is Just and true in every particular to the best of his Knowledge and that the Real Property therein Contain'd was free and clear from all incumbrance whatsoever, excepting a Yearly Rent of Four Pounds p Year for ever, &c

Sworn before me at Montreal the 7th day of January in the year 1784 —

James Finlay C.P.

[illegible] witness

We the Subscribers do Solemnly and sincerely affirm and upon Oath declare, that the within Accompt of Losses of Phillips Emis is to the best of our Knowledge Just and true; and that such Losses were actually Incurred by Reason of his Loyalty to his Majesty and Attachment to the Government of Great Britain [illegible] that his Wife and five Children are now in Canada.

Martin [illegible]
his
Chris + Galnger
Mark

443 E
Philip Emis

Fig. 34 A & B Philip Eamer's claim for losses during the Revolutionary War. 7 Jan 1784 at Montreal, Quebec. The National Archives of the UK; Kew, Surrey, England; American Loyalist Claims, Series II; Class: AO 13; Piece 012: New Claims C D E F, New York. The Memorial of Philip Emis.

The days lingered on after Philip swore his claim. Most days he and Catrina did one thing, stand vigil outside the barrack hospital for news of Martin's condition. Nothing changed. Any news they received was brief and was delivered with increasingly melancholic faces. On January 21st, they received a dreadful report from the Doctor. Catrina sat on the edge of her bed rocking back and forth weeping. Philip held her tight as his own tears streamed down his cheeks.

Philip tried to speak but only managed a few phrases every few minutes. He said, "God have mercy. God hold our son in your merciful arms." Catrina moaned and continued rocking.

Michael came and sat beside Philip. With one hand on his knee, he said, "Agatha and I ache with you friend. We pray God rests his grace upon Martin. We're here whenever you're in need. We'll be away for a few hours this afternoon. Our son Christopher is to marry Sarah Runnions, the widow of Henry Fykes.[723] They're to marry at the Anglican Church. John and Jane will stay with you."

Philip turned to his friend and said, "Michael, we must attend Christopher's wedding. We've known him since he was an infant. 'T'is important, and we'll be there. We will gather strength from witnessing this union."

A few days after Christopher and Sarah's marriage, Stephen DeLancey, inspector of all Loyalists victualled in Montreal and other refugee camps, ordered an inspection. This meant that Philip, Catrina, and Maria Catherine along with hundreds of others must line up and answer questions regarding the sex and age of family members and the number of rations received each day. Standing in the cold was wearisome at the best of times. Along with their burden of grief, Philip and Catrina knew Maria Catherine needed their help. Maria Catherine not only had Peter Jr. to look after, but she was due to deliver another child. Philip and Catrina saw her distress and found their daughter-in-law places to sit as the line moved along. On this particular day, Louis De Coigne oversaw the inspection at the camp.

Mr. De Coigne recorded Maria Catherine as Catherine Eamer junr., attached to the 2nd Battalion KRRNY with one male under six years of age. The total of her family was two, and they received ¾ of a ration every day. He recorded Catrina as Catherine Eamer Senr. and remarked that she was an old woman attached to the 2nd Battalion KRRNY with no children. She received ½ ration. Mr. De Coigne recorded no children with John Waite Sr. and Jane and noted they received 1 ½ rations. He remarked that John Waite Sr. was a poor, old, and infirm farmer. Michael Carman Sr., with one woman, received 1 ½ rations and was recorded as aged and infirm. Elizabeth Young, Andrew Millross's wife, was recorded as having one male above six years and one female above six years. She received 1 ½ rations and was attached to the 2nd Battalion KRRNY. William Kennedy's family consisted of one man, one woman, four boys above six and one female above six. They received four rations and were recorded as distressed. Philip Alguire was recorded by himself and received ½ ration. He was not recorded as attached to any regiment. Margaret Shuman, William's wife, received two rations for herself and two boys above six and one girl above six. She was attached to the 2nd Battalion KRRNY. Margaret Waldorf received 2 ¼ rations for one boy above six and one girl above six and one girl under six. Margaret was recorded as attached to the Indian Department. Catherine Wick, Michael Cline's wife, received ¾ ration for herself and one boy under six. Sophia Engolt, Nicholas Mattice's wife, received ½ ration for herself and was recorded as a pensioner's family. Catherine, Adam Klein's wife, received 2 ¾ rations for two boys over six, one boy under six and two girls over six. She was attached to the 2nd Battalion KRRNY. Margaret Carman, Michael Carman Jr.'s wife, received 1 ½ rations for herself, one boy over six and one girl over six. She was attached to the 1st Battalion KRRNY. Margaret and Michael Carman's daughter Magdalena married Jacob Coons and was recorded as Mary Madden Coons. She was married in this province and received ½ rations.[724]

Maria Catherine waited patiently in line with young Peter who was now almost four years old. She thought about the Gallingers who just recently moved to the camp at Saint Laurent just a few kilometres northwest of Montreal. She knew they would be standing in line too. Agatha Ade, Michael Gallinger Sr.'s wife, was recorded as Alyda Gallinger with one boy over six. She received one ration each day and was attached to the 2nd Battalion KRRNY. Sophia, John Farlinger Sr.'s wife, received 1 ½ rations for herself and two girls over six. She was attached to the 2nd Battalion and recorded as a newcomer. Anna Ruppert, the wife of Daniel Fykes, received 1 ¾ rations for herself, one boy under six and two girls over six. She was attached to the 2nd Battalion KRRNY and described as a distressed, sickly family.[725]

One week after the ordeal of the inspection of Loyalists, Philip, Catrina, Maria Catherine, and Anna Margaret stood outside the hospital barrack. The surgeon's assistant opened the door and slowly shook his head saying, "We're so sorry. Your son passed early this morning." Philip tried to hold Catrina on her feet, but she slipped from his arms and fell to the ground weeping. Maria Catherine reached to help her stand, but she wasn't strong enough to lift her weakened mother-in-law. The women sat on the steps of the hospital wrapped in each other's arms.

Philip asked the assistant surgeon, "When can we bury our son Sir?"

"You cannot. We bury all who are afflicted with the pox in a quarantined graveyard far from the city. I'm sorry Sir. 'T'is for the protection of others. Reverend Stuart performs his blessing prior to the burial and will come and pray with you. I will let him know that you wait."

For weeks in February, Philip did no work, and Catrina rarely left her bed. Old friends from the Mohawk Valley came to comfort Philip and Catrina. Little Peter stood beside his grandmother's bed and stroked her hair. Philip tried to offer Catrina encouragement.

Often, Philip sat by Catrina's side holding her hand, but she just repeated, "I wasn't with him as he suffered. I could do nothing! I couldn't even bury my own son! We didn't take watch over his body or make him a decent coffin. I don't even know if they gave him a coffin!"

"We're not to blame ourselves for this tragedy. God took his spirit and will bath it in eternal grace. And with God's blessing, in time our pain will ease."

Early in March 1784, helping Maria Catherine manage the long days of washing, cooking, and looking after Peter Jr. made it easier for Catrina to pass the days after Martin's death. Catrina's spirit lifted late in March after the birth of Peter and Maria Catherine's daughter Catherine Eamer.[726] The newborn brought a few more smiles each day and sounds of young life. More smiles came not long after. Early one morning, news came from L'Assomption. Henry Gallinger and Dorothy were proud parents of a baby girl whom they named Catherine Gallinger.

Philip brought Catrina encouraging news as often as he could. Everyone needed encouraging news. Many of the disbanded soldiers and their families knew that each day the season advanced meant their chances of survival in the coming winter less likely. Time to clear land, build shelter, and plant crops was running short. One afternoon Philip entered the hut, and while filling his pipe he announced, "Sir John Johnson departed for Long Sault to prepare for our arrival. The surveyor Mr. Patrick McNiff and near twenty six others left to survey our land. Lieutenant Walter Sutherland, Michael Cook, James Peachy, and Louis Kotté are with him. They say that the 1st Battalion is to settle on Township Numbers one to five and the 2nd Battalion on Townships three and four. Township Number one starts at the western end of Lake St. Francis and the other townships run up towards Cataraqui."[727]

Catharina asked, "Do they say when we leave Papa? What provisions do they provide for us? People say 't'is wilderness. There are so many children. What about our old people?"

John Waite Sr. leaned forward in his chair, and reaching for his wife's hand he said, "We'll be fine Catharina. Sir John and General Haldimand will provide for us. And, many of us are skilled woodsmen who've built cabins in the wilderness and lived through many harsh winters. We've all had fine farms in the Mohawk Valley, some of us in Pennsylvania, Vermont, and Connecticut. The old people will do what we can every day."

Philip turned to Catharina, and pointing at her with the stem of his pipe he said, "I overheard the stores-keeper say that new provisions are arriving soon. They're expecting boxes of short handled axes, hoes, and drawing knives. And, they're sending men down to Crown Point, into Vermont, and even into our Mohawk Valley for Indian corn and wheat seed."[728]

Young Philip Alguire piped up and said, "Mama, we should just get Corporal Adam P. Empey to get us supplies. He's just petitioned Governor Haldimand for permission to trade in dry goods and liquor from here to Cataraqui or to Niagara!"[729]

Through April, supply wagons came and went in a flurry. Philip and Peter spent many hours at the camp stores loading and unloading bales, bundles, barrels, and boxes.

One day near the end of April, Peter stood wiping sweat from his neck and brow. He saw a wagon approach and said, "Papa, 't'is Michael Gallinger Sr. driving that wagon."

"I see son. They must need supplies for the camp at Ile Jesus."

Philip and Peter approached the wagon and helped Michael from the driver's seat. "Good day friend. 'I'm heartily glad to see you and to see you well."

"'T'is good to see you both. Agatha and I were sorry to hear about Martin and have said many prayers for him and for all of you."

"For now, we manage with the goodness of our Lord. Catrina struggles."

"We've come for supplies, but I bring news too. Our friend Lucas Feader Sr. passed only a few days ago. His wife Maria Service, their sons Philip and John, and their daughters Elizabeth, Hannah, and Christina are at Ile Jesus. Maria will need our help these coming months. They only just arrived last fall, and she has only her son Lucas Jr. to help her settle. She still laments that her son

William and daughter Anna Catharine stayed in the valley, likely to never see them again."[730]

"Is there anyone at Ile Jesus who can help now?"

"Aye, a few. There's John Jeacock's wife Nancy, Nicholas Frymire's wife Elizabeth Borst, and Mary who is Martin Middaugh's wife. But Mary is looking after the three orphan children of Henry Busch of Brant's Volunteers and his wife Nelly Middagh. They died at Machiche in November '78."[731]

"We'll watch for them all when we gather to make our journey up the St. Lawrence. And watch too Edward Foster, the old soldier and Irish friend of Sir William. He's was wounded so many times he cannot fend for himself.[732]

"Have you any word of when we draw our lots?"

"We draw lots when we arrive at our settlement."

"As the Superintendent of all Loyalist settlements, Sir John makes ready for our assembly at Lachine. We've been told we assemble before the end of May.[733] Many of us go to Township Number two. Our Chaplain Reverend John Stuart just left to journey up the St. Lawrence. He wants to visit all the settlements, perform necessary baptisms or marriages, and he most wants to visit his friends at the Mohawk settlement near the Bay of Quinte. He expects to return in a few weeks. Perhaps he'll pass by our new settlement on his return."

"Aye. I heard that the Mohawks were granted land at the Bay of Quinte, but Joseph Brant and the Mohawks changed the plans and received land at the Grand River."[734]

"They say our new land is fine farm land. 'T'is good for our children and grandchildren. But you and I've had our time at breaking ground and building our farms near our beloved Johnstown. They will be greatly missed. The news of property confiscations reached so many this past year. You and your sons Michael Jr. and Christopher know this news well. I've not heard about mine own, but I've heard at least Jacob Waggoner, David Jeacocks Jr., Johannes P. Helmer lost their land. Rumors are that Henry Hart bought Jacob Crieghoof's farm, Captain Jelles Fonda bought Johannes Hartle Sr. farm for £240, and Jacob Myers and Michael Carman Jr. of Philadelphia Bush lost claim on their lots 43 and 44. Sir William willed those lots to his son George in '74.[735]

I hoped for so long 't'was just a bad dream from which I would wake. But, 't'is not so."

"We must plan to gather in the same fleet of bateaux. Aye, and the Alguire's and Silmsers. Agatha and I plan to make our way to Lachine near the end of May."

Every day in May, Philip and Peter watched the constant activity at the stores hut. Often, they helped unload wagons full of boxes of firelocks and ammunition, sacks of seed and Indian corn, bundles of blankets and bedding, bundles of canvas tents, and boxes of cook pots and buckets. For Catrina, Philip always asked what kinds of seeds were in the bags. He knew she would want to know what kind of food she could grow. He knew she'd be happy when he recited the list of seeds they unloaded: 4 lb of onion, 11 lbs of Norfolk turnip, 9 lbs early Dutch turnip, 12 lbs large Dutch cabbage, 13 lbs celery, 17 lbs orange carrot, 4 lbs short top radish, 3 lbs parsley seed, and one bushel of narrow fat peas. They also unloaded bags of potatoes and boxes of fruit saplings.[736] To Philip it seemed like plenty, but he knew there were going to be almost 500 settlers in Township Number two.

During their rest breaks, Philip and Peter talked about the work necessary to settle in for the winter. One day, while sitting in the shade, Peter put his feet up on a log and said, "Papa, if we don't draw lots next to each other and close to Jacob Henry and Martin Alguire, Martin and Nicholas Silmser, Henry Gallinger, and Jacob Myers and Michael Myers, we'll have to move about the crowd of people looking to exchange lots. 'T'is allowed is it not?"

"Aye. 'T'is allowed."[737] "If we're close to each other, we've enough men to work in groups. Some of us can build cabins, some can clear land to sow wheat and plant gardens, and some can chop wood. Even some of the grandchildren are old enough to do some of the heavy work. There are Michael's boys, Philip, Godfrey, and Christian Myers, and Martin Alguire's boys, Philip, John, Peter, and even eight year old Daniel Alguire can help."

"Do we know what rations will be provided for the first year?"

"To every man and woman in a family there's one treasury ration, to every child above ten one treasury ration, and to every child under ten ½ treasury ration. Each ration being 1 lb of flour, 1 lb beef, and 12 ozs of pork. Sir John directs the distribution of tools to each family. Each man is allowed one axe and one hoe. Drawing knives and other small tools are distributed according to need."

"What of guns and ammunition for hunting game and fowl?"

"Aye. For every five men one firelock is allowed, and Sir John has been allotted 2 lbs of powder, 4 lbs of ball and flint for each firelock."[738]

Late in May, everyone in camp was busy all day and all evening. Women were doing extra washing, and men were sharpening axes and draw knives. During the last days of May, Philip and Peter saw men rowing bateaux passed the city west toward La Chine. Every hour there were about ten almost empty bateaux. There was talk around camp that there were not enough boats to take all the settlers up the river. But, from the sight of the flotilla, Philip and Peter thought there seemed enough.[739]

For several days before the Eamer, Myer, Silmser, and Alguire families were to leave Montreal and gather at La Chine, Catrina walked to the Church of the Visitation in the village of Sault-au-Récollet north of the city or to the Chapel at the hospital Hotel Dieu. Reverend Stuart was away at Cataraqui and there was no Anglican Church in Montreal, so she spent many hours in places of Roman Catholic worship. It didn't matter to her. She needed to feel the presence of God. Since she left the Mohawk Valley, she had not been to the graves of her children. Even here, she could not visit Martin's grave. She knew, where they were going, there would be no place of worship for many years. She cherished those few hours of prayer.

Early one morning, Catrina, Anna Margaret, and Maria Catherine washed and put away their pots and dishes, gathered their blankets and their knapsacks, and, with the infants Dorothy Silmser and Catherine Eamer in their arms, they led the other children out the front door. It was time to leave Montreal. They met Philip, Peter, and Nicholas at the wagon that would take them to La Chine. Philip, Peter, and Nicholas were dressed in their 2nd Battalion KRRNY uniforms as they would not be disbanded until mid-June. But Martin Alguire was dressed in a hunting frock and linen breeches. Being in Major James Gray's Company of the 1st Battalion, he was discharged this past Christmas Eve. Martin Silmser and Elizabeth Margareta were waiting at the wagon with Michael Myers and his family.

Earlier, Martin Alguire and Catharina told everyone that she would wait at Montreal with little Daniel and Peter Alguire and their five year old sister Elizabeth. Martin and his boys Philip and John would come back to Montreal in the fall and bring them up to their lands. Catharina decided to wait because Martin's father, Jacob Henry, was still weak and tired from his recent imprisonment at Hartford, Connecticut and from the long journey north. Catharina wanted to stay and help Jacob Henry and his wife Maria Salome.

There were others who decided to stay in Montreal because of illness or wanting to bring in the crops they grew near Montreal. They would go to their land in the fall: George Bender, his wife and one boy under ten (Tunis or George Jr.), Anthony Walliser, his wife Magdelena and two boys above ten and two girls above ten (likely Anthony Jr., Christian, Magdelena, and Elizabeth), Hermanus Cryderman, Mattheus Snetsinger, Caleb Peck, Philip Empey, George Crites Jr., Christopher Empey, and Captain Patrick Daly stayed at Montreal. Others went to New York to collect family or possessions and returned to their new lands: Matheus Link, Francis Ruppert, and Martin Waldorf travelled to New York.[740] Regardless of how many decided to stay, there were still hundreds who made their way to La Chine for the journey up the river.

As their wagon rolled into La Chine, Catrina watched for Henry and Dorothy and their infant daughter Catherine. They were arriving from L'Assomption. The driver steered the wagon to a spot close to the wharf where batteaux sat bobbing in the water next to the dock. Philip was impressed with the number of young muscular Canadiens standing near the boats, each smoking a pipe. They all dressed in linen hunting frocks tied at the waist with a colorful sash, deer skin leggings, and moccasins. Some wore cotton head scarfs, and some wore red wool caps that flopped to one side of their head. Their long hair met their kerchiefs which laid snug against their necks.[741]

After collecting their knapsacks and blankets, everyone walked to one end of the wharf where they saw several KRRNY soldiers standing. Immediately, Philip recognized several soldiers. There was Corporal Philip Empey standing with a cane talking to Sergeant John Peascod and Joseph Hanes. A long table stood near the soldiers where a line of refugees stood. Philip, Peter, Nicholas Silmser, and Martin Alguire made their way to the line while their wives and children stood by their belongings. As they stood waiting, Catrina saw William Sheets in a wagon approaching the wharf. He was sitting next to Henry and Dorothy. She waved frantically until she saw Dorothy wave back. She smiled when she saw the tiny bundle in Dorothy's arms. Henry helped Dorothy out of the wagon and went to join the men at the line.

Captain Samuel Anderson sat at the table leaning over a large black book. Philip saw that each man who approached the table was asked a few questions, and the answers were recorded in the book. It wasn't long before Philip reached the front of the table.

He tipped his hat and nodded to Captain Anderson and said, "'T'is a good day Sir."

"Aye Sir. 'T'is a short journey up the river to your lands with good weather expected. What is your name, with what regiment do you serve, and who in your family are going to their lands?"

"Philip Eamer Sir. Private soldier in the 2nd Battalion KRRNY. 'T'is me and my wife Catrina who go to our lands."

"Fine. Are there a group of families going with you?"

"There are Sir. They're behind me in this line."

"Which families?"

"Gallinger, Alguire, Silmser, Myers, and my son Peter Eamer."

"You'll travel together in the same batteau. When you reach Township Number Two, you'll disembark and wait for Lieutenant Jeremiah French and Lieutenant Joseph Anderson to gather everyone to draw your lots."

"Aye Sir. Thank you. How long does it take to travel to Township Number Two?"

"Two days if the weather is good and the portages go well. Your batteau is loaded and waiting at the wharf. 'T'is batteau number seven."

Philip tipped his hat and turned to join the women and children.

The families gathered near batteau number seven waiting for the Canadien conductor to tell them to board. As they stood waiting, Catrina scurried from infant grandchild to infant grandchild. Sometimes she just stood and stared at their soft calm faces, and other times she played with their fingers and stroked their cheeks. The men stood pointing out all the people they recognized and hoped they too would be taking the journey to Township Number Two. They saw Captain David Jeacocks with his wife Hannah Alguire and their daughters Mary, Nancy Ann, and Elizabeth. And, they saw Corporal Jacob Countryman, David McEwan, Peter Ruppert, Conrad Snyder, and Henry Hawn.[742]

They hadn't waited long before they saw the conductor wave them toward the bateau. There were eight batteauxmen, two of whom helped each family member into the boat. The batteaumen took time to help Maria Catherine, Dorothy, and Anna Margaret with their infant daughters. The women were seated near the middle of the boat with the men and boys along the sides, each sitting still while the batteaumen moved bundles and boxes of provisions from side to side to balance the boat. With their knapsacks and blankets neatly tucked under the wooden seats and the small children tucked under the arms of the older children, the conductor gave the signal to cast off.

Their batteau was one of a brigade of twelve boats casting off that morning. There was a breeze on the river, but the water was calm. The batteauman at the stern moved the sweeping oar while the six middle men rowed the batteau toward the centre of the river. The batteauman at the bow called the rhythm of their strokes and the direction forward. These men were expert at paddling and digging the poles into the bottom of this wild and shallow river. They were Voyageurs who knew every rock and channel.[743] Soon, Philip felt the pull of the current and watched as the shore line drifted out of sight. Along the shoreline and its high banks, Philip saw creeks opening into the river through stands of oak, pine, hickory, and beech.

As the men paddled, they sang. Some of the songs were uplifting and, at times, made Philip want to join in the paddling. Other songs were quieter and soothing. All the songs had a mesmerizing rhythm which softened time as it passed.[744] One of the songs helped Maria Catherine settle little Catherine who was wrapped in the woolen shawl made from cloth distributed to the Loyalists. Despite the cold breeze off the river, everyone was warm in their linen frocks, breeches, stockings, and Canada shoes.[745] If needed, they wrapped themselves in a blanket or a woolen shawl.

After a few hours, the brigade of bateaux entered a narrow channel passing a waterfall. Not far up the channel, Philip saw rapids and watched their batteaumen sink deeper into their oars. Soon, at a place called Les Cèdres, the Conductor told them they had to portage. And, a little further up the river at Coteau du Lac, there was another portage. The portages were hard work for everyone. The batteauxmen unloaded the provisions and, with a strip of leather on their heads to hold the load, they carried it the length of the portage. Sometimes, there were carts to hold the load and to carry the passengers through the forests along the trail or along a narrow piece of land. During one portage, the batteauxmen hauled the boats along the shore of the river using long ropes.[746]

After the portages, the current and the water calmed as the brigade entered a wide section of the river called Lake St. Francis. They paddled twelve miles, which took them half way up the Lake, when the Conductor announced they would set ashore and camp for the night. For everyone, it was a welcome relief from the movement of the boat and having to trudge through brush and branches in the forests carrying or leading young children. The batteauxmen showed their delight when they danced, smoked their pipes, and sang well into the night.

The sun had barely risen when the Conductor ordered their parting. As the batteauxmen lifted their loads into the boat, the water level rose along its sides. Philip, Peter, Nicholas, Michael, and Martin were the last to board. They had been standing on shore seeming to contemplate the last few kilometres of a journey that began years before. Memories of their homes in the Mohawk Valley were agonizing, but the waves, rocks, and splashing water before them calmed their thoughts.

The journey up the last half of Lake St. Francis was easier. There were still channels the batteauxmen had to navigate and rocks they had to avoid, but the strong currents and rapids were behind them. Sometimes, the men stood and poled their boat through shallow sections. Late in the afternoon, the brigade exited Lake St. Francis and entered a narrower channel where they soon floated past several islands. Peter saw a group of Indians on shore and recognized them as Mohawk. Just as Peter was getting Philip's attention to point out the Indians, the batteauman at the bow of their boat hollered, "Row in men. Easy to shore." Peter and Philip turned and saw a quiet, broad, and spacious bay tucked between the mainland and a large island. Here, the river was shallow but not too rocky. The batteaumen announced their pleasure at not having to navigate the brutal rapids at Long Sault that day. They called this spot Grand Pointe Maligne. To them it was a navigation point where batteaux departed to navigate the rapids up the river.[747]

It was Sunday June 6, 1784 when one by one the batteauxmen rowed the twelve boats to shore. The men got off first and waded over the rocky bottom and through knee deep water. Once the men and most of the boxes and bundles were ashore, they dragged the boat to the pebbly beach, and the women climbed ashore. Right away Philip, Peter, Nicholas, Michael, and Martin walked a few hundred metres inland to find a good place to pitch their tents. Each family had an army tent made of white duck canvas cloth. The tents had three poles each two metres high. The ridge pole was two metres long. It was expected that five people would sleep in each tent. Martin Alguire and Catharina's tent held a family of eight, three of whom were under the age of ten. Still, it would be a crowded tent. Philip, Catrina, Peter, Maria Catherine and little Catherine and

Peter shared a tent. Nicholas and Anna Margaret and little Martin, Philip, and Dorothy fit nicely in their own tent. While Martin and Elizabeth Margareta Silmser shared a tent with Henry Gallinger and Dorothy and their newborn Catherine. Michael Myers and his wife Elizabeth Crieghoof had two tents. One tent was for the older children, Philip, Elizabeth Margaret, Godfrey, Christian, and Margaret, and the other tent was for Michael, Elizabeth, and their youngest children Maria and Michael Myers Jr.

The families found suitable flat, high ground not to close to the edge of the forest but under the shade of maple and black oak trees. They set up camp for a few days to draw their lots, collect their provisions, and organize work groups. There were several men of the 2nd Battalion who had to wait until they were given permission to go to their lands. The Battalion would not disband until 24 June 1784 which was a few weeks away. At that time, the men would receive their discharge certificates and pay owed to them. They would also return their firearms and receive one firelock for every five men.[748]

Fig. 35. "Encampment of the Loyalists at Johnstown, a New Settlement, on the Banks of the River St. Lawrence in Canada, taken June 6th 1784" Courtesy of Library and Archives Canada Item No: e008299655.

After the tents were raised and the blankets set inside, the men and boys collected firewood to prepare a fire for a meal, some warmth, and a bit of smoke to keep the mosquitoes away. They gathered a few large logs and rolled them close to the fire for a place to sit or rest a head. The young children ran about the crowd of people giggling and squealing when they met someone they knew. Maria Salome Alguire and Elizabeth Margaret Myers ran back to the camp shouting, "Papa! Mama! We saw Mr. Farlinger and his daughter Elizabeth Farlinger, and we saw Mr. Michael Warner and his daughter Maria Margareta Warner." Catching their breath they continued, "Tell Dorothy we saw Mr. Gallinger's father and mother and his brothers Michael, George, and Christopher, and his sister Dorothy!"[749] Before the sun set, everyone was in their tent, most of them too tired to sleep. Catrina lay awake still feeling the roll of the boat. The crickets and frogs nearly concealed the noise from tents not far away. It was the sound of the crickets and frogs that lulled her to sleep.

The next morning everyone at each camp was awake and busy as if no one had gone to sleep. Sergeant John Smith, Sergeant George Barnhardt, and Corporal Jacob Countryman marched through the camp telling everyone that at noon, near Captain Samuel Anderson's tent, they would draw their lots.

Close to noon, Philip reached for his pipe and his hat and said to Catrina, "Come with me dear wife. I need your luck this day. 'T'is our new home we draw for."

"Yes, I want to bring you luck, and I want to see a good lot come from your draw! There's no one more deserving than you dear husband."

Crowds gathered near Captain Anderson's tent. There was so much noise no one heard the sound of the river rushing past. Nor could anyone hear Sergeant Barnhart holler for quiet. Finally, the noise dulled. Philip pointed toward the tent as Captain Anderson climbed a makeshift platform. From there, Captain Anderson hoped he would be heard. He knew hard feelings could arise from this significant event if fairness was not enforced. Governor Haldimand had instructed all the officers regarding the process for distributing lots. He was resolute in his instructions. The draw was crucial. It was to be a random draw with no one person seen to be at an advantage, even the officers. Bitter feelings were to be avoided at all costs. Feelings of satisfaction was the goal. Settlers needed to feel there was fair and sufficient reward for their service to the King and the loss of all personal property whether it was land, life, limb, stock, or earnings.[750]

Captain Anderson announced the rules of the draw and surprised the crowd by telling them that their new settlement was to be called New Johnstown. This name not only honoured the memory of Sir William Johnson and the former home of so many families, but it also honoured their commanding officer and superintendent of the new settlements, Sir John Johnson. One by one, the men walked to a long table in front of Captain Anderson's tent. They drew a ticket from a hat, and Lieutenant Joseph Anderson wrote their name and lot number in the register and issued them a certificate for their land. After their lot was recorded, Lieutenant Jeremiah French recited an Oath of Allegiance to the King to which they swore. After twelve months, the registers for all the townships would be processed ensuring each settler met the rules of settlement. Only then would the men receive their deeds.[751]

One hour passed when Philip, Peter, Martin, Nicholas, and Michael Myers approached the table. Each of them took their turn drawing their lot and taking the oath. Philip drew part of lot 9 and 10 on the 4th concession on the eastern boundary. Peter drew lot 37 on concession 13. This lot was distant from his father's, so he spent a few hours that day trading lots with someone. Eventually, his name was registered in the book with his father's on part of lots 10 and 11 on the 4th concession. Later that day, Philip discovered that Johannes George Alguire and Michael Cline drew the remainder of lot 9. Peter also discovered that Martin Silmser drew the remainder of lots 10 and 11. Martin Alguire drew lot 12 on the 4th concession for himself and his father Jacob Henry who was still in Montreal and coming up in the fall. Next to them on lot 11 were George Gallinger and Michael Gallinger Jr.. Nicholas Silmser drew lot 7 on concession 3 with George Waite. And next to them were Jacob Waggoner and John Karn. Finally, Henry Gallinger and Dorothy drew lot 8 on concession 2.[752]

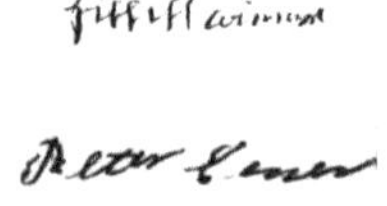

Fig 36 Signatures of Philip Eamer and Peter Eamer

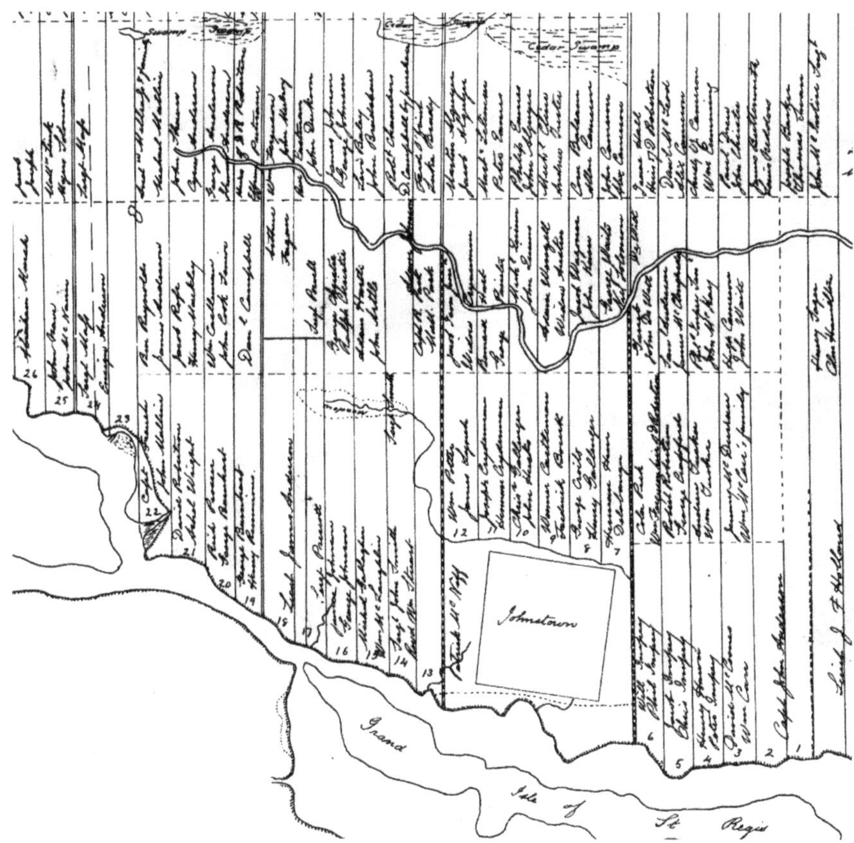

Fig. 37. Survey Map of New Johnstown (Cornwall, Ontario). A plan of part of the new settlements, on the north bank of the south-west branch of the St. Lawrence River. Patrick McNiff, 1786. Courtesy of the Library and Archives Canada, MIKAN No. 4159295

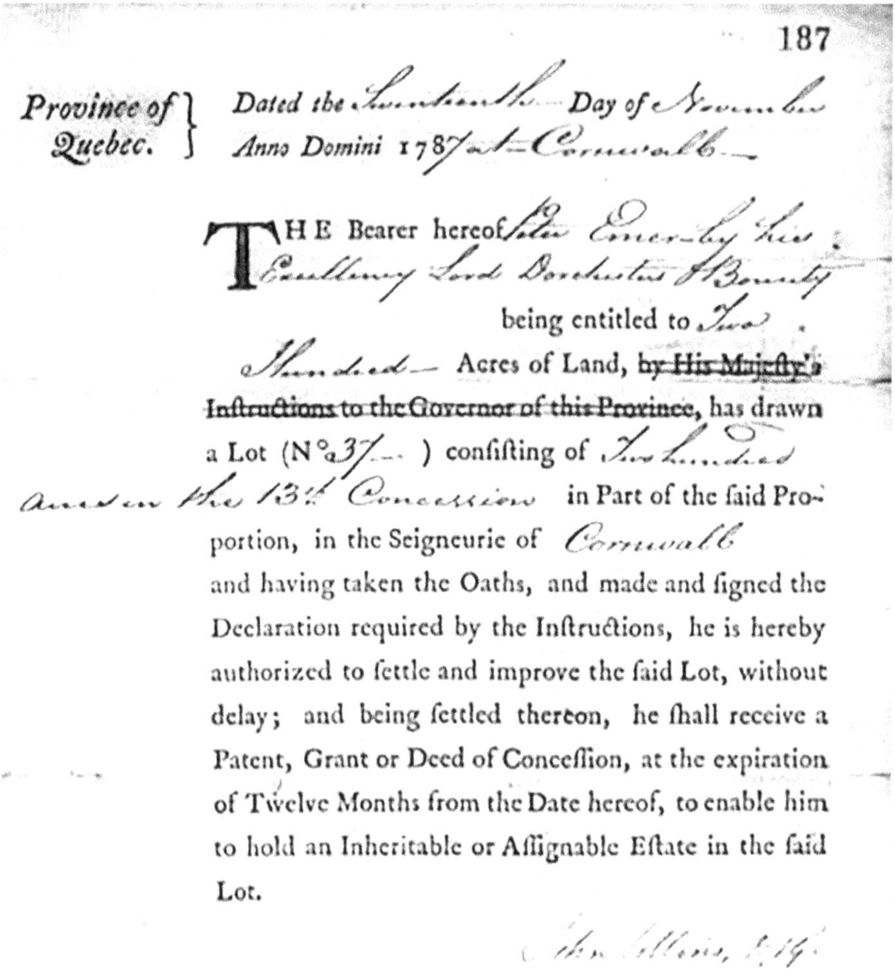

187

Province of Quebec. } Dated the Twentieth Day of November Anno Domini 1787 at Cornwall

THE Bearer hereof Peter Emer by his Excellency Lord Dorchester's Bounty being entitled to Two Hundred Acres of Land, ~~by His Majesty's Instructions to the Governor of this Province,~~ has drawn a Lot (N° 37) consisting of Two hundred and on the 13th Concession in Part of the said Proportion, in the Seigneurie of Cornwall and having taken the Oaths, and made and signed the Declaration required by the Instructions, he is hereby authorized to settle and improve the said Lot, without delay; and being settled thereon, he shall receive a Patent, Grant or Deed of Concession, at the expiration of Twelve Months from the Date hereof, to enable him to hold an Inheritable or Assignable Estate in the said Lot.

John Collins, D.S.G.

Fig. 38. Peter Eamer Land Certificate 20 November 1787, Lot No. 37, Concession 13. Courtesy of Library and Archives Canada. *Heir and Devisee Commission.* Lac_reel_h1135, H-1135, RG 1 L5, 205142, Image 441.

It wasn't until the evening that the commotion and confusion of the day's event diminished. The men gathered around the fire and planned the work for the next few months. While he stoked the fire, Nicholas turned to Philip and said, "Our lot is not far east of yours. I hope an easy path can be made through the forest and brush, but it seems there's a small river on the property for which I'm grateful."

Philip leaned forward and said, "Aye Nicholas. A path can be made, and the river will be a blessing. And George Waite and his wife Mary Cocker are your neighbours. 'T'is good. Before we departed from Lachine, Mary delivered an infant daughter whom they named Mary. And young Jacob Waggoner and Henry Gallinger are close too. Much can be done if you work together.[753] They'll find yours and Anna Margaret's company a blessing too. And John Waite Sr. and Jane are a short distance east of you and will be up this fall."

Peter nodded and said, "We'll start felling trees and digging a well as soon as we get there. We've Michael Cline and Johannes George Alguire close. There'll be a good working crew."

Martin Silmser turned to his son Nicholas and said, "Your mother and I'll come to your lot as soon as we walk our lot. We'll stay with you through the winter. I think we should head up to our lands day after tomorrow. We need only to collect our provisions, seeds, tools, pots, and buckets and maybe fish for a few hours. A bit of fresh fish will be tasty. Salt pork gets tiresome."

Two days later, after Philip and Peter took down their tent and packed their knapsacks with provisions, they went to Captain Anderson's tent to ask if the surveyors set a path to the back concessions. They learned that a path was set not far west of the camp. They were given instructions to go north past George Crites and Henry Gallinger's lot and on to Jacob Waggoner's and John Karn's lot then cross the narrow river. Once across the river, they'd walk west past two lots. They were told a surveyor's stick marked their lot.

The day was sunny and warm when the group gathered at the edge of the forest. Maria Catherine and Anna Margaret had a hard time keeping the children together. Martin Alguire's boys Philip, John, and Peter were jostling to be first on the trail. Peter and Martin Alguire took the lead with the boys, and the group started walking. It was a decent trail, not too much underbrush and a fine canopy of tall maple, hickory, and basswood. Near noon, the shade was welcome. Within an hour they'd come across Henry Gallinger and Dorothy. Their tent was set, and Henry was contemplating a good site for a cabin.

Philip waved, hailing Henry over. "Good day Henry. You rose early to be here so soon. Will your brother George be up this fall?"

"Aye. He will Mr. Eamer. I've no time to waste. We want to be warm and dry this winter. Have you far to go?"

"Nay, only a few lots northwest. We'll come by next week on our way back from collecting our provisions."

"Good. We'll watch for you."

Crossing the river was not a challenge. In fact, everyone took their shoes and stockings off and bathed their feet in the cool, fresh water. Peter sat on a rock dabbling his feet and said, "Papa, there'll be nice fish in this little river. Maybe turtles and frogs too. Ducks and their eggs won't be far away either.

'T'is good and not a day's walk from our land and less for Nicholas."

This was where the group parted with Nicholas, Anna Margaret, their two boys, and little Dorothy. Catrina was worried about Anna Margaret who was pregnant with her fourth child (See corrections); so they stayed to make sure they had a good spot for their tent and enough firewood.

It was only a two hour walk from the river to the surveyor's stake that marked lots 9 and 10 on the 4th concession. As they stood beside the stake, Martin Silmser and Elizabeth Margaret walked toward a clearing under three large basswood. The group followed and threw themselves and their load of knapsacks, buckets, pots, and tools under the spread of the giant trees. The spread of the tree limbs reached over them as if ready to scoop them up to savour the sweet fragrance of hundreds of dangling white flowers. For an hour, they feasted on a few corn cakes that Maria Catherine and Anna Margaret made while in camp. All that could be done for the rest of the day was to set up the tents and collect enough wood for a few days. Work would start early in the morning.

Philip and Peter spent the next morning walking their lot north to the cedar swamp at the back of the property and west towards Johannes George Alguire and Michael Cline's lot. They stopped to talk to Johannes and Michael about building six cabins. One for Johannes George Alguire, one for Michael Cline, one for Philip and Peter, one for Michael Myers, one for Martin Alguire, and one for George and Michael Gallinger Jr.. Snow would fall before seven men plus Michael Cline's teenage son George Cline could finish the work. They also talked about clearing a bit of land for this year's garden, digging six wells, and chopping firewood for winter. Michael Myers cabin would be first as he had several young children, Michael Cline's was next and then Philip and Peter's cabin.

Philip and Peter rose at dawn every day for the next week. After digging for three days, their well sprung water. For two more days, they lined the inside walls with rocks and set rocks around the outside. It was a good spot they chose. The well filled quickly, and the water was clear and fresh. Catrina walked over one afternoon and said, 'T'is good water. Our vegetable seeds will do well. 'T'will be a fine fall garden if the weather is good."

It was a fine garden. In mid-July, Catrina was picking radishes and watching the potatoes flower and the cabbage and turnip ripen. She assigned her grandchildren the job of weeding and keeping pests away. Young Philip and John Alguire went with their grandfather and Uncle Peter to the cedar swamp one day. The boys' job was to catch as many frogs as they could and cut willow sticks for a wattle fence to protect the garden from pests. By the time the green feathery carrot tops were blowing in the breeze, the wattle fence surrounded the garden.

By mid-July, the men were working on Philip and Peter's cabin. They marked the trees to fell, and Maria Catherine, Elizabeth Crieghoof, and Catherine Wick spent weeks picking stones for a foundation and a fireplace. While they picked stones, the children picked saskatoon berries, blueberries, gooseberries, and blackcurrents. What they didn't eat with their meals, they dried. The men worked six days a week from sunrise to sunset, but Catrina insisted they take one afternoon and evening off to rest. They also took a day every few weeks to hunt fowl, beaver, muskrat, squirrel, rabbit and sometimes deer. Fall was the best time to sit at dawn and dusk and hunt deer near the cedar swamp where deer were plentiful. With one gun between them, they hoped to shoot at least one deer.

One afternoon early in August, Philip was shaving a log with his drawing knife. He was making shingles for the roof. For a cabin 4 metres x 5.5 metres, plenty of shingles were needed.

Martin Alguire carried a small log to Philip and said, "In few weeks, I'll take my turn to go to New Johnstown and collect our provisions. I hope my father Jacob Henry will be there with my mother. I long to see Catharina, Peter, Daniel, and Elizabeth."

“’T’is good. I expect them in September. We’ll have your cabin finished near then and have a well dug. We can chop firewood in September and October. We’ve cleared an acre for a garden that’s doing well. There’ll be plenty of root vegetables to put away. If the bateaux at New Johnstown brought supplies, can you get some salt, tobacco, and a bit of rum? Catrina asked if there might be a few crocks. She wants to make sauerkraut. I would wish a few fruit saplings. Getting them in the ground early fall is best.”

“Aye. I’ll get what is allowed.”

Catrina wandered over with a bucket of water for her garden and said, “You’ve a plan that requires me?”

“No Catrina. Martin tells me he’s to go to New Johnstown in a few weeks to collect Catharina and the children.”

“”T’is good. Thank you Martin. You must want to see your mother and father too. And, I wish Maria Salome to help me and the children pick nuts in the forest. We need to fill our root cellar.”

“What root cellar Mrs. Eamer?”

“The one that’s to be dug at the perfect site I’ve chosen. The children are busy drying berries for it.”

Catrina pointed to a large rise in the ground near the well. “All we’ll need is a solid door of shaven logs. Just like the ones you’re working on with that drawing knife dear husband!”

“We shall dig it as soon as Martin and Catharina’s cabin is built. ‘T’will be October before George and Michael Gallinger can move into theirs.”

Catrina turned to Martin and said, “The cabin you’ve made us is a fine home. The three rooms will suit all of us fine. There’s room for Philip and I and Peter, Maria Catherine, and our two beautiful grandchildren. The hearth is big enough for a pot and a kettle if they arrive in a batteau this fall. The large fire will keep most of the frost off the walls. I see no spaces between the logs. That moss we collected was of good use. And, ‘t’is the door you’ve finished that’ll keep the wolves out.”[754]

Fig. 39. Representation of the Eamers' Cabin on the 4th Concession, Royal Township #2. Sketch by Anne Hill, Sixth great- granddaughter of Philip and Catrina Eamer.

It was easy to know September was near. There was a chill in the morning and again as the sun set. During one of Philip and Peter's afternoons of rest, they sat by the fire chewing on a few of the last carrots. Philip was busy whittling a latch for the cabin and root cellar doors, and Peter was whittling spoons and peeling cattail leaves to weave birch branches into a broom.

Philip picked up a piece of wood next to him and said, "This would make a nice handle for that broom son."

"Aye, it would. Don't know why Mama wants a broom. The floors in the cabin are dirt."

"She'll sweep inside and out son. She's been sweeping for near sixty years."

"Papa, I think we should visit Nicholas and Anna Margaret. Anna Margaret has little Dorothy to look after, and she'll deliver another child before winter."

"Aye. We'll go next week and spend the day fishing with Nicholas. He's had time to find the best spot for fishing in that river. And, we'll make sure their wood pile is ready for winter."

"Fishing sounds good. We can add to Mama's pile of dried fish and have a meal of fresh walleye or pike, perhaps some trout."

One evening, Martin knocked on his father-in-law's door. When it opened, he handed Philip a carved wooden dish full of hickory nuts saying, "'T'is a good year for hickory. They're falling off the tree in handfuls."

"Thank you Martin. Come in for a hot rose hip drink."

"Aye. T'will be a good rest, but just a few minutes. I can't leave the children long. I've come to say that I'm leaving day after tomorrow to New Johnstown. Will you watch the children while I'm gone? Should be about four days. I hear several brigades of bateaux are arriving soon. I hope Catharina is on one of them."

"We'll watch them. Peter and I'll be gone deer hunting for a day. We're going up to the cedar swamp and hope to be lucky. A deer will feed us all through winter, and the hide will be of great use. We can make snowshoes. We'll need them to check the traps we set in the snow."

One week later, Martin walked up the trail to the cabin with Catharina and little Elizabeth beside him. Young Daniel walked with his grandfather and grandmother, Jacob Henry and Maria Salome Alguire. It was four months since Catrina and Philip saw their daughter and grandchildren. Their greeting was full of hugs, kisses, smiles, and laughs. Now, Catrina thought, "My four living children are here near me and six are in my heart and the heart of God. I can be easy. No bitter, hateful words near us and no guns in our faces. We've shelter, food, fire, water, and the love of our grandchildren." Counting to herself, she thought, "Nineteen and one coming soon!"

Peter reached to hug his sister and said, "You've just come, and 't'is time for us to go to New Johnstown for the township muster! Martin can come with us. You stay and rest. Visit with Mama. I know she won't let those children out of her sight."

It was mid-October when Philip, Peter, Martin, Michael, and Nicholas walked along the trail picking up Henry Gallinger just north of the village. When they walked out of the forest, in front of them were crowds of people, many tents, and even a cabin and a few small huts. They walked toward Captain Anderson's tent which stood beside the small cabin. In front of the cabin was a long table. Peter thought, "Muster must be there. We'll answer their questions, get our provisions, and I think I'll visit with a few of my old friends. I see Adam and Henry Hartle by the cabin and George Sheets and Henry Runnion. I know

Papa will want to talk to the widow Cryderman, Mr. Michael Warner and the old soldiers John Farlinger and Frederick Goose.[755]

Peter took his spot in line. When he reached the table, he answered their questions, "'T'is me and my wife on our land. I am of the disbanded 2nd Battalion KRRNY. We've one boy under ten, his name is Peter, and we've one girl under ten, her name is Catherine. The man behind the table handed Peter a note for three rations per day.

Philip was next. He answered the same questions. "'T'is me and my dear wife Catrina on our lands. I am of the disbanded 2nd Battalion KRRNY.[756.] Our children are all grown with lands of their own." The man handed Philip a note for two provisions per week.

The lines moved quickly, but the visiting went on until late in the afternoon. Peter, Martin, Michael, and Nicholas found each other in the crowd. Now it was time to find Philip and start the walk home. It would be dark the last ½ kilometre.

Winter grew closer as the men worked. One day, Catrina sat in the chair Philip made and looked toward the window. She strained to see through it. She rose, and peering through the oil papered window she said, "'T'is snowing!"

Philip turned sharply and chuckled as he answered, "Well, we'll soon see if Canada gets as much snow as New York. I think our record in New York was 1½ metres!"

"You may'n't laugh in December husband. I'm thinking of Anna Margaret soon to deliver."

"Of course. We're here to help if need be."

Philip leaned back in his chair enjoying a drag of his pipe and thinking, "I'm blessed to have found enough tobacco to last me through the winter. Every puff will be savoured."

Peter leaned toward the fire and stoked it with a stick. "Papa, I hear the Governor extended the deadline to make claims for losses in the war with the Americans. Commissioner Thomas Dundas is still hearing claims and will for a while longer."

"'T'is a good thing. So many didn't know about submitting their claims and missed the deadline. Our King will be fair and will reward those who were loyal to him and Great Britain."

"Have you heard about your claim Papa?"

"No son. I've not heard anything since it was given to Captain Anderson. 'T'will have to wait until spring 'til I can inquire."

"Perhaps you'll have to submit another?"

"Perhaps. I hope I don't have to travel all the way to Montreal to stand before the Commissioner."

Just as Philip finished his sentence, Catrina jumped out of her chair and said, "I hear someone coming up the trail. Philip, Peter look."

Peter rose from his chair as the door flew open. It was Nicholas Silmser. Breathless he said, "Maria Catherine, Mrs. Eamer come quickly. Anna Margaret is heavy with labour."

Maria Catherine grabbed her woolen coat and a blanket from the bed in their room. As she wrapped her coat and the blanket over her shoulders, she followed Nicholas out the door saying, "I'll help her. I'll be back in the morning!" As she walked away from the cabin, Catharina met her along the path. Holding a basket, she turned toward the forest and said, "I'll come too. Anna Margaret may need us both."

Catrina couldn't believe she slept that night, but she was up pacing the kitchen floor before the sun rose. She kept herself busy putting wood on the fire and separating rations for breakfast. She put a few potatoes in the pot over the fire and took some nuts and dried berries out of their containers. The morning dragged on and on. To keep her occupied, Philip gave her potatoes to scrub for supper. Finally, just before noon, the cabin door slowly opened, and Maria Catherine walked in taking the blanket off her shoulder as she entered. Catharina followed.

Catharina smiled at her mother and said, "She's fine Mama. She delivered a fine healthy baby girl. They call her Elizabeth Silmser."

"Oh so blessed we are. And Nicholas and Anna Margaret!"

"They are blessed Mama. I need to sit for a while."

Guiding her daughter toward the chair, Catrina said, "Rest dear. Let me fix you something hot to drink."

"Thank you Mama."

Catharina sat down and started to sob into her hands.

"Oh daughter! Catrina said as she hugged Catharina's shoulders. What's wrong?"

"Mama. My sister Elizabeth was all I could think of when Anna Margaret's dear child was born. I miss Elizabeth."

Catrina lowered her head, and her eyes softened. She reached for Catharina's hand and said, "Our dear Elizabeth brought many smiles and gave us five beautiful children."

Catharina squeezed her mother's hand and rose from her chair saying, "I want to show you something Mama."

With furrowed brows, Catrina watched her daughter walk through her bedroom door. As Catharina walked back into the kitchen, Catrina saw something in her hand, and she gasped, "Oh my dear child! You've kept it all these years! 'T'is worn badly."

"Aye, Mama. 'T'is Poppy. I tucked her in your blanket chest for safe keeping. The day we left our New York home, Papa yelled for us to pack our things quickly. The first thing I put at the bottom of my sack was Poppy. I could not leave her for the Rebels. She's been with me across the great sea, through Pennsylvania, near twenty five years in New York, through the Adirondacks, up Lake Champlain, in the camps at Pointe Claire and Montreal, up the St. Lawrence River, and along the trail to our new home. Always, Elizabeth made sure I had Poppy near me. I remember her fussing on the ship and along the roads from Philadelphia. You know, I offered Poppy to Elizabeth when she married Michael. I thought she might be lonely. She refused to take her because she knew the little doll meant so much to me. Maybe Papa will carve new legs for her. Hers are marked and worn. And, if you don't mind to make her a new cape and cap. These are tattered and have lost their colour."

"I'd like to do that for you daughter."

"Thank you Mama. I'm going to keep Poppy on the shelf in our kitchen where we can see her. When the spirits of my brothers and sister come, they'll recognize her and stay to watch over us. Maybe one day, when we show the little doll to our grandchildren and great-grandchildren we'll tell them stories of all the little doll endured.

APPENDICES

APPENDIX A
Proving Origins of Johannes Philip Eamer and Maria Catherine Leser

When I started the research for this book, I knew only that Philip Eamer and Maria Catherine Leser came from Germany to America in 1755. Therefore, attempting to prove their place of origin and from whom they descended was a daunting task. This task involved several years of research at various archives and searching thousands of names on FamilySearch.org. I cannot say with certainty that what I found proves the origins of Philip Eamer, but the following process and documentation provides an explanation for my claim of their origins and their descendant chart.

Knowing that the spelling of names in eighteenth century documents varied, some spellings looking or sounding nothing like the name one was searching, I found a myriad of spellings for Eamer such as: Wimmer/Weemer/Wemer/Weamer/Weimer/Amer/Amor/Aimer/Aymer/Emer/Emir/Ener/Beemer. After a period of time, I realized that the original spelling of Eamer was Wimmer or Wiemer. Overtime, through phonetics, translation, or transcription, the surname evolved to Eamer.

1. Philip's Loyalist claim for losses during the Revolutionary War stated that he came from Germany in 1755. On one page, he signed the document 'Philip Wimmer'. Records found at the Eberstadt church archives record Adam Wiemer's name as Wimmer, just as Philip spelled his name on his loyalist claim in 1788. The archivist at Auerbach states that Adam Wiemer is considered the patriarch of all Wiemer's in that area of Hesse, Germany. In the 1775 baptismal record of Peter Alguire, son of Martin and Catharina, Petrue Weimer is one of the sponsors.

   Ancestry.com. *UK, American Loyalist Claims, 1776-1835* [database on-line]. Provo, UT. American Loyalist Claims, 1776–1835. AO 12–13. The National Archives of the United Kingdom, Kew, Surrey, England. Piece 079: Letters, Etc. 181.; The National Archives of the UK; Kew, Surrey, England;

American Loyalist Claims, Series I; Class: AO 13; Piece 031: Evidence, New York, 1787-1788. 276-278.

Evangelishce Kirche in Hessen Und Nassau, Zentral Archive. Records of Darmstadt-Eberstadt, 1690. Burial records of Thomas Wimmer and his wife Ottilia. Records of Darmstadt-Eberstadt, 1706. Marriage record of Johann Adam Wimmer and Elizabeth Dorothea Rau. Written communication with Archive Researcher 24 March 2017.

Claudia Sosniak's, archivist of Auerbach church records, email message to Vicki Holmes with attachment of Johannes Philip Wiemer's baptism from Auerbach Church records, December 20, 2016; *Deutschland Geburten und Taufen, 1558-1898," database,* 17; *FamilySearch* (https://familysearch.org/ark:/61903/1:1:VHQ5-9PC : 28 November 2014), Johann Adam Wiemer in entry for Johann Philipp Wiemer, 26 Dec 1722; citing ; FHL microfilm 1,340,361

Ancestry.com. *U.S., Dutch Reformed Church Records in Selected States, 1639-1989* [database on-line]. Provo, UT. The Archives of the Reformed Church in America; New Brunswick, New Jersey; Reformed Church of Fonda, Baptisms, Marriages, Members, Consistory Minutes, 1758-1839. 1775 June 4, Entry No. 214. Martinus Algyre, Catrina Weemer, Petrue, born May 29, Sponsors Petrue Weimer, Maragrita Algyre.

a. I searched online ship lists for immigrants from Germany in 1755, hoping that a document might provide information of his place of origin. I found nothing for Philip Eamer/Wimmer/Wiemer or Wemer. Research of ship lists at the Pennsylvania Archives generated no results.

b. I requested research from the Albany Land Records Office hoping that Philip's New York land lease from Harmans Wendell might provide a place of origin. No record was found.

2. A military muster roll of Colonel James Gray's Company of the Upper Canada Militia 10 Feb 1789 revealed that, on this date, Philip's age was recorded as 66 years, and his country of origin was Germany.

> Upper Canada Militia Col. James Gray's Co. Feb. 10, 1789. National Archives Canada. N.A.C Reference: M.G. 19 F 35 Series 1, Lot 727, Entries 1 - 73 Philip Eamer, 66, (marital status not shown), concession 3, lot 9, 3 yrs service, country (of origin) Ger

a. Knowing that Philip's name was spelled Wimmer/Wiemer/Wemer, and he was born in Germany ca. 1723, I searched the FamilySearch.org database. I used Germany as the place of origin and searched for any Philip Wimmer/Wiemer/Wemer born near that date. After months of searching thousands of names, I found an entry for a Philip Wiemer. Philip's father's name was Adam and his mother's name was Elisabeth Dorothea. The archivist at Darmstadt found Adam and Elisabetha's marriage record in the church records of Eberstadt. Her surname was Rau. Records show that Adam was a Miller at Eberstadt and moved with Elisabeth Dorothea to Auerbach ca. 1710. Adam and Elisabeth Dorothea had seven children: George, Daniel, Peter, Jacob, Johannes, Philip, and Anna Elizabeth. With Adam's second wife Elizabeth Barbara Muetz, they had six children: Johannes Valentin, Anna Barbara, Anna Margareta, Johannes Mattheus (2, one died), and Anna Catharina.

> Johann Philipp Wiemer Gender: Male Baptism/Christening Date: 26 Dec 1722 Baptism/Christening Place: Evangelisch, Birkenau, Starkenburg, Hesse-Darmstadt. Birth Date: 23 Dec 1722 Birthplace: Death Date: Name Note: Race: Father's Name: Johann Adam Wiemer Father's Birthplace:

Father's Age: Mother's Name: Elisabetha Dorothea Mother's Birthplace: Mother's Age: "Deutschland, Geburten und Taufen 1558-1898," index, FamilySearch (https://familysearch.org/pal:/MM9.1.1/VHQ5-9PC: accessed 15 May 2013), Johann Adam Wiemer in entry for Johann Philipp Wiemer, 23 Dec 1722.

Claudia Sosniak's, archivist of Auerbach church records, email message to Vicki Holmes with attachment of Johannes Philip Wiemer's baptism from Auerbach Church records, December 20, 2016; *Deutschland Geburten und Taufen, 1558-1898," database,* 17; *FamilySearch* (https://familysearch.org/ark:/61903/1:1:VHQ5-9PC : 28 November 2014), Johann Adam Wiemer in entry for Johann Philipp Wiemer, 26 Dec 1722; citing ; FHL microfilm 1,340,361

b. In the FamilySearch database, I searched for a death record of this Philip in Hesse. I found none. I searched for a record of baptisms after 1755 for Philip Wimmer/Wiemer named as father and Maria Catherine (Catrina) named as mother. I found none.

c. I searched records in the FamilySearch.org database using Philip Wiemer/Wimmer to find a marriage record and/or baptism records of children before 1755. I found a baptism for Elisabetha Catharina Wiemer born 28 Sept 1752. Her parents were Philip Wiemer and Maria Catharina. Christina Wiemer was the child's godmother. According to the archivist of the Eberstadt church records, Christina (born 1682) was a sister of Adam Wiemer, Philip's father. (The Auerbach church record archivist stated that the FamilySearch notation of Birkenau as the place of baptism is incorrect. All records listing Birkenau are actually baptisms that took place at Auerbach.) I knew Philip and Maria Catherine had a daughter named Catharina who married Martin Alguire 26 Nov 1769. At the baptism of their son Peter in 1775, her name is recorded as Catriena Weemer. In fact, all of the baptismal records of their children record her name as

Catherine. None give the full name Elizabeth Catherine. If she was born in 1752, she would have been 17 years old when she married.

> Elisabetha Catharina Wiemer Gender: Female Christening Date: 29 Sep 1752 Christening Place: Evangelisch, Birkenau, Starkenburg, Hesse-Darmstadt. Birth Date: 28 Sep 1752 Birthplace: Death Date: Name Note: Race: Father's Name: Johann Philipp Wiemer Father's Birthplace: Father's Age: Mother's Name: Maria Catharina Mother's Birthplace: Mother's Age:
>
> Evangelishce Kirche in Hessen Und Nassau, Zentral Archive. Records of Darmstadt-Auerbach 1752. Baptismal record of Elizabeth Catharina Wiemer. 29 September 1752. Die Bergkirche, Auerbach, Hesse. Written communication with archive researcher 24 March 2017.
>
> Records of the Lutheran Trinity Church of Stone Arabia: in the town of Palatine, Montgomery County, N.Y. Vol 1 page 280. 1769 November den 26ten Martin Algejer & Catharina Emeri.

d. In the FamilySearch database, I searched for a marriage or death record in Hesse, Germany after 1752 for Elisabetha Catharina Wiemer. I found none.

e. Philip and Catrina named one daughter Dorothy, one Elizabeth, and one Anna Margaret, one son Peter, one Johannes, and one Mattheus. Dorothy and Elizabeth were Philip's mother's names and the others are names of Philip's brothers and sisters. From records found, Philip and Catrina did not name any of their children Adam.

3. I searched the FamilySearch database for a marriage record for Philip and Catrina but found none. I requested a search by the archivist at Darmstadt and Auerbach. No record was found.

4. I looked for manumission records (emigrants required this as a release from feudal obligations to Lords of the district) online for Hesse, Germany ca. 1755 hoping to find information about Philip's family and departure to America. I found none.

5. I wondered if Philip and Catrina were married in her village. In New York documents, Catrina is recorded as Catherina Lyser. Therefore, I searched Maria Catherine Lyser/Liser in the FamilySearch database and found no records. I listened to recordings of various spellings of the name Lyser and phonetically Leser is like Lyser/Liser. I searched the FamilySearch database for Maria Catherine Leser born ca. 1720-1735 in areas in Hesse. I found the family name Leser in Arheilgen, Darmstadt, but a search by the Darmstadt archivist revealed no results. There were records on the FamilySearch database for a Leser family at Spachbrucken, Reinheim, Hesse, which is 18.5 kilometres east of Eberstadt and about thirty six kilometres northeast of Auerbach. I have not requested a record search of that area yet.

Locating the record of Philip Wiemer, born 23 Dec 1722 at Auerbach, who married Maria Catherine (Catrina) and who had a daughter Elizabeth Catharina baptized 29 Sept 1752 at Auerbach led me to conclude that this Philip Wiemer and Maria Catherine were my sixth great-grandparents. I make this claim with reasonable certainty. However, a search of records could prove this claim wrong. I will continue to search German and North American records to find more conclusive evidence or evidence that disproves my claim.

APPENDIX B

Johannes Philip Eamer And Maria Catherine Leser Descendant Chart

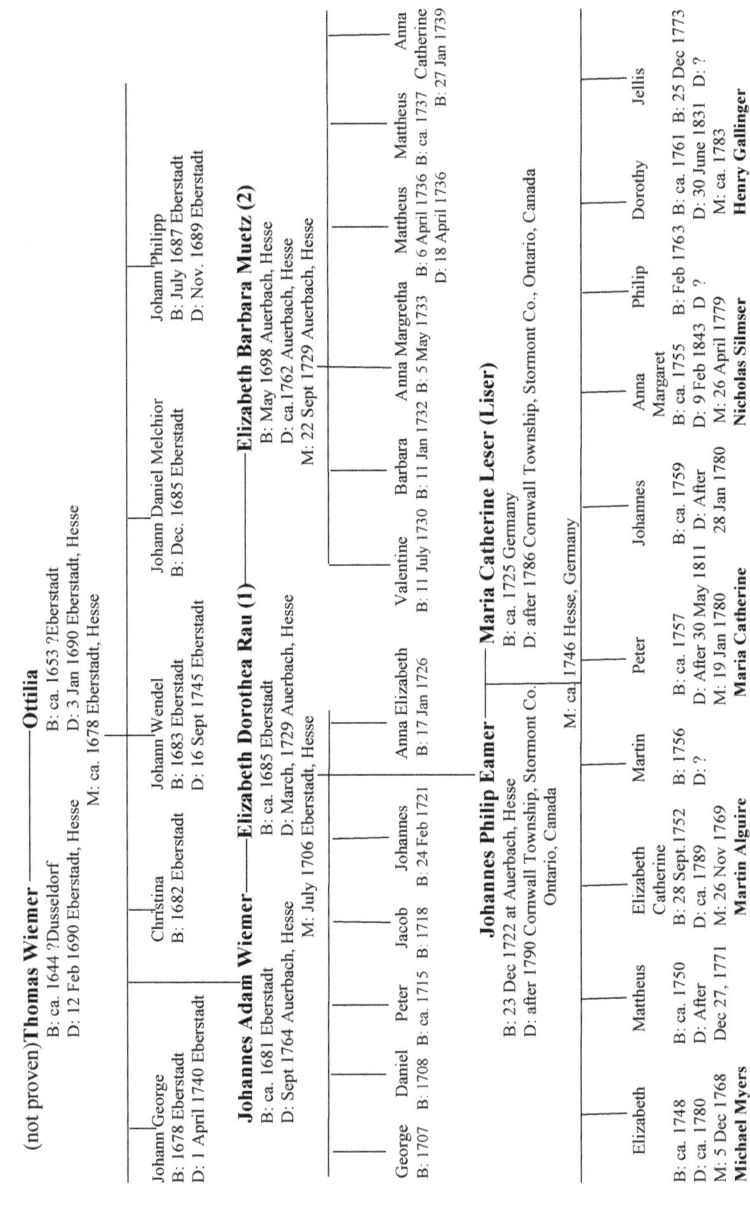

APPENDIX C

Michael Myers And Elizabeth Eamer Descendant Chart

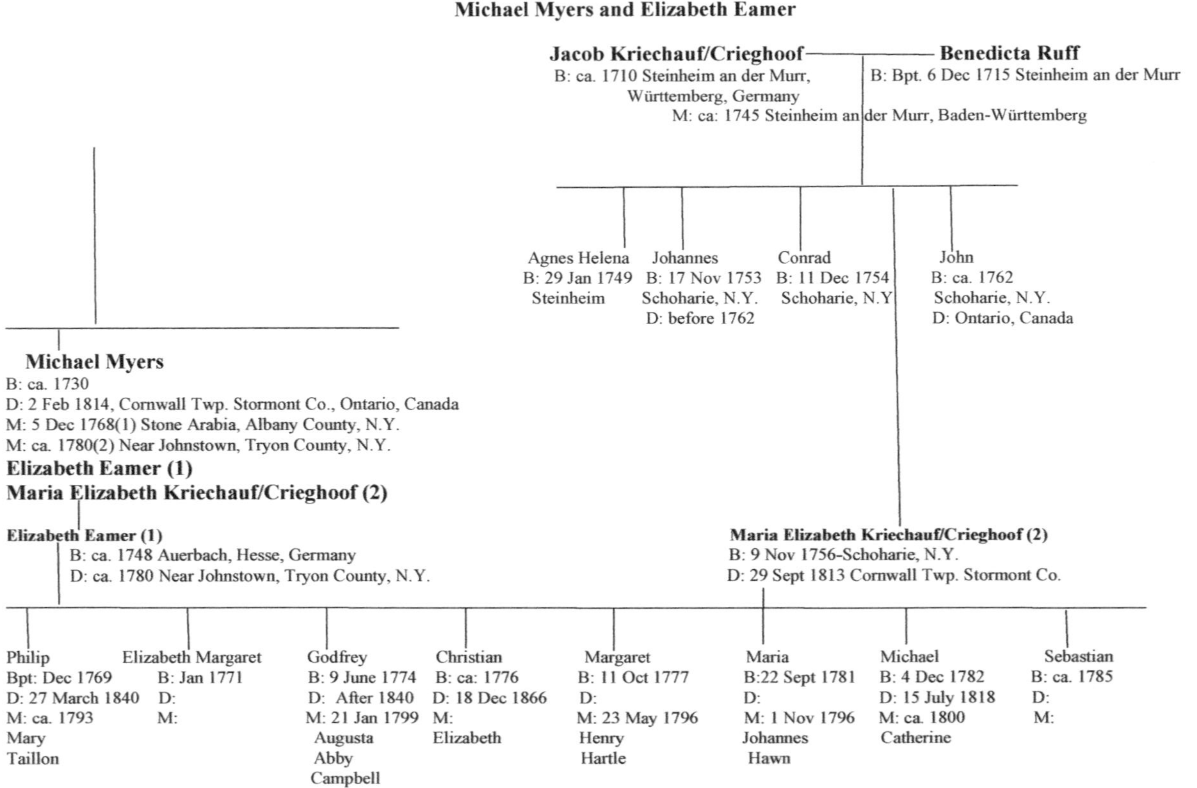

Descendant Chart
Michael Myers and Elizabeth Eamer
Jacob Kriechauf/Crieghoof
B: ca. 1710 Steinheim an der Murr, Württemberg, Germany
M: ca: 1745 Steinheim an der Murr, Baden-Württemberg
Benedicta Ruff
B: Bpt. 6 Dec 1715 Steinheim an der Murr
Agnes Helena
B: 29 Jan 1749
Steinheim
Johannes
B: 17 Nov 1753
Schoharie, N.Y.
D: before 1762
Conrad
B: 11 Dec 1754
Schoharie, N.Y
John
B: ca. 1762
Schoharie, N.Y.
D: Ontario, Canada
Michael Myers
B: ca. 1730
D: 2 Feb 1814, Cornwall Twp. Stormont Co., Ontario, Canada
M: 5 Dec 1768(1) Stone Arabia, Albany County, N.Y.
M: ca. 1780(2) Near Johnstown, Tryon County, N.Y.
Elizabeth Eamer (1)
Maria Elizabeth Kriechauf/Crieghoof (2)
Elizabeth Eamer (1)
B: ca. 1748 Auerbach, Hesse, Germany
D: ca. 1780 Near Johnstown, Tryon County, N.Y.
Maria Elizabeth Kriechauf/Crieghoof (2)
B: 9 Nov 1756-Schoharie, N.Y.
D: 29 Sept 1813 Cornwall Twp. Stormont Co.
Philip
Bpt: Dec 1769
D: 27 March 1840
M: ca. 1793
Mary
Taillon
Elizabeth Margaret
B: Jan 1771
D:
M:
Godfrey
B: 9 June 1774
D: After 1840
M: 21 Jan 1799
Augusta
Abby
Campbell
Christian
B: ca: 1776
D: 18 Dec 1866
M:
Elizabeth
Margaret
B: 11 Oct 1777
D:
M: 23 May 1796
Henry
Hartle
Maria
B:22 Sept 1781
D:
M: 1 Nov 1796
Johannes
Hawn
Michael
B: 4 Dec 1782
D: 15 July 1818
M: ca. 1800
Catherine
Sebastian
B: ca. 1785
D:
M:

Family Record Sheet: Michael Myers and Elizabeth Eamer

Reference

Husband: _Michael Myers____ 2
Born: ___ca. 1730______________________ Place ___________________________ 1
Married __5 Dec 1768____________________ Place _____ Stone Arabia, Albany County, 2
New York ____
Died: __Buried 2 Feb 1814_______________ Place ___Cornwall Twp. Stormont County, 1
Ontario, Canada ____
Father: _______unknown____
Mother: _______unknown____

Wife: (1) _Elizabeth Eamer____ 2
Born: __ca. 1748 ______________ Place _ Auerbach, Hesse, Germany ______________
Died: __ca. 1780_______________ Place _Near Johnstown, Tryon County, New York, USA. 3
Father: ____Johannes Philip Wiemer/Eamer___________________________________
Mother: ___Maria Catherine Leser/Liser_____________________________________

Wife: _(2) Maria Elizabeth Kriechauf /Crieghoof______________________________ 3
Born: __9 Nov 1756_____________ Place ______Schoharie, Schoharie County, New York 4
Died: __Buried 29 Sept 1813_______ Place ______Cornwall Twp. Stormont County, Ontario, 5
Canada ____
Married ____ca. 1780_____________ Place Near Johnstown, Tryon County, New York, USA. 3
Father: ____Jacob Kriechauf/Crieghoof_B: ca. 1715_Steinheim an der Murr, Baden-Wurttemburg, 4/6
Germany. Father: unkown Mother: unkown
Mother: __Benedicta Ruff_Bpt: 6 Dec 1715, Steinheim an der Murr, Baden-Wurttemburg,_____ 4/6
Germany. Father: Theodorus Rueff. Mother: Magdalena___________________________ 7

References

1. "Family Search" Church Records 1803-1846. Church of England in Canada, Trinity Church Cornwall, Ontario. Public Archives of Canada no.: MG9, D7, v.3. 1814 Entry 32, Febr. 2nd Michael Myers buried aged 84. **2.** Ancestry.com. *Records of the Lutheran Trinity Church of Stone Arabia: in the town of Palatine, Montgomery County, N.Y.* [database on-line]. Provo, UT. Vol.1 Marriages, 1763 to 1778; 1790; 1810 to 1815; 1827 to 1830. P. 279. Register der copulirten. Anno 1768, December den 5ten, Michael Majer & Elisabetha Vermerin. Ancestry.com. *U.S., Dutch Reformed Church Records in Selected States, 1639-1989* [database on-line]. Provo, UT. The Archives of the Reformed Church in America; New Brunswick, New Jersey; Reformed Church of Fonda, Baptisms, Marriages, Members, Consistory Minutes, 1758-1839. P. 21. 1777, Nov 2, Michal Myers, Elizabeth Emer, Maragriet, Born Oct 11, Sponsors, Daniel McGregory, Maragriet Emer. **3.** Ancestry.com. *U.S., Dutch Reformed Church Records in Selected States, 1639-1989* [database on-line]. Provo, UT. The Archives of the Reformed Church in America; New Brunswick, New Jersey; Fonda Church, Baptisms, Marriages, 1797-1872. P. 56 of 324. 1781, Dec 26. Michael Myers, Elizabeth Chichogf, Maria Born: Sept 22, Sponsors, Hendr. Simson, Maria. Ancestry.com. *Records of the Reformed Protestant Dutch Church of Caughnawaga* [database on-line]. Provo, UT. Volume one. Baptisms and births, 1758 to 1797. P. 64. Jan. 4, 1783 Entry no: 767 Michel Myers & Elizabeth Criehoof. Michel 4 weeken Sponsors Godfrey Anie & Maria Anie. **4.** "Schoharie County NY GenWeb" Baptism Records St. Paul's Evangelical Lutheran Church Schoharie, New York 1743-1757. Maria Elisabeth 1756 Nov 9 Jacob Krieshauf & Benedista. Sponsors: Salomon and Maria Elisabeth Yorck. Conrad Born: 1754 Dec 11 Baptized: Dec 12 Father: Jacob Kriechauf Mother: Benedicta Sponsors: Conrad Freymäuer and his wife. **5.** "Family Search" Church Records 1803-1846. Church of England in Canada, Trinity Church Cornwall, Ontario. Public Archives of Canada no.: MG9, D7, v.3. 1813, Septr. 29, was buried Elizabeth Myers aged 55. **6.** Deutschland Geburten und Taufen, 1558-1898," database, *FamilySearch* https://familysearch.org/ark:/61903/1:1:NL3F-9RL: 10 February 2018, Jacob Kreichauff in entry for Agnes Helena Kreichauff, 29 Jan 1749; citing Steinheim/Murr (OA. Marbach) Württemberg, Germany; FHL microfilm 1,187,116. Father: Jacob Kreichauff. Mother: Benedicta Ruff. **7.** Deutschland Geburten und Taufen, 1558-1898," database, *FamilySearch* https://familysearch.org/ark:/61903/1:1:NCWF-RMK: 10 February 2018, Benedicta Rueff, 06 Dec 1715; citing; FHL microfilm 1,187,116. Father: Theodorus Rueff. Mother: Magdalena.

Children

Name	Born	Married	Died
1. Philip	Bpt: 21 Dec 1769, Schenectady, Albany Co. N.Y.	Mary Taillon, ca. 1793, Cornwall Twp. Stormont Co.	27 March 1840, Cornwall Twp., Stormont Co.
2. Elizabeth Margaret	Bpt: 29 Jan 1771, Near Johnstown, Tryon Co. N.Y.		
3. Godfrey	9 June 1774, Near Johnstown, Tryon Co. N.Y.	Augusta Abby Campbell, 21 Jan 1799, Cornwall Twp., Stormont Co.	After 1840, Madrid, St. Lawrence Co. N.Y.
4. Christian	ca. 1776, Near Johnstown, Tryon Co. N.Y.	Elizabeth,	18 Dec 1866, Waddington, St. Lawrence Co. N.Y.
5. Margaret	11 Oct 1777, Near Johnstown, Tryon Co. N.Y.	Henry Hartle, 23 May 1796, Cornwall Twp., Stormont Co.	Cornwall Twp., Stormont Co.
6. Maria	22 Sept 1781, Near Johnstown, Tryon Co. N.Y.	Johannes Hawn, 1 Nov 1796, Cornwall Twp., Stormont Co.	After 1815, Niagara, Niagara, Ontario, Canada
7. Michael	4 Dec 1782, Near Johnstown, Tryon Co. N.Y.	Catherine, ca. 1800, Cornwall Twp., Stormont Co.	15 July 1818, Cornwall Twp., Stormont Co. (accidental drowning)
8. Sebastian	ca. 1785, Cornwall Twp., Stormont County		Cornwall Twp. Stormont Co.

APPENDIX D
Martin Alguire And Elizabeth Catherine Eamer Descendant Chart

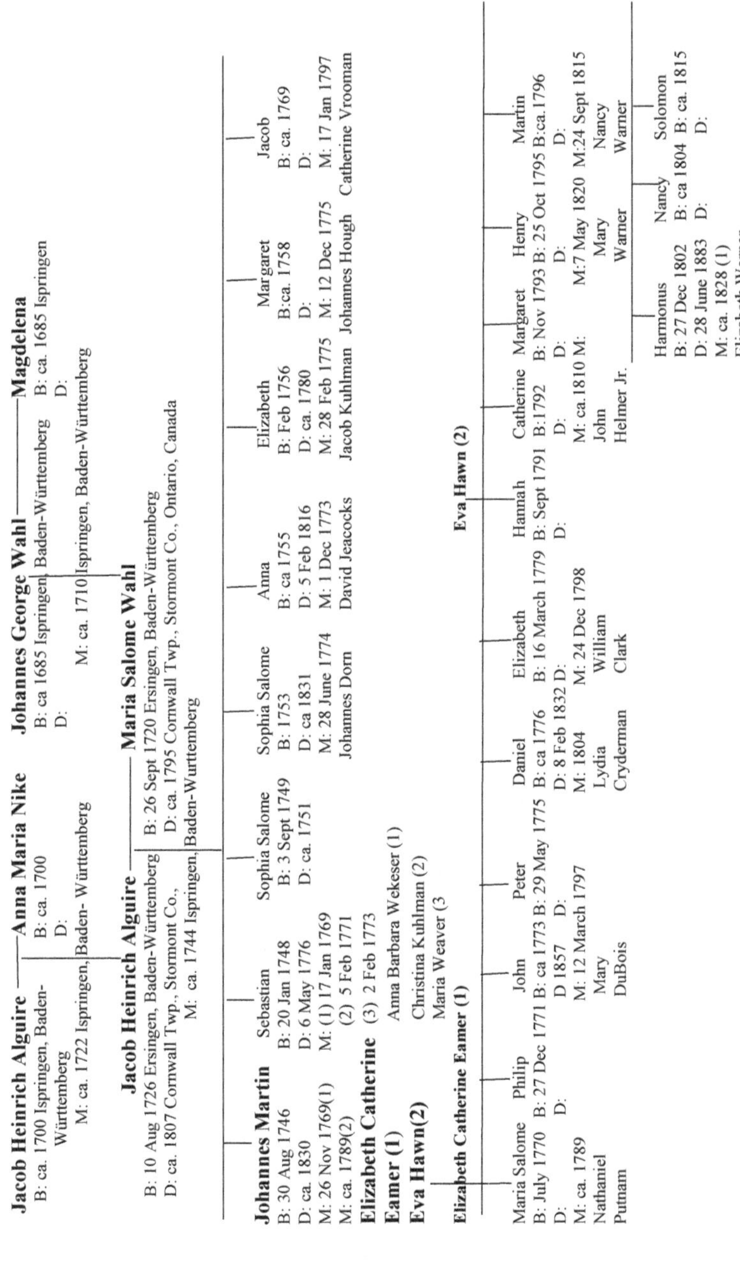

Descendant Chart
Martin Alguire and Elizabeth Catherine Eamer
Jacob Heinrich Alguire
B: ca. 1700 Ispringen, Baden-Württemberg
M: ca. 1722 Ispringen, Baden- Württemberg
Anna Maria Nike
B: ca. 1700
D:
Johannes George Wahl
B: ca 1685 Ispringen, Baden-Württemberg
D:
M: ca. 1710 Ispringen, Baden-Württemberg
Magdelena
B: ca. 1685 Ispringen
D:
Jacob Heinrich Alguire
B: 10 Aug 1726 Ersingen, Baden-Württemberg
D: ca. 1807 Cornwall Twp., Stormont Co.,
M: ca. 1744 Ispringen, Baden-Wurttemberg
Maria Salome Wahl
B: 26 Sept 1720 Ersingen, Baden-Württemberg
D: ca. 1795 Cornwall Twp., Stormont Co., Ontario, Canada
Johannes Martin
B: 30 Aug 1746
D: ca. 1830
M: 26 Nov 1769(1)
M: ca. 1789(2)
Elizabeth Catherine
Eamer (1)
Eva Hawn(2)
Sebastian
B: 20 Jan 1748
D: 6 May 1776
M: (1) 17 Jan 1769
(2) 5 Feb 1771
(3) 2 Feb 1773
Anna Barbara Wekeser (1)
Christina Kuhlman (2)
Maria Weaver (3
Sophia Salome
B: 3 Sept 1749
D: ca. 1751
Sophia Salome
B: 1753
D: ca 1831
M: 28 June 1774
Johannes Dorn
Anna
B: ca 1755
D: 5 Feb 1816
M: 1 Dec 1773
David Jeacocks
Elizabeth
B: Feb 1756
D: ca. 1780
M: 28 Feb 1775
Jacob Kuhlman
Margaret
B:ca. 1758
D:
M: 12 Dec 1775
Johannes Hough
Jacob
B: ca. 1769
D:
M: 17 Jan 1797
Catherine Vrooman
Elizabeth Catherine Eamer (1)
Eva Hawn (2)
Maria Salome
B: July 1770
D:
M: ca. 1789
Nathaniel
Putnam
Philip
B: 27 Dec 1771
D:
John
B: ca 1773
D 1857
M: 12 March 1797
Mary
DuBois
Peter
B: 29 May 1775
D:
Daniel
B: ca 1776
D: 8 Feb 1832
M: 1804
Lydia
Cryderman
Elizabeth
B: 16 March 1779
D:
M: 24 Dec 1798
William
Clark
Hannah
B: Sept 1791
D:
Catherine
B:1792
D:
M: ca.1810
John
Helmer Jr.
Margaret
B: Nov 1793
D:
M:
Henry
B: 25 Oct 1795
D:
M:7 May 1820
Mary
Warner
Martin
B:ca.1796
D:
M:24 Sept 1815
Nancy
Warner
Harmonus
B: 27 Dec 1802
D: 28 June 1883
M: ca. 1828 (1)
Elizabeth Warner
Nancy
B: ca 1804
D:
Solomon
B: ca. 1815
D:

Family Record Sheet: Martin Alguire and Elizabeth Catherine Eamer

	Reference
Husband: ____Johann Martin Alguire________________________________	1/6
Born: _30 August 1746_Bpt. 1 Sept 1746_ Place: _Ersingen, Baden-Württemberg, Germany__________	1
Married: __26 Nov 1769______________ Place: Stone Arabia, Albany County, New York__________	4
Died: ____Before 24 April 1833________ Place: Osnabruck Twp., Stormont Co., Ontario, Canada ____	5
Father: Jacob Heinrich Algeer B: 10 Aug 1726 Bpt 11 Aug 1726, Ispringen, Baden-Württemburg, (Parish Ersingen)__________	2/3/6
Mother: Maria Salome Wahl Bpt. 26 Sept. 1720, Ispringen, Baden-Württemburg, (Parish Ersingen)_______	1/6
Wife (1): _Elizabeth Catherine Eamer__________________________	
Born: _28 Sept. 1752_Bpt. 29 Sept 1752_ Place Auerbach, Hesse, Germany_____________________	7
Died: ____ca. 1789________________ Place Cornwall Twp., Stormont County, Ontario, Canada_____	
Father: ___Johannes Philip Wiemer/Eamer__________________________	7
Mother: __Maria Catherine Leser/Liser__________________________	7
Wife: (2) _Eva Hawn__________________________________	8
Born: _ca. 1765 __________________ Place ___Near Johnstown, Albany County, N.Y.____________	
Married: ca. 1790_________________ Place __Cornwall Twp., Stormont Co., Ontario, Canada_______	8
Died: _________________________ Place __Osnabruck Twp., Stormont Co., Ontario, Canada _____	
Father: __Henry Hawn_(not proven)____________________________	9/10
Mother: __Ann Hezy (not proven)_____________________________	10/11

References

1. Ancestry.com. *Baden, Germany, Lutheran Baptisms, Marriages, and Burials, 1502-1985* [database on-line]. Provo, UT. Johann Martin Augejer, Father: Jacob Heinrich Augejer Mother: Salome Wahl, P. 297. **2.** Ibid. Jacob Heinrich Algeeer, Father: Jacob Heinrich Algeeer, Mother: Anna Maria, P. 54:55. **3.** Ibid, Jacob Heinrich Alyeers, Spouse: Anna Maria Nike, Father: Jacob Fridrich Alyeers, 11:535. **4.** Ancestry.com. *Records of the Lutheran Trinity Church of Stone Arabia: in the town of Palatine, Montgomery County, N.Y.* [database on-line]. Provo, UT. Vol.1 Marriages, 1763 to 1778; 1790; 1810 to 1815; 1827 to 1830. P.280. **5.** Upper Canada Land Petitions (1763-1865), Mikan Number: 205131, Microform: c-1613, P. 229-230. **6.** Ancestry.com. *U.S. and Canada, Passenger and Immigration Lists Index, 1500s-1900s* [database on-line]. Provo, UT. Original data: Filby, P. William, ed. *Passenger and Immigration Lists Index, 1500s-1900s*. Farmington Hills, MI, USA. Jacob Heinrich Allgeyer, age 27, Arrival year 1753, Child Johann Martin; Wife Salome Wahl; Child Sebastian; Child Sophia Salome. Ancestry.com. *Baden, Germany, Lutheran Baptisms, Marriages, and Burials, 1502-1985* [database on-line]. Provo, UT. Maria Salome Wahl, Bpt. 26 Sept, 1720, Ispringen, Baden-Württemberg, Parish Ersingen. P. 30/31. Father: Johann George Wahl, Mother: Magdelena Wahl. Ancestry.com. *Baden, Germany, Lutheran Baptisms, Marriages, and Burials, 1502-1985* [database on-line]. Provo, UT. Jacob Heinrich Algeeer, B: 10 Aug 1726, Bpt: 11 Aug 1726, Ispringen, Baden-Württemberg, Parish Ersingen, Father: Jacob Heinrich Algeeer, Mother: Anna Maria Algeer, P. 54/55. **7.** Deutschland Geburten und Taufen, 1558-1898," database, *FamilySearch* (https://familysearch.org/ark:/61903/1:1:VHQP-Y23 : 11 February 2018), Elisabetha Catharina Wiemer, 29 Sep 1752; citing ; FHL microfilm 1,340,361. **8**. Fraser, Alex, & Ross Rhoda, St. Andrews Presbyterian Church, Williamstown, Ontario. (1999). P. 64, 189. Baptisms 1791, Hannah Algire, Daughter of Martin Algire of Cornwall and of Eve Bone his wife was baptised on the 11th September 1791 Note from transcriber states Bone could be Hone. "Baptism Registers of the Parishes of Williamsburg, Matilda, Osnabruck and Edwardsburg." Wayne Bower 2017. **9.** Ancestry.com. *UK, American Loyalist Claims, 1776-1835* [database on-line]. Provo, UT. The National Archives of the UK; Kew, Surrey, England; *American Loyalist Claims, Series I;* Class: *AO 13;* Piece: *029. Evidence, New York, 1787-1788. Evidence on the claim of Henry Horn.* **10.** British Library, formerly British Museum, Additional Manuscripts 21804-21834, Haldimand Papers, Lac_reel_h1655, 105513, 2034239, MG 21, Image 55. Ann Hawn, 1 woman, 1 female above 6 1 Ration per day, 1st Battn Rl Yorkers. **11.** Ancestry.com. *U.S., Dutch Reformed Church Records in Selected States, 1639-1989* [database on-line]. Provo, UT. Holland Society of New York; New York, New York; *Albany, Vol III, Book 3. P. 161.* 1764 Sep. 2. B. Zacharias Hendrik Haan and Annatje Hezy, at Niskatha. (Niskayuna).

Children - Elizabeth Catherine Eamer

Name	Born	Married	Died
1. Maria Salome	Bpt: 7 July 1770, Lutheran Trinity Church Stone Arabia, NY.	Nathaniel Putnam ca. 1789, Cornwall Twp, Stormont Co.	
2. Philip	Bpt: 27 Dec 1771, Lutheran Trinity Church Stone Arabia, N.Y.		After Oct 1840, Osnabruck Twp, Stormont Co.
3. John	B: ca. 1773, Near Johnstown, Tryon Co., N.Y.	Mary DuBois 12 March 1797, Cornwall Twp, Stormont Co.	After 1851, Roxborough Twp, Stormont Co.
4. Peter	B: 29 May 1775, Bpt: 4 June 1775, Caughnawaga, Tryon Co. N.Y.	Catherine Helmer ca. 1804 Cornwall Twp, Stormont Co.	After 1851, Osnabruck Twp, Stormont Co.
5. Daniel	B: ca. 1776, Near Johnstown, Tryon Co., N.Y.	Lydia Cryderman 1804, Cornwall Twp, Stormont Co.	8 Feb 1832, Yonge Twp, Leeds Co.
6. Elizabeth	B: 16 March 1779, Bpt: 25 March 1779, Lutheran Trinity Church Stone Arabia, N.Y.	William Clark 24 Dec 1798, Cornwall Twp, Stormont Co.	

Children – Eva Hawn

Name	Born	Married	Died
7. Hannah	Bpt. 11 Sept 1791, Cornwall Twp, Stormont Co.		
8. Catherine	B: ca. 1792	John Helmer, Osnabruck Twp, Stormont Co.	
9. Margaret	Bpt. 17 Nov 1793, Cornwall Twp, Stormont Co.		
10. Henry	B: 25 Oct 1795, Bpt. 26 Dec 1795, Cornwall Twp. Stormont Co.	Mary Warner, 7 May 1820, Osnabruck Twp. Stormont Co.	After 1851, Osnabruck Twp. Stormont Co.
11. Martin	B: ca. 1796	Nancy Warner 24 Sept 1815, Osnabruck Twp. Stormont Co.	Osnabruck Twp. Stormont Co.
12. Harmonius	B: 27 Dec 1802, Osnabruck Twp. Stormont Co.	Elizabeth Warner, Osnabruck Twp. Stormont Co.	28 June 1883, Yonge, Leeds Co. Ontario
13. Nancy	B: ca. 1804, Osnabruck Twp. Stormont Co.		
14. Solomon	B: ca. 1808, Osnabruck Twp.		

APPENDIX E

Peter Eamer And Maria Catherine Gallinger Descendant Chart

Descendent Chart
Maria Catherine Gallinger and Peter Eamer

Johannes George Gallinger — **Anna Barbara Kubler**
B: ca. 1705 Hopfau, Baden-Württemberg
D: 22 April 1762 Hopfau, Baden-Württemberg

Anna Barbara Kubler
B: 1703 Neuneck, Baden-Wurttemberg
D:

M: ca. 1725 Hopfau, Baden- Württemberg

Christian Ade — **Maria Catherine Kohler**
B: ca. 1685 ?Sindelfingen, Baden-Württemberg
D:

Maria Catherine Kohler
B: ca 1685
D:

M: ca. 1712, Dürrenmettstetten, Baden-Württemberg

Anna Maria
Bpt. 12 Nov 1730 Hopfau
M: 19 Nov 1754
Mattheus Steinwand

Michael Gallinger — **Agatha Ade**
B: 10 Jan 1726 Hopfau
D: 23 Oct 1797 Cornwall Twp. Stormont Co., Ontario

Agatha Ade
B: 20 Sept 1727 Dürrenmettstetten
D: After 22 Feb 1794, Cornwall Twp., Stormont Co., Ontario

M: 2 Nov 1751 Hopfau, Baden- Württemberg

Christian
Bpt: 12 Aug 1722

Maria Barbara
Bpt: 12 Aug 1719

Anna Maria
Bpt: 7 Nov 1717

Anna Barbara
Bpt: 5 Feb 1714

Barbara
B: ca 1752
D: March 1753

Christian
B: Oct 1756
D:
M: ca. 1780
John Philip Helmer

Michael
B: ca. 1751
D: 3 May 1827
M: ca. 1785(1)
1809(2)
Catherine Cryderman (1)
Rosanne St. Maurice (2)

Christopher
B: ca. 1758
D: 1837
M: Jan 1784(1)
Sarah Fykes (nee Runnions)

Maria Catherine
Bpt: 25 Feb 1759
D: 27 Oct 1839
M: 19 Jan 1780
Peter Eamer

Henry
B: 4 Sept 1761
D: 16 Sept 1835
M: ca. 1783
Dorothy Eamer

Johannes George
B: 5 April 1764
D: 13 Jan 1833
M: 20 Oct 1788
Maria Margaret Warner

Elizabeth
B: ca. 1765
D:
M: 20 Jan 1785
James Thompson

Dorothy
B: 9 Dec 1767
D: ca. 1853
M: ca. 1781(1)
ca. 1805 (2)
Solomon Tuttle (1)
Solomon Noble (2)

Peter
B: ca.1780
D: 1859
M: 22 Oct 1805
Catherine Cline

Catherine
B: ca. 1783
D:
M: ca. 1809
William Nokes

Philip
B: Feb 1786
D: 1846
M: 10 March 1807
Mary Cryderman

Allinder (Olive)
B: ca 1789
D:
M: ca. 1810
Philip Empey

Mary (Polly)
B: ca. 1790
D:
M: 24 Jan 1810
William Noble

Barbara
Bpt: 23 June 1793
D: 18 March 1873
M: ca. 1810
Israel Bugbey

Jacob
Bpt: 7 May 1797
D: 26 July 1878
M: 11 May 1820 (1)
M: 1826 (2)
Hannah Cryderman (1)
Ann McQuay (2)

Michael
B: 16 Mar 1798
D: 26 May 1886
M: ca. 1824
Sarah Ann Alguire

Daniel David
B: ca. 1802
D:14 Dec 1838
M: ca. 1824
M: 1837 (2)
Mary Amanda Bender (1)
Elizabeth Isabel (2)

Elias Mattheus
B: ca. 1808
D: 10 June 1848
M: ca. 1835
Elizabeth Barkley

Family Record Sheet: Maria Catherine Gallinger and Peter Eamer

Reference

Husband: _Peter Eamer____ 2
Born: ___ca. 1757__________________ Place _Lot 59, Sacandaga Patent, Near Johnstown, 1
Albany County, New York
Married _19 Jan 1780_______________ Place _Caughnawaga, Tryon County, New York__ 2
Died: ___After 1811________________ Place Cornwall Twp. Stormont Co., Ontario, Canada 3
Father: __Johannes Philip Wiemer/Eamer_________________________________
Mother: _Maria Catherine Leser/Liser___________________________________

Wife: __Maria Catherine Gallinger_______________________________________
Born: _Bpt. 25 Feb 1759_____________ Place _ Lot 85 Kingsborough Patent East, Near_____ 4
Johnstown, Albany County, New York
Died: _27 Oct 1839_______________ Place Cornwall Twp. Stormont Co., Ontario, Canada 3
Father: _____Michael Gallinger_B: 10 Jan 1726, Hopfau, Württemberg, Germany. Father: ____4/5/6/7/8
George Gallinger, Mother: Anna Barbara Kübler. M: 2 Nov 1751,
Hopfau, Wurttemberg, D: 23 Oct 1797, Cornwall Twp. Stormont Co.
Mother: ___Agatha Ade B; 20 Sept 1727, Durrenmettstetten, Baden, Germany. Father: 4/5/6/7/9/10
Christian Ade, Mother: Maria Catherine Kohler. D: After 22 Feb 1794, Cornwall Twp. Stormont Co.

References

1. Fryer, Mary & Smy, W. (Lieutenant-Colonel), *Rolls of the Provincial (Loyalist) Corps, Canadian Command American Revolutionary Period*, (Toronto, Dundurn Press, 1981), P. 37. 25 April, 1783 Earner, Peter Age 26, Size 5'11", Country America, Total Servitude 3 years. The Global Gazette, Militia Rolls of Upper Canada Colonel James Gray's Company February 10, 1789. Peter Eamer, 32, married, concession 3, lot, 10, 4 years service, country (of origin) is America, Royal Regiment of New York. **2.** Ancestry.com. *U.S., Dutch Reformed Church Records in Selected States, 1639-1989* [database on-line]. Provo, UT. The Archives of the Reformed Church in America; New Brunswick, New Jersey; Reformed Church of Fonda, Baptisms, Marriages, Members, Consistory Minutes, 1758-1839. Reid, William D. *The Loyalists in Ontario: The Sons and Daughters of the American Loyalists of Upper Canada*. Lambertville, NJ, USA: Genealogical Publishing Co., 1973. P. 97. **3.** "Family Search" Church Records 1803-1846. Church of England in Canada, Trinity Church Cornwall, Ontario. Public Archives of Canada no.: MG9, D7, v.3. P. 107. Died on the 27th and was buried on the 29th of Oct 1839. Mrs Catherine Eamer, wife of Mr. Peter Eamer of the Township of Cornwall. Age 84 years. **4.** Register of Baptisms Rev John Olglivie Trinity Church New York, New York USA. Ancestry.com. *Württemberg, Germany, Lutheran Baptisms, Marriages, and Burials, 1500-1985* [database on-line]. Provo, UT. Taufen, Tote, Heiraten u Konfirmationen 1709-1876. Hofau.2 Nov 1751. Ancestry.com. *Württemberg, Germany, Family Tables, 1550-1985* [database on-line]. Lehi, UT. Konfirmationen, Kommunionen, Familienbuch u· Seelenregister 1726-1876. Hopfau u. Neunthausen. P. 57. **5.** Ancestry.com. *Canada, Find A Grave Index, 1600s-Current* [database on-line]. Provo, UT. Ancestry.com. *Records of the Lutheran Trinity Church of Stone Arabia: in the town of Palatine, Montgomery County, N.Y.* [database on-line]. Provo, UT. Vol.1. Birth and baptisms, 1751 to 1815. P. 20. 1756. **6.** Worall, L. & Frolick, A., *The Gallinger Family: Ancestors and Descendants in Germany, the United States and Canada.* (Stormont, Dundas and Glengarry Genealogical Society, 2001). **7.** Ancestry.com. *Canada, Find A Grave Index, 1600s-Current* [database on-line]. Provo, UT. Militia Rolls of Upper Canada Roll of Captain Jeremiah French's Company April 3 1790. (Global Genealogy, 15 April 1998), Original Source: National Archives of Canada: NAC Reference M.G. 19 F 35 Series 2, Lot 679, Pages 18-21. (Age) 68, Michel Gallinger, Royal Regiment of New York, 0,0,0,1,0. 1=infirm. Ancestry.com. *Württemberg, Germany, Lutheran Baptisms, Marriages, and Burials, 1500-1985* [database on-line]. Provo, UT. Taufen, Tote, Heiraten u Konfirmationen 1709-1876. Hopfau u. Neunthausen. OA Sulz. P. 288;289. 2 Nov 1751. Georg Gallingers, Child: Michael Household Members: Michael Gallinger, Georg Gallinger, Agatha Adn, Christian Adn. **8.** Ancestry.com. *Württemberg, Germany, Lutheran Baptisms, Marriages, and Burials, 1500-1985* [database on-line]. Provo, UT. *Taufen, Tote, Heiraten u Konfirmationen 1709-1876.* Hopfau u Neunthausen. Anna Maria Gallinger, Bpt. 12 Nov 1730. **9.** 22 Feb 1794, Agatha and George Gallinger Sponsors at the Baptism of her Grandson Henrich, son of Henry Gallinger and Dorothea Eamer. **10.** Ancestry.com. *Württemberg, Germany, Family Tables, 1550-1985* [database on-line]. Lehi, UT. *Konfirmationen, Kommunionen, Familienbuch u· Seelenregister 1726-1876.* Hopfau u. Neunthausen. Christian Ade. P. 104.

Ancestry.com. *Württemberg, Germany, Lutheran Baptisms, Marriages, and Burials, 1500-1985* [database on-line]. Provo, UT. *Familienbuch, Taufen, Heiraten, Tote u Familienbücher 1558-1912.* Dürrenmettstetten u Vierundzwanzig Höfe. Christianus Ade. 12 Aug 1722.

Children

Name	Born	Married	Died
1. Peter	B: ca. 1780, Montreal, Quebec	Catherine Cline, 22 Oct 1805, Cornwall Twp. Stormont Co.	D: 5 May 1859, Cornwall Twp. Stormont Co.
2. Catherine	B: ca. 1783, Montreal, Quebec	William Nokes, ca. 1809,	D: After Feb 1811, Cornwall Twp. Stormont Co.
3. Philip	Bpt. 11 Feb 1786, Cornwall Twp. Stormont Co.	Mary Cryderman, 10 March 1807, Cornwall Twp. Stormont Co.	D: 1846, Cornwall Twp. Stormont Co.
4. Olive (Allinder)	B: ca. 1789	Philip Empey, ca. 1810, Cornwall Twp. Stormont Co.	
5. Mary (Polly)	B: ca. 1790	William Noble, 24 Jan 1810, Cornwall Twp. Stormont Co.	D: After 28 Jan 1811, Cornwall Twp. Stormont Co.
6. Barbara	Bpt. 23 June 1793, Cornwall Twp. Stormont Co.	Never married	D: 18 March 1873, Cornwall Twp., Stormont Co.
7. Jacob	Bpt: 7 May 1797, Cornwall Twp. Stormont Co.	1. Hannah Cryderman, 11 May 1820. 2. Anne McQuay, 1826.	D: 26 July 1878, Brussels, Huron Co. Ontario
8. Michael	B: 16 March 1798, Cornwall Twp. Stormont Co.	Sarah Ann Alguire, 1824, Cornwall Twp. Stormont Co.	D: 28 May 1886, Cornwall Twp. Stormont Co.
9. Daniel David	B: 1802, Cornwall Twp. Stormont Co.	1. Mary Amanda Bender, 1824 2. Elizabeth Isabel, 1837	D: 14 Dec 1838, St. Eustache, Quebec
10. Elias Mattheus	B: ca. 1808, Cornwall Twp. Stormont Co.	Elizabeth Barkley, ca. 1835	D: 10 June 1848, Cornwall Twp. Stormont Co.

APPENDIX F
Henry Gallinger And Dorothy Eamer Descendant Chart

Descendent Chart
Henry Gallinger and Dorothy Eamer

Johannes George Gallinger — **Anna Barbara Kubler**

Johannes George Gallinger	**Anna Barbara Kubler**
B: ca. 1705 Hopfau, Baden-Württemberg	B: 1703 Neuneck, Baden-Wurttemberg
D: 22 April 1762 Hopfau, Baden-Württemberg	D:

M: ca. 1725 Hopfau, Baden- Württemberg

Christian Ade — **Maria Catherine Kohler**

Christian Ade	**Maria Catherine Kohler**
B: ca. 1685 ?Sindelfingen, Baden-Württemberg	B: ca 1685
D:	D:

M: ca. 1712 Dürrenmettstetten, Baden-Württemberg

Children of Johannes George Gallinger and Anna Barbara Kubler:

Anna Maria	**Michael Gallinger**
Bpt. 12 Nov 1730 Hopfau	B: 10 Jan 1726 Hopfau
M: 19 Nov 1754	D: 23 Oct 1797 Cornwall Twp. Stormont Co., Ontario
Mattheus Steinwand	

Children of Christian Ade and Maria Catherine Kohler:

Agatha Ade	Christian	Maria Barbara	Anna Maria	Anna Barbara
B: 20 Sept 1727 Dürrenmettstetten	Bpt: 12 Aug 1722	Bpt: 12 Aug 1719	Bpt: 7 Nov 1717	Bpt: 5 Feb 1714
D: After 22 Feb 1794, Cornwall Twp., Stormont Co., Ontario				

Michael Gallinger — **Agatha Ade**
M: 2 Nov 1751 Hopfau, Baden- Württemberg

Children of Michael Gallinger and Agatha Ade:

Barbara	Christian	Michael	Christopher	Maria Catherine	**Henry**	Johannes George	Elizabeth	Dorothy
B: ca 1752	B: Oct 1756	B: ca. 1751	B: ca. 1758	Bpt: 25 Feb 1759	B: 4 Sept 1761	B: 5 April 1764	B: ca. 1765	B: 9 Dec 1767
D: March 1753	D:	D: 3 May 1827	D: 1837	D: 27 Oct 1839	D: 16 Sept 1835	D: 13 Jan 1833	D:	D: ca. 1853
	M: ca. 1780	M: ca. 1785(1) 1809(2)	M: Jan 1784(1)	M: 19 Jan 1780	M: ca. 1783	M: 20 Oct 1788	M: 20 Jan 1785	M: ca. 1781(1) ca. 1805 (2)
	John Philip Helmer	Catherine Cryderman (1) Rosanne St. Maurice (2)	Sarah Fykes (nee Runnions)	Peter Eamer	**Dorothy Eamer**	Maria Margaret Warner	James Thompson	Solomon Tuttle (1) Solomon Noble (2)

Children of Henry Gallinger and Dorothy Eamer:

Catherine	Mary	Margaret	Michael H.	Philip	Allinder (Alia)	Henry	Christian (Christopher)	Elizabeth
B: ca. 1783	B: Feb 1786	B: 1788	B: ca. 1789	B: 1791	Bpt: 25 Nov 1792	B: 14 Feb 1794	B: 12 Nov 1795	B: June 1797
D: 1864	D:	D: 6 Sept 1860	D:	D:	D:	D:	D:	D:
M: ca. 1802	M:	M: ca. 1808	M: 19 Nov 1817	M:26 Aug 1823	M: ca. 1809	M: 20 Oct 1818	M: 3 Feb 1829	M:
John Farlinger	William Millroy	James Baker	Mary Switzer	Mary Morrison	John Johnson	Olive Alguire	Hannah Runnions	

Harriet	William	John	Jacob	Dorothy	Frances (Fanny)
B: ca. 1799	B: ca. 1801	B: ca. 1803	B: ca. 1805	B: 20 March 1807	Bpt: 1 May 1808
D:	D:	D:	D: 18 March 1889	D: 9 July 1862	D: 7 Jan 1879
M:	M:	M: ca. 1827	M: ca. 1829	M: ca. 1830	M: 26 Aug 1826
		Lucy	Warrender Leach	George Gordon Ross	William Bender

Family Record Sheet: Henry Gallinger and Dorothy Eamer

Reference

Husband: _Henry Gallinger____ 2
Born: _4 Sept 1761_Bpt. 14 Nov 1761____ Place Lot 85 Kingsborough Patent East,__________ 1
Near Johnstown, Albany County, New York.
Married _ca. 1783__________________ Place L'Assumption, Lower Canada, Quebec, Canada 2
Died: __16 Sept 1835________________ Place Concession 1, Lot 8 Cornwall Twp., Stormont Co. 3
Father: _Michael Gallinger B: 10 Jan 1726, Hopfau, Württemberg, Germany. Father: George 4/5/6/7/8
Gallinger, Mother: Anna Barbara Kübler. M: 2 Nov 1751,
Mother: ___Agatha Ade_ B; 20 Sept 1727, Durrenmettstetten, Baden, Germany. Father: Christian Ade,
Mother: Maria Catherine Kohler. D: After 22 Feb 1794, Cornwall Twp. Stormont Co. 4/5/6/7/9/10

Wife: _Dorothy Eamer____ 2
Born: __ca. 1761___________________ Place _Lot 59, Sacandaga Patent, Near Johnstown,___ 3
Albany Co., New York.
Died: __30 June 1831______________ Place _Concession 1, Lot 8 Cornwall, Stormont Co.__ 3
Father: ___Johannes Philip Wiemer/Eamer____
Mother: __Maria Catherine Leser/Liser____

References

1. Ancestry.com. *U.S., Dutch Reformed Church Records in Selected States, 1639-1989* [database on-line]. Provo, UT. The Archives of the Reformed Church in America; New Brunswick, New Jersey; *Stone Arabia Church, Baptisms, Members, Deaths, 1739-1987.* Henrich Galinger, B: 4 Sept. Bpt. 15 Nov 1761. Father: Michael, Mother: Agatha. Sponsors Henrich Dachstader, and Barbara Dachstader his daughter. **2.** Watt, Gavin K, Loyalist Refugees: Non-Military Refugees in Quebec 1776-1784. (Milton, On: Global Genealogy Press, 2014), The Refugee Roll, P. 165. Given Name: Gallinger Hendrick, Dorothy; Spouse: Wife Dorothea; Children 1F < 10; Locations Reported: L'Assumption, 24 Jan 1784, RT2, 1 Oct 1784; Remarks: Married in this province; Rank or Reg't Henry PTE 1 KRR, 1779-1783. Crowder, Norman, Early Ontario Settlers, A Source Book. (Baltimore, Genealogical Publishing, 1993), P. 42. Return of the Disbanded Troops and Loyalists settled in Township No. 2. Index No. B320 Hendrick Gollinger 1 man, 1 woman, 1 girl under 10, Rations per day 2 ½. Library and Archives Canada, British Library, formerly British Museum, Additional Manuscripts 21804-21834, Haldimand Papers. Lac_reel H 1655, Image 226. **3.** "Family Search" Church Records 1803-1846. Church of England in Canada, Trinity Church Cornwall, Ontario. Public Archives of Canada no.: MG9, D7, v.3. Died on the 16th and was buried on the 18th Sept. 1835. Henry Gollinger of the Township of Cornwall, aged 76. "Family Search" Church Records 1803-1846. Church of England in Canada, Trinity Church Cornwall, Ontario. Public Archives of Canada no.: MG9, D7, v.3. 1831, Dorothea Gallinger, wife of Henry Gollinger, age 70 years, died on 30th June and was buried on the 2d July 1831. D. Robertson Officiating Minister. P. 56 (472 of 519). **4.** Register of Baptisms Rev John Olgilvie Trinity Church New York, New York USA. Gallanger; 1759 2/25; District: Mohawks; Maria Cathrine, dau of Michael and Alida (Ady). Ancestry.com. *Württemberg, Germany, Lutheran Baptisms, Marriages, and Burials, 1500-1985* [database on-line]. Provo, UT. Taufen, Tote, Heiraten u Konfirmationen 1709-1876. Hopfau 2 Nov 1751. Ancestry.com. *Württemberg, Germany, Family Tables, 1550-1985* [database on-line]. Lehi, UT. Konfirmationen, Kommunionen, Familienbuch u· Seelenregister 1726-1876. Hopfau u. Neunthausen. P. 57. **5.** Ancestry.com. *Canada, Find A Grave Index, 1600s-Current* [database on-line]. Provo, UT. Ancestry.com. *Records of the Lutheran Trinity Church of Stone Arabia: in the town of Palatine, Montgomery County, N.Y.* [database on-line]. Provo, UT. Vol.1. Birth and baptisms, 1751 to 1815. P. 20. 1756. **6.** Worall, L. & Frolick, A., *The Gallinger Family: Ancestors and Descendants in Germany, the United States and Canada.* (Stormont, Dundas and Glengarry Genealogical Society, 2001). **7.** Ancestry.com. *Canada, Find A Grave Index, 1600s-Current* [database on-line]. Provo, UT. Militia Rolls of Upper Canada Roll of Captain Jeremiah French's Company April 3 1790. (Global Genealogy, 15 April 1998), Original Source: National Archives of Canada: NAC REference M.G. 19 F 35 Series 2, Lot 679, Pages 18-21. (Age) 68, Michel Gallinger, Royal Regiment of New York, 0,0,0,1,0. 1=infirm. Ancestry.com. *Württemberg, Germany, Lutheran Baptisms, Marriages, and Burials, 1500-1985* [database on-line]. Provo, UT. Taufen, Tote, Heiraten u Konfirmationen 1709-1876. Hopfau u. Neunthausen. OA Sulz. P. 288; 289. 2

Nov 1751. Georg Gallingers, Child: Michael Household Members: Michael Gallinger, Georg Gallinger, Agatha Adn, Christian Adn.

8. Ancestry.com. *Württemberg, Germany, Lutheran Baptisms, Marriages, and Burials, 1500-1985* [database on-line]. Provo, UT. *Taufen, Tote, Heiraten u Konfirmationen 1709-1876.* Hopfau u Neunthausen. Anna Maria Gallinger, Bpt. 12 Nov 1730.
9. 22 Feb 1794, Agatha and George Gallinger Sponsors at the Baptism of her Grandson Henrich, son of Henry Gallinger and Dorothea Eamer.
10. Ancestry.com. *Württemberg, Germany, Family Tables, 1550-1985* [database on-line]. Lehi, UT. *Konfirmationen, Kommunionen, Familienbuch u·Seelenregister 1726-1876.* Hopfau u. Neunthausen. Christian Ade. P. 104. Ancestry.com. *Württemberg, Germany, Lutheran Baptisms, Marriages, and Burials, 1500-1985* [database on-line]. Provo, UT. *Familienbuch, Taufen, Heiraten, Tote u Familienbücher 1558-1912.* Dürrenmettstetten u Vierundzwanzig Höfe. Christianus Ade. 12 Aug 1722.

Children

Name	Born	Married	Died
1. Catherine	ca. 1783, L'Assumption, Quebec	John Farlinger, ca. 1801, Cornwall Twp., Stormont Co.	Feb 1864, Charlottenburg, Glengarry Co.
2. Mary	Bpt: 11 Feb 1786, Cornwall Twp., Stormont Co	William Millroy, ca. 1804, Cornwall Twp., Stormont Co	
3. Margaret	ca. 1788, Cornwall Twp., Stormont Co.	James Baker, ca. 1806, Osnabruck Township, Stormont Co.	6 Sept 1860, Osnabruck Twp., Stormont Co.
4. Michael H.	ca. 1789, Cornwall Twp., Stormont Co.	Mary Switzer, 19 Nov 1817, Cornwall Twp., Stormont Co Catherine Barnhart, ca. 1830, Cornwall Twp., Stormont Co	After 1852, Cornwall Twp. Stormont Co.
5. Philip	1791, Cornwall Twp., Stormont Co.	Mary Morrison, (widow of Alexander Morrison) 26 Aug 1823, Cornwall Township, Stormont Co.	
6. Allinder (Alia)	Bpt: 25 Nov 1792, Cornwall Twp., Stormont Co.	John Johnson, ca. 1809, Cornwall Twp., Stormont Co	
7. Henry	14 Feb 1794, Bpt: 22 Feb 1794, Cornwall Twp., Stormont Co.	Olive Alguire, 20 Oct 1818, Cornwall Twp. Stormont Co.	ca. 1859 Bathurst Twp., Lanark Co., Ontario
8. Christian (Christopher)	12 Nov 1795, Bpt: 28 Dec 1795, Cornwall Twp., Stormont Co.	Hannah Runnions (widow of Benjamin Barnhart), 3 Feb 1829, Cornwall Twp., Stormont Co.	
9. Elizabeth	Bpt: 4 June 1797, Cornwall Twp., Stormont Co.		
10. Harriet	ca. 1799 Cornwall Twp. Stormont Co.		

11. William	ca. 1801, Cornwall Twp., Stormont Co.		
12. John	ca. 1803, Cornwall Twp., Stormont Co.	Lucy, ca. 1827, Brockville, Leeds and Grenville Cos., Ontario	Brockville, Leeds and Grenville Cos., Ontario
13. Jacob	ca. 1805, Cornwall Twp., Stormont co.	Warrender Leach, ca. 1829	18 March 1889, North Branch Twp., Lapeer Co., Michigan, USA
14. Dorothy	20 March 1807, Cornwall Twp., Stormont Co.	George Gordon Ross, ca. 1830, Cornwall Twp., Stormont Co.	9 July 1862, Cornwall Twp., Stormont Co.
15. Frances	Bpt: 1 May 1808, Cornwall Twp. Stormont Co.	William Bender, 29 Aug 1826, Cornwall Twp., Stormont Co.	7 Jan 1879, Cornwall Twp., Stormont Co.

APPENDIX G
Nicholas Silmser And Anna Margaret Eamer Descendant Chart

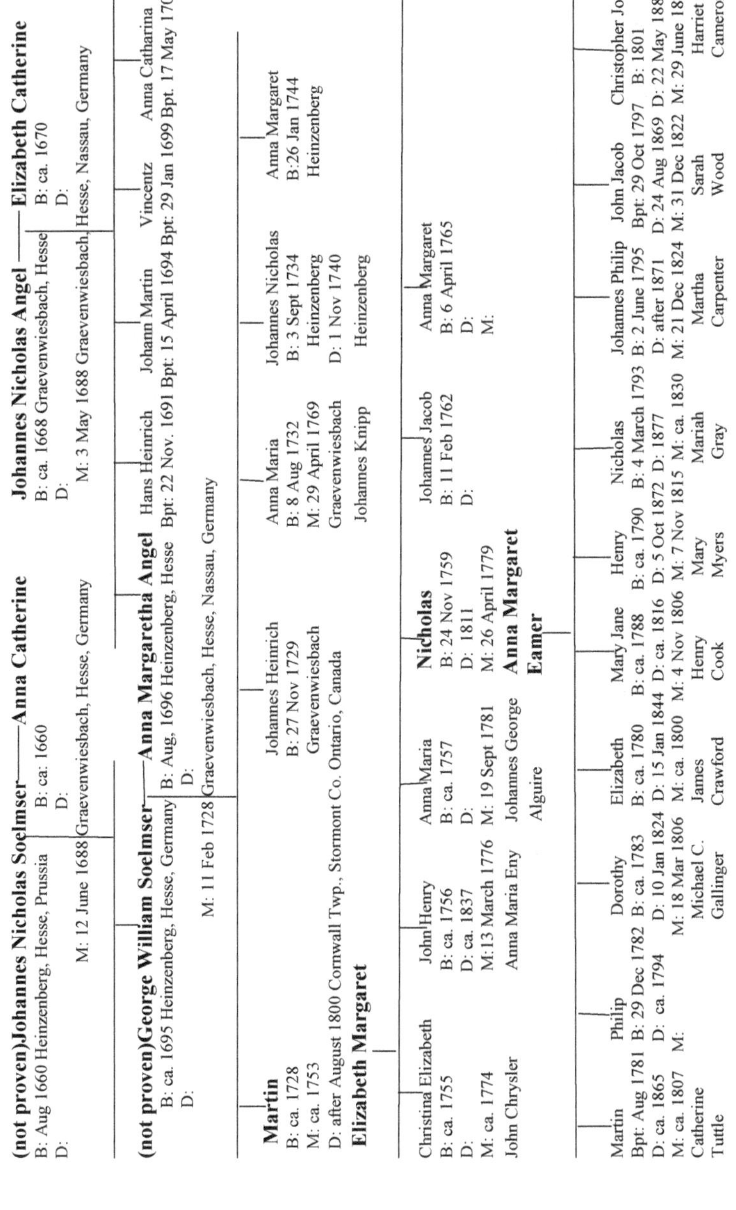

Family Record Sheet: Nicholas Silmser and Anna Margaret Eamer

		Reference
Husband: __Nicholas Silmser		2
Born: ___ca, 1758	Place Near Frankford, Philadelphia Co. Pennsylvania_	1/4
Married ___26 April 1779	Place __Caughnawaga, Tryon County, N.Y.	2
Died: _____1811	Place __Cornwall Twp. Stormont Co. Ontario	3
Father: __Martin Silmser_B: ca. 1728 ?Heinzenberg, Hesse, Germany		3/4/6/7/8
Mother: _Elizabeth Margareth_B: ca. 1724		5/6
Wife: _Anna Margaret Eamer		2/3
Born: ____ca. 1755	Place __Near Johnstown, Albany County, N.Y.	3
Died: ____9 Feb 1843	Place __Cornwall Township, Stormont Co.	3
Father: ___Johannes Philip Wiemer/Eamer		
Mother: __Maria Catherine Leser/Liser		

References

1. National Archives Canada, Militia Rolls of Upper Canada Rolls Captain Joseph Andersons April 2, 1790. National Archives of Canada. N.A.C. Reference: M.G. 19 F 35 Series 2, Lot 679, Pages 12-15. Nicholas Selemser Age 31, U.E., 1,0,0,0,1. **2.** Ancestry.com. *Records of the Reformed Protestant Dutch Church of Caughnawaga* [database on-line]. Provo, UT. Volume one. Marriages, 1772 to Jan. 31, 1818. P. 162. **3.** Will of Nicholas Silmser 23 June 1811. "Family Search" Church Records 1803-1846. Church of England in Canada, Trinity Church Cornwall, Ontario. Public Archives of Canada no.: MG9, D7, v.3. P. 119 (506 of 519). Burials from 1843 to 1845. Margaret Silmser died on the 9th of Feb 1843, aged 88 years and was buried on the 11th Feb 1843 by Mr. Alex Williams Rector of Cornwall. **4.** Ancestry.com. *Pennsylvania and New Jersey, Church and Town Records, 1669-2013* [database on-line]. Lehi, UT. Historical Society of Pennsylvania; Philadelphia, Pennsylvania; *Historic Pennsylvania Church and Town Records;* Reel: *1040. St Michael's Congregation. P. 42 Of 149.* 1758, Entry No: 29, Elizabethe Margretha Silmserin; How long in country: 4 yrs; How many children: 2; Age: ?. Ibid, 1758, Entry No. 138, Martin Simser, 4 years, Age 32. Ibid, 1759, Entry No. 90, Martin Silmser, 5 years, 3 children, Age 32. Ibid, 1756, Entry No. 19, Martin Simser, Frankford, 1 child, Age 29, Entry 20, Elisabeth Margretha, Age 32. Ibid, 1756, Entry No. 53, Martin Silmser, Frankfurth. **5.** Pennsylvania, Births and Christenings, 1709-1950," index, FamilySearch (https://familysearch.org/pal:/MM9.1.1/V2NZ-YCC: accessed 03 Sep 2012), Martin Silmser in entry for Anna Margreth Silmser, 14 Apr 1765; citing reference, FHL microfilm 1312257. Anna Margreth Silmser, Female, Christening, 14 Apr 1765 Philadelphia Philadelphia, Pennsylvania, Birth Date: 6 April 1765, Father's Name: Martin Silmser, Mother's Name: Elisabeth. **6.** Will of Martin Silmser, Stormont, Dundas and Glengarry Surrogate Court Records: Register Book A, pages 197-198. Microfilm Reel 862333. **7.** The Global Gazette, Militia Rolls of Upper Canada Colonel James Gray's Company February 10, 1789. Martin Silemser, 61, (marital status not shown), concession 3, lot 10, (no years of service shown), country (of origin) is Germany. **8.** Ancestry.com. *Germany, Select Marriages, 1558-1929* [database on-line]. Provo, UT. FHL Film Number: 943.41 V26K V. 1, 943.41 V26K V. 2. George Wilhelm Soelmser, Spouse: Anna Margaretha Angel, M: 11 Feb 1728, Graevenwiesbach, Hessen, Nassau, Prussia. **9.** Deutschland Geburten und Taufen, 1558-1898," database, *FamilySearch* (https://familysearch.org/ark:/61903/1:1:N89D-M7H: 10 February 2018), Johann Nickel Soelmser, 19 Aug 1660; citing; FHL microfilm 1180127 IT 2, 1180127 IT 3. Johann Nickel Soelmser, Bpt. 19 Aug 1660, Heinzenberg, Father: Hans George Soelmser. **10.** Deutschland Heiraten, 1558-1929," database, *FamilySearch* (https://familysearch.org/ark:/61903/1:1:V5PJ-8W2 : 11 February 2018), Johann Niclass Soelmser and Anna Catharina, 12 Jun 1688; citing Graevenwiesbach, Hessen-Nassau, Prussia; FHL microfilm 943.41 V26K V. 1, 943.41 V26K V. 2. Johann Niclass Soelmser, M. 12 June 1688. Graevenwiesbach, Hessen-Nassau, Prussia, Spouse, Anna Catherina.

Children

Name	Born	Married	Died
1. Elizabeth	B: ca. 1780 Near Johnstown, Tryon Co. N.Y.	James Crawford, ca. 1800, Cornwall Twp. Stormont Co.	15 Jan 1844, Cornwall Twp. Stormont Co.
2. Martin	Bpt. 25 Aug 1781, Schenectady, N.Y.	Catherine Tuttle, ca. 1807, Cornwall Twp. Stormont Co.	After 1850, Wilna Jefferson Co. N.Y.

3. Philip	B: 29 Dec 1782, Bpt. 10 Jan 1783, Caughnawaga, Tryon Co. N.Y.		ca. 1794 Cornwall Twp. Stormont Co.
4. Dorothy	B. ca. 1783 Montreal, Quebec	Michael Gallinger, 18 Mar, 1806, (s/o Christopher Gallinger & Sarah Fykes/Runnions) Cornwall Twp. Stormont Co.	10 Jan 1824, Barnhart's Island, Cornwall Twp. Stormont Co.
5. Mary Jane	B: ca. 1788, Cornwall Twp. Stormont Co.	Henry Cook, 4 Nov 1806,	ca. 1816, Cornwall Twp. Stormont Co.
6. Henry	B: ca. 1790, Cornwall Twp. Stormont Co.	Mary Myers, 7 Nov 1815, Cornwall Twp. Stormont Co.	5 Oct 1872, Cornwall Twp. Stormont Co.
7. Nicholas	B: 4 March 1793, Cornwall Twp. Stormont Co.	Mariah Gray, ca. 1830, Barnhart's Island, N.Y. USA	1877, Massena, St. Lawrence Co. N.Y.
8. Johannes Philip	B: 2 June 1795, Cornwall Twp. Stormont Co.	Martha Carpenter, 21 Dec 1824, Cornwall Twp. Stormont Co.	After 1871, Cornwall Twp. Stormont Co.
9. John Jacob	Bpt: 29 Oct 1797, Cornwall Twp. Stormont Co.	Sarah Wood, 31 Dec, 1822, Cornwall Twp. Stormont Co.	24 Aug 1869, Osnabruck Twp. Stormont Co.
10. Christopher John	B: 1801, Cornwall Twp. Stormont Co.	Harriet Cameron, 29 June, 1822, Cornwall Twp. Stormont Co.	22 May 1885, near Limoges, Prescott-Russell Co.

Will of Nicholas Silmser – 23 June 1811

In the Name of God Amen I Nicholas Silmser of the Township of Cornwall in the Eastern District of the Province of Upr. Canada Yeoman being sick in body but of perfect mind & memory thanks to God. Calling to mind the Morality of my body & knowing that is appointed for all men once to die, do make this my last will and Testament viz. First I Recommend my soul to God that gave it and my body I recommend to the earth to be buried in a Christian like manner at the discretion of my Friend Nothing Doubting but at the General Resurrections, I shall receive the same again by the mighty Power of God, and as Touching such world by estate with which it has pleased God to bless me in this life. I give, devise, and dispose of in the following Manner and form.

First I give and bequeath to Margaret my beloved wife all the Produce and grain and all the stock upon farm Whereon I now dwell being lott No 7 Second concession in the rear of Cornwall. Together with all the household Furniture and Utensils the aforesaid farm and Stock to remain in her hand and for her use during her widowhood.

Second I give and bequeath to Martin Silmser my eldest son Five Shillings and Six pence. Third I give and bequeath to Henry Silmser my second son Fifty acres of the aforesaid lott No 7 in the Second concession to be at his disposal on the day of her my widows Marriage if that should ever happen or on the day of my said widows decease. Fourthly I give and bequeath to Nicolas Silmser my Third son Fifty acres of land of the said lott No 7 in the second Concession to be at his disposal on the day of my aforesaid widows Marriage or her decease. Fifthly I give and bequeath to Philip Silmser my Fourth son Sixty Six acres of land being part of lott No 33 Fourth concession of Osnaburg. Sixthly I give and bequeath to John Silmser my Fifth son Sixty Six acres of land being part of lott No. 33 in the Fourth Concession of Osnaburg. Seventhly I give and bequeath to Christopher Silmser my sixth son sixty six acres of land being part of lott No 33 in the Fourth Concession of Osnaburg aforesaid. Eightly I give and bequeath to Elizabeth my eldest daughter and wife to James Crawford, Fifty acres land being part lott No 5 Third Concession of Cornwall. Ninethly I give and bequeath to Dorothy my Second daughter wife to Michael Gallinger One Cow. Tenthly I give and bequeath to Mary my Third daughter and wife to Henry Cook, One Cow... Not forgetting that all my lawfull debts shall be paid out of my aforesaid effects and Thereby Confirm that my Farm whereon I now live already described shall remain in Margaret Silmers my wifes lawfull posesson as long as she remains my widow, and Thereby Ordain Constitute and appoint Margaret my wife also Henry Wagoner & Matthias Snitsinger my executors of this my last will and testament and I hereby ratify and confirm this to be my last will and Testament... In witness whereof I have hereunto set my hand and Seal this Twenty Third day of June in the year of Our Lord one Thousand and Eight Hundred and Eleven.

Will of Martin Silmser
20 August 1800
Cornwall Township, Stormont County, Ontario, Canada
Stormont, Dundas and Glengarry Surrogate Court Records: Register Book A, pages 197-198
Microfilm Reel 862333
In the name of God Amen the 20th day of August Anni Domini one thousand Eight hundred 1 martin Silmser of the Town of Cornwall and County of Stormont and province of upper Canada. Farmer being very sick and weak in body but of perfect mind and Memory thanks be unto God...therefore calling unto Mind the Mortality of my Body and Knowing that it is appointed for all men once to die, do make and ordain this my last will and testament, that is to say principally, and first of all I give and recommend my soul into the hands of God that gives it and my Body I recommend to the Earth to be buried in decent Christian Burial at the discretion of my Executors nothing doubting but at the General resurrection I shall receive the same again by the Power of God and as touching such worldly estate wherewith it hath pleased God to bless me in this life. I give demise and dispose of in the following manner and form... Imprimis I give and bequeath to Elizabeth Margarate my dearly beloved wife of this my last will and testament all and singular my lands, My wages and Tinaments together with all my Household Goods, Debts and Moveable Effects by her freely to be possessed and enjoyed during her life and after my said beloved wife has departed this life thin the whole estate shall be divided unto my four Children as follows, my son John Henry shall have five Shilling Sterling and my son John Nicolas the half of my estate the other half of my estate shall equally divided unto my two Daughters Christina Elizabeth wife of John Crysler and Anna Mary the wife of John Algire.
And I do hereby utterly disallow revoke and dis an ull all and every other former Testaments wills legacies and bequeaths and Executors by me in any ways before named willed and bequeathed ratifying and confirming this and no other to be my last Will and Testament. In witness where of I have here unto Set my hand and seal the day and year above writtend.
(signed) Martin Silmser
Signed sealed Published pronounced and declared by ....

APPENDIX H
Tenants Of The Kingsborough And Sacandaga Patents

Residences of Tenants on the Kingsborough Patent

Name	Patent and Lot No.	Initial	Source
Christopher Service Sr.	Kingsborough West - No. 398	CS	1. Duncan Fraser
Peter Service Sr.	West – No. 400	PS	"
Martin Waldorf	West – No. 78	MW	"
Simon Clark	West – No. 95	SC	
Adam Ruppert Sr.	West –No. 77	AR	"
Christian Wert	West – No. 65	CW	"
Johannes Wert	West – No. 66	JW	"
Johannes Albrandt	West – No 75	JA	"
Johannes Dorn Sr.	West – No. 74	JD	"
Andrew Snyder	West – No. 67	AS	"
Nicholas Shaver	West – No. 73	NS	"
David Jeacocks	West – No. 68	DJ	"
George Schenck Sr.	West – No. 63	GS	"
Peter Fykes Sr.	West – No. 70	PF	"
Johannes Buys	West – No. 98	JB	"
Peter Buys	West – No. 71	PB	"
Jeremey Buys	West – No. 145	JB	
Johannes Hawn	West – No. 83	JH	"
Johannes Hertle Sr.	West – No. 43	JH	"
Edward Foster	West – No. 58	EF	"
Johannes Van Koughnot	West – No. 16	JVK	"
Johannes Shaver	West – No. 13	JS	"
Jacob Seeber	West – No. 72	JS	"
Johannes Ault	West – No. 42	JA	"
William Lottridge	West – No. 15	WL	"
Michael Byrne	West – No 76	MB	"
Henry Hough Jr.	West – No. 61	HH	"
Michael Galllinger Sr.	Kingsborough East – No 85	MG	"
Lawrence Eaman	East – No. 91	LE	2. New York State Archives
Mattheaus Link Sr.	East – No. 84	ML	1. Duncan Fraser 2. New York State Archives
Johannes Pickle	East – No. 84	JP	1. Duncan Fraser
John Farlinger Sr.	East – No. 90	JF	"
Philip Hendrick Klein	East – No. 95	PK	"
George Crites Sr.	East No. 87	GC	"
Dr. William Adams	East No. 86	WA	"
Henry Hawn	East No. 82	HH	
Robert Adams	East No. 80	RA	"
John Butler	East No. 92	JB	"
Anthony Walliser/Philip Pitet	East No. 83	AW/PP	"
John Friel	East No. 114	JF	"
Frederick Waggoner	East No. 115	FW	"
Jacob Crieghoof	East No. 112	JC	"
William Fraser	East No. 122	WF	
Hugh Fraser	East No. 123	HF	
Lodowyck Putnam	East No. 124	LP	"
Peter Young	East No. 125	PY	"
Joseph Hanes Sr.	East No. 157	JH	"
Michael Harps	East No. 167	MH	

Jacob Sheets Sr.	East No. 190	JS	"
Michael Carmen Sr.	East No. 191	MC	"
James Bennet	East No. 148	JB	1. Duncan Fraser 3. Maryly Penrose
Nathaniel Davis	East No. 107	ND	2. New York State Archives
George Adam Dachstader	Kingsborough East No lot given		1. Duncan Fraser
George Bender	Kingsborough West No lot given		"
Hans Jury (Johannes George) Crites	No lot given		"
Peter Service Jr.	No lot given		"
Jacob Waggoner	No lot given		"
Henry Fikes	No lot given		"
John Wait	No lot given		"
Jacob Van Koughnot	No lot given		"
Christian Sheek	No lot given		"
John Jeacocks	No lot given		"
David McEwan	No lot given		"
John Murchison Jr.	No lot given		"
Thomas Allen	No lot given		"
George Ruppert	Kingsborough East No lot given		"
Lucas Feader Sr.	No lot given		1. Duncan Fraser 4. Ancestry.com. UK, American Loyalist Claims 5. Library and Archives Canada

Sources

1. Duncan Fraser, Papers and Records of the Ontario Historical Society, Volume LII, 1960, Original Source, Public Record Office, London, England AC 13/114. *Sir John Johnson's Rent Roll of the Kingsborough Patent.*

2. New York State Archives, *Maps of Lots in the Village of Johnstown, Fulton County,* New York (State). State Engineer and Surveyor. Survey maps of lands in New York State, ca. 1711-1913. Series A0273-78, Map #875, Identifier NYSA_A0273-78_875.

3. Maryly B. Penrose, *Compendium of Early Mohawk Valley Families.* Vol 1 (Baltimore, Genealogical Publishing Co., 1990), 30.

4. Ancestry.com. *UK, American Loyalist Claims, 1776-1835* [database on-line]. Provo, UT. Piece 021: Evidence, New York, 1785-1786. 417. Evidence on the Foregoing Memorial of Lieut. Col. John Butler.

5. Library and Archives Canada, *Upper Canada Land Petitions (1763-1865),* Mikan Number: 205131 Microform: c-1893, Image 489.

Residences of Tenants on the Sacandaga Patent

Name	Patent and Lot No.	Initial	Source
Philip Eamer	Sacandaga - Lot No. 59	PE	1. Ancestry.com. UK, American Loyalist Claims
Martin Loefler Sr.	Sacandaga – Lot No. 84	ML	2. William Stone
Jacob Myers Sr.	Sacandaga – Lot No. 44	JM	3. Duncan Fraser 2. William Stone 4. Ancestry.com. New York, Sales of Loyalist Land
Michael Carman Jr.	Sacandaga – Lot No. 43	MC	4. Ancestry.com. New York, Sales of Loyalist Land. 5. Ancestry.com. UK, American Loyalist Claims 6. "Three Rivers"
Jacob Ross	Sacandaga – Lot No. 43	JR	6. "Three Rivers"
Hans Jury (Johannes George) Hough	Sacandaga – No lot given		3. Duncan Fraser
Valentine Cryderman	Sacandaga – No lot given		7. Ancestry.com. UK, American Loyalist Claims
Angus McDonell	Sacandaga – Lot No. 55	AM	3. Duncan Fraser

Sources

1. Ancestry.com. *UK, American Loyalist Claims, 1776-1835* [database on-line]. Provo, UT. Piece 031: Evidence, New York, 1787-1788. Evidence on the Claim of Philip Eamer. 276.

2. William Stone, *The Life and Times of Sir William Johnson, Bart., Vol II* (Albany, J. Munsell, 1865), 499, 497.

3. Duncan Fraser, Papers and Records of the Ontario Historical Society, Volume LII, 1960, Original Source, Public Record Office, London, England AC 13/114. *Sir John Johnson's Rent Roll of the Kingsborough Patent.*

4. Ancestry.com. *New York, Sales of Loyalist Land, 1762-1830* [database on-line]. Provo, UT. Original data: New York State Engineer and Surveyor. Records of Surveys and Maps of State Lands, 1686–1892, Series A4016, Vols. 7–10 and 17. New York State Archives, Albany, New York. 169.

5. Ancestry.com. *UK, American Loyalist Claims, 1776-1835* [database on-line]. Provo, UT. *Piece 027: Evidence, New York, 1787. Evidence on the Claim of Michl Carman. 409-411.*

6. "Three Rivers Hudson, Mohawk, Schoharie, History From America's Most Famous Valleys." http://threeriversshms.com/simmswillswj.htm

7. Ancestry.com. *UK, American Loyalist Claims, 1776-1835* [database on-line]. Provo, UT. Piece 029: Evidence, New York, 1787-1788. 323. Evidence on the Claim of Cathrine Cryderman Widow of Valentine Cryderman.

APPENDIX I
Tenants Of Johnstown Ca. 1777

Tenants of Johnstown ca. 1777

Name	Lot	Source
St. John's Church and Cemetery		2. Fulton County NYGenWeb
Christian Sheek – Blacksmith	Lot 1 and 2, 18 acres	1. Loyalist Claim
Court House	Lot 3	2. Fulton County NYGenWeb
Robert Picken – Surveyor	Lot 4	3. Sales of Loyalist Land 4. Duncan Fraser
John Lonie - Shoemaker	5 acres	4. Duncan Fraser 5. Loyalist Claim
Brian Lafferty – Lawyer	Lot 6	6. Sales of Loyalist Lands 4. Duncan Fraser
Johannes Eberhardt Van Koughnot Sr. – Tanner	Lot 7	7. Loyalist Claim 4. Duncan Fraser
Michael Cline – Gunsmith/Blacksmith	1 acre	8. Loyalist Claim 4. Duncan Fraser
Donald Ross	15 acres	9. Loyalist Claim
Randel McDonell		10. Loyalist Claim
John Fraser – Weaver		11. Loyalist Claim
School House	Lot 11	2. Fulton County NYGenWeb
John Little	Lot 12	12. Fulton County NYGenWeb
William Wallace		13. Pension Application
Gilbert Tice	Lot 13	14. Loyalist Claim 2. Fulton County NYGenWeb 4. Duncan Fraser
William Philips Jr. - Miller		15. Loyalist Claim 4. Duncan Fraser
Edward Wall – School Teacher	Lot 17	2. Fulton County NYGenWeb
Angus McDonell	8 acres	16. Loyalist Claim
Jail – Fort Johnstown		2. Fulton County NYGenWeb
James Bennett	Lot	17. Loyalist Claim American Loyalist Migrations
John McDonell	6 acres	18. Loyalist Claim

Sources

1. Ancestry.com. *UK, American Loyalist Claims, 1776-1835* [database on-line]. Provo, UT. The National Archives of the UK; Kew, Surrey, England; American Loyalist Claims, Series I; Class: AO 13; Piece 029: Evidence, New York, 1787-1788. 367-369. Evidence on the Claim of Christian Schick late of Tryon County.

2. "Fulton County NYGenWeb" Jeanette Shiel, Johnstown Historical Society Visitor's Guide. 2001. http://fulton.nygenweb.net/history/johnsvisit.html

3. Ancestry.com. *New York, Sales of Loyalist Land, 1762-1830* [database on-line]. Provo, UT. Original data: New York State Engineer and Surveyor. Records of Surveys and Maps of State Lands, 1686–1892, Series A4016, Vols. 7–10 and 17. New York State Archives, Albany, New York. *Page* 182 a-b.

4. Duncan Fraser, Papers and Records of the Ontario Historical Society, Volume LII, 1960, Original Source, Public Record Office, London, England AC 13/114. *Sir John Johnson's Rent Roll of the Kingsborough Patent.*

5. Ancestry.com. *UK, American Loyalist Claims, 1776-1835* [database on-line]. Provo, UT. *Piece 032: Evidence, New York, 1788. 234.* Original data: American Loyalist Claims, 1776–1835. AO 12–13. The National Archives of the United Kingdom, Kew, Surrey, England. Evidence on the claim of John Lonnie. John Lonnie's house and lot was a gift from Sir. William Johnson.

6. Ancestry.com. *New York, Sales of Loyalist Land, 1762-1830* [database on-line]. Provo, UT. New York State Engineer and Surveyor. Records of Surveys and Maps of State Lands, 1686–1892, Series A4016, Vols. 7–10 and 17. *Page 170.*

7. Ancestry.com. *UK, American Loyalist Claims, 1776-1835* [database on-line]. Provo, UT. Original data: American Loyalist Claims, 1776–1835. AO 12–13. The National Archives of the United Kingdom, Kew, Surrey, England. 354-356. Evidence on the Claim of Michael VanKoughnet late of Tryon County.

8. Ancestry.com. *UK, American Loyalist Claims, 1776-1835* [database on-line]. Provo, UT. The National Archives of the UK; Kew, Surrey, England; American Loyalist Claims, Series I; Class: AO 13; Piece 031: Evidence, New York, 1787-1788. 268-269. Evidence on the Claim of Michal Clene late of Tryon Co.

9. Ancestry.com. *UK, American Loyalist Claims, 1776-1835* [database on-line]. Provo, UT. The National Archives of the UK; Kew, Surrey, England; American Loyalist Claims, Series I; Class: AO 13; Piece 029: Evidence, New York, 1787-1788. 53-54. Evidence on the Claim of Donald Ross late of Tryon County.

10. Ancestry.com. *UK, American Loyalist Claims, 1776-1835* [database on-line]. Provo, UT. The National Archives of the UK; Kew, Surrey, England; American Loyalist Claims, Series I; Class: AO 13; Piece 031: Evidence, New York, 1787-1788. 26. Evidence on the claim of Ronald McDonell.

11. Ancestry.com. *UK, American Loyalist Claims, 1776-1835* [database on-line]. Provo, UT, USA: Ancestry.com Operations, Inc., 2013. Evidence on the claim of John Fraser. Original data: American Loyalist Claims, 1776–1835. AO 12–13. The National Archives of the United Kingdom, Kew, Surrey, England.

12. James F. Morrison. Captain John Little. https://fulton.nygenweb.net/military/little.html

13. The National Archives. *Revolutionary War Pension and Bounty Land Warrant Application Files.* M804. Pension No. S.26,849. Record Group 15. Roll 2480. Page 79. Pension Application of William Wallace.

14. Ancestry.com. *UK, American Loyalist Claims, 1776-1835* [database on-line]. Provo, UT. Original data: American Loyalist Claims, 1776–1835. AO 12–13. The National Archives of the United Kingdom, Kew, Surrey, England. The National Archives of the UK; Kew, Surrey, England; American Loyalist

Claims, Series I; Class: AO 12; Piece 086: Documents Communicated by New York State Government, 1786.

15. Ancestry.com. *UK, American Loyalist Claims, 1776-1835* [database on-line]. Provo, UT. The National Archives of the UK; Kew, Surrey, England; *American Loyalist Claims, Series I;* Class: *AO 13; Piece 027: Evidence, New York, 1787. 405-406. Evidence on the Claim of Wm Philips late of New York.*

16. Ancestry.com. *UK, American Loyalist Claims, 1776-1835* [database on-line]. Provo, UT. Original data: American Loyalist Claims, 1776–1835. AO 12–13. The National Archives of the United Kingdom, Kew, Surrey, England. *Piece 031:* Evidence, New York, 1787-1788. 92-93. Evidence on the Claim of Angus McDonell late of Tryon County.

17. Ancestry.com. *American (Loyalist) Migrations, 1765-1799* [database on-line]. Provo, UT. Original data: Coldham, Peter Wilson. *American Migrations 1765-1799: The lives, times, and families of colonial Americans who remained loyal to the British Crown before, during and after the Revolutionary War, as related in their own words and through their correspondence*. James Bennett, *New York*. 180. Baltimore, MD, USA: Genealogical Publishing Co., 2000.

18. Ancestry.com. *UK, American Loyalist Claims, 1776-1835* [database on-line]. Provo, UT. The National Archives of the UK; Kew, Surrey, England; American Loyalist Claims, Series I; Class: AO 13; Piece: 031. Evidence, New York, 1787-1788. 179-180. Evidence on the claim of John McDonel.

CORRECTIONS

Just before publication of the book, I located the online parish records of Trinity Anglican Church in Cornwall, Ontario. Finding burial records that gave the age at death allowed me to correct some inaccurate birth dates in this book.

1. Anna Margaret Silmser (nee Eamer) died on 9 Feb 1843 at the age of 88. Therefore, she was born ca. 1755 and not 1762 as told in this book. Perhaps she was born just prior to Philip and Catrina's journey and crossed the ocean as an infant.
2. Dorothy Gallinger (nee Eamer) died on 30 June 1831 at the age of 70. Therefore, she was born ca. 1761 and not 1765 as told in this book.
3. Michael Gallinger Jr. died 3 May 1827 at the age of 76. Therefore, he was born ca. 1751 and not 1757 as told in this book. He too would have made the journey across the ocean with his parents in 1754.
4. Elizabeth Silmser, daughter of Nicholas and Anna Margaret, died on 15 Jan 1844 at the age of 63. Elizabeth's brother Martin was baptized 25 August 1781. Therefore, Elizabeth must have been born ca. 1780 and not 1784 as told in this book.

WORKS CITED

Abler, Thomas S. "KAIEÑ?KWAAHTOÑ," in *Dictionary of Canadian Biography*. Vol. 4, University of Toronto/Université Laval, 2003. http://www.biographi.ca/en/bio/kaienkwaahton_4E.html

Access Genealogy. "Mohawk Indian Villages and Towns." Last Modified, October 11, 2013. https://www.accessgenealogy.com/native/mohawk-indian-villages-and-towns.htm

Allen, Thomas B. *Tories Fighting for the King in America's First Civil War*. Toronto: Harper, 2010.

"American Archives. Documents of the American Revolutionary Period, 1774-1776." Address of Governour Tryon to the Inhabitants of the Colony of New York. Address of Inhabitiants of New York to Governour Tryon. Affidavit of Johnathan French of Tryon County, Jan 11, 1776. http://amarch.lib.niu.edu/islandora/object/niu-amarch%3A89441

Ancestry.com. "England, Select Marriages, 1538–1973." [database on-line]. Provo, UT. England, Marriages, 1538–1973. Salt Lake City, Utah: FamilySearch, 2013.

Ancestry.com. New York State Archives. "New York, Sales of Loyalist Land, 1762-1830." [database on-line]. Provo, UT, USA: 2013. Original data: New York State Engineer and Surveyor. Records of Surveys and Maps of State Lands, 1686–1892, Series A4016, Vols. 7–10 and 17. New York State Archives. Albany: New York.

Ancestry.com. "The Old United Empire Loyalists List [database on-line]. Provo, UT. Appendix B." Original data: Centennial Committee. The Old United Empire Loyalists List. Baltimore: 1969.

Ancestry.com. "Pennsylvania and New Jersey, Church and Town Records, 1669-1999." [database on- line]. Lehi, UT, USA: Ancestry.com Operations, Inc., 2011. Historical Society of Pennsylvania; Philadelphia, Pennsylvania; Collection Name: Historic Pennsylvania Church and Town Records; Reel: 1040. St Michael's Congregation.

Ancestry.ca. Online publication Provo, UT: "Records of the Lutheran Trinity Church of Stone Arabia: in the town of Palatine, Montgomery County, N.Y." New York, unknown, 1914, Vol I Marriages.

Ancestry.com. Early Families of Herkimer County, New York. [database on-line]. Provo, UT.

Ancestry.com. "Records of the Lutheran Trinity Church of Stone Arabia: in the town of Palatine, Montgomery County, N.Y." [database on-line]. Provo, UT. Vol.1. Introduction. xxi.

Ancestry.com. "Records of the Lutheran Trinity Church of Stone Arabia: in the town of Palatine, Montgomery County, N.Y." [database on-line]. Provo, UT. Vol.1. Birth and baptisms, 1751 to 1815.

Ancestry.com. "Records of the Reformed Dutch Church of Stone Arabia: in the town of Palatine, Montgomery County, N.Y." [database on-line]. Provo, UT. Vol.1. Marriages, Oct. 16, 1739 to 1795.

Ancestry.com. "Records of the Reformed Dutch Church of Stone Arabia: in the town of Palatine, Montgomery County, N.Y." [database on-line]. Provo, UT. Vol.1. Register of members, Jan. 13, 1739 to 1795.

Ancestry.com. "Records of the Lutheran Trinity Church of Stone Arabia: in the town of Palatine, Montgomery County, N.Y." [database on-line]. Provo, UT: Ancestry.com Operations Inc, 2005.

Ancestry.com. "Records of the Reformed Dutch Church of Stone Arabia: in the town of Palatine, Montgomery County, N.Y." [database on-line]. Provo, UT: Ancestry.com Operations Inc, 2005.

Ancestry.com. "Register of baptisms, marriages, communicants, & funerals begun by Henry Barclay at Fort Hunter, January 26th, 1734 /5": regist [database on-line]. Provo, UT. Register book. 20.

Ancestry.com. "U.S., Dutch Reformed Church Records in Selected States, 1639-1989." [database on- line]. Provo, UT. Holland Society of New York; New York, New York; Schenectady Baptisms, Vol 3, Book 43. 276.

Ancestry.com. "UK, American Loyalist Claims, 1776-1835 [database on-line]. Provo, UT. Original data: American Loyalist Claims, 1776–1835. AO 12–13. The National Archives of the United Kingdom, Kew, Surrey, England. The National Archives of the UK; Kew, Surrey, England; American Loyalist Claims, Series I; Class: AO 12; Piece 086: Documents Communicated by New York State Government, 1786.

Ancestry.com. "UK, American Loyalist Claims, 1776-1835." [database on-line]. Provo, UT. Original data: American Loyalist Claims, 1776–1835. AO 12–13. The National Archives of the United Kingdom, Kew, Surrey, England. Piece 086: Documents Communicated by New York State Government, 1786. 128. Schedule of Convictions in the State of New York.

Ancestry.com. "UK, American Loyalist Claims, 1776-1835" [database on-line]. Provo, UT, USA: Ancestry.com Operations, Inc., 2013. Original data: American Loyalist Claims, 1776–1835. AO 12–13. The National Archives of the United Kingdom, Kew, Surrey, England. UK, American Loyalist Claims, 1776-1835 for Philip Eamer AO 12: American Loyalists Claims, Series I Piece 031: Evidence, New York, 1787-1788.

Ancestry.com. "UK, American Loyalist Claims, 1776-1835." [database on-line]. Provo, UT. American Loyalist Claims, 1776–1835. AO 12–13. The National Archives of the United Kingdom, Kew, Surrey, England. Piece 054: Temporary Assistance B-V, New York. Claim of Daniel Claus Esq.

Ancestry.com. "U.S., Dutch Reformed Church Records in Selected States, 1639-1989." [database on- line]. Provo, UT, USA: Ancestry.com Operations, Inc., 2014. Holland Society of New York; New York, New York; Schenectady Baptisms, Vol 2, Book 42.

Ancestry.com. "U.S., Dutch Reformed Church Records in Selected States, 1639-1989." [database on- line]. Provo, UT, USA: Ancestry.com Operations, Inc., 2014. The Archives of the Reformed Church in America; New Brunswick, New Jersey; Reformed Church of Fonda, Baptisms, Marriages, Members, Consistory Minutes, 1758-1839.

Ancestry.com. "U.S., Dutch Reformed Church Records in Selected States, 1639-1989." [database on- line]. Provo, UT. Holland Society of New York; New York, New York; New York City Lutheran, Vol III, Book 87.

Ancestry.com. "U.S., Dutch Reformed Church Records in Selected States, 1639-1989."[database on- line]. Provo, UT, USA: Ancestry.com Operations, Inc., 2014. The Archives of the Reformed Church in America; New Brunswick, New Jersey; Stone Arabia Church, Baptisms, Members, Deaths, 1739-1987.

Ancestry.com. "U.S., Dutch Reformed Church Records in Selected States, 1639-1989." [database on- line]. Provo, UT, USA: Ancestry.com Operations, Inc., 2014. Albany, Vol III, Book 3. 221.

Ancestry.com. "Württemberg, Germany, Family Tables, 1550-1985." [database on-line]. Lehi, UT, USA: Ancestry.com Operations, Inc., 2016. Konfirmationen, Kommunionen, Familienbuch u· Seelenregister 1726-1876.

The Annotated Newspapers of Harbottle Dorr Jr. "The Boston-Gazette, and Country Journal." 12 March 1770. 27 June 1774. Massachusetts Historical Society, 2018. http://www.masshist.org/dorr/volume/3/sequence/101

Atkinson, Sam. *The Casket. Flowers of Literature, Wit & Sentiment for 1829*. Philadelphia: Sam Atkinson, 1829.

Bannerman, Gordon. *Merchants and the Military in Eighteenth Century Britain: British Army Contracts and Domestic Supply, 1739-1763.* New York: Routledge, 2016.

Barber, J.W. & Howe, H. *Historical Collections of the State of New York.* New York, S. Tuttle, 1846. https://archive.org/stream/historicalcollec00barbny#page/170/mode/2up

Berry, Joyce, "Witch Hunts." Original documents at the Montgomery County Department of History and Archives, Fonda, New York. www.hvv.org

Berry, Stephen. *A Path in the Mighty Waters: Shipboard Life and Atlantic Crossings to the New World.* New Haven: Yale University Press, 2015.

Bibliothèque et Archives Nationales Quebec. *Mariages non catholiques de la région de Montréal, 1766- 1899.* Centre d'archives de Montréal, CE601,S63.

Bielinski, Stephan. "The People of Colonial Albany Live Here," *Abraham H Wendell.* Last modified, October 4, 2007. http://exhibitions.nysm.nysed.gov/albany/bios/w/abwendell2740.html

Bielinski, Stephan. "The People of Colonial Albany Live Here," *The Sacandaga Patent.* Last modified, December 10, 2009. http://exhibitions.nysm.nysed.gov/albany/na/sacandaga.html

The Book of Names Especially Relating to the Early Palatines and the First Settlers in the Mohawk Valley. "The Kocherthal Records: A Translation of the Kocherthal Records of the West Camp Lutheran Church," Translated by Christian Kramer. St. Johnsville: The Enterprise and News, 1933. http://www.threerivershms.com/nameskocherthal.htm

Boonshoft, Mark. *Dispossessing Loyalists and Redistributing Property in Revolutionary New York,* (New York Public Library, 19 September 2016) https://www.nypl.org/blog/2016/09/19/loyalist-property-confiscation

Borneman, Walter. *The French and Indian War: Deciding the Fate of North America.* Toronto: Harper Perennial, 2007.

Bower, Wayne. "Registers of the Parishes of Williamsburg, Matilda, Osnabruck, and Edwardsburg." Burial Registers of the Parishes of Williamsburg, Matilda, Osnabruck, and Edwardsburg. Last modified February 27, 2016.

Bowler, R. "JESSUP, EDWARD," in *Dictionary of Canadian Biography*, Vol. 5. Toronto, University of Toronto/Université Laval, 2003. http://www.biographi.ca/en/bio/jessup_edward_5E.html

Boyd, Julian, P. "Joseph Galloway's Plans of Union for the British Empire, 1774-1788." *The Pennsylvania Magazine of History and Biography 64,* no. 4 (1940): 492-515. http://www.jstor.org/stable/20087321.

Braisted, Todd. "Refugees & Others: Loyalist Families in the American War for Independence." *The Brigade Dispatch, Parts 1 & 2* Volume XXVI no. 4, 2-7; Vol XXVII no 2, 2-6.

Carver, Jonathan, and Robert Sayer and John Bennett. *A new map of the Province of Quebec, according to the Royal Proclamation, of the 7th of October*. London, Printed for Robt. Sayer and John Bennett, 1776. Map. https://www.loc.gov/item/74694799/.

Colonial Williamsburg Digital Library. Vineyard, Ron. "Stage Wagons and Coaches". Last Modified August, 2000. Colonial Willamsburg Foundation Library Research Report Series RR0380. Colonial Williamsburg Foundation Library, Williamsburg, Virginia, August 2002. http://research.history.org/DigitalLibrary/View/index.cfm?doc=ResearchReports%5CRR0380.xml

Cruikshank, E.A. and Watt, Gavin K. *The History and Master Roll of the King's Royal Regiment of New York, Appendix III.* Revised ed., image reprint CD. Milton, Ont: Global Heritage Press, 2006, 2010.

Cruikshank, E.A., *The King's Royal Regiment of New York.* Gavin Watt, ed. Toronto: The Ontario Historical Society, 1931 Reprinted Toronto, 1984.

Cruickshank, E.A. *Butler's Rangers. The Revolutionary Period.* Welland Ont: Tribune Printing House, 1893. https://www.gutenberg.ca/ebooks/cruikshank-butlers/cruikshank-butlers-00-h-dir/cruikshank-butlers-00-h.html

Bonaparte, Darren. "Wampum Chronicles. The Mohawk Longhouse." http://www.wampumchronicles.com/mohawklonghouses.html

Boston Tea Party Ships Museum. "Boston Tea Party: A Revolutionary Experience." The Committees of Correspondence: The Voice of the Patriots. 2018. https://www.bostonteapartyship.com/committees-of-correspondence

Campbell, William W. *Annals of Tryon County; or, The Border Warfare of New York, During The Revolution.* New York: J. & J. Harper, 1831. https://archive.org/stream/annalsoftryoncou00camp#page/n37/mode/2up

Cannon, Richard. *Historical Records of the British Army, Historical Record of the Forty Second, or, The Royal Highland Regiment of Foot.* London: Parker, Furnivall, and Parker, 1845.

Carleton, Sir Guy, 1724-1808. *Condition of the Indian Trade In North America, 1767: As Described In a Letter to Sir William Johnson.* Brooklyn, N.Y.: Historical Printing Club, 1890. https://hdl.handle.net/2027/aeu.ark:/13960/t9959tv86

Carman, William, *Yeoman's Service. Being an Account of the First Carman's From Kehl Germany to Come to America, Their Sojourn in Pennsylvania and New York, and Their Activities as Loyalist Pioneers in Canada. (1708-1840).*

Centennial Committee, *The Old United Empire Loyalists List: The Centennial of the Settlement of Upper Canada by the United Empire Loyalists, 1784-1884.* (Baltimore, Genealogical Publishing Co., 2003), Appendix B

Countryman, Alvin. *Countryman Genealogy Part I.* Lux Bros. & Heath Publishers, 1925.

Creutzburg, von, Karl Adolf Christoph (* ca. 1733) "in: Hessische Truppen in Amerika https://www.lagis-hessen.de/en/subjects/idrec/sn/hetrina/id/60235 (Stand: 20.1.2015).

Dailey, W.N.P. "Three Rivers Hudson, Mohawk, Schoharie: History From America's Most Famous Valleys, Excerpt from History of Montgomery Classis, R.C.A., Stone Arabia Reformed Church," Recorder Press, Amsterdam, NY, 1916. http://threeriversshms.com/StoneArabia.htm

Dempster, Rev. James, A Record of Marriages and Baptisms in Vicinity of Tryon County, 1778-1803. 25.

"Des Recollets" About the Recollets. http://www.vieux.montreal.qc.ca/tour/etape14/eng/14text4a.htm

Dickinson, John. *Empire and Nation: Letters from a Farmer in Pennsylvania (John Dickinson). Letters from the Federal Farmer (Richard Henry Lee),* ed. Forrest McDonald. Indianapolis, Liberty Fund 1999. [Online] available from http://oll.libertyfund.org/titles/690; accessed 12/22/2017; Internet.

Diffenderffer, Frank. *The German Immigration Into Pennsylvania Through the Port of Philadelphia 1700-1775 Part II The Redemptioners.* Lancaster PA: Pennsylvania- German Society, 1900. https://archive.org/details/germanimmigratio00diffuoft

Diffenderffer, Frank. *The German Exodus to England in 1709.* Lancaster PA: Pennsylvania- German Society, 1897.

Diffenderffer, Frank. *The Story of a Picture.* Philadelphia: 1905. https://archive.org/stream/storyofpicture00diffrich#page/n17/mode/2up

Digitalcompassshop. Sprague, Dan. "2 points abaft the beam: Pirate Talk." Last Modified, March 11, 2012. https://digitalcompassshop.wordpress.com/2012/03/11/2-points-abaft-the-beampirate-talk/

Dillenbeck, Andrew Luther D.D. *Lutheran Trinity Church of Stone Arabia, N.Y.* St. Johnsville, N.Y.: Enterprise and News, 1931.

Dotzert, Roland, Engels, Peter, and Leonhardt, Anke. *Stadtlexikon Darmstadt, Muhlen in Eberstadt.* Darmstadt: Konrad Theiss, 2006.

Dunbar, Seymour. *A History of Travel in America, Vol I.* nd.

Durant, S.W.and Peirce, H.B. *History of St. Lawrence County, New York.* Philadelphia: L.H. Everts & Co., 1878. https://archive.org/stream/cu31924028833015#page/54/mode/2up

Edwards, Ron. "McNIFF, PATRICK," in *Dictionary of Canadian Biography*. Vol. 5, University of Toronto/Université Laval, 2003. http://www.biographi.ca/en/bio/mcniff_patrick_5E.html

"Extract of a Letter From Governor Wentworth to the Right Hon. Sir Thomas Robinson" *London Magazine and Monthly Chronologer*, 24, 1755, London: C. Ackers, 1755,

"Extract of a Private Letter From New York dated June 2." *The Public Advertiser*, 13 July 1758, #7396. London: Greater London, England. *Newspapers.com*

FamilySearch. "New York, Births and Christenings, 1640-1962," index, https://familysearch.org/pal:/MM9.1.1/V2CS-P7H: Joseph Kriderman, 22 Nov 1761; citing reference, FHL microfilm 534201.

FamilySearch. Deutschland Geburten und Taufen, 1558-1898. Thomas W. male, christened 7 Nov 1647 at Evangelisch Duesseldorf Stadt, Rheinland, Prussia. Father: G.W. Mother: Margaretha Tilmans. https://www.familysearch.org/search/ark:/61903/1:1:NF2D-78D

FamilySearch. "New York Land Records, 1630-1975," images, https://familysearch.org/ark:/61903/3:1:3QS7-99WC-DV5W?cc=2078654&wc=M7HP-BP8%3A358134701%2C358236401: 22 May 2014, Fulton Deeds 1772-1801 vol 1 image 10, 39 of 296; county courthouses, New York. https://www.familysearch.org/ark:/61903/3:1:3QS7-99WC-DV5W?i=38&wc=M7HP-BP8%3A358134701%2C358236401&cc=2078654

"Fifty Acres of Beach and Wood. Discovering the Adirondack Heritage of Indian Point." Tom Thacher, Sir John Johnson's Escape. A Tale Retold. And Why Indian Point? November 25, 2014. https://fiftyacresofbeachandwood.org/tag/mohawk-indians/

Find a Grave Memorials. "Jacob Link, Birth 3 July 1766, Montgomery County, New York, USA, Death 23 May 1842 Herkimer, Herkimer County, New York, USA, Burial Garlock Cemetery, Little Falls, Herkimer County, New York, USA, Memorial ID 25663220." https://www.findagrave.com/memorial/25663220.

Flick, Alexander. *The Papers of Sir William Johnson, Vol VIII.* Albany, The University of the State of New York, 1933.

Flick, Alexander. *The Papers of Sir William Johnson Vol VII.* Albany, The University of the State of New York, 1931. https://archive.org/stream/papersofsirwilli07johnuoft#page/892/mode/2up

Flick, Alexander. *The Papers of Sir William Johnson, Vol IV.* Albany, The University of the State of New York, 1925.

Flick, Alexander. *Loyalism in New York During the Revolution. Vol 14, no. 1.* Columbia University Press, London, 1901. https://archive.org/stream/loyalisminnewyor00flic#page/24/mode/2up

Fitz, Caitlin A. ""Suspected on Both Sides": Little Abraham, Iroquois Neutrality, and the American Revolution." *Journal of the Early Republic* 28, no. 3 (2008): 299-335. http://www.jstor.org/stable/40208153.

Folgleman, Aaron. *Hopeful Journeys: German Immigration, Settlement and Political Culture in Colonial America 1717-1775.* Philadelphia: University of Pennsylvania Press, 1996.

Fraser, Duncan. Papers and Records of the Ontario Historical Society, Volume LII, 1960. *Sir John Johnson's Rent Roll of the Kingsborough Patent.* Original Source, Public Record Office, London, England AC 13/114. http://freepages.genealogy.rootsweb.ancestry.com/~wjmartin/kingsbor.htm

Friends of Schoharie Crossing. Friday, August 28, 2015. "Exploring Fort Hunter Through Maps – NYS Archives Part II." Last modified, August 28, 2015. http://friendsofschohariecrossing.blogspot.ca/2015/08/exploring-fort-hunter-through-maps-nys.html

Fraser, Alexander. Provincial Archivist. Digital Edition of the Second Report of the Bureau of Archives For the Province of Ontario. 1904. *United Empire Loyalists Enquiry Into The Losses and Services in Consequence of Their Loyalty Evidence in the Canadian Claims,*1904. Toronto: Global Heritage Press, 2010.

Frolick, Arlene, ed. *The Gallinger Family: Gallinger Ancestors in Germany and Their Descendants in Canada and the U.S.A.* 2nd ed. (Worall, L., 2004) https://books.google.ca/books/about/The_Gallinger_Family.html?id=R24MnwEACAAJ&redir_esc=y

Fryer, Mary & W. Smy (Lieutenant-Colonel), *Rolls of the Provincial (Loyalist) Corps, Canadian Command American Revolutionary Period.* Toronto: Dundern Press, 1981.

"Fulton County Courthouse, Johnstown, New York." https://www.nycourts.gov/history/legal-history-new-york/documents/Courthouse_History-Fulton-County.pdf

Fulton County, NYGenWeb. Burch, Wanda. "He was bought at public sale…, Slavery At Johnson Hall." The Sunday Leader-Herald, 27 Feb, 2000.

"Fulton County, NY GenWeb." James F. Morrison, A History of Fulton County in the Revolution, The Soldiers and Their Story. https://fulton.nygenweb.net/military/FCinRev5.html

"Fulton County NYGenWeb." James F. Morrison, Jellis Fonda. http://fulton.nygenweb.net/military/jellis.html

"Fulton County NYGenWeb." Loveday, William Jr. "The Birth of a County." 2002. Last modified 8 May 2008. http://www.fulton.nygenweb.net/history/WLbirth.html

"Fulton County NYGenWeb." Loveday, William A Shot of History." The Sunday Leader Herald, 10 March, 2002, 8A.

Fulton County Republican. (Johnstown, N.Y.), "Ancient Lease in Gloversville." Thursday, May 13, 1909.

Gale Research. "Passenger and Immigration Lists Index, 1500s-1900s." Online publication - Provo, UT, USA: Ancestry.com Operations, Inc, 2010.Original data - Filby, P. William, ed. Passenger and Immigration Lists Index, 1500s-1900s. Farmington Hills, MI, USA: Gale Research, 2010.

Greene, Nelson. The Story of Old Fort Plain and the Middle Mohawk Valley. Fort Plain, NY.: O'Connor Brothers, 1915. http://scans.library.utoronto.ca/pdf/3/21/storyofoldfortpl00greeuoft/storyofoldfortpl00greeuoft.pdf

Grubb, Farley. "The Market Structure of Shipping German Immigrants to Colonial America," University of Delaware, 1987. https://journals.psu.edu/pmhb/article/viewFile/44187/43908

Grubb, Farley. "Morbidity and Mortality on the North Atlantic Passage: Eighteenth Century German Immigration", *Journal of Interdisciplinary History* 17 no.3, 1987. DOI: 10.2307/204611

Gagliardo, John. *Germans and Agriculture in Colonial Pennsylvania.* Yale University, April, 1959. https://journals.psu.edu/pmhb/article/viewFile/41466/41187The

GlobalGenealogy.com. "Militia Rolls of Upper Canada Colonel James Gray's Company, February 10, 1789." The Global Gazette, 15 April 1998. Original data: National Archives of Canada. N.A.C Reference: M.G. 19 F 35 Series 1, Lot 727, Entries 1 – 73. globalgenealogy.com/globalgazette/List001/list46.htm

Graymont, Barbara, "KOÑWATSIˀTSIAIÉÑNI (Mary Brant)," in *Dictionary of Canadian Biography*, Vol. 4. University of Toronto/Université Laval, 2003. http://www.biographi.ca/en/bio/konwatsitsiaienni_4E.html

Graymont, Barbara, "THAYENDANEGEA," in *Dictionary of Canadian Biography*, vol. 5, University of Toronto/Université Laval, 2003. http://www.biographi.ca/en/bio/thayendanegea_5E.html

Greene County, New York History & Genealogy, *Baptismal Records of Zion's Lutheran Church, Athens, NY 1703-1789.*

Grems-Doolitte Library Collections. "Taverns and Inns of Schenectady Part I." Last modified, July 21, 2015. http://gremsdoolittlelibrary.blogspot.ca/2015/07/taverns-and-inns-of-schenectady-part-i.html

Gurgoyne, Bruce, E. trans., *Hesse-Hanau Order Books, A Diary And Rosters. A Collection of Items Concerning the Hesse-Hanau Contingent of "Hessians" Fighting Against the American Colonists in the Revolutionary War.* Maryland: Heritage Books, 2006.

Haberlein, Mark "German Communities in 18th Century Europe and North America," In *European Migrants, Diasporas and Indigenous Ethnic Minorities,* eds. Matjaz Klemencic and Mary Harris, Pisa: Pisa University Press, 2009.

Hallett, Christine. The Attempt to Understand Puerperal Fever in the Eighteenth and Early Nineteenth Centuries: The Influence of Infammation Theory, *Med Hist,* 49(1), 2005. https://www.ncbi.nlm.nih.gov/pmc/articles/PMC1088248/

Hal Stead Van Tyne, Claude. *The Loyalists in the American Revolution* (New York, The MacMillan Company, 1902. http://www.archive.org/stream/loyalistsinamer00vantrich#page/n207/mode/2up

Hamilton, Milton & Corey, Albert. *The Papers of Sir William Johnson, Vol XIII.* Albany: The University of the State of New York, 1962. https://archive.org/stream/papersofsirwilli13johnuoft#page/632/mode/2up

Hamilton, Milton & Corey, Albert. *The Papers of Sir William Johnson, Vol XII.* Albany: The University of the State of New York, 1957. https://archive.org/stream/papersofsirwilli12johnuoft#page/892/mode/2up

Heinemeier, Dan. *A Social History of Hesse Roman Times to 1900.* Arlington: Heinemeier Publications, 2002.

Herman, Bernard. *Town House: Architecture and Material Life in the Early American City, 1780-1830.* Chapel Hill: The University of North Carolina Press, 2009.

"Heritage." Library and Archives Canada, Great Britain War Office, *A List of Colonel Johnson's Department of Indian Affairs,* WO 28, lac_reel_c10861 C-10861, 158960, 125090, MG13WO http://heritage.canadiana.ca/view/oocihm.lac_reel_c10861/1440?r=0&s=3

"Heritage." Library and Archives Canada. Great Britain War Office (WO 28): *America.* Lac_reel_c10860, C10860, 158960, 125090, 105016, MG 13 WO. http://heritage.canadiana.ca/view/oocihm.lac_reel_c10860/1122?r=0&s=3

"Heritage." Library and Archives Canada. Great Britain, War Office (WO 28): *America.* Lac_reel_c10862, C10862, 158960, 125090, MG 13 WO. http://heritage.canadiana.ca/view/oocihm.lac_reel_c10862/371?r=1&s=6

"Héritage." Library and Archives Canada. *Amherst papers 12843.* Great Britain, War Office. Lac_reel_c12843 C-12843 105019 MG 13 WO 34.

"Heritage." Library and Archives Canada, MIKAN No. 4159295, Cartographic material. Patrick McNiff, A plan of part of the new settlements, on the north bank of the southwest branch of the St. Lawrence River. 1786.

"Heritage." Library and Archives Canada, *Daniel Claus and Family Fonds*: C-1478, Claus Papers. Lac_reel_c1478, C1478, 103767, MG 19 F1. http://heritage.canadiana.ca/view/oocihm.lac_reel_c1478/257?r=0&s=5

"Heritage." Library and Archives Canada. British Library, formerly British Museum, Additional Manuscripts 21804-21834, *Haldimand Papers.* Lac_reel_h1652, H-1652, 105513, 2034239, MG 21. http://heritage.canadiana.ca/view/oocihm.lac_reel_h1652/279?r=0&s=5

"Heritage." Library and Archives Canada, British Library, formerly British Museum, Additional Manuscripts 21804-21834, *Haldimand Papers.* Lac_reel_h1654, H-1654, 105513, 2034139, MG21. http://heritage.canadiana.ca/view/oocihm.lac_reel_h1654/729?r=0&s=5

"Heritage." Library and Archives Canada, British Library, formerly British Museum, Additional Manuscripts21804-21834, *Haldimand Papers.* Lac_reel_ h1655, H-1655, 105513, 2034239, MG 21. http://heritage.canadiana.ca/view/oocihm.lac_reel_h1655/28?r=1&s=4

"Heritage." Library and Archives Canada, *Haldimand Loyalist Lists (Index)*. Lac_reel c1475, C1475, 105513, 2034239, MG 21 Add.MSS.21661-21892. http://heritage.canadiana.ca/view/oocihm.lac_reel_c1475/360?r=3&s=4

"Héritage." Library and Archives Canada, Great Britain, War Office, *Haldimand Papers From the British Library*. Lac_reel_h1428 H-1428 105513 2034239 MG 21. http://heritage.canadiana.ca/view/oocihm.lac_reel_h1428

"Héritage." Library and Archives Canada. *Haldimand Papers From the British Library*. Lac_reel_h1429 1055132034239 MG 21. http://heritage.canadiana.ca/view/oocihm.lac_reel_h1429/978?r=0&s=5

"Heritage." Library and Archives Canada, *Heir and Devisee Commission*. Lac_reel_h1135, H-1135, RG 1 L5, 205142, Image 441. http://heritage.canadiana.ca/view/oocihm.lac_reel_h1135/441?r=0&s=2

"Héritage." Library and Archives Canada. *Indian Affairs, selections from the Claus Papers – 11773*. Lac_reel_c11773, C-11773, 102179, 135619, MG55. Image 12. http://heritage.canadiana.ca/view/oocihm.lac_reel_c11773/12?r=0&s=1

"Heritage." Library and Archives Canada, *Registres de paroisses, Québec*. Lac_reel_c3023, C3023, 101567, 98023, 98022. Image 498. Register of the Parish of Montreal.

"Héritage." Library and Archives Canada. *Upper Canada Land Petitions (1763-1865)*. Mikan Number 205131. Microform: c-1609. Image 1231.

"Heritage." Library and Archives of Canada, *Upper Canada Sundries*, Vol 18, July-August 1813. Item 46. 7413-7533. Petition of George McGinnis of Amherst Island, Lennox and Addington Counties, District of Midland. https://www.ancestry.ca/mediaui-viewer/collection/1030/tree/42428022/person/19923999976/media/ac0de139-1b6f-47a8-8adc-1a4942bf5d21?_phsrc=tLm6326&usePUBJs=true

"Hesse-Kassel Jäger Corps." Uniform Item Description. http://www.jaegerkorps.org/Uniforms2.html

"History of the Mohawk Valley: Gateway to the West 1614-1925." Chapter 76: 1775-1783. Roster of Mohawk Valley Revolutionary Militia. http://www.schenectadyhistory.org/resources/mvgw/history/076.html

"History of the 1747 Nellis Tavern." St. Johnsville, NY. http://www.palatinesettlementsociety.org/Documents/HistoryofNellisTavern4072015.pdf

HistoryofMassachusetts.org Brooks, Rebecca. "The Sons of Liberty: Who Were They and What Did They Do?" November 24, 2014.

Hochstadt, Steve. "Migration in Preindustrial Germany," *Central European History 16,* no.3. 1983.

Hodge, Adam. "Vectors of Colonialism: The Smallpox Epidemic of 1780-1782 and Northern Great Plains Indian Life." Masters Thesis, Kent State University, 2009. https://etd.ohiolink.edu/rws_etd/document/get/kent1239393701/inline

Holden, James. *Halfway Brook in History.* New York State Historical Association, 1905. https://archive.org/stream/halfwaybrookinhi00hold#page/2/mode/2up

Hough, Franklin, B. *Gazetteer of the State of New York. Embracing a Comprehensive Account of the History and Statistics of the State.* Albany: Andrew Boyd, 1872. https://archive.org/stream/gazetteerofstate00houg#page/311/mode/2up

Hough, Franklin. The Northern Invasion of 1780. New York: The Bradford Club, 1866. https://archive.org/stream/northerninvasion00houguoft#page/132/mode/2up

Irvin, Benjamin H. "Tar, Feathers, and the Enemies of American Liberties, 1768-1776." *The New England Quarterly* 76, no. 2 (2003): 197-238. doi:10.2307/1559903.

I Spy in Johnstown. "Jimmy Burke Inn." http://www.mvls.info/ispy/johnstown/joh_site09.html

J Stor Academic.edu. "The History Files European Kingdoms Central Europe Chatti (Hessians) (Germans)." http://www.historyfiles.co.uk/KingListsEurope/GermanyHesse.htm

Jackson, Joseph. *Market Street Philadelphia*. Philadelphia: Joseph Jackson, 1918.

Jasanoff, Maya. *Liberty's Exiles. American Loyalists in the Revolutionary War.* New York, Alfred A. Knopf, 2011

Jeffreys, Thomas. *An east prospect of the city of Philadelphia, taken by George Heap from the Jersey shore, under the direction of Nicholas Scull surveyor general of the Province of Pennsylvania. Engraving, 1771*. Library of Congress Prints and Photographs Division, Washington, D.C. http://hdl.loc.gov/loc.pnp/pp.print

Johnson, Crisfield. *The History of Washington County New York*. Philadelphia: Everts & Ensign, 1878. http://archive.org/stream/historyofwashing00john#page/28/mode/1up

Johnson, Ken D. "Fort Plank Bastion of My Freedom," The Burning of Caughnawaga by Henry Glen. http://www.fortplank.com/1780_Burning_of_Caughnawaga_By_Henry_Glen_Endnoted.pdf

Johnson, Ken D. "The Bloodied Mohawk: The Story of the American Revolution in the Words of Fort Plank's Defenders and Other Mohawk Valley Partisans". Recent Discoveries in Mohawk Valley History. *Certificate of Quit Rent Remission for the Conrad Countryman Patent.* http://www.fort-plank.com/QRRC_4_Countryman_Patent.html

Johnson, Ken D. "Fort Plank Bastion of my Freedom, Colonial Canajoharie, New York." Last Modified 6 October 2016. http://www.fort-plank.com/V_Maps/Canajoharie_Patent_1764_.jpg

Johnson, Ken, D. "Fort Plank Bastion of My Freedom, Colonial Canajoharie, New York."Last modified October 6, 2016.http://www.fort-plank.com/Warrensburgh_1738.html

Johnson, Ken D. "The Bloodied Mohawk: The Story of the American Revolution in the Words of Fort Plank's Defenders and Other Mohawk Valley Partisans." *A Return of Men Women and Children Distinguishing their Age & Sex which came by the Flag with C Yates from the Christopher Yates.* Papers housed in the Special Collections of the Bird Library of Syracuse University dated Isle Aux Noix March 17th 1780. http://www.fort-plank.com/Loyalists_Exchanged_March_1780.pdf

Johnston, C.M. "DESERONTYON, JOHN," in *Dictionary of Canadian Biography*. Vol. 5, University of Toronto/Université Laval, 2003, accessed April 4, 2018, http://www.biographi.ca/en/bio/deserontyon_john_5E.html

Johnston, S.A., and Garver, J.I., "Record of flooding on the Mohawk River from 1634 to 2000 based on historical Archives." *GSA Abstracts with Programs v. 33,* n.1 (2001): 73. http://minerva.union.edu/garverj/mohawk/1831_floods.html

Jones, Henry Z. Jr. *The Palatine Families of New York: A Study of the German Immigrants Who Arrived in Colonial New York in 1710, Vol. I.* Universal City, CA: Author, 1985.

Jones, J. Kelsey. Loyalist Plantations on the Susquehanna. http://www.seeleycreekvalleyfarm.com/loyalist_seeley.pdf

Kemp, Peter. *The Oxford Companion to Ships and the Sea,* ed. Oxford: Oxford University Press, 1976.

"The King's Royal Yorkers." James L. Kochan, Uniforms and Arms of the King's Royal Regiment of New York. http://royalyorkers.ca/regiment_recreating.php

"The King's Royal Yorkers." Allan S Joyner, Recreating the KRR: A Research Driven Interpretation. http://royalyorkers.ca/regiment_recreating.php

"The King's Royal Yorkers," Gavin Watt, The Companies of the 1st Battalion KRRNY. http://royalyorkers.ca/companies_1bn.php

"The King's Royal Yorkers" Captain Stephen Watts. http://royalyorkers.ca/lights/lc_cp_watts.htm

Kirschner, Friedrich, ed. "Eberstadt-Frankenstein Geschichtsverein Eberstadt-Frankenstein *Die Muhlen mit ihrem Erbauungsjahr im Uberblick"* http://www.eberstadt-frankenstein.de/content/011_muehlen.pdf

Knittle, Walter. *Early Eighteenth Century Palatine Emigration,* Philadelphia: Dorrance and Company, 1937. https://archive.org/stream/earlyeighteenthc00knit#page/n5/mode/2up

Kopperman, Paul E. "The Medical Dimension in Cornwallis' Army, 1780-1781." *The North Carolina Historical Review* 89, no. 4 (2012): 367-98. http://www.jstor.org/stable/23523993

Kronoskaf Virtual Time Machine. "Project Seven Years War, 1758 British Expedition Against Carillon." Last Modified 10 May 2017. http://www.kronoskaf.com/syw/index.php?title=1758_-_British_expedition_against_Carillon

Kyte, Elinor. *Christmas Eve in Montreal 1783-A Bleak Mid-Winter.* The Loyalist Gazette, 1986. 15- 16.

Lambert, James H. "CHABRAND DELISLE, DAVID," in *Dictionary of Canadian Biography*. Vol. 4, University of Toronto/Université Laval, 2003. http://www.biographi.ca/en/bio/chabrand_delisle_david_4E.html

Larson, Neil. Building a Stone House in Ulster County, New York in 1751. https://www.arct.cam.ac.uk/Downloads/ichs/vol-2-1867-1882-larson.pdf

Library of Congress. Digital Collections. *Documents From the Continental Congress and the Constitutional Convention 1774-1789, Articles and Essays.* https://www.loc.gov/collections/continental-congress-and-constitutional-convention-from-1774-to-1789/articles-and-essays/timeline/1766-to-1767/ ;

Library of Congress. Manuscript/Mixed Material. *George Washington Papers, Series 4, General Correspondence: Abraham Wempel, Interrogation of Two British Prisoners Captured by Oneida Indians.* 1781. https://www.loc.gov/item/mgw428504/

Loescher, Burt Garfield. *The History of Rogers Rangers Vol I.* San Fransisco: Author, 1946. https://archive.org/stream/historyofrogersr01loes#page/228/mode/2up

Loescher, Burt Garfield. *The History of Rogers Rangers Vol II*, 1st ed. San Mateo: 1969. http://heritage.canadiana.ca/view/oocihm.lac_reel_c12843/52?r=0&s=4

Lord, Phil. "Poles and Steam: An Experiment on the Mohawk River." October, 2012. http://www.living-in-the-past.com/steam.html

Lossing, Benson, J. *Pictorial Field Book of the Revolution. Volume 1 Chapter X.* New York: Harper & Brothers, 1859. https://archive.org/stream/pictorialfieldb00lossgoog#page/n243/mode/2up

Macwethy, Lou. *West Camp; Statement of Heads of Palaten Famileys and Number of Persons in Both Towns of ye West Side Hudsons River. Winter, 1710.* In The Book of Names. St. Johnsville [**NY**]: The Enterprise and News, 1933, Baltimore: Genealogical Publishing Co.. 1985.

Maerschalck, Francis and Duyckinck, Geraldus. *The Maerschalck Map: A Plan of the City of New York from an Acutual Survey Anno Domini MDCCLV, 1755.* Washington D.C.: Library of Congress. http://www.nyc99.org/1700/maerschalck.html

The Magazine of American History With Notes and Queries. Vol VI. *Orderly Book For Lieut. Col. Sir John Johnson's Company* 1776-1777. 283-284. https://archive.org/stream/magazineofameric06stev#page/282/mode/2up

Malcombson, Robert. "Nothing More Uncomfortable Than Our Flat Bottomed Boats:" Batteaux in the British Service During the War of 1812. *The Northern Mariner, XIII, No. 4,* (October, 2003), 17- 28. https://www.cnrs-scrn.org/northern_mariner/vol13/tnm_13_4_17-28.pdf

Manthey Central, 18th Century Reenacting. Manthey, David William. "Items in Day and Account Books." http://orbitals.com/self/history/daybook.htm

Marlett-Taft, Jane. *Gideon Marlett A Huguenot of Staten Island N.Y. With Some Account of the Descendants in the United States and Canada.* Burlington Vermont: 1907. https://archive.org/stream/gideonmarlettged00taft#page/n147/mode/2up

Martin, John Hill. *Martin's Bench and Bar of Philadelphia.* Philadelphia: Rees Welsh & Co., 1883.

"Marriages at St Paul's Lutheran Church Schoharie. 1773-1776." http://web.archive.org/web/20101120045734/http://bettyfink.com/mstp10.htm

"Martyn Cornell's Zythofile, Beer Now and Then." A Short History of Spruce Beer Part Two: The North American Connection. http://zythophile.co.uk/2016/04/20/a-short-history-of-spruce-beer-part-two-the-north-american-connection/

McCulloch, Ian. "Within Ourselves:" The Development of British Light Infantry in North America During the Seven Years War", *Canadian Military History,* 7, (2), 1998, 47. http://scholars.wlu.ca/cgi/viewcontent.cgi?article=1244&context=cmh

Mendel, Mesick, Cohen Architects, *Fort Johnston Amsterdam, New York: A Historic Structure Report 1974-1975.* Washington, D.C., Technical Preservation Services Division Office of Archeology and Historic Preservation US Department of the Interior, 1978. http://npshistory.com/publications/fort-johnson-hsr.pdf

Military History Now. Mallett, N. H.. ed. "Hessians For Hire: Meet the 18th Century's Busiest Mercenaries." 15 June 2013. http://militaryhistorynow.com/2013/06/15/hired-guns-ten-amazing-facts-about-the-hessians/

Millman, T.R. "Stuart, John (1740/41-1811)," in *Dictionary of Canadian Biography,* vol. 5, University of Toronto/Université Laval, 2003. http://www.biographi.ca/en/bio/stuart_john_1740_41_1811_5E.html

Mittelberger, Gottlied. *Gottlieb Mittelberger's Journey to Pennsylvania in the Year 1750 and His Return to Germany in 1754*. Translated by Eben Carl, Philadelphia: John Jos. McVey, 1898. https://archive.org/stream/gottliebmittelbe00gott#page/12/mode/2up

Montgomery County. History and Archives. Yacobucci Farqhar, Kelly. "The Trinity Lutheran Church." 2008. https://www.co.montgomery.ny.us/web/sites/departments/historian/articles_TrinityLutheranChurch.asp

Montgomery County NY GenWeb Genealogy & History. Lathrop, Elsie. Early "American Inns and Taverns." New York: R.M. McBride & Company, 1926.

Montgomery County NY GenWeb Genealogy & History. "The Loss-Claim of Johannes Veeder. An Account of the Damage Which Johannes Veeder Sustained by the Enemy Under the Comman of Sir John Johnson, 22 May, 1780 at Caugnawaga." Last Modified, 11, December, 1998.

Montgomery County NY GENWEB. Genealogy & History. Reid, Max. "The Story of Old Fort Johnson, Chapter XV. Land Grants: Royal, Kingsborough, Sacandaga, Johnson Hall." Last Modified, 10 December 1999.

Montgomery County NY GenWeb" The Town of Mohawk Montgomery County, NY. "History of the Town of Mohawk Part I." Last Modified, 1 January 1999. http://montgomery.nygenweb.net/mohawk/mohistory1.html

Moody, Kevin, and Fisher, Charles. "Archeological Evidence of Colonial Occupation at Schoharie Crossing Historic Site, Montgomery County, New York." *The Bulletin Journal of the New York State Archeological Association.* Fall, no. 99, 1989. http://nysarchaeology.org/download/nysaa/bulletin/number_099.pdf

Morrison, James F. *Capt. John Little. 3rd Battalion of Tryon County Militia.* http://www.littellfamiliesofamerica.com/secure/21st/2004LLA/Sect04H.htm

Morrison, James F. "Fulton County NYGenWeb." About Captain John Little http://fulton.nygenweb.net/military/little.html

Morrison, James F. "Fulton County NYGenWeb" The Great Conflagration of May 1780. Part I, II https://fulton.nygenweb.net/military/greatconflag1.html

Morrison, James F. *A Hanging in Canajoharie,* http://revwarny.com/hanging.pdf

The National Archives, *Compiled Service Records of Soldiers Who Served in the American Army During the Revolution documenting the period 1775-1784,* M881 National Archives Catalog ID: 570910 Record Group: 93 Roll: 0736, New York Regiment: Fisher's Regiment, Militia Record Type: Individual Surname: Gallenger Given Name: Henry.

The National Archives, *Papers of the Continental Congress, 1774-1789,* Letters From Maj. Gen. Philip Schuyler, Vol II, June 1775- December 1776, 47, NARA M247, Item No. 153, Record Group 360, Roll pcc_345148_0001.

The National Archives, *Revolutionary War Pension and Bounty-Land Warrant Application Files* M804, Record Group 15, Roll 0961. Pg. 5. Pension application of William Feeter. https://www.fold3.com/image/246/18314480

The National Archives, *Revolutionary War Pension and Bounty Land Warrant Application Files,* M804, Pension No. S. 22985, Record Group 15, Roll 2175, 10. Pension Application of Jacob Shew. https://www.fold3.com/image/246/15632041?xid=1945

The National Archives, *Revolutionary War Rolls 1775-1783,* A Muster Roll of Captain Andrew Finck's Co. in Colonel Van Schaick's Battalion of Forces, December 17 1776, in the Barracks at Saratoga. M246, Record Group 93, Roll 0077, Folder 163. Private Bastian Algoyer, enlisted March 6, 1776. https://www.fold3.com/image/10188403

The National Archives, *Revolutionary War Rolls 1775-1783,* Wemple's Regiment of Militia, Folder 170, page 33. August 1778, Captain Jelles Fonda's Company. Jacob Algaier. https://www.fold3.com/image/246/10195207

The National Archives, *Revolutionary War Rolls,* 1775-1783, M246, Record Group 93, Roll 0074, Folder 100, 118-119. Payroll of Capt. Jellis Fonda's company of Associated Exempts. Aug 10-Aug15 1777. https://www.fold3.com/image/10074302

The National Archives, *Revolutionary War Rolls,* 1775-1783, M246, Folder 170, Record Group 93, Roll 0077, Wemple's Regiment of Militia, List of Capt. Jelles Fonda's Company of Associated Exempts. https://www.fold3.com/image/10195239

The National Archives, *Revolutionary War Rolls, 1775-1783,* Wemple's Regiment of Militia, Folder 170, page 35. August 1778, Captain Jelles Fonda's Company. Martian Samser. https://www.fold3.com/image/246/10195239

The National Archives, *Revolutionary War Rolls, 1775-1783,* M246, Record Group 93, Roll 0077, Page 11, A Pay Roll of Captain Jelles Fonda's Company, May 1780, https://www.fold3.com/image/246/10194819

The National Archives of the UK. *American Loyalist Claims, Series I;* Class: *AO 13;* Piece: *03.* Kew, Surrey, England.

"National Humanities Center America in Class." Making The Revolution: 1763-1791. Alexander Hamilton & Isaac Ledyard, A Pamphlet War on the Post War Treatment of Loyalists. http://americainclass.org/sources/makingrevolution/independence/text4/hamiltonledyard.pdf

"National Humanities Center. America in Class." Making the Revolution: America 1763-1791. "Crisis."

"National Humanities Center. America in Class." Making the Revolution: America 1763-1791. "Crisis. 1764: Loyal Subjects?" "Stamp Act Crisis." http://americainclass.org/sources/makingrevolution/crisis/text2/text2.htm

New Netherland and Beyond. Colonial Church Records. "Reverend John Ogilvie Records Eastern NY State, Hudson Valley Area. 1750-1760. Baptisms Extracted from Trinity Church Records, NYC; *NYGBR,* 67. 1936." Last modified 2012. http://www.rootsweb.ancestry.com/~nycoloni/chrecalb03.html

New York Heritage Digital Collections, "Map of Service Patent and Part of Cosby's Manor. 1798?" http://nyheritage.nnyln.org/digital/collection/XFM001/id/17/

New York Historical Society. *Collections of the New York Historical Society. Muster Rolls of New York Provincial Troops 1751-1764*. New York: New York Historical Society, 1892. https://archive.org/stream/musterrollsnewy00socigoog#page/n70/mode/2up

New York Historical Society, *Minutes of the Committee and of the First Commission For Detecting and Defeating Conspiracies in the State of New York December 11, 1776-September 23, 1778*. Vol I New York, Collections of the New York Historical Society For the Year 1924. http://archive.org/stream/minutesofcommitt571newy#page/28/mode/2up

New York Historical Society, *Register of Lands in Three Parts 1761-1789, Series IV: Bound volumes, 1754-1843, undated. 2267-268.* Schnevis's Creek and Cobus Kill. http://digitalcollections.nyhistory.org/islandora/object/islandora%3A121904

"New York History Blog" Glenn Pearsall, French and Indian War Bayonet Discovered in the Adirondacks. August 2, 2017. https://newyorkhistoryblog.org/2017/08/02/french-indian-war-bayonet-discovered-near-loon-lake/ New York Public Library. Digital Collections. Manuscripts and Archives Division. Theodorus Bailey Myers Collection *Series II. "Prominent Civilians and Officials During the Colonial Period.* Johnson, Sir William. Johnson Hall" [New York], NYPL catalog ID b11868620 MSS Unit ID: 2091: Myers#262Archives EADID 478689, UUID: ddfeae00-2e59-0133-58a3-58d385a7b928, https://digitalcollections.nypl.org/items/e41b50e0-3320-0133-8520-58d385a7b928/book?parent=db55e2d0-2e58-0133-1b29-58d385a7b928#page/63/mode/2up

The New York Public Library. Digital Collections. Manuscripts and Archives Division, *The Memorial of Lieut. Col John Butler, Butler, John. Niagara, Quebec.* http://digitalcollections.nypl.org/items/4a8f9c00-3321-0133-4e41-58d385a7b928

The New York Public Library. Digital Collections. Manuscripts and Archives Division, *Carleton, Guy. Quebec.* Walter Butler's Commission as Captain in the corp of rangers. http://digitalcollections.nypl.org/items/be1faf30-348c-0133-fdc8-58d385a7b928 The New York Public Library. Digital Collections. Manuscripts and Archives Division. "Johnson, Sir John" Theodorus Bailey Myers Collection. *Series II. Prominent Civilians and Officials During the Colonial Period.* Account of Contingent Expenses Incurred by Sir John Johnson. https://digitalcollections.nypl.org/items/a2a42ef0-349f-0133-b9a7-58d385a7b928 The New York Public Library. Manuscripts and Archives Division. *List of loyalists against whom judgments were given under the Confiscation Act.* (UUID): 554d98e0-cc5f-0133-9fc2-00505686a51c. https://digitalcollections.nypl.org/items/931a49e0-0e2f-0134-a66c-00505686a51c

The New York Public Library. Digital Collections Manuscripts and Archives Division. *Butler, John. Tryon County.* http://digitalcollections.nypl.org/items/9ff20570-3321-0133-b461-58d385a7b928

The New York Public Library. Digital Collections. Manuscripts and Archives Division, *Frey, Hendrick.* http://digitalcollections.nypl.org/items/95c14a90-349d-0133-6c0f-58d385a7b928

The New York Public Library. Digital Collections. Manuscripts and Archives Division, *List of Loyalists against whom judgments were given under the Confiscation Act.* http://digitalcollections.nypl.org/items/92737eb0-0e2f-0134-64ed-00505686a51c

The New York Public Library. Digital Collections. Manuscripts and Archives Division. *Penn, John. Philadelphia. To Sir William Johnson* http://digitalcollections.nypl.org/items/86ceb390-34a5-0133-ef09-58d385a7b928

New York State, *Calendar of Historical Manuscripts Relating to the War of the Revolution, Vol I* Albany: Weed, Parsons & Company, 1868. 161-162. https://archive.org/stream/calendarofhistor01newy#page/160/mode/2up

New York State. General Assembly. *Journal of the Votes And Proceedings of the General Assembly of the Colony of New York: From 1766 to 1776, Inclusive.* Albany: Printed by J. Buel, 1820.

New York State. *Laws of the State of New York Passed At the Sessions of the Legislature Held In the Years 1777 [to 1801]* Albany: Weed, Parsons and Co, 188687. https://babel.hathitrust.org/cgi/pt?id=hvd.32044011878063;view=1up;seq=72

New York State. Legislature. *Journals of the Provincial Congress, Provincial Convention, Committee of Safety And Council of Safety of the State of New-York: 1775-1775-1777.* Albany: Printed by Thurlow Weed, printer to the State, 1842. https://babel.hathitrust.org/cgi/pt?id=nnc1.ar01406256;view=1up;seq=244

New York State, The Office of the State Comptroller, *New York in the Revolution as Colony and State Vol 1.* Albany: J.B. Lyon, 1904. 179-182. Tryon County Militia, Third Regiment;

New York State. The Office of the State Comptroller. *New York in the Revolution as Colony and State.* Raid of Sir John Johnson of the Schoharie and Mohawk Valleys, in October 1780. Albany: Weed-Parsons, 1897. xiii-xviii. https://archive.org/stream/newyorkinrevolu00robegoog#page/n24/mode/2up

New York State. The Office of the State Comptroller, *New York In the Revolution As Colony And State: Supplement.* Albany: O.A. Quayle, 1901. 242-250. https://babel.hathitrust.org/cgi/pt?id=coo.31924032737938;view=1up;seq=246

New York State, *Public Papers of George Clinton, First Governor of New York, 1777 1795, 1801-1804, Military Vol I.* Albany: Wynkoop Hallenbeck Crawford Co., 1899. https://archive.org/stream/publicpapersofge01newy1#page/120/mode/2up

New York State Archives, A0870-77, *Copies of accounts audited by the auditor general for bills presented to the state, 1780-1794.* NYSA_A0870-77_Book B Page 23, 84.

New York State Archives. Instructional glass lantern slides, ca. 1856-1939. Series A3045-78, No. 732. NYSA_A3045-78_732. Route of Col. Sir John Johnson in his Raid through the Schoharie and the Mohawk Valleys. http://digitalcollections.archives.nysed.gov/index.php/Detail/Object/Show/object_id/1280

New York State Archives. New York (State). *State Engineer and Surveyor. Survey maps of lands in New York State, ca. 1711-1913.* Series A0273-78, Map #147A.1769 NYSA_A0273-78_147A. Map of the Western Boundary Line of the Third Tract, Granted to John Morine Scott http://digitalcollections.archives.nysed.gov/index.php/Detail/Object/Show/object_id/36677#

New York State Archives. New York (State). *State Engineer and Surveyor. Survey maps of lands in New York State, ca. 1711-1913.* Series A0273-78, Map #681. 1755-1770. NYSA_A0273-78_681. Survey of Land for J.N. Mathias, William Bauch, Lawrence Lawyer, and Wm. Wood. http://digitalcollections.archives.nysed.gov/index.php/Detail/Object/Show/object_id/37246

New York State Archives. New York (State). *State Engineer and Surveyor. Survey maps of lands in New York State, ca. 1711-1913.* Series A0273-78, Map #618, 875. http://digitalcollections.archives.nysed.gov/index.php/Detail/Object/Show/object_id/37137 http://digitalcollections.archives.nysed.gov/index.php/Detail/Object/Show/object_id/37452#

New York State Archives. Engineer and Surveyor. *Records of Surveys and Maps of State Lands, 1686-1892.* Series A4016-77, Volume 7, Folder 161. NYSA_A4016-77_V7_F161 Printed Copy of an act for the forfeiture and sale of estates.

New York State Archives. *Maps of State Lands, 1686–1892.* Series A4016, Vols. 7–10 and 17.

New York State Archives. *State Engineer and Surveyor. Survey maps of lands in New York State, ca. 1711-1913.* NYSA_A0273-78_193. Series A0273-78, Map #193. Map of Staley's Patent in Herkimer CountyNYSA_A0273-78_181_Copy Series A0273-78, Map #181 (copy). Map of Burnet's Field (copy). [Herkimer County]. http://digitalcollections.archives.nysed.gov/index.php/Detail/Object/Show/object_id/36720 ;

New York State Archives. *State Engineer and Surveyor. Survey maps of lands in New York State, ca. 1711-1913.* Series A0273-78, NYSA_A0273-78_894, Map #894. Map of Grants to Philip Livingston and Frederick Young. http://digitalcollections.archives.nysed.gov/index.php/Detail/Object/Show/object_id/37479

New York State Archives. *State Engineer and Surveyor. Survey maps of lands in New York State, ca. 1711-1913.* Series A0273-78, Map #875. Map of Lots in the Village of Johnstown, Fulton County. *http://digitalcollections.archives.nysed.gov/index.php/Detail/Object/Show/object_id/37452*

New York State Archives. *State Engineer and Surveyor. Survey maps of lands in New York State, ca. 1711-1913.* NYSA_A0273-78_640Series A0273-78, Map #640. Survey of Land for Lendert Gansevoort and James Stewart Map #640. http://digitalcollections.archives.nysed.gov/index.php/Detail/Object/Show/object_id/37318

New York (State). General Assembly. *Journal of the Votes And Proceedings of the General Assembly of the Colony of New York: From 1766 to 1776, Inclusive.* Albany: Printed by J. Buel, 1820. 13-14.

New York State Historical Association, Fenimore Art Museum, Special Collections. *Jellis Fonda Papers, Coll. No. 157, 1750-1791.* Cooperstown, New York. http://n94057.eos-intl.net/N94057/OPAC/Details/Record.aspx?BibCode=4384088

New York (State). Legislature. *Journals of the Provincial Congress, Provincial Convention, Committee of Safety And Council of Safety of the State of New-York: 1775-1775-1777.* (Albany: Printed by Thurlow Weed, printer to the State, 1842), 1006-1007.

Newman, Peter C. *Hostages to Fortune. The United Empire Loyalists and the Making of Canada.* Toronto: Simon & Schuster, 2016.

"North American Forts" Eastern USA, Mohawk River Valley. https://www.northamericanforts.com/East/ny.html

"Northern Illinois University Digital Library." American Archives. V6:1073. List of Tories from Tryon County sent to Hartford, June 25, 1776. Document ID: S4-V6-P02-sp13-D0213.

O'Callaghan, E. B. *Documents Relative to the Colonial History of the State of New York, Vol VIII.* Albany: Weed, Parsons and Company, 1857. https://archive.org/stream/documentsrelativ08brod#page/484/mode/2up

O'Callaghan, E.B. *The Documentary History of the State of New York,* Vol I. Chapter XVII Papers Relating to the First Settlement and Capture of Oswego 1727-1756. Albany: Weed, Parsons and Co. 1849.

O'Callaghan, E.B. *The Documentary History of the State of New York Vol IV.* Chapter XII Papers Relating to the Six Nations, List of Scholars at the Free School, Johnstown, May 1769. Albany: Weed Parsons & Co. 1851. https://archive.org/stream/documentaryhist04ocal#page/260/mode/2up

O'Callaghan, E.B. *The Documentary History of the State of New York, A Memorial Concering the Iroquois, or Five Confederate Nations of Indians in the Province of New York, Vol IV,* Chapter XXIII, Albany: Charles Van Benthuysen, 1851.

O'Callaghan, E.B. *The Documentary History of the State of New York, Papers Principally Relating to Conversion and Civilization of the Six Nations Indians,* Chapter XXII. Albany: Charles Van Benthuysen, 1851. https://archive.org/stream/documentaryhisto04ocal#page/472/mode/2up

"The Online Institute For Advanced Loyalist Studies." Loyalist Muster Rolls Kings Royal Regiment of New York. http://www.royalprovincial.com/military/musters/krrny/mrkrrmain.htm

Onondaga Nation People of the Hills. "Dress." http://www.onondaganation.org/culture/dress/

Onondaga and Oswego Masonic District Historical Society. Heinmiller, Gary. "Loyalist Freemasons From the State of New York." August/September, 2010. http://www.omdhs.syracusemasons.com/sites/default/files/history/Loyalist%20Freemasons.pdf

O'Reilly, William. *Competition for Colonists: Europe and Her Colonies in the Eighteenth Century*. University of Galway, nd. http://www.histecon.magd.cam.ac.uk/docs/o'reilly_competition_oct04.pdf

O'Toole, Fintan. *White Savage: William Johnson and the Invention of America*, Albany: State University of New York, 2005.

Otterness, Philip. *Becoming German: The 1709 Palatine Migration to New York*, Ithaca: Cornell University Press, 2004.

Parliament of Canada, *Sessional Papers of the Dominion of Canada*, Vol 23, Issue 6. Ottawa: 1890. 13 Nov 1781.

Pastore, Ralph T. "TEIORHÉÑHSERE?," in *Dictionary of Canadian Biography*. Vol. 4, University of Toronto/Université Laval, 2003. http://www.biographi.ca/en/bio/teiorhenhsere_4E.html

Pearson, Johnathan. *A History of the Schenectady Patent in the Dutch and English Times; Being Contributions Towards a History of the Lower Mohawk Valley*, Albany: Joel Munsell's Sons, 1885. https://archive.org/stream/historyofschenec00pe#page/6/mode/2up

Pease, R.H. (Engraver) and DeWitt, Simeon (Surveyor). "A Plan of the City of Albany". Albany: Albany Institute of History & Art. Published in Joel Munsell, The Annals of Albany, vol. 3. 1852. http://www.albanyinstitute.org/details/items/a-plan-of-the-city-of-albany.html

Pennsylvania Historical and Museum Commission Bureau of Archives and History, Pennsylvania State Archives. MG-19 Sequestered Baynton, Wharton, and Morgan Papers, Series Descriptions. #19m.14 http://www.phmc.state.pa.us/bah/dam/mg/sd/m019sd.htm

Pennsylvania Historical & Museum Commission: Department of the Interior. "Pennyslvania Architectural Field Guide. Pennsylvania German Traditional 1700-1870." The Preservation of Historic Architecture. The U.S. Government's Official Guidelines for Preserving Historic Homes. Guildford: The Lyons Press. 2004. Last modified 26 August 2015. http://www.phmc.state.pa.us/portal/communities/architecture/styles/pa-german.html

Penrose, Maryly, B. *Compendium of Early Mohawk Valley Families Vol I & II.* Baltimore: Genealogical Publishing Co., 1990.

"The People of Colonial Albany Live Here." Excerpts From Peter Kalm on Albany. Last Modified November 1, 2010. http://exhibitions.nysm.nysed.gov/albany/art/kalm.html#ch

"The People of Colonial Albany Live Here." The Fort at Albany. https://exhibitions.nysm.nysed.gov/albany/loc/fortalbany.html

Petrin, Guylaine. "Rupert of Osnabruck Chronology," 1. http://www.uelac.org/Loyalist-Info/extras/Rupert-Adam/Rupert-Adam-Family-of-Osnabruck-Chronology-by-Guylaine-Petrin.pdf

Petrin, Guylaine. *Disentangting a loyalist family tree.* The Free Library. 2011 United Empire Loyalists' Association. The Rupert Families in New York. https://www.thefreelibrary.com/Disentangting+a+loyalist+family+tree.-a0275310916

Phelps, Richard. *Newgate of Connecticut; Its Origin and Early History.* American Publishing Company, 1876. 25-58. https://archive.org/stream/newgateofconnect00pheliala#page/n9/mode/2up

Pound, Arthur, 1884-1966. *Johnson of the Mohawks: a Biography of Sir William Johnson, Irish Immigrant, Mohawk War Chief, American Soldier, Empire Builder.* New York: The Macmillan Company, 1930.

Pringle, J. F. *Lunenburgh or the Old Eastern District Its Settlement and Early Progress.* Cornwall, ON: Standard Printing House, 1890. https://archive.org/stream/lunenburgh00prinuoft#page/n397/mode/2up

Promotions Civil and Military. *"London Magazine and Monthly Chronologer."* November, 1755, 24, 550. London: C. Ackers, 1755. https://hdl.handle.net/2027/mdp.39015021267748?urlappend=%3Bseq=584

"Records of the Reformed Dutch Church of Albany, New York, 1683-1809." (Excerpted from the Year Books of the Holland Society of New York).

Reid, Max. *The Mohawk Valley. Its Legends and Its History*. New York: G.P. Putnam's Sons. 1901. http://archive.org/stream/mohawkvalley00reid#page/194/mode/2up

Reid, William. *The Loyalists in Ontario: The Sons and Daughters of the American Loyalists of Upper Canada*. Lambertville, NJ: Genealogical Publishing Co., 1973. https://catalog.hathitrust.org/Record/002896808

"Rivard: Voyageur's World." Clothing. http://www.rendezvousvoyageurs.ca/en/world/worklife/index.html

Roach, Hannah. "Advice to German Emigrants 1749," in *Pennsylvania German Roots Across the Ocean*, ed. Marion Egge. Philadelphia: Genealogical Society of Pennsylvania, Special Publication No. 8, 2000.

Roscoe, William. *History of Schoharie County, New York*. Syracuse: D. Mason & Co., 1882. https://archive.org/stream/cu31924028834541#page/36/mode/2up

Rose, Robert. *The Bordentown and New York Stage*. nd.. http://www.hamiltonphilatelic.org/presentations/bordentown.pdf

Ross, John. *War on the Run. The Epic Story of Robert Rogers and the Conquest of America's Frontier*. New York: Bantam Books, 2011.

Rupp, I. Daniel 1803-1878. *A Collection of Upwards of Thirty Thousand Names of German, Swiss, Dutch, French And Other Immigrants In Pennsylvania From 1727-1776*. Chronologisch Geordnete Sammlung Von Mehr Als 30,000 Namen Von Einwanderern In Pennsylvanien Aus Deutschland, Der Schweiz, Holland, Frankreich U. A. St. Von 1727 Bis 1776 2nd rev. and enl. ed. with German translation. Philadelphia: Leary, Stuart, 1898. 267. https://hdl.handle.net/2027/yale.39002001155903?urlappend=%3Bseq=285

Sauthier, Claude Joseph, Bernard Ratzer, and William Faden. *A map of the Province of New-York reduc'd from the large drawing of that Province, compiled from actual surveys by order of His Excellency William Tryon, Esqr., Captain General & Governor of the same, by Claude Joseph Sauthier; to which is added New Jersey*. London, Wm. Faden, 1776. Map. https://www.loc.gov/item/74692660/.

Schenectady Digital History Archives. "History of the Mohawk Valley Gateway to the West 1614- 1925." Chapter 44: 1757 Massacre at German Flats. http://www.schenectadyhistory.org/resources/mvgw/history/044.html

"Schoharie County Genealogy and History" Schoharie County NY, Revolutionary War Soldiers. http://genealogytrails.com/ny/schoharie/revwar_roster.html

Schoolcraft, Henry. *Historical Considerations on the Siege and Defense of Fort Stanwix 1777*. New York: New York Historical Society, 1846. https://archive.org/stream/historicalconsid01scho#page/n9/mode/2up

Secretary of State of New York. *Calendar of Colonial Manuscripts Indorsed Land Papers*. Albany: Weed, Parsons & Co. 1864. https://archive.org/stream/calendarofnycolo00alba#page/184/mode/2up

Sewall, Samuel. *The History of Woburn, Middlesex County, Mass, Appendix IX*. Boston: Wiggin & Lunt, 1868. https://archive.org/stream/historyofwoburnm00sewa#page/n581/mode/2up

Shepard, Catherine. "FRASER, THOMAS," in *Dictionary of Canadian Biography*. Vol. 6, University of Toronto/Université Laval, 2003. http://www.biographi.ca/en/bio/fraser_thomas_6E.html.

Shortt, Adam & Doughty, Arthur G. eds. Documents Relating to the Constitutional History of Canda, 1759-1791. Sessional Paper No. 18. Ottawa: S.E. Dawson, 1907. 494-495. https://archive.org/stream/documentsrelatin00shor#page/494

Simms, Jeptha Root. *The Frontiersmen of New York: Showing Customs of the Indians, Vicissitudes of the Pioneer White Settlers, And Border Strife In Two Wars. Vol I and II*. Albany: G.C. Riggs, 188283. https://hdl.handle.net/2027/mdp.39015008573084?urlappend=%3Bseq=335

Smith, Abbott. *Some New Facts About Eighteenth Century German Immigration*. New York: Columbia University, nd. https://journals.psu.edu/phj/article/viewFile/21422/21191

Smith, James. *An Account of the Remarkable Occurrences in the Life and Travels of Col. James Smith*. Lexington: 1799. https://archive.org/stream/accountofremarka00smit#page/14/mode/2up

Smith, William. *The History of the Late Province of New York From Its Discovery, to the Apppointment of Governor Colden 1762. Vol 1.* New York: New York Historical Society, 1830. https://archive.org/stream/historyoflatepro01smit_0#page/312/mode/2up

St. John's Episcopal Church. "Our History." http://www.stjohnsjohnstown.org/custompage2.php

St. Pauls Evangelical Lutheran Church. Vernon Benjamin and Karlyn Knaust Elia. "History of the Palatines." http://www.stpaulswestcamp.com/page/history_of_the_palatines

Starbuck, David. *Excavating the Sutler's House: Artifacts of the British Armies in Fort Edward and Lake George.* Lebanon: University Press of New England, 2010.

The State of New York, *The colonial laws of New York from the year 1664 to the Revolution, including the charters to the Duke of York, the commissions and instructions to colonial governors, the Duke's laws, the laws of the Dongan and Leisler Assemblies, the charters of Albany and New York and the acts of the colonial legislatures from 1691 to 1775 inclusive. Transmitted to the Legislature by the Commissioners of Statutory Revision, pursuant to chapter 125 of the Laws of 1891.* Vol 5. Chapters 1584, 1595,1638, 1624. Ithica: Cornell University Library, nd.

The State of New York. *Public Papers of George Clinton, First Governor of New York, 1777-1795, - 1801-1804.* Albany, Wynkoop, Hallenbeck, Crawford Co. 290-292. https://archive.org/stream/cu31924014576684#page/n349/mode/2up

Stephenson, R.S. *Pennsylvania Provincial Soldiers in the Seven Year's War.* Charlottesville: University of Virginia, nd. https://journals.psu.edu/phj/article/viewFile/25220/24989

Stone, William. *Life of Joseph Brant – Thayendanegea. Including the Border Wars of the American Revolution. Vol I.* New York: Alexander V. Blake, 1838. 52-53. https://archive.org/stream/lifeofjosephbran01ston#page/52/mode/2up

Stone, William. *Orderly Book of Sir John Johnson During the Oriskany Campaign 1776-1777.* Albany: Joel Munsell's Sons, 1882. https://archive.org/stream/orderlybooksirj00stongoog#page/n240/mode/

Stone, William, *The Life and Times of Sir William Johnson, Bart.*. Albany: J. Munsell, 1865. https://archive.org/stream/lifetimesofsirwi02stonuoft#page/394/mode/2up

Stormont, Dundas and Glengarry Surrogate Court Records Register Book A, 197-198. Microform Reel 862333. Will of Martin Silmser, 20 August 1800.

Strassburger, Ralph. *Pennsylvania German Pioneers, I, 1727-1775.* Norristown: Pennsylvania German Society Vol. 42 of the Proceedings of the Society, 1934.

Struzinski, Steven. "The Colonial Tavern in America." *The Gettysburg Historical Journal* Vol I, 7. (2002): http://cupola.gettysburg.edu/cgi/viewcontent.cgi?article=1026&context=ghj

Sullivan, James. *The Papers of Sir William Johnson, Vol II.* Albany: The University of the State of New York, 1921.

Sullivan, James. *Minutes of the Albany Committee of Correspondence 1775-1778.* Albany: The University of the State of New York, 1923. 3-4. https://archive.org/stream/MinutesOfTheAlbanyCommitteeOfCorrespondence1775-1778Vol1#page/n19/mode/2up

Third Annual Report of the State Historian of the State of New York. Albany: Wynkoop, Hallenbeck Crawford Co., 1898. https://archive.org/details/annualreportofst02newy

Three Rivers Hudson, Mohawk, Schoharie, History From America's Most Famous Valleys. "Following the Old Mohawk Trail. The Old Palatine Church and the Cochran House" http://threeriversshms.com/oldpalch.htm

Three Rivers Hudson, Mohawk, Schoharie, History From America's Most Famous Valleys. Dean R. Snow, Dean, R. & Guldenzopf, David B. "Indian Castle Church The Mohawk Upper Castle Historic District National Historic Landmark." 2001. https://web.archive.org/web/20060622142738/http://indiancastle.com/ICNHL.htm

Three Rivers Hudson, Mohawk, Schoharie, History From America's Most Famous Valleys. "Johnson's Ledger Names of Retainers of The Great Sir William." http://www.threerivershms.com/namesjohnson.htm

"Three Rivers Hudson, Mohawk, Schoharie. History From America's Most Famous Valleys." Roster of Oriskay Heroes. http://www.threerivershms.com/namesoriskany.htm

"Three Rivers." Towns and Villages of Fulton County. Johnstown Village. Frothingham, Washington. ed. The History of Fulton County. Syracuse: D. Mason & Co., 1892.

"Three Rivers Hudson Mohawk Schoharie. History From America's Most Famous Valleys." Krahmer, Christian. The Kocherthal Records. A Translation of the Kocherthal Records of the West Camp Lutheran Church, October 1926. In Lou MacWethy, The Book of Names Especially Relating to The Early Palatines and the First Settlers in the Mohawk Valley. St. Johnsville, New York, Enterprise and News, 1933.

"Three Rivers Hudson, Mohawk, Schoharie. History From America's Most Famous Valleys." Lou D. McWethy, The Book of Names Especially Relating to the Early Palatines and the First Settlers in the Mohawk Valley, (St. Johnsville, NY, The Enterprise and News, 1933), Johnson's Ledger Names of Retainers of The Great Sir William. The Battle of Klock's Field.

"Three Rivers Hudson, Mohawk, Schoharie. History From America's Most Famous Valleys." Klock's Churchyard Preservation Group, 1780-1980 The Bicentennial of the Schoharie and Mohawk Valley Raids. http://threerivershms.com/schoharie.htm

Thompson Kelsay, Isabel. *Joseph Brant 1743-1807 Man of Two Worlds.* Syracuse: Syracuse University Press, 1984.

Todd, Malcolm. *The Early Germans,* 2d ed. Malden, MA: Blackwell, 2004.

"UEALC St Lawrence Branch" McNiff Maps. Edward Kipp & George Anderson, An Index to the 1786 McNiff Maps of the Townships of Lancaster, Charlottenburg, Cornwall, Osnabruck, Williamsburg, and Matilda (The Loyalist Maps). 2007. http://uelac.org/st-lawrence/wp content/uploads/2017/12/2_CORNWALL.pdf ;

University of Massachusetts History Club. "Stamp Act the Origins, Implementation and Consequences." http://www.stamp-act-history.com

"United Empire Loyalists Association of Canada," Loyalist Trails, 2017-44, 29 October 2017, Alida Vrooman Hare UEL, http://www.uelac.org/Loyalist-Trails/2017/Loyalist-Trails-2017.php?issue=201744

"Upper Canada East Marriage Indexes." Michael Stephenson. Last Updated 2018. Gallinger, Michael, Selismer? Dorothy. 1806. https://www.ontariogenealogy.com/easternontariomarriages.html

Van Laer, A. J. F. *Early Records of the City and County of Albany and Colony of Rensselaerswyck, Vol 2 (Deeds 3 and 4, 1678-1704).* Albany: The University of the State of New York, 1916. https://archive.org/stream/earlyrecordsofc02alba#page/354/mode/2up

Van Schaack, Henry C. *The Life of Peter Van Schaack, LL.D.* New York: D. Appleton & Co., 1842. https://archive.org/stream/lifeofpetervan00vans#page/n35/mode/2up

Van Schaack, Henry C. *Memoirs of the Life of Henry Van Schaack. Embracing Selections From His Correspondence During the American Revolution.* Chicago: A.C. McClurg & Company, 1892. https://archive.org/stream/memoirslifehenr00schagoog#page/n33/mode/2up ;

VerPlanck, William & Collyer, Moses. *The Sloops of the Hudson*. New York: G.P. Putnam's Sons, 1908. https://archive.org/stream/sloopsofhudsonhi00verp#page/14/mode/2up

Village of Barneveld. "History & Maps, 1793 Village Map." http://villageofbarneveld.org/content/History/Home/:field=documents;/content/Documents/File/59.pdf

Vrooman, John, J. "Three Rivers Hudson, Mohawk, Schoharie. History From America's Most Famous Valleys." From Forts & Firesides of The Mohawk County, Queen Anne's Chapel Parsonage, Fort Hunter." 1951. http://www.threeriversshms.com/qanne.htm

Watt, Gavin & Morrison, James F. *The Burning of The Valleys. Daring Raids From Canada Against The New York Frontier in the Fall of 1780,* rev. ed. Toronto: Dundern Press, 1997.

Watt, Gavin. *Rebellion in the Mohawk Valley. The St. Leger Expedition of 1777.* Toronto: Dundern Press, 2002.

Watt, Gavin. *A Dirty, Trifling, Piece of Business Volume I: The Revolutionary War as Waged From Canada in 1781.* Toronto: Dundern Press, 2009.

Watt, Gavin. *Loyalist Refugees: Non-Military Refugees in Quebec 1776-1784.* Milton ON: Global Heritage Press, 2014.

Watt, Gavin. *Poisoned By Lies and Hypocrisy. America's First Attempt to Bring Liberty To Canada, 1775-1776.* Toronto: Dundern Press, 2014.

Watt, Gavin. *Fire & Desolation. The Revolutionary War's 2778 Campaign as Waged from Quebec and Niagara Against the American Frontiers.* Toronto: Dundurn, 2017.

Welch, Steven. "1775 The Montresor Plan Surveyed in the Winter of 1775" Last Modified 16 June 2014. http://stevenwarranresearch.blogspot.ca/2014/06/1775-montresor-plan-surveyed-in-winter.html

Whittemore, Henry. *The Abeel And Allied Families.* New York: 1899. https://hdl.handle.net/2027/wu.89062958707 ;

Witthoft, Herman Wellington Sr. & Empie Greene, Barbara. *The Descendants of Johan Ernst Emichen Emigrant to America Volume II The Loyalist Canadian Empey Family.* Orleans, ON: Edward, Kipp, 2003.

Wokeck, Marianne. *Trade in Strangers: The Beginnings of Mass Migration to North America.* University Park PA: Pennsylvania State Press, 1999.

Yates, Austin. *Schenectady County New York: Its History to the Close of the Nineteenth Century.* New York History Company, 1902. https://archive.org/stream/schenectadycount00yate#page/n33/mode/2up

Christopher Yates Papers, Special Collections Research Center, Sryacuse, N.Y. Transcribed by Ken D. Johnson, 2012. http://www.fort-plank.com/Loyalists_Exchanged_March_1780.pdf

Zeichner, Oscar. "The Loyalist Problem in New York After the Revolution." *New York History* 21, no. 3 (1940): 284-302. http://www.jstor.org/stable/23135069.

ENDNOTES

1 Ancestry.com. *UK, American Loyalist Claims, 1776-1835 [database on-line]*. Provo, UT, USA: Ancestry.com Operations, Inc., 2013. Original data: American Loyalist Claims, 1776–1835. AO 12–13. The National Archives of the United Kingdom, Kew, Surrey, England. UK, American Loyalist Claims, 1776-1835 for Philip Eamer AO 12: American Loyalists Claims, Series I Piece 031: Evidence, New York, 1787-1788, 156. 277-278. There were two Commissioners to hear Philip's claim on February 14, Mr. Pemberton and Colonel Dundas. http://heritage.canadiana.ca/view/oocihm.lac_reel_c12904/2102?r=0&s=3

2 Although there were several dates and routes Philip and Catrina could have taken in 1781. I believe the Sacandaga/Schroon lake route in October was the most likely. For many years, this was a well-travelled military and trade route from Johnstown, New York to Quebec, Canada. And, I believe they waited until the last possible moment to leave due to their age, or due to hopes they could remain in their home despite the outcome of the war. However, after the Johnstown Battle October 25, 1781, American forces were firm in removing anyone suspected of being loyal to the crown. William Stone, *Orderly Book of Sir John Johnson During the Oriskany Campaign 1776-1777* (Albany: Joel Munsell's Sons, 1882), 18. https://archive.org/stream/orderlybooksirj00stongoog#page/n240/mode/2up ; Gavin Watt, *A dirty, trifling, piece of business Volume I: The Revolutionary War as Waged From Canada in 1781* (Toronto: Dundern Press, 2009), 178, 314,358.

3 Ancestry.com. *UK, American Loyalist Claims, 1776-1835*, 156.

4 Ancestry.com. *UK, American Loyalist Claims, 1776-183,* American Loyalist Claims, 1776-1835 for Philip Emis AO 13: American Loyalists Claims, Series II Piece 012: New Claims C. D. E. F., New York, 425-26.

5 Alexander Fraser, Provincial Archivist. Digital Edition of the Second Report of the Bureau of Archives For the Province of Ontario. 1904. *United Empire Loyalists Enquiry Into The Losses and Services in Consequence of Their Loyalty Evidence in the Canadian Claims, 1904* (Toronto: Global Heritage Press, 2010), No 49, 402, 406, 407.

6 Frank Diffenderffer, *The German Immigration Into Pennsylvania Through the Port of Philadelphia 1700-1775 Part II The Redemptioners,* (Lancaster: Pennsylvania-German Society, 1900), 50.

CHAPTER ONE
Home in the Upper Rhine Valley

7 Thomas Wiemer was most likely born in Dusseldorf and believed to be the son of Gregor Wimmer. Claudia Sosniak of Hochstadten, Hesse, "Questions-Eamer/Wiemer" email message to Vicki Holmes with attachment of Johannes Philip Wiemer's baptism from Auerbach Church records, December 20, 2016; Claudia Sosniak, "Summary of Wiemer Family" email message to Vicki Holmes, December 20, 2016; Hessen Arcinsys, 16841685, HstAD fonds E 10 No 1577, E10 Nr. 167/8.

8 Dan Heinemeier, *A Social History of Hesse Roman Times to 1900,* (Arlington: Heinemeier Publications, 2002), 16.

9 Ibid, 6.

10 Malcolm Todd, *The Early Germans, 2nd ed.* (Malden: Blackwell, 2004), 53.

11 "J Stor Academic.edu" *The history files: European Kingdoms Central Europe Chatti (Hessians) (Germans)* http://www.historyfiles.co.uk/KingListsEurope/GermanyHesse.htm.

12 Dan Heinemeier, *A Social History of Hesse Roman Times to 1900*, (Arlington: Heinemeier Publications, 2002), 151.

13 Archives in Hessen, E-10 Policey-Angelegenheiten. Hessen Arcinsys, 16841685, HstAD fonds E 10 No 1577, E10 Nr. 167/8. 1684-1685. "Enter the Miller Hans George Frolich to Eberstadt for permission on the construction of a new mill. Please severed for permission to build a ship mill at Erfelden. Enter the Miller Thomas Wiemer of Dusseldorf on the Eschollmuhle against the mill building." The only record that might belong to Thomas Wiemer I found in the FamilySearch database was: Deutschland Geburten und Taufen, 1558-1898. Thomas W. male, christened 7 Nov 1647 at Evangelisch Duesseldorf Stadt, Rheinland, Prussia. Father: G.W. Mother: Margaretha Tilmans. https://www.familysearch.org/search/ark:/61903/1:1:NF2D-78D

14 Claudia Sosniak, "Summary of Wiemer Family" email message to Vicki Holmes, December 20, 2016. *The Eschollmule*; CityLexicon Darmstadt: Mills in Eberstadt http://www.darmstadt-stadtlexikon.de/m/muehlen-in-eberstadt.html; Stadtlexikon Darmstadt, eds. Roland Dotzert, Peter Engels, Anke Leonhardt, *Muhlen in Eberstadt*, (Darmstadt, Konrad Theiss, 2006), 647; Friedrich Kirschner, ed., Geschichtsverein Eberstadt-Frankenstein *Die Muhlen mit ihrem Erbauungsjahr im Uberblick* Eberstadt-Frankenstein, http://www.eberstadt-frankenstein.de/content/011_muehlen.pdf ; Katja Shafer, *Swantes Geneology, Escholmulle (Wambolts Mill)*, https://translate.google.ca/translate?hl=en&sl=de&u=http://www.swantes.de/index.php/muehlenforschung/mue%20hlenverzeichnis-alle/63-muehle-64297-eschollmuehl&prev=search Aaron Folgleman, *Hopeful Journeys: German Immigration, Settlement and Political Culture in Colonial America 1717-1775*, (Philadelphia: University of Pennsylvania Press, 1996), 18.

15 Stadtlexikon Darmstadt, eds. Roland Dotzert, Peter Engels, Anke Leonhardt, *Muhlen in Eberstadt*, (Darmstadt, Konrad Theiss, 2006), 647; Friedrich Kirschner, ed., Geschichtsverein Eberstadt-Frankenstein *Die Muhlen* ; Wikipedia *Eschcollmule* https://translate.

google.ca/translate?hl=en&sl=de&u=https://de.wikipedia.org/wiki/Eberstadt&prev=search

16 Friedrich Kirschner, ed., Geschichtsverein Eberstadt-Frankenstein *Die Muhlen*; Archives in Hessen, E-10 Policey-Angelegenheiten. Hessen Arcinsys, 16841685, HstAD fonds E 10 No 1577, E10 Nr. 167/8. 1684-1685. https://arcinsys.hessen.de/arcinsys/detailAction.action?detailid=v3656615&icomefrom=search

17 Claudia Sosniak, "Summary of Wiemer Family" email message to Vicki Holmes, December 20, 2016. The Eschollmule; *Deutschland Geburten und Taufen, 1558-1898," database, FamilySearch* (https://familysearch.org/ark:/61903/1:1:N5VT-6PP: 28 November 2014), Thomas Wimmer in entry for Johann Daniel Wimmer, 21 Dec 1685; citing ; FHL microfilm 1,190,527. Evangelishce Kirche in Hessen Und Nassau, Zentral Archive. Records of Darmstadt-Eberstadt, 1690. Birth records of Christina, Johann Wendel, Johann Daniel Melchior, Johann Philipp. Written communication with Archive Researcher 24 March 2017.

18 Evangelishce Kirche in Hessen Und Nassau, Zentral Archive. Records of Darmstadt-Eberstadt, 1690. Burial records of Thomas Wimmer and his wife Ottilia. Written communication with Archive Researcher 24 March 2017. *Deutschland Tote und Beerdigungen, 1582-1958," database, FamilySearch* (https://familysearch.org/ark:/61903/1:1:JW5G-YPV: 28 November 2014), Thomas Wimer, 12 Feb 1690; citing, reference; FHL microfilm 1,190,527.; *Deutschland Geburten und Taufen, 1558-1898," database, FamilySearch* (https://familysearch.org/ark:/61903/1:1:N5VT-W88 : 28 November 2014), Thomas Wimmar in entry for Joh. Philippus Wimmar, 31 Jul 1687; citing; FHL microfilm 1,190,527; *Deutschland Tote und Beerdigungen,* 1582-1958," database, FamilySearch (https://familysearch.org/ark:/61903/1:1:JW5G-YLZ : 28 November 2014), Thomas Wimmer in entry for Joan Philippus Wimmer, 01 Dec 1689; citing , reference ; FHL microfilm 1,190,527.

19 Friedrich Kirschner, ed., Geschichtsverein Eberstadt-Frankenstein *Die Muhlen mit ihrem Erbauungsjahr im Uberblick* Eberstadt-Frankenstein, http://www.eberstadt-frankenstein.de/content/011_muehlen.pdf

20 Evangelishce Kirche in Hessen Und Nassau, Zentral Archive. Records of Darmstadt-Eberstadt, 1706. Marriage record of Johann Adam Wimmer and Elizabeth Dorothea Rau. Written communication with archive researcher, 24 March 2017.

21 *Deutschland Geburten und Taufen, 1558-1898," database, FamilySearch* (https://familysearch.org/ark:/61903/1:1:NL46-P8V : 28 November 2014), Joh. Adam Wiemar in entry for Johann Georg Wiemar, 02 Oct 1707; citing ; FHL microfilm 1,190,527; *Deutschland Geburten und Taufen, 1558-1898," database, FamilySearch* (https://familysearch.org/ark:/61903/1:1:NL46-YM8 : 28 November 2014), Johann Adam Wiemar in entry for Johann Daniel Wiemar, 24 Oct 1708; citing ; FHL microfilm 1,190,527.*Deutschland Heiraten, 1558-1929, database, FamilySearch* (https://familysearch.org/ark:/61903/1:1:J4GS-MB4 : 26 December 2014), Johann Peter Wiemar and Maria Elissabetha Barbara Roth, 22 Jan 1737; citing Evangelisch, Birkenau, Starkenburg, Hesse-Darmstadt; FHL microfilm 1,340,362.; *Deutschland Geburten und Taufen, 1558-1898," database, FamilySearch* (https://familysearch.org/ark:/61903/1:1:VHQ5-8GG : 28 November 2014), Johann Jacob Wiemer, 07 Sep 1718; citing ; FHL microfilm 1,340,361.; *Deutschland Geburten und Taufen, 1558-1898," database, FamilySearch* (https://familysearch.org/ark:/61903/1:1:VHQ5-7LJ : 28 November 2014), Johann Adam Wiemer in entry for Johannes Wiemer, 28 Feb 1721; citing ; FHL microfilm 1,340,361.

22 Claudia Sosniak, "Questions-Eamer/Wiemer" email message to Vicki Holmes with attachment of Johannes Philip Wiemer's baptism from Auerbach Church records, December 20, 2016; *Deutschland Geburten und Taufen, 1558-1898," database,* 17; *FamilySearch* (https://familysearch.org/ark:/61903/1:1:VHQ5-9PC : 28 November 2014), Johann Adam Wiemer in entry for Johann Philipp Wiemer, 26 Dec 1722;

citing ; FHL microfilm 1,340,361; Personal communication with Claudia Sosniak, holder of the Auerbach Church Records, she stated that the records indicating 'Birkenau' in the family search database are incorrect. The records in the database are from the Auerbach Church records.

23 *Deutschland Geburten und Taufen, 1558-1898," database, FamilySearch* (https://familysearch.org/ark:/61903/1:1:VHQ5-WHQ: 28 November 2014), Anna Elisabetha Wiemar, 20 Jan 1726; citing FHL microfilm 1,340,361.

24 Evangelishce Kirche in Hessen Und Nassau, Zentral Archive. Records of Darmstadt-Auerbach 1729. Burial record of Elizabeth Dorothea Rau. Marriage record of Johann Adam Wimmer and Elizabeth Barbara Muetz. Written communication with Archive Researcher 24 March 2017; *Deutschland Heiraten, 1558-1929," database, FamilySearch* (https://familysearch.org/ark:/61903/1:1:VC13-M5D : 26 December 2014), Johann Adam Wiemar and Elisbetha Barbara Muetzen, 22 Sep 1729; citing Evangelisch, Birkenau, Starkenburg, Hesse-Darmstadt; FHL microfilm 1,340,361.; Claudia Sosniak, "Summary of Wiemer Family" email message to Vicki Holmes, December 20, 2016.

25 *Deutschland Geburten und Taufen, 1558-1898,"* database, *FamilySearch* (https://familysearch.org/ark:/61903/1:1:VHQ5-ZMD: 28 November 2014), Johann Valentin Wiemer, 14 Jul 1730; citing; FHL microfilm 1,340,361; Ancestry.com. *Germany, Select Births and Baptisms, 1558-1898* [database on-line]. Provo, UT, USA: Ancestry.com Operations, Inc., 2014. Original data: *Germany, Births and Baptisms, 1558-1898.* Salt Lake City, Utah: FamilySearch, 2013. (Anna Barbara Wiemar); Ancestry.com. *Germany, Select Births and Baptisms, 1558-1898* [database on-line]. Provo, UT, USA: Ancestry.com Operations, Inc., 2014. Original data: *Germany, Births and Baptisms, 1558-1898*. Salt Lake City, Utah: FamilySearch, 2013. (Anna Margretha Wiemar); *Deutschland Geburten und Taufen, 1558-1898," database, FamilySearch* (https://familysearch.org/ark:/61903/1:1:VHQP-1RV: 28 November 2014), Johann Adam Wiemar in entry for Johann Mathaeus Wiemar, 08 Apr 1736; citing; FHL microfilm 1,340,361; Ancestry.com. *Germany,*

Select Births and Baptisms, 1558-1898 [database on-line]. Provo, UT, USA: Ancestry.com Operations, Inc., 2014. Original data: *Germany, Births and Baptisms, 1558-1898.* Salt Lake City, Utah: FamilySearch, 2013. (Death Johann Mathaeus Wiemar 18 April 1736); *Deutschland Geburten und Taufen, 1558-1898,"* database, *FamilySearch*(https://familysearch.org/ark:/61903/1:1:VHQP-1RV : 28 November 2014), Johann Adam Wiemar in entry for Johann Mathaeus Wiemar, 08 Apr 1736; citing ; FHL microfilm 1,340,361; *Deutschland Heiraten, 1558-1929,"* database, *FamilySearch*(https://familysearch.org/ark:/61903/1:1:J4GS-9R5 : 26 December 2014), Johann Adam Wiemer in entry for Johann Matthaeus Wiemer and Anna Margretha Weinreich, 25 Nov 1757; citing Evangelisch, Birkenau, Starkenburg, Hesse-Darmstadt; FHL microfilm 1,340,362; *Deutschland Geburten und Taufen, 1558-1898,"* database, *FamilySearch*(https://familysearch.org/ark:/61903/1:1:VHQ5-XQF : 28 November 2014), Johann Adam Wiemar in entry for Anna Catharina Wiemar, 30 Jan 1739; citing ; FHL microfilm 1,340,361.

26 Dan Heinemeier, *A Social History of Hesse Roman Times to 1900,* (Arlington: Heinemeier Publications, 2002), 192; Philip Otterness, *Becoming German: The 1709 Palatine Migration to New York,* (Ithaca: Cornell University Press, 2004), 17.

27 Philip Otterness, *Becoming German,* 17; Dan Heinemeier, *A Social History of Hesse Roman Times to 1900,* 129; Steve Hochstadt, "Migration in Preindustrial Germany," *Central European History* 16, no.3 (1983), 210, 223. https://www.uzh.ch/cmsssl/suz/dam/jcr:ffffffff-866d-1ee0-ffff-ffff9b28ba23/11.08_hochstadt_83.pdf

28 N.H. Mallett, ed., Military History Now. *Hessians For Hire: Meet the 18th Century's Busiest 'Mercenaries'* http://militaryhistorynow.com/2013/06/15/hired-guns-ten-amazing-facts-about-the-hessians/ ; Frank Diffenderffer, *The German Immigration Into Pennsylvania Through the Port of Philadelphia 1700-1775 Part II The Redemptioners,* (Lancaster: Pennsylvania-German Society, 1900), 17 https://archive.org/details/germanimmigratio00diffuoft

29 Steve Hochstadt, "Migration in Preindustrial Germany," *Central European History* 16, no.3 (1983), 203. https://www.uzh.ch/cmsssl/suz/dam/jcr:ffffffff-866d-1ee0-ffff-ffff9b28ba23/11.08_hochstadt_83.pdf

30 Marianne Wokeck, *Trade in Strangers: The Beginnings of Mass Migration to North America,* (University Park: Pennsylvania State Press, 1999); Aaron Folgleman, *Hopeful Journeys: German Immigration, Settlement and Political Culture in Colonial America 1717-1775,* (Philadelphia: University of Pennsylvania Press, 1996), 6.

31 Evangelishce Kirche in Hessen Und Nassau, Zentral Archive. Records of Darmstadt-Auerbach 1752. Baptismal record of Elizabeth Catharina Wiemer. Written communication with Archive Researcher 24 March 2017; *Deutschland Geburten und Taufen, 1558-1898,*" database, *FamilySearch* (https://familysearch.org/ark:/61903/1:1:VHQP-Y23: 28 November 2014), Elisabetha Catharina Wiemer, 29 Sep 1752; citing ; FHL microfilm 1,340,361; Ancestry.com. *Germany, Select Births and Baptisms, 1558-1898* [database on-line]. Provo, UT, USA: Ancestry.com Operations, Inc., 2014. Original data: *Germany, Births and Baptisms, 1558-1898*. Salt Lake City, Utah: FamilySearch, 2013.

32 I do not know the owner of the ship that brought Philip and Catrina to America; however, the process of recruiting and transporting emigrants is fact. The statement that John Henry Keppele's Company brought them is fiction, although he was a very real business man in Philadelphia at the time they arrived in America. He was a German born entrepreneur who came to Pennsylvania in 1738. He was a successful businessman, trader and part owner in dozens of ships that brought German emigrants to Pennsylvania. Birte Pfleger, "Immigrant Entrepreneurship: German-American Business Biographies," *John Henry Keppele (1716-1797), https://www.immigrantentrepreneurship.org/entry.php?rec=7* William O'Reilly, *Competition for Colonists: Europe and Her Colonies in the Eighteenth Century,* (University of Galway, nd), 14; 21-23. http://www.histecon.magd.cam.ac.uk/docs/o'reilly_competition_oct04.pdf; Farley Grub, "Morbidity and Mortality on the North Atlantic Passage:

Eighteenth Century German Immigration," *Journal of Interdisciplinary History,* 17(3), 1987, 566, DOI: 10.2307/204611

33 William O'Reilly, *Competition for Colonists;* 12, 14; Boyd, James. "Merchants of Migration: Keeping the German Atlantic Connected in America's Early National Period." In *Immigrant Entrepreneurship: German-American Business Biographies, 1720 to the Present,* vol. 1, edited by Marianne S. Wokeck. German Historical Institute, 2-3, Last modified February 12, 2015; Mark Haberlein, "German Communities in 18th Century Europe and North America" in Matjaz Klemencic and Mary Harris eds, *European Migrants, Diasporas and Indigenous Ethnic Minorities,* (Pisa: Pisa University Press, 2009) 22; Frank Diffenderffer, *The German Immigration Into Pennsylvania Through the Port of Philadelphia 1700-1775 Part II The Redemptioners* (Lancaster: Pennsylvania-German Society, 1900), 18, 22, 32-33. https://archive.org/details/germanimmigratio00diffuoft ; Albert Gerberich trans., *Well Meant Information as to How the Germans, Who Wish to Travel Pennsylvania Should Conduct Themselves,* James Dwight Hartsell 1749 Pamphlet for German Emigrants, http://www.jdhartsell.com/HansGeorg/1749_pamphlet/index.html ; Carl Eben, trans., *Gottlieb Mittelberger's Journey to Pennsylvania in the Year 1750 and His Return to Germany in 1754* (Philadelphia: John Jos. McVey, 1898), 11-12, 17, 26. https://archive.org/stream/gottliebmittelbe00gott#page/12/mode/2up ; Frank Diffenderffer, *The German Exodus to England in 1709* (Lancaster, Pennsylvania-German Society, 1897), 288; Philip Otterness, *Becoming German: The 1709 Palatine Migration to New York* (Ithaca: Cornell University Press, 2004), 26-27; Walter Knittle, *Early Eighteenth Century Palatine Emigration* (Philadelphia: Dorrance and Company, 1937), 20, https://archive.org/stream/earlyeighteenthc00knit#page/n5/mode/2up Marianne Wokeck, *Trade in Strangers: The Beginnings of Mass Migration to North America,* (University Park: Pennsylvania State Press, 1999), ; Marion Egge, ed., *Pennsylvania German Roots Across the Ocean,* (Philadelphia: Genealogical Society of Pennsylvania, Special Publication No. 8, 2000), 46,48-49.

34 Farley Grub, "Morbidity and Mortality on the North Atlantic Passage: Eighteenth Century German Immigration," *Journal of Interdisciplinary History,* 17(3), 1987, 565, DOI: 10.2307/204611; Frank Diffenderffer, *The German Immigration Into Pennsylvania Through the Port of Philadelphia 1700-1775 Part II The Redemptioners* (Lancaster: Pennsylvania-German Society, 1900), 57-70; Carl Eben, trans., *Gottlieb Mittelberger's Journey to Pennsylvania in the Year 1750 and His Return to Germany in 1754* (Philadelphia: John Jos. McVey, 1898), 20-28.

35 Philip Otterness, *Becoming German: The 1709 Palatine Migration to New York* (Ithaca: Cornell University Press, 2004), 23.

36 Ibid, *25-30;* Walter Knittle, *Early Eighteenth Century Palatine Emigration,* (Philadelphia: Dorrance and Company, 1937), 14-15. https://archive.org/stream/earlyeighteenthc00knit#page/n5/mode/2up

37 Philip Wiemer and Adam Hertle's son Johannes lived a few miles from each other near Johnstown, New York about 1769; Philip's son Peter and Adam's son Johannes were in the same British regiment during the revolutionary war; they were also cousins in Canada in the late 1790s. The Barnhardt family leased Barnhardt Island near Cornwall, Ontario from the St. Regis Mohawk Indians about 1800. Christian Kramer, trans., *The Kocherthal Records: A Translation of the Kocherthal Records of the West Camp Lutheran Church,* The Book of Names Especially Relating to the Early Palatines and the First Settlers in the Mohawk Valley, (St. Johnsville: The Enterprise and News, 1933), 45. http://www.threeriversshms.com/nameskocherthal.htm . "Deutschland Geburten und Taufen, 1558-1898," database, *FamilySearch* (https://familysearch.org/ark:/61903/1:1:NCX5-68Y: 10 February 2018), Adam Hertel, 21 Aug 1662; Birkenau, Hessen. Father: Hans Hertel, Mother: Margreth. Citing; FHL microfilm 1,340,344.; "Deutschland Geburten und Taufen, 1558-1898," database, *FamilySearch* (https://familysearch.org/ark:/61903/1:1:NNFC-Z6F: 10 February 2018), Philips Jacob Bernhardt in entry for Johannes Bernhardt, 11 Sep 1678; Gros Zimmern, Hesse. Citing; FHL microfilm 1,190,553.

38 Carl Eben, trans., *Gottlieb Mittelberger's Journey to Pennsylvania in the Year 1750 and His Return to Germany in 1754,* (Philadelphia: John Jos. McVey, 1898), 18. https://archive.org/stream/gottliebmittelbe00gott#page/12/mode/2up

39 Hannah Roach, "Advice to German Emigrants 1749," in *Pennsylvania German Roots Across the Ocean,* Marion Egge, ed. (Philadelphia: Genealogical Society of Pennsylvania, Special Publication No. 8, 2000), 46; Marianne Wokeck, *Trade in Strangers: The Beginnings of Mass Migration to North America,* (University Park: Pennsylvania State Press, 1999); Ralph Strassburger, *Pennsylvania German Pioneers Vol I 1727-1775,* (Norristown: Pennsylvania German Society Vol. 42 of the Proceedings of the Society, 1934), xxxvii; Frank Diffenderffer, *The German Immigration Into Pennsylvania Through the Port of Philadelphia 1700-1775 Part II The Redemptioners,* (Lancaster: Pennsylvania-German Society, 1900), 30-31, 57. https://archive.org/details/germanimmigratio00diffuoft

40 Marianne Wokeck, *Trade in Strangers: The Beginnings of Mass Migration to North America,* (University Park: Pennsylvania State Press, 1999),

41 Documentation of Philip's good character from the Pastor and his manumission record have not been located. William O'Reilly, *Competition for Colonists: Europe and Her Colonies in the Eighteenth Century,* (University of Galway, nd), 6; http://www.histecon.magd.cam.ac.uk/docs/o'reilly_competition_oct04.pdf ; Aaron Folgleman, *Hopeful Journeys: German Immigration, Settlement and Political Culture in Colonial America 1717-1775,* (Philadelphia: University of Pennsylvania Press, 1996), 19-20. Ralph Strassburger, *Pennsylvania German Pioneers Vol I 1727-1775,* (Norristown: Pennsylvania German Society Vol. 42 of the Proceedings of the Society, 1934), xxxviii

42 Marion Egge, ed., *Pennsylvania German Roots Across the Ocean,* (Philadelphia: Genealogical Society of Pennsylvania, Special Publication No. 8, 2000), 49-50; Frank Diffenderffer, *The German Immigration Into Pennsylvania Through the Port of Philadelphia 1700-1775 Part II*

The Redemptioners, (Lancaster: Pennsylvania-German Society, 1900), 59, 62-6.

43 A Scow was a common type of sailboat that was used to carry cargo and passengers. Its flat bottom allowed it to sail in shallow water and dock at multiple stops along the river. Boyd, James. "Merchants of Migration: Keeping the German Atlantic Connected in America's Early National Period." In *Immigrant Entrepreneurship: German-American Business Biographies, 1720 to the Present,* vol. 1, edited by Marianne S. Wokeck. German Historical Institute, 3. Last modified February 12, 2015. https://www.immigrantentrepreneurship.org/entry.php?rec=229

44 Frank Diffenderffer, *The German Immigration Into Pennsylvania Through the Port of Philadelphia 1700-1775 Part II The Redemptioners,* (Lancaster: Pennsylvania-German Society, 1900), 32.

45 I chose Gernsheim as the port that Philip departed from because it was the closest port to Auerbach. He might have sailed from Worms which is directly west of Auerbach and only a few miles further than Gernsheim. Carl Eben, trans., *Gottlieb Mittelberger's Journey to Pennsylvania in the Year 1750 and His Return to Germany in 1754,* (Philadelphia: John Jos. McVey, 1898), 26. https://archive.org/stream/gottliebmittelbe00gott#page/12/mode/2up

46 Carl Eben, trans., *Gottlieb Mittelberger's Journey to Pennsylvania in the Year 1750 and His Return to Germany in 1754,* (Philadelphia: John Jos. McVey, 1898), 18. https://archive.org/stream/gottliebmittelbe00gott#page/12/mode/2up

CHAPTER TWO
The Journey to America (1755)

47 Carl Eben, trans., *Gottlieb Mittelberger's Journey to Pennsylvania in the Year 1750 and His Return to Germany in 1754,* (Philadelphia: John Jos. McVey,

1898), 18. https://archive.org/stream/gottliebmittelbe00gott#page/12/mode/2up

48 The Weise family is fictional; however it was common for emigrants to travel in groups up the Rhine and in Rotterdam.

49 Boyd, James. "Merchants of Migration: Keeping the German Atlantic Connected in America's Early National Period." In *Immigrant Entrepreneurship: German-American Business Biographies, 1720 to the Present,* vol. 1, ed. Marianne S. Wokeck. German Historical Institute, 3. Last modified February 12, 2015. http://www.immigrantentrepreneurship.org/entry.php?rec=229

50 Jolly boats were rowboats and the smallest type of ship's boats used to transport goods and people to and from ships. They were also used to transport a small number of people from the ships to shore. Peter Kemp, *The Oxford Companion to Ships and the Sea,* ed. (Oxford: Oxford University Press, 1976), 434.

51 Although Ingrid is a fictional Innkeeper, many Innkeepers in Rotterdam were women and served as agents for the merchants and shipping companies. William O'Reilly, *Competition for Colonists: Europe and Her Colonies in the Eighteenth Century,* (University of Galway, nd), 12. http://www.histecon.magd.cam.ac.uk/docs/o'reilly_competition_oct04.pdf

52 In his claim to the British government in 1788, Philip stated he came to America in 1755. There is evidence of two ships arriving in Philadelphia in 1755. The first is the Neptune, Captain George Smith Master, arriving from Rotterdam and Gosport, 7 October 1755 with 226 passengers. The surviving passenger list is only partial and lists 90 names. Unfortunately, Philip's name is not one of them. I believe this is the ship on which Philip and Catrina arrived. The other ship, the Pennsylvania, arriving from London, 6 November 1755 carried 36 passengers. Ralph Strassburger, *Pennsylvania German Pioneers Vol I 1727-1775,* (Norristown: Pennsylvania German Society Vol. 42 of the Proceedings of the Society, 1934), 677-682. https://archive.org/stream/pennsylvaniagerm03penn_2#page/676/mode/2up

53 Farley Grubb, "The Market Structure of Shipping German Immigrants to Colonial America," (University of Delaware, 1987), 37, https://journals.psu.edu/pmhb/article/viewFile/44187/43908 ; Carl Eben, trans., *Gottlieb Mittelberger's Journey to Pennsylvania in the Year 1750 and His Return to Germany in 1754,* (Philadelphia: John Jos. McVey, 1898), 18-21. https://archive.org/stream/gottliebmittelbe00gott#page/12/mode/2up ; Abbott Smith, *Some New Facts About Eighteenth Century German Immigration,* (New York, Columbia University, nd), 107-108. https://journals.psu.edu/phj/article/viewFile/21422/21191

54 Tween decks is the space between decks. On an emigrant ship tween decks is between the upper deck and the hold. Stephen Berry, *A Path in the Mighty Waters: Shipboard Life and Atlantic Crossings to the New World,* (New Haven: Yale University Press, 2015), 24; Carl Eben, trans., *Gottlieb Mittelberger's Journey to Pennsylvania,* 19, 32: Abbott Smith, *Some New Facts,* 110.

55 Klaus Wust, "Feeding the Palatines: Shipboard Diet in the Eighteenth Century," (nd), 39. http://loyolanotredamelib.org/php/report05/articles/pdfs/Report39Wustp32-42.pdf

56 Ibid., 34.

57 Carl Eben, trans., *Gottlieb Mittelberger's Journey to Pennsylvania in the Year 1750 and His Return to Germany in 1754,* (Philadelphia: John Jos. McVey, 1898), 20-24. https://archive.org/stream/gottliebmittelbe00gott#page/12/mode/2up ; Abbott Smith, *Some New Facts About Eighteenth Century German Immigration,* (New York, Columbia University, nd), 110. https://journals.psu.edu/phj/article/viewFile/21422/21191

58 Carl Eben, trans., *Gottlieb Mittelberger's Journey to Pennsylvania, 26*

59 Stephen Berry, *A Path in the Mighty Waters: Shipboard Life and Atlantic Crossings to the New World,* (New Haven: Yale University Press, 2015), 17-18.

60 From 1727 to 1776, approximately 324 ships sailed into Philadelphia carrying approximately 65,000 German emigrants. And, in the 1708-1709 mass emigration about 15,000 Germans emigrated to New York. Ralph Strassburger, *Pennsylvania German Pioneers Vol I 1727-1775,* (Norristown: Pennsylvania German Society Vol. 42 of the Proceedings of the Society, 1934), xxix-xxx.; Philip Otterness, *Becoming German: The 1709 Palatine Migration to New York* (Ithaca: Cornell University Press, 2004), 35.

61 Stephen Berry, *A Path in the Mighty Waters: Shipboard Life and Atlantic Crossings to the New World,* (New Haven: Yale University Press, 2015), 62; James Beilder, *Chronological Bibliography of 18th Century Voyage Narratives,* (2012), http://jamesmbeidler.com/documents/germans2pa.pdf; Martin Grove Brumbaugh, *A History of the German Brethren in Europe and America,* (Letter from John Nass to his son regarding the voyage from Rotterdam to Pennsylvania, 17 Oct 1733), (Mount Morris, Illinois: Brethren Publishing House, 1899), 108-123. https://archive.org/stream/historyofgerman00brum#page/108/mode/2up

62 Carl Eben, trans., *Gottlieb Mittelberger's Journey to Pennsylvania in the Year 1750 and His Return to Germany in 1754,* (Philadelphia: John Jos. McVey, 1898), 20-22, 24. https://archive.org/stream/gottliebmittelbe00gott#page/12/mode/2up

63 This prayer is the most common mealtime prayers of North American Lutherans published in 1753. It is sometimes attributed to Martin Luther, "Wikipedia" *Common Table Prayer,* (28 December 2016) https://en.wikipedia.org/wiki/Common_table_prayer

64 Philip Parker, "Q-files: The Great Illustrated Encyclopedia," *Pirates and Galleons: Navigation, 16th-18th century,* https://www.q-files.com/history/pirates-galleons/navigation-16th%E2%80%9318th-centuries/

65 John Newton "Christian Classics Ethereal Library: Olney Hymns," *John 6:16-21 Hymn 114 The Disciples at Sea,* (1779), http://www.ccel.org/ccel/newton/olneyhymns.Book1.JHN.h1_114.html

66 Dan Sprague, "Digitalcompassshop *2 points abaft the beam: Pirate Talk*", (March 11, 2012) https://digitalcompassshop.wordpress.com/2012/03/11/2-points-abaft-the-beampirate-talk/

67 Carl Eben, trans., *Gottlieb Mittelberger's Journey to Pennsylvania in the Year 1750 and His Return to Germany in 1754*, (Philadelphia: John Jos. McVey, 1898), 48.

68 Carl Eben, trans., *Gottlieb Mittelberger's Journey to Pennsylvania in the Year 1750 and His Return to Germany in 1754*, (Philadelphia: John Jos. McVey, 1898), 49-50.

69 Thomas Jeffreys, An east prospect of the city of Philadelphia taken by George Heap from the Jersey shore, under the direction of Nicholas Scull surveyor general of the Province of Pennsylvania, Engraving, 1771, Library of Congress Prints and Photographs Division Washington, D.C. 20540 USA http://hdl.loc.gov/loc.pnp/pp.print

70 Joseph Jackson, *Market Street Philadelphia: The Most Historic Highway in America: Its Merchants and Its Story*, (Philadelphia, Joseph Jackson, 1918), 3. https://archive.org/stream/marketstreetphil00jack#page/n33/mode/2up

71 Carl Eben, trans., *Gottlieb Mittelberger's Journey to Pennsylvania in the Year 1750 and His Return to Germany in 1754*, (Philadelphia: John Jos. McVey, 1898), 25-26.

72 Farley Grub, "Morbidity and Mortality on the North Atlantic Passage: Eighteenth Century German Immigration," *Journal of Interdisciplinary History* 17, no. 3, (1987): 573-577, DOI: 10.2307/204611; Ralph Strassburger, *Pennsylvania German Pioneers Vol I 1727-1775*, (Norristown: Pennsylvania German Society Vol. 42 of the Proceedings of the Society, 1934), 681. Doctors' certificate of the ship Neptune. https://archive.org/stream/pennsylvaniagerm03penn_2#page/n771/mode/2up

73 William Perrine, "US History.org, Philadelphia History, *Dock Street. From the Evening Bulletin, Jan 27, 1919*", (Independence Hall Association,

1995), http://www.ushistory.org/philadelphia/street_dock.htm; Farley Grub estimates that males suffered a 3.8% mortality rate and children 9%. He adds that typhoid, dysentery, and most commonly seasickness were the causes of most morbidity. Between 1727 and 1754. A 3.49% rate of morbidity was the average. Farley Grub, "Morbidity and Mortality on the North Atlantic Passage: Eighteenth Century German Immigration," *Journal of Interdisciplinary History* 17, no. 3, (1987): 574, 567, 573-577, DOI: 10.2307/204611; Marianne Wokeck, *Trade in Strangers: The Beginnings of Mass Migration to North America,* (University Park: Pennsylvania State Press, 1999); Frank Diffenderffer, *The German Immigration Into Pennsylvania Through the Port of Philadelphia 1700-1775 Part II The Redemptioners,* (Lancaster: Pennsylvania-German Society, 1900), 60; 144-145. https://archive.org/stream/germanimmigratio107diff#page/n321/mode/2up ; Carl Eben, trans., *Gottlieb Mittelberger's Journey to Pennsylvania in the Year 1750 and His Return to Germany in 1754,* (Philadelphia: John Jos. McVey, 1898), 23-24, 26-27, 38-40. https://archive.org/stream/gottliebmittelbe00gott#page/26/mode/2up ; Ralph Strassburger, *Pennsylvania German Pioneers Vol I 1727-1775,* (Norristown: Pennsylvania German Society Vol. 42 of the Proceedings of the Society, 1934), xxxvii https://archive.org/stream/pennsylvaniagerm03penn_2#page/n49/mode/2up

74 Ralph Strassburger, *Pennsylvania German Pioneers Vol I 1727-1775,* (Norristown: Pennsylvania German Society Vol. 42 of the Proceedings of the Society, 1934), 681.

75 "Art to Zoo, *A Ticket to Philly – In 1769: Thinking about Cities, Then and Now",* (Washington D.C., Smithsonian Institute,1990); http://www.smithsonianeducation.org/educators/lesson_plans/ticket_to_philly/ATZ_ATickettoPhilly_May1990.pdf ; *Gottlieb Mittelberger's Journey to Pennsylvania in the Year 1750 and His Return to Germany in 1754,* (Philadelphia: John Jos. McVey, 1898), 49-51. https://archive.org/stream/gottliebmittelbe00gott#page/50/mode/2up Milton Hamilton, The Papers of Sir William Johnson, Vol.XIII, (Albany, The University of the State of New York, 1962), 181. https://archive.org/stream/papers

ofsirwilli13johnuoft#page/180/mode/2up ; Carl Eben, trans., *Gottlieb Mittelberger's Journey to Pennsylvania in the Year 1750 and His Return to Germany in 1754,* (Philadelphia: John Jos. McVey, 1898), 49. https://archive.org/stream/gottliebmittelbe00gott#page/48/mode/2up

76 Carl Eben, trans., *Gottlieb Mittelberger's Journey to Pennsylvania,* 50. https://archive.org/stream/gottliebmittelbe00gott#page/50/mode/2up ; Joseph Jackson, *Market Street Philadelphia: The Most Historic Highway in America: Its Merchants and Its Story,* (Philadelphia, Joseph Jackson, 1918), 22.

77 The 'usual qualifications' were the Oaths of Allegiance and Abjuration. In his statistical analysis of the number of ships arriving in Philadelphia and the number of passengers taking the Oath of Allegiance, Ralph Strassburger determined that 324 ships and 65,040 passengers arrived in America from Germany between 1727-1775. Strassburger states that this number included only those passengers labeled 'whole freight' which meant adults above the age of 16. There must have been many children under the age of 16. The number also did not include women. The Neptune cited 226 'whole freight'. If women and children were included, the number of passengers on that ship must have been close to 300. Strassburger also states that the list for the ship Neptune was incomplete. Of the 226 'whole freights' listed, only 90 were on the list. Johannes Philip Wiemer was not one of the 90. Also, merchants who owned the ships used the number of 'whole freight' to calculate provisions needed for the journey. Consequently, many ships did not carry enough provisions. Ralph Strassburger, *Pennsylvania German Pioneers Vol I 1727-1775,* (Norristown: Pennsylvania German Society Vol. 42 of the Proceedings of the Society, 1934), 3-6, xxiii, 679. https://archive.org/stream/pennsylvaniagerm03penn_2#page/n71/mode/2up ; John Hill Martin, *Martin's Bench and Bar of Philadelphia,* (Philadelphia, Rees Welsh & Co., 1883), 32-33.

78 Rev. Heinzelman was a respected Lutheran clergyman in Philadelphia who married Margaretha Catharina, a daughter of Conrad Weiser. Conrad Weiser was a German emigrant who came to New York in 1709.

He was a native interpreter and diplomat who had significant influence in the Schoharie Valley, New York and in Pennsylvania. "History of Old Zion Church Philadelphia, The Beginnings of Old Zion 1740-1820", (28 July, 2011), http://oldzionhistory.blogspot.ca/2011/07/beginnings-of-old-zion-1740-1820.html; Samuel Hazard, ed., *The Register of Pennsylvania,* Vol IV (Philadelphia, 1829) 370.

79 Pennsylvania and New Jersey, Church and Town Records, 1707-1985, Lutheran St Michael's Congregation, 26 May 1756, Entry 19 Martin Silmser, age 29, residence Frankford, 1 child, Entry 20 Elizabeth Margretha, age 32, 'lines through columns indicate residence, and children, are the same as Martin'; Pennsylvania and New Jersey, Church and Town Records, 1707-1985, Lutheran St Michael's Congregation, 1758, Martin Simser, in America 4 years, 3? Children, age 32; Pennsylvania and New Jersey, Church and Town Records, 1707-1985, Lutheran St Michael's Congregation, 1759, Entry 90, 5 years in America, 3 children; Retrieved from Online publication – Provo, UT, USA. Ancestry.com Operations, Inc., 2011. Original data – Historic Pennsylvania Church and Town Records. Philadelphia Pennsylvania: Historical Society of Pennsylvania. Original data: Historic Pennsylvania Church and Town Records.

80 By 1756, this revolt cost the lives of 2500 settlers. In January 1756, citizens of Kingston sent a letter to Sir William Johnson of the Mohawk Valley appealing for assistance in quieting the Indians. Samuel Hazard, ed. *Pennsylvania Archives Series I, Vol II* (Philadelphia, Pennsylvania Historical & Museum Commisssion, 1755), 443-445, 455. https://www.fold3.com/image/1/1181001 ; RS Stephenson, Pennsylvania Provincial Soldiers in the Seven Year's War, (University of Virginia, nd) 196-212. https://journals.psu.edu/phj/article/viewFile/25220/24989 ; Frank Diffenderffer, *The Story of a Picture,* (Philadelphia, Lancaster, 1905), 191-194, https://archive.org/stream/storyofpicture00diffrich#page/n17/mode/2up Fintan O'Toole, *White Savage: William Johnson and the Invention of America,* (Albany, State University of New York, 2005), 109-110, 160.

81 "Pennsylvania Assembly: Reply to the Governor, 28 July 1755," *Founders Online,* National Archives, last modified March 30, 2017, http://founders.archives.gov/documents/Franklin/01-06-02-0060. [Original source: *The Papers of Benjamin Franklin,* vol. 6, *April 1, 1755, through September 30, 1756,* ed. Leonard W. Labaree. New Haven and London: Yale University Press, 1963, pp. 111–112.]

82 Frank Diffenderffer, *The German Immigration Into Pennsylvania Through the Port of Philadelphia 1700-1775 Part II The Redemptioners,* (Lancaster: Pennsylvania-German Society, 1900), 96. https://archive.org/details/germanimmigratio00diffuoft

83 "Historicbridges.org *Pennypack Creek Bridge: Frankford Avenue Bridge,*" (31 May 2010), http://historicbridges.org/bridges/browser/?bridgebrowser=pennsylvania/frankford/

84 Richard Castor, "Passing of the Old Jolly Post Hotel." The Frankford Dispatch, 33 no. 32, (Friday, January 13, 1911), https://www.scribd.com/document/111276979/Passing-of-the-Jolly-Post-Hotel

85 Robert Rose, *The Bordentown and New York Stage.* (nd.), http://www.hamiltonphilatelic.org/presentations/bordentown.pdf ; Seymour Dunbar, *A History of Travel in America Vol 1,* (nd,), 183.

86 On April 29, 1779, in New York, Martin Silmser's son Nicholas married Philip's daughter Anna Margaretha Wiemer becoming Philip's son in law. Seymour Dunbar, *A History of Travel in America,* Vol 1, (nd,), 183.

87 Phil Lord, "Poles and Steam: An Experiment on the Mohawk River," (October, 2012), http://www.living-in-the-past.com/steam.html

88 Ron Vineyard, "Colonial Williamsburg Digital Library, *Stage Wagons and Coaches*" (August, 2000) Colonial Williamsburg Foundation Library Research Report Series RR0380. (Colonial Williamsburg Foundation Library, Williamsburg, Virginia, August 2002), http://research.history.org/DigitalLibrary/View/index.cfm?doc=ResearchReports%5CRR0380.xml

89 Sam Atkinson, *The Casket. Flowers of Literature, Wit & Sentiment for 1829*, (Philadelphia, Sam Atkinson, 1829), 231.

90 Great Britain, War Office: Amherst papers Lac_reel_c12837 C-12837 105019 MG13W034, Library and Archives Canada. http://heritage.canadiana.ca/view/oocihm.lac_reel_c12837/1?r=0&s=1

91 William VerPlanck & Moses Collyer, *The Sloops of the Hudson*, (New York, G.P. Putnam's Sons, 1908), 14, 17. https://archive.org/stream/sloopsofhudsonhi00verp#page/14/mode/2up

92 Francis Maerschalck and Geraldus Duyckinck, The Maerschalck Map: A Plan of the City of New York from an Acutual Survey Anno Domini MDCCLV, 1755 (Washington D.C., Library of Congress) http://www.nyc99.org/1700/maerschalck.html Steven Welch, "1775 The Montresor Plan Surveyed in the Winter of 1775" (16 June 2014) http://stevenwarranresearch.blogspot.ca/2014/06/1775-montresor-plan-surveyed-in-winter.html

93 "The People of Colonial Albany Live Here. Peter Kalm on Albany", (Albany, New York State Museum, 1 November 2010). http://exhibitions.nysm.nysed.gov/albany/art/kalm.html#ch

94 Richard Cartwright was a successful merchant and Tavern/Inn owner of Albany for many decades. For loyalties to the King, he was banished from Albany 20 July 1778 and escorted under guard to Canada on 19 August 1778. He is listed in the Montreal refugee camp with his wife on 01 July 1779 through to September 1784, eventually settling in Kingston Ontario. He claimed damages and losses of over £1500 and claimed support of the British through providing money for loyalist refugees, prisoners, and for assisting in the escape of Captain Butler. His son Richard became a Judge of the Court at Kingston and a member of the Legislative Council.; Gavin Watt, *Loyalist Refugees: Non-Military Refugees in Quebec 1776-1784*, (Milton ON: Global Heritage Press, 2014), 127.; Ancestry.com, *The National Archives of the UK; Kew, Surrey, England; American Loyalist Claims*, Series II; Class: AO 13; Piece: 011; Stefan Bielinski, "The People of Colonial Albany Live Here.

City Streets", (Albany, New York State Museum, 1 November 2010). http://exhibitions.nysm.nysed.gov//albany/streets.html#court; Stefan Bielinski, "The People of Colonial Albany Live Here. Richard Cartwright", (Albany, New York State Museum, 1 November 2010). http://exhibitions.nysm.nysed.gov//albany/bios/c/ricartwright6508.html; RH Pease (Engraver) and Simeon DeWitt (Surveyor), "A Plan of the City of Albany",(Albany, Joel Munsell, 1852), Published in Joel Munsell, The Annals of Albany, vol. 3 (1852), opposite page 156, Albany Institute of History & Art, http://www.albanyinstitute.org/details/items/a-plan-of-the-city-of-albany.html

95 Walter Borneman, *The French and Indian War. Deciding the Fate of North America,* (New York, Harper, 2006), 26. "The People of Colonial Albany Live Here. Peter Kalm on Albany", (Albany, New York State Museum, 1 November 2010). http://exhibitions.nysm.nysed.gov/albany/art/kalm.html#ch

96 Born in 1716, Mr. Abraham Harmanus Wendel was a successful Albany merchant and land holder. He was one of the proprietors of the Sacandaga Patent in 1741. The Wendels descend from the first settler in Albany in 1653, Evert Janse Wendel. Stefan Bielinski, "The People of Colonial Albany Live Here. The Sacandaga Patent," (10 December 2009) http://exhibitions.nysm.nysed.gov/albany/na/sacandaga.html ; Stefan Bielinski, "The People of Colonial Albany Live Here. Abraham H Wendell," (4 October 2007) http://exhibitions.nysm.nysed.gov/albany/bios/w/abwendell2740.html ; New York State Archives. New York (State). State Engineer and Surveyor. Survey maps of lands in New York State, ca. 1711-1913. NYSA_A0273-78_640Series A0273-78, Map #640. Survey of Land for Lendert Gansevoort and James Stewart Map #640. http://digitalcollections.archives.nysed.gov/index.php/Detail/Object/Show/object_id/37318 ; Lewis (Ludovicus Cobes) Clement was the son of Joseph Clement and Anna Peek, daughter of Jacob Peek. Joseph and Anna were among the earliest settlers of the Tribes Hill area. They are noted in a land patent as early as 1706 and again in 1731 in a land deed with William Powell at Maquasland (Mohawk Territory). New York Land Records, 1630-1975," images, *FamilySearch* (https://familysearch.

org/ark:/61903/3:1:3QS7-99WC-CHS8?cc=2078654&wc=M7H5-M38%3A358136301%2C358240201: 22 May 2014), Montgomery Deeds 1772-1788 vol 1 image 8 of 278; county courthouses, New York.

97 "Onondaga Nation People of the Hills. Dress," http://www.onondaganation.org/culture/dress/

98 Ancestry.com.*UK, American Loyalist Claims, 1776-1835* [database on-line]. Provo, UT, USA: Ancestry.com Operations, Inc., 2013. *Piece 031: Evidence, New York, 1787-1788.* Original data: American Loyalist Claims, 1776–1835. AO 12–13. The National Archives of the United Kingdom, Kew, Surrey, England.; Ancestry.com. *UK, American Loyalist Claims, 1776-1835* [database on-line]. Provo, UT, USA: Ancestry.com Operations, Inc., 2013. The National Archives of the UK; Kew, Surrey, England; *American Loyalist Claims, Series II;* Class: *AO 13;*Piece: *079* Original data: American Loyalist Claims, 1776–1835. AO 12–13. The National Archives of the United Kingdom, Kew, Surrey, England.

99 William Smith, The History of the Late Province of New York From Its Discovery, to the Appointment of Governor Colden, in 1762 Vol 1, (New York, New York Historical Society, 1830), 312-315. https://archive.org/stream/historyoflatepro01smit_0#page/312/mode/2up ; RH Pease (Engraver) and Simeon DeWitt (Surveyor), "A Plan of the City of Albany",(Albany, Joel Munsell, 1852), Published in Joel Munsell, The Annals of Albany, vol. 3 (1852), opposite page 156, Albany Institute of History & Art, http://www.albanyinstitute.org/details/items/a-plan-of-the-city-of-albany.html Walter Borneman, *The French and Indian War. Deciding the Fate of North America,* (New York, Harper, 2006), 26. "The People of Colonial Albany Live Here. Excerpts From Peter Kalm on Albany," (revised November 1, 2010) http://exhibitions.nysm.nysed.gov/albany/art/kalm.html#ch

100 Stefan Bielinski, *How Cities Worked: Occupations in Colonial Albany,* Selected Rensselaerswijck Seminar Papers, Colonial Albany Social History Project, New York State Museum (Albany, nd) http://www.newnetherlandinstitute.org/files/3713/5067/3662/4.4.pdf

101 Ancestry.com. *UK, American Loyalist Claims, 1776-1835* [database on-line]. Provo, UT, USA: Ancestry.com Operations, Inc., 2013. The National Archives of the UK; Kew, Surrey, England; *American Loyalist Claims, Series I*; Class: *AO 13*; Piece: *028* ; Records of the Reformed Protestant Dutch Church of Caughnawaga: now the Reformed Church of Fonda, in the village of Fonda, Montgomery County, New York, USA. Volume one. Baptisms and births, 1758 to 1797, 39.

102 Don Rittner, *The King's Highway: Schenectady's First Road Travel Guide,* (Schenectady, Schenectady County Department of Historical Services, nd). http://www.donrittner.com/kingshighway.pdf

103 Alice Morse Earle, "18th Century History –The Light of Other Days", (nd), http://northernwoodlands.org/articles/article/tarheels-pitch-pine-colonial-america ; Emery Gluck, "Northern Woodlands – Yankee Tarheels: Remembering the Pitch Pine Industry of Colonial America", (30 June 2015), http://www.history1700s.com/index.php/articles/156-home-life-in-colonial-days/806-the-light-of-other-days.html

104 Fintan O'Toole, *White Savage: William Johnson and the Invention of America,* (Albany, State University of New York, 2005), 111-112. Walter Borneman, *The French and Indian War. Deciding the Fate of North America,* (New York, Harper, 2006), 42.

105 The State of New York, The colonial laws of New York from the year 1664 to the Revolution, including the charters to the Duke of York, the commissions and instructions to colonial governors, the Duke's laws, the laws of the Dongan and Leisler Assemblies, the charters of Albany and New York and the acts of the colonial legislatures from 1691 to 1775 inclusive. Transmitted to the Legislature by the Commissioners of Statutory Revision, pursuant to chapter 125 of the Laws of 1891 (Volume 3), 895; James Sullivan, *The Papers of Sir William Johnson, Vol I* (Albany, The University of the State of New York, 1921), 631-633, 636, 755-756, 784-785. https://archive.org/stream/papersofsirwilli01johnuoft#page/636/mode/2up

106 Fintan O'Toole, *White Savage: William Johnson and the Invention of America,* (Albany, State University of New York, 2005), 57, 66-69.

107 James Sullivan, *The Papers of Sir William Johnson, Vol I* (Albany, The University of the State of New York, 1921), 465-466. https://archive.org/stream/papersofsirwilli01johnuoft#page/464/mode/2up

108 Richard Berleth, *Bloody Mohawk: The French and Indian War & American Revolution on New York's Frontier,* (Delmar NY, Black Dome Press, 2010), 45-60.

109 New York Historical Society, Muster Rolls of New York Provincial Troops 1755-1764. (New York, New York Historical Society, 1891), 24 June 1755, 6-7. http://archive.org/stream/musterrollsnewy00socigoog#page/n26/mode/2up; Annual Report of the State Historian*, New York Colonial Muster Rolls, 1664-1775, Vol. I* [database on-line], 655-657.

110 London Magazine and Monthly Chronologer, Vol 24, 1755, (London, C. Ackers, 1755), *Extract of a Letter From Governor Wentworth to the Right Hon. Sir Thomas Robinson* 545. https://hdl.handle.net/2027/mdp.39015021267748?urlappend=%3Bseq=578 ; E.B. O'Callagahan, ed. *Documents Relative to the Colonial History of the State of New York Vol VI,* (Albany, Weed, Parsons and Co.,, 1855), 1005-1007, https://archive.org/stream/documentsrelativ06brod#page/1004/mode/2up

111 Austin Yates, Schenectady County New York: Its History to the Close of the Nineteenth Century, (New York History Company, 1902), 14-16. https://archive.org/stream/schenectadycount00yate#page/n33/mode/2up

112 "Grems-Doolitte Library Collections, Taverns and Inns of Schenectady Part I" 21 July 2015. http://gremsdoolittlelibrary.blogspot.ca/2015/07/taverns-and-inns-of-schenectady-part-i.html

113 "Manthey on 18th Century Reenacting: Items From Day Books," http://orbitals.com/self/history/daybook.htm

114 Johnathan Pearson, *A History of the Schenectady Patent in the Dutch and English Times; Being Contributions Towards a History of the Lower Mohawk Valley,* (Albany, Joel Munsell's Sons, 1885), 7-9. https://archive.org/stream/historyofschenec00pe#page/6/mode/2up

115 Mendel, Mesick, Cohen Architects, *Fort Johnston Amsterdam, New York: A Historic Structure Report 1974-1975,* (Washington, D.C., Technical Preservation Services Division Office of Archeology and Historic Preservation US Department of the Interior, 1978) http://npshistory.com/publications/fort-johnson-hsr.pdf ; The Miriam and Ira D. Wallach Division of Art, Prints and Photographs: Print Collection, The New York Public Library. *"A north view of Fort Johnson drawn on the spot by Mr. Guy Johnson, Sir Wm. Johnson's son."* New York Public Library Digital Collections. Accessed September 5, 2017. http://digitalcollections.nypl.org/items/510d47da-2444-a3d9-e040-e00a18064a99

116 James Sullivan, *The Papers of Sir William Johnson, Vol I* (Albany, The University of the State of New York, 1921), 638-641, 659, 669. https://archive.org/stream/papersofsirwilli01johnuoft#page/638/mode/2up Alexander Flick, The Papers of Sir William Johnson, Vol IV, *Memorandum on Six Nations and Other Confederacies,* (Albany, The University of the State of New York, 1925),240-246. https://archive.org/stream/papersofsirwilli04john#page/240/mode/2up ; George Croghan, *A Selection of Letters and Journals Relating to Tours Into the Western Country November 16 1750 – November 1765,* A list of the different nations and tribes of Indians in the northern district of North America, with the number of their fighting men, 167-169. https://archive.org/stream/selectionofgeorg00crogrich#page/166/mode/2up

117 James Sullivan, *The Papers of Sir William Johnson, Vol I,* (Albany, The University of the State of New York, 1921), 625. https://archive.org/stream/papersofsirwilli01johnuoft#page/624/mode/2up

118 "Reverend John Ogilvie Records, Eastern NY State, Hudson Valley Area 1750-1760 *Baptisms" Extracted from Trinity Church Records,* NYC; NYGBR Vol 67, ©1936, Clement 1755 3/9 Mohawks Jacomyntie, dau

of Lewis and Catalyntje (Potman), http://www.rootsweb.ancestry.com/~nycoloni/chrecalb03.html

119 Ken D. Johnson, "Fort Plank Bastion of My Freedom, Colonial Canajoharie, New York" The Charles Williams or Warrensburgh Patent, (26 November, 2015). http://www.fort-plank.com/Warrensburgh_1738.html ; Secretary of State of New York, Calendar of N.Y. Colonial Manuscripts Indorsed Land Papers, (Albany, Weed, Parsons & Co. 1864), Certificate to Henry Hoffe, 24 November 1726, 184. https://archive.org/stream/calendarofnycolo00alba#page/184/mode/2up ; New York State Archives. New York (State). State Engineer and Surveyor. Survey maps of lands in New York State, ca. 1711-1913. Series A0273-78, Map #618. http://digitalcollections.archives.nysed.gov/index.php/Detail/Object/Show/object_id/37137 A portion of Henry Hough's land on the north side of the river was purchased by Sir William Johnson and is known as the 'Guy Park Square Mile." Max Reid, "The Story of Old Fort Johnson," *Chapter XV Land Grants: Royal, Kingsborough, Sacandaga, Johnson Hall.* http://montgomery.nygenweb.net/johnson/Chap15.html

120 Ken D. Johnson, "Fort Plank Bastion of My Freedom, Colonial Canajoharie, New York" The Charles Williams or Warrensburgh Patent, (26 November, 2015). http://www.fort-plank.com/Warrensburgh_1738.html

121 The Pennsylvania Archives, Series 1 Vol 2 Pennsylvania Archives 1755, 436. https://www.fold3.com/image/1/1180992 ; James Sullivan, *The Papers of Sir William Johnson, Vol II,* (Albany, The University of the State of New York, 1921), 293, 298. https://www.ancestry.ca/media/viewer/viewer/f470cf38-43d8-4a4d-aff2-a337dcb0 20a1/44704820/24055182031

122 John J. Vrooman, "Three Rivers Hudson, Mohawk, Schoharie: History From America's Most Famous Valleys," *From Forts & Firesides of The Mohawk County, Queen Anne's Chapel Parsonage, Fort Hunter,* (1951) http://www.threeriversshms.com/qanne.htm ;"Friends of Schoharie

Crossing, *Exploring Fort Hunter Through Maps – NYS Archives Part II*," (28 August, 2015) http://friendsofschohariecrossing.blogspot.ca/2015/08/exploring-fort-hunter-through-maps-nys.html ; "Access Genealogy, *Mohawk Indian Villages and Towns*," (11 October, 2013) https://www.accessgenealogy.com/native/mohawk-indian-villages-and-towns.htm ; Darren Bonaparte, "Wampum Chronicles. The Mohawk Longhouse," http://www.wampumchronicles.com/mohawklonghouses.html ; Kevin Moody & Charles L. Fisher, Archeological Evidence of Colonial Occupation at Schoharie Crossing Historic Site, Montgomery County, New York, *The Bulletin Journal of the New York State Archeological Association, No. 99,* (Fall 1989), http://nysarchaeology.org/download/nysaa/bulletin/number_099.pdf

123 "Montgomery County New York, Kelly Yacobucci Farqhar, The Trinity Lutheran Church, 2008." Last Modified 2015 https://www.co.montgomery.ny.us/web/sites/departments/historian/articles_TrinityLutheranChurch.asp ; "Three Rivers Hudson, Mohawk, Schoharie: History From America's Most Famous Valleys, Excerpt from "History of Montgomery Classis, R.C.A.", 1916, by W.N.P. Dailey. Recorder Press, Amsterdam, NY, Stone Arabia Reformed Church." http://threeriversshms.com/StoneArabia.htm

124 Captain Peter Service received his commission as Captain in the New York Militia January 5, 1758. He lived on Lot 400 on the Western Allotment of the Kingsborough Patent. On 4 August 1768 he and others received a survey for 25,000 acres of land on the north side of the Mohawk River above German Flats. Peter Service must have sold some of this land to Sir William Johnson because in 1772, Sir William sold it to Lord Adam Gordon of Preston Hall, North Britain. Adam Ruppert was a Sergeant in Captain Service's Company in 1758. He lived on lot 77 on the Western Allotment of the Kingsborough Patent. His lot was north and next to Captain Service. Duncan Fraser, Papers and Records of the Ontario Historical Society, Volume LII, 1960, Original Source, Public Record Office, London, England AC 13/114. *Sir John Johnson's Rent Roll of the Kingsborough Patent.* http://freepages.genealogy.rootsweb.ancestry.com/~wjmartin/kingsbor.htm ; Secretary of State

of New York, *Calendar of Colonial Manuscripts Indorsed Land Papers,* (Albany, Weed, Parsons & Co., 1864), 461. https://archive.org/stream/calendarofnycolo00alba#page/460/mode/2up

125 The Colonial Government bought 20,000 acres of land from the Indians north of the Mohawk River. They paid the Indians "3 pieces of inen (shoddy wool), 6 pieces of gailing inen, 3 barrels of beer, 6 gallons of rum and a fatt "beast". The government issued this land as the Kingsborough Patent to Arent Stevens and others in 1753. A survey for this patent was issued on February 3, 1753. By 1762 William Johnson owned the land and had settled more than 100 families on the land. He eventually built Johnson Hall. This patent includes the towns of Johnstown, Ephratah, and Mayfield. Secretary of State of New York, Calendar of Colonial Manuscripts Indorsed Land Papers, Vol XV, (Albany, Weed, Parsons & Co. 1864), 272-273 https://archive.org/stream/calendarofnycolo00alba#page/272/mode/2up ; W. Max Reid, "The Story of Old Fort Johnson", Chapter XV, Land Grants: Royal, Kingsborough, Sacandaga – Johnson Hall. http://montgomery.nygenweb.net/johnson/Chap15.html; "Fulton County NYGenWeb," William Loveday Jr. The Birth of a County, 2002, Last modified 8 May 2008. http://www.fulton.nygenweb.net/history/WLbirth.html; James Sullivan, *The Papers of Sir William Johnson, Vol III* (Albany, The University of the State of New York, 1921), 954. https://archive.org/stream/paperssirwillia00unkngoog#page/n1022/mode/2up

126 Philip's son Peter Eamer would marry Michael Gallinger's daughter Maria Catharina on 19 January 1780. And Philip's daughter Dorothy would marry Michael Gallinger's son Henry about 1783. The Archives of the Reformed Church in America; New Brunswick, New Jersey; *Reformed Church of Fonda, Baptisms, Marriages, Members, Consistory Minutes, 1758-1839;* A. W. Fraser, & R. Ross, St. Andrews Presbyterian Williamstown, Ontario. Baptisms-Marriages-Deaths 1779-1804, 1999, Allinder Gallinger, Daughter of Henry Gallinger of Cornwall and of Dorothy Amer his wife, was Baptised on the 25th November 1792; The National Archives of the UK; Kew, Surrey, England; *American Loyalist Claims, Series I;* Class: *AO 13;* Piece: *03, 282;* New York State Archives.

New York (State). State Engineer and Surveyor. Survey maps of lands in New York State, ca. 1711-1913. Series A0273-78, Map #875. *Map of Lots in the Village of Johnstown, Fulton County, http://digitalcollections.archives.nysed.gov/index.php/Detail/Object/Show/object_id/37452* ; Duncan Fraser, Papers and Records of the Ontario Historical Society, Volume LII, 1960, Original Source, Public Record Office, London, England AC 13/114. *Sir John Johnson's Rent Roll of the Kingsborough Patent.http://freepages.genealogy.rootsweb.ancestry.com/~wjmartin/kingsbor.htm*

CHAPTER THREE
Settlement in New York 1755-1763

127 New York State Archives. New York (State). State Engineer and Surveyor. Survey maps of lands in New York State, ca. 1711-1913. "*Map of Lots in the Village of Johnstown, Fulton County*," Map #875, Series A0273-78. http://digitalcollections.archives.nysed.gov/index.php/Detail/Object/Show/object_id/37452#

128 Ibid; Wayne Bower. "Registers of the Parishes of Williamsburg, Matilda, Osnabruck, and Edwardsburg." Burial Registers of the Parishes of Williamsburg, Matilda, Osnabruck, and Edwardsburg. Last modified February 27, 2016. Snyder, Mary, Died 01/02/1840, Buried 03/02/1840, Age 85, Widow of the late Adam Snyder of Williamsburg. http://bowergenealogy.ca/resources/lutheran/Burial%20Register.htm ; Ancestry.com. *Württemberg, Germany, Family Tables, 1550-1985* [database on-line]. Lehi, UT, USA: Ancestry.com Operations, Inc., 2016. *Konfirmationen, Kommunionen, Familienbuch u-Seelenregister 1726-1876.* Matthias Link, Mannlich, Birthdate 9 Jan 1728, Residence Hopfau Neunthausen, Father Michael Link, Mother Katharina Link, FHL Film Number 1732292. Wife Maria Magdelena Kraft, Marriage date, 28 Nov 1753, Hopfau Neunthausen. FHL 1732292.

129 Philip and Catrina leased Lot 59 on the Sacandaga Patent from Harmanus Wendel. Ancestry.com. *UK, American Loyalist Claims,*

1776-1835 [database on-line]. Provo, UT, USA: Ancestry.com Operations, Inc., 2013. Original data: American Loyalist Claims, 1776–1835. AO 12–13. The National Archives of the United Kingdom, Kew, Surrey, England. UK, American Loyalist Claims, 1776-1835 for Philip Eamer AO 12: American Loyalists Claims, Series I Piece 031: Evidence, New York, 1787-1788, 139-140.; *"Map of the Sacondaga,"* Map #286, Series A0273-78. New York State Archives. New York (State). State Engineer and Surveyor. Survey maps of lands in New York State, ca. 1711-1913. http://digitalcollections.archives.nysed.gov/index.php/Detail/Object/Show/object_id/36827# The White Pine Tree is a significant symbol for the Haudenosaunee (Iroquois Confederacy of Six Nations). It is known to them as the tree of peace and was a major icon in the story of the creation of the Five Nation's Confederacy (Six, after the Tuscarora Nation joined the Confederacy). After decades of war, they created ways in which they could live together in peace. http://www.dec.ny.gov/docs/administration_pdf/1013treeofpeacewhitepine.pdf

130 Ancestry.com. *Records of the Lutheran Trinity Church of Stone Arabia: in the town of Palatine, Montgomery County, N.Y.* [database on-line] 1914. XXI; Provo, UT: Ancestry.com Operations Inc, 2005.; *UK, American Loyalist Claims, 1776-1835* [database on-line]. AO 12–13. *Series I;* Class: *AO 13;* Piece: *029, 361-362.* ; Gale Research, *Passenger and Immigration Lists Index, 1500s-1900s* Online publication - Provo, UT, USA: Ancestry.com Operations, Inc, 2010. Original data: Filby, P. William, ed. Passenge, Pennsylvania, 1753, 4. Jacob Heinrich Allgeyer, age 27, arrival 1753, Pennsylvania, Child Johann Martin, Wife Salome Wahl, Child Sebastian, Child Sophia Salome; "New Netherland and Beyond. Colonial Church Records." Reverend John Ogilvie Records Eastern NY State, Hudson Valley Area. 1750-1760 Baptisms. Extracted from Trinity Church Records, NYC; *NYGBR,* volume 67, ©1936. (2012). Alguyer, 1753, 10/19, Albany, Sophie, dau of Yancope and Shallame (Valey).

131 Department of the Interior, *The Preservation of Historic Architecture, The U.S. Government's Official Guidelines for Preserving Historic Homes.* (Guildford CT: The Lyons Press, 2004), 288. "Pennsylvania Historical & Museum Commission: Pennyslvania Architectural Field Guide.

Pennsylvania German Traditional 1700-1870." 26 August 2015. http://www.phmc.state.pa.us/portal/communities/architecture/styles/pa-german.html

132 Martin Alguire would become Philip and Catrina's son in law when he married their daughter Catharina on 26 November 1769. Online publication Ancestry.ca Provo, UT: The Generations Network, Inc., 2005.Original data - *Records of the Lutheran Trinity Church of Stone Arabia: in the town of Palatine, Montgomery County, N.Y.* New York, unknown, 1914, Vol I Marriages, 280. 1769 November den 26ten Martin Algejer & Catharina Emeri.

133 The National Archives of the UK; Kew, Surrey, England; *American Loyalist Claims, Series I;* Class: *AO 13;* Piece: *03,* 281.

134 Bernard Herman, *Town House: Architecture and Material Life in the Early American City, 1780-1830* (Chapel Hill, University of North Carolina Press, 2009), 85.

135 Secretary of State of New York, *Calendar of Colonial Manuscripts Indorsed Land Papers* (Albany, Weed, Parsons & Co., 1864), 183-186, https://archive.org/stream/calendarofnycolo00alba#page/182/mode/2up; *"Survey of land for Henry Hoofe and Wm York,"* Map #618, Series A0273-78, New York State Archives. New York (State). State Engineer and Surveyor. Survey Maps of Lands in New York State, ca. 1711-1913 http://digitalcollections.archives.nysed.gov/index.php/Detail/Object/Show/object_id/37137

136 Philip Otterness, *Becoming German: The 1709 Palatine Migration to New York* (Ithaca, Cornell University Press, 2004), 123-146.

137 London Magazine and Monthly Chronologer, "Promotions Civil and Military," *London Magazine and Monthly Chronologer, November, 1755,* 24, 550. https://hdl.handle.net/2027/mdp.39015021267748?urlappend=%3Bseq=584 ; James Sullivan, *The Papers of Sir William Johnson, Vol II* (Albany, The University of the State of New York, 1921), 343-350.

https://archive.org/stream/paperssirwillia00johngoog#page/n392/mode/2up 137.

138 "New Netherland and Beyond. Colonial Church Records." Reverend John Ogilvie Records Eastern NY State, Hudson Valley Area. 1750-1760 Baptisms. Extracted from Trinity Church Records, NYC; *NYGBR,* volume 67, ©1936. (2012). Weemer, 1756 2/11, Mohawks, Martin, son of Philip and Cathrine (Lyserin). http://www.rootsweb.ancestry.com/~nycoloni/chrecalb03.html

139 Ibid. Alguyr, 1756 2/11, Mohawks, Elizabeth, dau of Jacob and Salome (Wale). Alguyer, 1753, 10/19, Albany, Sophie, dau og Yancope and Shallame (Valey).

140 In standard European warfare, soldiers were seen as professionals and thus treated with honour whether they were the victors or the defeated. Soldiers were allowed the privileges of dignity. However, principles of Native warfare were different. Natives fought to bring honour to their Nations. They weren't professional soldiers. They required proof to validate honour brought to their Nation. Trophies brought back from the defeated, such as loot, scalps, and prisoners were proof of honour. Prisoners were not only considered loot, but they also replaced any brethren killed in battle. Brethren killed in battle were not only honoured through taking of prisoners, but also through subsequent acts of revenge. If Natives did not bring back these items of honour or allowed revenge, they were considered defeated. These fundamental differences in the principles of warfare led to Natives being seen as 'savages' or merciless, or their revenge seen as slaughter and butchery. The British and the French were often not able to subdue these significant principles of their Native allies' methods of warfare. Therefore, settlers' intense fear and panic was the consequence of living with the prospects of Native attack. Fintan O'Toole, *White Savage: William Johnson and the Invention of America* (Albany, State University of New York, 2005), 144, 268.

141 Ibid. 161; James Sullivan, *The Papers of Sir William Johnson, Vol II* (Albany, The University of the State of New York, 1921), 433, https://archive.org/stream/paperssirwillia00johngoog#page/n480/mode/2up

142 Fintan O'Toole, *White Savage:* 161-165.

143 Ancestry.com. *Records of the Lutheran Trinity Church of Stone Arabia: in the town of Palatine, Montgomery County, N.Y.* [database on-line]. Provo, UT: Ancestry.com Operations Inc, 2005. Original data: *Records of the Lutheran Trinity Church of Stone Arabia: in the town of Palatine, Montgomery County, N.Y.*. New York: unknown, 1914. 17. Vol.1. Birth and baptisms, 1751 to 1815. MDCCLVI, d 10 Apr. Mathes Linck c. ux Maria Magdalena Sponsors: Johannes Spangenberg, Johann Gottfried Klein, Catharina Kleinin. Child: Johann Gottfriedt.; Kelly Yacobucci Farquhar "Montgomery County History and Archives." *The Trinity Lutheran Church.* (2015). https://www.co.montgomery.ny.us/web/sites/departments/historian/articles_TrinityLutheranChurch.asp

144 Reverend Andrew Luther Dillenbeck, D.D., *Lutheran Trinity Church of Stone Arabia, N.Y.* (Enterprise and News, St. Johnsville, N.Y., 1931), 28-29. http://www.cregojones.com/Stories/trinity.pdf

145 Herman Wellington Witthoft Sr. & Barbara Empie Greene. *The Descendants of Johan Ernst Emichen Emigrant to America Volume II The Loyalist Canadian Empey Family.* (Kipp, Edward, Orleans, Ontario, 2003); Ancestry.com. *Records of the Reformed Dutch Church of Stone Arabia: in the town of Palatine, Montgomery County, N.Y.* [database on-line]. Provo, UT: Ancestry.com Operations Inc, 2005. Original data: *Records of the Reformed Dutch Church of Stone Arabia: in the town of Palatine, Montgomery County, N.Y.*. New York: unknown, 1916. Vol. 3. The History of the Reformed Dutch Church of Stone Arabia. 85.

146 Reverend Andrew Luther Dillenbeck, D.D. *Lutheran Trinity Church of Stone Arabia, N.Y.* (Enterprise and News, St. Johnsville, N.Y., 1931), 22. http://www.cregojones.com/Stories/trinity.pdf ; *Collections of the New York Historical Society 1891,* Muster Rolls of New York Provincial Troops

1751-1764. (New York, 1892), 51-52. https://archive.org/stream/musterrollsnewy00socigoog#page/n70/mode/2up

147 The State of New York, *The colonial laws of New York from the year 1664 to the Revolution, including the charters to the Duke of York, the commissions and instructions to colonial governors, the Duke's laws, the laws of the Dongan and Leisler Assemblies, the charters of Albany and New York and the acts of the colonial legislatures from 1691 to 1775 inclusive.* Transmitted to the Legislature by the Commissioners of Statutory Revision, pursuant to chapter 125 of the Laws of 1891 (Ithica, N.Y., Cornell University Library, 1894), 4, 432. http://ebooks.library.cornell.edu/cgi/t/text/pageviewer-idx?c=cdl;cc=cdl;idno=cdl182;node=cdl1823A3;view=image;seq=436;size=100;page=root

148 James Sullivan, *The Papers of Sir William Johnson, Vol II* (Albany, The University of the State of New York, 1921), 620. https://archive.org/stream/paperssirwillia00johngoog#page/n666/mode/2up

149 James Sullivan, *The Papers of Sir William Johnson, Vol II* (Albany, The University of the State of New York, 1921), 613, 622.

150 John G. Gagliardo, *Germans and Agriculture in Colonial Pennsylvania* (Yale University, April, 1959), 207-208. https://journals.psu.edu/pmhb/article/viewFile/41466/41187The

151 James Sullivan, *The Papers of Sir William Johnson, Vol II* (Albany, The University of the State of New York, 1921), 533, 526-527, https://archive.org/stream/paperssirwillia00johngoog#page/n578/mode/2up

152 Ibid, 502, 537-538. https://archive.org/stream/paperssirwillia00johngoog#page/n548/mode/2up ; Walter Borneman, *The French and Indian War: Deciding the Fate of North America* (Toronto, Harper Perennial, 2007), 68; E.B. O'Callaghan, *The Documentary History of the State of New York,* Vol I, Chapter XVII Papers Relating to the First Settlement and Capture of Oswego 1727-1756 (Albany, Weed Parsons & Co. 1849), 482-487. https://archive.org/stream/documentaryhist00morggoog#page/n506/mode/2up.; Richard

Cannon, *Historical Record of the Forty-Second, or, Royal Highland Regiment of Foot* (London, Parker, Furnivall & Parker, 1845), 45. https://archive.org/stream/cihm_48390#page/n61/mode/2up

153 Ibid, 488-495; James Sullivan, *The Papers of Sir William Johnson, Vol II,* 549, 884. https://archive.org/stream/paperssirwillia00johngoog#page/n594/mode/2up

154 Ibid, 543-545, 560-561 "Newspapers.com" The Public Advertiser (London, Greater London, England, 13 July 1758), #7396 Extract of a private letter from New York dated June 2; "Schenectady Digital History Archives" History of the Mohawk Valley Gateway to the West 1614-1925, Chapter 44: 1757 Massacre at German Flats. http://www.schenectadyhistory.org/resources/mvgw/history/044.html

155 Ancestry.com. *Records of the Lutheran Trinity Church of Stone Arabia: in the town of Palatine, Montgomery County, N.Y.* [database on-line]. Provo, UT: Ancestry.com Operations Inc, 2005. Original data: *Records of the Lutheran Trinity Church of Stone Arabia: in the town of Palatine, Montgomery County, N.Y.*. New York: unknown, 1914. Section: Vol.1. Birth and baptisms, 1751 to 1815, 20. MDCCVI, d3gt Michel Gallinger c. ux Agatha, Christian, Sponsors, Philip Henrich Klein, Ernst Spangenberg, Catharine Frederichin.

156 Ken D. Johnson, "Fort Plank Bastion of My Freedom, Colonial Canajoharie, New York" The Butlersbury Tract. (26 November 2015). http://www.fort-plank.com/Butlersbury_Tract.html

157 Ancestry.com. *New York, Sales of Loyalist Land, 1762-1830* [database on-line]. Provo, UT, USA: 2013. Original data: New York State Engineer and Surveyor. Records of Surveys and Maps of State Lands, 1686–1892, Series A4016, Vols. 7–10 and 17. New York State Archives, Albany, New York, 176 a-g, 19 September 1784, Lot 75 Western Allotment Kingsborough Patent. https://www.ancestry.com/interactive/5368/41763_1120704930_1301-00013; Duncan Fraser, Papers and Records of the Ontario Historical Society, Volume LII, 1960, Original Source, Public Record Office, London, England AC 13/114.

Sir John Johnson's Rent Roll of the Kingsborough Patent.http://freepages.genealogy.rootsweb.ancestry.com/~wjmartin/kingsbor.htm ; Fulton County Republican, *Ancient Lease in Gloversville,* Thursday, May 13, 1909, 3. http://fultonhistory.com/Newspaper%2011/Johnstown%20NY%20Fulton%20County%20Republican/Johnstown%20NY%20Fulton%20County%20Republican%201908-1909%20Grayscale/Johnstown%20NY%20Fulton%20County%20Republican%201908-1909%20Grayscale%20-%200286.pdf

158 Maryly B. Penrose, *Compendium of Early Mohawk Valley Families Vol II* (Genealogical Publishing Co., Baltimore, 1990), 903. Baptisms of Children of Johannes Wick & Dorothea: Margaretha, Michael, Johannes, Severines; Ancestry.com. *Records of the Lutheran Trinity Church of Stone Arabia: in the town of Palatine, Montgomery County, N.Y.* [database on-line]. Provo, UT: Ancestry.com Operations Inc, 2005. Original data: *Records of the Lutheran Trinity Church of Stone Arabia: in the town of Palatine, Montgomery County, N.Y.*. New York: unknown, 1914. *Vol.1. Birth and baptisms, 1751 to 1815,* MDCCVLVI 13 Sept Johannes Wick c. ux Dorodea, Margaretha, Sponsors Johannes Bart c. ux Margaretha, 19, *Vol.1. Death register, 1768 to 1779; 1811 to 1814,* 346. "July 22, 1769. They buried Hennrich son of Joannes Wicken".

159 "The Mohawk Valley." (n.d.) http://mohawkvalley-wiki.com/

160 No record of Peter's baptism has been found, but the following Militia Roll indicates he was 32 yrs old in February 1789 making his birthdate 1757. "GlobalGenealogy.com" Militia Rolls of Upper Canada Colonel James Gray's Company, February 10, 1789 Peter Eamer, age 32, married, concession 3, lot, 10, 4 years service, country (of origin) is America, Royal Regiment of New York. (The Global Gazette, 15 April 1998). Original source: National Archives of Canada. N.A.C Reference: M.G. 19 F 35 Series 1, Lot 727, Entries 1 - 73 globalgenealogy.com/globalgazette/List001/list46.htm

161 Fintan O'Toole, *White Savage: William Johnson and the Invention of America* (Albany, State University of New York, 2005), 184-185.

162 *New York Colonial Muster Rolls, 1664-1775, Vol. II [database on-line].* Supplemental Muster Roll, Capt. Mark Petry's Return Rec'd February 26, 1757, 781-782.

163 Fintan O'Toole, *White Savage: William Johnson and the Invention of America* (Albany, State University of New York, 2005), 186; James Sullivan, *The Papers of Sir William Johnson, Vol II* (Albany, The University of the State of New York, 1921, 884-885.; *New York Colonial Muster Rolls, 1664-1775, Vol. II* [database on-line]. Supplemental Muster Roll, Company of Soffrines Deychert, 783-784. Capt. Mark Petry's Return Rec'd February 26, 1757, 1781-782.

164 Martin Waldorf lived on lot 78 on the western allotment of the Kingsborough Patent, next to Adam Ruppert. Lawrence Eaman lived on lot 91 Eastern Allotment Kingsborough Patent. Lodowyck Putman lived on lot 124 on the Eastern Allotment of the Kingsborough Patent. Conrad Smith lived just southeast of Philip Hendrick Klein on the Butlersbury Tract. Duncan Fraser, Papers and Records of the Ontario Historical Society, Volume LII, 1960. Original Source, Public Record Office, London, England AC 13/114. *Sir John Johnson's Rent Roll of the Kingsborough Patent.http://freepages.genealogy.rootsweb.ancestry.com/~wjmartin/kingsbor.htm Division of Rare and Manuscripts Collection Cornell University Library." Collection Number: 1072. Rice Family Genealogy* http://hausegenealogy.com/stubbs-rice.htm

165 Fintan O'Toole, *White Savage: William Johnson and the Invention of America* (Albany, State University of New York, 2005), 186.

166 Erin Crissman "The Farmer's Museum" Glamour Shots for our Venerable Old Lady. http://thefarmersmuseum.blogspot.ca/2010/04/glamour-shots-for-our-venerable-old.html

167 "CanadianHeadstones.com" In Memory of Caty, Wife of John Waldorff who died April 15, 1809 aged 51 years 8 mos 15 ds.

168 Walter Borneman, *The French and Indian War: Deciding the Fate of North America* (Toronto, Harper Perennial, 2007), 93.; James Sullivan,

The Papers of Sir William Johnson, Vol II (Albany, The University of the State of New York, 1921), 885. https://archive.org/stream/paperssirwillia00johngoog#page/n932/mode/2up ; http://archive.org/stream/coloniallawsnew00nygoog#page/n295/mode/2up The State of New York, *The colonial laws of New York from the year 1664 to the Revolution, including the charters to the Duke of York, the commissions and instructions to colonial governors, the Duke's laws, the laws of the Dongan and Leisler Assemblies, the charters of Albany and New York and the acts of the colonial legislatures from 1691 to 1775 inclusive.* Transmitted to the Legislature by the Commissioners of Statutory Revision, pursuant to chapter 125 of the Laws of 1891, Vol 4, Chapter 1066 (Albany, N.Y., James B. Lyon, 1894), 281.

169 E.B. O'Callaghan, The Documentary History of the State of New York Vol I, Chapter XVIII *Papers Relating to the Oneida Country and Mohawk Valley 1756, 1757* (Albany, Weed, Parsons & Co., 1849), 515-518. https://archive.org/stream/documentaryhist00morggoog#page/n544/mode/2up: Herkimer Historical Society, Herkimer NY, August 2008., *Reese vertical file.* "About 1968 a Reese family genealogist transcribed the story from a Xeroxed copy of a newspaper account discovered in the library or historical society of Herkimer County. The copy had been submitted to the Enterprise & News newspaper in St. Johnsville, N.Y. by a family member. Susan Jennings is the granddaughter of Letitia Winchell Reese who related the following story to her." Susan Jennings is the great great granddaughter of Magdelena Helmer/Reese. https://www.ancestry.co.uk/boards/thread.aspx?mv=flat&m=2271&p=surnames.reese ; James Sullivan, *The Papers of Sir William Johnson, Vol II* (Albany, The University of the State of New York, 1921), 757, 759, 760. https://archive.org/stream/paperssirwillia00johngoog#page/n802/mode/2up

170 Ibid, 760, 762, 763, 769. https://archive.org/stream/paperssirwillia00johngoog#page/n808/mode/2up ; The State of New York, *The colonial laws of New York from the year 1664 to the Revolution, including the charters to the Duke of York, the commissions and instructions to colonial governors, the Duke's laws, the laws of the Dongan and Leisler Assemblies, the charters of Albany and New York and the acts of the colonial*

legislatures from 1691 to 1775 inclusive. Transmitted to the Legislature by the Commissioners of Statutory Revision, pursuant to chapter 125 of the Laws of 1891 (Ithica, N.Y., Cornell University Library, 1894), 4, 432.

171 James Sullivan, *The Papers of Sir William Johnson, Vol II, 897. https://archive.org/stream/paperssirwillia00johngoog#page/n944/mode/2up*

172 Ibid. 809, 897; *New York Colonial Muster Rolls, 1664-1775, Vol. II* [database on-line]. Supplemental Muster Roll, 786.

173 It is fact that Peter Service's regiment was raised with these officers and fourteen privates. I do not know who the privates were. The statement that Michael, George, Jacob, Philip Klein, Martin, Peter and Philip Wiemer joined is fiction. But it is very possible they were some of the fourteen privates as they all lived close to Peter Service. Guylaine Petrin, "Rupert of Osnabruck Chronology," 1. "A Return of the Commission/ NonCommission officers and private men of Captain Peter Servise Company over 20 and under 46 years old in the Manor of Kingsborough and County of Albany. 9 July 1758 Captain Peter Servise, Lieut Francis Ropper, Ensign George Russ, Sgts John Addam Roopert, Anthony Flower, Corporal: Andrew Snider, 14 privates. New York Historical Society, NYC. Manuscript Division French and Indian War Muster Rolls (Albany County uncatalogued. Copied by Penny Minter." http://www.uelac.org/Loyalist-Info/extras/Rupert-Adam/Rupert-Adam-Family-of-Osnabruck-Chronology-by-Guylaine-Petrin.pdf ; In Philip's Loyalist Claim in 1788, John Farlinger, a soldier in the 60th regiment, was a witness. John stated that he knew Philip from Charlotte County. To my knowledge Philip never lived in Charlotte County (now Washington County). He came to America in 1755, and the baptism of his son Martin was in the Mohawk River area in February, 1756. Many battles of the French Indian War were fought in areas that became Charlotte County in 1772, For example: Fort Ticonderoga, Fort Edward, and Fort George. The 60th regiment fought in many of these battles. I believe that Philip could have gone to these areas with Sir William's militia. This is how John Farlinger might have known Philip.

174 James Sullivan, *The Papers of Sir William Johnson, Vol II* (Albany, The University of the State of New York, 1921), 108-110. https://archive.org/stream/papersofsirwilli13johnuoft#page/108/mode/2up

175 Sir William Johnson appointed four officers to assist in the organization of Indian war parties. They were John Butler, Jelles Fonda, William Hare and Hendrick Nelles. Fintan O'Toole, *White Savage: William Johnson and the Invention of America* (Albany, State University of New York, 2005), 231.; James Sullivan, *The Papers of Sir William Johnson, Vol II* (Albany, The University of the State of New York, 1921), 837-838, 840. https://archive.org/stream/paperssirwillia00johngoog#page/n880/mode/2up.

176 James Austin Holden, *Halfway Brook in History* (New York State Historical Association, 1905), 2-3. https://archive.org/stream/halfwaybrookinhi00hold#page/2/mode/2up ; Samuel Sewall, *The History of Woburn, Middlesex County, Mass, Diary of Lieut Samuel Thompson of Woburn,* Appendix IX (Boston, Wiggin & Lunt, 1868), 547-558. https://archive.org/stream/historyofwoburnm00sewa#page/n581/mode/2up ; Crisfield Johnson, *The History of Washington County New York* (Philadelphia, Everts & Ensign, 1878), 27-28, http://archive.org/stream/historyofwashing00john#page/28/mode/1up

177 Gordon Bannerman, *Merchants and the Military in Eighteenth Century Britain: British Army Contracts and Domestic Supply, 1739-1763* (New York, Routledge, 2016), 60, 69.

178 Arlene Frolick, ed, *The Gallinger Family: Gallinger Ancestors in Germany and Their Descendants in Canada and the U.S.A.,* 2nd ed, (Worall, L., 2004)

179 David Starbuck, *Excavating the Sutler's House: Artifacts of the British Armies in Fort Edward and Lake George* (Lebanon, NH, University Press of New England, 2010), 8, 20-22.

180 Burt Garfield Loescher, *The History of Rogers Rangers Vol I* (San Fransisco, Author, 1946), 228.; https://archive.org/stream/historyofrogersr01loes#page/228/mode/2up ; Library Archives Canada, Great Britain War Office, *Amherst Papers 12843,* lac_reel_c12843,

105019, MG 13 WO 34, Image 52. http://heritage.canadiana.ca/view/oocihm.lac_reel_c12843/52?r=0&s=1 ; Burt Garfield Loescher, *The History of Rogers Rangers Vol II*, 1st ed, (San Mateo, 1969), 8, 94, 105. http://heritage.canadiana.ca/view/oocihm.lac_reel_c12843/52?r=0&s=4 ; Walter Bourneman, *The French and Indian War: Deciding the Fate of North America* (Toronto, Harper Perennial, 2007), 130. John Ross, *War on the Run. The Epic Story of Robert Rogers and the Conquest of America's Frontier* (New York, Bantam Books, 2011), 167, 177, 240, 258,

181 Ancestry.com. *U.S., Dutch Reformed Church Records in Selected States, 1639-1989* [database on-line]. Provo, UT, USA: Ancestry.com Operations, Inc., 2014. Holland Society of New York; New York, New York; Schenectady Baptisms, Vol 1, Book 41, 1734, 1737, 1740, 1745.

182 Crisfield Johnson, *The History of Washington County New York* (Philadelphia, Everts & Ensign, 1878), 29.

183 Ian McCulloch, "Within Ourselves:" The Development of British Light Infantry in North America During the Seven Years War", *Canadian Military History*, 7, (2), 1998, 47. http://scholars.wlu.ca/cgi/viewcontent.cgi?article=1244&context=cmh

184 "Kronoskaf Virtual Time Machine," Project Seven Years War, 1758 British Expedition Against Carillon. Last modified 10 May 2017. http://www.kronoskaf.com/syw/index.php?title=1758_-_British_expedition_against_Carillon

185 Daniel E. Wager, *Col. Marinus Willett: The Hero of the Mohawk Valley. An Address Before the Oneida Historical Society* (Utica, Utica Herald Publishing Company, 1891), 4. https://archive.org/stream/heroofmohawk00wagerich#page/4/mode/2up

186 Ibid. 5. ; "Schenectady Digital History Archives" History of the Mohawk Valley Gateway to the West 1614-1925, Chapter 47: 1758 Ticonderoga and Fort Frontenac. http://www.schenectadyhistory.org/resources/mvgw/history/047.html

187 Fintan O'Toole, *White Savage: William Johnson and the Invention of America* (Albany, State University of New York, 2005), 196-197. James Smith, *An Account of the Remarkable Occurrences in the Life and Travels of Col. James Smith.* (Lexington, 1799), 14. https://archive.org/stream/accountofremarka00smit#page/14/mode/2up

188 Guylaine Petrin, "Rupert of Osnabruck Chronology," 1. "A Return of the Commission/NonCommission officers and private men of Captain Peter Servise Company over 20 and under 46 years old in the Manor of Kingsborough and County of Albany. 9 July 1758 Captain Peter Servise, Lieut Francis Ropper, Ensign George Russ, Sgts John Addam Roopert, Anthony Flower, Corporal: Andrew Snider, 14 privates. New York Historical Society, NYC. Manuscript Division French and Indian War Muster Rolls (Albany County uncatalogued. Copied by Penny Minter." http://www.uelac.org/Loyalist-Info/extras/Rupert-Adam/Rupert-Adam-Family-of-Osnabruck-Chronology-by-Guylaine-Petrin.pdf

189 Richard Cannon, *Historical Records of the British Army, Historical Record of the Forty Second, or, The Royal Highland Regiment of Foot* (London, Parker, Furnivall, and Parker, 1845), 46-48. https://archive.org/stream/cihm_48390#page/n61/mode/2up; Daniel E. Wager, *Col. Marinus Willett: The Hero of the Mohawk Valley. An Address Before the Oneida Historical Society* (Utica, Utica Herald Publishing Company, 1891), 5-6.; Crisfield Johnson, *The History of Washington County New York* (Philadelphia, Everts & Ensign, 1878), 29.; Walter Borneman, *The French and Indian War: Deciding the Fate of North America* (Toronto, Harper Perennial, 2007), 135-136.

190 Wayne Bower. "Registers of the Parishes of Williamsburg, Matilda, Osnabruck, and Edwardsburg." Burial Registers of the Parishes of Williamsburg, Matilda, Osnabruck, and Edwardsburg. Last modified February 27, 2016. 1809 April 17, Catarina Walldorf, Consort of John Waldorf of Osnabruck, born July 20, 1758, died April 15th, aged 50 years, 8 months and 20 days. http://bowergenealogy.ca/resources/lutheran/A/180.jpg

191 John Ross, *War on the Run. The Epic Story of Robert Rogers and the Conquest of America's Frontier* (New York, Bantam Books, 2011), 258-262.; Walter Bourneman, *The French and Indian War: Deciding the Fate of North America* (Toronto, Harper Perennial, 2007), 227-233.

192 Milton Hamilton & Albert Corey, *The Papers of Sir William Johnson, Vol X* (Albany, The University of the State of New York, 1951), 33-34. https://archive.org/stream/papersofsirwilli10johnuoft#page/32/mode/2up ; E.B. O'Callaghan, *The Documentary History of the State of New York,* Vol IV, *Chapter XIII Fort Stanwix* (Albany, Charles Van Benthuysen, 1851), 520-528. https://archive.org/stream/documentaryhisto04ocal#page/520/mode/2up

193 Library and Archives Canada, Great Britain, War Office, *Amherst Papers 12843,* lac_reel_c12843 C-12843 105019 MG 13 WO 34, Image 452. http://heritage.canadiana.ca/view/oocihm.lac_reel_c12843 ; Library and Archives Canada, Great Britain, War Office, *Amherst Papers 12832,* lac_reel_c12842 C-12842 105019 MG 13 WO 34, Image 2035, http://heritage.canadiana.ca/view/oocihm.lac_reel_c12842

194 Milton Hamilton & Albert Corey, *The Papers of Sir William Johnson, Vol X* (Albany, The University of the State of New York, 1951), https://archive.org/stream/papersofsirwilli10johnuoft#page/30/mode/2up ; Library and Archives Canada, Great Britain, War Office, *Amherst Papers 12842,* lac_reel_c12842 C-12842 105019 MG 13 WO 34, Image 2034, http://heritage.canadiana.ca/view/oocihm.lac_reel_c12842

195 Maria Catherine Gallinger would become Philip and Catrina's daughter in law when she married Peter Eamer 19 Jan 1780 at Caugnawaga, New York. "New Netherland and Beyond. Colonial Church Records." Reverend John Ogilvie Records Eastern NY State, Hudson Valley Area. *1750-1760 Baptisms. Extracted from Trinity Church Records,* NYC; *NYGBR,* volume 67, ©1936. (2012). Gallanger, 1759 2/25, Mohawks, Maria Cathrine, dau of Michael and Alida (Ady). http://www.rootsweb.ancestry.com/~nycoloni/chrecalb03.html

196 Milton Hamilton & Albert Corey, *The Papers of Sir William Johnson, Vol X* (Albany, The University of the State of New York, 1951), 112-113. https://archive.org/stream/papersofsirwilli10johnuoft#page/112/mode/2up ; Library and Archives Canada, Great Britain, War Office, *Haldimand Papers,* lac_reel_h1428 H-1428 105513 2034239 MG 21, Image 462, http://heritage.canadiana.ca/view/oocihm.lac_reel_h1428 The State of New York, *The colonial laws of New York from the year 1664 to the Revolution, including the charters to the Duke of York, the commissions and instructions to colonial governors, the Duke's laws, the laws of the Dongan and Leisler Assemblies, the charters of Albany and New York and the acts of the colonial legislatures from 1691 to 1775 inclusive.* Transmitted to the Legislature by the Commissioners of Statutory Revision, pursuant to chapter 125 of the Laws of 1891 (Ithica, N.Y., Cornell University Library, 1894), 4, 343-345. http://ebooks.library.cornell.edu/cgi/t/text/pageviewer-idx?c=cdl;cc=cdl;idno=cdl182;node=cdl182%3A3;view=image;seq=347;size=100;page=root

197 James Sullivan, *The Papers of Sir William Johnson, Vol III* (Albany, The University of the State of New York, 1921), 27-30. https://archive.org/stream/paperssirwillia00unkngoog#page/n56/mode/2up

198 No baptism record has been found for Johannes Eamer, but he was a sponsor at the baptism of Johannes Service, son of Philip Service and Catrina Seever 28 March 1780. He must have been of an age to be a sponsor, at least 16 years old. Therefore, born before 1764. I've chosen 1759 as the approximate year of his birth. Ancestry.com. *Records of the Reformed Protestant Dutch Church of Caughnawaga*: now the Reformed Church of Fonda, in the village of Fonda, Mon [database on-line]. Provo, UT: Ancestry.com Operations Inc, 2005. Volume one. Baptisms and births, 1758 to 1797*, 56.*

199 The State of New York, *The colonial laws of New York from the year 1664 to the Revolution, including the charters to the Duke of York, the commissions and instructions to colonial governors, the Duke's laws, the laws of the Dongan and Leisler Assemblies, the charters of Albany and New York and the acts of the colonial legislatures from 1691 to 1775 inclusive. Transmitted*

to the Legislature by the Commissioners of Statutory Revision, pursuant to chapter 125 of the Laws of 1891 (Ithica, N.Y., Cornell University Library, 1894), Vol. 4, 357-359. http://ebooks.library.cornell.edu/cgi/t/text/pageviewer-idx?c=cdl;cc=cdl;idno=cdl182;node=cdl182%3A3;view=image;seq=361;size=100;page=root

200 Johannes Wert lived on lot 66 Western Allotment Kingsborough Patent. Corporal Andrew Snyder lived on lot 67, the lot next (south) to Johannes Wert. Duncan Fraser, Papers and Records of the Ontario Historical Society, Volume LII, 1960, Original Source, Public Record Office, London, England AC 13/114. *Sir John Johnson's Rent Roll of the Kingsborough Patent.* http://freepages.genealogy.rootsweb.ancestry.com/~wjmartin/kingsbor.htm

201 Milton Hamilton & Albert Corey, *The Papers of Sir William Johnson, Vol XIII* (Albany, The University of the State of New York, 1951), 114-157, 160, https://archive.org/stream/papersofsirwilli13johnuoft#page/114/mode/2up ; James Sullivan, *The Papers of Sir William Johnson, Vol III,* (Albany, The University of the State of New York, 1921), 108. https://archive.org/stream/paperssirwillia00unkngoog#page/n144/mode/2up Stone, William, *The Life and Times of Sir William Johnson, Bart.*, Vol II (Albany, J. Munsell, 1865), 394. https://archive.org/stream/lifetimesofsirwi02stonuoft#page/394/mode/2up

202 "New Netherland and Beyond. Colonial Church Records." Reverend John Ogilvie Records Eastern NY State, Hudson Valley Area. *1750-1760 Baptisms. Extracted from Trinity Church Records,* NYC; *NYGBR,* volume 67, ©1936. (2012). Clement 175(_) 10/28 Mohawks Joseph, son of Lewis and Catalyntje (Potman) http://www.rootsweb.ancestry.com/~nycoloni/chrecalb03.html

203 Ancestry.com. *U.S., Dutch Reformed Church Records in Selected States, 1639-1989* [database on-line]. Provo, UT, USA: Ancestry.com Operations, Inc., 2014.Original data: Dutch Reformed Church Records from New York and New Jersey. Holland Society of New York, New York, New York. Dutch Reformed Church Records from New Jersey.

The Archives of the Reformed Church in America, New Brunswick, New Jersey. *Reformed Church of Fonda, Baptisms, Marriages, Members, Consistory Minutes, 1758-1839.* February 25, 1760, Mathias Link, Maria Magdalena Kraaft, Julianna, Sponsors, Jacob Pikel and Julianna Pikel.

204 Martin Waldorf lived on lot 78 Western Allotment Kingsborough Patent. Peter Fykes lived on lot 70 Western Allotment Kingsborough Patent. Duncan Fraser, Papers and Records of the Ontario Historical Society, Volume LII, 1960, Original Source, Public Record Office, London, England AC 13/114. *Sir John Johnson's Rent Roll of the Kingsborough Patent.* http://freepages.genealogy.rootsweb.ancestry.com/~wjmartin/kingsbor.htm

205 This is John Bowen, son of William Bowen and Cornelia Putnam of Warrensburgh near Fort Hunter and brother of Sergeant William Bowen http://heritage.canadiana.ca/view/oocihm.lac_reel_c1478/635?r=0&s=6 James Sullivan, *The Papers of Sir William Johnson, Vol III* (Albany, The University of the State of New York, 1921), 233. https://archive.org/stream/paperssirwillia00unkngoog#page/n274/mode/2up

206 Ancestry.ca New York Colonial Muster Rolls, 1664-1775, Vol. II [database on-line]. Annual Report of the State Historian. *A Muster Roll of the Men Raised and Passed in the County of Albany for Captain Christopher Yate's Company May The 5th 1760.* 585-587. https://www.ancestry.ca/interactive/48600/NYMusterRollsII-003874-587#?imageId=NYMusterRollsII-003872-585

207 Ancestry.com. Register book, Register of baptisms, marriages, communicants, & funerals begun by Henry Barclay at Fort Hunter, January 26th, 1734 /5 : regist [database on-line]. Provo, UT: Ancestry.com Operations Inc, 2005. Original data: *Register of baptisms, marriages, communicants, & funerals begun by Henry Barclay at Fort Hunter, January 26th, 1734 /5 : register book, Fort Hunter 1734.* Albany, N.Y.: New York State Library, 1919, 22, 38. Joseph son of ....Powell and Elizabeth his wife. Will Johnson, Joseph Clement and Anna Clement, Surties. 11 May

1740, February 7, 1740, John son of Catherine Wysenbergh. Isaac Wemp, William Powell, Elizabeth Powell, Surties.

208 Ken D. Johnson, "Fort Plank Bastion of My Freedom, Colonial Canajoharie, New York." Mohawk Valley Maps and Sketches. The Butlersbury Tract. (Last modified, 26 Nov 2015). http://www.fort-plank.com/Butlersbury_Tract.html; Duncan Fraser, Papers and Records of the Ontario Historical Society, Volume LII, 1960, Original Source, Public Record Office, London, England AC 13/114. *Sir John Johnson's Rent Roll of the Kingsborough Patent.*http://freepages.genealogy.rootsweb.ancestry.com/~wjmartin/kingsbor.htm

209 No baptismal, marriage or death record of Catherine Waldorf has been found, but she is on the list of children attending the Johnstown school in 1769. I assume she was born about 1760. E.B. O'Callaghan, The Documentary History of the State of New York Vol IV, *Chapter XII Papers Relating to the Six Nations, List of Scholars at the Free School, Johnstown, May 1769* (Albany, 1851), 260-261. .https://archive.org/stream/documentaryhist04ocal#page/260/mode/2up

210 Milton Hamilton & Albert Corey, *The Papers of Sir William Johnson, Vol XIII, Journal of Warren Johnson* (Albany, The University of the State of New York, 1962), 180-214 https://archive.org/stream/papersofsirwilli13johnuoft#page/180/mode/2up

211 John G. Gagliardo, *Germans and Agriculture in Colonial Pennsylvania* (Yale University, April, 1959), 194. https://journals.psu.edu/pmhb/article/viewFile/41466/41187The

212 Fintan O'Toole, *White Savage: William Johnson and the Invention of America* (Albany, State University of New York, 2005), 214-215.; Milton Hamilton & Albert Corey, *The Papers of Sir William Johnson, Vol XIII, List of Indians* (Albany, The University of the State of New York, 1962), 170-171, 173-178. https://archive.org/stream/papersofsirwilli13johnuoft#page/172/mode/2up ; Library and Archives Canada, Great Britain War Office: *Amherst Papers* 12843, lac_reel-c12843 C-12843, 105019,

MG 13 WO 34, Image 106, 281-291. http://heritage.canadiana.ca/view/oocihm.lac_reel_c12843/106?r=0&s=4

213 James Sullivan, *The Papers of Sir William Johnson, Vol III* (Albany, The University of the State of New York, 1921), 343, 349. https://archive.org/stream/paperssirwillia00unkngoog#page/n400/mode/2up

214 Timothy (Teady) McGinnis was one of the soldiers killed at the battle of Bloody Pond near Lake George in 1755. He was a merchant, trader, and land owner in the Mohawk Valley. His wife Sarah Kast McGinnis was the daughter of Hans Jury Kast, a German immigrant of 1709. She was an Indian interpreter for the British during the Revolutionary War. Milton Hamilton & Albert Corey, *The Papers of Sir William Johnson, Vol X* (Albany, The University of the State of New York, 1951), 248-250. https://archive.org/stream/papersofsirwilli10johnuoft#page/248/mode/2up Secretary of State of New York, *Calendar of Colonial Manuscripts Indorsed Land Papers* (Albany, Weed, Parsons & Co., 1864), 302. https://archive.org/stream/calendarofnycolo00alba#page/302/mode/2up

215 Castle Cumberland is a summer house Sir William Johnson built about twelve miles north of Fort Johnson on the Sacandaga River, Milton Hamilton & Albert Corey, *The Papers of Sir William Johnson, Vol X* (Albany, The University of the State of New York, 1951), 223-229, https://archive.org/stream/papersofsirwilli10johnuoft#page/226/mode/2up; Fintan O'Toole, *White Savage: William Johnson and the Invention of America* (Albany, State University of New York, 2005), 236.

216 Milton Hamilton & Albert Corey, *The Papers of Sir William Johnson, Vol X* (Albany, The University of the State of New York, 1951), 223 250. https://archive.org/stream/papersofsirwilli10johnuoft#page/250/mode/2up

217 Library and Archives Canada, Great Britain, War Office, lac_reel_c12843 C-12843 105019 MG 13 WO 34, *Amherst Papers 12843*, Image 452. Image 118. 11 June 1761. http://heritage.canadiana.ca/view/oocihm.lac_reel_c12843/118?r=0&s=4 ; Library and Archives Canada, *Claus*

Papers 1478, lac_reel_c1478 C1478 103767 MG 19 F 1, Image 47, Castle Cumberland 23 March 1761. http://heritage.canadiana.ca/view/oocihm.lac_reel_c1478

218 New York Historical Society, *Muster Rolls of New York Provincial Troops 1755-1764, A Muster Roll of the Men Rais'd and Pass'd in the County of Albany for Captain Christopher Yates May 19th 1761* (New York, New York Historical Society, 1891), 368-373. Adam Fix, Inlisted May 18, Born Germany, Labourer, Capt Yates Inlisted, 5'51/4, Fair Complexion, Blue Eyes, Brown Hair. Joseph Powell, Inlisted April 29, Age 21, Born Mohawks, Labourer, 5' 4 ½, Fair Complexion, Blue Eyes, Brown Hair. http://archive.org/stream/musterrollsnewy00socigoog#page/n390/mode/2up

219 Ancestry.com. *UK, American Loyalist Claims, 1776-1835* [database on-line]. Provo, UT, USA: Ancestry.com Operations, Inc., 2013. Original data: American Loyalist Claims, 1776–1835. AO 12–13. The National Archives of the United Kingdom, Kew, Surrey, England. Piece 031: Evidence, New York, 1787-1788. Estimate of the Real and Personal Estate of Philip Eamer, 139.

220 Henry Gallinger would become Philip and Catrina's son in law when he married their daughter Dorothy at Quebec in 1783. Ancestry.com. *U.S., Dutch Reformed Church Records in Selected States, 1639-1989* [database on-line]. Provo, UT, USA: Ancestry.com Operations, Inc., 2014. Original data: Dutch Reformed Church Records from New York and New Jersey. Holland Society of New York, New York, New York. Dutch Reformed Church Records from New Jersey. The Archives of the Reformed Church in America, New Brunswick, New Jersey. Stone Arabia Church, Baptisms, Members, Deaths, 1739-1987. Henrich, 1761, born 4 Sept., baptized 15 Nov, Michael Galinger and Agatha, Sponsors: Henrich Dachstader and Barbara Dachstader, Henrich's legitimate daughter.

221 James Sullivan, *The Papers of Sir William Johnson, Vol III* (Albany, The University of the State of New York, 1962), 357. https://archive.org/stream/paperssirwillia00unkngoog#page/n408/mode/2up ; The State

of New York, *The colonial laws of New York from the year 1664 to the Revolution, including the charters to the Duke of York, the commissions and instructions to colonial governors, the Duke's laws, the laws of the Dongan and Leisler Assemblies, the charters of Albany and New York and the acts of the colonial legislatures from 1691 to 1775 inclusive. Transmitted to the Legislature by the Commissioners of Statutory Revision, pursuant to chapter 125 of the Laws of 1891,* Vol. 4 (Albany, James B. Lyon, 1894), 546-548. http://archive.org/stream/coloniallawsnew00nygoog#page/n561/mode/2up

222 Wayne Bower. "Registers of the Parishes of Williamsburg, Matilda, Osnabruck, and Edwardsburg." *Burial Registers of the Parishes of Williamsburg, Matilda, Osnabruck, and Edwardsburg.* Last modified February 27, 2016. 1801 Aug 31, Mathias Link of Osnabrug, Born Novemb. 28 in the year 1761. Died Aug 29th, 1801. His age was 39 years, 9 months and 7 days. http://bowergenealogy.ca/resources/lutheran/A/176.jpg

223 Milton Hamilton & Albert Corey, *The Papers of Sir William Johnson, Vol X* (Albany, The University of the State of New York, 1951), 357-371. https://archive.org/stream/papersofsirwilli10johnuoft#page/356/mode/2up; ; Ken D. Johnson, "Fort Plank Bastion of My Freedom, Colonial Canajoharie, New York." Mohawk Valley Maps and Sketches. A Traverse of the Schoharie Kill From Duanesburg to Kadoreto in 1768. (Last modified, 26 Nov 2015). http://www.fort-plank.com/Kadorte_NYSL_SC7004.html ; New Dorlach Patent https://www.ancestry.ca/mediaui-viewer/tree/44704820/person/6984991669/media/dd59a76b-f34d-4ccd-bc0a-4fadce79d135 ; Ancestry.com. *Register of baptisms, marriages, communicants, & funerals begun by Henry Barclay at Fort Hunter, January 26th, 1734 /5: regist* [database on-line]. Provo, UT. Register book. 15 July 1739, Barent son of Johann Peter Frederick and Anna Veronica his wife, Barent Vroman Jr., Engltie Hansen Surties.

224 Alexander Flick, The Papers of Sir William Johnson, Vol IV (Albany, The University of the State of New York, 1925), 40. https://archive.org/stream/papersofsirwilli04john#page/40/mode/2up

225 Ancestry.com. *U.S., Dutch Reformed Church Records in Selected States, 1639-1989* [database on-line]. Provo, UT, USA: Ancestry.com Operations, Inc., 2014. Original data: Dutch Reformed Church Records from New York and New Jersey. Holland Society of New York, New York, New York. Dutch Reformed Church Records from New Jersey. *The Archives of the Reformed Church in America*, New Brunswick, New Jersey. Cagnawaga or Fonda, Book 15. 1762, Philip March 18, Stephanus Jordan, Margaretha Bellony, Philip Beumer, Catharina his wife; Volume one. Baptisms and births, 1758 to 1797, 7. Maart 18 1762, (045), Stephanus Jordan, Margariet Bellong, Philip, Sponsors: Philip Beemener, Catarena Beemener.

226 George Schenck lived on lot 63 on the Western Allotment of the Kingsborough Patent. In 1761, he also owned 59 acres in Stone Arabia. Library and Archives Canada, Great Britain, War Office, lac_reel_c12843 C-12843 105019 MG 13 WO 34, *Amherst Papers 12843*, Image 858-894. http://heritage.canadiana.ca/view/oocihm.lac_reel_c12843/858?r=0&s=4; James Sullivan, *The Papers of Sir William Johnson, Vol III* (Albany, The University of the State of New York, 1962), 522. https://archive.org/stream/paperssirwillia00unkngoog#page/n580/mode/2up

227 Ancestry.com. *Records of the Reformed Protestant Dutch Church of Caughnawaga: now the Reformed Church of Fonda, in the village of Fonda, Mon* [database on-line]. Provo, UT: Ancestry.com Operations Inc, 2005. Original data: *Records of the Reformed Protestant Dutch Church of Caughnawaga: now the Reformed Church of Fonda, in the village of Fonda, Montgomery County, N.Y.*. New York,: unknown, 1917. Volume one. Baptisms and births, 1758 to 1797. 7. July 4, 1762, Hendrick Hof, Caterin Terrel; Maria, Sponsors, Nicholaes Gardenier, Maria Antes.

228 Milton Hamilton & Albert Corey, *The Papers of Sir William Johnson, Vol XIII* (Albany, The University of the State of New York, 1962), 278. https://archive.org/stream/papersofsirwilli13johnuoft#page/278/mode/2up ; James Sullivan, *The Papers of Sir William Johnson, Vol III* (Albany, The University of the State of New York, 1921), 834, 852.

https://archive.org/stream/paperssirwillia00unkngoog#page/n914/mode/2up; *New York Colonial Muster Rolls, 1664-1775, Vol. II* [database on-line]. *Supplemental Muster Rolls. 797-798.*

229 A tippling house is a place where liquor is sold without a license. James Sullivan, *The Papers of Sir William Johnson, Vol III* (Albany, The University of the State of New York, 1921), 855-856. https://archive.org/stream/paperssirwillia00unkngoog#page/n920/mode/2up

230 Kersey is a thick, sturdy, warm woolen cloth with a twill weave. New York State Historical Association, Fenimore Art Museum, Research Library Special Collections, *Jellis Fonda Papers,* Coll. No. 157, 1750-1791 (Cooperstown, New York). Algair, Jacob: 48B.

231 Philip's brother Mattheus married Anna Margaretha Weinreich at Auerbach, Hesse 25 Nov 1757. By 1763 they had three children: Johannes Peter, Elizabeth Catharina, and Elizabeth Barbara. Ancestry.com. *Germany, Select Marriages, 1558-1929* [database on-line]. Provo, UT. Original data: *Germany, Marriages, 1558-1929.* Salt Lake City, Utah: FamilySearch, 2013. FHL Film Number: 1340362.

232 No record has been found of Philip's marriage, death, or the birth of any children. Also, there is no record of his arrival in Canada with his parents in 1781-1786. Therefore, I assume he died between 1763 and 1781, age 0-18. Ancestry.com. *Records of the Reformed Protestant Dutch Church of Caughnawaga: now the Reformed Church of Fonda, in the village of Fonda, Mon* [database on-line]. Provo, UT: Ancestry.com Operations Inc, 2005. Original data: Records of the Reformed Protestant Dutch Church of Caughnawaga: now the Reformed Church of Fonda, in the village of Fonda, Montgomery County, N.Y.. New York: unknown, 1917. Volume one. Baptisms and births, 1758 to 1797, 9. Feb 6, 1763, Entry (063), Philip Weemer, Catarina Lyser; Philip, Sponsors, Philip Miller, Anna Visbach.

233 James Sullivan, *The Papers of Sir William Johnson, Vol III* (Albany, The University of the State of New York, 1921), 954. https://archive.org/stream/paperssirwillia00unkngoog#page/n1022/mode/2up; Milton

Hamilton & Albert Corey, *The Papers of Sir William Johnson, Vol XIII* (Albany, The University of the State of New York, 1962), 282-283, 285-286, 303-317. https://archive.org/stream/papersofsirwilli13johnuoft#page/282/mode/2up ; History of Montgomery and Fulton Counties N.Y. (F.W. Beers & Co., New York, 1878). https://archive.org/stream/historyofmontgom00beer#page/n485/mode/2up 188-200.; William, L. Stone, *The Life and Times of Sir William Johnson, Bart, Vol II* (Albany, J. Munsell, 1865), 478-479.https://archive.org/stream/lifetimesofsirwi02stonuoft#page/478/mode/2up

234 "Montgomery County GenWeb Geneology and History," *Montgomery County.* (1998). http://montgomery.nygenweb.net/mont1841b.html ; "Montgomery County GenWeb Geneology and History," Lillian Dockstader Van Dusen, *A History of the Reformed Church of Fonda N.Y.*, (2000). ; http://montgomery.nygenweb.net/mohawk/fondarefchurch1.html ; "Three Rivers, Hudson, Mohawk, Schoharie, History From America's Most Famous Valleys," W.N.P. Daily, *Fonda Reformed Church,* Recorder Press Amsterdam N.Y. 1916. http://threeriversshms.com/rcafonda.htm ; Benson, J. Lossing, *Pictorial Field Book of the Revolution.* Volume 1 Chapter X, (New York, Harper & Brothers, 1859), http://freepages.history.rootsweb.ancestry.com/~wcarr1/Lossing1/Chap10.html

235 The State of New York, *The colonial laws of New York from the year 1664 to the Revolution, including the charters to the Duke of York, the commissions and instructions to colonial governors, the Duke's laws, the laws of the Dongan and Leisler Assemblies, the charters of Albany and New York and the acts of the colonial legislatures from 1691 to 1775 inclusive. Transmitted to the Legislature by the Commissioners of Statutory Revision, pursuant to chapter 125 of the Laws of 1891,* Vol. 4 (Albany, James B. Lyon, 1894), 458-459. http://archive.org/stream/coloniallawsnew00nygoog#page/n473/mode/2up

236 Milton Hamilton & Albert Corey, *The Papers of Sir William Johnson, Vol XIII,* (Albany, The University of the State of New York, 1962),

370. https://archive.org/stream/papersofsirwilli13johnuoft#page/370/mode/2up

237 Lieutenant William Dillenbach was fined £300. Proceedings against Lieutenant Dillenbach continued until March 1765, unless there was a separate incident in 1765. Goal in Albany or seizure of property was considered as payment of the fine. "Three Rivers. Hudson, Mohawk Schoharie. History From America's Most Famous Valleys." Lou D. MacWethy, The Book of Names Especially Relating to the Early Palatines and the First Settlers in the Mohawk Valley (St. Johnsville, NY, The Enterprise and News, 1933), http://www.threeriversshms.com/namesfrindianwar.htm ; Alexander Flick, The Papers of Sir William Johnson, Vol IV (Albany, The University of the State of New York, 1925), 220, 702. https://archive.org/stream/papersofsirwilli04john#page/220/mode/2up ; Ancestry. ca. *New York Colonial Muster Rolls, 1664-1775, Vol. II* [database on-line]. Supplemental Muster Rolls. 1763, Captain Deyger's List of Delinquents.

238 Ancestry.com. *UK, American Loyalist Claims, 1776-1835* [database on-line]. Provo, UT, USA: Ancestry.com Operations, Inc., 2013. The National Archives of the UK; Kew, Surrey, England; American Loyalist Claims, Series I; Class: AO 13; Piece: 027 Evidence, New York, 1787; Ancestry.com. *UK, American Loyalist Claims, 1776-1835* [database on-line]. Provo, UT, USA: Ancestry.com Operations, Inc., 2013. The National Archives of the UK; Kew, Surrey, England; American Loyalist Claims, Series I; Class: AO 13; Piece: 031: Evidence, New York, *1787-1788.;* Duncan Fraser, Papers and Records of the Ontario Historical Society, Volume LII, 1960, Original Source, Public Record Office, London, England AC 13/114. *Sir John Johnson's Rent Roll of the Kingsborough Patent.* http://freepages.genealogy.rootsweb.ancestry.com/~wjmartin/kingsbor.htm

239 Milton Hamilton & Albert Corey, *The Papers of Sir William Johnson, Vol X* (Albany, The University of the State of New York, 1951), 977-985. https://archive.org/stream/papersofsirwilli10johnuoft#page/976/mode/2up

240 A gill equals one half cup. Stone, William, *The Life and Times of Sir William Johnson, Bart., Vol II* (Albany, J. Munsell, 1865), 486-490. https://archive.org/stream/lifetimesofsirwi02stonuoft#page/478/mode/2up

241 Col. James Smith, *An Account of the Remarkable Occurrences in the Life and Times of Col. James Smith During His Captivity With the Indians in the years 1755, 56, 57, 58 & 59* (Lexington, John Bradford, 1799), 14. https://archive.org/stream/accountofremarka00smit#page/14/mode/2up

242 Francis Whiting Halsey, *The Old New York Frontier. Its Wars With Indians and Tories, Its Missionary Schools, Pioneers and Land Titles. 1614-1800* (New York, Charles Scribner's Sons, 1801) 116. https://archive.org/stream/oldnewyorkfronti01hals#page/116/mode/2up

CHAPTER FOUR
Home in the Mohawk River Valley (1764-1774)

243 Stroud is a course woolen cloth used to make coats, jackets, or blankets. Penniston is a woolen cloth used to make clothing such as petticoats, jackets, or breeches. New York State Historical Association, Fenimore Art Museum, Research Library Special Collections, *Jellis Fonda Papers,* Coll. No. 157, 1750-1791. Wemer, Philip: 69A.

244 Ibid.

245 John Abeel was a gunsmith and trader, primarily with the Seneca. He was the son of Christophel Abeel. As a trader, John Abeel traveled through Pennsylvania and New York. He married a Seneca Princess of the Wolf Clan named Aliquipiso or Gah-hon-no-neh, 'She Who Goes To The River'. They lived along the Genesee River. Their son, born ca. 1742, was the famous Seneca War Chief Gaiänt'wakê , or 'Cornplanter'. When John Abeel moved to New York, he lived just west of Fort Plain (Minden) and married his second wife Mary Knouts. .About 1780, he became 'insane' and had to be chained to the floor. In later years, he was allowed to

wander about his property. Milton Hamilton & Albert Corey, *The Papers of Sir William Johnson, Vol XIII* (Albany, The University of the State of New York, 1962), 321-322. https://archive.org/stream/papersofsirwilli13johnuoft#page/320/mode/2up ; Henry Whittemore, *The Abeel And Allied Families.* (New York, 1899), 4-5. https://hdl.handle.net/2027/wu.89062958707 ; "Montgomery County NY GENWEB. Genealogy & History," Max Reid, The Story of Old Fort Johnson, Chapter XV. Land Grants: Royal, Kingsborough, Sacandaga-Johnson Hall. (Last Modified, 10 December 1999).

246 Milton Hamilton & Albert Corey, *The Papers of Sir William Johnson, Vol XIII* (Albany, The University of the State of New York, 1962), 322. https://archive.org/stream/papersofsirwilli13johnuoft#page/320/mode/2up; Alexander C. Flick, *The Papers of Sir William Johnson, Vol IV* (Albany, The University of the State of New York, 1925), 286. https://archive.org/stream/papersofsirwilli04john#page/286/mode/2up

247 New York Public Library Digital Collections, Theodorus Bailey Myers Collection Series II. Prominent Civilians and Officials During the Colonial Period, *Johnson, Sir William. Johnson Hall [New York]*, 1764, NYPL catalog ID b11868620 MSS Unit ID: 2091: Myers#262. Archives EADID 478689, UUID: ddfeae00-2e59-0133-58a3-58d385a7b928, https://digitalcollections.nypl.org/items/e41b50e0-3320-0133-8520-58d385a7b928/book?parent=db55e2d0-2e58-0133-1b29-58d385a7b928#page/63/mode/2up

248 "Mohawk River Flooding and Watershed Analysis Union College," History of Mohawk River Floods, (Schenectady, NY, Union College, nd.). http://minerva.union.edu/garverj/mohawk/history.html

249 *Ancestry.com. UK, American Loyalist Claims, 1776-1835 [database on-line]. Provo, UT, USA: Ancestry.com Operations, Inc., 2013. The National Archives of the UK; Kew, Surrey, England; American Loyalist Claims, Series I; Class: AO 13; Piece 027: Evidence, New York, 1787;* Duncan Fraser, Papers and Records of the Ontario Historical Society, Volume LII, 1960, Original

Source, Public Record Office, London, England AC 13/114. *Sir John Johnson's Rent Roll of the Kingsborough Patent.* http://freepages.genealogy.rootsweb.ancestry.com/~wjmartin/kingsbor.htm

250 Ancestry.com. *U.S., Dutch Reformed Church Records in Selected States, 1639-1989* [database on-line]. Provo, UT, USA. Ancestry.com Operations, Inc., 2014.The Archives of the Reformed Church in America; New Brunswick, New Jersey; Stone Arabia Church, Baptisms, Members, Deaths, 1739-1987. Anna Link, Born 22 March, Baptized 5 May, Mattheus Link and Maria Magdelena, Sponsor, Barbara, George Bayers widowed wife; Johann George, Born April 9, Baptized 5 May, Michael Kalyer and Agata, Sponsors, Johann George Schenck and Magdelena his wife.

251 Ancestry.com. *Records of the Reformed Dutch Church of Stone Arabia in the town of Palatine, Montgomery County, N.Y.* [database on-line]. Provo, UT: Ancestry.com Operations Inc, 2005. Vol.1. Baptisms and births. 45.

252 The map hanging on the wall was the map of Ireland. The painting was the 'Last Parting of Hector and Andromache'. Fintan O'Toole, *White Savage: William Johnson and the Invention of America* (Albany, State University of New York, 2005), 292-293, 303-304.

253 Thayendanegea 'He Sets or Places Together Two Bets' or Joseph and Gonwatsijayenni 'Someone Lends Her a Flower' or Molly (Mary) Brant were brother and sister of the Mohawk Wolf Clan near Canajoharie. Joseph was a War Chief, Translator, and British Indian Department Officer. Mary was the consort of Sir William Johnson and bore him eight children. She was also a Loyalist and Translator. They both settled in western Ontario after the war. http://www.carf.info/kingston-past/molly-brant Barbara Graymont, "KOÑWATSIˀTSIAIÉÑNI (Mary Brant)," in *Dictionary of Canadian Biography*, vol. 4, University of Toronto/Université Laval, 2003. http://www.biographi.ca/en/bio/konwatsitsiaienni_4E.html ; Barbara Graymont, "THAYENDANEGEA," in *Dictionary of Canadian Biography*, vol. 5, University of Toronto/Université Laval, 2003. http://www.biographi.ca/en/bio/

thayendanegea_5E.html ; Library and Archives Canada, Claus Papers, 1478, lac_reel_c1478, C-1478, 103767, MG 19 F 1, Image 360. http://heritage.canadiana.ca/view/oocihm.lac_reel_c1478

254 Fintan O'Toole, *White Savage: William Johnson and the Invention of America* (Albany, State University of New York, 2005), 292-293; "Fulton County, NYGenWeb." Wanda Burch, "He was bought at public sale…, Slavery At Johnson Hall (The Sunday Leader-Herald, 27 Feb, 2000).

255 In 1764, Philip Eamer had a lease forever of sixty six acres of land from Harmanus Wendell. The land was identified as being about three miles from Johnstown, lot 59 on the Sacandaga Patent. The Sacandaga Patent was surveyed for Lendert Gansevoort and others 7 Nov, 1741. Ancestry.com. *UK, American Loyalist Claims, 1776-1835* [database on-line]. Provo, UT, USA: Ancestry.com Operations, Inc., 2013. Piece 031: Evidence, New York, 1787-1788, 276-278.; "The People of Colonial Albany Live Here." Stefan Beilinski, *The Sacandaga Patent.* (Last modified 5 May 2017). *https://exhibitions.nysm.nysed.gov/albany/na/sacandaga.html* ; Secretary of State of New York, *Calendar of Colonial Manuscripts Indorsed Land Papers Vol XIII* (Albany, Weed, Parsons & Co., 1864), 245. https://archive.org/stream/calendarofnycolo00alba#page/244/mode/2up

256 Mendel, Mesick, Cohen Architects, *Fort Johnston Amsterdam, New York: A Historic Structure Report 1974-1975* (Washington, D.C., Technical Preservation Services Division Office of Archeology and Historic Preservation US Department of the Interior, 1978), 6. http://npshistory.com/publications/fort-johnson-hsr.pdf

257 Michael Carman lived on lot 191 and Jacob Sheets lived next to him on lot 190 on the eastern allotment of the Kingsborough Patent. Duncan Fraser, Papers and Records of the Ontario Historical Society, Volume LII, 1960, Original Source, Public Record Office, London, England AC 13/114. *Sir John Johnson's Rent Roll of the Kingsborough Patent.* http://freepages.genealogy.rootsweb.ancestry.com/~wjmartin/kingsbor.htm

258 Hugh Fraser lived on lot 123 of the eastern allotment of the Kingsborough Patent. John Fraser lived on lot 113 and William Jr. lived

on lot 122. William Sr. and Thomas lived on land they had in Ballstown, Albany County, New York. Duncan Fraser, Papers and Records of the Ontario Historical Society, Volume LII, 1960, Original Source, Public Record Office, London, England AC 13/114. *Sir John Johnson's Rent Roll of the Kingsborough Patent.* http://freepages.genealogy.rootsweb.ancestry.com/~wjmartin/kingsbor.htm ; Fintan O'Toole, *White Savage: William Johnson and the Invention of America* (Albany, State University of New York, 2005), 308. *http://freepages.genealogy.rootsweb.ancestry.com/~wjmartin/kingsbor.htm* ; Ancestry.com. *UK, American Loyalist Claims, 1776-1835* [database on-line]. Provo, UT, USA: Ancestry.com Operations, Inc., 2013. The National Archives of the UK; Kew, Surrey, England; American Loyalist Claims, Series I; Class: AO 13; Piece: 029, 1787-1788.

259 Alexander C. Flick, *The Papers of Sir William Johnson, Vol IV* (Albany, The University of the State of New York, 1925), 540-541. https://archive.org/stream/papersofsirwilli04john#page/540/mode/2up

260 Secretary of State of New York, *Calendar of Colonial Manuscripts Indorsed Land Papers Vol XIII* (Albany, Weed, Parsons & Co., 1864), 245. https://archive.org/stream/calendarofnycolo00alba#page/244/mode/2up ; James Sullivan, *The Papers of Sir William Johnson, Vol III* (Albany, The University of the State of New York, 1921), 634.

261 Alexander C. Flick, *The Papers of Sir William Johnson, Vol IV* (Albany, The University of the State of New York, 1925), 344-400, 392-394, 405-406. https://archive.org/stream/papersofsirwilli04john#page/392/mode/2up

262 Ibid. 466-481. https://archive.org/stream/papersofsirwilli04john#page/466/mode/2up ; Library and Archives Canada, *Indian Affairs, selections from the Claus Papers – 11773.* Lac_reel_c11773, C-11773, 102179, 135619, MG55. Image 12. http://heritage.canadiana.ca/view/oocihm.lac_reel_c11773/12?r=0&s=1

263 "Three Rivers, Hudson, Mohawk, Schoharie. History From America's Most Famous Valleys," Jeptha R. Simms, The Frontiersmen of New York, vol 1, 276 (Albany, New York, 1883).

264 Ancestry.com. *U.S., Dutch Reformed Church Records in Selected States, 1639-1989* [database on-line]. Provo, UT, USA: Ancestry.com Operations, Inc., 2014. The Archives of the Reformed Church in America; New Brunswick, New Jersey; Reformed Church of Fonda, Baptisms, Marriages, Members, Consistory Minutes, 1758-1839.

265 Fintan O'Toole, *White Savage: William Johnson and the Invention of America* (Albany, State University of New York, 2005), 283, 288-289.; http://www.threeritvershms.com/johnstownvillage.pdf ; Ancestry.com. *UK, American Loyalist Claims, 1776-1835* [database on-line]. AO 12–13. 18. Series I; Class: AO 13; Piece: 027: Evidence, New York, 1787. 183; Milton Hamilton & Albert Corey, *The Papers of Sir William Johnson, Vol XIII* (Albany, The University of the State of New York, 1962), 161-162. https://archive.org/stream/papersofsirwilli13johnuoft#page/160/mode/2up

266 Fintan O'Toole, *White Savage*, 288-289. "Three Rivers, Hudson, Mohawk, Schoharie. History From America's Most Famous Valleys." Jeptha R. Simms, The Frontiersmen of New York Vol I (Albany, 1883). 256.

267 Isabel Thompson Kelsay, *Joseph Brant 1743-1807 Man of Two Worlds* (Syracuse, Syracuse University Press, 1984), 321.

268 No record of Dorothy Eamer's birth or baptism has been found. She married Henry Gallinger who was born in 1761, and the first record of a child born to them was in 1786. Therefore, I assume Dorothy was born ca. 1765.

269 "Montgomery County NY GenWeb Genealogy & History." The Loss-Claim of Johannes Veeder. An Account of the Damage Which Johannes Veeder Sustained by the Enemy Under the Command of

Sir John Johnson, 22 May, 1780 at Caughnawaga. (Last modified 11, December, 1998).

270 "Immigrant Entrepreneurship. German-American Business Biographies. Peter Hasenclever (1716-1793)." (Last modified, 4 January 2016). https://www.immigrantentrepreneurship.org/entry.php?rec=224 ; Alexander C. Flick, *The Papers of Sir William Johnson, Vol IV* (Albany, The University of the State of New York, 1925), 11, 724, 772, 776, 850, 870. https://archive.org/stream/papersofsirwilli04john#page/724/mode/2up ; "The Town of Schuyler, Herkimer County, NY" Profile and History of the Town of Schuyler. (Last Modified 30 September 2017). http://herkimer.nygenweb.net/schuyler.html

271 National Humanities Center. "America in Class." Making the Revolution: America 1763-1791. Crisis. 1764: Loyal Subjects? http://americainclass.org/sources/makingrevolution/crisis/text2/text2.htm ; Ibid, 1765-1766: Stamp Act Crisis. http://americainclass.org/sources/makingrevolution/crisis/text3/text3.htm

272 Gilbert Tice also rented lot 93 on the eastern allotment of Kingsborough Patent. Dr. William Adams also owned lot 86 eastern allotment Kingsborough Patent. Duncan Fraser, Papers and Records of the Ontario Historical Society, Volume LII, 1960, Original Source, Public Record Office, London, England AC 13/114. *Sir John Johnson's Rent Roll of the Kingsborough Patent.* http://freepages.genealogy.rootsweb.ancestry.com/~wjmartin/kingsbor.htm ; Alexander C. Flick, *The Papers of Sir William Johnson, Vol V* (Albany, The University of the State of New York, 1927), 413-414. https://archive.org/stream/papersofsirwilli05johnuoft#page/412/mode/2up; "Montgomery County NY GenWeb Genealogy & History." Elsie Lathrop, Early American Inns and Taverns (New York, R.M. McBride & Company, 1926). http://montgomery.nygenweb.net/history/earlyamerinns.html ; Ancestry.com. *UK, American Loyalist Claims, 1776-1835* [database on-line]. Provo, UT, USA. The National Archives of the UK; Kew, Surrey, England; *American Loyalist Claims, Series I;* Class: *AO 13;* Piece: *027. Evidence, New York, 1787*. Claim of John Fraser. And *Piece 29*, Claim of Donald Ross. And *Series I;* Class: *AO*

13; Piece: *028*. Claim of Randel McDonell; Brian Lafferty's lot was sold by the Commissioners of Forteiture to Amaziah Rust of Montgomery County 17 Sept 1774. Ancestry.com. *New York, Sales of Loyalist Land, 1762-1830* [database on-line]. Provo, UT. New York State Engineer and Surveyor. Records of Surveys and Maps of State Lands, 1686–1892, Series A4016, Vols. 7–10 and 17. New York State Archives, Albany, New York. 170. "Three Rivers" Towns and Villages of Fulton County. Johnstown Village. In *The History of Fulton County,* ed. Washington Frothingham, 222-228. (Syracuse, D. Mason & Co., 1892) https://archive.org/stream/cu31924083983951#page/n257/mode/2up

273 Ancestry.com. *Records of the Lutheran Trinity Church of Stone Arabia : in the town of Palatine, Montgomery County, N.Y.* [database on-line]. Provo, UT. Vol.1. Introduction. xix.; Philip Otterness, *Becoming German: The 1709 Palatine Migration to New York* (Ithaca, Cornell University Press, 2004), 113-160.

274 Ancestry.com. *UK, American Loyalist Claims, 1776-1835* [database on-line]. Provo, UT, USA. The National Archives of the UK; Kew, Surrey, England; American Loyalist Claims, Series I; Class: AO 13; Piece: 031. 268-269. Michael Clene; "Making HistoryInspiration For The Modern Revolutionary." Brian Nesslage, Trading Secrets: The 18th Century Lock, Stock and Barrel. February 25, 2015. http://makinghistorynow.com/2015/02/trading-secrets-lock-stock-and-barrel/

275 "Interior Plaster Walls Explained." (2006-2017). https://www.practicaldiy.com/general-building/plaster-walls/walls-plaster.php#lathplaster

276 Martin Loefler Sr. lived on lot 84 on the Sacandaga Patent which joined Philip and Catrina's lot at their south east corner. William L. Stone, *The Life and Times of Sir William Johnson, Bart., Vol. II* (Albany, J. Munsell, 1865). 499. https://archive.org/stream/lifetimesofsirwi02stonuoft#page/498/mode/2up ; New York State Archives. New York (State). State Engineer and Surveyor. *Survey maps of lands in New York State,* ca. 1711-1913. Series A0273-78, Map #286.; http://digitalcollections.archives.

nysed.gov/index.php/Detail/Object/Show/object_id/36827#; Milton Hamilton & Albert Corey, *The Papers of Sir William Johnson, Vol XIII* (Albany, The University of the State of New York, 1962), 198. https://archive.org/stream/papersofsirwilli13johnuoft#page/198/mode/2up

277 Ancestry.com. *Pennsylvania and New Jersey, Church and Town Records, 1669-1999 [database on-line].* Lehi, UT, USA: Ancestry.com Operations, Inc., 2011. Historical Society of Pennsylvania; Philadelphia, Pennsylvania; Collection Name: Historic Pennsylvania Church and Town Records; Reel: 1040. *St Michael´s Congregation.* 1756, Item19, Martin Silmser (Jr.?), Lived at Frankfurt, number of children 1, age 29, unable to translate; Item 20, Elisabeth Margretha, age 32.; 1759, Item 90, Martin Silmser, years in county 5, number of children 3, age 32.; *Pennsylvania Births and Christenings, 1709-1950, database, FamilySearch* (https://familysearch.org/ark:/61903/1:1:V2NZ-YCC : 9 December 2014), Martin Silmser in entry for Anna Margreth Silmser, 14 Apr 1765; Christening, citing Philadelphia, Philadelphia, Pennsylvania; FHL microfilm 1,312,257.

278 A Peck is a measurement of dry volume that equals eight quarts. One bushel equals four pecks. A Rundlet was a barrel that held eighteen gallons. *New York Colonial Muster Rolls, 1664-1775, Vol. II* [database on-line]. *Annual Report of the State Historian,* 587.

279 "Th: Jefferson Monticello, Monticello.org" Hewe's Crab Apple" (Monticello, nd) https://www.monticello.org/site/house-and-gardens/in-bloom/hewes-crab-apple ; "Greenfield Village Open Air Museum" A Taste of History: A Fall Flavors Weekend (December 28, 2013); Alexander C. Flick, *The Papers of Sir William Johnson, Vol VII* (Albany, The University of the State of New York, 1931), 1059-1060. https://archive.org/stream/papersofsirwilli07johnuoft#page/1058/mode/2up ; Alexander C. Flick, *The Papers of Sir William Johnson, Vol VI* (Albany, The University of the State of New York, 1928), 169. https://archive.org/stream/papersofsirwilli06johnuoft#page/168/mode/2up

280 New York State Historical Association, Fenimore Art Museum, Research Library Special Collections, *Jellis Fonda Papers,* Coll. No. 157, 1750-1791. Algair, Jacob: 48B.

281 Johannes Hartle settled on lot 43 on the western allotment Kingsborough Patent. Duncan Fraser, Papers and Records of the Ontario Historical Society, Volume LII, 1960, Original Source, Public Record Office, London, England AC 13/114. *Sir John Johnson's Rent Roll of the Kingsborough Patent.* http://freepages.genealogy.rootsweb.ancestry.com/~wjmartin/kingsbor.htm; *Ancestry.com. Germany, Select Births and Baptisms, 1558-1898* [database on-line]. Provo, UT, USA: Ancestry.com Operations, Inc., 2014. Original data: *Germany, Births and Baptisms, 1558-1898.* Salt Lake City, Utah: FamilySearch, 2013. Adam Hertel, 21 Aug 1662, Baptism Place, Birkenau, Hessen, Germany, Father, Hans Hertel, Mother Margreth.; "Three Rivers, Hudson, Mohawk, Schoharie. History From America's Most Famous Valleys," *The Kocherthal Records: A Translation of the Kocherthal Records of the West Camp Lutheran Church,* In Lou MacWethy, The Book of Names Especially Relating to the Early Palatines and the First Settlers in the Mohawk Valley, (St. Johnsville: The Enterprise and News, 1933), 45. http://www.threeriversshms.com/nameskocherthal.htm Marriages: 1716 June 26th: Adam HERTEL, widower, of Georgetown, formerly of Liferspach, near Heppenheim, on the mountain-road (Bergstrasse), and Gertraud WAID, widow of the late Johann WAID, formerly of Wallwig, duchy of Nassau-Dillenburg.

282 Henry Z. Jones Jr., *The Palatine Families of New York: A Study of the German Immigrants Who Arrived in Colonial New York in 1710, Vol. I* (Universal City, CA: Author, 1985). 342.; Lou, Macwethy, *"West Camp; Statement of Heads of Palaten Fameleys and Number of Persons in Both Towns of ye West Side Hudsons River. Winter, 1710."* In The Book of Names. St. Johnsville [NY]: The Enterprise and News, 1933, (Reprinted by Genealogical Publishing Co., Baltimore, 1985.), 123-124.; Walter Allen Knittle, *"The New York Subsistence List." In Early Eighteenth Century Palatine Emigration.* (Philadelphia: Dorrance & Co., 1937) (Reprinted by Genealogical Publishing Co., Baltimore, 1982). 285.; "Three Rivers Hudson Mohawk Schoharie. History From America's Most Famous

Valleys." Christian Krahmer, The Kocherthal Records. A Translation of the Kocherthal Records of the West Camp Lutheran Church, October 1926, In Lou MacWethy, The Book of Names Especially Relating to The Early Palatines and the First Settlers in the Mohawk Valley, (St. Johnsville, New York, Enterprise and News, 1933). Item 82. 1716 June 26th: Adam HERTEL, widower, of Georgetown, formerly of Liferspach, near Heppenheim, on the mountain-road (Bergstrasse), and Gertraud WAID, widow of the late Johann WAID, formerly of Wallwig, duchy of Nassau-Dillenburg.; "St Pauls Evangelical Lutheran Church." Vernon Benjamin and Karlyn Knaust Elia, History of the Palatines. http://www.stpaulswestcamp.com/page/history_of_the_palatines

283 Alexander C. Flick, *The Papers of Sir William Johnson, Vol V* (Albany, The University of the State of New York, 1927), 201-202. https://archive.org/stream/papersofsirwilli05johnuoft#page/202/mode/2up ; James Sullivan, *The Papers of Sir William Johnson, Vol III* (Albany, The University of the State of New York, 1921), 531-535. https://archive.org/stream/paperssirwillia00unkngoog#page/n588/mode/2up

284 "HistoryofMassachusetts.org" Rebecca Brooks, The Sons of Liberty: Who Were They and What Did They Do? (November 24, 2014).

285 Henry Cruger Van Schaack, *Memoirs of the Life of Henry Van Schaack. Embracing Selections From His Correspondence During the American Revolution* (Chicago, A.C. McClurg & Company, 1892), 12-13. https://archive.org/stream/memoirslifehenr00schagoog#page/n33/mode/2up ; Alexander C. Flick, *The Papers of Sir William Johnson, Vol V* (Albany, The University of the State of New York, 1927), 5-6. https://archive.org/stream/papersofsirwilli05johnuoft#page/4/mode/2up

286 Alexander C. Flick, *The Papers of Sir William Johnson, Vol VII* (Albany, The University of the State of New York, 1931), 696. https://archive.org/stream/papersofsirwilli07johnuoft#page/696/mode/2up ; "HistoryofMassachusetts.org" Rebecca Brooks, The Sons of Liberty.

287 Ancestry.com. *U.S., Dutch Reformed Church Records in Selected States, 1639-1989* [database on-line]. Provo, UT, USA: The Archives of the

Reformed Church in America; New Brunswick, New Jersey; Stone Arabia Church, Baptisms, Members, Deaths, 1739-1987.1766. N. d. 16 Februar B. d. 19, April Johann Adam Ruppert und Anna Barbara, Johannes, Sponsor Johannes Ruppert.

288 New York State Historical Association, Fenimore Art Museum, Research Library Special Collections, *Jellis Fonda Papers,* Coll. No. 157, 1750-1791. Philip Wemer: 69A.

289 Jacob Crieghoof (Kriechauf) lived on lot 112 on the eastern allotment of the Kingsborough Patent, only one lot west of Philip. George Bender lived on the western allotment of the Kingsborough Patent, lot unknown. Duncan Fraser, Papers and Records of the Ontario Historical Society, Volume LII, 1960, Original Source, Public Record Office, London, England AC 13/114. *Sir John Johnson's Rent Roll of the Kingsborough Patent.* http://freepages.genealogy.rootsweb.ancestry.com/~wjmartin/kingsbor.htm

290 Henry Hawn lived on lot 82 on the eastern allotment Kingsborough Patent. Duncan Fraser, Papers and Records of the Ontario Historical Society, Volume LII, 1960, *Sir John Johnson's Rent Roll of the Kingsborough Patent.* http://freepages.genealogy.rootsweb.ancestry.com/~wjmartin/kingsbor.htm

291 Max Reid, *The Mohawk Valley. Its Legends and Its History* (New York, G.P. Putnam's Sons, 1901), 194. http://archive.org/stream/mohawkvalley00reid#page/194/mode/2up ; Alexander C. Flick, *The Papers of Sir William Johnson, Vol VIII* (Albany, The University of the State of New York, 1933), 376 https://archive.org/stream/papersofsirwilli08johnuoft#page/376/mode/2up

292 Milton Hamilton & Albert Corey, *The Papers of Sir William Johnson, Vol XIII* (Albany, The University of the State of New York, 1962), 633-635. https://archive.org/stream/papersofsirwilli13johnuoft#page/632/mode/2up; "Onondaga and Oswego Masonic District Historical Society." Gary Heinmiller, Loyalist Freemasons From the State of New York, (August/September, 2010). http://www.omdhs.syracusemasons.

com/sites/default/files/history/Loyalist%20Freemasons.pdf; Alexander C. Flick, *The Papers of Sir William Johnson, Vol V* (Albany, The University of the State of New York, 1927), 29. https://archive.org/stream/papersofsirwilli05johnuoft#page/28/mode/2up; Fintan O'Toole, *White Savage: William Johnson and the Invention of America* (Albany, State University of New York, 2005), 311-312.; "The New York History Blog." Wanda Burch, Johnstown: St. Patrick's Masonic Lodge. January 28, 2013. http://newyorkhistoryblog.org/2013/01/28/johnstown-st-patricks-masonic-lodge/

293 In 1774 in Sir William's will, Robert Adams received lots 1 and 8 in Johnstown. Perhaps he continued to rent lot 1 to Christian Sheeks. New York Land Records, 1630-1975," images, *FamilySearch* (https://familysearch.org/ark:/61903/3:1:3QSQ-G9WC-6SG?cc=2078654&wc=M7HP-BP8%3A358134701%2C358236401: 22 May 2014), Fulton Deeds 1772-1801 vol 1 image 25 of 296; county courthouses, New York; Ancestry.com. *UK, American Loyalist Claims, 1776-1835* [database on-line]. Provo, UT, USA: Ancestry.com Operations, Inc., 2013. The National Archives of the UK; Kew, Surrey, England; American Loyalist Claims, Series I; Class: AO 13; Piece: 029. 366-369; Duncan Fraser, Papers and Records of the Ontario Historical Society, Volume LII, 1960, Original Source, Public Record Office, London, England AC 13/114. *Sir John Johnson's Rent Roll of the Kingsborough Patent.* http://freepages.genealogy.rootsweb.ancestry.com/~wjmartin/kingsbor.htm

294 Ancestry.com. *UK, American Loyalist Claims, 1776-1835* [database on-line]. Provo, UT, USA: Ancestry.com Operations, Inc., 2013. Piece 032: Evidence, New York, 1788. 234-236. Claim of John Lonnie; Duncan Fraser, Papers and Records of the Ontario Historical Society, Volume LII, 1960, http://freepages.genealogy.rootsweb.ancestry.com/~wjmartin/kingsbor.htm

295 "Find a Grave Memorials." Jacob Link, Birth 3 July 1766, Montgomery County, New York, USA, Death 23 May 1842 Herkimer, Herkimer County, New York, USA, Burial Garlock Cemetery, Little Falls, Herkimer

County, New York, USA, Memorial ID 25663220. https://www.findagrave.com/memorial/25663220. Headstone reads: In Memory of Jacob Link, who died May 23, 1842, aged 86 years 10 months 20 days, Headstone Reads: Readers behold as you pass by, As you are now so once was I, As I am now, so you must be, Prepare for death and follow me.

296 E.B. O'Callaghan, *The Documentary History of the State of New York, Vol IV* (Albany, Charles Van Benthuysen, 1851), 348-350. https://archive.org/stream/documentaryhisto04ocal#page/348/mode/2up

297 Eberhard Van Koughnot arrived in Philadelphia October 7, 1751 aboard the ship 'Janet'. He was naturalized at Albany in 1761 with his son Eberhard Jr.. There is a John Koghnot listed as a Tanner at Johnstown ca. 1770. And, there is Johan Evert Koghnot at Kingsborough Patent lot 16 on the western allotment, Commencement of Rent: 25 March 1769, 100 Acres, Paid 6 Pounds 3 Shillings Rent Annually.; Rupp, I. Daniel 1803-1878. *A Collection of Upwards of Thirty Thousand Names of German, Swiss, Dutch, French And Other Immigrants In Pennsylvania From 1727-1776*: Chronologisch Geordnete Sammlung Von Mehr Als 30,000 Namen Von Einwanderern In Pennsylvanien Aus Deutschland, Der Schweiz, Holland, Frankreich U. A. St. Von 1727 Bis 1776 2nd rev. and enl. ed. with German translation. Philadelphia: Leary, Stuart, 1898. 267. https://hdl.handle.net/2027/yale.39002001155903?urlappend=%3Bseq=285 ; Duncan Fraser, Papers and Records of the Ontario Historical Society, Volume LII, 1960, Original Source, Public Record Office, London, England AC 13/114. *Sir John Johnson's Rent Roll of the Kingsborough Patent.* http://freepages.genealogy.rootsweb.ancestry.com/~wjmartin/kingsbor.htm

298 Alexander C. Flick, *The Papers of Sir William Johnson, Vol V* (Albany, The University of the State of New York, 1927), 11-14, 345.

299 Secretary of the State of New York, *Calendar of N.Y. Colonial Manuscripts Indorsed Land Papers 1643-1803* (Albany, Weed, Parsons & Co., 1864), 414, 418, 452. https://archive.org/stream/calendarofnycolo00alba#page/414/mode/2up

300 E.B. O'Callaghan, *The Documentary History of the State of New York, Vol IV* (Albany, Charles Van Benthuysen, 1851), 348-350. https://archive.org/stream/documentaryhisto04ocal#page/348/mode/2up

301 Samuel Runnions lived on the south side of the Mohawk River and across from Fort Hunter on the west side of the Schoharie River. His neighbor was Gideon Marlet. A note at the top of the document for Samuel Runion states he was living on Butler's land. Jane Marlett-Taft, *Gideon Marlett A Huguenot of Staten Island N.Y. With Some Account of the Descendants in the United States and Canada.* (Burlington Vermont, 1907), 67. https://archive.org/stream/gideonmarlettged00taft#page/n147/mode/2up ; New York State Archives. New York (State). State Engineer and Surveyor. *Survey maps of lands in New York State, ca. 1711-1913.* Series A0273-78, Map #759. 1725-1734. http://digitalcollections.archives.nysed.gov/index.php/Detail/Object/Show/object_id/37332;

302 New York State Historical Association, Fenimore Art Museum, Research Library Special Collections, *Jellis Fonda Papers,* Coll. No. 157, 1750-1791. Hendrick Hoff 142, 162B, 164B.

303 Fenimore Art Museum & The Farmers' Museum. *Jellis Fonda Papers.* Sam Runion 144A; Ancestry.com. *Records of the Reformed Protestant Dutch Church of Caughnawaga: now the Reformed Church of Fonda, in the village of Fonda, Mon* [database on-line]. Provo, UT: Ancestry.com Operations Inc, 2005. Volume one. Baptisms and births, 1758 to 1797. Birth of son Richard 1782; Ancestry.com. *Records of the Reformed Dutch Church of Stone Arabia: in the town of Palatine, Montgomery County, N.Y.* [database on-line]. Provo, UT. Vol.1. Marriages, Oct. 16, 1739 to 1795. 1765 22n Octobr, Sam Rennors und Denglas Davis. 177.

304 Ancestry.com. *Records of the Reformed Dutch Church of Stone Arabia : in the town of Palatine, Montgomery County, N.Y.* [database on-line]. Provo, UT: Ancestry.com Operations Inc, 2005. Vol.1. Marriages, Oct. 16, 1739 to 1795. 181. 1767 9n Mertz, Daniel Veith und Anna Ruppertin.

305 Alexander C. Flick, *The Papers of Sir William Johnson, Vol V* (Albany, The University of the State of New York, 1927), 490. http://archive.org/stream/papersofsirwilli05johnuoft#page/490/mode/2up

306 Michael Cline and Catherine Wick were married on 28 April 1767. Ancestry.com. *U.S., Dutch Reformed Church Records in Selected States, 1639-1989* [database on-line]. Provo, UT, USA: Ancestry.com Operations, Inc., 2014. Holland Society of New York; New York, New York; Stone Arabia and Staten Island, Book 48. 283.

307 New York State Historical Association, Fenimore Art Museum, Research Library Special Collections, *Jellis Fonda Papers,* Coll. No. 157, 1750-1791. Samuel Runion, 144A.

308 "Library of Congress Digital Collections." Documents From the Continental Congress and the Constitutional Convention 1774-1789, Articles and Essays. https://www.loc.gov/collections/continental-congress-and-constitutional-convention-from-1774-to-1789/articles-and-essays/timeline/1766-to-1767/ ; "Stamp Act the Origins, Implementation and Consequences." University of Massachusetts History Club. http://www.stamp-act-history.com ; National Humanities Center. "America in Class." Making the Revolution: America 1763-1791. Crisis. http://americainclass.org/sources/makingrevolution/crisis/text4/text4.htm

309 Nicholas Philips is related to William Philips the famous Robert's Ranger of the French Indian War and Wagonmaker at Johnstown, and to his son William Philips Jr., a Miller at Johnstown. From the late 1600s, the Philips family owned land on the north and south side of the Mohawk River at 'Willow Flats' (Today Cranesville, Amsterdam, N.Y.) between Schenectady and Fort Johnson. A. J. F. Van Laer, *Early Records of the City and County of Albany and Colony of Rensselaerswyck, Vol 2 (Deeds 3 and 4, 1678-1704)* (Albany, The University of the State of New York, 1916), 355-356. https://archive.org/stream/earlyrecordsofc02alba#page/354/mode/2up

310 New York State Historical Association, Fenimore Art Museum, Research Library Special Collections, *Jellis Fonda Papers,* Hendrick Hoff, 142, 162B, 164B.

311 "New York Land Records, 1630-1975," images, *FamilySearch* (https://familysearch.org/ark:/61903/3:1:3QS7-99WC-DV5W?cc=2078654&wc=M7HP-BP8%3A358134701%2C358236401 : 22 May 2014), Fulton Deeds 1772-1801 vol 1 image 39 of 296; county courthouses, New York. https://www.familysearch.org/ark:/61903/3:1:3QS7-99WC-DV5W?i=38&wc=M7HP-BP8%3A358134701%2C358236401&cc=2078654; New York State Historical Association, Fenimore Art Museum, Research Library Special Collections, *Jellis Fonda Papers,* Michael Doren, 138 B.

312 David Jeacocks Sr. lived on lot 68 on the western allotment of the Kingsborough Patent. Duncan Fraser, Papers and Records of the Ontario Historical Society, Volume LII, 1960, Original Source, Public Record Office, London, England AC 13/114. *Sir John Johnson's Rent Roll of the Kingsborough Patent.* http://freepages.genealogy.rootsweb.ancestry.com/~wjmartin/kingsbor.htm ; Ancestry.com. *UK, American Loyalist Claims, 1776-1835* [database on-line]. Provo, UT, USA. Piece 013: New Claims G· H· J·, New York. 441-442 ; Ancestry.com. *UK, American Loyalist Claims, 1776-1835* [database on-line]. Provo, UT, USA. The National Archives of the UK; Kew, Surrey, England; American Loyalist Claims, Series I; Class: AO 13; Piece: 032. Evidence, New York, 1788. 177-178.; Ancestry.com. *U.S., Dutch Reformed Church Records in Selected States, 1639-1989* [database on-line]. Provo, UT, USA. Holland Society of New York; New York, New York; Poughkeepsie and The Flats, Book 39. 147. 1749, Mar. 10, Reg. David Jekoks, y.m., bo. in Ulster County; Grietje Keuning, y.d., bo. at Tappan, Marr. Apr 3, Both liv at Pou.

313 The State of New York, Historical Manuscripts Collection, *The colonial laws of New York from the year 1664 to the Revolution, including the charters to the Duke of York, the commissions and instructions to colonial governors, the Duke's laws, the laws of the Dongan and Leisler Assemblies, the charters of Albany and New York and the acts of the colonial legislatures from 1691*

to 1775 inclusive. Transmitted to the Legislature by the Commissioners of Statutory Revision, pursuant to chapter 125 of the Laws of 189, Vol 4 Chapter 1121 Cornell University Library, nd), 456-466. http://ebooks.library.cornell.edu/cgi/t/text/pageviewer-idx?c=cdl&cc=cdl&idno=cdl182&node=cdl182%3A4&view=image&seq=460&size=100

314 New York State Historical Association, Fenimore Art Museum, Research Library Special Collections, *Jellis Fonda Papers,* Coll. No. 157, 1750-1791. Hendrick Hoff, 142, 162B, 164B.

315 Fintan O'Toole, *White Savage: William Johnson and the Invention of America* (Albany, State University of New York, 2005), 284, 304-305.

316 Johannes Adam Pabst arrived in Philadelphia 28 Sept 1753 aboard the ship 'Two Brothers', Captain Thomas Arnot.; Ralph Strassburger, *Pennsylvania German Pioneers, I, 1727-1775* (Norristown: Pennsylvania German Society Vol. 42 of the Proceedings of the Society, 1934). 565; Ancestry.com. *Records of the Reformed Dutch Church of Stone Arabia: in the town of Palatine, Montgomery County, N.Y.* [database on-line]. Provo, UT. Vol.1. Baptisms and births. 77; Pabst, Jno Adam,; Ancestry.com. *History of Gilead Evangelical Lutheran Church: Centre Brunswick, Rensselaer Co., N.Y. and the vicinity* [database on-line]. Provo, UT. Chapter VII. Addenda. 147.

317 New York State Historical Association, Fenimore Art Museum, Research Library Special Collections, *Jellis Fonda Papers,* Coll. No. 157, 1750-1791. Service, Cristofell, 190B.

318 Ibid.

319 John Dickinson, *Empire and Nation: Letters from a Farmer in Pennsylvania (John Dickinson). Letters from the Federal Farmer (Richard Henry Lee),* ed. Forrest McDonald (Indianapolis: Liberty Fund 1999). Online Library of Liberty, http://oll.libertyfund.org/titles/dickinson-empire-and-nation-letters-from-a-farmer

320 Ancestry.com. *U.S., Dutch Reformed Church Records in Selected States, 1639-1989* [database on-line]. Provo, UT, USA: Ancestry.com Operations, Inc., 2014. Stone Arabia Church, Baptisms, Members, Deaths, 1739-1987. 1767 N. d. 25 October, B. d. 19n December, Georg Bender u. Gertraud, Antoni, Sponsors, Gottfried Schue und Catharina. 1767, 9 Decembr, 28 Decembr, Michael Galiginger, Agata, Dorothea, Dorothea und Johannes Teughart.

321 Ancestry.com. *Records of the Reformed Dutch Church of Stone Arabia: in the town of Palatine, Montgomery County, N.Y.* [database on-line]. Provo, UT. Vol.1. Baptisms and births. 82. 1768, N. d. 29, Novembr, B. d. 10n. Januar, Wilhelm Schooman u. Margretha, Catharina, Jacob Aallcajer und Catharina.

322 William Casselman was the son of Dieterich Casselman and Anna Rinder. Dieterich was one of the first settlers on the Stone Arabia Patent, lot nos. 23 and 29. William married Anna Margaretha Salzman, daughter of George Salzman and Anna Margaretha Kaputzgi. William and Anna Margaretha lived on the north side of the Mohawk River opposite Canajoharie on the Hermanus Van Slyck and Abraham DePeyster Patent. "Three Rivers Hudson, Mohawk, Schoharie, History From America's Most Famous Valleys" *The Book of Names Especially Relating to the Early Palatines and the First Settlers in the Mohawk Valley, The Kocherthal Records: A Translation of the Kocherthal Records of the West Camp Lutheran Church,* Translated by Christian Kramer. St. Johnsville, NY: The Enterprise and News, 1933. http://www.threeriversshms.com/nameskocherthal.htm 1711, July 21st: Wilhelm, born July 19th, child of Johann Dietrich and Anna CASTELMANN: sponsor: Philip MUELLER, the sexton. ; Ken D. Johnson, "Fort Plank Bastion of my Freedom Colonial Canajoharie, New York" Mohawk Valley Maps and Sketches. The Hermanus Van Slyck & Abraham DePeyster Patent, (Last Modified 26 Nov 2015). http://www.fort-plank.com/Van_Slyck_Patent_COF.html

323 Alexander C. Flick, *The Papers of Sir William Johnson, Vol V* (Albany, The University of the State of New York, 1927) 516-518. http://archive.

org/stream/papersofsirwilli05johnuoft#page/516/mode/2up ; Guy Carleton, Sir, 1724-1808. *Condition of the Indian Trade In North America, 1767: As Described In a Letter to Sir William Johnson* (Brooklyn, N.Y.: Historical Printing Club, 1890). https://hdl.handle.net/2027/aeu.ark:/13960/t9959tv86

324 Isabel Thompson Kelsay, *Joseph Brant 1743-1807 Man of Two Worlds* (Syracuse, Syracuse University Press, 1984), 321.

325 New York Colonial Muster Rolls, 1664-1775, Vol. II [database on-line]. Supplemental Muster Rolls. *A List of Men Under the Command of Leut. John M. Veeder & Ensign Gerret Banker in the Colony of Rencelarswick.* 818 ; Third Annual Report of the State Historian of the State of New York, (Albany, Wynkoop, Hallenbeck Crawford Co., 1898). 842-856, 881-891.

326 Ancestry.com. *U.S., Dutch Reformed Church Records in Selected States, 1639-1989* [database on-line]. Provo, UT, USA: Ancestry.com Operations, Inc., 2014. Albany, Vol III, Book 3. 221.

327 New York State Historical Association, Fenimore Art Museum, Research Library Special Collections, *Jellis Fonda Papers,* Coll. No. 157, 1750-1791. Service, Christofell, 190B.

328 Ancestry.com. *Records of the Lutheran Trinity Church of Stone Arabia : in the town of Palatine, Montgomery County, N.Y.* [database on-line]. Provo, UT. Vol.1. Birth and baptisms, 1751 to 1815. 27.

329 "New York Land Records, 1630-1975," images, *FamilySearch* (https://familysearch.org/ark:/61903/3:1:3QS7-L9WC-DV6P?cc=2078654&wc=M7HP-BP8%3A358134701%2C358236401: 22 May 2014), Fulton Deeds 1772-1801 vol 1 image 10 of 296; county courthouses, New York.

330 New York State Historical Association, Fenimore Art Museum, Research Library Special Collections, *Jellis Fonda Papers,* Coll. No. 157, 1750-1791. Service, Christofell, 190B.

331 Alexander C. Flick, *The Papers of Sir William Johnson, Vol VI* (Albany, The University of the State of New York, 1928), 248. https://archive.org/stream/papersofsirwilli06johnuoft#page/248/mode/2up ; "Pennsylvania Historical and Museum Commission Bureau of Archives and History, Pennsylvania State Archives" MG-19 Sequestered Baynton, Wharton, and Morgan Papers, Series Descriptions. #19m.14 http://www.phmc.state.pa.us/bah/dam/mg/sd/m019sd.htm

332 Ancestry.com. *Records of the Reformed Dutch Church of Stone Arabia : in the town of Palatine, Montgomery County, N.Y.* [database on-line]. Provo, UT. Vol.1. Baptisms and births. 87. 1768 N. d. 3n Marty, B. d. 4n July, Adam Ruppert und Barbara, Margreth, Sponsors, Margretha, Franz Rupperts Ehle Haussfrau.

333 Francis Whiting Halsey, *The Old New York Frontier. Its Wars With Indians and Tories, Its Missionary Schools, Pioneers and Land Titles. 1614-1800* (New York, Charles Scribner's Sons, 1901), 99-103. https://archive.org/stream/oldnewyorkfronti01hals#page/98/mode/2up; Fintan O'Toole, *White Savage. William Johnson and the Invention of America* (Albany, State University of New York, 2005), 268-279, 297; E.B. O'Gallaghan, *The Documentary History of New York, Vol I Chapter XX* (Albany, Weed, Parsons & Co., 1849), 587 591. https://archive.org/stream/documentaryhist00morggoog#page/n622/mode/2up; Library and Archives Canada, *Haldimand Papers from the British Library,* lac_reel_h1429 105513 2034239 MG21 Image 806-866. http://heritage.canadiana.ca/view/oocihm.lac_reel_h1429/809?r=0&s=1 ; The New York Public Library. Manuscripts and Archives Division, The New York Public Library Digital Collections. *"Penn, John. Philadelphia. To Sir William Johnson" 1768.* http://digitalcollections.nypl.org/items/86ceb390-34a5-0133-ef09-58d385a7b928; Thomas S. Abler, "KAIEÑ?KWAAHTOÑ," in *Dictionary of Canadian Biography,* vol. 4, University of Toronto/Université Laval, 2003. http://www.biographi.ca/en/bio/kaienkwaahton_4E.html

334 Ancestry.com. *Records of the Lutheran Trinity Church of Stone Arabia: in the town of Palatine, Montgomery County, N.Y. [database on-line].* Provo,

UT. Vol.1 Marriages, 1763 to 1778; 1790; 1810 to 1815; 1827 to 1830. 279. 1768, December den 5ten, Michael Majer, Elisabetha Vemerin.

335 Ibid. 1768 December den 26ten Balthasar Breitenbach & Julianna Schnekin; 1769, January den 17ten, Sebastian Algejer & Anna Barbara Wekeserin.

336 Ancestry.com. *UK, American Loyalist Claims, 1776-1835* [database on-line]. Provo, UT, USA: Ancestry.com Operations, Inc., 2013. Piece 027: Evidence, New York, 1787. 405-406.

337 E.B. O'Callaghan, *The Documentary History of the State of New York, Vol IV* (Albany, Charles Van Benthuysen, 1851), 416-417. https://archive.org/stream/documentaryhisto04ocal#page/416/mode/2up

338 "Three Rivers Hudson, Mohawk, Schoharie, History From America's Most Famous Valleys" Dean R. Snow & David B. Guldenzopf, Indian Castle Church The Mohawk Upper Castle Historic District National Historic Landmark. (2001). https://web.archive.org/web/20060622142738/http://indiancastle.com/ICNHL.htm ; Isabel Thompson Kelsay, *Joseph Brant 1743-1807 Man of Two Worlds* (Syracuse, Syracuse University Press, 1984), 115.; Ken D. Johnson, ""Fort Plank Bastion of my Freedom Colonial Canajoharie, New York" Mohawk Valley Maps and Sketches. Canajoharie Patent, (Last Modified 6 October 2016). http://www.fort-plank.com/V_Maps/Canajoharie_Patent_1764_.jpg

339 Alexander C. Flick, *The Papers of Sir William Johnson, Vol VII* (Albany, The University of the State of New York, 1931), 666-668. https://archive.org/stream/papersofsirwilli07johnuoft#page/666/mode/2up

340 Alexander C. Flick, *The Papers of Sir William Johnson, Vol VI* (Albany, The University of the State of New York, 1928), 691. https://archive.org/stream/papersofsirwilli06johnuoft#page/690/mode/2up

341 Alvin Countryman, *Countryman Genealogy Part I* (Lux Bros. & Heath Publishers, 1925). Ken D. Johnson, "Fort Plank Bastion of my

Freedom Colonial Canajoharie, New York." The Hermanus Van Slyck and Abraham DePeyster Patent. The "Canajoharie" or Abraham Van Horne Patent. (Last Modified 6 October 2016). http://www.fort-plank.com/Van_Slyck_Patent_COF.html http://www.fort-plank.com/Canajoharie_Patent_1764.html ; Ken D. Johnson, "The Bloodied Mohawk" Recent Discoveries in Mohawk Valley History. Certificate of Quit Rent Remission for the Conrad Countryman Patent. http://www.fort-plank.com/QRRC_4_Countryman_Patent.html

342 William Stone, The Life and Times of Sir William Johnson, Bart., Vol II (Albany, J. Munsell, 1865), 176-185.

343 Alexander C. Flick, *The Papers of Sir William Johnson, Vol VI*, 769- 773. .https://archive.org/stream/papersofsirwilli06johnuoft#page/770/mode/2up ; William Stone, 323-325.; "Three Rivers Hudson, Mohawk, Schoharie, History From America's Most Famous Valleys" Johnson's Ledger Names of Retainers of The Great Sir William, http://www.threeriversHMS.com/namesjohnson.htm ; Ken D. Johnson, "Fort Plank Bastion of my Freedom Colonial Canajoharie, New York" 1764 Survey of the Royal Grant. Last Modified 6 October 2016.

344 Duncan Fraser, Papers and Records of the Ontario Historical Society, Volume LII, 1960, Original Source, Public Record Office, London, England AC 13/114. *Sir John Johnson's Rent Roll of the Kingsborough Patent.* http://freepages.genealogy.rootsweb.ancestry.com/~wjmartin/kingsbor.htm; "I Spy in Johnstown" Jimmy Burke Inn. http://www.mvls.info/ispy/johnstown/joh_site09.html ; "Fulton County NYGenWeb" William Loveday, A Shot of History (The Sunday Leader Herald, 10 March 2002, p. 8A) http://fulton.nygenweb.net/history/fultontaverns.html ; Milton Hamilton & Albert Corey, *The Papers of Sir William Johnson, Vol XIII* (Albany, The University of the State of New York, 1962), 521. https://archive.org/stream/papersofsirwilli13johnuoft#page/520/mode/2up ; Ancestry.com. *UK, American Loyalist Claims, 1776-1835* [database on-line]. Provo, UT, USA. American Loyalist Claims, 1776–1835. AO 12–13. The National Archives of the United Kingdom,

Kew, Surrey, England. Piece 020: Evidence, New York, 1784-1785. Sir John Johnson.

345 Secretary of State of New York, *Calendar of Colonial Manuscripts Indorsed Land Papers Vol XXIV* (Albany, Weed, Parsons & Co., 1864), 467-468. https://archive.org/stream/calendarofnycolo00alba#page/466/mode/2up ; Ken D. Johnson, "Fort Plank Bastion of my Freedom Colonial Canajoharie, New York" Mohawk Valley Maps and Sketches. The John Bowen or Stone Heap Patent. (Last Modified 6 October 2016). http://www.fort-plank.com/John_Bowen_Pat_2.html http://www.fort-plank.com/John_Bowen_Pat_1.html

346 Secretary of State of New York, *Calendar of Colonial Manuscripts Indorsed Land Papers Vol XXIV*, 461. https://archive.org/stream/calendarofnycolo00alba#page/460/mode/2up ; Milton Hamilton & Albert Corey, *The Papers of Sir William Johnson, Vol XIII* (Albany, The University of the State of New York, 1962), 491. http://archive.org/stream/papersofsirwilli13johnuoft#page/491/mode/1up ; "New York Heritage Digital Collections" Map of Service Patent and Part of Cosby's Manor. 1798?. http://nyheritage.nnyln.org/digital/collection/XFM001/id/17/ ; "Village of Barneveld" History & Maps, 1793 Village Map http://villageofbarneveld.org/content/History/Home/:field=documents;/content/Documents/File/59.pdf http://nyheritage.nnyln.net/cdm/singleitem/collection/XFM001/id/18/rec/15 http://villageofbarneveld.org/content/History

347 Secretary of State of New York, *Calendar of Colonial Manuscripts Indorsed Land Papers Vol XXV*, 468, 502. https://archive.org/stream/calendarofnycolo00alba#page/468/mode/2up

348 New York State Historical Association, Fenimore Art Museum, Research Library Special Collections, *Jellis Fonda Papers,* Coll. No. 157, 1750-1791. Service, Christofell, 190B, Doren, Johannes, 171A, Hoff, Hendrick, 142, 162B, 164B.

349 Alexander C. Flick, *The Papers of Sir William Johnson, Vol VII* (Albany, The University of the State of New York, 1931), 350-351. https://

archive.org/stream/papersofsirwilli07johnuoft#page/350/mode/2up ; Ibid. 32-33. https://archive.org/stream/papersofsirwilli07johnuoft#page/32/mode/2up

350 Ancestry.com. *UK, American Loyalist Claims, 1776-1835* [database on-line]. Provo, UT, USA: Ancestry.com Operations, Inc., 2013. The National Archives of the UK; Kew, Surrey, England; American Loyalist Claims, Series I; Class: AO 13; Piece: 031. 158-159.

351 No record of Jacob Alguire's baptism has been found, but the 1851 Canada Census states his year of birth as ca. 1771. Ancestry.com. *Records of the Lutheran Trinity Church of Stone Arabia: in the town of Palatine, Montgomery County, N.Y.* [database on-line]. Provo, UT. Vol.1. Birth and baptisms, 1751 to 1815. 26-27. Anno 1769. Junii d 15ten Michael Wern Sponsors: Jacob Kilman & Helena Morin Child: Maria Margaretha.; Anno 1769, Maii d18tn, Sevrenus Casselman, Anna Maria ux., Cunrad, Sponsors, Heinrich Dillenbach, Gottlib Nestel, Anna Eva Sprecherin.; Ken D. Johnson, "The Bloodied Mohawk: The Story of the American Revolution in the Words of Fort Plank's Defenders and Other Mohawk Valley Partisans". from the Christopher Yates Papers housed in the Special Collections of the Bird Library of Syracuse University dated Isle Aux Noix March 17th 1780 entitled a *Return of Men Women and Children Distinguishing their Age & Sex which came by the Flag with C Yates.* In this document, 17 March 1780, Henry Casselman is listed as 10 years old. http://www.fort-plank.com/Loyalists_Exchanged_March_1780.pdf

352 "New York Land Records, 1630-1975," images, *FamilySearch* (https://familysearch.org/ark:/61903/3:1:3QS7-99WC-C4KD?cc=2078654&wc=M7H5-M38%3A358136301%2C358240201: 22 May 2014), Montgomery Deeds 1772-1788 vol 1 image 47 of 278; county courthouses, New York. Image 47; Alexander C. Flick, *The Papers of Sir William Johnson, Vol VII* (Albany, The University of the State of New York, 1931), 213-214. https://archive.org/stream/papersofsirwilli07johnuoft#page/212/mode/2up

353 The State of New York, Historical Manuscripts Collection, *The colonial laws of New York from the year 1664 to the Revolution, including the charters to the Duke of York, the commissions and instructions to colonial governors, the Duke's laws, the laws of the Dongan and Leisler Assemblies, the charters of Albany and New York and the acts of the colonial legislatures from 1691 to 1775 inclusive.* Transmitted to the Legislature by the Commissioners of Statutory Revision, pursuant to chapter 125 of the Laws of 189, Vol 4 Chapter 1121 (Cornell University Library, nd), 1050-1052.

354 *New York Colonial Muster Rolls, 1664-1775, Vol. II* [database on-line]. Supplemental Muster Rolls. 880, 882, 886, 887, 890.

355 Ancestry.com. *U.S., Dutch Reformed Church Records in Selected States, 1639-1989* [database on-line]. Provo, UT. The Archives of the Reformed Church in America; New Brunswick, New Jersey; Stone Arabia Church, Baptisms, Members, Deaths, 1739-1987. 8. 1769, N. d. 19 April, B. d. 21 Octobr, Martin Waldorf, u. Margretha, Maria, Sponsors, Johannes Gotz, Maria Service.

356 Alexander C. Flick, *The Papers of Sir William Johnson, Vol VII* (Albany, The University of the State of New York, 1931), 115-116. https://archive.org/stream/papersofsirwilli07johnuoft#page/114/mode/2up

357 Ancestry.com. *Records of the Lutheran Trinity Church of Stone Arabia : in the town of Palatine, Montgomery County, N.Y.* [database on-line]. Provo, UT. Vol.1 Marriages, 1763 to 1778; 1790; 1810 to 1815; 1827 to 1830. 280. 1769, November den 26ten, Martin Algejer & Catharina Emeri.

358 Albany Bush is an area southeast of Johnstown sometimes referred to as the Albany Patent. Some of the properties comprising this area are located on the Sacandaga Patent. Ancestry.com. *UK, American Loyalist Claims, 1776-1835* [database on-line]. Provo, UT, USA: Ancestry.com Operations, Inc., 2013. The National Archives of the UK; Kew, Surrey, England; American Loyalist Claims, Series I; Class: AO 13; Piece: 029. 361-362. Claim of Martin Algier.

359 E.B. O'Callaghan, *The Documentary History of the State of New York, Vol IV* (Albany, Charles Van Benthuysen, 1851), 1059.

360 Ancestry.com. *U.S., Dutch Reformed Church Records in Selected States, 1639-1989* [database on-line]. Provo, UT, USA: Ancestry.com Operations, Inc., 2014. Holland Society of New York; New York, New York; Schenectady Baptisms, Vol 2, Book 42. 175. 1769, 21 December, Michael Meyer, Elizabeth Emmerin, Philip, Sponsors, Carol Schreffer, Anna Maria Schreffer.

361 New York State Historical Association, Fenimore Art Museum, Research Library Special Collections, *Jellis Fonda Papers,* Coll. No. 157, 1750-1791. Wemer, Philip, 69A, Hoff, Hendrick, 142, 162B, 164B.

362 Steven Struzinski, "The Colonial Tavern in America, 2002," *The Gettysburg Historical Journal,* Vol I, Article 7. http://cupola.gettysburg.edu/cgi/viewcontent.cgi?article=1026&context=ghj

363 New York State Historical Association, Fenimore Art Museum, Research Library Special Collections, *Jellis Fonda Papers,* Coll. No. 157, 1750-1791. Wick, Johannes 222B.

364 Alexander C. Flick, *The Papers of Sir William Johnson, Vol VII* (Albany, The University of the State of New York, 1931), 495, 611-621.

365 Ibid, 346, 395-396, 666-668. https://archive.org/stream/papersofsirwilli07johnuoft#page/346/mode/2up

366 T.R. Millman, "STUART, JOHN (1740/41-1811)," in *Dictionary of Canadian Biography,* vol. 5, University of Toronto/Université Laval, 2003. http://www.biographi.ca/en/bio/stuart_john_1740_41_1811_5E.html

367 Ancestry.com. *Records of the Lutheran Trinity Church of Stone Arabia : in the town of Palatine, Montgomery County, N.Y.* [database on-line]. Provo, UT. Vol.1. Introduction. xxi. "Three Rivers Hudson, Mohawk, Schoharie, History From America's Most Famous Valleys." Following the Old

Mohawk Trail. The Old Palatine Church and the Cochran House. http://threeriversHms.com/oldpalch.htm

368 Ancestry.com. *Records of the Reformed Dutch Church of Stone Arabia : in the town of Palatine, Montgomery County, N.Y.* [database on-line]. Provo, UT. Vol.1. Baptisms and births. 99. 1770 N.d. 29 November, B.d. 14 January, David SheCocks u. Margretha, Sara, Benjamin Atch*? U.? Sara. Ancestry.com. *Records of the Lutheran Trinity Church of Stone Arabia : in the town of Palatine, Montgomery County, N.Y.* [database on-line]. Provo, UT. Vol.1 Marriages, 1763 to 1778; 1790; 1810 to 1815; 1827 to 1830. 281. 1770 January den 10ten, Jacob Eberhard von Kochnat & Cath: Diexin.; Alexander C. Flick, *The Papers of Sir William Johnson, Vol VII* 1113-1115. https://archive.org/stream/papersofsirwilli07johnuoft#page/1112/mode/2up ; Ibid, 352-354, 1081-1090. https://archive.org/stream/papersofsirwilli07johnuoft#page/352/mode/2up

369 "New York Land Records, 1630-1975," images, *FamilySearch* (https://familysearch.org/ark:/61903/3:1:3QS7-L9WC-64Z?cc=2078654&wc=M7HP-BP8%3A358134701%2C358236401 : 22 May 2014), Fulton > Deeds 1772-1801 vol 1 > image 11 of 296; county courthouses, New York. https://www.familysearch.org/ark:/61903/3:1:3QS7-L9WC-64Z?i=10&wc=M7HP-BP8%3A358134701%2C358236401&cc=2078654 ; "Montgomery County NY GenWeb" The Town of Mohawk Montgomery County, NY. History of the Town of Mohawk Part I. (Last Modified 1 January 1999). http://montgomery.nygenweb.net/mohawk/mohistory1.html ; Ken D. Johnson, "Fort Plank Bastion of my Freedom Colonial Canajoharie, New York" Mohawk Valley Maps and Sketches. The John, Margaret & Edward Collins or Caughnawaga Patent. And Butlersbury Tract. (Last Modified 26 November 2015). http://www.fort-plank.com/Butlersbury_Tract.html http://fort-plank.com/Caughnawaga_Patent.html

370 New York State Historical Association, Fenimore Art Museum, Research Library Special Collections, *Jellis Fonda Papers,* Coll. No. 157, 1750-1791. Doren, Johannes 171A; Milton Hamilton & Albert Corey, *The Papers of Sir William Johnson, Vol XIII* (Albany, The University of the State of New

York, 1962), 557. http://archive.org/stream/papersofsirwilli13johnuo ft#page/556/mode/2up ; Alexander C. Flick, *The Papers of Sir William Johnson, Vol VII* (Albany, The University of the State of New York, 1931), 663. https://archive.org/stream/papersofsirwilli07johnuoft#page/660/mode/2up

371 Alexander C. Flick, *The Papers of Sir William Johnson, Vol VII* (Albany, The University of the State of New York, 1931), 687-688, 695-696, 704-705.

372 "The Annotated Newspapers of Harbottle Dorr Jr." The Boston-Gazette, and Country Journal, 12 March 1770. Massachusetts Historical Society, 2018. http://www.masshist.org/dorr/volume/3/sequence/101 ; History of the 1747 Nellis Tavern. St. Johnsville, NY. http://www.palatinesettlementsociety.org/Documents/HistoryofNellisTavern4072015.pdf ; "National Humanities Center." America in Class. Making the Revolution: America 1763-1791. Crisis. 1770: Violence and Pause. http://americainclass.org/sources/makingrevolution/crisis/text5/text5.htm

373 Alexander C. Flick, *The Papers of Sir William Johnson, Vol VII.* 680. https://archive.org/stream/papersofsirwilli07johnuoft#page/680/mode/2up

374 Alexander C. Flick, *The Papers of Sir William Johnson, Vol VII* (Albany, The University of the State of New York, 1931), 1055-1058.

375 Ibid., 611-621, 1004-1013, 1060-1062. https://archive.org/stream/papersofsirwilli07johnuoft#page/610/mode/2up ; Milton Hamilton & Albert Corey, *The Papers of Sir William Johnson, Vol XII* (Albany, The University of the State of New York, 1957), 787. https://archive.org/stream/papersofsirwilli12johnuoft#page/786/mode/2up ; Alexander C. Flick, *The Papers of Sir William Johnson, Vol VII,* 676-677. https://archive.org/stream/papersofsirwilli07johnuoft#page/676/mode/2up

376 Ancestry.com. *Records of the Lutheran Trinity Church of Stone Arabia : in the town of Palatine, Montgomery County, N.Y.* [database on-line]. Provo,

UT. Vol.1. Birth and baptisms, 1751 to 1815. 32. Anno 1770. Julii d7ten. Mattaus Algeier & Catharina ux., Maria Salome, Sponsors, Michael Majer & Elisabetha.

377 New York State Historical Association, Fenimore Art Museum, Research Library Special Collections, *Jellis Fonda Papers,* Coll. No. 157, 1750-1791. Waldorf, Martinus 262A, Hoff, Henry 142, 162B, 164B, Casselman, Sufrenes, 33B, Runion, Samuel 144A.

378 E.B. O'Callaghan, *The Documentary History of the State of New York, Vol VIII* (Albany, Weed, Parsons and Company, 1857), 227-244. https://archive.org/stream/documentsrelativ08brod#page/226/mode/2up ; Alexander C. Flick, *The Papers of Sir William Johnson, Vol VII* (Albany, The University of the State of New York, 1931), 817-818, 832-833. https://archive.org/stream/papersofsirwilli07johnuoft#page/832/mode/2up

379 E.B. O'Callaghan, *The Documentary History of the State of New York, A Memorial Concering the Iroquois, or Five Confederate Nations of Indians in the Province of New York,* Vol IV, Chapter XXIII, (Albany, Charles Van Benthuysen, 1851), 1085-1117.

380 Alexander C. Flick, *The Papers of Sir William Johnson, Vol VII* (Albany, The University of the State of New York, 1931), 892-893. ; See Footnote #5. Franklin, B. Hough, *Gazetteer of the State of New York. Embracing a Comprehensive Account of the History and Statistics of the State* (Albany, Andrew Boyd, 1872), 312, https://archive.org/stream/gazetteerofstate00houg#page/311/mode/2up

381 Alexander C. Flick, *The Papers of Sir William Johnson, Vol VII,* 649.

382 New York State Archives. New York (State). State Engineer and Surveyor. *Survey maps of lands in New York State, ca. 1711-1913.* NYSA_A0273-78_193. Series A0273-78, Map #193. Map of Staley's Patent in Herkimer County. http://digitalcollections.archives.nysed.gov/index.php/Detail/Object/Show/object_id/36720 ; Ibid. Map of Burnet's Field (copy). [Herkimer County] NYSA_A0273-78_181_Copy Series

A0273-78, Map #181 (copy). http://digitalcollections.archives.nysed.gov/index.php/Detail/Object/Show/object_id/36709 ; Ancestry.com. *Records of the Reformed Dutch Church of Stone Arabia : in the town of Palatine, Montgomery County, N.Y.* [database on-line]. Provo, UT. Vol.1. Marriages, Oct. 16, 1739 to 1795. 1771, d. 6, Januar. Bernard Friedrich und Dorothea Schenck.; Ancestry.com. *Records of the Reformed Dutch Church of Stone Arabia : in the town of Palatine, Montgomery County, N.Y.* [database on-line]. Provo, UT. Vol.1. Baptisms and births. 108.

383 *New York Colonial Muster Rolls, 1664-1775, Vol. II* [database on-line]. Supplemental Muster Rolls. 891.

384 New York State Historical Association, Fenimore Art Museum, Research Library Special Collections, *Jellis Fonda Papers,* Coll. No. 157, 1750-1791. Doren, Johannes 171 A.

385 Ibid. Runion, Samuel, 144A.; Alexander C. Flick, *The Papers of Sir William Johnson, Vol VII* (Albany, The University of the State of New York, 1931), 1050-1051. https://archive.org/stream/papersofsirwilli07johnuoft#page/1050/mode/2up

386 Ancestry.com. *Records of the Reformed Dutch Church of Stone Arabia: in the town of Palatine, Montgomery County, N.Y.* [database on-line]. Provo, UT. Vol.1. Marriages, Oct. 16, 1739 to 1795. 190. 1771 d. 5, Februar. Sebastian Alcajer, wittibber, und Christina Kulhmannin; Ibid. Vol.1. Register of members, Jan. 13, 1739 to 1795. 213.

387 Ancestry.com. *Records of the Lutheran Trinity Church of Stone Arabia: in the town of Palatine, Montgomery County, N.Y.* [database on-line]. Provo, UT. Vol.1. Birth and baptisms, 1751 to 1815. 35. Anno 1771 January d29tn Michael Majer Elisabetha ux; Sponsors: Martin Selmser & ux; Child: Elisabetha Margareta.

388 The State of New York, *The colonial laws of New York from the year 1664 to the Revolution, including the charters to the Duke of York, the commissions and instructions to colonial governors, the Duke's laws, the laws of the Dongan and Leisler Assemblies, the charters of Albany and New York and the acts*

of the colonial legislatures from 1691 to 1775 inclusive. Transmitted to the Legislature by the Commissioners of Statutory Revision, pursuant to chapter 125 of the Laws of 1891. Vol 5. Chapter 1508, 263-265 (Ithica, Cornell University Library, nd).

389 "St. John's Episcopal Church" Our History. http://www.stjohnsjohnstown.org/custompage2.php

390 Johannes Richtmeyer was born in the Schoharie Valley and baptized at Albany 20 April, 1729. He was the son of Conrad Richtmeyer and Catherine Hooftmensch. He married Gertraud Conrad 13 Jan 1757 at St. Paul's, Schoharie County. He lived on the south side of the Mohawk River in Schoharie County, now the town of Glen, Montgomery County.; Milton Hamilton & Albert Corey, *The Papers of Sir William Johnson, Vol XIII* (Albany, The University of the State of New York, 1962), 563, http://archive.org/stream/papersofsirwilli13johnuoft#page/562/mode/2up ; Milton Hamilton & Albert Corey, *The Papers of Sir William Johnson, Vol XII, 900.;* Alexander C. Flick, *The Papers of Sir William Johnson, Vol VIII* (Albany, The University of the State of New York, 1933), 103, 138. https://archive.org/stream/papersofsirwilli08johnuoft#page/102/mode/2up

391 Gavin Watt, *Rebellion in the Mohawk Valley: The St. Leger Expedition of 1777* (Toronto, The Dundurn Group, 2002).

392 Alexander C. Flick, *The Papers of Sir William Johnson, Vol VIII,* 219-220. https://archive.org/stream/papersofsirwilli08johnuoft#page/218/mode/2up

393 Milton Hamilton & Albert Corey, *The Papers of Sir William Johnson, Vol XIII* (Albany, The University of the State of New York, 1962), 715. http://archive.org/stream/papersofsirwilli13johnuoft#page/715/mode/1up ; Douglas Leighton, "CLAUS, CHRISTIAN DANIEL," in *Dictionary of Canadian Biography,* vol. 4, University of Toronto/Université Laval, 2003–, accessed January 25, 2018, http://www.biographi.ca/en/bio/claus_christian_daniel_4E.html.

394 Alexander C. Flick, *The Papers of Sir William Johnson, Vol VIII* (Albany, The University of the State of New York, 1933), 330-335, 384-386. https://archive.org/stream/papersofsirwilli08johnuoft#page/384/mode/2up

395 In March of 1772, John Cottgrove had an altercation with Thomas Flood, and in May of 1772, John Cottgrove wrote to Sir William with a version of his ideas that omitted slurs against the inhabitants. He suggested finishing the church with a gallery for the children so they do not 'mix' with the adults. He thought Sir William should clothe the children, particularily with uniforms worn on the Sabbath to ensure their attention. Finally, he suggested building a new free school complete with yard and bell which would attract the attention of Gentlemen of first rate to the community. He requested that Sir William keep his request a secret. Alexander C. Flick, *The Papers of Sir William Johnson, Vol VIII* (Albany, The University of the State of New York, 1933), 322-324. https://archive.org/stream/papersofsirwilli08johnuoft#page/322/mode/2up ; E.B. O'Callaghan, *The Documentary History of the State of New York, Papers Principally Relating to Conversion and Civilization of the Six Nations Indians,* Chapter XXII, (Albany, Charles Van Benthuysen, 1851), 473-475. https://archive.org/stream/documentaryhisto04ocal#page/472/mode/2up

396 Ancestry.com. *Records of the Lutheran Trinity Church of Stone Arabia : in the town of Palatine, Montgomery County, N.Y.* [database on-line]. Provo, UT. Vol.1. Birth and baptisms, 1751 to 1815. 41. Gebohren im Jahr und Tag Anno 1771 December d 27ten Father: Martin Algeier, Catharina ux; Sponsors: Mattaeus Emer, Sophia Algeier; Child: Philipp.

397 S.A. Johnston, and J.I. Garver, *Record of flooding on the Mohawk River from 1634 to 2000 based on historical Archives,* Geological Society of America, Abstracts with Programs 2001, v. 33, n.1, p.73. http://minerva.union.edu/garverj/mohawk/1831_floods.html

398 After December 1771, no record of Mattheus Eamer has been found. No marriage record or baptismal record of any children was found in

New York or Ontario records. There is no record of service in British or American forces during or after the revolutionary war. There was no record of his arrival in refugee camps or in Loyalist settlements in Canada during or after the Revolutionary war. Therefore, I assume Mattheus died in New York sometime after January 1772.

399 Alexander C. Flick, *The Papers of Sir William Johnson, Vol VIII* (Albany, The University of the State of New York, 1933), 384-386. https://archive.org/stream/papersofsirwilli08johnuoft#page/384/mode/2up ; Ibid. 413-415, 455-458, 477-479. ; The State of New York, *The colonial laws of New York from the year 1664 to the Revolution, including the charters to the Duke of York, the commissions and instructions to colonial governors, the Duke's laws, the laws of the Dongan and Leisler Assemblies, the charters of Albany and New York and the acts of the colonial legislatures from 1691 to 1775 inclusive. Transmitted to the Legislature by the Commissioners of Statutory Revision, pursuant to chapter 125 of the Laws of 1891.* Vol 5. Chapter 1552, (Ithica, Cornell University Library, nd), 383- 390. http://ebooks.library.cornell.edu/cgi/t/text/pageviewer-idx?c=cdl;cc=cdl;idno=cdl188;node=cdl188%3A3;view=image;seq=387;size=100;page=root

400 Alexander C. Flick, *The Papers of Sir William Johnson, Vol VIII*. 462-463. http://archive.org/stream/papersofsirwilli08johnuoft#page/462/mode/2up

401 Milton Hamilton & Albert Corey, *The Papers of Sir William Johnson, Vol XII* (Albany, The University of the State of New York, 1957), 892-895. https://archive.org/stream/papersofsirwilli12johnuoft#page/892/mode/2up

402 Fulton County Courthouse, Johnstown, New York. https://www.nycourts.gov/history/legal-history-new-york/documents/Courthouse_History-Fulton-County.pdf

403 Alexander C. Flick, *The Papers of Sir William Johnson, Vol VIII* (Albany, The University of the State of New York, 1933), 423-424.

404 The State of New York, *The colonial laws of New York from the year 1664 to the Revolution, including the charters to the Duke of York, the commissions and instructions to colonial governors, the Duke's laws, the laws of the Dongan and Leisler Assemblies, the charters of Albany and New York and the acts of the colonial legislatures from 1691 to 1775 inclusive. Transmitted to the Legislature by the Commissioners of Statutory Revision, pursuant to chapter 125 of the Laws of 1891.* Vol 5. Chapter 1551, (Ithica, Cornell University Library, nd). 369-383.; Alexander C. Flick, *The Papers of Sir William Johnson, Vol VIII,* 663.

405 "Three Rivers Hudson, Mohawk, Schoharie, History From America's Most Famous Valleys" The History of Montgomery County. Chapter V. " a List of the persons that are assessed above five pounds, with the sums they are to pay, and the number of days they are to work upon the King's highways, annexed."

406 Alexander C. Flick, *The Papers of Sir William Johnson, Vol VIII,* 944. https://archive.org/stream/papersofsirwilli08johnuoft#page/944/mode/2up

407 Milton Hamilton & Albert Corey, *The Papers of Sir William Johnson, Vol XIII* (Albany, The University of the State of New York, 1962), 590. http://archive.org/stream/papersofsirwilli13johnuoft#page/590/mode/1up

408 With License, a Philder Greyderman and Catharina Barrenton were married at the Lutheran church in New York City 18 December 1758. Ancestry.com. *U.S., Dutch Reformed Church Records in Selected States, 1639-1989* [database on-line]. Provo, UT. Holland Society of New York; New York, New York; New York City Lutheran, Vol III, Book 87. 75. Their son Joseph was baptized at Linlithgo. Joseph Kriderman gender: Male baptism/christening date: 22 Nov 1761 baptism/christening place: Reformed Church Linlithgo, Columbia, New York. Father's name: Velten Kriderman: mother's name: Cathrina Bernet. "New York, Births and Christenings, 1640-1962," index, FamilySearch (https://familysearch.org/pal:/MM9.1.1/V2CS-P7H), Joseph Kriderman, 22 Nov 1761; citing

reference, FHL microfilm 534201. ; Ancestry.com. *UK, American Loyalist Claims, 1776-1835* [database on-line]. Provo, UT, USA. American Loyalist Claims, 1776–1835. AO 12–13. The National Archives of the United Kingdom, Kew, Surrey, England. Piece 029: Evidence, New York, 1787-1788. 321-323.; Joseph Hanes lived on lot 157 on the eastern allotment of the Kingsborough Patent. Duncan Fraser, Papers and Records of the Ontario Historical Society, Volume LII, 1960, Original Source, Public Record Office, London, England AC 13/114. *Sir John Johnson's Rent Roll of the Kingsborough Patent.* http://freepages.genealogy.rootsweb.ancestry.com/~wjmartin/kingsbor.htm

409 Jeptha Root Simms, 1807-1883. *The Frontiersmen of New York: Showing Customs of the Indians, Vicissitudes of the Pioneer White Settlers, And Border Strife In Two Wars* (Albany G.C. Riggs, 188283), 323. https://hdl.handle.net/2027/mdp.39015008573084?urlappend=%3Bseq=335 ; Alexander C. Flick, *The Papers of Sir William Johnson, Vol VIII* (Albany, The University of the State of New York, 1933), 556. 583-584. https://archive.org/stream/papersofsirwilli08johnuoft#page/n585/mode/2up

410 Milton Hamilton & Albert Corey, *The Papers of Sir William Johnson, Vol XII* (Albany, The University of the State of New York, 1957), 999-1000. https://archive.org/stream/papersofsirwilli12johnuoft#page/1000/mode/2up

411 Richard Berleth, *Bloody Mohawk. The French and Indian War & American Revolution on New York's Frontier* (Delmar N.Y., Black Dome, 2010), 143-148.; Ralph T. Pastore, "TEIORHÉÑHSERE?," in *Dictionary of Canadian Biography*, vol. 4, University of Toronto/Université Laval, 2003. http://www.biographi.ca/en/bio/teiorhenhsere_4E.html

412 Alexander C. Flick, *The Papers of Sir William Johnson, Vol VIII* (Albany, The University of the State of New York, 1933), 653-656. https://archive.org/stream/papersofsirwilli08johnuoft#page/652/mode/2up

413 The State of New York, *The colonial laws of New York from the year 1664 to the Revolution, including the charters to the Duke of York, the commissions and instructions to colonial governors, the Duke's laws, the laws of the Dongan*

and Leisler Assemblies, the charters of Albany and New York and the acts of the colonial legislatures from 1691 to 1775 inclusive. Transmitted to the Legislature by the Commissioners of Statutory Revision, pursuant to chapter 125 of the Laws of 1891. Vol 5. Chapter 1584, (Ithica, Cornell University Library, nd). 464-465.

414 Ibid, Vol 5. Chapter 1595, 492-493.; Jeptha Root Simms, 1807-1883. *The Frontiersmen of New York: Showing Customs of the Indians, Vicissitudes of the Pioneer White Settlers, And Border Strife In Two War* (Albany, G.C. Riggs, 188283), 325. https://hdl.handle.net/2027/mdp.390150085730 84?urlappend=%3Bseq=335

415 Alexander C. Flick, *The Papers of Sir William Johnson, Vol VIII* (Albany, The University of the State of New York, 1933), 708-709. https://archive.org/stream/papersofsirwilli08johnuoft#page/708/mode/2up ; Max Reid, *The Mohawk Valley. Its Legends and Its History* (New York, G.P. Putnam's Sons, 1901), 206. http://archive.org/stream/mohawkvalley00reid#page/206/mode/2up ; The State of New York, *The colonial laws of New York from the year 1664 to the Revolution*, 491-492.

416 Ancestry.com. *U.S., Dutch Reformed Church Records in Selected States, 1639-1989* [database on-line]. Provo, UT, USA. Holland Society of New York; New York, New York; Fonda, Vol II, Book 16. 109.

417 Ancestry.com. *UK, American Loyalist Claims, 1776-1835* [database on-line]. Provo, UT, USA. The National Archives of the UK; Kew, Surrey, England; American Loyalist Claims, Series II; Class: AO 13; Piece: 011. New Claims A·B·C·, New York. 289; Ancestry.com. *UK, American Loyalist Claims, 1776-1835* [database on-line]. Provo, UT, USA. The National Archives of the UK; Kew, Surrey, England; American Loyalist Claims, Series I; Class: AO 13; Piece: 029. Evidence, New York, 1787-1788. 358-359.

418 The State of New York, *The colonial laws of New York from the year 1664 to the Revolution, including the charters to the Duke of York, the commissions and instructions to colonial governors, the Duke's laws, the laws of the Dongan and Leisler Assemblies, the charters of Albany and New York and the acts*

of the colonial legislatures from 1691 to 1775 inclusive. Transmitted to the Legislature by the Commissioners of Statutory Revision, pursuant to chapter 125 of the Laws of 1891. Vol 5. Chapter 1624, (Ithica, Cornell University Library, nd). 583-584.

419 Ibid, Vol 5. Chapter 1638, 600-603.; New York (State). General Assembly, *Journal of the Votes and Proceedings of the General Assembly of the Colony of New York: From 1766-1776,* Inclusive. Albany: Printed by J. Buel, 1820.

420 Duncan Fraser, Papers and Records of the Ontario Historical Society, Volume LII, 1960, Original Source, Public Record Office, London, England AC 13/114. *Sir John Johnson's Rent Roll of the Kingsborough Patent.* http://freepages.genealogy.rootsweb.ancestry.com/~wjmartin/kingsbor.htm; Ancestry.com. *American (Loyalist) Migrations, 1765-1799* [database on-line]. Provo, UT, USA. New York. 299; Ancestry.com. *UK, American Loyalist Claims, 1776-1835* [database on-line]. Provo, UT, USA. The National Archives of the UK; Kew, Surrey, England; American Loyalist Claims, Series I; Class: AO 13; Piece: 028. 405-407. Andrew Mehoss.

421 W.L. Scott, *The Macdonells of Leek, Collachie, and Aberchalder.* http://www.cchahistory.ca/journal/CCHA1934-35/Scott.html; Fintan O'Toole, *White Savage. William Johnson and the Invention of America* (Albany, State University of New York, 2005), 309-311.; Duncan Fraser, Papers and Records of the Ontario Historical Society, Volume LII, 1960, Original Source, Public Record Office, London, England AC 13/114. *Sir John Johnson's Rent Roll of the Kingsborough Patent.* http://freepages.genealogy.rootsweb.ancestry.com/~wjmartin/kingsbor.htm ; Alexander C. Flick, *The Papers of Sir William Johnson, Vol VIII* (Albany, The University of the State of New York, 1933), 816; Ancestry.com. *UK, American Loyalist Claims, 1776-1835* [database on-line]. Provo, UT. The National Archives of the UK; Kew, Surrey, England; *American Loyalist Claims, Series II;* Class: *AO 13;* Piece: *080.* Claims recieved too late, South Carolina, Pennsylvania. Claim of Captain Alexander MacDonnel.

422 Ibid, 833.

423 O'Callaghan, E. B. (Edmund Bailey), 1797-1880, Berthold Fernow, John Romeyn Brodhead, and New York (State). Legislature. *Documents Relative to the Colonial History of the State of New-York: Procured In Holland, England, And France* (Albany: Weed, Parsons, 18531887), 395. https://hdl.handle.net/2027/uiug.30112063015736?urlappend=%3Bseq=429

424 Jeptha Root Simms, 1807-1883. *The Frontiersmen of New York: Showing Customs of the Indians, Vicissitudes of the Pioneer White Settlers, And Border Strife In Two Wars,*(Albany, G.C. Riggs, 188283), 325. https://hdl.handle.net/2027/mdp.39015008573084?urlappend=%3Bseq=335

425 No baptismal record of John Alguire has been found. However, his petition for land in 1807 at Osnabruck, Stormont County, Ontario, Canada states he is the son of Martin Alguire a UE Loyalist. Martin and Catharina were married Nov, 1769. Their daughter Maria Salome was born 1770, son Philip was born 1771, son Peter was born 1775, son Daniel born ca. 1776 and daughter Elizabeth was born 1779. Therefore, I assume John was born ca. 1773. Library and Archives Canada. *Upper Canada Land Petitions (1763-1865)*. Mikan Number 205131. Microform: c-1609. Image 1231.

426 The State of New York, *The colonial laws of New York from the year 1664 to the Revolution, including the charters to the Duke of York, the commissions and instructions to colonial governors, the Duke's laws, the laws of the Dongan and Leisler Assemblies, the charters of Albany and New York and the acts of the colonial legislatures from 1691 to 1775 inclusive. Transmitted to the Legislature by the Commissioners of Statutory Revision, pursuant to chapter 125 of the Laws of 1891.* Vol 5. Chapter 1629, (Ithica, Cornell University Library, nd). 588-590. http://ebooks.library.cornell.edu/cgi/t/text/pageviewer-idx?c=cdl;cc=cdl;idno=cdl188;node=cdl188%3A3;view=image;seq=592;size=100;page=root

427 Ancestry.com. *U.S., Dutch Reformed Church Records in Selected States, 1639-1989* [database on-line]. Provo, UT, USA. The Archives of the

Reformed Church in America; New Brunswick, New Jersey; Reformed Church of Fonda, Baptisms, Marriages, Members, Consistory Minutes, 1758-1839. 12. 1773, Dec 1, David Jecocks met Anna Algire.; Will of Martin Silmser 20 August 1800. *Stormont, Dundas and Glengarry Surrogate Records*, Register Book A. Pages 197-198, Microfilm Reel 862333. "… .my two daughters, Christina Elizabeth wife of John Crysler and Anna Mary wife of John Algire … ."

428 Alexander C. Flick, *The Papers of Sir William Johnson, Vol VIII* (Albany, The University of the State of New York, 1933), 839. http://archive.org/stream/papersofsirwilli82john#page/1074/mode/2up

429 Ancestry.com. *UK, American Loyalist Claims, 1776-1835* [database on-line]. Provo, UT, USA. American Loyalist Claims, 1776–1835. AO 12–13. The National Archives of the United Kingdom, Kew, Surrey, England. 181-182.

430 Angus McDonell settled on lot 55 on the Sacandaga Patent. Ancestry.com. *UK, American Loyalist Claims, 1776-1835* [database on-line]. Provo, UT, USA. The National Archives of the UK; Kew, Surrey, England; American Loyalist Claims, Series I; Class: AO 13; Piece: 031. Evidence, New York, 1787-1788. 183-184. Claim of Angus McDonell.; Duncan Fraser, Papers and Records of the Ontario Historical Society, Volume LII, 1960, Original Source, Public Record Office, London, England AC 13/114. *Sir John Johnson's Rent Roll of the Kingsborough Patent.* http://freepages.genealogy.rootsweb.ancestry.com/~wjmartin/kingsbor.htm

431 The State of New York, *The colonial laws of New York from the year 1664 to the Revolution, including the charters to the Duke of York, the commissions and instructions to colonial governors, the Duke's laws, the laws of the Dongan and Leisler Assemblies, the charters of Albany and New York and the acts of the colonial legislatures from 1691 to 1775 inclusive. Transmitted to the Legislature by the Commissioners of Statutory Revision, pursuant to chapter 125 of the Laws of 1891.* Vol 5. Chapter 1632, (Ithica, Cornell University Library, nd), 592-593.

432 Ancestry.com. *U.S., Dutch Reformed Church Records in Selected States, 1639-1989* [database on-line]. Provo, UT, USA. Holland Society of New York; New York, New York; Cagnawaga or Fonda, Book 15. 39. Jellis, Jan 16 1774, bo. Dec 25, 1773, Philip Beemer, Catriena Lyserin, Sponsors, Jellis Fonda, Jannitjie.

433 Ancestry.com. *U.S., Dutch Reformed Church Records in Selected States, 1639-1989* [database on-line]. Provo, UT, USA. The Archives of the Reformed Church in America; New Brunswick, New Jersey; Reformed Church of Fonda, Baptisms, Marriages, Members, Consistory Minutes, 1758-1839. 12. Jany 4, 1774. Johannis Algire met Maragrita Eenie.; Frank Reid Diffenderffer, *The German Exodus to England in 1709* (Lancaster, Pennsylvania German Society, 1897), 549. http://archive.org/stream/germanexodustoen07diff#page/548/mode/2up .1746, Ahlgeyer, Johan George, s Johannes and Catharina Margretha; b. Sept 11; bap. Sept. 14; Sp. Mathias Leher and w. Catharina, Hans Jurg Appel and w Julianna; Reverend John Ogilvie Records Eastern NY State, Hudson Valley Area 1750-1760 Baptisms. *Register of Baptisms Rev John Olgilvie Trinity Church New York.* Eneeg 1755 11/30 Albany Mary Margaret, dau of David and Marie (Huysmet).; "Deutschland Heiraten, 1558-1929," database, *FamilySearch* (https://familysearch.org/ark:/61903/1:1:J451-4SJ : 26 December 2014), David Ehni and Anna Maria Heuschmid, 08 Feb 1752; citing Gutenberg, Wuerttemberg, Germany; FHL microfilm 1,055,850. https://www.familysearch.org/pal:/MM9.1.1/J451-4SJ

434 "National Humanities Center." America in Class. Making the Revolution: America 1763-1791. Crisis: 1763-1775. 1772-1773: Crisis Renewed "THAT Worst of plagues, the detested TEA." http://americainclass.org/sources/makingrevolution/crisis/text6/teaactresponse.pdf

435 Joyce Berry, *Witch Hunts. Original documents at the Montgomery County Department of History and Archives, Fonda New York.* www.hvv.org https://www.ancestry.ca/mediaui-viewer/collection/1030/tree/44704820/person/24020814310/media/ee9dd5ac-ce22-495d-91c7-eec3dd5d0834?_phsrc=JTx9729&usePUBJs=true ; Jeptha Root Simms, 1807-1883. *The Frontiersmen of New York: Showing Customs of the*

Indians, Vicissitudes of the Pioneer White Settlers, And Border Strife In Two Wars (Albany, G.C. Riggs, 188283), 325.

436 Ancestry.com. *U.S., Dutch Reformed Church Records in Selected States, 1639-1989* [database on-line]. Provo, UT, USA. The Archives of the Reformed Church in America; New Brunswick, New Jersey; Reformed Church of Fonda, Baptisms, Marriages, Members, Consistory Minutes, 1758-1839. 13. 1774, June 26, Michael Mier, Elizabeth Wemell, Godfree, June 9, Godfree Aney, Margaret Aney.

437 No record of Jelles Eamer's death has been found, and there are no marriage records nor birth records for any children. He does not appear in any of the military rolls during the revolution, and he does not appear in any American Military pension rolls or any Loyalist claims or settlement records. I assume Jelles died young.

438 Manuscripts and Archives Division, The New York Public Library. "Butler, John. Tryon County" New York Public Library Digital Collections. Accessed February 10, 2018. http://digitalcollections.nypl.org/items/9ff20570-3321-0133-b461-58d385a7b928 ; Manuscripts and Archives Division, The New York Public Library. "Frey, Hendrick" New York Public Library Digital Collections. http://digitalcollections.nypl.org/items/95c14a90-349d-0133-6c0f-58d385a7b928 ; New York Public Library Collections, Theodorus Bailey Myers Collection, NYPL catalog ID (B-number): b11868620 MSS Unit ID: 2091, Arichives collections id: archives_collections_2091, Universal Unique Identifier (UUID): 8e0e4fd0-2e58-0133-2fde-58d385a7b928 https://digitalcollections.nypl.org/items/5773f620-349e-0133-6fd8-58d385a7b928/book?parent=db55e2d0-2e58-0133-1b29-58d385a7b928#page/69/mode/2up

439 Jane Marlett Taft, *Gideon Marlett (Gedeon Merlett) A Huguenot of Staten Island, N.Y. With Some Account of His Descendents in the United States and Canada* (Burlington, 1907), 58. https://archive.org/stream/gideonmarlettged00taft#page/n129/mode/2up

440 Alexander C. Flick, *The Papers of Sir William Johnson, Vol VIII* (Albany, The University of the State of New York, 1933), 1094, 1185. http://archive.org/stream/papersofsirwilli82john#page/1788/mode/2up

441 Alexander C. Flick, *The Papers of Sir William Johnson, Vol VIII* (Albany, The University of the State of New York, 1933), 1074-1077, 1178-1180, 1182-1183 http://archive.org/stream/papersofsirwilli82john#page/1772/mode/2up ; Richard Berleth, *Bloody Mohawk. The French and Indian War & American Revolution on New York's Frontier* (Delmar N.Y., Black Dome, 2010), 151-153.

442 "National Humanities Center." America in Class. Making the Revolution: America 1763-1791. Crisis: 1763-1775. 1772-1773: Crisis Renewed. Colonies United. http://americainclass.org/sources/makingrevolution/crisis/text6/text6.htm ; Gavin Watt, Poisoned By Lies and Hypocrisy. America's First Attempt to Bring Liberty To Canada, 1775-1776. (Toronto, Dundern Press, 2014), 23.

443 Alexander Clarence Flick, *Loyalism in New York During the Revolution.* Vol 14, No. 1 (London, Columbia University Press, 1901), 24-26. https://archive.org/stream/loyalisminnewyor00flic#page/24/mode/2up

444 Isabel Thompson Kelsay, *Joseph Brant 1743-1807 Man of Two Worlds* (Syracuse, Syracuse University Press, 1984), 135; Fintan O'Toole, *White Savage. William Johnson and the Invention of America* (Albany, State University of New York, 2005),323; Alexander C. Flick, *The Papers of Sir William Johnson, Vol VIII* (Albany, The University of the State of New York, 1933), 1195-1196, 1198-1200. http://archive.org/stream/papersofsirwilli82john#page/1808/mode/2up; Milton Hamilton & Albert Corey, *The Papers of Sir William Johnson, Vol XIII* (Albany, The University of the State of New York, 1962), 638-639 https://archive.org/stream/papersofsirwilli13johnuoft#page/638/mode/2up

445 William L. Stone, *The Life and Times of Sir William Johnson, Bart., Vol. II* (Albany, J. Munsell, 1865), 376-381. https://archive.org/stream/lifetimesofsirwi02stonuoft#page/376/mode/2up

446 William L. Stone, *The Life and Times of Sir William Johnson, Bart., Vol. II,* 379.; Henry C. Van Schaack, *The Life of Peter Van Schaack, LL.D* (New York, D. Appleton & Co., 1842), 14-15. https://archive.org/stream/lifeofpetervan00vans#page/n35/mode/2up ; Fintan O'Toole, *White Savage. William Johnson and the Invention of America* (Albany, State University of New York, 2005), 324-325.

447 E. B. O'Callaghan, *Documents Relative to the Colonial History of the State of New York, Vol VIII* (Albany, Weed, Parsons and Company, 1857), 485-486. https://archive.org/stream/documentsrelativ08brod#page/484/mode/2up ; Milton Hamilton & Albert Corey, *The Papers of Sir William Johnson, Vol XIII* (Albany, The University of the State of New York, 1962), 640-643. https://archive.org/stream/papersofsirwilli13johnuoft#page/640/mode/2up; Library and Archives Canada, *Haldimand Papers From the British Library,* lac_reel_h1429 105513 2034239 MG 21, Image 978. http://heritage.canadiana.ca/view/oocihm.lac_reel_h1429/978?r=0&s=5

448 "The Annotated Newspapers of Harbottle Dorr Jr." The Boston-Gazette, and Country Journal, 12 March 1770. Massachusetts Historical Society, 2018. http://www.masshist.org/dorr/volume/3/sequence/101 ; Ibid, 27 June 1774 http://www.masshist.org/dorr/volume/4/sequence/603 ; John Dickinson, *Empire and Nation: Letters from a Farmer in Pennsylvania (John Dickinson). Letters from the Federal Farmer (Richard Henry Lee),* Forrest McDonald, ed. (Indianapolis: Liberty Fund, 1999). http://oll.libertyfund.org/titles/690

449 "Boston Tea Party: A Revolutionary Experience." The Committees of Correspondence: The Voice of the Patriots. Boston Tea Party Ships Museum, 2018. https://www.bostonteapartyship.com/committees-of-correspondence

450 "Boston Tea Party: A Revolutionary Experience." The Committees of Correspondence: The Voice of the Patriots. Boston Tea Party Ships Museum, First Continental Congress: The Patriots React to the Intolerable Acts.; E. B. O'Callaghan, *Documents Relative to the*

Colonial History of the State of New York, Vol VIII (Albany, Weed, Parsons and Company, 1857), 485-487. https://archive.org/stream/documentsrelativ08brod#page/484/mode/2up ; Julian P. Boyd, "Joseph Galloway's Plans of Union for the British Empire, 1774-1788." *The Pennsylvania Magazine of History and Biography* 64, n4 (1940): 492-515. http://www.jstor.org/stable/20087321. Maya Jasanoff, Liberty's Exiles. American Loyalists in the Revolutionary War (New York, Alfred A. Knopf, 2011), 25.

451 Ancestry.com. *U.S., Dutch Reformed Church Records in Selected States, 1639-1989* [database on-line]. Provo, UT, USA. Holland Society of New York; New York, New York; Cagnawaga or Fonda, Book 15. 47.

452 Ancestry.com. *Records of the Lutheran Trinity Church of Stone Arabia : in the town of Palatine, Montgomery County, N.Y.* [database on-line]. Provo, UT. Section: Vol.1. Birth and baptisms, 1751 to 1815. 46. Maryly B. Penrose, *Compendium of Early Mohawk Valley Families. Vol. I.* (Baltimore, Genealogical Publishing Co., 1990). 233, 469.

453 Montgomery County Historical Society, *The Minute Book of the Committee of Saftey of Tryon County* (New York, Dodd, Mead and Company, 1905), 1-4. https://archive.org/stream/minutebookcommi00freygoog#page/n32/mode/2up ; William W. Campbell, *Annals of Tryon County; or, The Border Warfare of New York, During The Revolution* (New York, J. & J. Harper, 1831), 30-33. https://archive.org/stream/annalsoftryoncou00camp#page/n37/mode/2up

454 Gavin Watt, Poisoned By Lies and Hypocrisy. America's First Attempt to Bring Liberty To Canada 1775-1776 (Toronto, Dundern Press, 2014), 55.

CHAPTER FIVE
The Revolutionary War (1775-1781)

455 James Sullivan, *Minutes of the Albany Committee of Correspondence 1775-1778* (Albany, The University of the State of New York, 1923), 3-4. https://archive.org/stream/MinutesOfTheAlbanyCommitteeOfCorrespondence1775-1778Vol1#page/n19/mode/2up; William Roscoe, *History of Schoharie County, New York* (Syracuse, D. Mason & Co., 1882), 36-37. https://archive.org/stream/cu31924028834541#page/36/mode/2up

456 James Sullivan, *Minutes of the Albany Committee of Correspondence,*7-8. https://archive.org/stream/minutebookcommi00freygoog#page/n36/mode/2up

457 Ancestry.com. *UK, American Loyalist Claims, 1776-1835* [database on-line]. Provo, UT. American Loyalist Claims, 1776–1835. AO 12–13. The National Archives of the United Kingdom, Kew, Surrey, England. Piece 054: Temporary Assistance B-V, New York. Claim of Daniel Claus Esq.

458 Gavin Watt, *Poisoned By Lies and Hypocrisy. America's First Attempt to Bring Liberty To Canada 1775-1776* (Toronto, Dundern Press, 2014), 124-125.; New York (State). General Assembly. *Journal of the Votes And Proceedings of the General Assembly of the Colony of New York: From 1766 to 1776, Inclusive* (Albany, J. Buel, 1820). 13-14.

459 Alexander C. Flick, *The Papers of Sir William Johnson, Vol VIII* (Albany, The University of the State of New York, 1933), 1202 http://archive.org/stream/papersofsirwilli82john#page/1824/mode/2up ; William W. Campbell, *Annals of Tryon County; or, The Border Warfare of New York, During The Revolution* (New York, J. & J. Harper, 1831), 33, 36-37.

460 Caitlin A. Fitz, "Suspected on Both Sides: Little Abraham, Iroquois Neutrality, and the American Revolution." *Journal of the Early Republic* 28, no. 3 (2008): 299-300. http://www.jstor.org/stable/40208153

461 Isabel Thompson Kelsay, *Joseph Brant 1743-1807 Man of Two Worlds* (Syracuse, Syracuse University Press, 1984), 146.

462 No baptism, marriage, or death record was found for Christian. He resided in Mountain Township, Dundas County, Ontario ca. 1789 and moved to Madrid St. Lawrence County ca. 1810. His brother Godfrey is also on the Madrid St. Lawrence census of 1810. Centennial Committee, *The Old United Empire Loyalists List: The Centennial of the Settlement of Upper Canada by the United Empire Loyalists, 1784-1884. Supplementary List* Appendix B (Baltimore, Genealogical Publishing Co., 2003), 310. Myers, Christian of Mountain, son of Michl. Myers, N.E., N.McL.; United States Census, 1860", database with images, *FamilySearch* (https://familysearch.org/ark:/61903/1:1:MC41-CK3: 13 December 2017), Christian Myres in entry for Chas Myres, 1860.

463 Montgomery County Historical Society, *The Minute Book of the Committee of Safety of Tryon County* (New York, Dodd, Mead and Company, 1905), 16. https://archive.org/stream/minutebookcommi00freygoog#page/n48/mode/2up ; Alexander Flick, *Minutes of the Schenectady Committee 1775-1779, Vol II* (Albany, The University of the State of New York, 1925), 1009. https://archive.org/stream/minutes1775177802albauoft#page/1008/mode/2up

464 Gavin Watt, *Poisoned By Lies and Hypocrisy. America's First Attempt to Bring Liberty To Canada 1775-1776* (Toronto, Dundern Press, 2014), 36-37. William W. Campbell, *Annals of Tryon County; or, The Border Warfare of New York, During The Revolution* (New York, J. & J. Harper, 1831), 33-36. Montgomery County Historical Society, *The Minute Book of the Committee of Saftey of Tryon County*, 6-9.

465 Richard Berleth, *Bloody Mohawk. The French and Indian War & American Revolution on New York's Frontier* (Delmar N.Y., Black Dome, 2010), 169. William Stone, *Life of Joseph Brant – Thayendanegea. Including the Border Wars of the American Revolution. Vol I* (New York, Alexander V. Blake, 1838), 52-53. https://archive.org/stream/lifeofjosephbran01ston#page/52/mode/2up

466 Isabel Thompson Kelsay, *Joseph Brant 1743-1807 Man of Two Worlds* (Syracuse, Syracuse University Press, 1984), 147-153.; Montgomery County Historical Society, *The Minute Book of the Committee of Saftey of Tryon County* (New York, Dodd, Mead and Company, 1905), 18-25. https://archive.org/stream/minutebookcommi00freygoog#page/n52/mode/2up ; Gavin Watt, *Poisoned By Lies and Hypocrisy. America's First Attempt to Bring Liberty To Canada 1775-1776* (Toronto, Dundern Press, 2014), 54-55. ; William W. Campbell, *Annals of Tryon County; or, The Border Warfare of New York, During The Revolution* (New York, J. & J. Harper, 1831), 36-43. https://archive.org/stream/annalsoftryoncou00camp#page/n43/mode/2up ; James Sullivan, *Minutes of the Albany Committee of Correspondence 1775-1778, Vol I* (Albany, The University of the State of New York, 1923), 35-37. https://archive.org/stream/MinutesOfTheAlbanyCommitteeOfCorrespondence1775-1778Vol1#page/n53/mode/2up ; Richard Berleth, *Bloody Mohawk. The French and Indian War & American Revolution on New York's Frontier*, 169-170.

467 Isabel Thompson Kelsay, *Joseph Brant 1743-1807 Man of Two Worlds* (Syracuse, Syracuse University Press, 1984), 149-150.; C.M. Johnston, "DESERONTYON, JOHN," in *Dictionary of Canadian Biography*, vol. 5, University of Toronto/Université Laval, 2003, accessed April 4, 2018, http://www.biographi.ca/en/bio/deserontyon_john_5E.html ; Library and Archives Canada, Great Britain War Office, *A List of Colonel Johnson's Department of Indian Affairs*, WO 28, lac_reel_c10861 C-10861, 158960, 125090, MG13WO http://heritage.canadiana.ca/view/oocihm.lac_reel_c10861/1440?r=0&s=3 ; Ancestry.com. *UK, American Loyalist Claims, 1776-1835* [database on-line]. Provo, UT. The National Archives of the UK; Kew, Surrey, England; American Loyalist Claims, Series I; Class: AO 13; Piece 029: Evidence, New York, 1787-1788. 22. Claim of William Fraser Sr. and Captains William and Thomas Fraser.

468 Ancestry.com. *U.S., Dutch Reformed Church Records in Selected States, 1639-1989* [database on-line]. Provo, UT. The Archives of the Reformed Church in America; New Brunswick, New Jersey; Reformed Church of Fonda, Baptisms, Marriages, Members, Consistory Minutes, 1758-1839.

1775 June 4, Entry No. 214. Martinus Algyre, Catrina Weemer, Petrue, born May 29, Sponsors Petrue Weimer, Maragrita Algyre.

469 Ancestry.com. *UK, American Loyalist Claims, 1776-1835* [database on-line]. Provo, UT. The National Archives of the UK; Kew, Surrey, England; American Loyalist Claims, Series I; Class: AO 13; Piece 029: Evidence, New York, 1787-1788. 32. Claim of Alexander White.; Library and Archives Canada, Audit Office: AO 12. *Claims, American Loyalists Series I* 12904. Lac_reel_c12904, C-12904, 105765, 128170, 128171, 128173, MG 14 AO 12. Claim of Alexander Campbell. 158, 162 http://heritage.canadiana.ca/view/oocihm.lac_reel_c12904/1341?r=0&s=3; "American Archives. Documents of the American Revolutionary Period, 1774-1776." Address of Governour Tryon to the Inhabitants of the Colony of New York. http://amarch.lib.niu.edu/islandora/object/niu-amarch%3A89441; Ibid, Address of Inhabitiants of New York to Governour Tryon. http://amarch.lib.niu.edu/islandora/object/niu-amarch%3A105687; Gavin Watt, *Poisoned By Lies and Hypocrisy. America's First Attempt to Bring Liberty To Canada 1775-1776* (Toronto, Dundern Press, 2014), 157.

470 Library and Archives Canada, Great Britain War Office (WO 28): *America,* 10860, lac_reel_c10860,C-10860,158960, 125090, 105016, MG 13 WO lac_reel_c10860, Image 1039, http://heritage.canadiana.ca/view/oocihm.lac_reel_c10860/1039?r=0&s=3 Library and Archives Canada, Great Britain War Office (WO 28): *America,* 10861, lac_reel_c10861, C10861, 158906, 125090, MG 13 WO, Image 1253-1256. http://heritage.canadiana.ca/view/oocihm.lac_reel_c10861/1253?r=0&s=3 ; "The Kings Royal Yorkers" Captain Stephen Watts, http://royalyorkers.ca/lights/lc_cp_watts.htm

471 New York State, *Public Papers of George Clinton, First Governor of New York, 1777 1795, 1801-1804, Military Vol I* (Albany, Wynkoop Hallenbeck Crawford Co., 1899), 120-121 https://archive.org/stream/publicpapersofge01newy1#page/120/mode/2up "History of the Mohawk Valley: Gateway to the West 1614-1925." Chapter 76: 1775-1783. Roster of Mohawk Valley Revolutionary Militia. http://www.

schenectadyhistory.org/resources/mvgw/history/076.html "Schoharie County Genealogy and History" Schoharie County NY, Revolutionary War Soldiers. http://genealogytrails.com/ny/schoharie/revwar_roster.html

472 The National Archives, *Revolutionary War Rolls 1775 – 1783,* M246, Record Group 93, Roll 0074, Folder 100, New York, Fisher's Regiment of Militia. https://www.fold3.com/image/246/10073586

473 Montgomery County Historical Society, *The Minute Book of the Committee of Safety of Tryon County* (New York, Dodd, Mead and Company, 1905), 49-51, 55-58, 67.; James Sullivan, *Minutes of the Albany Committee of Correspondence 1775-1778, Vol I* (Albany, The University of the State of New York, 1923),165-167. https://archive.org/stream/MinutesOfTheAlbanyCommitteeOfCorrespondence1775-1778Vol1#page/n183/mode/2up ; Alexander C. Flick, *The Papers of Sir William Johnson, Vol VIII* (Albany, The University of the State of New York, 1933), 1204-1206. http://archive.org/stream/papersofsirwilli82john#page/1828/mode/2up ; Ancestry.com. *UK, American Loyalist Claims, 1776-1835* [database on-line]. Provo, UT. The National Archives of the UK; Kew, Surrey, England; American Loyalist Claims, Series I; Class: AO 13; Piece 029: Evidence, New York, 1787-1788. 27-28. Claim of Alexander White.

474 Ancestry.com. *UK, American Loyalist Claims, 1776-1835* [database on-line]. Provo, UT. The National Archives of the UK; Kew, Surrey, England; *American Loyalist Claims, Series I;* Class: AO 13; Piece 029: Evidence, New York, 1787-1788. 28. Claim of Alexander White.; Library and Archives Canada, British Library (Formerly British Museum) Haldimand Papers. Lac_reel_h1743, H-1743, 105513, 2034239, Image 1343. http://heritage.canadiana.ca/view/oocihm.lac_reel_h1743/1337?r=0&s=4 ; New York State, *Calendar of Historical Manuscripts Relating to the War of the Revolution, Vol I* (Albany, Weed, Parsons & Company, 1868), 161-162. https://archive.org/stream/calendarofhistor01newy#page/160/mode/2up

475 Montgomery County Historical Society, *The Minute Book of the Committee of Safety of Tryon County* (New York, Dodd, Mead and Company, 1905), 58, 68, 74-76, 85, 91, 97.; The National Archives, Revolutionary War Pension and Bounty-Land Warrant Application Files, M804, Pension Number S. 11350, Record Group 15, Roll 2112. Page 33. Sammons, Frederick. https://www.fold3.com/image/246/14669581?xid=1945

476 Ibid, 76-79.; Ancestry.com. *UK, American Loyalist Claims, 1776-1835* [database on-line]. Provo, UT. The National Archives of the UK; Kew, Surrey, England; American Loyalist Claims, Series I; Class: AO 13; Piece 027: Evidence, New York, 1787. 86. Claim of Philip Shover.; Ancestry.com. *UK, American Loyalist Claims, 1776-1835* [database on-line]. Provo, UT. The National Archives of the UK; Kew, Surrey, England; *American Loyalist Claims, Series I;* Class: AO 13; Piece 026: Evidence, New York, 1787. 285-287. Claim of Jane the Widow of John Waite.; The New England Historical and Genealogical Register, Vols 62, 63, 64, 65. *Emigrants From England 1773-1776* (Boston, New England Historic Genealogical Society, 1914), 160. *https://archive.org/stream/emigrantsfromeng00bost#page/160/mode/2up*

477 Montgomery County Historical Society, *The Minute Book of the Committee of Safety of Tryon County* (New York, Dodd, Mead and Company, 1905), 81-82, 84-85. William L. Stone, *The Life and Times of Sir William Johnson, Bart., Vol. II* (Albany, J. Munsell, 1865), 504-505. https://archive.org/stream/lifetimesofsirwi02stonuoft#page/504/mode/2up

478 Gavin Watt, *Poisoned By Lies and Hypocrisy. America's First Attempt to Bring Liberty To Canada 1775-1776* (Toronto, Dundern Press, 2014), 84, 86, 97-98, Montgomery County Historical Society, *The Minute Book of the Committee of Safety of Tryon County,* 99-104. https://archive.org/stream/minutebookcommi00freygoog#page/n150/mode/2up; Alexander Flick, *Minutes of the Schenectady Committee 1775-1779, Vol II* (Albany, The University of the State of New York, 1925), 1016, 1045. https://archive.org/stream/minutes1775177802albauoft#page/1016/

mode/2up ; Ancestry.com. *UK, American Loyalist Claims, 1776-1835* [database on-line]. Provo, UT. The National Archives of the UK; Kew, Surrey, England; American Loyalist Claims, Series I; Class: AO 13; Piece 028: Evidence, New York, 1787. 13. Claim of John Freel.

479 Montgomery County Historical Society, *The Minute Book of the Committee of Safety of Tryon County*, 67, 91-93. https://archive.org/stream/minutebookcommi00freygoog#page/n142/mode/2up

480 Ancestry.com. *U.S., Dutch Reformed Church Records in Selected States, 1639-1989* [database on-line]. Provo, UT. The Archives of the Reformed Church in America; New Brunswick, New Jersey; Reformed Church of Fonda, Baptisms, Marriages, Members, Consistory Minutes, 1758-1839. Entry 256, Dec 10, Jacob Keelman, Elizabeth Algire, Jacob born Dec 2, Sponsors Jacob Algire, Catrina Algire.; Ancestry.com. *U.S., Dutch Reformed Church Records in Selected States, 1639-1989* [database on-line]. Provo, UT. Holland Society of New York; New York, New York; Fonda, Vol II, Book 16. 1775 Dec 12, Johannes Hoogh to Margrieta Algire.

481 Alexander Flick, *Minutes of the Schenectady Committee 1775-1779, Vol II* (Albany, The University of the State of New York, 1925), 1035. https://archive.org/stream/minutes1775177802albauoft#page/1034/mode/2up

482 The National Archives, Papers of the Continental Congress, *Letters From Major General Philip Schuyler, Vol I June 1775-December 1776,* Item No. 153, M247, Roll 172, Record Group 360. Narrative of an Excersion to Tryon County. 414-443. https://www.fold3.com/image/1/345766 ; "American Archives. *Documents of the American Revolutionary Period, 1774-1776.* Affidavit of Johnathan French of Tryon County, Jan 11, 1776. http://amarch.lib.niu.edu/islandora/object/niu-amarch%3A103853 ; The National Archives, *Revolutionary War Pension and Bounty-Land Warrant Application Files.,* M804, Record Group 15, Roll 0945, pg. 24. Pension application of Adam Everson (Dorothy Dachstader); Ibid, Record Group 15, Roll 0824, pg. 4. Pension application of George Dachstader (Barbara Schultz); Ibid, Record Group 15, Roll 1987, pg 7.

Pension application of Richard Putman (Nelly Van Brakelen) https://www.fold3.com/image/246/16342948 https://www.fold3.com/image/246/17230630 https://www.fold3.com/image/246/27763482

483 Alexander Flick, *Minutes of the Schenectady Committee 1775-1779, Vol II* (Albany, The University of the State of New York, 1925), 1037. https://archive.org/stream/minutes1775177802albauoft#page/1036/mode/2up ; Library and Archives Canada, Audit Office: AO 12. Claims, *American Loyalists - Series I* – 12904. Lac_reel_c12904, C-12904, 105765, 128170, 128171, 128173, MG 14 A0 12. 162. http://heritage.canadiana.ca/view/oocihm.lac_reel_c12904/1345?r=0&s=3 Claim of Alex Campbell.

484 The National Archives, Papers of the Continental Congress, *Letters From Major General Philip Schuyler, Vol I June 1775-December 1776,* Item No. 153, M247, Roll 172, Record Group 360. Narrative of an Excersion to Tryon County, 432-434. https://www.fold3.com/image/1/345784 ; Library and Archives Canada, British Library (Formerly British Museum) Haldimand Papers, Lac_reel_h1743, H-1743, 105513, 2034239, Image 1076 http://heritage.canadiana.ca/view/oocihm.lac_reel_h1743/1076?r=0&s=4

485 The National Archives, Papers of the Continental Congress, *Letters From Major General Philip Schuyler, Vol I June 1775-December 1776,* Item No. 153, M247, Roll 172, Record Group 360, Narrative of an Excersion to Tryon County. 415-430, 440-443.; Richard Berleth, *Bloody Mohawk. The French and Indian War & American Revolution on New York's Frontier* (Delmar N.Y., Black Dome, 2010), 178-180.; J. P. McLean, *An Historical Account of the Settlements of Scotch Highlanders in America Prior to the Peace of 1783.* (Glasgow, John McKay, 1900), Chapter 8 Highland Settlement on the Mohawk. http://www.electricscotland.com/history/highlands/chapter8.htm ; Library and Archives Canada, Great Britain, War Office (WO 28): *America,* 10861. Lac_reel_c10861, C10861, 158960, 12590, MG 13 WO, Image 1369. The Memorials of Messrs Allan and Ranald McDonell. http://heritage.canadiana.ca/view/oocihm.lac_reel_c10861/1369?r=0&s=3 ; Ancestry.com. *UK, American*

Loyalist Claims, 1776-1835 [database on-line]. Provo, UT. Original data: American Loyalist Claims, 1776–1835. AO 12–13. The National Archives of the United Kingdom, Kew, Surrey, England. Piece 014: New Claims K·M N·O, New York. 124. Affadavit of Sir John Johnson for Ranald McDonell. 124. Ancestry.com. *UK, American Loyalist Claims, 1776-1835* [database on-line]. Provo, UT. The National Archives of the UK; Kew, Surrey, England; American Loyalist Claims, Series I; Class: AO 13; Piece 024: Evidence, New York, 1786-1787. 243. The Memorial of Revd. John McKenna.; Ibid, Series II; Class: AO 13; Piece 080: Claims recieved too late, South Carolina, Pennsylvania. The Memorial of Alexander McDonell, Late Captain in the Provincial Corps, called the Kings Royal Regt of New York.; Ancestry.com. *UK, American Loyalist Claims, 1776-1835* [database on-line]. Provo, UT. Piece 022: Evidence, New York, 1786. 231-239. The Memorial of John Thompson.; Library and Archives of Canada, *Upper Canada Sundries,* Vol 18, July-August 1813. Item 46. 7413-7533. Petition of George McGinnis of Amherst Island, Lennox and Addington Counties, District of Midland.

486 Ancestry.com. *UK, American Loyalist Claims, 1776-1835* [database on-line]. Provo, UT. The National Archives of the UK; Kew, Surrey, England; American Loyalist Claims, Series I; Class: AO 13; Piece 032: Evidence, New York, 1788. 177. Claim of David Jeacocks, 486.

487 The National Archives, *Papers of the Continental Congress, Letters From Major General Philip Schuyler, Vol I June 1775-December 1776,* Item No. 153, M247, Roll 172, Record Group 360. Narrative of an Excersion to Tryon County, 444; Secretary of State, *Calendar of Historical Manuscripts, Relating to the War of the Revolution, Vol I* (Albany, Weed, Parsons and Company, 1868), 583. https://archive.org/stream/calendarofhistor01newy#page/582/mode/2up ; Library and Archives Canada, British Library (Formerly British Museum) Haldimand Papers, Lac_reel_h1743, H-1743, 105513, 2034239, Image 1264-1266. http://heritage.canadiana.ca/view/oocihm.lac_reel_h1743/1264?r=0&s=4 ; Ancestry.com. *UK, American Loyalist Claims, 1776-1835* [database on-line]. Provo, UT. The National Archives of the UK; Kew, Surrey, England; American Loyalist Claims, Series I; Class: AO 13; Piece

031: Evidence, New York, 1787-1788. 315. Evidence on the Claim of Jacob Romborgh.

488 Ancestry.com. *UK, American Loyalist Claims, 1776-1835* [database on-line]. Provo, UT. The National Archives of the UK; Kew, Surrey, England; American Loyalist Claims, Series I; Class: AO 13; Piece 033: Evidence, North Carolina, 1788. 69. Claim of William Shewman.

489 The National Archives, *Revolutionary War Rolls 1775-1783,* A Muster Roll of Captain Andrew Finck's Co. in Colonel Van Schaick's Battalion of Forces, December 17 1776, in the Barracks at Saratoga. M246, Record Group 93, Roll 0077, Folder 163. Private Bastian Algoyer, enlisted March 6, 1776. https://www.fold3.com/image/10188403 ; The National Archives, *Revolutionary War Pension and Bounty-Land Warrant Application Files.,* M804, Record Group 15, Roll 0961. Pg. 5. Pension application of William Feeter. https://www.fold3.com/image/246/18314480

490 Papers of the Continental Congress, 1774-1789, *Letters From Maj. Gen. Philip Schuyler, Vol II, June 1775- December 1776,* 47, 177. NARA M247, Item No. 153, Record Group 360, Roll pcc_345148_0001. https://www.fold3.com/image/1/345957; Papers of the Continental Congress, 1774-1789, *Letters From Maj. Gen. Philip Schuyler, Vol II, June 1775- December 1776,* 81, NARA M247, Item No. 153, Record Group 360, Roll pcc_345148_0001. https://www.fold3.com/image/1/345988 ; Alexander Flick, *Minutes of the Schenectady Committee 1775-1779, Vol II* (Albany, The University of the State of New York, 1925), 1059-1060. https://archive.org/stream/minutes1775177802albauoft#page/1058/mode/2up

491 Ancestry.com. *Records of the Reformed Protestant Dutch Church of Caughnawaga: now the Reformed Church of Fonda, in the village of Fonda, Mon* [database on-line]. Provo, UT. Volume one. Marriages, 1772 to Jan. 31, 1818. 161. 1776, Meert 13, Hendrk Selmser met Anna Maria Ehanisin.

492 Ancestry.com. *UK, American Loyalist Claims, 1776-1835* [database on-line]. Provo, UT. Title: Piece 012: New Claims C·D·E·F, New York. 193. The Memorial of Captain Thomas Gumersall.

493 Ancestry.com. *UK, American Loyalist Claims, 1776-1835* [database on-line]. Provo, UT. The National Archives of the UK; Kew, Surrey, England; American Loyalist Claims, Series II; Class: AO 13; Piece 013: New Claims G·H·J·, New York. 214. The Memorial of Jost Harkimer. Ancestry.com. *UK, American Loyalist Claims, 1776-1835* [database on-line]. Provo, UT. The National Archives of the UK; Kew, Surrey, England; American Loyalist Claims, Series I; Class: AO 13; Piece 031: Evidence, New York, 1787-1788. 315 Claim of Jacob Romborgh.; Ancestry.com. *UK, American Loyalist Claims, 1776-1835* [database on-line]. Provo, UT. The National Archives of the UK; Kew, Surrey, England; American Loyalist Claims, Series I; Class: AO 13; Piece 032: Evidence, New York, 1788. 235. Claim of John Lonnie.; Ancestry.com. *UK, American Loyalist Claims, 1776-1835* [database on-line]. Provo, UT. The National Archives of the UK; Kew, Surrey, England; American Loyalist Claims, Series I; Class: AO 13; Piece 026: Evidence, New York, 1787. 217-219. Claim of Julius Bush. New York State, Calendar of Historical Manuscripts Relating to the War of the Revolution, Vol I (Albany, Weed, Parsons and Company, 1898), 304. https://archive.org/stream/calendarofhistor01newy#page/304/mode/2up ; Ancestry.com. *UK, American Loyalist Claims, 1776-1835* [database on-line]. Provo, UT. The National Archives of the UK; Kew, Surrey, England; American Loyalist Claims, Series I; Class: AO 13; Piece 028: Evidence, New York, 1787. 28. Memorial of Joseph Clement.; Ancestry.com. *UK, American Loyalist Claims, 1776-1835* [database on-line]. Provo, UT. The National Archives of the UK; Kew, Surrey, England; American Loyalist Claims, Series I; Class: AO 13; Piece 029: Evidence, New York, 1787-1788. 160 Claim of John Annable.

494 The National Archives, *Revolutionary War Rolls 1775-1783*, A Muster Roll of Captain Andrew Finck's Co. in Colonel Van Schaick's Battalion of Forces, December 17 1776, in the Barracks at Saratoga. M246, Record

Group 93, Roll 0077, Folder 163. Private Bastian Algoyer, enlisted March 6, 1776, died May 6. https://www.fold3.com/image/10188403

495 Papers of the Continental Congress, 1774-1789, *Letters From Maj. Gen. Philip Schuyler, Vol II, June 1775- December 1776,* 51, 54-55, 59, 77, 85-92. NARA M247, Item No. 153, Record Group 360, Roll pcc_345148_0001. https://www.fold3.com/image/1/345957

496 Papers of the Continental Congress, 1774-1789, *Letters From Maj. Gen. Philip Schuyler, Vol II, June 1775- December 1776,* 153. https://www.fold3.com/image/1/346053

497 Ibid, 150, 157, 158, 169, 171; https://www.fold3.com/image/1/346069 ; Richard Berleth, *Bloody Mohawk. The French and Indian War & American Revolution on New York's Frontier* (Delmar N.Y., Black Dome, 2010), 181-184.

498 Library and Archives Canada, Great Britain War Office (WO 28): *America,* 10860, lac_reel_c10860, C10860, 158960, 125090, 105016, MG 13 WO, 1122-1123, 1140. Muster Rolls of the Royal Regiment of New York. Point Claire 23 Feb 1777. http://heritage.canadiana.ca/view/oocihm.lac_reel_c10860/1122?r=0&s=4; Library and Archives Canada, British Library, formerly British Museum, Additional Manuscripts 21804-21834, *Haldimand Papers,* lac_reel_h1652, H-1652, 105513, 2034239, MG 21. Image 481. A Roll of Non Commissioned Officers, Drummers & Privatemen Inlisted for the 1st Battalion of the King's Royal Regt. Of New York. Point Claire, 17 May 1781. http://heritage.canadiana.ca/view/oocihm.lac_reel_h1652/page/n401/mode/481?r=0&s=5 ; Gavin Watt, *Poisoned By Lies and Hypocrisy. America's First Attempt to Bring Liberty To Canada 1775-1776* (Toronto, Dundern Press, 2014), 163-164.; "The Kings Royal Yorkers." Major John Ross. http://royalyorkers.ca/john_ross.php ; Fryer, Mary & W. Smy (Lieutenant-Colonel), *Rolls of the Provincial (Loyalist) Corps, Canadian Command American Revolutionary Period,* Muster Roll 1st Battalion KRRNY. Enlisted Men, First and Second Battalions, Captain Samuel Anderson's Company. Montreal, December, 1782. 38 (Toronto,

Dundern Press, 1981), Private, Captain Samuel Anderson's Light Company, 1st Battalion King's Royal Regiment of New York. Entry No.11 George Bendor, Born: America, Age: 20; Library and Archives Canada, Audit Office: AO 12. Claims, *American Loyalists Series I* 12904, lac_reel_c12904, C-12904, 105765, 128170, 128171, 128173, MG 14 AO 12, Claim of Michl Carman. http://heritage.canadiana.ca/view/oocihm.lac_reel_c12904/1506?r=0&s=3

499 Library and Archives Canada, *Claus Papers* 1478, lac_reel_c1478, C-1478, 103767, MG 19 F 1, http://heritage.canadiana.ca/view/oocihm.lac_reel_c1478/257?r=0&s=4 "Fifty Acres of Beach and Wood. Discovering the Adirondack Heritage of Indian Point." Tom Thacher, Sir John Johnson's Escape. A Tale Retold. And Why Indian Point? November 25, 2014. https://fiftyacresofbeachandwood.org/tag/mohawk-indians/

500 Papers of the Continental Congress, 1774-1789, *Letters From Maj. Gen. Philip Schuyler, Vol II, June 1775- December 1776,* 161, 163-165, 174, NARA M247, Item No. 153, Record Group 360, Roll pcc_345148_0001. https://www.fold3.com/image/1/346063

501 Ancestry.com. *UK, American Loyalist Claims, 1776-1835* [database on-line]. Provo, UT. The National Archives of the UK; Kew, Surrey, England; American Loyalist Claims, Series I; Class: AO 13; Piece 029: Evidence, New York, 1787-1788.156. Claim of Cathrine Cryderman widow of Valentine Cryderman.

502 Papers of the Continental Congress, 1774-1789, *Letters From Maj. Gen. Philip Schuyler, Vol II, June 1775- December 1776.* 173-174.; Ancestry.com. *UK, American Loyalist Claims, 1776-1835* [database on-line]. Provo, UT. Piece 012: New Claims C·D E·F, New York. 193. Memorial of Captain Thomas Gumersall.

503 Ancestry.com. *UK, American Loyalist Claims, 1776-1835* [database on-line]. Provo, UT. The National Archives of the UK; Kew, Surrey, England; American Loyalist Claims, Series I; Class: AO 13; Piece 028: Evidence, New York, 1787. 51-52. Claim of Margt Hare W of John Hare late of New York; Papers of the Continental Congress, 1774-1789, *Letters*

From Maj. Gen. Philip Schuyler, Vol II, June 1775- December 1776, 159. https://www.fold3.com/image/1/346059 ; Nelson Greene, *The Story of Old Fort Plain and the Middle Mohawk Valley* (Fort Plain, O'Connor Brothers, 1915), 32. http://scans.library.utoronto.ca/pdf/3/21/storyofoldfortpl00greeuoft/storyofoldfortpl00greeuoft.pdf

504 Ancestry.com. *UK, American Loyalist Claims, 1776-1835* [database on-line]. Provo, UT. The National Archives of the UK; Kew, Surrey, England; American Loyalist Claims, Series I; Class: AO 13; Piece 027: Evidence, New York, 1787. 171. Claim of Philip Shover.; Ancestry.com. *U.S., Dutch Reformed Church Records in Selected States, 1639-1989* [database on-line]. Provo, UT. The Archives of the Reformed Church in America; New Brunswick, New Jersey; Fonda Church, Baptisms, Marriages, 1797-1872. 257. 1776 Oct 29, Philip Shaver, Elizabeth Angst; Peter, born Sept 27; Ancestry.com. *UK, American Loyalist Claims, 1776-1835* [database on-line]. Provo, UT. The National Archives of the UK; Kew, Surrey, England; American Loyalist Claims, Series I; Class: AO 13; Piece 029: Evidence, New York, 1787-1788. Claim of Cathrine Cryderman widow of Valentine Cryderman.

505 "Records of the Reformed Dutch Church of Albany, New York, 1683-1809." (Excerpted from the Year Books of the Holland Society of New York)." Baptismal Record Since the Year 1725. 1738 May 28. Johannes, of Johannes and Catharyna Hogh. Wit: Lodewyck and Hiltje Schriddel. https://mathcs.clarku.edu/~djoyce/gen/albany/part3.html#marriage ; Ancestry.com. *UK, American Loyalist Claims, 1776-1835* [database on-line]. Provo, UT. The National Archives of the UK; Kew, Surrey, England; American Loyalist Claims, Series I; Class: AO 13; Piece 028: Evidence, New York, 1787. 213-214. Claim of John Hough.; Library and Archives Canada, *Upper Canada Land Petitions (1763-1865).* Mikan No. 205131, Microform c-2043, 924. Memorial of John Hough Private Soldier in the late 2nd Battalion KR Reg of NewYork. Fredericksburg, 21 March 1797.

506 New York State, *Calendar of Historical Manuscripts Relating to the War of the Revolution, Vol I* (Albany, Weed, Parsons & Company, 1868),

525. https://archive.org/stream/calendarofhistor01newy#page/524/mode/2up

507 Library and Archives Canada, *Daniel Claus and Family Fonds*: C-1478, Claus Papers, 1478. Lac_reel_c1478, C1478, 103767, MG 19 F1. Image 257. http://heritage.canadiana.ca/view/oocihm.lac_reel_c1478/257?r=0&s=5 ; "Fifty Acres of Beach and Wood. Discovering the Adirondack Heritage of Indian Point." Tom Thacher, Sir John Johnson's Escape. A Tale Retold. And Why Indian Point? November 25, 2014. https://fiftyacresofbeachandwood.org/tag/mohawk-indians/

508 E. A. Cruikshank, *The King's Royal Regiment of New York*. ed. Gavin Watt, (Toronto, The Ontario Historical Society, 1931) Reprinted Toronto, 1984, 10. Gavin Watt, *Rebellion in the Mohawk Valley. The St. Leger Expedition of 1777*. Toronto: Dundern Press, 2002). 32-33.

509 "The King's Royal Yorkers." Allan S Joyner, Recreating the KRR: A Research Driven Interpretation. James Kochan, Uniforms and Arms of the King's Royal Regiment of New York. http://royalyorkers.ca/regiment_recreating.php

510 New York State, *Calendar of Historical Manuscripts Relating to the War of the Revolution, Vol I* (Albany, Weed, Parsons & Company, 1868), 520. https://archive.org/stream/calendarofhistor01newy#page/520/mode/2up ; "Three Rivers, Hudson, Mohawk, Schoharie, History From America's Most Famous Valleys." Lead http://threeriversshms.com/nyrevlead.htm

511 No baptismal record for Daniel Alguire was found; however, he petitioned for land as the son of a UE Loyalist on 12 May 1800. He would have had to be at least 21 years old to petition for land which means he was born by 1779. There is a record of his sister Maria Salome's birth in 1770 and Elizabeth's birth in 1779 and his brothers Philip 1771, John 1773 and Peter 1775; therefore, I assume Daniel was born ca. 1776. ; No Baptismal record was found for Johannes Alguire. It was difficult to determine his date of birth; however his parents were married 4 Jan 1774 and had a daughter Dorothy Victoria in 1779; therefore, I assume

he was born ca. 1776. Determining correct documentation of his arrival in Canada or his marriage or death was also difficult as there were four John Alguires in Cornwall Township: John Alguire brother of Johannes George, both sons of John Alguire, and John son of Martin Alguire.

512 James Sullivan, *Minutes of the Albany Committee of Correspondence 1775-1778, Vol I* (Albany, The University of the State of New York, 1923), 502-503. https://archive.org/stream/MinutesOfTheAlbanyCommitteeOfCorrespondence1775-1778Vol1#page/n523/mode/2up; Ancestry.com. *UK, American Loyalist Claims, 1776-1835* [database on-line]. Provo, UT. *Piece 011: New Claims A·B·C, New York.* Memorial of Joseph Anderson late Capt in the Kings Royal Regt of New York. 30. Correspondence between prisoners and the Committee, 31-35. List of prisoners and their crimes, 35-39. Ancestry.com. *Register of baptisms, marriages, communicants, & funerals begun by Henry Barclay at Fort Hunter, January 26th, 1734 /5: regist* [database on-line]. Provo, UT. Register book. 20. February 24, 1739/40, Owen, son of Owen Conner deceased, baptized 2 March 1739/40. Capt. Walter Butler, Walter Butler Jr., Rebecca Wemp, Surties. "Northern Illinois University Digital Library." Amerian Archives. V6:1073. List of Tories from Tryon County sent to Hartford, June 25, 1776. Document ID: S4-V6-P02-sp13-D0213.

513 Library and Archives Canada, British Library, formerly British Museum, Additional Manuscripts 21804-21834, Haldimand Papers, 1652. Lac_reel_h1652, H-1652, 105513, 2034239, MG 21. Image 279. A List of New Names Arrived From Johnstown, April 1777. http://heritage.canadiana.ca/view/oocihm.lac_reel_h1652/279?r=0&s=5 ; Richard Phelps, *Newgate of Connecticut; Its Origin and Early History* (American Publishing Company, 1876), 25-58. https://archive.org/stream/newgateofconnect00pheliala#page/n9/mode/2up "The People of Colonial Albany Live Here," The Fort at Albany. https://exhibitions.nysm.nysed.gov/albany/loc/fortalbany.html

514 Alexander Flick, The Papers of Sir William Johnson, Vol VI (Albany, The University of the State of New York, 1928), 70. https://archive.org/stream/papersofsirwilli06johnuoft#page/70/mode/2up; New York

Historical Society, *Minutes of the Committee and of the First Commission For Detecting and Defeating Conspiracies in the State of New York December 11, 1776-September 23, 1778. Vol I* (New York, Collections of the New York Historical Society For the Year 1924), 28. http://archive.org/stream/minutesofcommitt571newy#page/28/mode/2up

515 New York Historical Society, *Minutes of the Committee and of the First Commission For Detecting and Defeating Conspiracies in the State of New York December 11, 1776-September 23, 1778. Vol I* (New York, Collections of the New York Historical Society For the Year 1924), 50-51. http://archive.org/stream/minutesofcommitt571newy#page/50/mode/2up "The Online Institute For Advanced Loyalist Studies." Return of Department of Indian Affairs. 4 Oct 1776. Original Source: Great Britain, Public Record Office, Headquarters Papers of the British Army in America, PRO 30/55/10209. http://www.royalprovincial.com/military/rhist/dian/dianretn5.htm

516 Jepha R. Simms, *The Frontiersmen of New York. Showing Customs of the Indians, Vicissitudes of the Pioneer White Settlers and Border Strife in Two Wars* (Albany, Geo. C. Riggs, 1888), 12; Isabel Thompson Kelsay, *Joseph Brant 1743-1807 Man of Two Worlds* (Syracuse, Syracuse University Press, 1984), 186-187. https://archive.org/stream/frontiersmennew00simmgoog#page/n15/mode/2up ; "American Archives. Documents of the American Revolutionary Period, 1774-1776." A True Copy of a Letter Wrote by Aaron Kanonaron, a Mohawk Chief From Niagara, to his Brother David. http://amarch.lib.niu.edu/islandora/object/niu-amarch%3A94663; Ibid, A Speech of Ojistarale, the Grasshopper, an Oneida Chief to Colonel Elmore, Commandant of Fort Schuyler. http://amarch.lib.niu.edu/islandora/object/niu-amarch%3A90375 R. Arthur Bowler and Bruce G. Wilson, "BUTLER, JOHN (d. 1796)," in *Dictionary of Canadian Biography*, vol. 4, University of Toronto/Université Laval, 2003, accessed April 20, 2018, http://www.biographi.ca/en/bio/butler_john_1796_4E.html

517 Library of Archives Canada, Audit Office: AO 12. *Claims, American Loyalists,* Series I, 12904, lac_reel_c12904, 105765, 128170,

128171, 128173, MG 14 AO 12, Image 1313, Claim of Philip Shaver; http://heritage.canadiana.ca/view/oocihm.lac_reel_c12904/1313?r=0&s=3;Ibid, Claim of John Fraser, http://heritage.canadiana.ca/view/oocihm.lac_reel_c12904/1327?r=0&s=3; Ancestry.com. *UK, American Loyalist Claims, 1776-1835* [database on-line]. Provo, UT. The National Archives of the UK; Kew, Surrey, England; American Loyalist Claims, Series II; Class: AO 13; Piece 013: New Claims G H J, New York. 214-215. The Memorial of Jost Harkimer.

518 Library and Archives Canada, Great Britain War Office (WO 28): *America,* lac_reel_c10860, C10860, 158960, 125090, 105016, MG 13 WO, Image 420, His Majesty's Royal Regiment of New York, Commanded by Lt. Col. Sir John Johnson, Point Clare, 23 Febry 1777. Muster Roll. http://heritage.canadiana.ca/view/oocihm.lac_reel_c10860/1122?r=0&s=3 ; The Magazine of American History With Notes and Queries. Vol VI. *Orderly Book For Lieut. Col. Sir John Johnson's Company* 1776-1777. 283-284. https://archive.org/stream/magazineofameric06stev#page/282/mode/2up; Library and Archives Canada, *Great Britain, War Office* (WO 28) lac_reel_c10861, 158960, 125090, MG 13 WO. Image 1093, The Memorial of the Volunteers Under the Command of Lieut. Col. Jessup. http://heritage.canadiana.ca/view/oocihm.lac_reel_c10861/1093?r=0&s=3 ; Ibid, British Library, formerly British Museum, *Additional Manuscripts 21804-21834, Haldimand Papers,* Lac_reel_h1654, H-1654, 105513, 2034239, MG 21, Image 944. Subsistence Roll Jessups' Corp. http://heritage.canadiana.ca/view/oocihm.lac_reel_h1654/944?r=0&s=5

519 New York (State). *Comptroller's Office. New York In the Revolution As Colony And State: Supplement.* (Albany, N.Y.: O.A. Quayle, 1901), 242-250. https://babel.hathitrust.org/cgi/pt?id=coo.31924032737938;view=1up;seq=246

520 Ancestry.com. *UK, American Loyalist Claims, 1776-1835* [database on-line]. Provo, UT. The National Archives of the UK; Kew, Surrey, England; American Loyalist Claims, Series II; Class: AO 13; Piece 012:

New Claims C D E F·, New York. 382-385. Account of the Losses of John Farlinger.

521 New York (State). *Comptroller's Office. New York In the Revolution As Colony And State: Supplement.* (Albany, N.Y.: O.A. Quayle, 1901), 246-249.

522 State of New York, *Public Papers of George Clinton, First Governor of New York, 1777-1795, - 1801-1804* (Albany, Wynkoop, Hallenbeck, Crawford Co.), 290-292. https://archive.org/stream/cu31924014576684#page/n349/mode/2up ; Library and Archives Canada, British Library (Formerly British Museum) *Haldimand Papers,* Lac_reel_h1743, H-1743, 105513, 2034239, Image 1264, The Petition of Michael Carman Loyalist. http://heritage.canadiana.ca/view/oocihm.lac_reel_h1743/1264?r=0&s=4 ; Ancestry.com. *UK, American Loyalist Claims, 1776-1835* [database on-line]. Provo, UT. The National Archives of the UK; Kew, Surrey, England; American Loyalist Claims, Series II; Class: AO 13; Piece 081: New Claims, Canada.74-75. The Memorial of Christian Dillebach.

523 Library and Archives Canada, Great Britain, War Office (WO 28): *America,* Lac_reel_c10861, 158960, 125090, MG 13 WO. Image 1165; http://heritage.canadiana.ca/view/oocihm.lac_reel_c10861/1165?r=0&s=3 ; Ancestry.com. *UK, American Loyalist Claims, 1776-1835* [database on-line]. Provo, UT. The National Archives of the UK; Kew, Surrey, England; American Loyalist Claims, Series I; Class: AO 13; Piece 029: Evidence, New York, 1787-1788. 42-44. Claim of William Fraser Sr.; Ancestry.com. *UK, American Loyalist Claims, 1776-1835* [database on-line]. Provo, UT. The National Archives of the UK; Kew, Surrey, England; American Loyalist Claims, Series II; Class: AO 13; Piece: 012. New Claims C D E·F, New York. 502-508. The Memorial of William Fraser Senior, a Loyalist and William and Thomas Fraser late Captains in His Majesty's Loyal Rangers.; "The Online Institute For Advanced Loyalist Studies." McAlpin's Corps of Royalists. Batteau Men. 16 Aug 1777. Original Source: Great Britain, British Library, Additional

Manuscripts, No. 21827, folio 122. http://www.royalprovincial.com/military/rhist/mcalpin/mcform.htm

524 Gavin Watt, *Rebellion in the Mohawk Valley: The St. Leger Expedition of 1777* (Toronto, The Dundurn Group, 2002), 143.

525 Library and Archives Canada, British Library, formerly British Museum, Additional Manuscripts 21804-21834, *Haldimand Papers,* Lac_reel_h1652, H-1652, 105513, 2034239, MG 21, Image 279-282; 283-285. http://heritage.canadiana.ca/view/oocihm.lac_reel_h1652/280?r=0&s=6 ; Ken D. Johnson, "Fort Plank Bastion of My Freedom, Colonial Canajoharie, New York." Mohawk Valley Maps and Sketches. The Hermanus Van Slyck & Abraham Depeyster Patent. Lot 22 Peter Davis. http://www.fort-plank.com/Van_Slyck_Patent_COF.html

526 Library and Archives Canada, British Library, formerly British Museum, Additional Manuscripts 21804-21834, *Haldimand Papers,* Lac_reel_h1652, H-1652, 105513, 2034239, MG 21, Image 286. http://heritage.canadiana.ca/view/oocihm.lac_reel_h1652/286?r=0&s=6 ; E.A. Cruikshank, E.A., *The King's Royal Regiment of New York.* ed. Gavin Watt (Toronto, The Ontario Historical Society, 1931) Reprinted Toronto, 1984, Enlistment dates in KRRNY, 6 May 1777, Conradt Snyder, Michael Ault, John Hartle, George Wait, Joseph Wait, Michael Warner, Jacob A. Waggoner, John Peascod.

527 Ancestry.com. *UK, American Loyalist Claims, 1776-1835* [database on-line]. Provo, UT. The National Archives of the UK; Kew, Surrey, England; American Loyalist Claims, Series I; Class: AO 13; Piece 024: Evidence, New York, 1786-1787. 243-247. The Meml of the Rev. John M. McKenna.; Ancestry.com. *UK, American Loyalist Claims, 1776-1835* [database on-line]. Provo, UT. The National Archives of the UK; Kew, Surrey, England; American Loyalist Claims, Series I; Class: AO 13; Piece 019: Evidence, New York, 1783-1784. 32-33.Evidence on the foregoing Memorial of the Revd. John Doty.; Alexander Flick, *Minutes of the Schenectady Committee 1775-1779, Vol II* (Albany, The University of the State of New York, 1925),1098-1099. https://archive.org/stream/minu

tes1775177802albauoft#page/1098/mode/2up ; Library and Archives Canada, British Library (Formerly British Museum) Haldimand Papers. Lac_reel_h1743, H-1743, 105513, 2034239, Image 1337. http://heritage.canadiana.ca/view/oocihm.lac_reel_h1743/1337?r=0&s=4

528 For enlistment dates of many of the soldiers of the 1st Battalion see: "The Online Institute For Advanced Loyalist Studies." Kings Royal Regiment of New York Muster Rolls. http://www.royalprovincial.com/military/musters/krrny/mrkrrmain.htm ; Ancestry.com. *UK, American Loyalist Claims, 1776-1835* [database on-line]. Provo, UT. The National Archives of the UK; Kew, Surrey, England; American Loyalist Claims, Series II; Class: AO 13; Piece 079: Letters, Etc. The Memorial of John McDonel Capt. Late of the 1st Batn. K.R.Rt. of New York. 398-399.; Ancestry.com. *UK, American Loyalist Claims, 1776-1835* [database on-line]. Provo, UT. The National Archives of the UK; Kew, Surrey, England; American Loyalist Claims, Series I; Class: AO 13; Piece 032: Evidence, New York, 1788. 227-228. Evidence on the Claim of John Ault.; Ancestry.com. *UK, American Loyalist Claims, 1776-1835* [database on-line]. Provo, UT. Piece 032: Evidence, New York, 1788. 224-225. Evidence on the Claim of Luke Bowen.; Maryly B. Penrose, *Compendium of Early Mohawk Valley Families. Vol I* (Baltimore, Genealogical Publishing Co., 1990), 233; E.A. Cruikshank, *The King's Royal Regiment of New York.* ed. Gavin Watt, (Toronto, The Ontario Historical Society, 1931) Reprinted Toronto, 1984, 179, 194-195.; Alexander Flick, *The Papers of Sir William Johnson, Vol VIII* (Albany, The University of the State of New York, 1933), 172. https://archive.org/stream/papersofsirwilli08johnuoft#page/172/mode/2up ; Ken D. Johnson, "Fort Plank Bastion of My Freedom, Colonial Canajoharie, New York." Mohawk Valley Maps and Sketches. The Hermanus Van Slyck & Abraham Depeyster Patent. Lot 26 Wilhelmes Kasselman, Lot 16 Sufrenes Kasselman. http://www.fort-plank.com/Van_Slyck_Patent_COF.html ; Ken D. Johnson, "Fort Plank Bastion of My Freedom, Colonial Canajoharie, New York." Additional Partisans H-M. "Seferenus Kasselman, Map #12 drawn for the Commissioners of Forfeitures by New York Deputy Surveyor General Isaac Vrooman shows that at the time of the American Revolution,

Sefernus occupied a house in Woodland Lot 3 of the DePeyster Division of the Harmanus Van Slyck/Abraham DePeyster Patent (Surveyor General's Maps, #872)." http://www.fort-plank.com/Additional_Partisans_H_M.html

529 Many tenants of Kingsborough and Philadelphia Bush enlisted in Fonda's Associated Exempts. This company was for men between the age of 50 and 60 and were only called for service during an invasion. Maya Jasanoff, *Liberty's Exiles. American Loyalists in the Revolutionary World* (New York, Alfred A. Knopf, 2011), 8-9, 23; The National Archives, *Revolutionary War Rolls, 1775-1783*, M246, Record Group 93, Roll 0074, Folder 100, 118-119. Payroll of Capt. Jellis Fonda's company of Associated Exempts. Aug 10-Aug15 1777. https://www.fold3.com/image/10074302 ; "Fulton County NYGenWeb" James F. Morrison, Jellis Fonda. http://fulton.nygenweb.net/military/jellis.html

530 Isabel Thompson Kelsay, *Joseph Brant 1743-1807 Man of Two Worlds* (Syracuse, Syracuse University Press, 1984), 188-192. Gavin Watt, *Rebellion in the Mohawk Valley: The St. Leger Expedition of 1777* (Toronto, The Dundurn Group, 2002), 57-63.

531 Ancestry.com. *UK, American Loyalist Claims, 1776-1835* [database on-line]. Provo, UT. The National Archives of the UK; Kew, Surrey, England; American Loyalist Claims, Series I; Class: AO 13; Piece 033: Evidence, North Carolina, 1788. 213-215. Evidence on the claim of Jonas Wood.; Library and Archives Canada, *Upper Canada Land Petitions (1763-1865)*, Mikan Number 205131, Microform c-2045, 350-351, 312-313, Mikan Number 205131, Microform c-2107, 747. Petition of John Huff/Hough.; Library and Archives Canada, British Library (Formerly British Museum) *Haldimand Papers.* Lac_reel_h1743, H-1743, 105513, 2034239. Image 1401. Memorial of Hendrick Huff of Tryon County. Recommended by Captain Brant. http://heritage.canadiana.ca/view/oocihm.lac_reel_h1743/1401?r=0&s=3 ; Secretary of State, *Calendar of Historical Manuscripts Relating to the War of the Revolution, Vol II* (Albany, Weed, Parsons and Company, 1868), 135. https://archive.org/stream/cu31924092740640#page/134/mode/2up ; Hugh Hastings,

Public Papers of George Clinton, First Governor of New York, 1777-1795, 1801-1804, For Treason Against the State, More Traitors Sentenced to Death (New York, Wynkoop, Hallenback Crawford Company, 1899), 749-762, 765-782. https://archive.org/stream/publicpapersofge01newy1#page/762/mode/2up ; Neil Larson, *Building a Stone House in Ulster County, New York in 1751*. https://www.arct.cam.ac.uk/Downloads/ichs/vol-2-1867-1882-larson.pdf ; Ancestry.com. *UK, American Loyalist Claims, 1776-1835* [database on-line]. Provo, UT. The National Archives of the UK; Kew, Surrey, England; American Loyalist Claims, Series I; Class: AO 13; Piece 029: Evidence, New York, 1787-1788. 272-275. Evidence on the claim of Geo. Barnhart.; Ancestry.com. *UK, American Loyalist Claims, 1776-1835* [database on-line]. Provo, UT. The National Archives of the UK; Kew, Surrey, England; American Loyalist Claims, Series I; Class: AO 13; Piece 032: Evidence, New York, 1788. 24-27. Evidence on the Claim of Martin Middagh on behalf of Henry, Charles, Rachel, & Mary Bush children of the late Henry Bush.; Ancestry.com. *UK, American Loyalist Claims, 1776-1835* [database on-line]. Provo, UT. The National Archives of the UK; Kew, Surrey, England; American Loyalist Claims, Series II; Class: AO 13; Piece 014: New Claims K· M· N· O·, New York. 322. The Memorial of Martin Middock on behalf of Henry, Charles, Rachel and Mary orphaned children of Henry Bush and Nelly his wife; Ancestry.com. *UK, American Loyalist Claims, 1776-1835* [database on-line]. Provo, UT. The National Archives of the UK; Kew, Surrey, England; American Loyalist Claims, Series I; Class: AO 13; Piece 029: Evidence, New York, 1787-1788. 337-338.Evidence on the Claim of John Glasford Jr.; Ancestry.com. *UK, American Loyalist Claims, 1776-1835* [database on-line]. Provo, UT. The National Archives of the UK; Kew, Surrey, England; American Loyalist Claims, Series II; Class: AO 13; Piece 015: New Claims P·Q·R S·, New York.327. The Memorial of Daniel Servos late of Charlotte River.

532 Isabel Thompson Kelsay, *Joseph Brant 1743-1807, Man of Two Worlds* (Syracuse, Syracuse University Press, 1984), 193-195.

533 Gavin Watt, *Rebellion in the Mohawk Valley: The St. Leger Expedition of 1777* (Toronto, The Dundurn Group, 2002), 116-117, 136-137.

Richard Berleth, *Bloody Mohawk. The French and Indian War & American Revolution on New York's Frontier* (Delmar N.Y., Black Dome, 2010), 207.

534 Isabel Thompson Kelsay, *Joseph Brant 1743-1807 Man of Two Worlds,* 200-201.; New York (State). Legislature. *Journals of the Provincial Congress, Provincial Convention, Committee of Safety And Council of Safety of the State of New-York: 1775-1775-1777.* (Albany: Thurlow Weed, 1842), 1006-1007. https://babel.hathitrust.org/cgi/pt?id=nnc2.ark:/13960/t1sf5hz5r;view=1up;seq=1019

535 The National Archives, Revolutionary War Rolls, 1775-1783, M246, Record Group 93, Roll 0074, Folder 100, 118-119. *Payroll of Capt. Jellis Fonda's company of Associated Exempts. Aug 10-Aug15 1777.* https://www.fold3.com/image/10074294 ; Gavin Watt, *Rebellion in the Mohawk Valley.* 143.; The National Archives, *Revolutionary War Pension and Bounty Land Warrant Application Files,* NARA M804, Record Group 15, Roll 1987, pg 2-3, Declaration Nelly Putman. https://www.fold3.com/image/246/27763463 ; Ibid, Roll 0945, pg 24-25. Adam Everson. https://www.fold3.com/image/246/17230630?xid=1945

536 William L. Stone, *The Orderly Book of Sir John Johnson During the Oriskany Campaign 1776-1777* (Albany, Joel Munsell's Sons, 1882), 3-98. https://archive.org/stream/orderlybookofsir00johnuoft#page/n209/mode/2up;"The King's Royal Yorkers." Articles - The Companies of the 1st Battalion KRRNY. http://royalyorkers.ca/companies_1bn.php ; Captain Richard Duncan's Coy. http://royalyorkers.ca/duncans.php; "The Online Institute For Advanced Loyalist Studies." Loyalist Muster Rolls Kings Royal Regiment of New York. http://www.royalprovincial.com/military/musters/krrny/mrkrrmain.htm ; Gavin Watt, *Rebellion in the Mohawk Valley: The St. Leger Expedition of 1777* (Toronto, The Dundurn Group, 2002), 148-149, 155-171, 317; Library and Archives Canada, *Haldimand Loyalist Lists (Index),* lac_reel c1475, C1475, 105513, 2034239, MG 21 Add.MSS.21661-21892, List to draw pay of the undermentioned persons, officers now serving in the Indian Department in the Indian Country and at Niagara, 1777. http://heritage.canadiana.ca/view/oocihm.lac_reel_c1475/360?r=3&s=4 ; E.A.

Cruikshank, E.A., *The King's Royal Regiment of New York.* ed. Gavin Watt (Toronto, The Ontario Historical Society, 1931) Reprinted Toronto, 1984, 259.; Ancestry.com. *UK, American Loyalist Claims, 1776-1835* [database on-line]. Provo, UT. The National Archives of the UK; Kew, Surrey, England; American Loyalist Claims, Series I; Class: AO 13; Piece 028: Evidence, New York, 1787. Evidence on the claim of Margt. Hare W. of John Hare late of New York.; "Three Rivers Hudson, Mohawk, Schoharie. History From America's Most Famous Valleys." Roster of Oriskay Heroes. http://www.threerivershms.com/namesoriskany.htm ; Ken D. Johnson, "Fort Plank Bastion of my Freedom. Colonial Canajoharie, New York." Recent Discoveries in Mohawk Valley History. Tryon County List of Prisoners of War, February 20, 1782. http://www.fort-plank.com/1782_POW_List.html ; The State of New York, *Public Papers of George Clinton, First Governor of New York, 1777-1795-1801-1804,* Further Particulars From Oriskany (Albany, Wynkoop, Hallenback, Crawford Co., 1900), 203-204. https://archive.org/stream/cu31924014576684#page/n261/mode/2up ; Richard Berleth, *Bloody Mohawk. The French and Indian War & American Revolution on New York's Frontier* (Delmar N.Y., Black Dome, 2010), 212-237, 243; "Find A Grave." Pvt. Jacob Empie https://www.findagrave.com/memorial/94927959 ; The National Archives, *Revolutionary War Rolls 1775-1783,* Folder 103, Page 3, 1776, Gettman's Company of Rangers. https://www.fold3.com/image/246/10074457?xid=1945 ; Henry Schoolcraft, *Historical Considerations on the Siege and Defense of Fort Stanwix 1777* (New York, New York Historical Society, 1846), 3-29. https://archive.org/stream/historicalconsid01scho#page/n9/mode/2up

537 Richard Berleth, *Bloody Mohawk. The French and Indian War & American Revolution on New York's Frontier*, 200, 242-243; Ken D. Johnson, "Fort Plank Bastion of my Freedom. Colonial Canajoharie, New York." Memorandum of Indians Killed in the Battle of Oriskany. http://www.fort-plank.com/Fondas_Memo_Of_Indians_Killed.html ; Isabel Thompson Kelsay, *Joseph Brant 1743-1807 Man of Two Worlds* (Syracuse, Syracuse University Press, 1984), 205-206.

538 State of New York, *Public Papers of George Clinton, First Governor of New York, 1777-1795, - 1801-1804,* Desolation in Tryon County, Tryon County in a Deplorable Condition (Albany, Wynkoop, Hallenbeck, Crawford Co.), 262-264, 283-286. https://archive.org/stream/cu31924014576684#page/n341/mode/2up; Gavin Watt, *Rebellion in the Mohawk Valley: The St. Leger Expedition of 1777* (Toronto, The Dundurn Group, 2002), 224-229, 233-234, 236-238.; The National Archives, Revolutionary War Pension and Bounty Land Warrant Application Files, M804, Pension No. S. 13013, Record Group 15, Roll 0961, page 6. William Feeter; https://www.fold3.com/image/246/18314481 ; Gavin Watt, *Fire & Desolation. The Revolutionary War's 1778 Campaign as Waged from Quebec and Niagara Against the American Frontiers* (Toronto, Dundurn, 2017), 103-104.; Isabel Thompson Kelsay, *Joseph Brant 1743-1807 Man of Two Worlds,* 222.; E.A. Cruikshank, *The King's Royal Regiment of New York.* Gavin Watt, ed. (Toronto, The Ontario Historical Society, 1931) Reprinted Toronto, 1984, 172, 181.

539 Gavin Watt, *Rebellion in the Mohawk Valley: The St. Leger Expedition of* 1777, 226-227, 392; Library and Archives Canada, British Library (Formerly British Museum) *Haldimand Papers,* Lac_reel_h1743, H-1743, 105513, 2034239, Image 1122-1123, 1253-1256. The humble Petition of Philip Empy. http://heritage.canadiana.ca/view/oocihm.lac_reel_h1743/1122?r=0&s=4

540 Ken D. Johnson, "Fort Plank Bastion of My Freedom, Colonial Canajoharie, New York." Mohawk Valley Maps and Sketches. The Hermanus Van Slyck & Abraham Depeyster Patent. Lot 26 Wilhelmes Kasselman, Lot 16 Sufrenes Kasselman. http://www.fort-plank.com/Van_Slyck_Patent_COF.html; Ancestry.com. *UK, American Loyalist Claims, 1776-1835* [database on-line]. Provo, UT. The National Archives of the UK; Kew, Surrey, England; American Loyalist Claims, Series I; Class: AO 13; Piece 033: Evidence, North Carolina, 1788. 163-165. Evidence on the Claim of Warner Casselman.; Ancestry.com. *UK, American Loyalist Claims, 1776-1835* [database on-line]. Provo, UT. The National Archives of the UK; Kew, Surrey, England; American Loyalist Claims, Series I; Class: AO 13; Piece 028: Evidence,

New York, 1787. 413-415. Evidence on the Claim of Philip Impey Sr.; The National Archives, *Revolutionary War Rolls, 1775-1783,* Folder 121, p. 2, Klock's Regiment of Militia. https://www.fold3.com/image/246/10239918?xid=1945

541 Gavin Watt, *Fire & Desolation. The Revolutionary War's 1778 Campaign as Waged from Quebec and Niagara Against the American Frontiers* (Toronto, Dundurn, 2017), 98-100.; Library and Archives Canada, *Haldimand papers from the British Library,* Lac_reel_h1431, H1431, 105513, 2034239, MG 21. Image 239-240. http://heritage.canadiana.ca/view/oocihm.lac_reel_h1431/239?r=0&s=5.; E. Cruickshank, *Butler's Rangers. The Revolutionary Period* (Welland Ont, Tribune Printing House, 1893). https://www.gutenberg.ca/ebooks/cruikshank-butlers/cruikshank-butlers-00-h-dir/cruikshank-butlers-00-h.html ; Manuscripts and Archives Division, The New York Public Library. *The Memorial of Lieut. Col John Butler, Butler, John. Niagara, Quebec,* New York Public Library Digital Collections. Accessed April 29, 2018. http://digitalcollections.nypl.org/items/4a8f9c00-3321-0133-4e41-58d385a7b928 ; Manuscripts and Archives Division, The New York Public Library. "Carleton, Guy. Quebec" Walter Butler's Commission as Captain in the corp of rangers. New York Public Library Digital Collections. Accessed April 29, 2018. http://digitalcollections.nypl.org/items/be1faf30-348c-0133-fdc8-58d385a7b928

542 Ancestry.com. UK, *American Loyalist Claims, 1776-1835* [database on-line]. Provo, UT. The National Archives of the UK; Kew, Surrey, England; American Loyalist Claims, Series I; Class: AO 13; Piece 027: Evidence, New York, 1787. 204-205. Evidence on the Claim of Wm Philips late of New York; Audit Office: AO 12. *Claims, American Loyalists, Series I,* Lac_reel_c12904, C-12904, 105765, 128170, 128171, 128173, MG 14, AO 12, An Estimate of Losses Sustained by William Philips Late of Johnstown. http://heritage.canadiana.ca/view/oocihm.lac_reel_c12904/1503?r=0&s=3

543 The Archives of the Reformed Church in America; New Brunswick, New Jersey; *Reformed Church of Fonda, Baptisms, Marriages, Members,*

Consistory Minutes, 1758-1839, 21. 1777, Nov 2, Michael Myers, Elizabeth Emer, Maragriet b. Oct 11, Daniel McGregory, Maragriet Emer.

544 Gavin Watt, *Rebellion in the Mohawk Valley: The St. Leger Expedition of 1777* (Toronto, The Dundurn Group, 2002), 250-261.

545 Ancestry.com. *UK, American Loyalist Claims, 1776-1835* [database on-line]. Provo, UT. The National Archives of the UK; Kew, Surrey, England; American Loyalist Claims, Series I; Class: AO 13; Piece 028: Evidence, New York, 1787. 413-415. Evidence on the Claim of Philip Impey Sr.; Maya Jasanoff, *Liberty's Exiles. American Loyalists in the Revolutionary World* (New York, Alfred A. Knopf, 2011), 40; Library and Archives Canada, British Library (Formerly British Museum) *Haldimand Papers,* Lac_reel_h1743, H-1743, 105513, 2034239, Image 1122-1123. The humble Petition of Philip Empy. http://heritage.canadiana.ca/view/oocihm.lac_reel_h1743/1122?r=0&s=4

546 The National Archives, *Revolutionary War Pension and Bounty Land Applications,* NARA M804, Record Group 15, Roll 2175, pg 12. Henry Shew. https://www.fold3.com/image/246/15631303 ; Ibid, Roll 2112, pg 20, Frederick Sammons.; Ibid, Roll 2151, pg 7, 14. John Servoss, https://www.fold3.com/image/246/14424468?xid=1945; "The Town of Mohawk" 138, http://threeriversshms.com/twnmohawk.pdf

547 Ancestry.com. *UK, American Loyalist Claims, 1776-1835* [database on-line]. Provo, UT. The National Archives of the UK; Kew, Surrey, England; American Loyalist Claims, Series I; Class: AO 13; Piece 021: Evidence, New York, 1785-1786. The Memorial of Philip Cooke, late of Canajoharie.

548 Library and Archives Canada, Great Britain War Office (WO 28) *America,* Lac_reel_c10860, C-10860, 158960, 125090, 105016, MG 13 WO, Image 1144, 1156. http://heritage.canadiana.ca/view/oocihm.lac_reel_c10860/1156?r=0&s=3; Ibid, Lac_reel 10861, Image 1493. http://heritage.canadiana.ca/view/oocihm.lac_reel_c10861/1493?r=0&s=3; Gavin Watt, *Fire & Desolation. The Revolutionary War's 1778 Campaign as*

Waged from Quebec and Niagara Against the American Frontiers (Toronto, Dundurn, 2017), 32, 110.

549 Isabel Thompson Kelsay, *Joseph Brant 1743-1807 Man of Two Worlds* (Syracuse, Syracuse University Press, 1984), 214.

550 Gavin Watt, *Fire & Desolation. The Revolutionary War's 1778 Campaign as Waged from Quebec and Niagara Against the American Frontiers* (Toronto, Dundurn, 2017), 137-142.; The affidavit of Hendrik Matthias states that Nicholas and Philip Frymire were seen with Butler on 4 June 1778. However, a petition written at Beauport, Quebec on 13 June 1778 by the men of Captain John McDonells contains the signatures of Nicholas and Philip Frymire indicating they were in Quebec with the KRRNY. The State of New York, Hugh Hastings, *Public Papers of George Clinton, First Governor of New York, 1777-1795, 1801-1804, Vol III,* (Albany, James B. Lyon, 1900), Affidavit of Hendrik Matthias. The Invasion of Tryon County (New York, Wynkoop, Hallenback Crawford Company, 1899), 413-415, 423-425. https://archive.org/stream/georgeclinton03newy#page/422/mode/2up; New York Historical Society, *Register of Lands in 3 Parts, 1761-1789,* Series IV: Bound volumes, 1754-1843, undated. 2267-268. Schnevis's Creek and Cobus Kill. http://digitalcollections.nyhistory.org/islandora/object/islandora%3A121904

551 Gavin Watt, *Fire & Desolation. The Revolutionary War's 1778 Campaign as Waged from Quebec and Niagara Against the American Frontiers,* 126.; The State of New York, Hugh Hastings, *Public Papers of George Clinton,* 414.; New York State Archives. New York (State). State Engineer and Surveyor. *Survey maps of lands in New York State, ca. 1711-1913.* Series A0273-78, NYSA_A0273-78_894, Map #894. Map of Grants to Philip Livingston and Frederick Young. http://digitalcollections.archives.nysed.gov/index.php/Detail/Object/Show/object_id/37479

552 The State of New York, Hugh Hastings, *Public Papers of George Clinton,* Brant and His Allies on the Warpath. Springfield Destroyed. Colonel

Klock Sounds a Cry of Alarm. 475-476, 555-557, 559. https://archive.org/stream/georgeclinton03newy#page/474/mode/2up

553 The National Archives, *Revolutionary War Rolls, 1775-1783*, M246, Folder 100, Record Group 93, Roll 0074, p. 17-18. Fisher's Regiment of Militia. Petition of Godfrey Shew https://www.fold3.com/image/246/10073627; The State of New York, Hugh Hastings, *Public Papers of George Clinton, First Governor of New York, 1777-1795, 1801-1804, Vol III* (Albany, James B. Lyon, 1900), 395-396, 415-416, 474. https://archive.org/stream/georgeclinton03newy#page/414/mode/2up Ibid, 565. https://archive.org/stream/georgeclinton03newy#page/564/mode/2up ; The State of New York, Hugh Hastings, *Public Papers of George Clinton, First Governor of New York, 1777-1795, 1801-1804, Vol IV* (Albany, James B. Lyon, 1900), 721-724. https://archive.org/stream/publicpapersgeo00histgoog#page/n797/mode/2up

554 The State of New York, Hugh Hastings, *Public Papers of George Clinton, First Governor of New York, 1777-1795, 1801-1804, Vol III*, Ten Broeck Reports to Governor Clinton, A Man of Spirit Wanted, An Appeal to the Governor, 562-564, 570,571, 581-583, 591. https://archive.org/stream/georgeclinton03newy#page/562/mode/2up

555 Documentation shows that Martin Alguire enlisted in the KRRNY on 5 May 1779. Martin states in his Loyalist claim that he was on his march to join when he was taken prisoner. He was held for about 5 months then released or escaped to serve in Major James Gray's Co. 1st Battalion KRRNY. He must have been taken prisoner sometime in the fall of 1778. Ancestry.com. *UK, American Loyalist Claims, 1776-1835* [database on-line]. Provo, UT. The National Archives of the UK; Kew, Surrey, England; American Loyalist Claims, Series I; Class: AO 13; Piece 029: Evidence, New York, 1787-1788. 361-362. Evidence on the Claim of Martin Algier.; Library and Archives Canada, Upper Canada Land Petitions (1763-1865), Mikan Number 205131, Microform c-1612, Page 396, Affadavit of Henry Gallinger.; The National Archives, *Revolutionary War Rolls 1775-1783*, Wemple's Regiment of Militia, Folder 170, page

33. August 1778, Captain Jelles Fonda's Company. Jacob Algaier. https://www.fold3.com/image/246/10195207

556 Library and Archives, Great Britain, War Office (WO 28): *America,* Lac_reel_c10861, C10861, 158960, 125090, MG 13 WO, Image 1303-1313 http://heritage.canadiana.ca/view/oocihm.lac_reel_c10861/1311?r=0&s=3

557 The State of New York, Hugh Hastings, *Public Papers of George Clinton, First Governor of New York, 1777-1795, 1801-1804, Vol III* (Albany, James B. Lyon, 1900), 630-632. https://archive.org/stream/georgeclinton03newy#page/630/mode/2up ; The Office of the State Comptroller, *New York in the Revolution as Colony and State, Vol II* (Albany, J.B. Lyon Co., 1904), 240. http://archive.org/stream/newyorkinrevolut02newyuoft#page/240/mode/2up ; New York State, *Minutes of the Commissioners for Detecting and Defeating Conspiracies in the State of New York,* (Albany, J.B. Lyon Co., 1909), 213-214. https://archive.org/stream/cu31924088942523#page/n221/mode/2up

558 Ancestry.com. *U.S., Dutch Reformed Church Records in Selected States, 1639-1989* [database on-line]. Provo, UT. Holland Society of New York; New York, New York; Cagnawaga or Fonda, Book 15, 93. 1778, Jacob b. Sept 5, John Hoog, Maragrieta Algire, Witnesses, John Keelman, Elizabeth d.

559 New York State, *Minutes of the Commissioners for Detecting and Defeating Conspiracies in the State of New York,* (Albany, J.B. Lyon Co., 1909), 232-234. https://archive.org/stream/cu31924088942523#page/n241/mode/2up; John Becksted lived near Berne, Albany County. He was a prisoner at Greenbush with his wife Helena McDonald and their children Alexander, John, Francis, Jacob, Henry and infant Maurice until 1783. He settled in Williamsburg, Dundas County, Ontario in 1792. *Upper Canada Land Petitions (1763-1865),* Mikan No. 205131, Microform, c-1631, Image 450-451, 456, 460; Ancestry.com. *U.S., Dutch Reformed Church Records in Selected States, 1639-1989* [database on-line]. Provo, UT, Holland Society of New York; New York, New York; Church Records

of Niskayuna and Schoharie, Book 36. 219. 1778, Mauitz bo. Aug 22, baptized Sept, 9, John Bedstead, Helena d of, Sponsors Stoffel Hoth & wife Hannatjie. Manuscripts and Archives Division, The New York Public Library. *"Johnson, Sir John"* New York Public Library Digital Collections. Accessed May 3, 2018. http://digitalcollections.nypl.org/items/a2a42ef0-349f-0133-b9a7-58d385a7b928 ; William Roscoe, History of Schoharie County New York (Sryacuse, D. Mason & Co., 1882), 39-43. https://archive.org/stream/cu31924028834541#page/42/mode/2up

560 New York State, *Minutes of the Commissioners for Detecting and Defeating Conspiracies in the State of New York,* (Albany, J.B. Lyon Co., 1909), 234. https://archive.org/stream/cu31924088942523#page/n241/mode/2up ; Ancestry.com. *UK, American Loyalist Claims, 1776-1835* [database on-line]. Provo, UT. The National Archives of the UK; Kew, Surrey, England; American Loyalist Claims, Series I; Class: AO 13; Piece 029: Evidence, New York, 1787-1788. 367. Evidence on the Claim of Christian Schick.

561 Isabel Thompson Kelsay, *Joseph Brant 1743-1807 Man of Two Worlds* (Syracuse, Syracuse University Press, 1984), 225-226.; The State of New York, Hugh Hastings, *Public Papers of George Clinton, First Governor of New York, 1777-1795, 1801-1804, Vol IV* (Albany, James B. Lyon, 1900), Another Foray in the Mohawk Valley, Destruction of German Flats, George Clinton to Washington, 39, 47-50, 78-79. https://archive.org/stream/publicpapersofge04newyiala#page/78/mode/2up ; Gavin Watt, *Fire & Desolation. The Revolutionary War's 1778 Campaign as Waged from Quebec and Niagara Against the American Frontiers* (Toronto, Dundurn, 2017), 272-273. "The Online Institute For Advanced Loyalist Studies." Butler's Rangers, Caldwell's Coy. 24 Dec. 1777- 24 Oct 1778. Original Source. Great Britain, British Library, Additional Manuscripts, No. 21765, folios 64-65. http://www.royalprovincial.com/military/musters/brangers/brcald1.htm

562 Ancestry.com. *U.S., Dutch Reformed Church Records in Selected States, 1639-1989* [database on-line]. Provo, UT. Holland Society of New York;

New York, New York; Cagnawaga or Fonda, Book 15. 97. 1778 20 Dec. Caty, Adam Snyder, Maria Link, Sponsor Nicholas Ault, Caty Link.; On 12 January 1795, Mattheus Link was witness to the probate of Andrew Snyder's will at Johnstown, New York. Maryly B. Penrose, *Compendium of Early Mohawk Valley Families, Vol II* (Baltimore, Genealogical Publishing Co., 1990), 758.

563 Isabel Thompson Kelsay, *Joseph Brant 1743-1807 Man of Two Worlds* (Syracuse, Syracuse University Press, 1984), 230-234.; The State of New York, Hugh Hastings, *Public Papers of George Clinton, First Governor of New York, 1777-1795, 1801-1804, Vol IV* (Albany, James B. Lyon, 1900), Albany Citizens Appeal to the Governor in Behalf of the Sufferers of Cherry Valley, A Threatening Letter to Colonel Cantine From Four Indian Chiefs (Demanding that the Colonel not molest and kill the Indians of the Delaware), Lists of Suffers in Tryon County, A list of Sufferers in Canajoharie District Entitled to State Reflief, Destitute Inhabitants of Cobleskill Appeal to General James Clinton For Assistance, List of Distressed Families in Mohawk District, List of Cherry Valley Sufferers, Colonel Harper's Letter, 363-364, 721-723, 786-788, 474-475, 700, 674-675, 412-417, https://archive.org/stream/publicpapersofge04newyiala#page/362/mode/2up ; Library and Archives Canada, *Haldimand Loyalist Lists* (Index), Lac_reel_c1475, C-1475, 105513, 2034239, MG 21 Add.MSS. 21661-21892, Images 405-408, 362. A List of Persons Sent Back 12 Nov 1778 to General Schuyler, taken prisoners at Cherry Valley, A List of Prisoners in the Hands of the Congress Belonging to the Corps of Rangers, Royalists & Their Families. http://heritage.canadiana.ca/view/oocihm.lac_reel_c1475/407?r=0&s=6 ; The State of New York, Hugh Hastings, *Public Papers of George Clinton, First Governor of New York, 1777-1795, 1801-1804, Vol VII*, 457-459. Walter Butler Scored. https://archive.org/stream/publicpapersofge04newyiala#page/456/mode/2up

564 Ancestry.com. *Records of the Lutheran Trinity Church of Stone Arabia: in the town of Palatine, Montgomery County, N.Y.* [database on-line]. Provo, UT. Vol.1. Birth and baptisms, 1751 to 1815. 56. Tauf Verzeichniss 1779, Entry No. 9, Johann Allgeier, Margaretha, Sponsors Gottfried Ehring,

Maria Mohrin, b. 26 Jan 1779, baptized 31 Jan 1779, Dorothea Victoria. ; Entry No. 8, Micael Schaab, Dorothea, Sponsors Heinrich Gallinger, Susanna Hickertin, b. 18 May 1778, baptized 31 Jan 1779, Dorothea.

565 "The Online Institute For Advanced Loyalist Studies." Indian Department Property Losses Sustained. Original Source Great Britain, Public Record Office, Audit Office, Class 13, Volume 54, folio 92. Martin Waldroff, 1 woman, 2 males over 16, 1 male under 16, 2 females over 16., Simon Clark, 1 woman, 1 male under 7. http://www.royalprovincial.com/military/rhist/dian/dianprop.htm; Ancestry.com. *UK, American Loyalist Claims, 1776-1835* [database on-line]. Provo, UT. The National Archives of the UK; Kew, Surrey, England; American Loyalist Claims, Series I; Class: AO 13; Piece 032: Evidence, New York, 1788. 131-132. Evidence on the Claim of Simon Clark. Ancestry.com. *UK, American Loyalist Claims, 1776-1835* [database on-line]. Provo, UT. The National Archives of the UK; Kew, Surrey, England; American Loyalist Claims, Series II; Class: AO 13; Piece 011: New Claims A·B·C, New York. 583. Account of Losses Sustained by the Rebles; the property of Simon Clark.

566 Ancestry.com. *Records of the Lutheran Trinity Church of Stone Arabia: in the town of Palatine, Montgomery County, N.Y.* [database on-line]. Provo, UT. Vol.1. Birth and baptisms, 1751 to 1815. 56. Tauf Verzeichniss 1779, Entry No. 18, Martin Allgeier, Catharina, Jacob Killmann, Elizabeth, Elizabeth born 16 Mertz 1779, baptized 25 Mertz 1779.

567 Ancestry.com. *U.S., Dutch Reformed Church Records in Selected States, 1639-1989* [database on-line]. Provo, UT. Holland Society of New York; New York, New York; Fonda, Vol II, Book 16. 119. 1779, April 26. Nicholas Simser to Margrieta Emmer. Ancestry.com. *Records of the Reformed Protestant Dutch Church of Caughnawaga: now the Reformed Church of Fonda, in the village of Fonda, Mon* [database on-line]. Provo, UT. Volume one. Marriages, 1772 to Jan. 31, 1818. 162. 1779, April 26, Nicholas Simser met Maragrita Emmer.

568 The State of New York, Hugh Hastings, *Public Papers of George Clinton, First Governor of New York, 1777-1795, 1801-1804, Vol IV* (Albany, James

B. Lyon, 1900), 709-710, 717-718, 809. For the Aid of the Frontier Sufferers, Commissary Cuyler Urges the Seizure of Wheat in Albany County, George Clinton Gives Directions for the Distribution of £1800 Among the Tryon County Sufferers. https://archive.org/stream/publicpapersofge04newyiala#page/716/mode/2up ; Ancestry.com. *UK, American Loyalist Claims, 1776-1835* [database on-line]. Provo, UT. The National Archives of the UK; Kew, Surrey, England; American Loyalist Claims, Series I; Class: AO 13; Piece 031: Evidence, New York, 1787-1788. 142. Evidence on the Claim of Michal Gollinger.

569 The State of New York, Hugh Hastings, *Public Papers of George Clinton, First Governor of New York, 1777-1795, 1801-1804, Vol IV.* 646-648, 669-670. Clinton to Washington, Jelles Fonda Offers Suggestions https://archive.org/stream/publicpapersofge04newyiala#page/668/mode/2up

570 Ibid, 713; Secretary of State, *Calendar of Historical Manuscripts, Relating to the War of the Revolution Vol II,* (Albany, Weed, Parsons and Company, 1868), 248. http://archive.org/stream/cu31924092740640#page/248/mode/2up ; The National Archives, *Revolutionary War Pension and Bounty Land Warrant Application Files,* M804, Record Group 15, Roll 2151, 7, 14, 22, 26. John Servoss.; Ibid, Roll 2175, 12, Henry Shew; E. A. Cruikshank, *The King's Royal Regiment of New York.* ed. Gavin Watt, (Toronto, The Ontario Historical Society, 1931) Reprinted Toronto, 1984, 208.

571 The State of New York, Hugh Hastings, *Public Papers of George Clinton, First Governor of New York, 1777-1795, 1801-1804, Vol IV* (Albany, James B. Lyon, 1900), 669-670. Manuscripts and Archives Division, The New York Public Library. "Johnson, Sir John" New York Public Library Digital Collections. Accessed May 9, 2018. http://digitalcollections.nypl.org/items/a2a42ef0-349f-0133-b9a7-58d385a7b928; Ancestry.com. *UK, American Loyalist Claims, 1776-1835* [database on-line]. Provo, UT. The National Archives of the UK; Kew, Surrey, England; American Loyalist Claims, Series II; Class: AO 13; Piece 012: New Claims C D E F, New York. The Memorial of Daniel Phoyk; "Three Rivers Hudson, Mohawk, Schoharie, History From America's Most Famous Valleys."

Lou D. McWethy, The Book of Names Especially Relating to the Early Palatines and the First Settlers in the Mohawk Valley, (St. Johnsville, NY, The Enterprise and News, 1933), "Johnson's Ledger Names of Retainers of The Great Sir William." Faix, Hendrick, Faix, Jr., Peter, Tenant http://www.threeriversbms.com/namesjohnson.htm; The National Archives, *Revolutionary War Rolls, 1775-1783,* M246, Folder 121, Record Group, 93, Roll 0075. Philip Fikes. https://www.fold3.com/image/246/10239986?xid=1945 ; Duncan Fraser, Papers and Records of the Ontario Historical Society, Volume LII, 1960, Original Source, Public Record Office, London, England AC 13/114. *Sir John Johnson's Rent Roll of the Kingsborough Patent.* Adam (Fikes?), Hendk Fikes. http://freepages.genealogy.rootsweb.ancestry.com/~wjmartin/kingsbor.htm

572 To be pinioned is to have ones arms restrained or tied to ones body. The State of New York, Hugh Hastings, *Public Papers of George Clinton, First Governor of New York, 1777-1795, 1801-1804, Vol IV,* 712-717. Experiences of Vather and Rodingburg.

573 E.A. Cruikshank, *The King's Royal Regiment of New York.* ed. Gavin Watt, (Toronto, The Ontario Historical Society, 1931) Reprinted Toronto, 1984, 166, 201, 215, 255, 269. Library and Archives Canada, *Upper Canada Land Petitions (1763-1865),* Mikan Number, 205131, Microform c-1893, 491. Affadavit of Capt. Allan McDonell for Lucas Feader Sr.

574 Secretary of State, *Calendar of Historical Manuscripts, Relating to the War of the Revolution Vol II* (Albany, Weed, Parsons and Company, 1868), 361. Muster Roll of Captain John Kasselman's Company of Rangers Raised out of Col. Jacob Klock's Regiment of Tryon County Militia. https://archive.org/stream/cu31924092740640#page/361/mode/2up

575 The Sullivan Expedition left only two Seneca towns standing throughout the whole Susquehanna, Mohawk, and Alleghany country destroying forty towns, 160,000 bushels of corn, and vast quantities of vegetables. Over 3700 Mohawk, Onondaga, Tutelos, Oneidas, Tuscaroras, Mahicans, Nanticokes, Conoys, Shawnee and Delaware all fled to Niagara with no food or possessions. Isabel Thompson Kelsay, *Joseph Brant*

1743-1807 Man of Two Worlds (Syracuse, Syracuse University Press, 1984), 232-233, 254-264.; The State of New York, Hugh Hastings, *Public Papers of George Clinton, First Governor of New York, 1777-1795, 1801-1804, Vol IV* (Albany, James B. Lyon, 1900), 615-618, 689-690, 702-704, 777. Preparing for the Sullivan Expedition, The Defense of New York's Frontiers, War Against the Onondagas. https://archive.org/stream/publicpapersofge04newyiala#page/702/mode/2up ; Library and Archives Canada, *Haldimand Loyalist Lists (Index),* Lac_reel_c1475, C-1475, 105513, 2034239, MG 21 Add.MSS.21661-21892. Image 364. http://heritage.canadiana.ca/view/oocihm.lac_reel_c1475/364?r=0&s=4

576 Library and Archives Canada, *Claus Papers,* Lac_reel_c1478, C-1478, 103767, MG 19 F 1, Image 402. Captain Tice to General Haldimand 6 May 1779. http://heritage.canadiana.ca/view/oocihm.lac_reel_c1478/403?r=0&s=6; Isabel Thompson Kelsay, *Joseph Brant 1743-1807 Man of Two Worlds,* 232-233.

http://heritage.canadiana.ca/view/oocihm.lac_reel_c1475/362?r=1&s=4; "United Empire Loyalists Association of Canada," Loyalist Trails, 2017-44, 29 October 2017, Alida Vrooman Hare UEL, http://www.uelac.org/Loyalist-Trails/2017/Loyalist-Trails-2017.php?issue=201744

577 James F. Morrison, *A Hanging in Canajoharie,* http://revwarny.com/hanging.pdf ; The National Archives, *Revolutionary War Pension and Bounty Land Warrant Application Files,* M804, Pension No. R. 7623, Record Group 15, Roll 1812, 7. Pension Application of William J. Newkirk. https://www.fold3.com/image/246/25339862 ; Library and Archives Canada, Great Britain, War Office (WO 28): *America,* Lac_reel_c10861, C-10861, 158960, 125090, MG 13 WO, Image 1493, A Return of the Officers and Rangers of the 5 Nations Indian Department, Montreal, March 30 1778, http://heritage.canadiana.ca/view/oocihm.lac_reel_c10861/1493?r=0&s=3 ; Maryly B. Penrose, *Compendium of Early Mohawk Valley Families Vol 1* (Baltimore, Genealogical Publishing Co., 1990), 92; The State of New York, Hugh Hastings, *Public Papers of George Clinton, First Governor of New York, 1777-1795, 1801-1804, Vol V* (Albany, James B. Lyon, 1901), 122-123. https://archive.org/

stream/georgeclinton05newy#page/122/mode/2up; Nelson Greene, *The Story of Old Fort Plain and the Middle Mohawk Valley* (Fort Plain, O'Connor Brothers, 1915), 71-72. https://archive.org/stream/storyofoldfortpl00gree#page/70/mode/2up ; Jeptha Root Simms, *The Frontiersmen of New York: Showing Customs of the Indians, Vicissitudes of the Pioneer White Settlers, And Border Strife In Two Wars, Vol II* (Albany, N.Y.: G.C. Riggs, 1883), 242-244.; Library and Archives Canada, *Haldimand Loyalist Lists (Index),* Lac_reel_c1475, C-1475, 105513, 2034239, MG 21 Add.MSS. 21661-21892. Image 362.

578 The State of New York, *Minutes of the Commissioners for Detecting and Defeating Conspiracies in the State of New York* (Albany, State of New York, 1909), 364, 371, 382-383, 385, 388, 396. http://archive.org/stream/cu31924088942523#page/n381/mode/2up; Ancestry.com. *UK, American Loyalist Claims, 1776-1835* [database on-line]. Provo, UT. The National Archives of the UK; Kew, Surrey, England; American Loyalist Claims, Series I; Class: AO 13; Piece 026: Evidence, New York, 1787. 434. Evidence on the Claim of Julius Bush; The State of New York, Hugh Hastings, *Public Papers of George Clinton, First Governor of New York, 1777-1795, 1801-1804, Vol VI* (Albany, James B. Lyon, 1902), 451. William Empey exchange November, 1780. https://archive.org/stream/publicpapersofge06innewy#page/450/mode/2up

579 "North American Forts" Eastern USA, Mohawk River Valley. https://www.northamericanforts.com/East/ny.html

580 Ancestry.com. *UK, American Loyalist Claims, 1776-1835* [database on-line]. Provo, UT. The National Archives of the UK; Kew, Surrey, England; American Loyalist Claims, Series I; Class: AO 13; Piece 028: Evidence, New York, 1787. 406. Evidence on the Claim of Andrew Mehoss.; Ancestry.com. *UK, American Loyalist Claims, 1776-1835* [database on-line]. Provo, UT. Original data: American Loyalist Claims, 1776–1835. AO 12–13. The National Archives of the United Kingdom, Kew, Surrey, England. Piece 031: Evidence, New York, 1787-1788. 280-282. Evidence on the Claim of Michal Gollinger.

581 New York (State). *Laws of the State of New York Passed At the Sessions of the Legislature Held In the Years 1777 [to 1801]* Albany, N.Y.: Weed, Parsons and Co, 188687. 62-71. https://babel.hathitrust.org/cgi/pt?id=hvd.32044011878063;view=1up;seq=72; The State of New York, Hugh Hastings, *Public Papers of George Clinton, First Governor of New York, 1777-1795, 1801-1804, Vol IV* (Albany, James B. Lyon, 1900), 726-727.; "NY GenWeb Fulton County" James F. Morrison, A History of Fulton County in the Revolution, The Soldiers and Their Story. John Little. https://fulton.nygenweb.net/military/FCinRev5.html

582 Ancestry.com. *UK, American Loyalist Claims, 1776-1835* [database on-line]. Provo, UT. The National Archives of the UK; Kew, Surrey, England; American Loyalist Claims, Series I; Class: AO 13; Piece 143: Losses of Divers Persons, 1784. 23; Ancestry.com. *UK, American Loyalist Claims, 1776-1835* [database on-line]. Provo, UT. The National Archives of the UK; Kew, Surrey, England; American Loyalist Claims, Series I; Class: AO 13; Piece 027: Evidence, New York, 1787. 354-355. Account of the Losses Sustained by Michael Van Koughnet.

583 Many tenants of Kingsborough and Philadelphia Bush enlisted in Fonda's Associated Exempts. This company was for men between the age of 50 and 60 and were only called for service during an invasion. The following men are on Fonda's list: Conrad Smith, Johannes Ault, Nicholas Shaver, Johannes Hertel, Mattheus Link, Jacob Henry Alguire, William Philips, Edward Connor, Joseph Hanes, George Ruppert, William Kennedy, George Schenck, Lawrence Eaman, Johannes Wert, and Jacob Sheets. The National Archives, *Revolutionary War Rolls, 1775-1783,* M246, Folder 170, Record Group 93, Roll 0077, page 35. Wemple's Regiment of Militia, List of Capt. Jelles Fonda's Company of Associated Exempts. https://www.fold3.com/image/10195239

584 "NY GenWeb Fulton County" James F. Morrison, A History of Fulton County in the Revolution, Lieutenant Peter Vrooman of Captain John Little's Company. Grog Shenk Sr., Grog Shenk Jr. http://fulton.nygenweb.net/military/vrooman.html

585 Mary Fryer, & W. Smy, (Lieutenant-Colonel), *Rolls of the Provincial (Loyalist) Corps, Canadian Command American Revolutionary Period* (Toronto, Dundern, 1981), 37. Captain Patrick Daly's Company (9th company) Entry 4 Private Henry Gallinger Country A (America) Age 21; National Archives, *Compiled Service Records of Soldiers Who Served in the American Army During the Revolution documenting the period 1775-1784,* M881 National Archives Catalog ID: 570910 Record Group: 93 Roll: 0736, New York Regiment: Fisher's Regiment, Militia Record Type: Individual Surname: Gallenger Given Name: Henry.; E.A. Cruikshank, *The King's Royal Regiment of New York.* ed. Gavin Watt, (Toronto, The Ontario Historical Society, 1931) Reprinted Toronto, 1984, 201.

586 Ancestry.com. *UK, American Loyalist Claims, 1776-1835* [database on-line]. Provo, UT. Piece 031: Evidence, New York, 1787-1788. 276. Evidence on the Claim of Philip Eamer late of Tryon Co.; New York State, The Office of the State Comptroller, *New York in the Revolution as Colony and State, Vol 1* (Albany, J.B. Lyon, 1904) 179-182. Tryon County Militia, Third Regiment, Peter Ener, Peter Weener.; National Archives, *Compiled Service Records of Soldiers Who Served in the American Army During the Revolution documenting the period 1775-1784,* M881 National Archives Catalog ID: 570910 Record Group: 93 Roll: 0736, New York Regiment: Fisher's Regiment, Militia Record. Page 1. Peter Ener, Peter Weener https://www.fold3.com/image/19566728

587 The State of New York, Hugh Hastings, *Public Papers of George Clinton, First Governor of New York, 1777-1795, 1801-1804, Vol V* (Albany, James B. Lyon, 1901), 297, 320. https://archive.org/stream/georgeclinton05newy#page/296/mode/2up

588 Mark Boonshoft, *Dispossessing Loyalists and Redistributing Property in Revolutionary New York,* (New York Public Library, 19 September 2016) https://www.nypl.org/blog/2016/09/19/loyalist-property-confiscation ; New York (State). *Comptroller's Office. New York In the Revolution As Colony And State: Supplement.* Albany, N.Y.: O.A. Quayle, 1901. 248-249. https://babel.hathitrust.org/cgi/pt?id=coo.31924032737938;view=1up;seq=252; New York (State). *Laws of the State of New York Passed At the*

Sessions of the Legislature Held In the Years 1777 to 1801 (Albany, N.Y.: Weed, Parsons and Company) 188687 173-185. https://babel.hathitrust.org/cgi/pt?id=mdp.39015068627960;view=1up;seq=181 ; New York State Archives, New York State Engineer and Surveyor. *Records of Surveys and Maps of State Lands, 1686-1892.* Series A4016-77, Volume 7, Folder 161. NYSA_A4016-77_V7_F161 http://digitalcollections.archives.nysed.gov/index.php/Detail/Object/Show/object_id/41931; Ancestry.com. *UK, American Loyalist Claims, 1776-1835* [database on-line]. Provo, UT. Original data: American Loyalist Claims, 1776–1835. AO 12–13. The National Archives of the United Kingdom, Kew, Surrey, England. Piece 086: Documents Communicated by New York State Government, 1786. 128. Schedule of Convictions in the State of New York.

589 Library and Archives Canada, British Library, formerly British Museum, Additional Manuscripts 21804-21834, *Haldimand Papers,* Lac_reel_h1654, H-1654, 105513, 2034239, MG 21. Image 618-620, 624-630. Subsistence return for Royalists attached to Kings Royal Regiment of New York, An Effective List of all the loyalists in Canada, 1 July 1779. http://heritage.canadiana.ca/view/oocihm.lac_reel_h1654/630?r=0&s=4

590 National Archives, *Revolutionary War Pension and Bounty Land Warrant Application Files,* M804, Pension No. S. 22985, Record Group 15, Roll 2175, 10. Pension Application of Jacob Shew. https://www.fold3.com/image/246/15632041?xid=1945

591 Mary Fryer, & W. Smy, (Lieutenant-Colonel), *Rolls of the Provincial (Loyalist) Corps, Canadian Command American Revolutionary Period* (Toronto, Dundern, 1981), 37. Entry 24 Major's Co. Private Martin Algire, Country A (America) Age 37, Major James Gray's Company; Ancestry.com. *UK, American Loyalist Claims, 1776-1835* [database on-line]. Provo, UT. The National Archives of the UK; Kew, Surrey, England; American Loyalist Claims, Series I; Class: AO 13; Piece 029: Evidence, New York, 1787-1788. 361-362. Evidence on the Claim of Martin Algier late of Tryon County.

592 Ancestry.com. *Records of the Reformed Protestant Dutch Church of Caughnawaga: now the Reformed Church of Fonda, in the village of Fonda, Mon* [database on-line]. Provo, UT. Volume one. Marriages, 1772 to Jan. 31, 1818. 162. Janry 19, 1780, Peter Emer met Catrina Gollinger, No. 120.

593 The State of New York, *Minutes of the Commissioners for Detecting and Defeating Conspiracies in the State of New York*, Vol II, 1780-1781 (Albany, State of New York, 1909), 432-433. https://archive.org/stream/detectingdefecting02paltrich#page/432/mode/2up

594 The State of New York, Hugh Hastings, *Public Papers of George Clinton, First Governor of New York, 1777-1795, 1801-1804, Vol V*, 521-525. https://archive.org/stream/georgeclinton05newy#page/520/mode/2up ; Christopher Yates Papers, Special Collections Research Center, Sryacuse, N.Y. Transcribed by Ken D. Johnson, 2012. http://www.fort-plank.com/Loyalists_Exchanged_March_1780.pdf; Library and Archives Canada, *Haldimand Loyalist Lists (Index)*, Lac_reel_c1475, C-1475, 105513, 2034239, MG 21 Add.MSS.21661-21892 http://heritage.canadiana.ca/view/oocihm.lac_reel_c1475/362?r=1&s=3; The State of New York, Hugh Hastings, *Public Papers of George Clinton, First Governor of New York, 1777-1795, 1801-1804, Vol IV* (Albany, James B. Lyon, 1900), 412-417. https://archive.org/stream/publicpapersofge04newyiala#page/412/mode/2up ; Library and Archives Canada, Claus Papers, Lac_reel_1478, C-1478, 103767, 103767, MG 19 F 1, 488-489, 498-502, http://heritage.canadiana.ca/view/oocihm.lac_reel_c1478/489?r=0&s=4

595 E.A. Cruikshank, *The King's Royal Regiment of New York*. ed. Gavin Watt, (Toronto, The Ontario Historical Society, 1931) Reprinted Toronto, 1984, 36-37.; New York (State). Governor (1777-1795: Clinton). *Public Papers of George Clinton, First Governor of New York, 1777-1795, 1801-1804* (Albany, 18991914), 26.

596 Ken D. Johnson, "The Bloodied Mohawk: The Story of the American Revolution in the Words of Fort Plank's Defenders and Other Mohawk

Valley Partisans". from the Christopher Yates Papers housed in the Special Collections of the Bird Library of Syracuse University dated Isle Aux Noix March 17th 1780 entitled a *Return of Men Women and Children Distinguishing their Age & Sex which came by the Flag with C Yates.* In this document, 17 March 1780, Henry Casselman is listed as 10 years old. http://www.fort-plank.com/Loyalists_Exchanged_March_1780.pdf

597 State of New York, Calendar of Historical Manuscripts, Relating to the War of the Revolution, Vol II (Albany, Weed, Parsons and Company, 1868), 361. Muster Roll of Captain John Kasselman's Company of Rangers. https://archive.org/stream/cu31924092740640#page/361/mode/2up The National Archives, *Revolutionary War Rolls 1775-1783,* M 246, Record Group 93, Roll 0077, page 35-36. https://www.fold3.com/image/246/10191871 ; "Fulton County NYGenWeb." James F. Morrison, Lieutenant Peter Vrooman. http://fulton.nygenweb.net/military/vrooman.html ;The State of New York, Hugh Hastings, *Public Papers of George Clinton, First Governor of New York, 1777-1795, 1801-1804, Vol V* (Albany, James B. Lyon, 1901), 538. https://archive.org/stream/georgeclinton05newy#page/538/mode/2up

598 Ancestry.com. *Records of the Reformed Protestant Dutch Church of Caughnawaga: now the Reformed Church of Fonda, in the village of Fonda, Mon* [database on-line]. Provo, UT. *Volume one. Baptisms and births, 1758 to 1797.* 56. 1780, 28 March, Philip Service, Catrina Seever, Joannis, Meert 14, Johannes Emer, Maria Service.

599 Claude Hal Stead Van Tyne, *The Loyalists in the American Revolution* (New York, The MacMillan Company, 1902), 192. http://www.archive.org/stream/loyalistsinamer00vantrich#page/n207/mode/2up ; *Pennsylvania Packet,* August 5, 1779 ; reprinted in Frank Moore, *Diary of the American Revolution* (New York, etc., 1860). II, 166-168. https://archive.org/stream/diaryofamericanr02moor#page/166/mode/2up

600 Benjamin H. Irvin, "Tar, Feathers, and the Enemies of American Liberties, 1768-1776." *The New England Quarterly* 76, no. 2 (2003): 197-238. doi:10.2307/1559903

601 New York (State). Legislature. *Journals of the Provincial Congress, Provincial Convention, Committee of Safety And Council of Safety of the State of New-York: 1775-1775-1777* (Albany: Printed by Thurlow Weed, printer to the State, 1842), 232. https://babel.hathitrust.org/cgi/pt?id=nnc1.ar01406256;view=1up;seq=244; Peter C. Newman, Hostages to Fortune. The United Empire Loyalists and the Making of Canada (Toronto, Simon & Schuster, 2016), 48-56.

602 There is no record of Johannes Eamer's death. The last record for him was as a sponsor at the Baptism of Johannes Service, son of Philip Service and Catherine Seeber on 28 March 1780. No record of Johannes arriving in Canada has been found nor any record of him in the Mohawk Valley after 1780. Therefore, I assume he died after 28 March 1780.

603 Library and Archives Canada, British Library, formerly British Museum, Additional Manuscripts 21804-21834, *Haldimand Papers*, Lac_reel_h1652, H-1652, 105513, 2034239, MG 21, Image 370-373; 375-378, 380-381, 385. http://heritage.canadiana.ca/view/oocihm.lac_reel_h1652/370?r=0&s=5 ; E.A. Cruikshank, *The King's Royal Regiment of New York*. ed. Gavin Watt, (Toronto, The Ontario Historical Society, 1931) Reprinted Toronto, 1984, 36-37, 188; Gavin Watt & James F. Morrison, *The Burning of The Valleys. Daring Raids From Canada Against The New York Frontier in the Fall of 1780*, rev. ed. (Toronto, Dundern Press, 1997), 75. "The Kings Royal Yorkers," Gavin Watt, The Companies of the 1st Battalion KRRNY. http://royalyorkers.ca/companies_1bn.php "The Online Institue for Advanced Loyalist Studies," Loyalist Muster Rolls, Kings Royal Regiment of New York. http://www.royalprovincial.com/military/musters/krrny/mrkrrmain.htm ; Ancestry.com. *Records of the Lutheran Trinity Church of Stone Arabia: in the town of Palatine, Montgomery County, N.Y.* [database on-line]. Provo, UT. Original data: Records of the Lutheran Trinity Church of Stone Arabia: in the town of Palatine, Montgomery County, N.Y.. New York: unknown, 1914. Vol.1.

Birth and baptisms, 1751 to 1815. 17. MDCCLVI, d. 29 Feb, Niclas Schäfer, c ux, Elisabetha; Sponsors, Jerg Adam Dagstetter, Eva Berletin; Jerg Adam.

604 Ancestry.com. *U.S., Find A Grave Index, 1600s-Current* [database on-line]. Provo, UT. Original data: *Find A Grave*. Find A Grave. http://www.findagrave.com/cgi-bin/fg.cgi. George Valentine Cryderman, date of death , 1780; Ancestry.com. *UK, American Loyalist Claims, 1776-1835* [database on-line]. Provo, UT. Piece 029: Evidence, New York, 1787-1788. 323. Evidence on the Claim of Cathrine Cryderman Widow of Valentine Cryderman late of Tryon County.

605 James F. Morrison, *Capt. John Little. 3rd Battalion of Tryon County Militia.* http://www.littellfamiliesofamerica.com/secure/21st/2004LLA/Sect04H.htm ; James F. Morrison, "Fulton County NYGenWeb." About Captain John Little, http://fulton.nygenweb.net/military/little.html ; James F. Morrison, "Fulton County NYGenWeb" The Great Conflagration of May 1780. Part I, II, https://fulton.nygenweb.net/military/greatconflag1.html ; The National Archives, *Revolutionary War Pension and Bounty Land Warrants,* M804, Pension No. W.19000, Record Group 15, Roll 2112, Page 7, Thomas Sammons, https://www.fold3.com/image/246/14669841; Ibid, Roll 0824, Pension No. W. 16,241, Page 6, Leonard Dochstader https://www.fold3.com/image/246/16343288 ; Ibid, Roll 2112, Pension No. 2112, Page 16, Frederick Sammons, https://www.fold3.com/image/246/14669525 ; The National Archives, *Revolutionary War Rolls 1775-1783,* M246, Record Group 93, Roll 0077, Page 11, A Pay Roll of Captain Jelles Fonda's Company, May 1780, https://www.fold3.com/image/246/10194819 ; "Fort Plank Bastion of My Freedom," The Burning of Caughnawaga by Henry Glen. http://www.fort-plank.com/1780_Burning_of_Caughnawaga_By_Henry_Glen_Endnoted.pdf

606 Gavin Watt & James F. Morrison, *The Burning of The Valleys. Daring Raids From Canada Against The New York Frontier in the Fall of 1780,* rev. ed. (Toronto, Dundern Press, 1997), 75-76.

607 Library and Archives Canada, British Library, formerly British Museum, Additional Manuscripts 21804-21834, *Haldimand Papers,* Lac_reel_h1652, H-1652, 105513, 2034239, MG 21, Image 387-390, 491. http://heritage.canadiana.ca/view/oocihm.lac_reel_h1652/387?r=0&s=5 ; The State of New York, Hugh Hastings, *Public Papers of George Clinton, First Governor of New York, 1777-1795, 1801-1804, Vol V* (Albany, James B. Lyon, 1901), 669-670. 736-749. https://archive.org/stream/georgeclinton05newy#page/768/mode/2up "Fort Plank Bastion of My Freedom," The Burning of Caughnawaga by Henry Glen. http://www.fort-plank.com/1780_Burning_of_Caughnawaga_By_Henry_Glen_Endnoted.pdf

608 "The Online Institue for Advanced Loyalist Studies," Loyalist Muster Rolls, Kings Royal Regiment of New York. Johnson's Company 21 January 1778. http://www.royalprovincial.com/military/musters/krrny/krrjohnson.htm ; Guylaine Petrin, *Disentangling a Loyalist Family Tree.* The Free Library. 2011 United Empire Loyalists' Association. The Rupert Families in New York. https://www.thefreelibrary.com/Disentangting+a+loyalist+family+tree.-a0275310916 ; E.A. Cruikshank, *The King's Royal Regiment of New York.* ed. Gavin Watt, (Toronto, The Ontario Historical Society, 1931) Reprinted Toronto, 1984, 183. Kline (Clyne, Cline, Klyn) Michael Born Germany 1744 2nd Battalion Private 22 May 1780 Settled Township #2 (Cornwall) Wife Catherine 4 sons 2 daughters 5' 2".; Ancestry.com. *UK, American Loyalist Claims, 1776-1835* [database on-line]. Provo, UT. The National Archives of the UK; Kew, Surrey, England; American Loyalist Claims, Series I; Class: AO 13; Piece 027: Evidence, New York, 1787. 405-406. Evidence on the Claim of Wm. Philips late of New York.

609 Library and Archives Canada, British Library, formerly British Museum, Additional Manuscripts 21804-21834, *Haldimand Papers,* Lac_reel_h1652, 105513, 2034239, MG 21, Image 722, http://heritage.canadiana.ca/view/oocihm.lac_reel_h1652/722?r=0&s=4 ; The National Archives, *Revolutionary War Pension and Bounty-Land Warrant Application Files,* M804, Pension Number S. 11350, Record Group 15, Roll 2112. Page 16, 29-30. Sammons, Frederick. This application includes the story of

his capture, imprisonment, development of scurvy, and his miraculous escape. https://www.fold3.com/image/246/14669581?xid=1945 ; Ibid, Pension Number W. 19000, Page 7. Thomas Sammons, https://www.fold3.com/image/246/14669841; http://digitalcollections.archives.nysed.gov/index.php/Detail/Object/Show/object_id/41660 New York State Archives, A0870-77, Copies of accounts audited by the auditor general for bills presented to the state, 1780-1794. NYSA_A0870-77_Book B, Page 84; John W. Barber & Henry Howe, Historical Collections of the State of New York, (New York, S. Tuttle, 1846), 170-171. https://archive.org/stream/historicalcollec00barbny#page/170/mode/2up; Gavin Watt & James F. Morrison, *The Burning of The Valleys. Daring Raids From Canada Against The New York Frontier in the Fall of 1780,* rev. ed. (Toronto, Dundern Press, 1997), 78.

610 Gavin Watt & James F. Morrison, *The Burning of The Valleys. Daring Raids From Canada Against The New York Frontier in the Fall of 1780,* rev. ed. (Toronto, Dundern Press, 1997), 77-79.; John W. Barber & Henry Howe, Historical Collections of the State of New York, (New York, S. Tuttle, 1846), 170-171. https://archive.org/stream/historicalcollec00barbny#page/170/mode/2up ; 769-770, The State of New York, Hugh Hastings, *Public Papers of George Clinton, First Governor of New York, 1777-1795, 1801-1804, Vol V* (Albany, James B. Lyon, 1901), 736-747. https://archive.org/stream/georgeclinton05newy#page/736/mode/2up; E.A. Cruikshank, *The King's Royal Regiment of New York.* ed. Gavin Watt, (Toronto, The Ontario Historical Society, 1931) Reprinted Toronto, 1984, 180-181.; Ancestry.com. *UK, American Loyalist Claims, 1776-1835* [database on-line]. Provo, UT. The National Archives of the UK; Kew, Surrey, England; American Loyalist Claims, Series I; Class: AO 13; Piece 032: Evidence, New York, 1788. 201-201. Evidence on the Claim of Simeon Christie late of Mayfield, Tryon County, New York. ; "Fort Plank Bastion of My Freedom," The Burning of Caughnawaga by Henry Glen. http://www.fort-plank.com/1780_Burning_of_Caughnawaga_By_Henry_Glen.pdf ; "Bill Martin's Genealogy Pages." Extracts From Canadian Archives Haldimand Papers, Series B, Vol 158, page 128. St. Johns 3 June 1780. http://my.tbaytel.net/bmartin/aid.htm

611 William Stone, Orderly Book of Sir John Johnson During the Oriskany Campaign, 1776-1777 (Albany, Joel Munsell's Sons, 1882), 18. http://archive.org/stream/orderlybooksirj00myergoog#page/n231/mode/2up ; "New York History Blog" Glenn Pearsall, French and Indian War Bayonet Discovered in the Adirondacks. August 2, 2017. https://newyorkhistoryblog.org/2017/08/02/french-indian-war-bayonet-discovered-near-loon-lake/ ; Arhtur Pound, *Johnson of the Mohawks: a Biography of Sir William Johnson, Irish Immigrant, Mohawk War Chief, American Soldier, Empire Builder* (New York: The Macmillan Company, 1930), 191. https://babel.hathitrust.org/cgi/pt?id=mdp.39015027039430;view=1up;seq=243

612 "Bill Martin's Genealogy Pages." Extracts From Canadian Archives Haldimand Papers, Series B, Vol 158, page 128. St. Johns 3 June 1780. http://my.tbaytel.net/bmartin/aid.htm ; E.A. Cruikshank, *The King's Royal Regiment of New York*. ed. Gavin Watt, (Toronto, The Ontario Historical Society, 1931) Reprinted Toronto, 1984, 42-43.; New York State, The Office of the State Comptroller, *New York in the Revolution as Colony and State, Vol 1* (Albany, J.B. Lyon, 1904) 176, 178-183, 736-742.; "Montgomery County NYGenWeb" Montgomery County NY Military Index Page. The Loss Claim of Johannes Veeder. http://montgomery.nygenweb.net/mohawk/jveeder.html ; "Find A Grave" Pvt Lodowyck Arentse Putman. https://www.findagrave.com/memorial/83490121/put ; "Fort Plank Bastion of My Freedom," The Burning of Caughnawaga by Henry Glen. http://www.fort-plank.com/1780_Burning_of_Caughnawaga_By_Henry_Glen.pdf ; Gavin Watt & James F. Morrison, *The Burning of The Valleys. Daring Raids From Canada Against The New York Frontier in the Fall of 1780*, rev. ed. (Toronto, Dundern Press, 1997), 79-80.

613 The National Archives, *Revolutionary War Rolls 1775-1783*, Wemple's Regiment of Militia, Folder 170, page 35. August 1778, Captain Jelles Fonda's Company. Martian Samser. https://www.fold3.com/image/246/10195239 ; The State of New York, *Minutes of the Commissioners for Detecting and Defeating Conspiracies in the State of New*

York, Vol II, 1780-1781 (Albany, State of New York, 1909), 563. http://archive.org/stream/detectingdefecting02paltrich#page/562/mode/2up

614 New York State Archives, *Copies of accounts audited by the auditor general for bills presented to the state, 1780-1794*. NYSA_A0870-77_Book B. 58. http://digitalcollections.archives.nysed.gov/index.php/Detail/Object/Show/object_id/41660 ; Catherine Shepard, "FRASER, THOMAS," in *Dictionary of Canadian Biography*, vol. 6, University of Toronto/Université Laval, 2003, http://www.biographi.ca/en/bio/fraser_thomas_6E.html ; Library and Archives Canada, British Library (Formerly British Museum) *Haldimand Papers*, Lac_ree_h1743, H-1743, 105513, 2034239, Image 1074-1075. http://heritage.canadiana.ca/view/oocihm.lac_reel_h1743/1074?r=0&s=4

615 New York (State). *Comptroller's Office. New York In the Revolution As Colony And State: Vol II* (Albany, J.B. Lyon, 1904), 253. https://archive.org/stream/newyorkinrevolut02newyuoft#page/252/mode/2up

616 Ancestry.com. *UK, American Loyalist Claims, 1776-1835* [database on-line]. Provo, UT. The National Archives of the UK; Kew, Surrey, England; American Loyalist Claims, Series I; Class: AO 13; Piece 029: Evidence, New York, 1787-1788. 360-362. Evidence on the Claim of Martin Algier Late of Tryon County.

617 Ancestry.com. *UK, American Loyalist Claims, 1776-1835* [database on-line]. Provo, UT. Original data: American Loyalist Claims, 1776–1835. AO 12–13. Piece 031: Evidence, New York, 1787-1788. 141-143. The National Archives of the United Kingdom, Kew, Surrey, England. Evidence on the Claim of Michael Gollinger late of Tryon County. "Northern Illinois University Digital Library." Amerian Archives. V6:1073. List of Tories from Tryon County sent to Hartford, June 25, 1776. Document ID: S4-V6-P02-sp13-D0213.

618 The State of New York, Hugh Hastings, *Public Papers of George Clinton, First Governor of New York, 1777-1795, 1801-1804, Vol VI* (Albany, James B. Lyon, 1902), 276-277. https://archive.org/stream/publicpapersofge06innewy#page/278/mode/2up

619 Ancestry.com. *Records of the Lutheran Trinity Church of Stone Arabia: in the town of Palatine, Montgomery County, N.Y.* [database on-line]. Provo, UT. Vol.1. Birth and baptisms, 1751 to 1815. 30. Anno 1770, Januarii d 7ten, Michael Klein & Catharina, Sponsors Joannes Wik & Ux, Johannes.; The State of New York, Hugh Hastings, *Public Papers of George Clinton, First Governor of New York, 1777-1795, 1801-1804, Vol VI*, 77-84, 88-90. https://archive.org/stream/publicpapersofge06innewy#page/76/mode/2up ; Isabel Thompson Kelsay, *Joseph Brant 1743-1807 Man of Two Worlds* (Syracuse, Syracuse University Press, 1984), 292-294.; Gavin Watt & James F. Morrison, *The Burning of The Valleys. Daring Raids From Canada Against The New York Frontier in the Fall of 1780,* rev. ed. (Toronto, Dundern Press, 1997), 81-82.; The State of New York, Hugh Hastings, *Public Papers of George Clinton, First Governor of New York, 1777-1795, 1801-1804, Vol VI*, 93-94. https://archive.org/stream/publicpapersofge06innewy#page/92/mode/2up ; The National Archives, *Revolutionary War Rolls 1775-1783*, M246, Folder 167, Record Group 93, Roll 0077, Page 39. Vrooman's Regiment of Militia, https://www.fold3.com/image/246/10191920

620 New York State Archives. New York (State). *State Engineer and Surveyor. Survey maps of lands in New York State*, ca. 1711-1913. Series A0273-78, Map #147A.1769 NYSA_A0273-78_147A. Map of the Western Boundary Line of the Third Tract, Granted to John Morine Scott http://digitalcollections.archives.nysed.gov/index.php/Detail/Object/Show/object_id/36677# ; New York State Archives. New York (State). *State Engineer and Surveyor. Survey maps of lands in New York State,* ca. 1711-1913. Series A0273-78, Map #681. 1755-1770. NYSA_A0273-78_681. Survey of Land for J.N. Mathias, William Bauch, Lawrence Lawyer, and Wm. Wood. http://digitalcollections.archives.nysed.gov/index.php/Detail/Object/Show/object_id/37246 ; Library and Archives Canada, *Audit Office: AO 12. Claims, American Loyalists-Series I*, Lac_reel_c12904, C-12904, 105765, 1281700, 128171, 128173, MG 14 AO 12, Image 1514. The Memorial of Adam Chrysler late of Schoharie.

621 Library and Archives Canada, Haldimand papers from the British Library, Lac_reel_h1435, H-1435, 105513, 2034239, MG21,

Image 22. http://heritage.canadiana.ca/view/oocihm.lac_reel_h1435/22?r=0&s=4 ; E.A. Cruikshank, *The King's Royal Regiment of New York*. ed. Gavin Watt, (Toronto, The Ontario Historical Society, 1931) Reprinted Toronto, 1984, 43-44.; Gavin Watt, *A dirty, trifling, piece of business Volume I, The Revolutionary War as Waged From Canada in 1781* (Toronto, Dundern Press, 2009), 46-48.; The State of New York, Hugh Hastings, *Public Papers of George Clinton, First Governor of New York, 1777-1795, 1801-1804, Vol VI* (Albany, James B. Lyon, 1902), 136-137. https://archive.org/stream/publicpapersofge06innewy#page/136/mode/2up

622 No record of Elizabeth's death has been found. However, Michael Myers and Elizabeth Eamer's last child Margaret was born Oct 1777 and the first child born to Michael Myers and his second wife Elizabeth Crieghoof was Maria born 22 Sept 1781. Therefore, Michael's first wife Elizabeth Eamer must have died between October 1777 and approximately December 1780. Christine Hallett, The Attempt to Understand Puerperal Fever in the Eighteenth and Early Nineteenth Centuries: The Influence of Infammation Theory, *Med Hist,* 49(1), 2005. https://www.ncbi.nlm.nih.gov/pmc/articles/PMC1088248/

623 The State of New York, Hugh Hastings, *Public Papers of George Clinton, First Governor of New York, 1777-1795, 1801-1804, Vol VI* (Albany, James B. Lyon, 1902), 276-277, 456-457. https://archive.org/stream/publicpapersofge06innewy#page/456/mode/2up

624 "The King's Royal Yorkers" Gavin Watt, The Companies of the 1st Battalion, KRRNY, http://royalyorkers.ca/companies_1bn.php

625 J.F. Pringle, Lunenburgh or the Old Eastern District Its Settlement and Early Progress (Cornwall, ON, Standard Printing House, 1890), 372. https://archive.org/stream/lunenburgh00prinuoft#page/n397/mode/2up ; Ancestry.com. *The Old United Empire Loyalists List* [database on-line]. Provo, UT. *Appendix B. 131.* Original data: Centennial Committee. The Old United Empire Loyalists List. Baltimore: 1969.

"Amor, Peter Residence: E. District A Grenadier Royl. Yorkers, J.B. say Philip."

626 Thomas B. Allen, *Tories Fighting for the King in America's First Civil War* (Toronto, Harper, 2010), 267.

627 E.A. Cruikshank, *The King's Royal Regiment of New York.* ed. Gavin Watt, (Toronto, The Ontario Historical Society, 1931) Reprinted Toronto, 1984, 51-54.; Thomas B. Allen, *Tories Fighting for the King in America's First Civil War* (Toronto, Harper, 2010),267-270.; Isabel Thompson Kelsay, *Joseph Brant 1743-1807 Man of Two Worlds* (Syracuse, Syracuse University Press, 1984), 292-299.; Gavin Watt & James F. Morrison, *The Burning of The Valleys. Daring Raids From Canada Against The New York Frontier in the Fall of 1780,* rev. ed. (Toronto, Dundern Press, 1997), 157-184, 191-243. "Three Rivers Hudson, Mohawk, Schoharie: History From America's Most Famous Valleys, Klock's Churchyard Preservation Group, 1780-1980 The Bicentennial of the Schoharie and Mohawk Valley Raids. http://threerivershms.com/schoharie.htm ; Ibid, Lou D. MacWethy, The Battle of Klock's Field. http://www.threerivershms.com/klockfield.htm New York State Archives. Instructional glass lantern slides, ca. 1856-1939. Series A3045-78, No. 732. NYSA_A3045-78_732. *Route of Col. Sir John Johnson in his Raid through the Schoharie and the Mohawk Valleys.* http://digitalcollections.archives.nysed.gov/index.php/Detail/Object/Show/object_id/1280 ; National Archives, *Revolutionary War Rolls 1775-1783,* M246, Folder 167, Record Group 93, Roll 0077. Vrooman's Regiment of Militia. Page 39. https://www.fold3.com/image/246/10191920 ; James A. Roberts (Comptroller), *New York in the Revolution as Colony and State,* Raid of Sir John Johnson of the Schoharie and Mohawk Valleys, in October 1780 (Albany, Weed-Parsons, 1897), xiii-xviii. https://archive.org/stream/newyorkinrevolu00robegoog#page/n24/mode/2up; Franklin Hough, *The Northern Invasion of 1780* (New York, The Bradford Club, 1866), 133-137. https://archive.org/stream/northerninvasion00houguoft#page/132/mode/2up ; Library and Archives Canada, British Library (Formerly British Museum) *Haldimand Papers,* Lac_reel_h1743, H-1743, 105513, 2034239, Image 1618. Memorial of Lieut George Mcginn. http://heritage.canadiana.ca/view/oocihm.

lac_reel_h1743/1618?r=0&s=3 ; National Archives, *Revolutionary War Pension and Bounty Land Warrant Application Files*, M804, Pension W.16563, Record 15, Roll 0824, Page 5. George Dockstader. https://www.fold3.com/image/246/16342951

628 Ancestry.com. *U.S., Dutch Reformed Church Records in Selected States, 1639-1989* [database on-line]. Provo, UT. The Archives of the Reformed Church in America; New Brunswick, New Jersey; Fonda Church, Baptisms, Marriages, 1797-1872. 29. 1781, Nov 26, Michel Meyers, Elizabeth Criehoof, Maria b. Sept 22, Sponsors, Hendk Simson, Maria.

629 Library and Archives Canada, British Library, formerly British Museum, Additional Manuscripts 21804-21834, *Haldimand Papers*. Lac_reel_h1654, H-1654, 105513, 2034239, MG 21, Image 665, 672, 674. http://heritage.canadiana.ca/view/oocihm.lac_reel_h1654/663?r=0&s=6 ; Ibid, 660.

630 Isabel Thompson Kelsay, *Joseph Brant 1743-1807 Man of Two Worlds* (Syracuse, Syracuse University Press, 1984), 301-305. "Horton's Articles," Gerald Horton, What Happened to 7000 People? http://threerivershms.com/hh7thousand.htm

631 The State of New York, *Minutes of the Commissioners for Detecting and Defeating Conspiracies in the State of New York*, Vol II, 1780-1781 (Albany, State of New York, 1909), 672-673. March 1781 Recognizance Forfeited: Philip Empey, Johannes Staring, Nicholas Ault, Peter Fykes and Adam Shaver. http://archive.org/stream/cu31924021474782#page/n253/mode/2up ; The State of New York, Hugh Hastings, *Public Papers of George Clinton, First Governor of New York, 1777-1795, 1801-1804, Vol VI* (Albany, James B. Lyon, 1902), List of Prisoners of War, Albany and Tryon. 731. https://archive.org/stream/publicpapersofge06innewy#page/730/mode/2up

632 Library and Archives Canada, British Library, formerly British Museum, *Additional Manuscripts 21804-21834, Haldimand Papers*. Lac_reel_h1654, H-1654, 105513, 2034239, MG 21, Image 675, 676, 677, 678, 680. General Return of Unincorporated Families, 25

March-24 April 1781. ,http://heritage.canadiana.ca/view/oocihm.lac_reel_h1654/663?r=0&s=6 ; Library and Archives Canada, British Library, formerly British Museum, *Additional Manuscripts 21804-21834, Haldimand Papers,* Lac_Reel, h1652, 105513, 2034239, MG21, Image 487-488. http://heritage.canadiana.ca/view/oocihm.lac_reel_h1652/487?r=0&s=4; New York (State), *Public Papers of George Clinton, First Governor of New York, 1777-1795,* 1801-1804. (Albany, 18991914), Proclamation by Sir John Johnson, 27. https://babel.hathitrust.org/cgi/pt?id=nyp.33433062495811;view=1up;seq=99

633 The State of New York, *Minutes of the Commissioners for Detecting and Defeating Conspiracies in the State of New York,* Vol II, 1780-1781 (Albany, State of New York, 1909), 733 http://archive.org/stream/cu31924021474782#page/n313/mode/2up ; Ancestry.com. *UK, American Loyalist Claims, 1776-1835* [database on-line]. Provo, UT. The National Archives of the UK; Kew, Surrey, England; American Loyalist Claims, Series I; Class: AO 13; Piece 026: Evidence, New York, 1787. 285-287. Evidence on the claim of John Waite.; http://archive.org/stream/detectingdefecting02paltrich#page/732/mode/2up ; New England Historical and Genealogical Register, *Emigrants from England 1773-1776, Vol 62-65* (Boston, New England Historic Genealogical Society, 1913), 160. https://archive.org/stream/emigrantsfromeng00bost#page/160/mode/2up

634 The State of New York, *Minutes of the Commissioners for Detecting and Defeating Conspiracies in the State of New York,* Vol II, 1780-1781 (Albany, State of New York, 1909), 728, 737-739, http://archive.org/stream/cu31924021474782#page/n317/mode/2up ; *George Washington Papers, Series 4, General Correspondence: Abraham Wempel, Interrogation of Two British Prisoners Captured by Oneida Indians.* 1781. Manuscript/Mixed Material. https://www.loc.gov/item/mgw428504/

635 "Fulton County NYGenWeb" James F. Morrison, Canadian Regiments in the Continental Army. http://fulton.nygenweb.net/military/CanReg.html ; Gavin Watt, *A dirty, trifling, piece of business Volume I: The*

Revolutionary War as Waged From Canada in 1781 (Toronto: Dundern Press, 2009), 182-186.

636 Gavin Watt, *A dirty, trifling, piece of business Volume I: The Revolutionary War as Waged From Canada in 1781* (Toronto: Dundern Press, 2009), 162-163.174.; National Archives, *Revolutionary War Pension and Bounty Land Warrant Application Files,* M804, Pension Number, W. 16687, Record Group 15, Roll 1987, Garret Putman, Rebecca Putman https://www.fold3.com/image/246/27763379 ; Ibid, Pension Number, S. 22944, Victor Putman https://www.fold3.com/image/246/27763552

637 Library and Archives Canada, British Library, formerly British Museum, Additional Manuscripts 21804-21834, Haldimand Papers, Lac_reel_h1652, H-1652, 105513, 2034239, MG21, Image 626-627. http://heritage.canadiana.ca/view/oocihm.lac_reel_h1652/626?r=0&s=4

638 Gavin Watt, *A dirty, trifling, piece of business Volume I: The Revolutionary War as Waged From Canada in 1781* (Toronto: Dundern Press, 2009), 198-199.; The State of New York, Hugh Hastings, *Public Papers of George Clinton, First Governor of New York, 1777-1795, 1801-1804, Vol VI* (Albany, James B. Lyon, 1902), 78-81. Colonel Willett Sends to the Governor a Report, an Affidavit and a Statement Regarding Depredations Near Schoharie, 15 July 1781. (The affidavit lists many Tories near Schoharie many of whom were apprehended including Christopher Reddick, Henry Frauts, and Michael Frederick.) https://archive.org/stream/publicpapersgeo00unkngoog#page/n144/mode/2up ; The State of New York, *Minutes of the Commissioners for Detecting and Defeating Conspiracies in the State of New York,* Vol II, 1780-1781 (Albany, State of New York, 1909), 751-752. http://archive.org/stream/cu31924021474782#page/n331/mode/2up

639 Ancestry.com. *U.S., Dutch Reformed Church Records in Selected States, 1639-1989* [database on-line]. Provo, UT. Holland Society of New York; New York, New York; Cagnawaga or Fonda, Book 15. 93. 1778, Jacob, bo. Sept 5, John Hoog, Maragrieta Algire, Sponsors, John Keelman, Elizabeth d of.; Ancestry.com. *U.S., Dutch Reformed Church Records in Selected*

States, 1639-1989 [database on-line]. Provo, UT. Holland Society of New York; New York, New York; Schenectady Baptisms, Vol 3, Book 43. 276. 1781, Aug 25, Nicholass Simser, Margariet Beemer; Martinus, Sponsors, Henderick Simser, Maria Simser.

640 Ancestry.com. *U.S., Dutch Reformed Church Records in Selected States, 1639-1989* [database on-line]. Provo, UT. The Archives of the Reformed Church in America; New Brunswick, New Jersey; Fonda Church, Baptisms, Marriages, 1797-1872. 27. 1780, Dec 7, John Hoogh, Maragrita Algire; Martinus Dec 2, Jacob Algire, Catrina Algire.

641 Maryly Penrose, Compendium of Early Mohawk Valley Families Volume I (Baltimore, Genealogical Publishing Co., 1990), 5. Original Source: Records of the Reformed Protestant Dutch Church of German Flatts, ed. by R.W. Vosburgh. Collections of the New York genealogical and Biographical Society, Vol. I 1918. 195. Alcajer, Johannes m. Maria Semser, 19 September 1781.

642 E.A. Cruikshank, *The King's Royal Regiment of New York*. ed. Gavin Watt, (Toronto, The Ontario Historical Society, 1931) Reprinted Toronto, 1984, 45-51.; Manuscripts and Archives Division, The New York Public Library. "Johnson, Sir John" New York Public Library Digital Collections. Theodorus Bailey Myers Collection. *Series II. Prominent Civilians and Officials During the Colonial Period.* Account of Contingent Expenses Incurred by Sir John Johnson. 1781 Sept. 10. To cash to Sergeant Haines and party for their services on a scout to the county of Tryon. https://digitalcollections.nypl.org/items/a2a42ef0-349f-0133-b9a7-58d385a7b928

643 Todd W. Braisted, Refugees & Others: Loyalist Families in the American War for Independence, "The Brigade Dispatch," Parts 1 & 2 Volume XXVI no. 4, 2-7; Vol XXVII no 2, 2-6.; Gavin Watt, *Loyalist Refugees: Non-Military Refugees in Quebec 1776-1784,* (Milton ON: Global Heritage Press, 2014), 28.

644 New York State Archives, *Copies of accounts audited by the auditor general for bills presented to the state, 1780-1794.* NYSA_A0870-77_Book B.

Page 23, 24. For wheat impressed for the use of the public by Johnathan Douglass by order of General Marinus Willett. October 17, George Ruppert, Adam Ruppert, Johannes Dorn, Johannes Albrandt, Johannes Wert Sr., Johannes Wert Jr., Mattheus Link, Andrew Snyder, George Schenck, Godfrey Eney, George Adam Dachstader, Frederick Dachstader, Jacob Kitts. Sept 25, Beef, John Servis, Sept 28, Oct 22 Wheat for use of the troops, Michael & John Lingenfelder, Sept 30, Transporting Flour, Anthony van Veghten. http://digitalcollections.archives.nysed.gov/index.php/Detail/Object/Show/object_id/41660

645 Library and Archives Canada, British Library (Formerly British Museum) *Haldimand Papers,* Lac-reel_h1743, H-1743, 105513, 2034239, Image 1275-1276. http://heritage.canadiana.ca/view/oocihm.lac_reel_h1743/1275?r=0&s=4 Memorial of Joseph Hanes.

646 Gavin Watt, *A dirty, trifling, piece of business Volume I: The Revolutionary War as Waged From Canada in 1781* (Toronto: Dundern Press, 2009), 332.

647 Gavin Watt, *A dirty, trifling, piece of business Volume I: The Revolutionary War as Waged From Canada in 1781* (Toronto: Dundern Press, 2009), 320-333.; "The King's Royal Yorkers" Major John Ross. http://royalyorkers.ca/john_ross.php ; Ibid, Gavin K. Watt, The Companies of the 1st Battalion, KRRNY. http://royalyorkers.ca/companies_1bn.php ; Library and Archives Canada, *Upper Canada Land Petitions (1763-1865),* Mikan Number 205131, Microform c-2033, Page 446. Affidavit of Captain Samuel Anderson supporting Michael Gallinger Jr. service as a Grenadier in the KRRNY. The National Archives, *Revolutionary War Rolls 1775-1783,* M246, Record Group 93, Roll 0077, Folder 170. Page 24. Wemple's Regiment of Militia. https://www.fold3.com/image/246/10195046 ; "Fulton County NYGenWeb." Douglas J. Weaver, Roster of the Men in the Battle of Johnstown. 26 April 1999. http://fulton.nygenweb.net/military/roster1781.html

648 Gavin Watt, *A dirty, trifling, piece of business Volume I: The Revolutionary War as Waged From Canada in 1781* (Toronto: Dundern Press, 2009), 321.

649 Ancestry.com. *UK, American Loyalist Claims, 1776-1835 [database on-line]*. Provo, UT, USA: Ancestry.com Operations, Inc., 2013. Original data: American Loyalist Claims, 1776–1835. AO 12–13. The National Archives of the United Kingdom, Kew, Surrey, England. UK, American Loyalist Claims, 1776-1835 for Philip Eamer AO 12: American Loyalists Claims, Series I Piece 031: Evidence, New York, 1787-1788, 156. 277-278.

650 Library and Archives Canada, British Library (Formerly British Museum) *Haldimand Papers*, Lac_reel_h1743, H-1743, 105513, 2034239. Image 1244-1248. Statement of William Kennedy 6 Nov 1782. http://heritage.canadiana.ca/view/oocihm.lac_reel_h1743/1244?r=0&s=4 ; Ibid, Image 1264-1265. The Petition of Michael Carman Loyalist.1782. ; Ancestry.com. *UK, American Loyalist Claims, 1776-1835* [database on-line]. Provo, UT. The National Archives of the UK; Kew, Surrey, England; American Loyalist Claims, Series II; Class: AO 12; Piece 116: Temporary Assistance N-R, New York. 137-139. A Memorial and Petition humbly presented by William Parker.; Manuscripts and Archives Division, The New York Public Library. "Johnson, Sir John" New York Public Library Digital Collections. Theodorus Bailey Myers Collection. *Series II. Prominent Civilians and Officials During the Colonial Period.* Account of Contingent Expenses Incurred by Sir John Johnson. To cash to William Parker Senr. ..., To cash William Kennedy. https://digitalcollections.nypl.org/items/a2a42ef0-349f-0133-b9a7-58d385a7b928

651 Gavin Watt, *A dirty, trifling, piece of business Volume I: The Revolutionary War as Waged From Canada in 1781* (Toronto: Dundern Press, 2009), 358.; Ancestry.com. *UK, American Loyalist Claims, 1776-1835* [database on-line]. Provo, UT. The National Archives of the UK; Kew, Surrey, England; American Loyalist Claims, Series I; Class: AO 13; Piece 026: Evidence, New York, 1787. 285-287. Evidence on the Claim of

John Waite.; Ancestry.com. *UK, American Loyalist Claims, 1776-1835* [database on-line]. Provo, UT. The National Archives of the UK; Kew, Surrey, England; American Loyalist Claims, Series I; Class: AO 13; Piece 031: Evidence, New York, 1787-1788. 282. Evidence on the Claim of Michael Gollinger.

652 Ancestry.com. *Records of the Reformed Protestant Dutch Church of Caughnawaga : now the Reformed Church of Fonda, in the village of Fonda, Mon* [database on-line]. Provo, UT. Volume one. Marriages, 1772 to Jan. 31, 1818. 164. 1785, Jan 20. James Thompson met Elizabeth Gollinger.; Ancestry.com. *UK, American Loyalist Claims, 1776-1835* [database on-line]. Provo, UT. The National Archives of the UK; Kew, Surrey, England; American Loyalist Claims, Series I; Class: AO 13; Piece 026: Evidence, New York, 1787. 285-287. Evidence on the claim of John Waite late of New York.; Library and Archives Canada, *Upper Canada Land Petitions (1763-1865),* Mikan No. 205131, Microform c2106. Image 987. The Petition of John Hanes late of the County of Trion, York Province.; Ancestry.com. *UK, American Loyalist Claims, 1776-1835* [database on-line]. Provo, UT. The National Archives of the UK; Kew, Surrey, England; American Loyalist Claims, Series I; Class: AO 13. Piece 028: Evidence, New York, 1787. 355-356. Evidence on the Claim of Jospeh Hanes.

653 Arthur R. Bowler, "JESSUP, EDWARD," in *Dictionary of Canadian Biography,* vol. 5 (Toronto, University of Toronto/Université Laval, 2003). http://www.biographi.ca/en/bio/jessup_edward_5E.html ; Gavin Watt & Todd A. Braisted, A Service History and Master Roll of Major Edward Jessup's Loyal Rangers (Ottawa, Global Heritage Press, 2017); Centennial Committee, *The Old United Empire Loyalists List: The Centennial of the Settlement of Upper Canada by the United Empire Loyalists, 1784-1884* (Baltimore, Genealogical Publishing Co., 2000). Appendix B 253, Silmeser, Martin, Residence: Eastern District, Cornwall A soldier in Jessup's corps, Land Board Lunenburg, Provision List 1786.; Library and Archives Canada, *Upper Canada: Land Board Minutes and Records, 1765-1804,* Lac_reel_c14027, C-14027, 205141, RG 1 L 4, Image 780, Rec'd a petition from Martin Selemzer praying for

two hundred acres of land as a reduced soldier in Jessup's Corps which the board granted him. http://heritage.canadiana.ca/view/oocihm.lac_reel_c14027/780?r=0&s=3

654 The National Archives, *Revolutionary War Pension and Bounty Land Warrant Application Files,* M804, Record Group 15, Roll 2151, 15. John Servoss. https://www.fold3.com/image/246/14424494 ; Jane Marlett-Taft, *Gideon Marlett A Huguenot of Staten Island N.Y. With Some Account of the Descendants in the United States and Canada.* (Burlington Vermont, 1907), 72-73.; Gavin Watt, *A dirty, trifling, piece of business Volume I: The Revolutionary War as Waged From Canada in 1781* (Toronto: Dundern Press, 2009), 314-357. ; "Fulton County, NYGenWeb" Roster of the Men in the Battle of Johnstown on October 25, 1781. http://fulton.nygenweb.net/military/roster1781.html ; The State of New York, Hugh Hastings, *Public Papers of George Clinton, First Governor of New York, 1777-1795, 1801-1804, Vol VI* (Albany, James B. Lyon, 1902), 472-475. Defeat of Major Ross at Johnson Hall. https://archive.org/stream/publicpapersgeo00unkngoog#page/n550/mode/2up Letters to Headquarters. http://fulton.nygenweb.net/military/HQletters.html ; New York State Archives, Copies of accounts audited by the Auditor General for obligations incurred by the state during years 1775-1794. Book A, A0870-77, page 16. http://digitalcollections.archives.nysed.gov/index.php/Detail/Object/Show/object_id/46580 ; The National Archives, Revolutionary War Pension and Bounty Land Warrant Application Files, M804, Pension No. S. 14,312, Record Group 15, Roll 2048. Henry Rightmyer.; The Rev. James Dempster, a Record of Marriages and Baptisms in Vicinity of Tryon County, 1778-1803. 25. Lewis, of John Bowman, Warrens, h, 15th Oct 1781; Library and Archives Canada, Haldimand Loyalist Lists (Index), Lac_reel_c1475, C-1475, 105513, 2034239, MG 21 Add.MSS. 21661-21892. Image 333. http://heritage.canadiana.ca/view/oocihm.lac_reel_c1475/333?r=1&s=4 ; Upper Canada Land Petitions (1763-1865), Mikan No. 205131, c-1635, Image 553. Petition of Willliam Bush, son of William Bush.

New York State Archives, State Engineer and Surveyor. Survey maps of lands in New York State, ca. 1711-1913. Series A0273-78, Map #147A. Map of the Western Boundary Line of the third tract, granted to John Morine Scott and others, in 1769. http://digitalcollections.archives.nysed.gov/index.php/Detail/Object/Show/object_id/36677# ; Secretary of State of New York, Calendar of N.Y. Colonial Manuscripts Indorsed Land Papers, (Albany, Weed, Parsons & Co. 1864), Vol XII, 236. August 22, 1738. https://archive.org/stream/calendarofnycolo00alba#page/236/mode/2up

655 William Stone, *Orderly Book of Sir John Johnson During the Oriskany Campaign 1776-1777* (Albany: Joel Munsell's Sons, 1882), 18. https://archive.org/stream/orderlybooksirj00stongoog#page/n240/mode/2up

CHAPTER SIX
Home in the St. Lawrence River Valley (1781-1784)

656 Library and Archives Canada, British Library, formerly British Museum, Additional Manuscripts 21804-21834, *Haldimand Papers,* Lac_reel_h1654, H-1654, 105513, 2034239, MG21, Gerneral Return of Unincorporated Loyalists 25 August-24 Sept 1781. Image 710 http://heritage.canadiana.ca/view/oocihm.lac_reel_h1654/710?r=0&s=6 Image 619 Subsistence Return for Royalists Attached to the King's Royal Regiment of New York. http://heritage.canadiana.ca/view/oocihm.lac_reel_h1654/619?r=0&s=6 ; "The King's Royal Yorkers" Gavin K. Watt, The Recreated King's Royal Yorkers-Uniform Research. http://royalyorkers.ca/regiment_recreating.php

657 Library and Archives Canada, British Library, formerly British Museum, Additional Manuscripts 21804-21834, *Haldimand Papers,* Lac_reel_h1654, H-1654, 10513, 2034239, MG 21, Image 705, General Return of Unincorporated Royalists 25 August – 24 Sept 1781. Barnabas Hough, Peter's Corps, St. Johns. http://heritage.canadiana.ca/view/oocihm.lac_reel_h1654/705?r=0&s=6 ; "The Online Institute of Advanced Loyalist Studies." Queens Royal Rangers Effective Roll 1 May 1781. http://www.royalprovincial.com/military/musters/

Queens_Loyal_Rangers/1781-05-01_Queens_Loyal_Rangers.htm; T. R. Millman, "STUART, JOHN (1740/41-1811)," in *Dictionary of Canadian Biography*, vol. 5, University of Toronto/Université Laval, 2003. http://www.biographi.ca/en/bio/stuart_john_1740_41_1811_5E.html

658 After 1784, Bernhard Doenge's name changed to Bernhard Tinkess. In German, the letters d and t were interchangeable. Bernhard, or Barney, was the patriarch of the Tinkess family of Cornwall Township. On 28 June 1910, Sadie Ethel Tinkess, Daughter of James Bergin Tinkess and Mary Margaret Norman, married Arden Elzie Eamer, son of Peter Eamer and Mary Elizabeth Armstrong. "Hesse-Kassel Jäger Corps." Uniform Item Description http://www.jaegerkorps.org/Uniforms2.html ; Creutzburg, von, Karl Adolf Christoph (* ca. 1733) "in: *Hessische Truppen in Amerika* https://www.lagis-hessen.de/en/subjects/idrec/sn/hetrina/id/60235 (Stand: 20.1.2015); Doenges, Bernhard (* ca. 1756)", in: Hessische Truppen in Amerika https://www.lagis-hessen.de/en/subjects/idrec/sn/hetrina/id/61059 (Stand: 20.1.2015); Library and Archives Canada, *Upper Canada: Land Board Minutes and Records, 1765-1804.* Lac_reel_c14027, C-14027, 205141, RG 1 L 4. Image 777. Petition From Barnhart Dungus Late Soldier in Col: De Cruetzburg's Regt. http://heritage.canadiana.ca/view/oocihm.lac_reel_c14027/777?r=0&s=4 ; Ibid, Upper Canada Land Petitions (1763-1865). Mikan No. 205131, Microform c-1885. Page 399. The Memorial of Barnhard Donges of Cornwall.

659 Bruce E. Gurgoyne, trans., *Hesse-Hanau Order Books, A Diary And Rosters. A Collection of Items Concerning the Hesse-Hanau Contingent of "Hessians" Fighting Against the American Colonists in the Revolutionary War.*251-255.; Gavin Watt, I am heartily ashamed Volume II: The Revolutionary War's Final Campaign As Waged From Canada in 1782 (Toronto, Dundern Press, 2010), 431.

660 Robert Malcombson, "Nothing More Uncomfortable Than Our Flat Bottomed Boats:" Batteaux in the British Service During the War of

1812. *The Northern Mariner, XIII, No. 4,* (October, 2003), 17-28. https://www.cnrs-scrn.org/northern_mariner/vol13/tnm_13_4_17-28.pdf

661 The description of the Loyalist camp being near the Recollet's gate west of the city of Montreal is fiction. However, there were large loyalist settlements very near Montreal. In one source, the army barracks are placed just above the wharf at what is now known as Jacques Cartier Square. "Wikimedia Commons" Montreal 1725." https://commons.wikimedia.org/wiki/File:Montreal_1725.jpg ; "Des Recollets" Order of the Friar Recollects were once brothers to the French Army in Montreal. About the Recollets. http://www.vieux.montreal.qc.ca/tour/etape14/eng/14text4a.htm

662 Parliament of Canada, *Sessional Papers of the Dominion of Canada,* Vol 23, No. 6, (Ottawa, 1890), 13 Nov 1781.

663 A Sutler is a person who follows an army and sells provisions to soldiers. "The King's Royal Yorkers" Nancy Watt, "Spirited Women" KRRNY Loyalist Refugees. http://royalyorkers.ca/distaff.php ; Library and Archives Canada, British Library, formerly British Museum, Additional Manuscripts 21804-21834, *Haldimand Papers,* Lac_reel_h1654, H-1654, 10513, 2034239, MG 21, Image 728, Recapitulation Return of the Unincorporated Loyalists who Received Provisions Gratis From 25 Dec 1781-24 Jan 1782. http://heritage.canadiana.ca/view/oocihm.lac_reel_h1654/728?r=0&s=5

664 Alexander Cain, The Loyalist Refugee Experience in Canada, *Journal of the American Revolution,* January 26, 2015. https://allthingsliberty.com/2015/01/the-loyalist-refugee-experience-in-canada/ ; Gavin Watt, *Loyalist Refugees: Non-Military Refugees in Quebec 1776-1784,* (Milton ON: Global Heritage Press, 2014), 70-71. "Three Rivers Hudson, Mohawk, Schoharie, History From America's Most Famous Valleys" Horton's Historical Articles What Happened to 7000 People? http://threeriversshms.com/hh7thousand.htm

665 Library and Archives Canada, British Library, formerly British Museum, Additional Manuscripts 21804-21834, *Haldimand Papers,*

Lac_reel_h1654, H-1654, 10513, 2034239, MG 21, 715. Return of Unincorporated Loyalists and Families Who Received Their Provisions Gratis, 25 Dec 1781-24 Jan 1782. http://heritage.canadiana.ca/view/oocihm.lac_reel_h1654/718?r=0&s=5 ; Wayne Bower. "Registers of the Parishes of Williamsburg, Matilda, Osnabruck, and Edwardsburg." Burial Registers of the Parishes of Williamsburg, Matilda, Osnabruck, and Edwardsburg. Last modified February 27, 2016. 1803 buried, Dec 6th, William Empy Sen. of Osnabruck, born Apr. 29th 1728. Dec 5th, 78 yrs 7 months, 6 days. http://bowergenealogy.ca/resources/lutheran/A/178.jpg ; Ancestry.com. *Records of the Lutheran Trinity Church of Stone Arabia: in the town of Palatine, Montgomery County, N.Y.* [database on-line]. Provo, UT. Section: *Vol.1.* Birth and baptisms, 1751 to 1815. 12. MDCCLV d 28 Mart. Wilhelm Emige, c. ux. Maria Margaretha; Sponsors, Dieterich Loucks, Catharina Capernollin; Johann Dieterich.; Henry Z. Jones, Jr., *The Palatine Familes of New York: A Study of the German Immigrants Who Arrived in Colonial New York in 1710.,* Vol. I (Universal City, CA: H.Z. Jones, 1985), 535. 11749, 17 Dec, Wilhelmus Emmerich md. Margaretha Loucks, (daughter of Johannes Peter Loucks and Neltjie Leg), Athens (Loonenburg) Lutheran Church.

666 Library and Archives Canada, British Library, formerly British Museum, Additional Manuscripts 21804-21834, *Haldimand Papers.* Lac_reel_h1654, H-1654, 105513, 2034239, MG 21. 668, 674. http://heritage.canadiana.ca/view/oocihm.lac_reel_h1654/674?r=0&s=5 ; Library and Archives Canada, *Haldimand Loyalist Lists (Index),* lac_reel c1475, C1475, 105513, 2034239, MG 21 Add.MSS.21661-21892, 362. A List of Prisoners in the Hands of Congress Belonging to the Corps of Rangers Royalist and Their Families. Mrs Henry Hare, 1 woman, 4 boys, 3 girls. http://heritage.canadiana.ca/view/oocihm.lac_reel_c1475/362?r=1&s=3 ; "United Empire Association of Canada," Loyalist Trails, 44, 2017. Alida Vrooman Hare. http://www.uelac.org/Loyalist-Trails/2017/Loyalist-Trails-2017.php?issue=201744

667 Ancestry.com. *U.S., Dutch Reformed Church Records in Selected States, 1639-1989* [database on-line]. Provo, UT. The Archives of the Reformed Church in America; New Brunswick, New Jersey; Reformed Church of

Fonda, Baptisms, Marriages, Members, Consistory Minutes, 1758-1839. 15. Entry 191, 1775, April 16, Peter Service, Lena Millar. Philip get Febrary 8, Sponsors, John Service, Catrina Service.; Ancestry.com. *U.S., Dutch Reformed Church Records in Selected States, 1639-1989* [database on-line]. Provo, UT. Holland Society of New York; New York, New York; Stone Arabia and Staten Island, Book 48. 287. 1769, Oct 1, Johannis Serves to Catharina Schenck.; Ancestry.com. *U.S., Dutch Reformed Church Records in Selected States, 1639-1989* [database on-line]. Provo, UT. The Archives of the Reformed Church in America; New Brunswick, New Jersey; Stone Arabia Church, Baptisms, Members, Deaths, 1739-1987. 1763, 6 Januar, Johann Adam Helmer und Maria Beersch.; Ancestry.com. *Early Families of Herkimer County, New York* [database on-line]. Provo, UT. Barsh/Bretsch/Borsch 6. #306 pr. Maria b. say 1744, m. 1763 Adam Helmer Jr.; Ancestry.com. *Records of the Reformed Dutch Church of Stone Arabia: in the town of Palatine, Montgomery County, N.Y.* [database on-line]. Provo, UT. Vol.1. Baptisms and births. 67. 1766, N. d. 4n August, B. d. 9n August, Georg Adam Dachstaeder u. Eva.; Johannes, Sponsors, Johannes Berlet, und Sara Dachstaeder.

668 Library and Archives Canada, British Library, formerly British Museum, Additional Manuscripts 21804-21834, *Haldimand Papers.* Lac_reel_h1652, H-1652, 105513, 2034239, MG 21, A Roll of Men Inlisted for the Second Battalion of the Kings Royal Regt. Of New York. http://heritage.canadiana.ca/view/oocihm.lac_reel_h1652/487?r=0&s=3

669 I believe the following gravestone record belongs to Peter Eamer Jr. son of Peter Eamer and Maria Catherine Gallinger. The gravestone indicates he was born 11 July 1777; however, Peter and Maria Catherine were not married until January of 1780. I don't believe they would have waited 3 years to legitimize a son born in 1777. I think Peter Eamer Jr. was born ca. Nov. 1780 which would mean his age in 1859 was 79. I think there is an error in the birthdate and age on this gravestone and record. "Find A Grave" https://www.findagrave.com/memorial/103272760

670 Library and Archives Canada, British Library, formerly British Museum, Additional Manuscripts 21804-21834, *Haldimand*

Papers, Lac_reel_h1654, H-1654, 105513, 2034239, MG 21, Image 797. Estimate of Supplies of Provisions for the use of Loyalists. 16 October 1784. http://heritage.canadiana.ca/view/oocihm.lac_reel_h1654/797?r=1&s=6 ; "The King's Royal Yorkers." Captain Singleton's Light Company. A Brief History of the 2nd Battalion KRRNY. http://royalyorkers.ca/singletons.php ; Ibid, James L. Kochan, Uniforms and Arms of the King's Royal Regiment of New York. http://royalyorkers.ca/regiment_recreating.php ; "Canadian War Museum" Service Dress Coatee. https://www.warmuseum.ca/collections/artifact/1059136/?q=&page_num=1&item_num=0&media_irn=5389692&mode=artifact

671 Library and Archives Canada, Great Britain, War Office (WO 28). *America.* Lac_reel_c10861, C-10861, 158960, 125090, MG 13 WO. 366, 368. http://heritage.canadiana.ca/view/oocihm.lac_reel_c10861/366?r=0&s=3

672 E. A. Cruikshank, *The King's Royal Regiment of New York.* ed. Gavin Watt, (Toronto, The Ontario Historical Society, 1931) Reprinted Toronto, 1984, 201, 205-206, 269.

673 Library and Archives Canada, Great Britain War Office (WO 28): *America,* Lac_reel_c10860, C-10860, 158960, 125090, 105016, MG 13 WO, Image 1376. http://heritage.canadiana.ca/view/oocihm.lac_reel_c10860/1376?r=1&s=4 ; Ibid, Lac_reel_c10861, Image 366; Library and Archives Canada, *Heir and Devisee Commission,* Lac_reel_h1133, H-1133, RG 1 L5, 205142, Image 557. Land Certificate of Nicholas Barnhart Quebec, 1785. http://heritage.canadiana.ca/view/oocihm.lac_reel_h1133/557?r=0&s=4 ; Greene County, New York History & Genealogy, *Baptismal Records of Zion's Lutheran Church, Athens, NY 1703-1789.* Sons of Johannes Barnhardt and Gertraud Rau.: 1740 Mar 25 Niclas Bernhard, Joh*s & Gertryd.; Extracted from J.B. Beers "History of Greene County", published in 1884, by Ann Clapper Website: © Copyright 2000-2012 Sylvia Hasenkopf. Ancestry.com. U.S., *Dutch Reformed Church Records in Selected States, 1639-1989* [database on-line]. Provo, UT. Holland Society of New York; New York, New

York; Germantown NY, Book 81. 31. Georg, Jan 29 1744, J. Bernhardt Gertroudt; Sponsors, George Barnhardt, Marytche Rau.

674 Library and Archives Canada, British Library, formerly British Museum, Additional Manuscripts 21804-21834, *Haldimand Papers*, Lac_reel_h1654, H-1654, 10513, 2034239, MG 21, Image 721, 725. Return of Unincorporated Loyalists and Families Who Received Their Provisions Gratis, 25 Dec 1781-24 Jan 1782. http://heritage.canadiana.ca/view/oocihm.lac_reel_h1654/721?r=0&s=5 ; Gavin Watt, *I am heartily ashamed Volume II: The Revolutionary War's Final Campaign As Waged From Canada in 1782* (Toronto, Dundern Press, 2010), 131, 134-135, 142.; Library and Archives Canada, British Library, formerly British Museum, Additional Manuscripts 21804-21834, *Haldimand Papers*. Lac_reel_h1655, H-1655, 105513, 2034239, MG21. Image 955, http://heritage.canadiana.ca/view/oocihm.lac_reel_h1655/955?r=0&s=5 ; E. A. Cruikshank, *The King's Royal Regiment of New York*. ed. Gavin Watt, (Toronto, The Ontario Historical Society, 1931) Reprinted Toronto, 1984, 85-86.

675 Don J. Durzan, "Arginine, scurvey and Cartier's "tree of life" *Journal of Ethnobiology and Ethnomedicine*, 5, No. 5 (2009) doi 10.1186/1746-4269. https://www.ncbi.nlm.nih.gov/pmc/articles/PMC2647905/ ; "Martyn Cornell's Zythofile, Beer Now and Then." A Short History of Spruce Beer Part Two: The North American Connection. http://zythophile.co.uk/2016/04/20/a-short-history-of-spruce-beer-part-two-the-north-american-connection/ ; E.A. Cruikshank, Gavin K. Watt, *The History and Master Roll of the King's Royal Regiment of New York, Revised* Edition, image reprint CD, (Milton, Ontario: Global Heritage Press, 2006, 2010), Appendix III.; Paul E. Kopperman, "The Medical Dimension in Cornwallis's Army, 1780-1781." *The North Carolina Historical Review*, 89, No. 4 (2012): 367-98. http://www.jstor.org/stable/23523993. Jail fever was a term used to describe Typhus.

676 E. A. Cruikshank, *The King's Royal Regiment of New York*. ed. Gavin Watt, (Toronto, The Ontario Historical Society, 1931) Reprinted Toronto, 1984, 93.; Library and Archives Canada, Great Britain, War Office

(WO 28) : *America.* Lac_reel_c10861, C-10861, 158960, 125090, MG 13 WO. Image 54, 59, 87, 89. State of the Garrison of Carleton Island, 1 Jan 1782, 1 May 1782. Present State of the Garrison of Oswego 23 April 1782, 1 June 1782. http://heritage.canadiana.ca/view/oocihm.lac_reel_c10861/91?r=0&s=2

677 Library and Archives Canada, British Library (Formerly British Museum) Haldimand Papers. Lac_reel_h1743, H-1743, 105513, 2034239. Image 1198-1199. http://heritage.canadiana.ca/view/oocihm.lac_reel_h1743/1198?r=0&s=4; Duncan Fraser, Papers and Records of the Ontario Historical Society, Volume LII, 1960, Original Source, Public Record Office, London, England AC 13/114. *Sir John Johnson's Rent Roll of the Kingsborough Patent.* http://freepages.genealogy.rootsweb.ancestry.com/~wjmartin/kingsbor.htm ; Ancestry.com. *U.S., Dutch Reformed Church Records in Selected States, 1639-1989* [database on-line]. Provo, UT. Holland Society of New York; New York, New York; Stone Arabia and Staten Island, Book 48. 93. 1765, Andreas, bo. Jan 29; Jacob Andries Kumerling, Barbara; Sponsor, Catharina wife of Andries Dillenbach.

678 Library and Archives Canada, British Library (Formerly British Museum) Haldimand Papers. Lac_reel_h1743, H-1743, 105513, 2034239. Image 1244-1248. Petition of William Kennedy. http://heritage.canadiana.ca/view/oocihm.lac_reel_h1743/1244?r=0&s=4; Ibid, Image 1264-1266. Petition of Michael Carman Praying for Relief. Affidavit of Sir John Johnson. On 24 Dec 1782 Michael Carman Sr. was ordered a bounty of 3 dollars per month for house, hire, and fuel. http://heritage.canadiana.ca/view/oocihm.lac_reel_h1743/1244?r=0&s=4

679 Margaret's parents are possibly Ludovicus (Lewis) Davis and Maria Clement of Fort Hunter, or William Davis of Schenectady. Ancestry.com. *U.S., Dutch Reformed Church Records in Selected States, 1639-1989* [database on-line]. Provo, UT. The Archives of the Reformed Church in America; New Brunswick, New Jersey; Reformed Church of Fonda, Baptisms, Marriages, Members, Consistory Minutes, 1758-1839. 1764, May 13, John Hare, Margarita Davis; William geb May 6, Sponsors William Hare, Elizabeth Hare.; Library and Archives

Canada, British Library (Formerly British Museum) Haldimand Papers. Lac_reel_h1743, H-143, 105513, 2034239. Image 1625-1627. Petition of Margaret Hare. http://heritage.canadiana.ca/view/oocihm.lac_reel_h1743/1625?r=0&s=4

680 Library and Archives Canada, Upper Canada Land Petitions (1763-1865), Mikan Number, 20531, Microform c-1625, Image 394. Petition of Anne Bender of Kingston, wife of George Bender, daughter of John Wait. Kingston 28 July 1819.; Library and Archives Canada, *Haldimand Loyalist Lists (Index),* Lac_reel_c1475, C-1475, 105513, 2034239, MG 21 Add.MSS. 21661-21892. Image 405-406. A List of Prisoners in the Hands of Congress Belonging to the Corps of Rangers. http://heritage.canadiana.ca/view/oocihm.lac_reel_c1475/406?r=0&s=5 ; British Library, formerly British Museum, Additional Manuscripts 21804-21834, *Haldimand Papers,* Lac_reel_h1654, H-1654, 105513, 2034239, MG 21. Image 627. http://heritage.canadiana.ca/view/oocihm.lac_reel_h1654/627?r=0&s=6 ; E.A. Cruikshank, Gavin K. Watt, *The History and Master Roll of the King's Royal Regiment of New York, Revised* Edition, image reprint CD, (Milton, Ontario: Global Heritage Press, 2006, 2010), Appendix III.; Guylaine Petrin, *The Free Library.* S.v. Disentangting a loyalist family tree." (United Empire Loyalists Association) https://www.thefreelibrary.com/Disentangting+a+loyalist+family+tree.-a0275310916 ; J. Kelsey Jones, Loyalist Plantations on the Susquehanna. http://www.seeleycreekvalleyfarm.com/loyalist_seeley.pdf

681 National Archives, *Revolutionary Rolls 1775-1783,* M246, Record Group 93, Roll 0067, Folder 22. A Description Roll of Deserters of the 2nd New York Regiment of Foot. Commanded by Col Philip Cortlandt. No. 10 John Crieghoff, Age 19, 5'6", Weaver, Where born: New York, Albany, Schenectady; Place of Residence, Tryon, Johnstown; Color of Hair, Brown; Complexion, Brown; When deserted 8 July 1781.

682 Library and Archives Canada, British Library, formerly British Museum, Additional Manuscripts 21804-21834, *Haldimand Papers.* Lac_reel_h1652, H-1652, 105513, 2034239, MG 21. Image 630. http://heritage.canadiana.ca/view/oocihm.lac_reel_h1652/630?r=0&s=6

683 In Reid, William D. *The Loyalists in Ontario: The Sons and Daughters of the American Loyalists of Upper Canada,* the wife of Martin Waldorf is listed as Leana. However, in the baptism record for their son Martin Jr. her name is listed as Margaretha. Ancestry.com. *Records of the Lutheran Trinity Church of Stone Arabia: in the town of Palatine, Montgomery County, N.Y.* [database on-line]. Provo, UT. Vol.1. Birth and baptisms, 1751 to 1815. 42. Anno 1772, Februy 27ten; Martin Waldorff & Margaretha ux; Sponsors, Peter Servis. Capit & ux; Martin.

684 Ancestry.com. *UK, American Loyalist Claims, 1776-1835* [database on-line]. Provo, UT. The National Archives of the UK; Kew, Surrey, England; American Loyalist Claims, Series I; Class: AO 13. Piece 032: Evidence, New York, 1788. 170. Evidence on the Claim of Martin Waldroff late of Tryon County.

685 Simon Clark and Ann Eve Waldorf married ca. 1782. Reid, William D. *The Loyalists in Ontario: The Sons and Daughters of the American Loyalists of Upper Canada.* (Lambertville, NJ, Genealogical Publishing Co., 1973) 329.

686 Library and Archives Canada, British Library, formerly British Museum, Additional Manuscripts 21804-21834, *Haldimand Papers.* Lac_reel) h1655, H-1655, 105513, 2034239, MG 21. Image 28. Return of Distressed Families of Loyalists in the District of Montreal. 26 April 1782. lhttp://heritage.canadiana.ca/view/oocihm.lac_reel_h1655/28?r=1&s=4 ; Library and Archives of Canada, *Heir and Devisee Commission.* Lac_reel_h1135, H-1135, RG 1 L5, 205142. Image 352. Land Certificate of Adam Casselman of Williamsburg, Drummer KRRNY. http://heritage.canadiana.ca/view/oocihm.lac_reel_h1135/352?r=0&s=2 ; Ancestry.com. *Records of the Lutheran Trinity Church of Stone Arabia: in the town of Palatine, Montgomery County, N.Y.* [database on-line]. Provo, UT. *Vol.1.* Birth and baptisms, 1751 to 1815. 27. Anno 1769, Maii d 28ten, William Casselmann & Catharina ux.; Sponsors, Adam Forry & Margaretha Sprechetin; Adam.; Ancestry.com. *U.S., Dutch Reformed Church Records in Selected States, 1639-1989* [database on-line]. Provo, UT. Holland Society of New York; New

York, New York; Church Records of Niskayuna and Schoharie, Book 36. 363. 1753, Sept. 29, Reg. John Nicohlas Matheese, son of Nicholas, and Sophia dau. of Johannis Enckhold. Both bo. & liv here; The New York Public Library. Manuscripts and Archives Division, *List of loyalists against whom judgments were given under the Confiscation Act.* New York Public Library Digital Collections. http://digitalcollections.nypl.org/items/92737eb0-0e2f-0134-64ed-00505686a51c ; Ancestry.com. *New York, Sales of Loyalist Land, 1762-1830* [database on-line]. Provo, UT. Original data: New York State Engineer and Surveyor. Records of Surveys and Maps of State Lands, 1686–1892, Series A4016, Vols. 7–10 and 17. New York State Archives, Albany, New York. Page 100 a-f. Nicholas Mathias 2000 acres.

687 E.A. Cruikshank, Gavin K. Watt, *The History and Master Roll of the King's Royal Regiment of New York, Revised* Edition, image reprint CD, (Milton, Ontario: Global Heritage Press, 2006, 2010), Appendix III.; Library and Archives Canada, British Library, formerly British Museum, Additional Manuscripts 21804-21834, *Haldimand Papers.* Lac_reel_h1652, H1652, 105513, 2034239, MG 21. Image 513, 514. Roll of Men, 2nd Battn KRRNY Enlisted Since 25 Oct 1781. http://heritage.canadiana.ca/view/oocihm.lac_reel_h1652/513?r=0&s=5

688 Library and Archives Canada, *Registres de paroisses, Québec.* Lac_reel_c3023, C3023, 101567, 98023, 98022. Image 498. Register of the Parish of Montreal. 1782 Sept Philip Mauk and Helen Walderf; James H. Lambert, "CHABRAND DELISLE, DAVID," in *Dictionary of Canadian Biography*, vol. 4, University of Toronto/Université Laval, 2003, http://www.biographi.ca/en/bio/chabrand_delisle_david_4E.html; "Bill Martin's Genealogy Pages." Extracts From Canadian Archives Haldimand Papers, Series B, Vol 158, page 365. A list of men inlisted by orders of the late Mr. Hewetson for Sir John Johnson's (Bart.) Brigade, and joined Joseph Brant's Volunteers of their own accord: Philip Moake. http://my.tbaytel.net/bmartin/aid.htm

689 Library and Archives Canada, British Library (Formerly British Museum) *Haldimand Papers*, Lac_reel_h1743, H-1743, 105513,

2034239, Image 1255. http://heritage.canadiana.ca/view/oocihm.lac_reel_h1743/1255?r=0&s=4

690 Library and Archives Canada, British Library, formerly British Museum, Additional Manuscripts 21804-21834, *Haldimand Papers.* Lac_reel_h1655, H-1655, 105513, 2034239, MG 21. Image 955. Effective strength of the Garrison at Oswego as fixed for the winter. http://heritage.canadiana.ca/view/oocihm.lac_reel_h1655/955?r=0&s=5 ; Library and Archives Canada, Great Britain, War Office (WO 28): *America.* Lac_reel_c10861, C10861, 158960, 125090, MG 13 WO. Image 70. http://heritage.canadiana.ca/view/oocihm.lac_reel_c10861/70?r=0&s=3 ; E. A. Cruikshank, *The King's Royal Regiment of New York.* ed. Gavin Watt, (Toronto, The Ontario Historical Society, 1931) Reprinted Toronto, 1984, 97.; Fryer, Mary & W. Smy (Lieutenant-Colonel), *Rolls of the Provincial (Loyalist) Corps, Canadian Command American Revolutionary Period,* Muster Roll 1st Battalion KRRNY. Enlisted Men, First and Second Battalions, (Toronto, Dundern Press, 1981), 26.

691 Fryer, Mary & W. Smy (Lieutenant-Colonel), *Rolls of the Provincial (Loyalist) Corps, Canadian Command American Revolutionary Period.* Muster Roll 1st Battalion KRRNY. Enlisted Men, First and Second Battalions, Montreal, December, 1782. (Toronto, Dundern Press, 1981), 26.

692 Library and Archives Canada. Great Britain, War Office (WO 28): *America.* Lac_reel_c10862, C10862, 158960, 125090, MG 13 WO. Image 371. A Roll of the Age, Size, Country's, and Time of Service of the Sergeants, Corporals, Drummers, and privates of the 2nd Bn KRRt New York. #97 Peter Earner, Years 26 Months 0, Feet 5, Inches 11, Regt. -, Former Servitude -, Servitude in this, 3, Total 3. http://heritage.canadiana.ca/view/oocihm.lac_reel_c10862/371?r=1&s=6

693 Library and Archives Canada, British Library, formerly British Museum, Additional Manuscripts 21804-21834, *Haldimand Papers.* Lac_reel_h1654, H-1654, 105513, 2034139, MG21, Image 326, 729. Return of Royalists who are entitled to House rent and Firewood from

the Government. Montreal 1 Jan. 1782; 1 Jan 1783. http://heritage.canadiana.ca/view/oocihm.lac_reel_h1654/729?r=0&s=5

694 This is Henry Bowen of Butler's Rangers the only son of John Bowen of London England. Library and Archives Canada, Great Britain, War Office (WO 28): *America*. Lac_reel_c10861, C-10861, 158960, 125090, MG 13 WO. Image 1520. http://heritage.canadiana.ca/view/oocihm.lac_reel_c10861/1520?r=0&s=2 ; Library and Archives Canada, *Registres de paroisses, Québec*. Lac_reel_c3023, C-3023, 101567, 98023, 98022. Image 398. Bridgroom, Bone Henry. Bride, Commerly Catherine. http://heritage.canadiana.ca/view/oocihm.lac_reel_c3023/398?r=0&s=5 ; Bibliothèque et Archives Nationales Quebec. Mariages non catholiques de la région de Montréal, 1766-1899. Centre d'archives de Montréal, CE601,S63. Henry Bone, Catherine Cammerly, 1783, Christ Anglican Church (Montreal), page 26.

695 "America in Class" Making The Revolution: 1763-1791. Alexander Hamilton & Isaac Ledyard, A Pamphlet War on the Post War Treatment of Loyalists. http://americainclass.org/sources/makingrevolution/independence/text4/hamiltonledyard.pdf ; Oscar Zeichner, "The Loyalist Problem in New York After the Revolution." *New York History* 21, no. 3 (1940): 284-302. http://www.jstor.org/stable/23135069; E. A. Cruikshank, *The King's Royal Regiment of New York*. ed. Gavin Watt, (Toronto, The Ontario Historical Society, 1931) Reprinted Toronto, 1984, 103.

696 Alexander Fraser, Provincial Archivist. Digital Edition of the Second Report of the Bureau of Archives For the Province of Ontario. 1904. *United Empire Loyalists Enquiry Into The Losses and Services in Consequence of Their Loyalty Evidence in the Canadian Claims, 1904* (Toronto: Global Heritage Press, 2010), 11-12.; Maya Jasanoff, Liberty's Exiles. American Loyalists in the Revolutionary War (New York, Alfred A. Knopf, 2011), 87.

697 Ancestry.com. *UK, American Loyalist Claims, 1776-1835* [database on-line]. Provo, UT. The National Archives of the UK; Kew, Surrey,

England; American Loyalist Claims, Series I; Class: AO 12; Piece: 86. Documents Communicated by New York State Government, 1786. Kline, Adam of Caghnuaga, Tryon. Indicted County of Albany, When Indicted March 8th 1781, Date of Judgment Aug 3 1782.; E.A. Cruikshank, Gavin K. Watt, *The History and Master Roll of the King's Royal Regiment of New York, Revised* Edition, image reprint CD, (Milton, Ontario: Global Heritage Press, 2006, 2010), Appendix III.

698 Library and Archives Canada, British Library, formerly British Museum, Additional Manuscripts 21804-21834, *Haldimand Papers.* Lac_reel_h1654, H-1654, 105513, 2034239, MG 21. Image 731. Return of distressed unincorporated Loyalists that are victualled by the bounty of Government in the Province of Quebec, 24 March 1783. Eamer, Cathrine, 1 woman, 1 boy above 6 years. Total 2, Number of rations per day 1. To what corps attached, Ryl Yks 2nd Bn. Remarks, Montreal. http://heritage.canadiana.ca/view/oocihm.lac_reel_h1654/731?r=0&s=5

699 Ibid, 733. http://heritage.canadiana.ca/view/oocihm.lac_reel_h1654/733?r=0&s=5

700 Maya Jasanoff, *Liberty's Exiles. American Loyalists in the Revolutionary War.* 85, 92.

701 Isabel Thompson Kelsay, *Joseph Brant 1743-1807 Man of Two Worlds* (Syracuse, Syracuse University Press, 1984), 339, 348.; C. M. Johnston, "DESERONTYON, JOHN," in *Dictionary of Canadian Biography,* vol. 5, University of Toronto/Université Laval, 2003. http://www.biographi.ca/en/bio/deserontyon_john_5E.html ; *Haldimand papers from the British Library.* Lac_reel_h1437, H-1437, 105513, 2034239, MG 21. Image 1322. Letter from Frederick Haldimand to Sir John Johnson. http://heritage.canadiana.ca/view/oocihm.lac_reel_h1437/1322?r=0&s=4

702 Gavin Watt, *I am heartily ashamed Volume II: The Revolutionary War's Final Campaign As Waged From Canada in 1782* (Toronto, Dundern Press, 2010), 141,142, 161; Library and Archives of Canada, *Haldimand*

Papers B2/3, 63. Jacob Countryman and Sefrenis Casselman request reward for scouting.

703 Library and Archives Canada, British Library, formerly British Museum, Additional Manuscripts 21804-21834, *Haldimand Papers.* Lac_reel_h1655, H-1655, 105513, 2034239, MG 21, Image 1000-1001. Number of British and Provincial Troops in the Lower Part of the Province of Quebec. http://heritage.canadiana.ca/view/oocihm.lac_reel_h1655/1000?r=0&s=5 ; Ibid, Lac_reel_h1654, H-1654, 105513, 2034239, MG 21, Image 763. Recapitulation. http://heritage.canadiana.ca/view/oocihm.lac_reel_h1654/763?r=0&s=5

704 Ibid, Lac_reel_h1654, H-1654, 105513, 2034239, MG 21. Image 749-764. Return of distressed unincorporated Loyalists that are victualled by the bounty of Government in the Province of Quebec, 24 July 1783. http://heritage.canadiana.ca/view/oocihm.lac_reel_h1654/749?r=0&s=5 ; Source: S00124 Author: LDS film # N39035 0862340 Title: *Estate Files Stormont, Dundas, Glengarry Counties Repository*: #R00047. NOTELDS film # N39035 0862340, 1812, Estate Files Stormont, Dundas, Glengarry Counties, the will of David McCuen. Source: *WikiTree* profile McEwen. Ruth Pharoah.; Alex W. Fraser & Rhoda Ross, ed. *St. Andrews Presbyterian Church, Willamstown, Ontario, Baptisms and Marriages From 1779-1804.* (1999), 72; Library and Archives Canada, Great Britain War Office (WO 28): *America.* Lac_reel_c10860, C-10860, 158960, 125090, 105016, MG 13 W0, Image 909. Monthly Return of Loyalists Names and the dates of their arrival from the Colonies. St. Johns 1 June 1782. http://heritage.canadiana.ca/view/oocihm.lac_reel_c10860/909?r=0&s=4

705 Philip Eamer and Micheal Gallinger Sr. enlisted in the 2nd battalion KRRNY on March 23, 1783. E.A. Cruikshank, *The King's Royal Regiment of New York.* ed. Gavin Watt, (Toronto, The Ontario Historical Society, 1931) Reprinted Toronto, 1984, 104, 193, 201; Adam Shortt & Arthur G. Doughty, ed. *Documents Relating to the Constitutional History of Canda, 1759-1791.* Sessional Paper No. 18. (Ottawa, S.E. Dawson, 1907), 494-495. https://archive.org/stream/documentsrelatin00shor#page/494 ;

David T. Moorman, *The First Business of Government: The Land Granting Administration of Upper Canada,* (Ottawa, The National Library of Canada, 1997), 12-16. http://collectionscanada.gc.ca/obj/s4/f2/dsk2/tape17/PQDD_0014/NQ28362.pdf

706 Library and Archives Canada, British Library, formerly British Museum, Additional Manuscripts 21804-21834, *Haldimand Papers.* Lac_reel_h1655, H-1655, 105513, 2034239, MG 21. Image 253. http://heritage.canadiana.ca/view/oocihm.lac_reel_h1655/253?r=0&s=5

707 Library and Archives Canada, Ibid, Lac_reel_h1743, H-1743, 105513, 2034239, Image 1321. The Memorial of John Monier late Postmaster & Contractor's Agent at Albany. http://heritage.canadiana.ca/view/oocihm.lac_reel_h1743/1321?r=0&s=4 ; Ibid, Lac_reel_h1655, H-1655, 105513, 2034239, MG 21, Image 1006. Strength of the 1st Battalion Royal Regiment New York doing garrison duty, Montreal, 1st August 1783. Staff of the Garrison, Lewis Geneway Barrack Master http://heritage.canadiana.ca/view/oocihm.lac_reel_h1655/1006?r=0&s=5

708 Stormont, Dundas and Glengarry Surrogate Court Records Register Book A, 197-198. Microform Reel 862333. Will of Martin Silmser, 20 August 1800. "….unto my two daughters Christina Elizabeth wife of John Chrysler and Anna Mary wife of John Algire."

709 Centennial Committee, *The Old United Empire Loyalists List: The Centennial of the Settlement of Upper Canada by the United Empire Loyalists, 1784-1884.* (Baltimore, Genealogical Publishing Co., 2003), Appendix B Page 130, 253. Algire, Junior, Jacob, Residence: E. District Son of Jacob, Senr. not U.E. in his own right. p. Petition, 1798; Algire, Martin, E. District, Soldier, Royal Yorkers, Muster Roll, P.L. 2d 1786.; Algire, Senior, Jacob, E. District, R.R.N.Y. P.L. 2d 1786 I.F.; Silmeser, Martin, Eastern District, Cornwall A soldier in Jessup's corps, Land Board Lunenburg, Provision List 1786.; Ancestry.com. *Records of the Reformed Protestant Dutch Church of Caughnawaga: now the Reformed Church of Fonda, in the village of Fonda, Mon* [database on-line]. Provo, UT. Volume

one. Baptisms and births, 1758 to 1797. 64; Entry No: 768. Jan. 10 1783 Nichllas Simson & Maragrita Beemer, Philip bo: Decr. 29 1782 Sponsors Martin Simson & Elizabeth Simson; G.B. Alguire 1920. *New Claim No AO 13/81*, 1 March 1788, Estimate of the real and personal estate of Jacob Algier in the County of Tryone.; Ancestry.com. *U.S., Dutch Reformed Church Records in Selected States, 1639-1989* [database on-line]. Provo, UT. The Archives of the Reformed Church in America; New Brunswick, New Jersey; Reformed Church of Fonda, Baptisms, Marriages, Members, Consistory Minutes, 1758-1839. Nov 3 1782, Johannes Algyre, Anna Maria; Elizabeth Maragreta, b. Oct 20; Sponsors Martin Shave, Elizabeth Maragrita.; Ibid. Jan 4 1783, Michel Myers, Elizabeth Criehoof; Michel 4 weeken; Sponsors, Godfrey Anie, Maria Anie.; Ibid, Dec 20 1783, Johannes Wart, Dorothy Eman; Nichlas, Oct 28, Sponsors, Nichlaas Wert, Anna Albrant.; Ancestry.com. *U.S., Dutch Reformed Church Records in Selected States, 1639-1989* [database on-line]. Provo, UT. The Archives of the Reformed Church in America; New Brunswick, New Jersey; Fonda Church, Baptisms, Marriages, 1797-1872. 26. 1781, Nov 26, Michel Myers, Elizabeth Chiehogf; Maria bo. Sept 22; Sponsors Hendr Simson, & Maria.

710 Library and Archives Canada, British Library, formerly British Museum, Additional Manuscripts 21804-21834, *Haldimand Papers*. Lac_reel_h1655, H-1655, 105513, 2034239, MG 21, Image 44. Return of Unincorporated Loyalists Victualled in the Province of Quebec. 24 Jan 1784. http://heritage.canadiana.ca/view/oocihm.lac_reel_h1655/44?r=1&s=5 ; Ancestry.com. *The Loyalists in Ontario* [database on-line]. Provo, UT. Original data: Reid, William D. *The Loyalists in Ontario: The Sons and Daughters of the American Loyalists of Upper Canada*. Lambertville, NJ, USA: Genealogical Publishing Co., 1973. Section: V, 326. Van Koughnet, Michael of Cornwall, Sgt. RRNY.

711 No record of Dorothy Silmser's birth was found; however there is a record of her marriage to Michael Gallinger in 1806. Assuming she was over 18 when married, she was born before 1788. "Upper Canada East Marriage Indexes." Michael Stephenson. Last Updated 2018. Gallinger, Michael, Selismer? Dorothy. 1806. https://www.ontariogenealogy.com/

easternontariomarriages.html ; Library and Archives Canada. British Library, formerly British Museum, Additional Manuscripts 21804-21834, Haldimand Papers. Lac_reel_h1655, H-1655, 105513, 2034239, MG 21. Image 228. Muster of Township No. 2., 1784. Nichlas Sellemser, 1 man, 1 woman, 1male under 10, 2 females under 10. Total 5, Rations per day, 3 ½. Family on their lands.

712 Ancestry.com. *Records of the Reformed Protestant Dutch Church of Caughnawaga: now the Reformed Church of Fonda, in the village of Fonda, Mon* [database on-line]. Provo, UT. Volume one. Marriages, 1772 to Jan. 31, 1818. 160. 1774, May 21. Francis Jecoks, met Nelly Allen, numb 30; Ancestry.com. *England, Select Marriages, 1538–1973* [database on-line]. Provo, UT. *England, Marriages, 1538–1973.* Salt Lake City, Utah: FamilySearch, 2013. John Pescod, Marriage date: 30 May 1765, Marriage Place: Saint Nicholas, White Haven, Cumberland England, Spouse: Mary Johnson.FHL Film Number: 90658, 90682; Library and Archives Canada, British Library, formerly British Museum, Additional Manuscripts 21804-21834, *Haldimand Papers.* Lac_reel_h1655, H-1655, 105513, 2034239, MG 21, Image 52. Return of Unincorporated Loyalists Victualled in the Province of Quebec. 24 Jan 1784; Dorothy Gallinger, Remarks, R, Y, 1st Bn, married in this province.

713 Library and Archives Canada, British Library, formerly British Museum, Additional Manuscripts 21804-21834, *Haldimand Papers.* Lac_reel_h1655, H-1655, 105513, 2034239, MG 21. Image 253. http://heritage.canadiana.ca/view/oocihm.lac_reel_h1655/253?r=0&s=5 ; Library and Archives Canada, Great Britain War Office (WO 28): *America.* Lac_reel_c10860, C-10860, 158960, 125090, 105016, MG 13, WO. Image 954. http://heritage.canadiana.ca/view/oocihm.lac_reel_c10860/954?r=0&s=3

714 Ron Edwards, "McNIFF, PATRICK," in *Dictionary of Canadian Biography*, vol. 5, University of Toronto/Université Laval, 2003. http://www.biographi.ca/en/bio/mcniff_patrick_5E.html; Library and Archives Canada, British Library (Formerly British Museum) *Haldimand Papers.* Lac_reel_h1743, H-1743, 105513, 2034239. Image 1358.

Memorial of Patrick McNiff. http://heritage.canadiana.ca/view/oocihm.lac_reel_h1743/1358?r=0&s=4 ; Adam Shortt & Arthur G. Doughty, ed. *Documents Relating to the Constitutional History of Canda, 1759-1791.* Sessional Paper No. 18. (Ottawa, S.E. Dawson, 1907), 494-495. https://archive.org/stream/documentsrelatin00shor#page/494

715 Alexander Fraser, Provincial Archivist. Digital Edition of the Second Report of the Bureau of Archives For the Province of Ontario. 1904. *United Empire Loyalists Enquiry Into The Losses and Services in Consequence of Their Loyalty Evidence in the Canadian Claims, 1904* (Toronto: Global Heritage Press, 2010), 12-14.; Ancestry.com. *UK, American Loyalist Claims, 1776-1835* [database on-line]. Provo, UT. The National Archives of the UK; Kew, Surrey, England; American Loyalist Claims, Series I; Class: AO 13; Piece 031: Evidence, New York, 1787-1788. 143. Evidence on the Claim of Michal Gollinger.

716 Ancestry.com. *UK, American Loyalist Claims, 1776-1835* [database on-line]. Provo, UT. The National Archives of the UK; Kew, Surrey, England; American Loyalist Claims, Series I; Class: AO 13; Piece 031: Evidence, New York, 1787-1788. 427. Evidence on the claim of Sarah Gollinger widow of Henry Fykes.

717 Although there is no baptismal record for Catherine Gallinger, Henry Gallinger and Dorothy are listed as having a daughter under 10. Library and Archives Canada, British Library, formerly British Museum, Additional Manuscripts 21804-21834, *Haldimand Papers,* Lac_reel_h1655, H-1655, 105513, 2034239, MG 21. Image 226.

718 Library and Archives Canada, *Upper Canada Land Petitions (1763-1865),* Mikan Number 205131, Microform c-1888, Image 22. Discharge certificate of Jacob Eaman of Captain Archibald Mcdonell's Company. 25 yrs old, born in the parish of Johnstown in the County Tryon. Montreal, 24 Dec 1783. Signed by John Johnson.; Ibid, Microform c-2044, Image 551-552. Discharge certificate of Henry Hoople of Captain Archibald Mcdonell's Company, born in the parish of Cherry Valley in the County of Tryon, aged 24. Montreal, 24 Dec 1783; Library and Archives Canada,

Upper Canada Land Petitions (1763-1865) Mikan Number: 205131 Microform: c-2033. 446. Affidavit from Captain Samuel Anderson certifying Michael Gallinger Jr.s discharge from the Grenadier Company of the KRRNY.

719 Elinor Kyte, *Christmas Eve in Montreal 1783-A Bleak Mid-Winter.* (The Loyalist Gazette, 1986). 15-16. http://www.uelac.org/education/QuebecResource/Chapters/Christmas%20Eve%20in%20Montreal%201783.html

720 Library and Archives Canada, British Library, formerly British Museum, Additional Manuscripts 21804-21834, *Haldimand Papers.* Lac_reel_h1655, H-1655, 105513, 2034239, MG 21. Image 1006. Strength of the 1st Battalion Royal Regiment New York doing garrison duty, Montreal, 1st August 1783. Staff of the Garrison, Charles Blake, Surgeon; Library and Archives Canada, British Library, formerly British Museum, Additional Manuscripts 21804-21834, *Haldimand Papers.* Lac_reel_h1654, H-1654, 105513, 2034239, MG 21. Image 508, 527. http://heritage.canadiana.ca/view/oocihm.lac_reel_h1654/508?r=0&s=4

721 Elinor Kyte, *Christmas Eve in Montreal 1783-A Bleak Mid-Winter.*; Adam R. Hodge, Vectors of Colonialism: The Smallpox Epidemic of 1780-1782 and Northern Great Plains Indian Life. Masters Thesis, Kent State University, 2009. 67-70. https://etd.ohiolink.edu/rws_etd/document/get/kent1239393701/inline

722 Ancestry.com. *UK, American Loyalist Claims, 1776-1835* [database on-line]. Provo, UT. The National Archives of the UK; Kew, Surrey, England; American Loyalist Claims, Series II; Class: AO 13; Piece 012: New Claims C D E F, New York. The Memorial of Philip Emis.

723 Ancestry.com. *Quebec, Canada, Vital and Church Records (Drouin Collection), 1621-1968* [database on-line]. Provo, UT. Institut Généalogique Drouin; Montreal, Quebec, Canada; Drouin Collection; Author: Gabriel Drouin, comp. Year or Year Range: 1766-1795. 30. Christopher Callinger and Sarah Ronion were married by publication the 21st of Jan.

724 Library and Archives Canada, British Library, formerly British Museum, Additional Manuscripts 21804-21834, *Haldimand Papers.* Lac_reel_h1655, H-1655, 105513, 2034239, MG 21, Image 44. Return of Unincorporated Loyalists Victualled in the Province of Quebec. 24 Jan 1784. http://heritage.canadiana.ca/view/oocihm.lac_reel_h1655/44?r=1&s=6

725 Ibid, Image 47-48. http://heritage.canadiana.ca/view/oocihm.lac_reel_h1655/48?r=1&s=6

1784 is an estimate of Catherine's birth. No birth record of Catherine has been found. Catherine received her 'Daughter of a U.E. Loyalist' land grant on Oct. 11, 1811. To receive this grant she had to be 21 years of age. Therefore; she was born before 1790. Her sisters Olive, Mary, and Barbara also received their land grants on Oct 11, 1811. Ancestry.com. *The Loyalists in Ontario* [database on-line]. Provo, UT. Original data: Reid, William D. *The Loyalists in Ontario: The Sons and Daughters of the American Loyalists of Upper Canada.* Lambertville, NJ, USA: Genealogical Publishing Co., 1973. Section: E. 97. Eamer, Catherine m. William Nokes of Cornwall O.C. 16 Feb. 1811.; Library and Archives Canada. British Library, formerly British Museum, Additional Manuscripts 21804-21834, Haldimand Papers. Lac_reel_h1655, H-1655, 105513, 2034239, MG 21. Image 224. Muster of Township No. 2. Peter Emer, 1 man, 1 woman, 1 male under 10, 1 female under 10. Total 4, Rations per day 3, on their lands. http://heritage.canadiana.ca/view/oocihm.lac_reel_h1655/224?r=0&s=4

727 J.F. Pringle, Lunenburgh or the Old Eastern District Its Settlement and Early Progress (Cornwall, ON, Standard Printing House, 1890), 32. https://archive.org/stream/lunenburgh00prinuoft#page/n55/mode/2up ; E. A. Cruikshank, *The King's Royal Regiment of New York.* ed. Gavin Watt, (Toronto, The Ontario Historical Society, 1931) Reprinted Toronto, 1984, 116; Library and Archives Canada, *Haldimand papers from the British Library.* Lac_reel_h1437, H-1437, 105513, 2034239, MG 21. Image 1208, 1226, 1514. http://heritage.canadiana.ca/view/oocihm.lac_reel_h1437/1226?r=0&s=5; Library

and Archives Canada, Heir and Devisee Commission. Lac_reel_h1134, H-1134, RG 1 L5, 205142. Image 58. http://heritage.canadiana.ca/view/oocihm.lac_reel_h1134/58?r=0&s=2 ; British Library, formerly British Museum, Additional Manuscripts 21804-21834, *Haldimand Papers.* Lac_reel_h1655, H-1655, 105513, 2034239, MG 21. Image 142. General Abstract of Men, Women, and Children settled on the New Townships. Montreal, July 1784. http://heritage.canadiana.ca/view/oocihm.lac_reel_h1655/142?r=1&s=4

728 Ibid, Image 121, 129, 136. http://heritage.canadiana.ca/view/oocihm.lac_reel_h1655/121?r=0&s=4 ; Ibid, Lac_reel_h1653, H-1653, 105513, 2034239, MG 21. Image 492. Major Matthews to Captain Sherwood regarding Indian Corn.

729 Library and Archives Canada, British Library (Formerly British Museum) Haldimand Papers. Lac_reel_h1743, H-1743, 105513, 2034239. Image 1447-1448. Petition of Adam Empey late a Corporal in the 1st batn Kings Royal Regt. N. York. http://heritage.canadiana.ca/view/oocihm.lac_reel_h1743/1447?r=0&s=3

730 British Library, formerly British Museum, Additional Manuscripts 21804-21834, *Haldimand Papers.* Lac_reel_h1655, H-1655, 105513, 2034239, MG 21. Image 51. Mary Fater, 1 male above 6, 1 male under 6, 3 females above 6. Isle Jesu. Rt. Yorkers, 1st Batn. Newcomers. http://heritage.canadiana.ca/view/oocihm.lac_reel_h1655/51?r=1&s=5 ; Library and Archives Canada, Upper Canada Land Petitions (1763-1865). Mikan Number, 205131, Microform c-1893, Image 485-491. Petition of Lucas Feader of the Township of Matilda (includes the military service and will of Lucas Feader Sr.).

731 Library and Archives Canada. British Library, formerly British Museum, Additional Manuscripts 21804-21834, *Haldimand Papers.* Lac_reel_h1655, H-1655, 105513, 2034239, MG 21. Image 5-51.; Ancestry.com. *UK, American Loyalist Claims, 1776-1835* [database on-line]. Provo, UT. The National Archives of the UK; Kew, Surrey, England; American Loyalist Claims, Series II; Class: AO 13; Piece 014: New Claims

K·M·N·O·, New York. 322. The memorial of Martin Middock on behalf of Henry, Charles, Rachel, and Mary Bush, Orphan children of the late Henry Bush and Nelly his wife.; "Marriages at St Paul's Lutheran Church Schoharie. 1773-1776." 1775, Oct. 18. Nicolas Freymauer, Elizabeth Borst. http://web.archive.org/web/20101120045734/http://bettyfink.com/mstp10.htm

732 Library and Archives Canada. British Library (Formerly British Museum) *Haldimand Papers*. Lac_reel_h1743, H-1743, 105513, 2034239. Image 1456. Memorial of Edward Foster Past Private Soldier in first Battn King's Royal Regiment of New York. http://heritage.canadiana.ca/view/oocihm.lac_reel_h1743/1456?r=0&s=4

733 Ancestry.com. *UK, American Loyalist Claims, 1776-1835* [database on-line]. Provo, UT. Original data: American Loyalist Claims, 1776–1835. AO 12–13. The National Archives of the United Kingdom, Kew, Surrey, England. *Piece 016: New Claims T·V·W·Y, New York. 217.* Estimation of the losses sustained by Jacob Waggoner.

734 Library and Archives Canada. *Haldimand papers from the British Library*. Lac_reel_h1437, H-1437, 105513, 2034239, MG 21. Image 1432, 1437. http://heritage.canadiana.ca/view/oocihm.lac_reel_h1437/1437?r=0&s=4 ; Library and Archives Canada, British Library, formerly British Museum, Additional Manuscripts 21804-21834, *Haldimand Papers*. Lac_reel_ h1653, H-1653, 105513, 2034239, MG 21. Image 510, 605. ; Library and Archives Canada. *Haldimand papers from the British Library*. Lac_reel_h1437, H-1437, 105513, 2034239, MG 21. Image 1309-1310. http://heritage.canadiana.ca/view/oocihm.lac_reel_h1437/1309?r=0&s=4 ; Isabel Thompson Kelsay, *Joseph Brant 1743-1807 Man of Two Worlds* (Syracuse, Syracuse University Press, 1984), 350-351.

735 Ancestry.com. *New York, Sales of Loyalist Land, 1762-1830* [database on-line]. Provo, UT. Original data: New York State Engineer and Surveyor. Records of Surveys and Maps of State Lands, 1686–1892, Series A4016, Vols. 7–10 and 17. New York State Archives, Albany,

New York. Page 185; Memorandum of Agreement between Commys Western District and Henry Hart for Lot No. 112 Eastern Allotment of Kingsborough Patent. 16 Sept, 1784; Ibid page 176 a-g. Memorandum of Agreement Coms. Of Forfeitures W. District and Jelles Fonda Esq. of palatine district county of Montgomery For the Rent and Reversions of Lot No. 43 in W. allotment of Kingsborough. Consideration £240. Sept 17, 1784.; Ibid page 169, To George, brother of the former, Lots No. 43 & 44 in Sacondaga Patent, 250 ac. each.; New York Public Library. Manuscripts and Archives Division. *List of loyalists against whom judgments were given under the Confiscation Act.* (UUID): 554d98e0-cc5f-0133-9fc2-00505686a51c. https://digitalcollections.nypl.org/items/931a49e0-0e2f-0134-a66c-00505686a51c

736 Library and Archives Canada. *Haldimand papers from the British Library*. Lac_reel_h1437, H-1437, 105513, 2034239, MG 21. Image 1433. http://heritage.canadiana.ca/view/oocihm.lac_reel_h1437/1433?r=0&s=4

737 Ibid, Image 1429. Frederick Haldimand to John Collins. 17 May 1784. Image 1533, Frederick Haldimand to Sir John Johnson. 14 June 1784. Image 1457, Frederick Haldimand to Major Ross. 24 May 1784. http://heritage.canadiana.ca/view/oocihm.lac_reel_h1437/1429?r=0&s=4

738 Ibid, Image 1276, 1437, 1449, 1520 http://heritage.canadiana.ca/view/oocihm.lac_reel_h1437/1433?r=0&s=4

739 Library and Archives Canada, *Haldimand papers from the British Library*. Lac_reel_h1437, H-1437, 105513, 2034239, MG 21. Image 1524, 1527. http://heritage.canadiana.ca/view/oocihm.lac_reel_h1437/1524?r=0&s=5

740 Library and Archives Canada. British Library, formerly British Museum, Additional Manuscripts 21804-21834, Haldimand Papers. Lac_reel_h1655, H-1655, 105513, 2034239, MG 21. Image 224. Muster of Township No. 2. http://heritage.canadiana.ca/view/oocihm.lac_reel_h1655/224?r=0&s=4 ; Library and Archives Canada. British Library, formerly British Museum, Additional Manuscripts 21804-21834,

Haldimand Papers. Lac_reel_h1655, H-1655, 105513, 2034239, MG 21. Image 154. Return of Refugees, Loyalists, and Disbanded Troops, Lodged and Victualled in & about Montreal Mustered this day, 17 Sept. 1784. Refugee, Jacob Alguire & sons.... 1 man, 1 woman, 2 boys over 10, 1 boy under 10. Total 5, Rations 41/2. Going up to their lands this fall. I'm not sure who the boy under 10 is in this victualling list. From the records I've located, Jacob Henry Alguire Sr.and Salome Wahl had 3 sons: Martin, Sebastian (d. 1776), and Jacob Jr. Unless the boy under 10 was a grandchild belonging to Sebastian and one of his three wives. I did not find any records in New York of children born to Sebastian Alguire. In the 1786 victualling list at Cornwall, Jacob Alguire is listed as having 1 boy over 10, who would be Jacob Alguire Jr. Johannes Alguire Sr. and Catherine Margaretha Mueller had 3 sons: Johannes George, Johannes, and Philip. I did not locate any record of a son Jacob who could have been the boy Alguire under 10.

741 "Rivard: Voyageur's World." Clothing. http://www.rendezvousvoyageurs.ca/en/world/worklife/index.html

742 Library and Archives Canada. British Library, formerly British Museum, Additional Manuscripts 21804-21834, *Haldimand Papers.* Lac_reel_h1655, H-1655, 105513, 2034239, MG 21. Image 224. Muster of Township No. 2. http://heritage.canadiana.ca/view/oocihm.lac_reel_h1655/224?r=0&s=4 ; Ibid, Image 161. Return of the Refugee Loyalists & disbanded troops in and about Lachine. 19 Sept 1784. http://heritage.canadiana.ca/view/oocihm.lac_reel_h1655/161?r=0&s=6

743 Robert Malcombson, "Nothing More Uncomfortable Than Our Flat Bottomed Boats:" Batteaux in the British Service During the War of 1812. *The Northern Mariner, XIII, No. 4,* (October, 2003), 19-20, 25. https://www.cnrs-scrn.org/northern_mariner/vol13/tnm_13_4_17-28.pdf

744 "Rivard: Voyageur's World." Songs of the Voyageur. A la Claire fontaine, C'est l'aviron, Dans le mois de mai, V'la l'bon vent. http://www.rendezvousvoyageurs.ca/en/world/worklife/index.html

745 Library and Archives Canada, British Library, formerly British Museum, Additional Manuscripts 21804-21834, *Haldimand Papers*. Lac_reel_h1654, H-1654, 105513, 2034239, MG 21. Image 780. Loyalist receipt for clothing. Machiche, 1 December 1783. http://heritage.canadiana.ca/view/oocihm.lac_reel_h1654/780?r=0&s=4

746 Ken D. Johnson, "Fort Plank Bastion of My Freedom, Colonial Canajoharie, New York" Slack's Report on Batteauxing, Montreal, 9 April, 1777. http://www.fort-plank.com/B-Slacks_Report_on_Batteauxing_1777.pdf ; S.W. Durant & H. B. Peirce, History of St. Lawrence County, New York, Chapter III French Occupation. The Journal of Isaac Weld Jr. 1799 (Philadelphia, L.H. Everts & Co., 1878). 54-55. https://archive.org/stream/cu31924028833015#page/54/mode/2up

747 "Cornwall Community Museum" Historic Cornwall Square Mile. https://cornwallcommunitymuseum.wordpress.com/2016/11/08/historic-cornwall-square-mile/

748 Library and Archives Canada, *Haldimand papers from the British Library*. Lac_reel_h1437, H1437, 105513, 2034239, MG 21. Image 1457. Frederick Haldimand to Major Ross, Headquarters Quebec, 24 May 1784. http://heritage.canadiana.ca/view/oocihm.lac_reel_h1437/1457?r=0&s=5

749 Library and Archives Canada, British Library, formerly British Museum, Additional Manuscripts 21804-21834, *Haldimand Papers*. Lac_reel_h1655, H-1655, 105513, 2034239, MG 21. Image 224-230. Muster of Township No. 2. http://heritage.canadiana.ca/view/oocihm.lac_reel_h1655/224?r=0&s=4

750 Library and Archives Canada. *Haldimand papers from the British Library*. Lac_reel_h1437, H1437, 105513, 2034239, MG 21. Image 1434-1436. Frederick Haldimand to Major Samuel Holland, Surveyor General of the Province. http://heritage.canadiana.ca/view/oocihm.lac_reel_h1437/1435?r=0&s=4

751 Ibid, Image 1435, 1461-1462.

752 "UEALC St Lawrence Branch" McNiff Maps. Edward Kipp & George Anderson, An Index to the 1786 McNiff Maps of the Townships of Lancaster, Charlottenburg, Cornwall, Osnabruck, Williamsburg, and Matilda (The Loyalist Maps). 2007. http://uelac.org/st-lawrence/wp-content/uploads/2017/12/2_CORNWALL.pdf ; Library and Archives Canada, MIKAN No. 4159295, Cartographic material. Patrick McNiff, A plan of part of the new settlements, on the north bank of the southwest branch of the St. Lawrence River. 1786.; Library and Archives Canada, Heir and Devisee Commission. Lac_reel_h1135, H-1135, RG 1 L5, 205142, Image 441. Land certificate of Peter Emer for Lot 37, concession 13.. Issued at Cornwall, 17 November 1787. http://heritage.canadiana.ca/view/oocihm.lac_reel_h1135/441?r=0&s=2

753 Alex W. Fraser & Rhoda Ross, ed. *St. Andrews Presbyterian Church, Willamstown, Ontario, Baptisms and Marriages From 1779-1804.* (1999), 19. Mary Wert, Daughter of George Wert, Taylor at Lachine, was Baptised on the 27th Day of June 1784.

754 Peter C. Newman, Hostages to Fortune. The United Empire Loyalists and the Making of Canada (Toronto, Simon & Schuster, 2016), 120-121, 169-171.

755 *Early Ontario Settlers* [database on-line], 1784 Provisioning Lists: Cornwall.

756 *Early Ontario Settlers* [database on-line], 1784 Provisioning Lists: Cornwall.

INDEX

A

B

C

D

E

H

I

J

N

O

P

R

S

T